HARDYBOYS
ADVENTURES™

D1133580

PAPERCUTZ™

MORE GREAT GRAPHIC NOVEL SERIES AVAILABLE FROM PAPERCUTZ

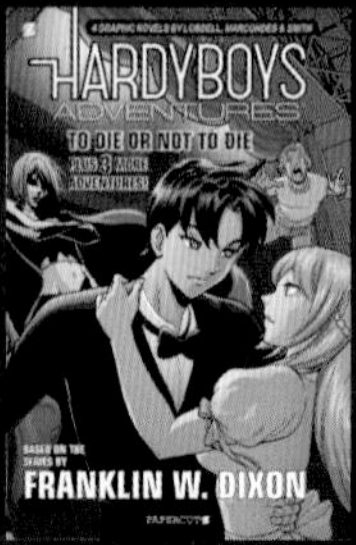
HARDYBOYS
ADVENTURES
TO DIE OR NOT TO DIE
PLUS 3 MORE ADVENTURES!
BASED ON THE SERIES BY
FRANKLIN W. DIXON
PAPERCUTZ

HARDY BOYS
ADVENTURE #1
"To Die Or Not To Die?"

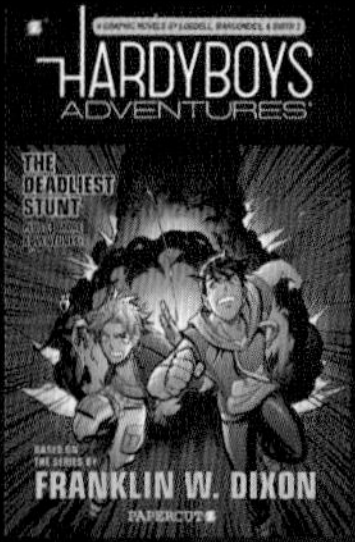
HARDYBOYS
ADVENTURES
THE DEADLIEST STUNT
FRANKLIN W. DIXON
PAPERCUTZ

HARDY BOYS
ADVENTURE #2
"The Deadliest Stunt"

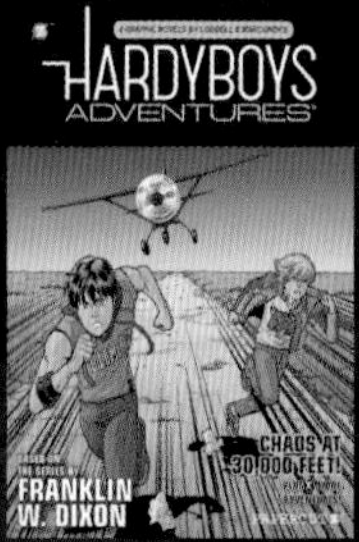
HARDYBOYS
ADVENTURES
CHAOS AT 30,000 FEET!
FRANKLIN W. DIXON
PAPERCUTZ

HARDY BOYS
ADVENTURE #3
"Chaos at 30,000 Feet!"

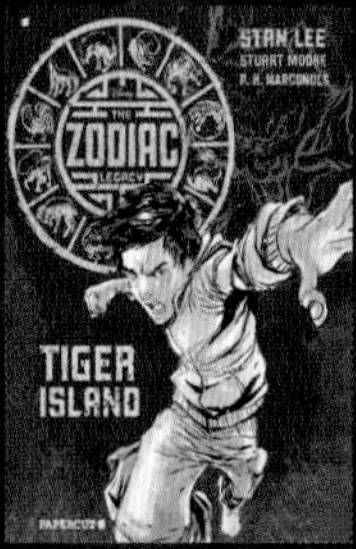
STAN LEE
STUART MOORE
P. H. MARCONDES
THE ZODIAC LEGACY
TIGER ISLAND
PAPERCUTZ

THE ZODIAC LEGACY #1
"Tiger Island"

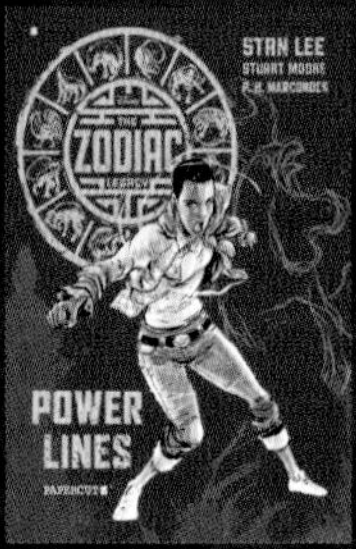
STAN LEE
STUART MOORE
P. H. MARCONDES
THE ZODIAC LEGACY
POWER LINES
PAPERCUTZ

THE ZODIAC LEGACY #2
"Power Line"

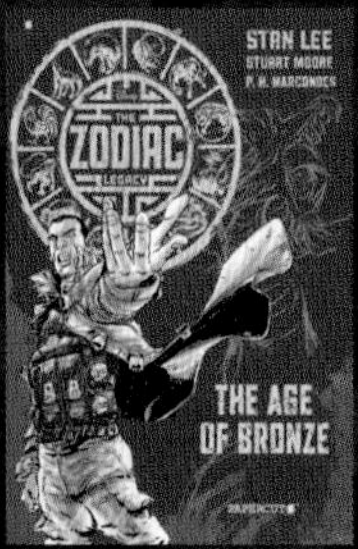
STAN LEE
STUART MOORE
P. H. MARCONDES
THE ZODIAC LEGACY
THE AGE OF BRONZE
PAPERCUTZ

THE ZODIAC LEGACY #3
"The Age of Bronze"

COMING SOON

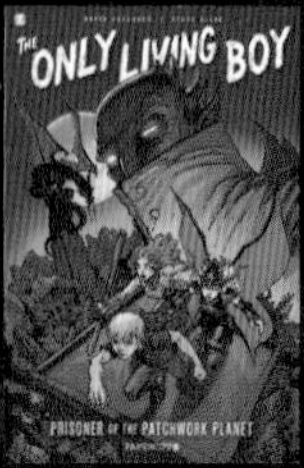
THE ONLY LIVING BOY
PRISONER OF THE PATCHWORK PLANET

THE ONLY
LIVING BOY #1
"Prisoner of the
Patchwork Planet"

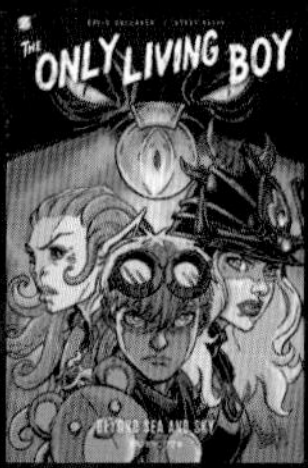
THE ONLY LIVING BOY
BEYOND SEA AND SKY

THE ONLY
LIVING BOY #2
"Beyond Sea
and Sky"

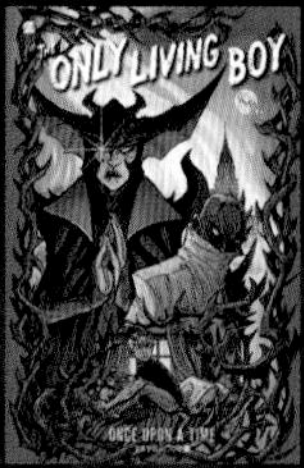
THE ONLY LIVING BOY
ONCE UPON A TIME

THE ONLY
LIVING BOY #3
"Once Upon
a Time"

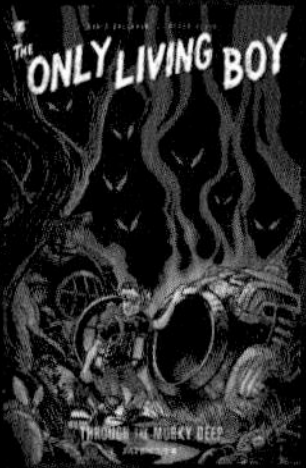
THE ONLY LIVING BOY
THROUGH THE MURKY DEEP

THE ONLY
LIVING BOY #4
"Through the
Murky Deep"

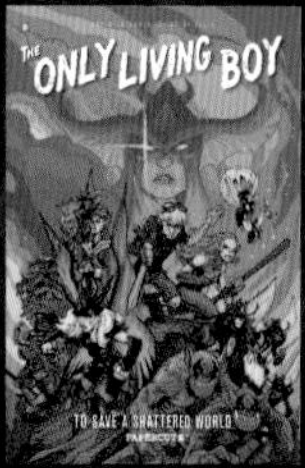
THE ONLY LIVING BOY
TO SAVE A SHATTERED WORLD
PAPERCUTZ

THE ONLY
LIVING BOY #5
"To Save a
Shattered World"

THE ZODIAC LEGACY graphic novels are available for $7.99 in paperback, and $12.99 in hardcover. THE ONLY LIVING BOY graphic novels are $8.99 in paperback, and $13.99 in hardcover. HARDY BOYS ADVENTURES graphic nnovels are $15.99 in paperback only. Available from booksellers everywhere. You can also order online from www.papercutz.com.
Or call 1-800-886-1223, Monday through Friday, 9–5 EST. MC, Visa, and AmEx accepted. To order by mail, please add $4.00 for postage and handling for first book ordered, $1.00 for each additional book and make check payable to NBM Publishing.
Send to: Papercutz, 160 Broadway, Suite 700, East Wing, New York, NY 10038.

HARDY BOYS ADVENTRUES and THE ONLY LIVING BOY graphic novels are also available wherever e-books are sold.

HARDYBOYS
ADVENTURES™

SCOTT LOBDELL – Writer
PAULO HENRIQUE MARCONDES – Artist
Based on the series by
FRANKLIN W. DIXON

PAPERCUTZ™

NEW YORK

TABLE OF CONTENTS

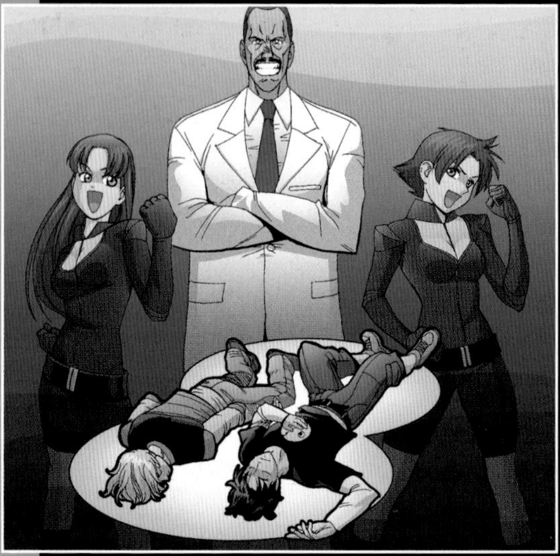

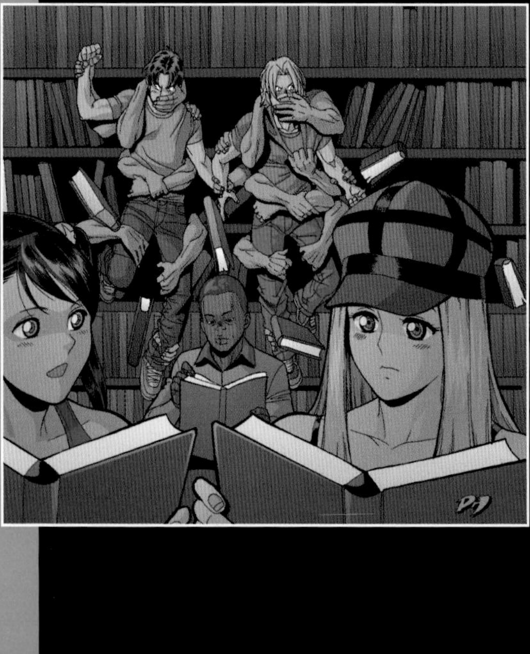

TABLE OF CONTENTS

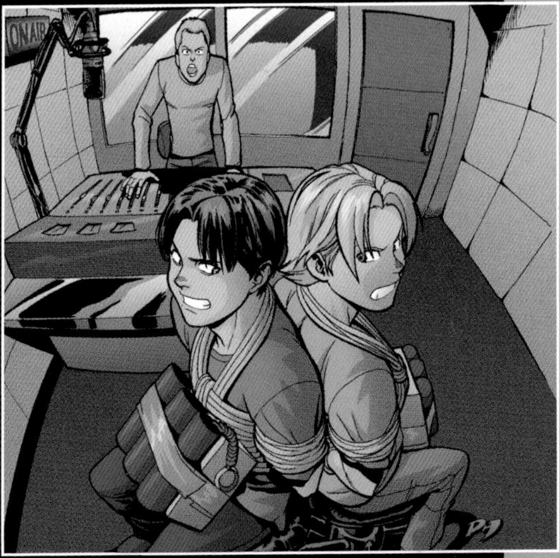
ONAIR

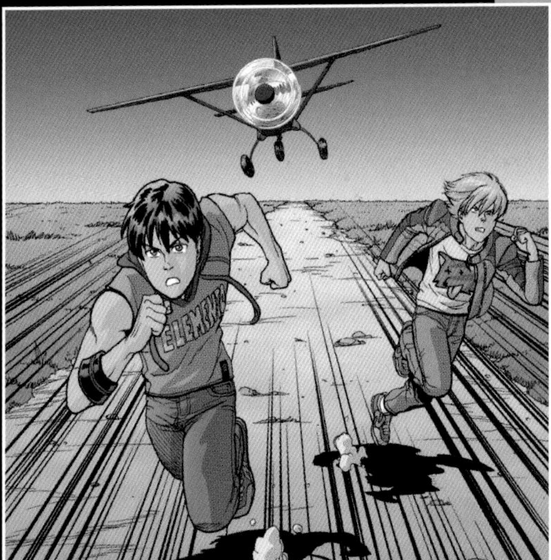

THE HARDY BOYS ADVENTURES #3

"LIVE FREE, DIE HARDY," "SHHHHHH!" "WORD UP!" and "CHAOS AT 30,000 FEET"

SCOTT LOBDELL – Writer
PAULO HENRIQUE MARCONDES – Artist
MARK LERER – Letterer
LAURIE E. SMITH – Colorist
BIG BIRD ZATRYB – Production
DAWN GUZZO – Production Coordinator
JEFF WHITMAN – Assistant Managing Editor
ROBERT V. CONTE – Editor
JIM SALICRUP
Editor-in-Chief

ISBN: 978-1-62991-754-2

Printed in China
August 2017

Distributed by Macmillian
First Printing

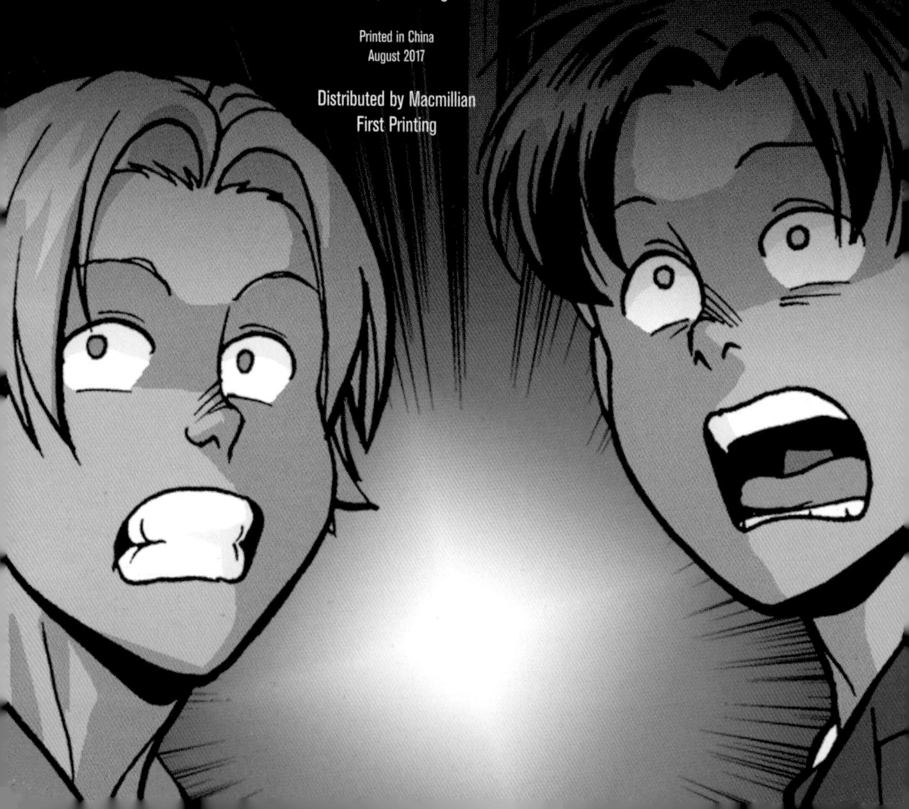

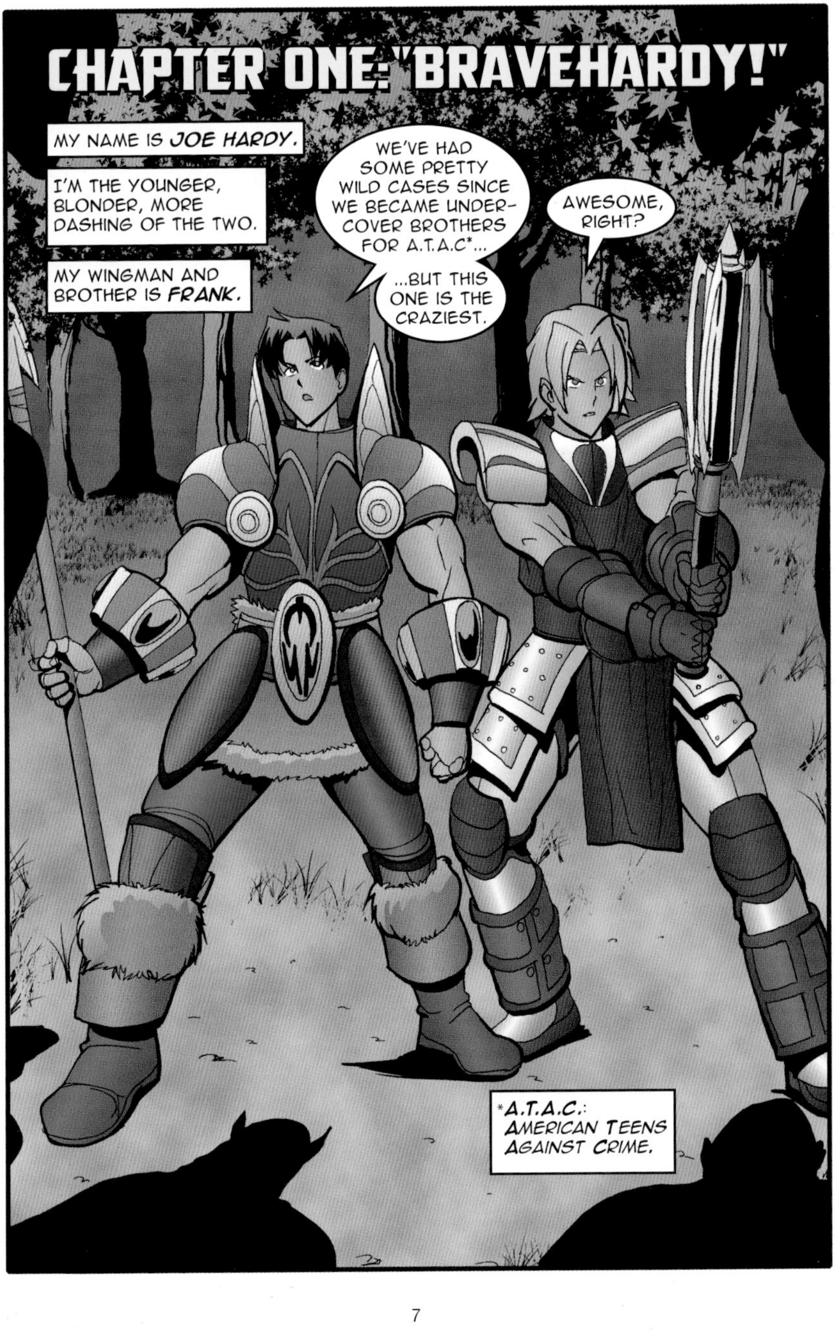
CHAPTER ONE: "BRAVEHARDY!"
MY NAME IS JOE HARDY.
I'M THE YOUNGER, BLONDER, MORE DASHING OF THE TWO.
MY WINGMAN AND BROTHER IS FRANK.
WE'VE HAD SOME PRETTY WILD CASES SINCE WE BECAME UNDER-COVER BROTHERS FOR A.T.A.C*...
...BUT THIS ONE IS THE CRAZIEST.
AWESOME, RIGHT?
*A.T.A.C.: AMERICAN TEENS AGAINST CRIME.

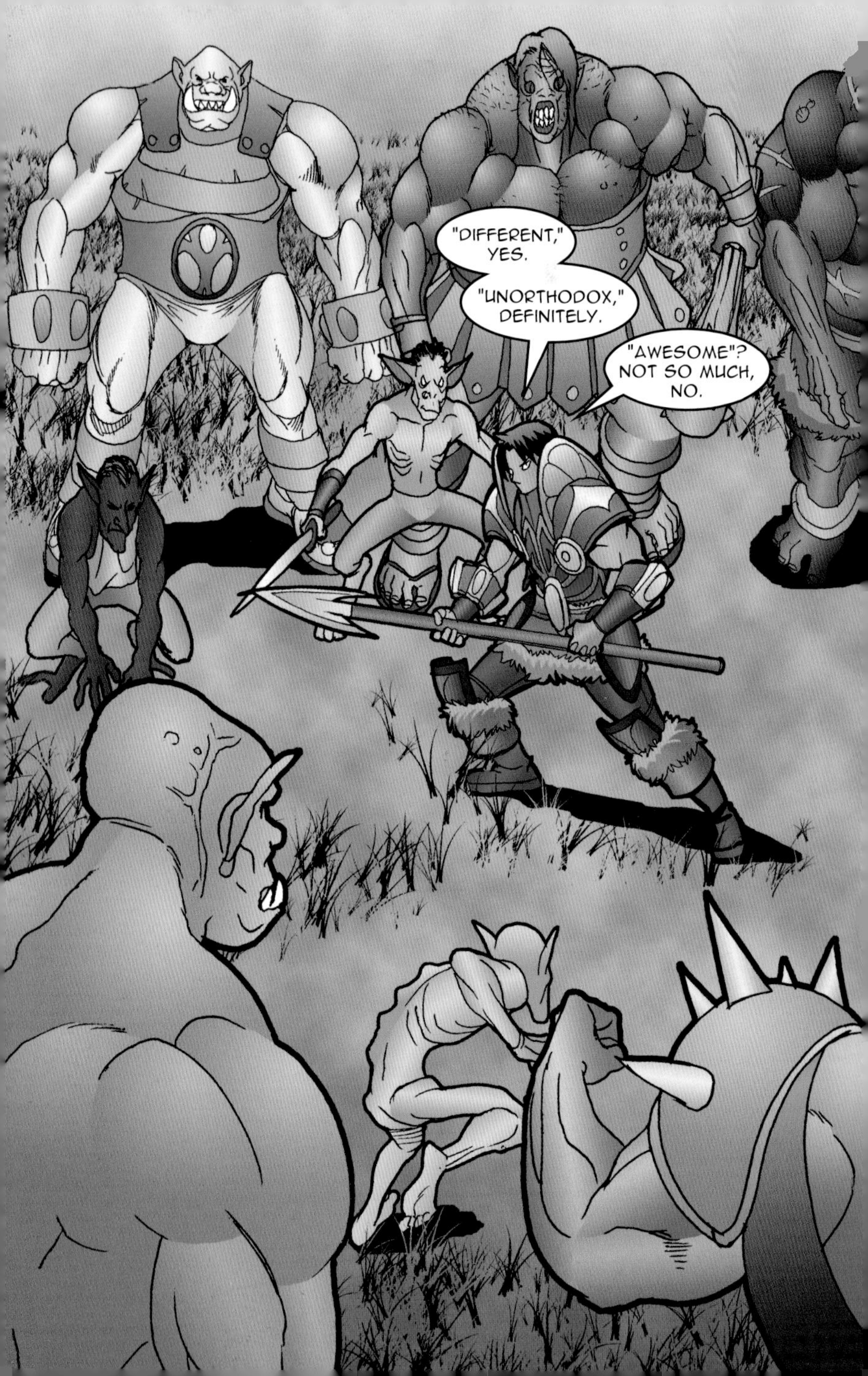

"DIFFERENT," YES.
"UNORTHODOX," DEFINITELY.
"AWESOME"? NOT SO MUCH, NO.

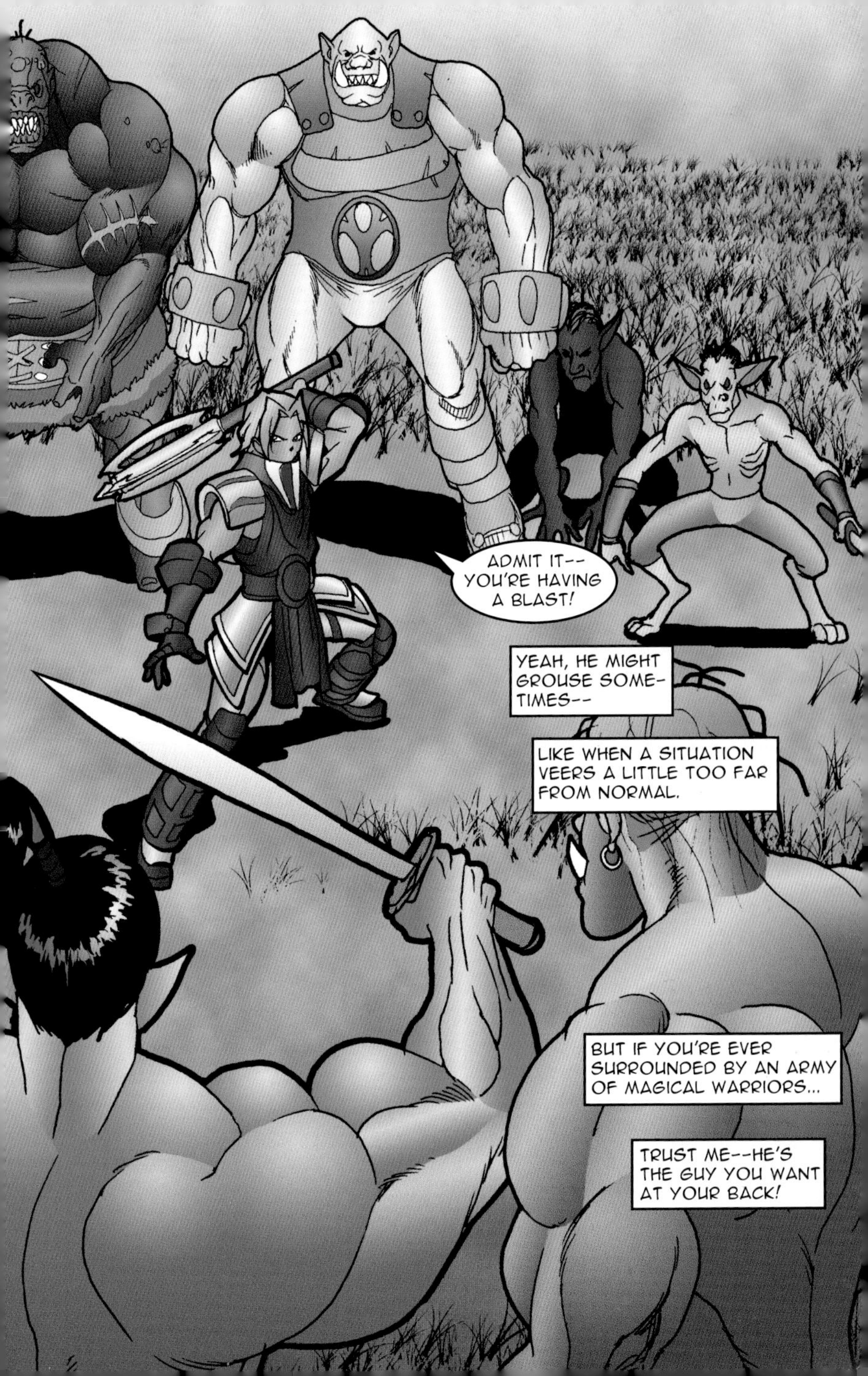
ADMIT IT--
YOU'RE HAVING
A BLAST!
YEAH, HE MIGHT
GROUSE SOME-
TIMES--
LIKE WHEN A SITUATION
VEERS A LITTLE TOO FAR
FROM NORMAL.
BUT IF YOU'RE EVER
SURROUNDED BY AN ARMY
OF MAGICAL WARRIORS...
TRUST ME--HE'S
THE GUY YOU WANT
AT YOUR BACK!

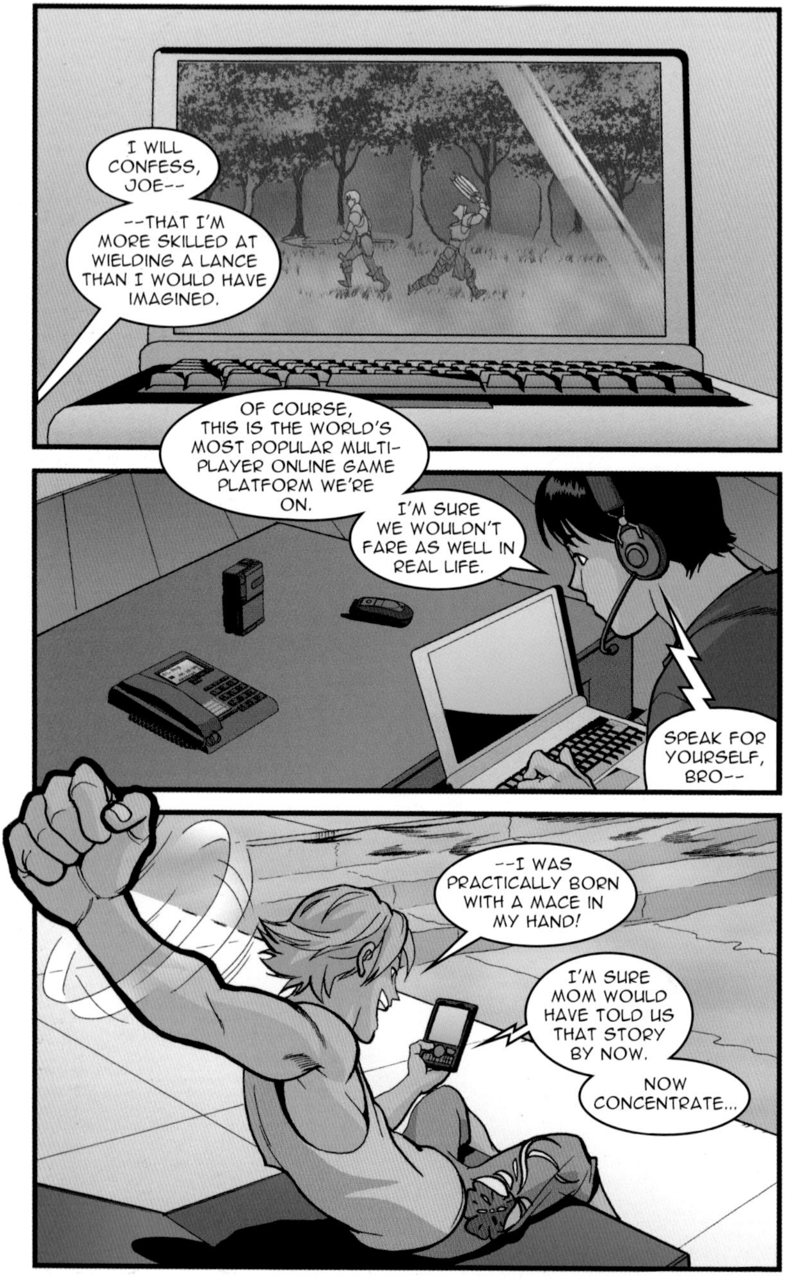
I WILL CONFESS, JOE--
--THAT I'M MORE SKILLED AT WIELDING A LANCE THAN I WOULD HAVE IMAGINED.
OF COURSE, THIS IS THE WORLD'S MOST POPULAR MULTI-PLAYER ONLINE GAME PLATFORM WE'RE ON.
I'M SURE WE WOULDN'T FARE AS WELL IN REAL LIFE.
SPEAK FOR YOURSELF, BRO--
--I WAS PRACTICALLY BORN WITH A MACE IN MY HAND!
I'M SURE MOM WOULD HAVE TOLD US THAT STORY BY NOW.
NOW CONCENTRATE...

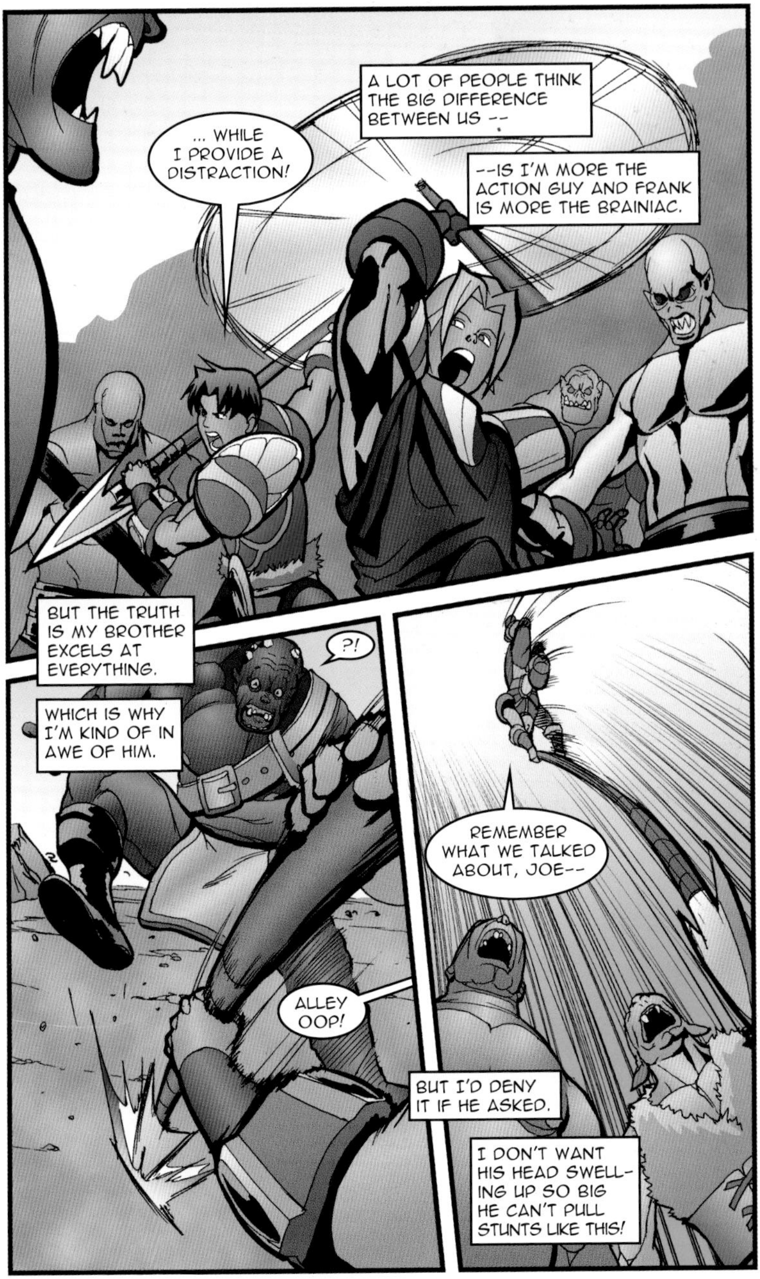
A LOT OF PEOPLE THINK THE BIG DIFFERENCE BETWEEN US --
... WHILE I PROVIDE A DISTRACTION!
--IS I'M MORE THE ACTION GUY AND FRANK IS MORE THE BRAINIAC.
BUT THE TRUTH IS MY BROTHER EXCELS AT EVERYTHING.
?!
WHICH IS WHY I'M KIND OF IN AWE OF HIM.
REMEMBER WHAT WE TALKED ABOUT, JOE--
ALLEY OOP!
BUT I'D DENY IT IF HE ASKED.
I DON'T WANT HIS HEAD SWELL-ING UP SO BIG HE CAN'T PULL STUNTS LIKE THIS!

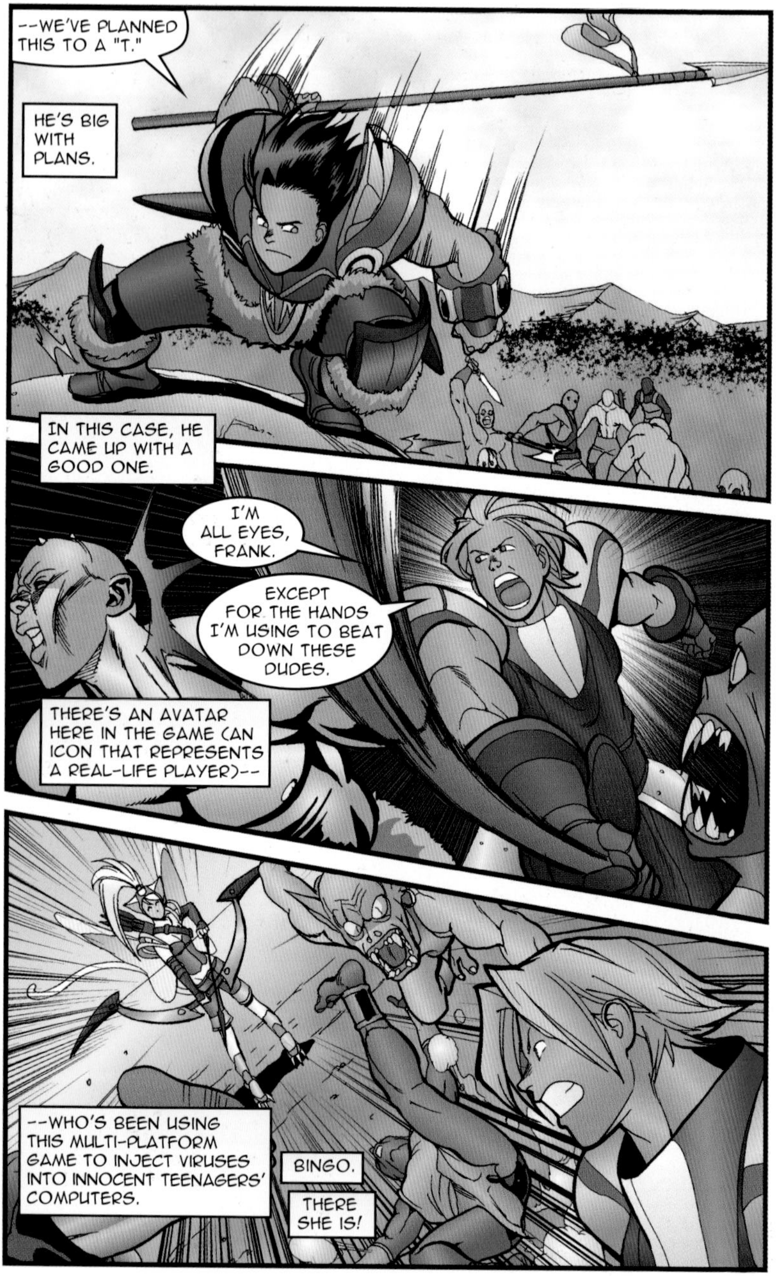
--WE'VE PLANNED THIS TO A "T."
HE'S BIG WITH PLANS.
IN THIS CASE, HE CAME UP WITH A GOOD ONE.
I'M ALL EYES, FRANK.
EXCEPT FOR THE HANDS I'M USING TO BEAT DOWN THESE DUDES.
THERE'S AN AVATAR HERE IN THE GAME (AN ICON THAT REPRESENTS A REAL-LIFE PLAYER)--
--WHO'S BEEN USING THIS MULTI-PLATFORM GAME TO INJECT VIRUSES INTO INNOCENT TEENAGERS' COMPUTERS.
BINGO.
THERE SHE IS!

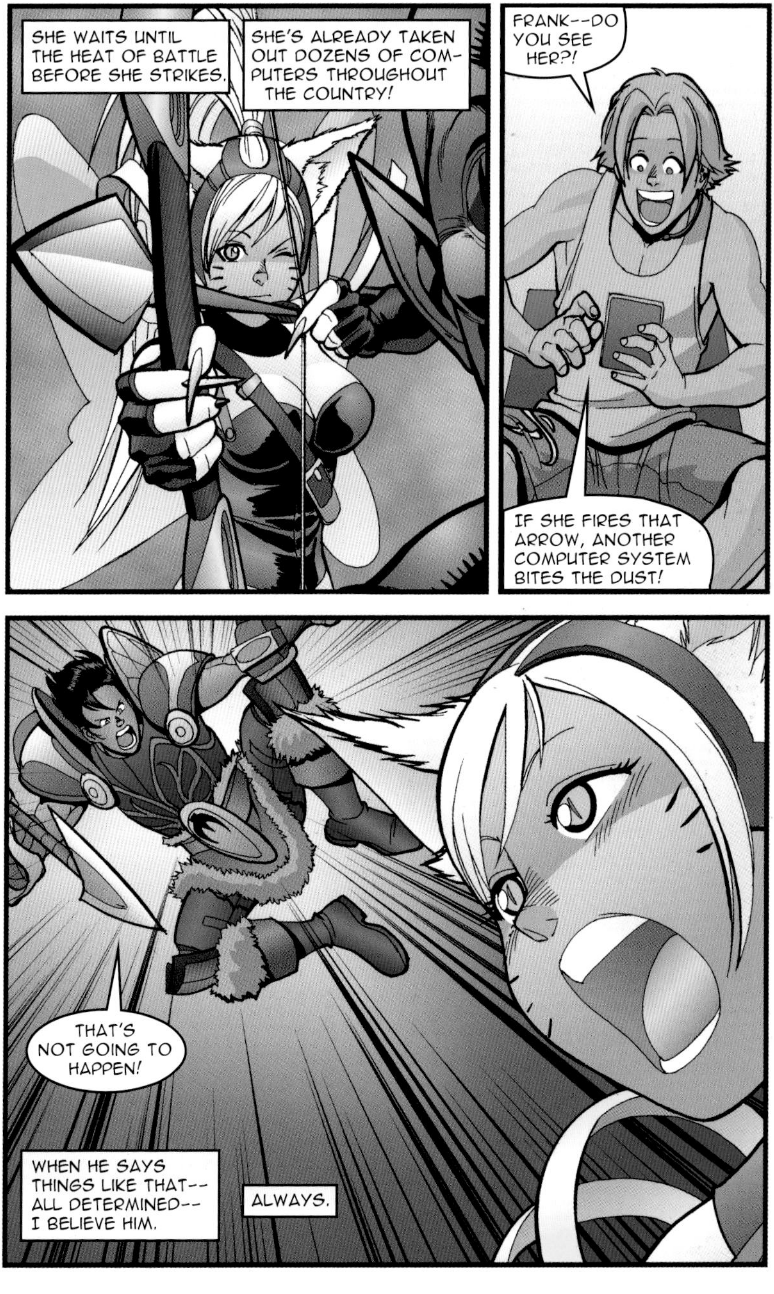
SHE WAITS UNTIL THE HEAT OF BATTLE BEFORE SHE STRIKES.
SHE'S ALREADY TAKEN OUT DOZENS OF COM-PUTERS THROUGHOUT THE COUNTRY!
FRANK--DO YOU SEE HER?!
IF SHE FIRES THAT ARROW, ANOTHER COMPUTER SYSTEM BITES THE DUST!
THAT'S NOT GOING TO HAPPEN!
WHEN HE SAYS THINGS LIKE THAT--ALL DETERMINED--I BELIEVE HIM.
ALWAYS.

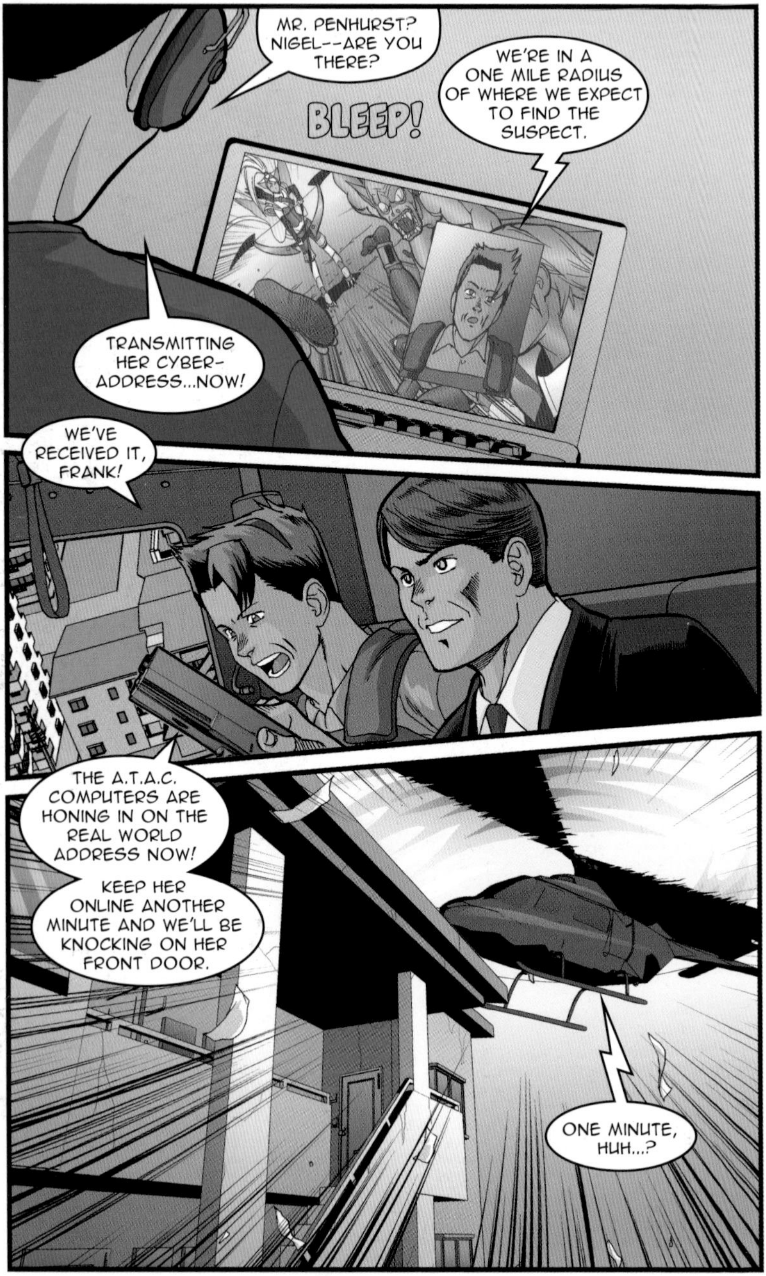
MR. PENHURST? NIGEL--ARE YOU THERE?
BLEEP!
WE'RE IN A ONE MILE RADIUS OF WHERE WE EXPECT TO FIND THE SUSPECT.
TRANSMITTING HER CYBER-ADDRESS...NOW!
WE'VE RECEIVED IT, FRANK!
THE A.T.A.C. COMPUTERS ARE HONING IN ON THE REAL WORLD ADDRESS NOW!
KEEP HER ONLINE ANOTHER MINUTE AND WE'LL BE KNOCKING ON HER FRONT DOOR.
ONE MINUTE, HUH...?

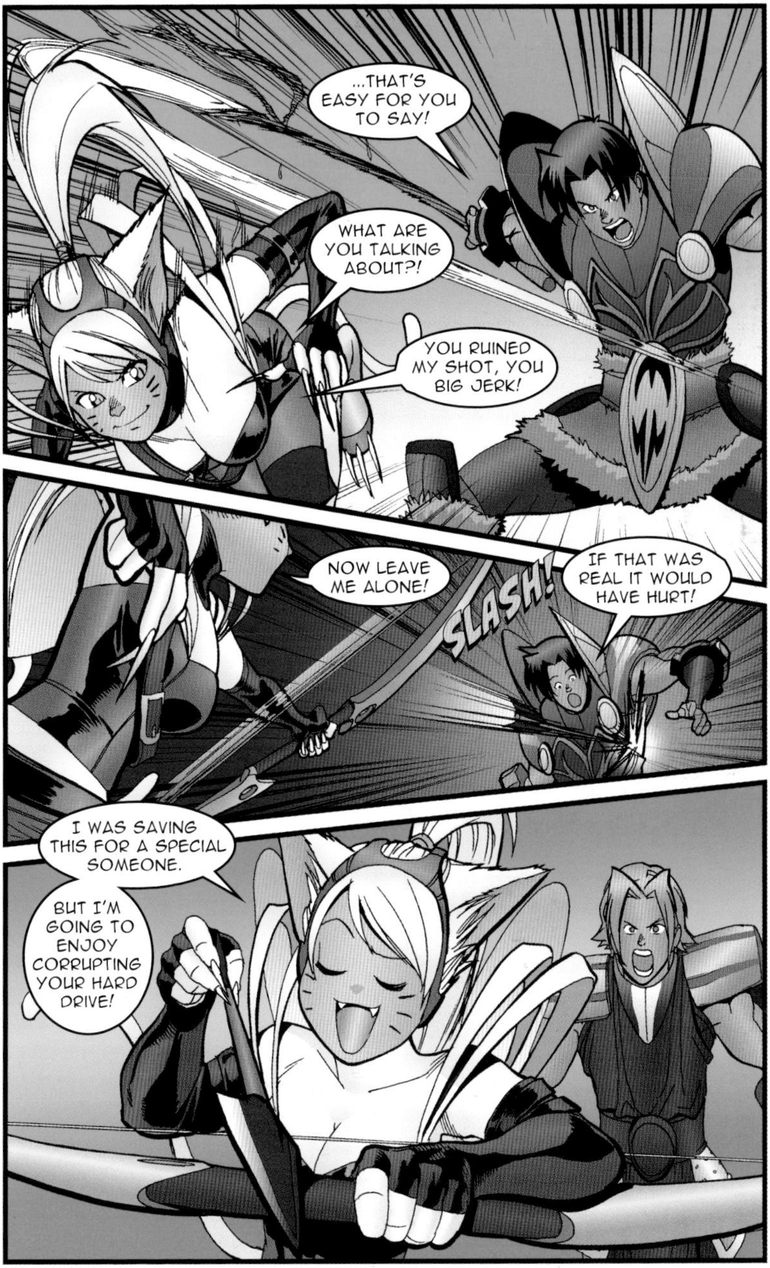
...THAT'S EASY FOR YOU TO SAY!
WHAT ARE YOU TALKING ABOUT?!
YOU RUINED MY SHOT, YOU BIG JERK!
NOW LEAVE ME ALONE!
SLASH!
IF THAT WAS REAL IT WOULD HAVE HURT!
I WAS SAVING THIS FOR A SPECIAL SOMEONE.
BUT I'M GOING TO ENJOY CORRUPTING YOUR HARD DRIVE!

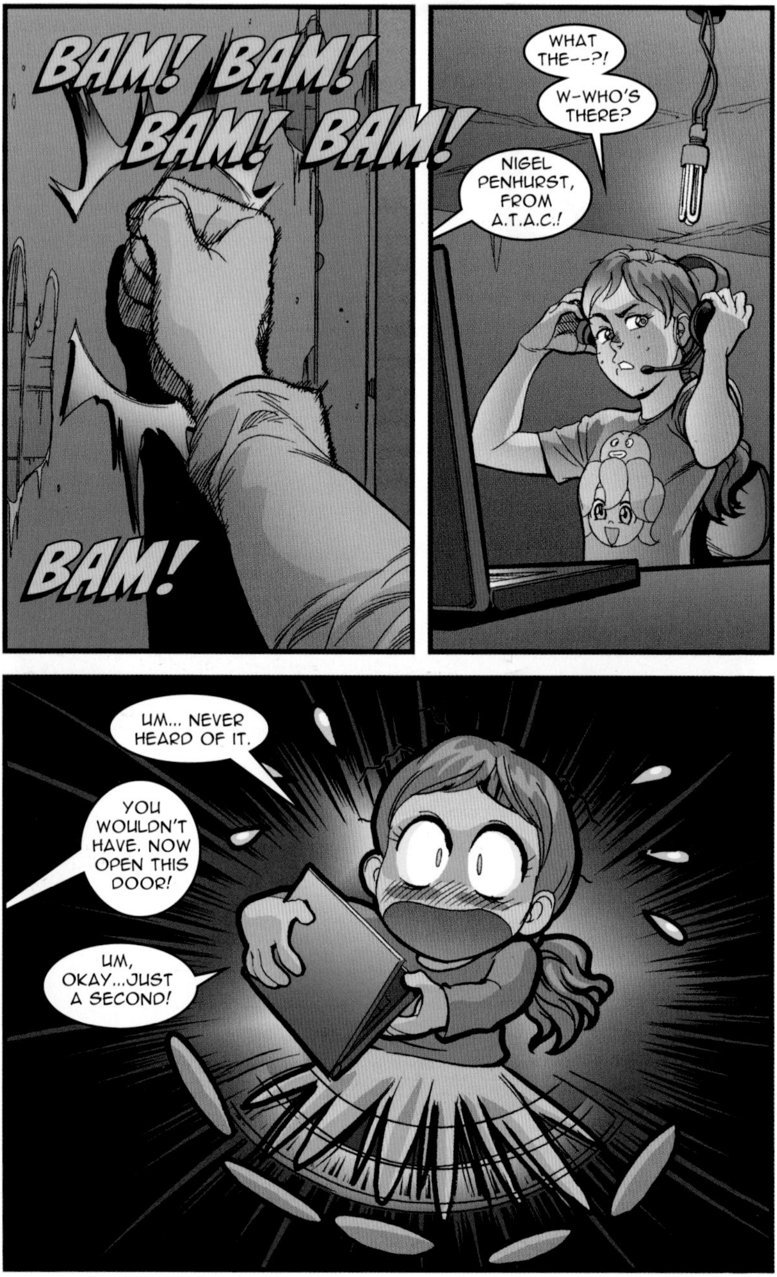
BAM! BAM!
BAM! BAM!
BAM!
WHAT THE--?!
W-WHO'S THERE?
NIGEL PENHURST, FROM A.T.A.C.!
UM... NEVER HEARD OF IT.
YOU WOULDN'T HAVE. NOW OPEN THIS DOOR!
UM, OKAY...JUST A SECOND!

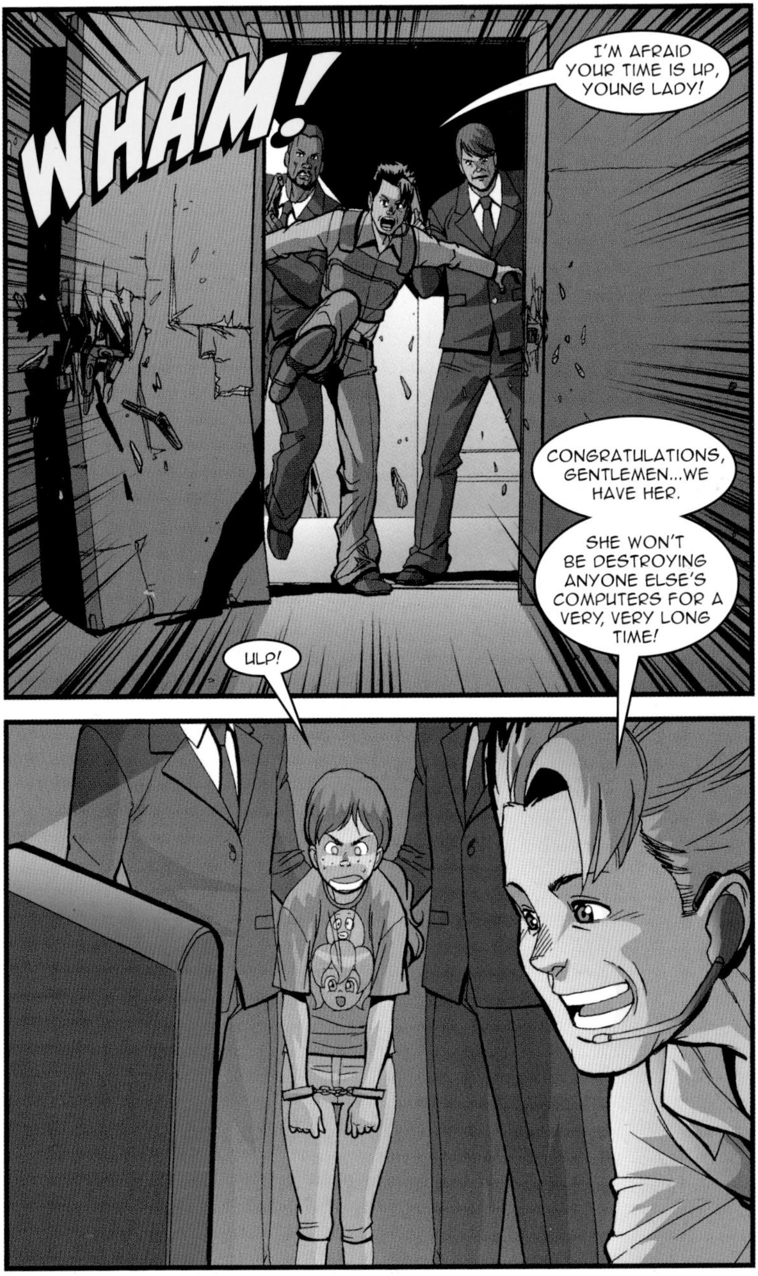
WHAM!
I'M AFRAID YOUR TIME IS UP, YOUNG LADY!
CONGRATULATIONS, GENTLEMEN...WE HAVE HER.
SHE WON'T BE DESTROYING ANYONE ELSE'S COMPUTERS FOR A VERY, VERY LONG TIME!
ULP!

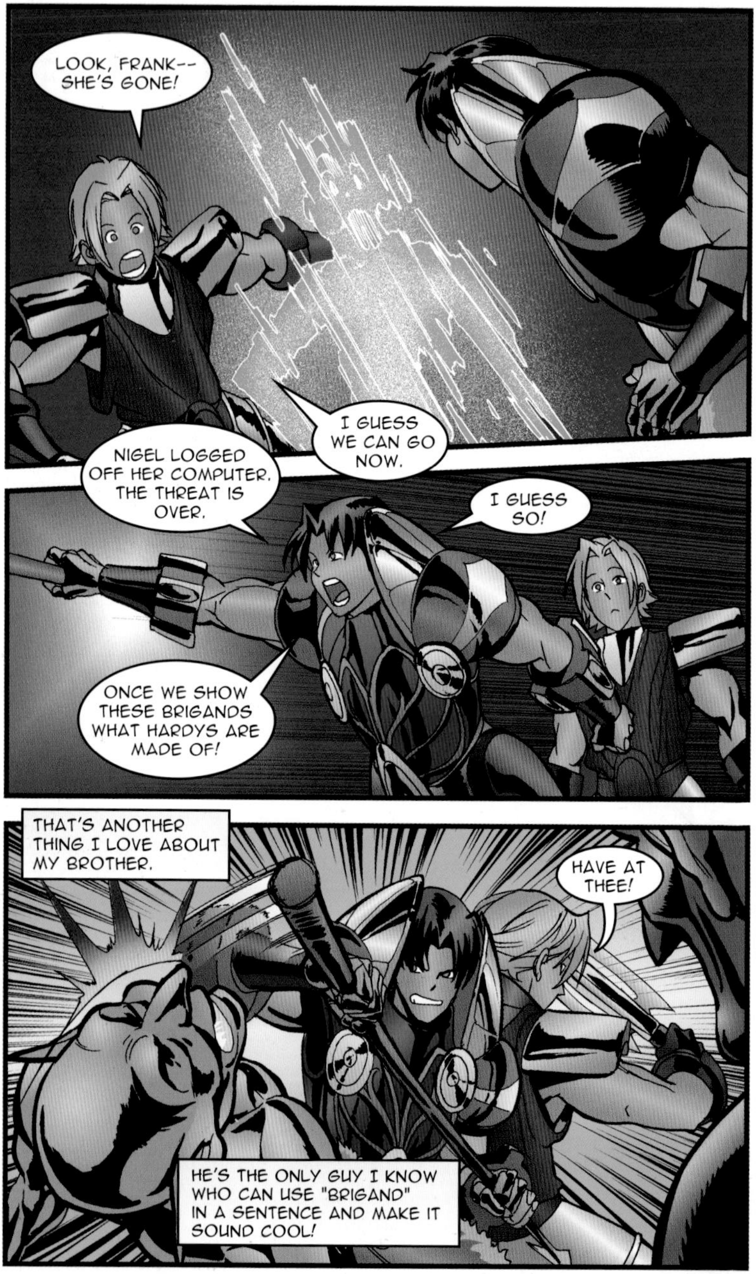
LOOK, FRANK-- SHE'S GONE!
I GUESS WE CAN GO NOW.
NIGEL LOGGED OFF HER COMPUTER. THE THREAT IS OVER.
I GUESS SO!
ONCE WE SHOW THESE BRIGANDS WHAT HARDYS ARE MADE OF!
THAT'S ANOTHER THING I LOVE ABOUT MY BROTHER.
HAVE AT THEE!
HE'S THE ONLY GUY I KNOW WHO CAN USE "BRIGAND" IN A SENTENCE AND MAKE IT SOUND COOL!

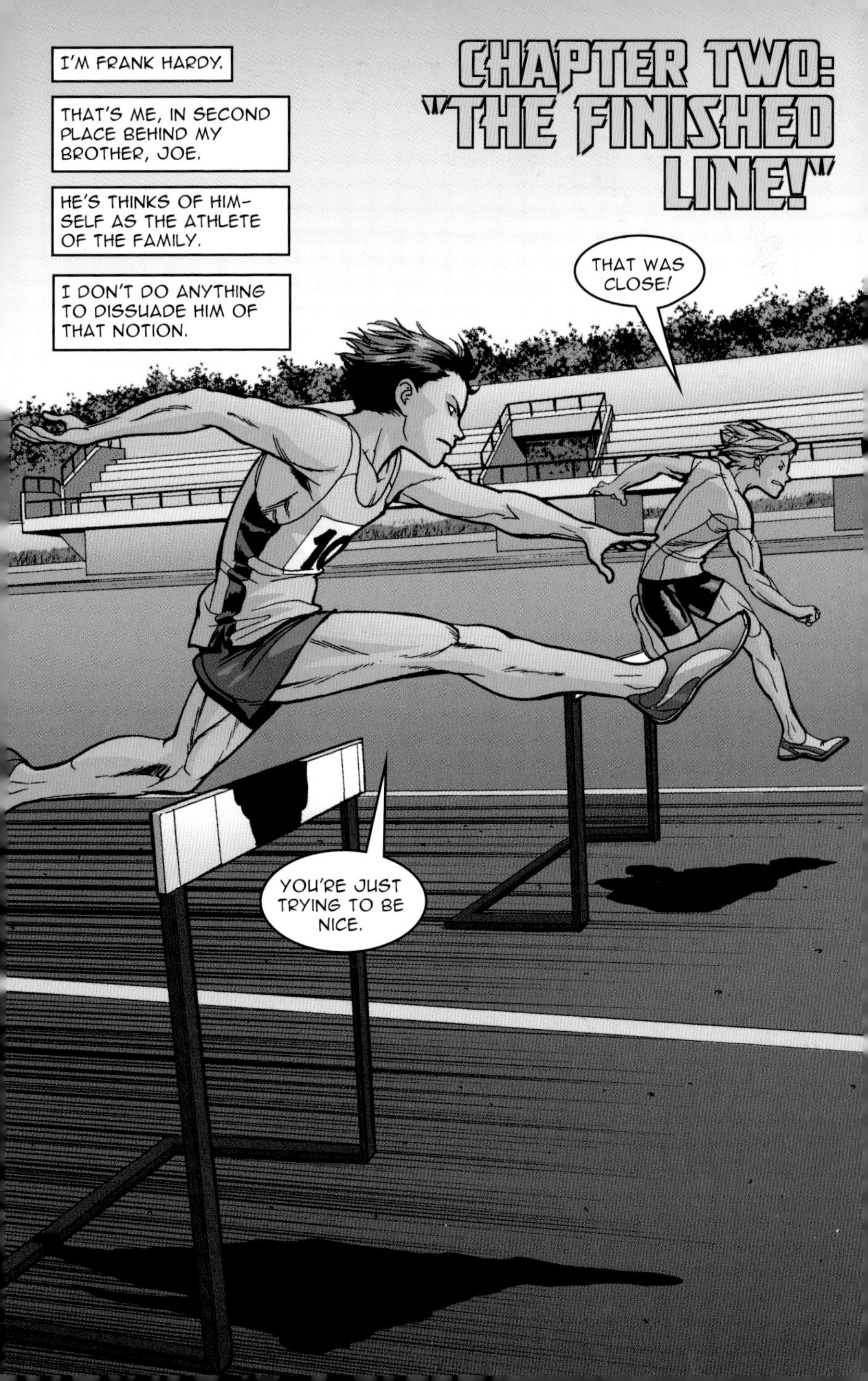

CHAPTER TWO: "THE FINISHED LINE!"
I'M FRANK HARDY.
THAT'S ME, IN SECOND PLACE BEHIND MY BROTHER, JOE.
HE'S THINKS OF HIM-SELF AS THE ATHLETE OF THE FAMILY.
I DON'T DO ANYTHING TO DISSUADE HIM OF THAT NOTION.
THAT WAS CLOSE!
YOU'RE JUST TRYING TO BE NICE.

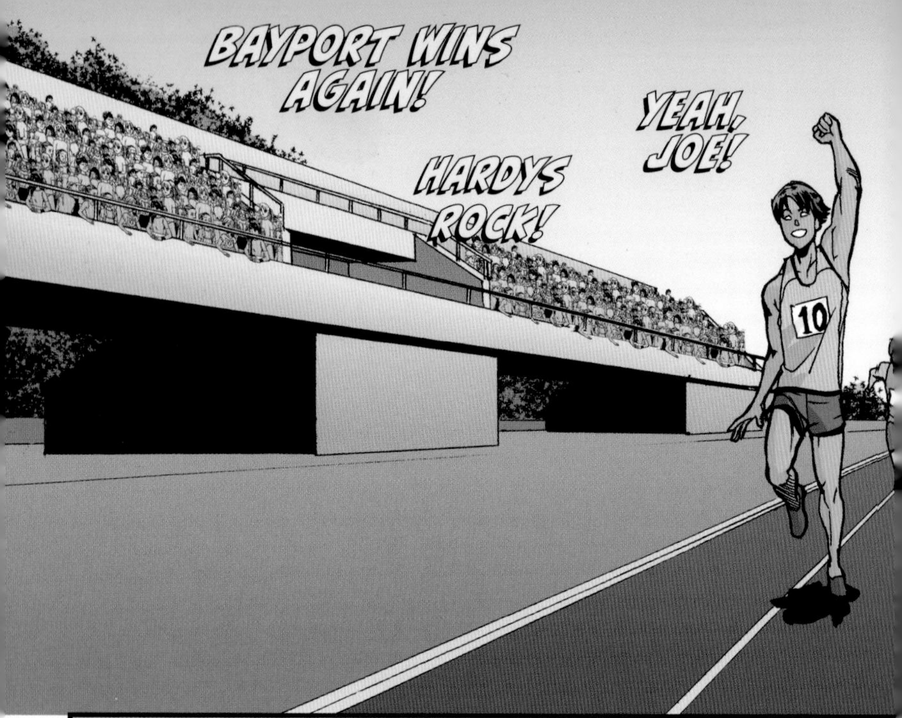
BAYPORT WINS AGAIN!
HARDYS ROCK!
YEAH, JOE!
10

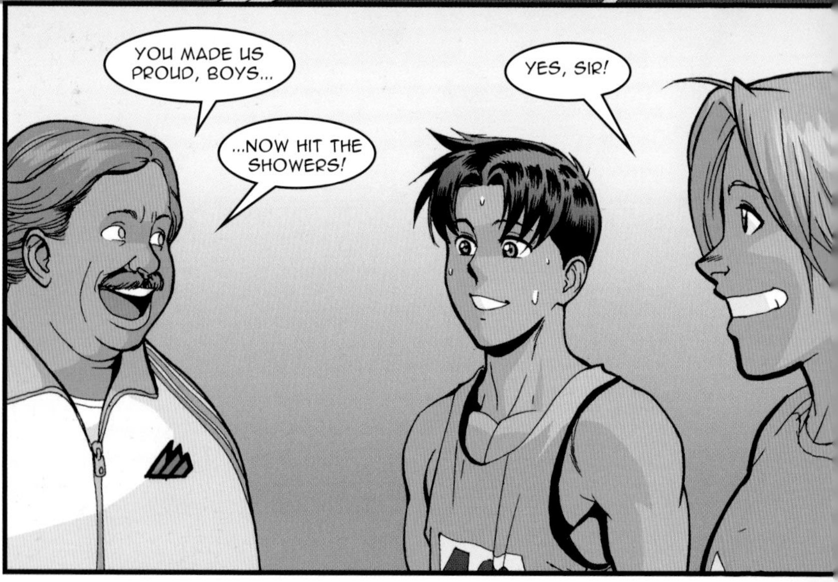
YOU MADE US PROUD, BOYS...
...NOW HIT THE SHOWERS!
YES, SIR!

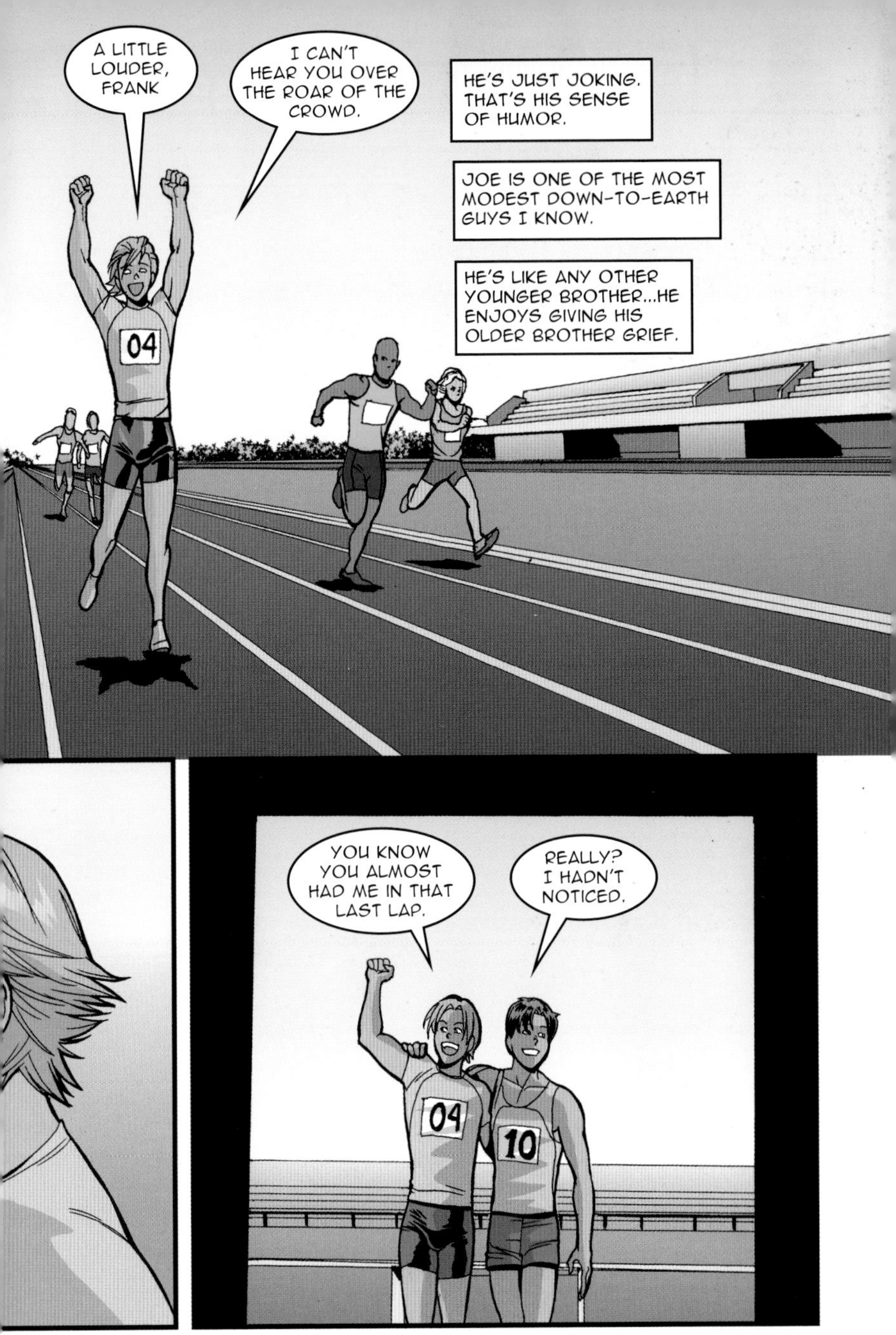
A LITTLE LOUDER, FRANK
I CAN'T HEAR YOU OVER THE ROAR OF THE CROWD.
HE'S JUST JOKING. THAT'S HIS SENSE OF HUMOR.
JOE IS ONE OF THE MOST MODEST DOWN-TO-EARTH GUYS I KNOW.
HE'S LIKE ANY OTHER YOUNGER BROTHER...HE ENJOYS GIVING HIS OLDER BROTHER GRIEF.
04
YOU KNOW YOU ALMOST HAD ME IN THAT LAST LAP.
REALLY? I HADN'T NOTICED.
04
10

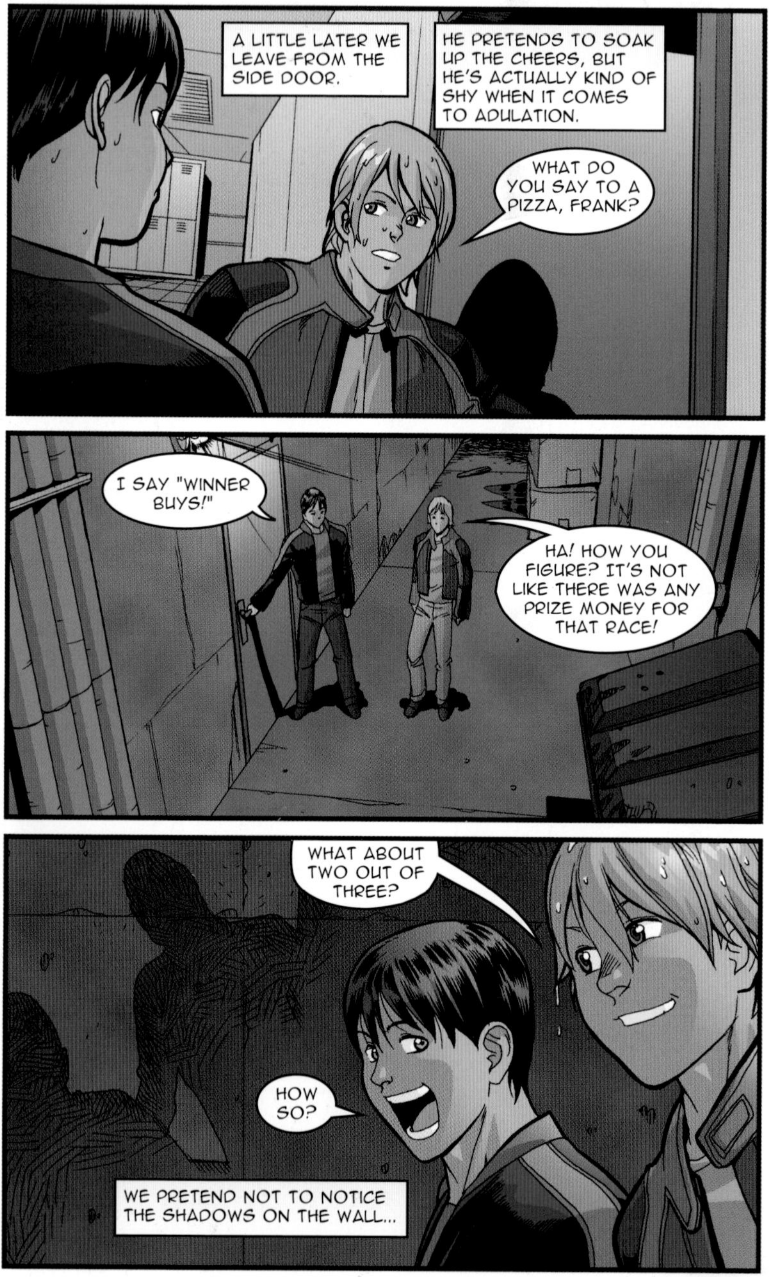
A LITTLE LATER WE LEAVE FROM THE SIDE DOOR.
HE PRETENDS TO SOAK UP THE CHEERS, BUT HE'S ACTUALLY KIND OF SHY WHEN IT COMES TO ADULATION.
WHAT DO YOU SAY TO A PIZZA, FRANK?
I SAY "WINNER BUYS!"
HA! HOW YOU FIGURE? IT'S NOT LIKE THERE WAS ANY PRIZE MONEY FOR THAT RACE!
WHAT ABOUT TWO OUT OF THREE?
HOW SO?
WE PRETEND NOT TO NOTICE THE SHADOWS ON THE WALL...

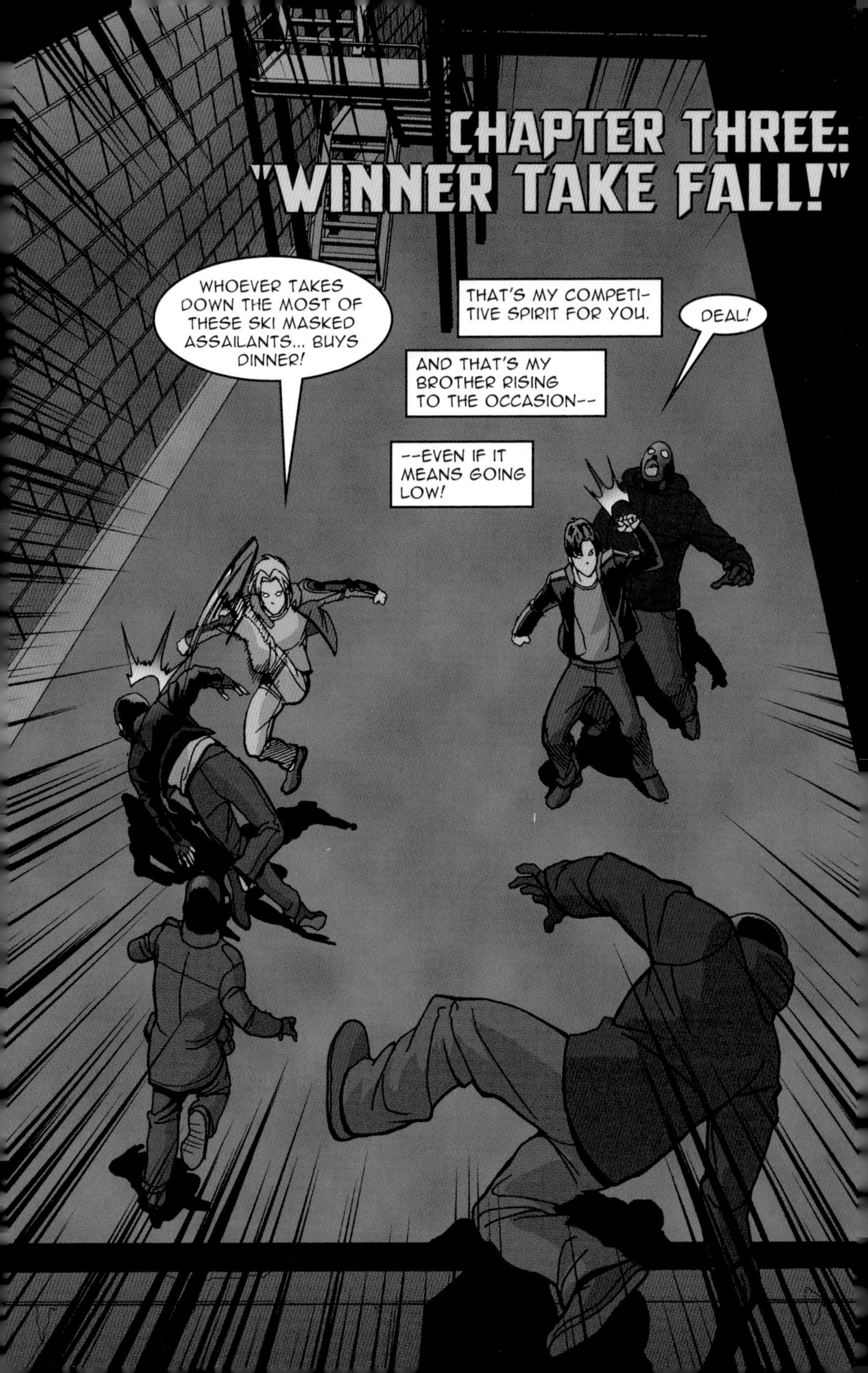
CHAPTER THREE:
"WINNER TAKE FALL!"
WHOEVER TAKES DOWN THE MOST OF THESE SKI MASKED ASSAILANTS... BUYS DINNER!
THAT'S MY COMPETITIVE SPIRIT FOR YOU.
AND THAT'S MY BROTHER RISING TO THE OCCASION--
DEAL!
--EVEN IF IT MEANS GOING LOW!

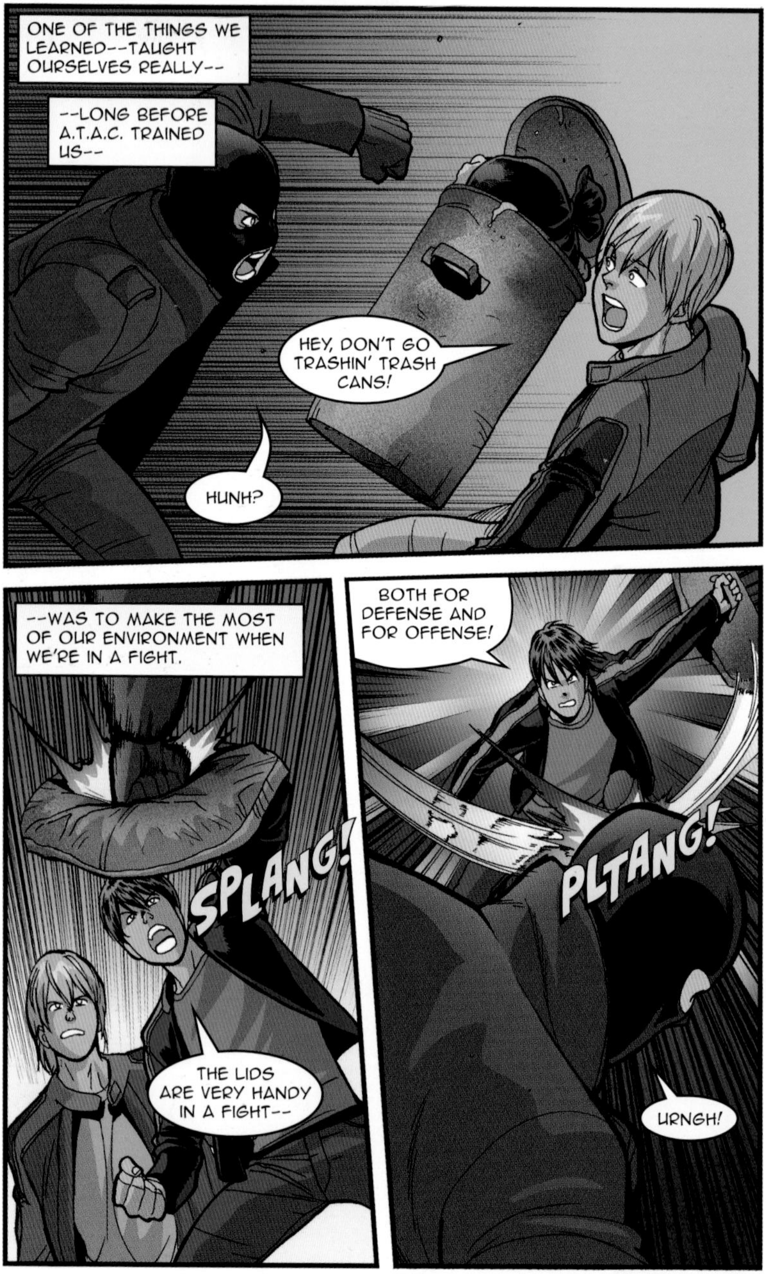
ONE OF THE THINGS WE LEARNED--TAUGHT OURSELVES REALLY--
--LONG BEFORE A.T.A.C. TRAINED US--
HEY, DON'T GO TRASHIN' TRASH CANS!
HUNH?
--WAS TO MAKE THE MOST OF OUR ENVIRONMENT WHEN WE'RE IN A FIGHT.
SPLANG!
THE LIDS ARE VERY HANDY IN A FIGHT--
BOTH FOR DEFENSE AND FOR OFFENSE!
PLTANG!
URNGH!

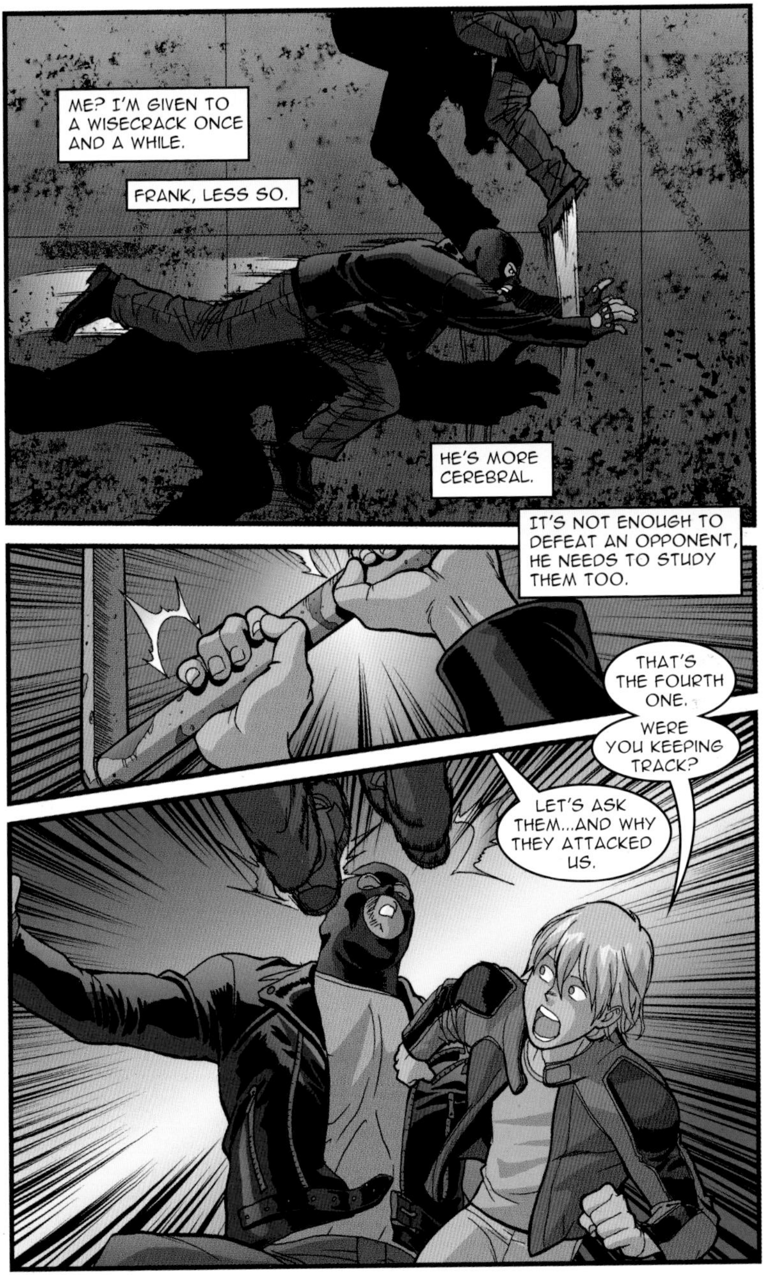
ME? I'M GIVEN TO A WISECRACK ONCE AND A WHILE.
FRANK, LESS SO.
HE'S MORE CEREBRAL.
IT'S NOT ENOUGH TO DEFEAT AN OPPONENT, HE NEEDS TO STUDY THEM TOO.
THAT'S THE FOURTH ONE.
WERE YOU KEEPING TRACK?
LET'S ASK THEM...AND WHY THEY ATTACKED US.

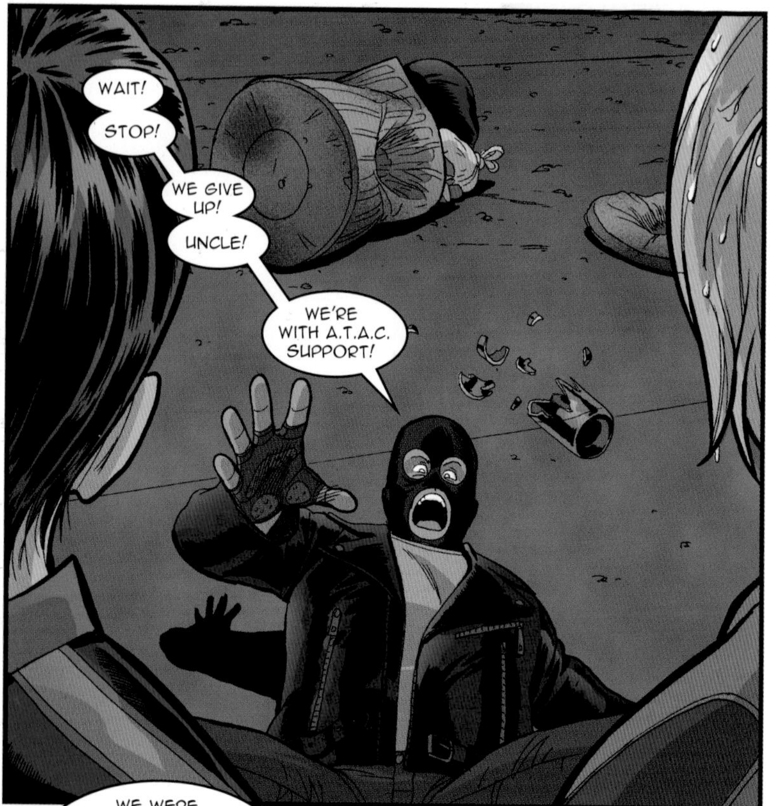
WAIT!
STOP!
WE GIVE UP!
UNCLE!
WE'RE WITH A.T.A.C. SUPPORT!

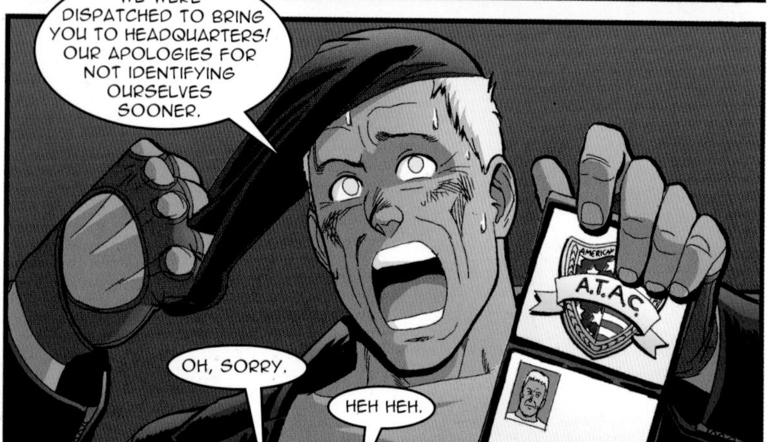
WE WERE DISPATCHED TO BRING YOU TO HEADQUARTERS! OUR APOLOGIES FOR NOT IDENTIFYING OURSELVES SOONER.
A.T.A.C.
OH, SORRY.
HEH HEH.

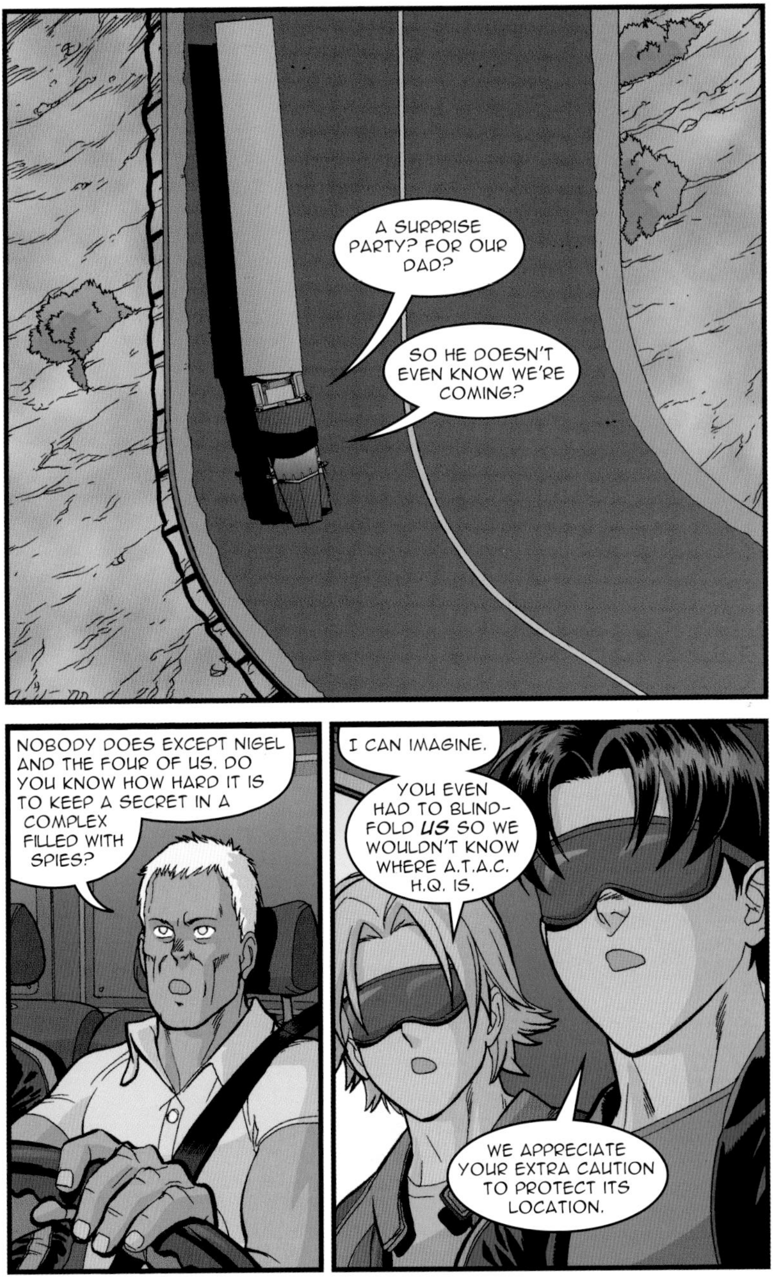
A SURPRISE PARTY? FOR OUR DAD?
SO HE DOESN'T EVEN KNOW WE'RE COMING?
NOBODY DOES EXCEPT NIGEL AND THE FOUR OF US. DO YOU KNOW HOW HARD IT IS TO KEEP A SECRET IN A COMPLEX FILLED WITH SPIES?
I CAN IMAGINE.
YOU EVEN HAD TO BLINDFOLD US SO WE WOULDN'T KNOW WHERE A.T.A.C. H.Q. IS.
WE APPRECIATE YOUR EXTRA CAUTION TO PROTECT ITS LOCATION.

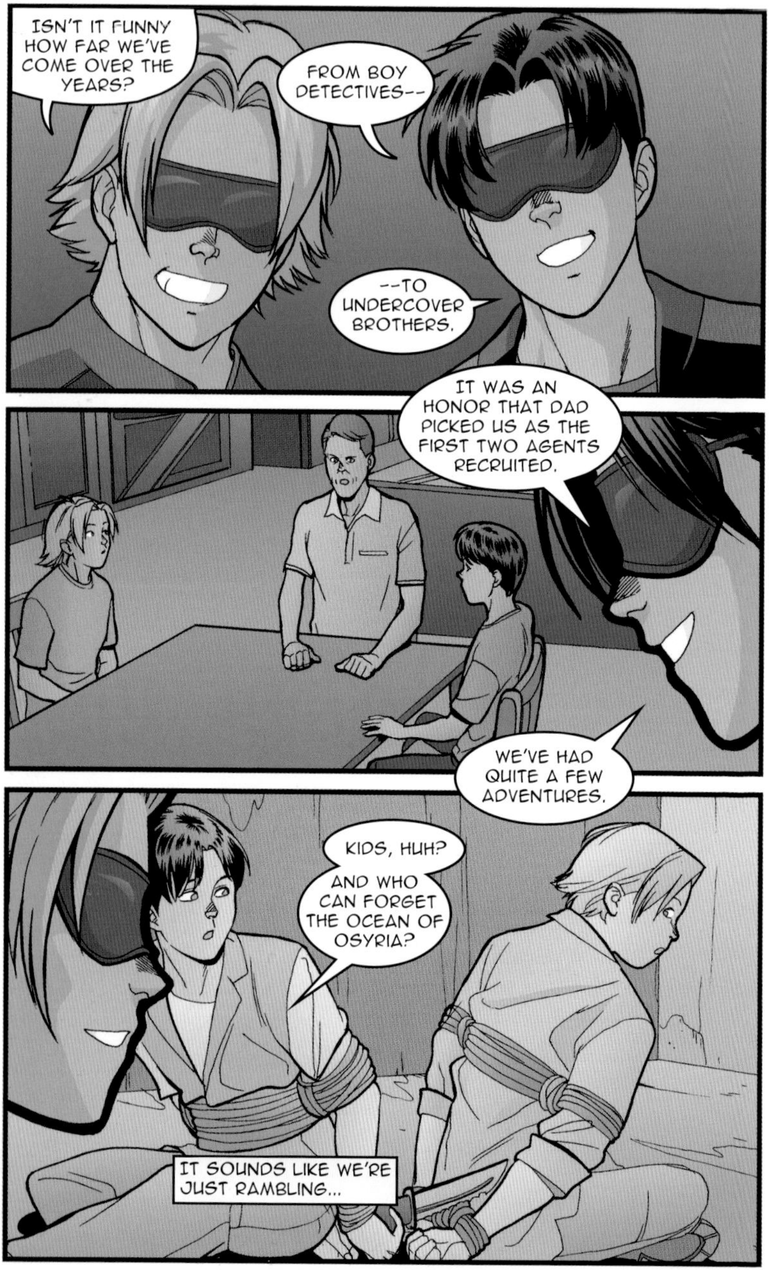
ISN'T IT FUNNY HOW FAR WE'VE COME OVER THE YEARS?
FROM BOY DETECTIVES--
--TO UNDERCOVER BROTHERS.
IT WAS AN HONOR THAT DAD PICKED US AS THE FIRST TWO AGENTS RECRUITED.
WE'VE HAD QUITE A FEW ADVENTURES.
KIDS, HUH?
AND WHO CAN FORGET THE OCEAN OF OSYRIA?
IT SOUNDS LIKE WE'RE JUST RAMBLING...

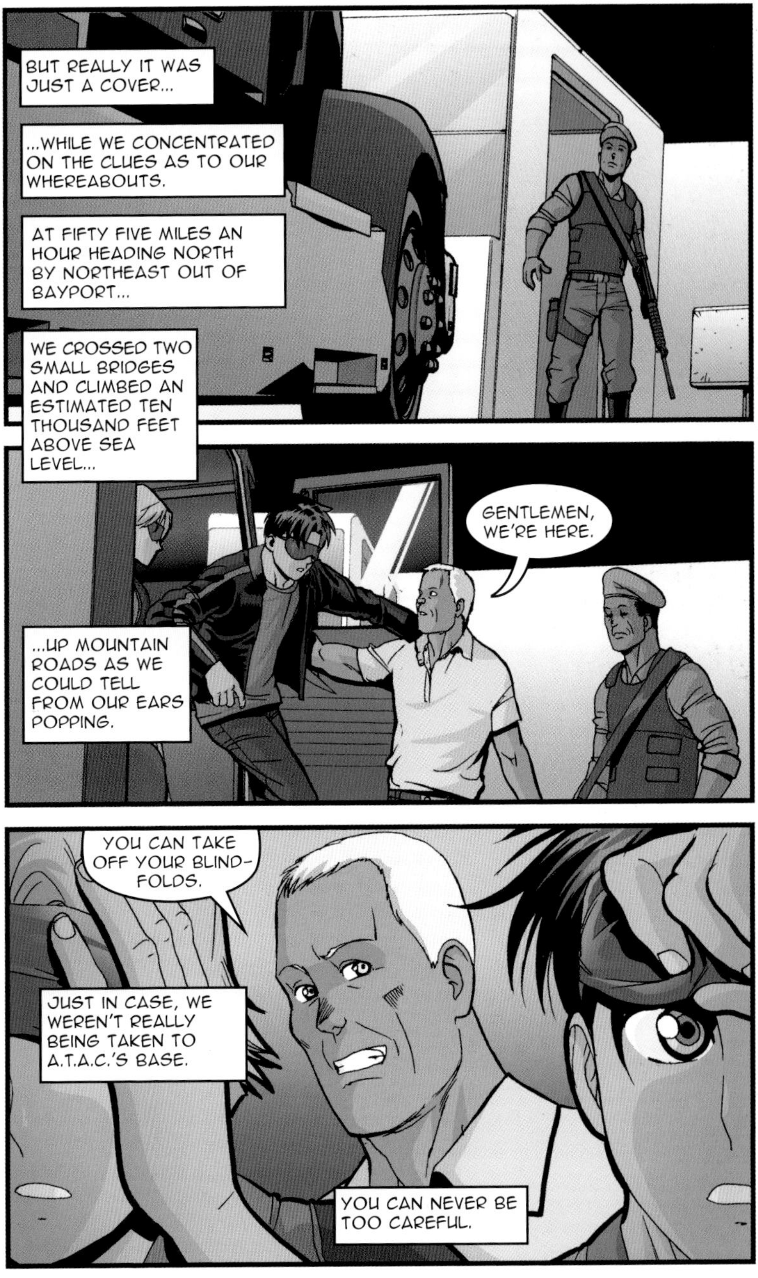
BUT REALLY IT WAS JUST A COVER...
...WHILE WE CONCENTRATED ON THE CLUES AS TO OUR WHEREABOUTS.
AT FIFTY FIVE MILES AN HOUR HEADING NORTH BY NORTHEAST OUT OF BAYPORT...
WE CROSSED TWO SMALL BRIDGES AND CLIMBED AN ESTIMATED TEN THOUSAND FEET ABOVE SEA LEVEL...
GENTLEMEN, WE'RE HERE.
...UP MOUNTAIN ROADS AS WE COULD TELL FROM OUR EARS POPPING.
YOU CAN TAKE OFF YOUR BLIND-FOLDS.
JUST IN CASE, WE WEREN'T REALLY BEING TAKEN TO A.T.A.C.'S BASE.
YOU CAN NEVER BE TOO CAREFUL.

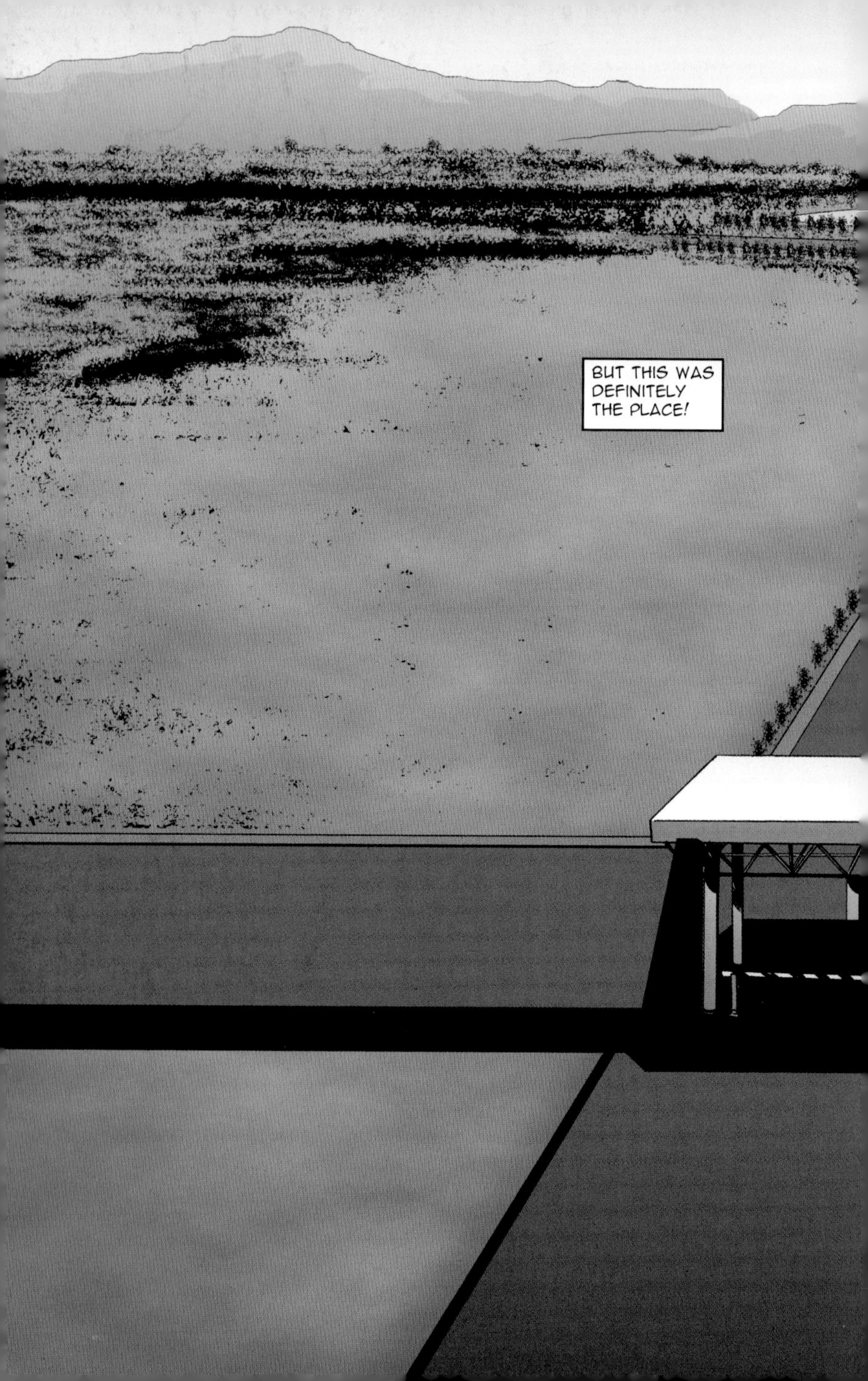
BUT THIS WAS DEFINITELY THE PLACE!

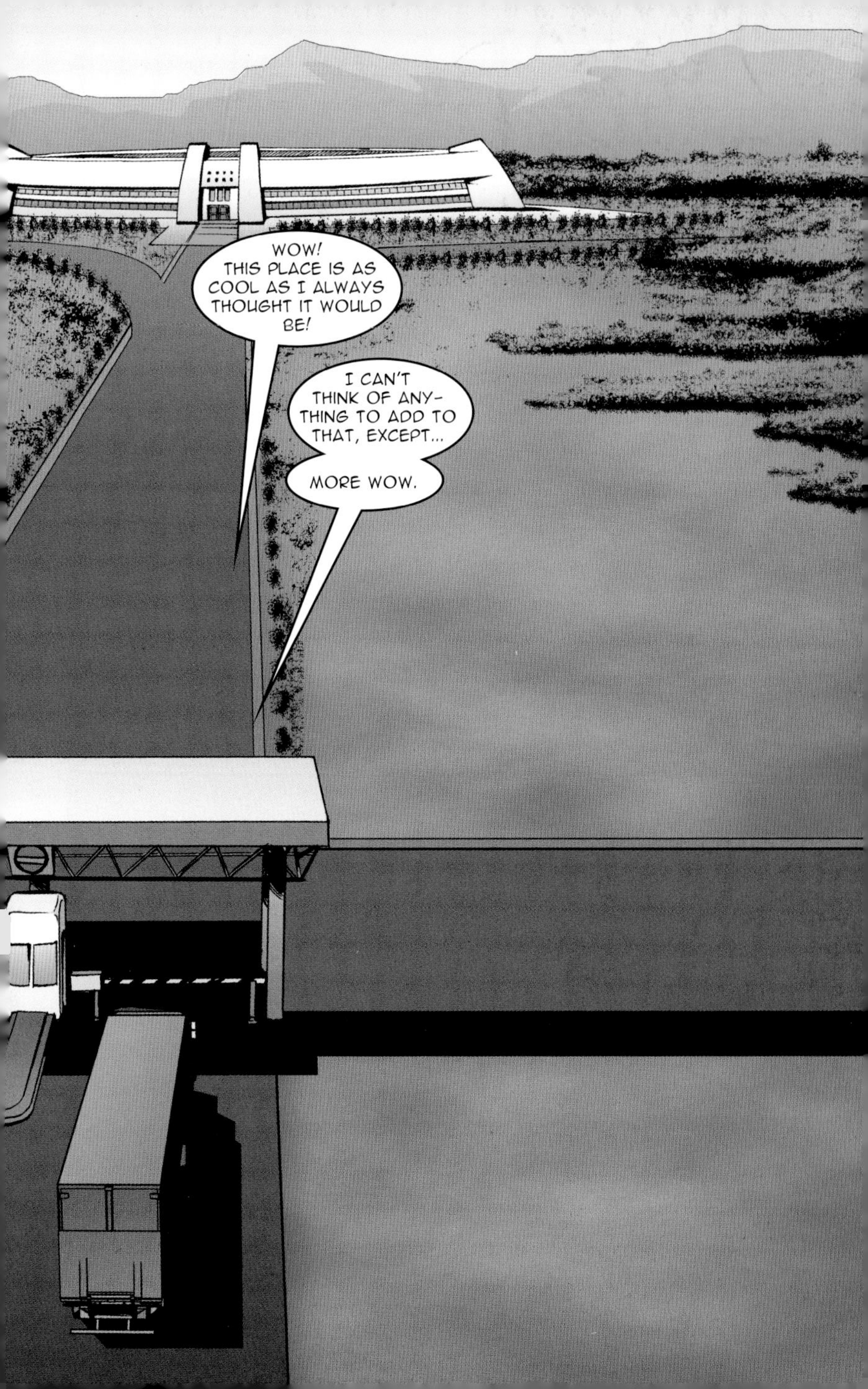
WOW! THIS PLACE IS AS COOL AS I ALWAYS THOUGHT IT WOULD BE!
I CAN'T THINK OF ANY-THING TO ADD TO THAT, EXCEPT...
MORE WOW.

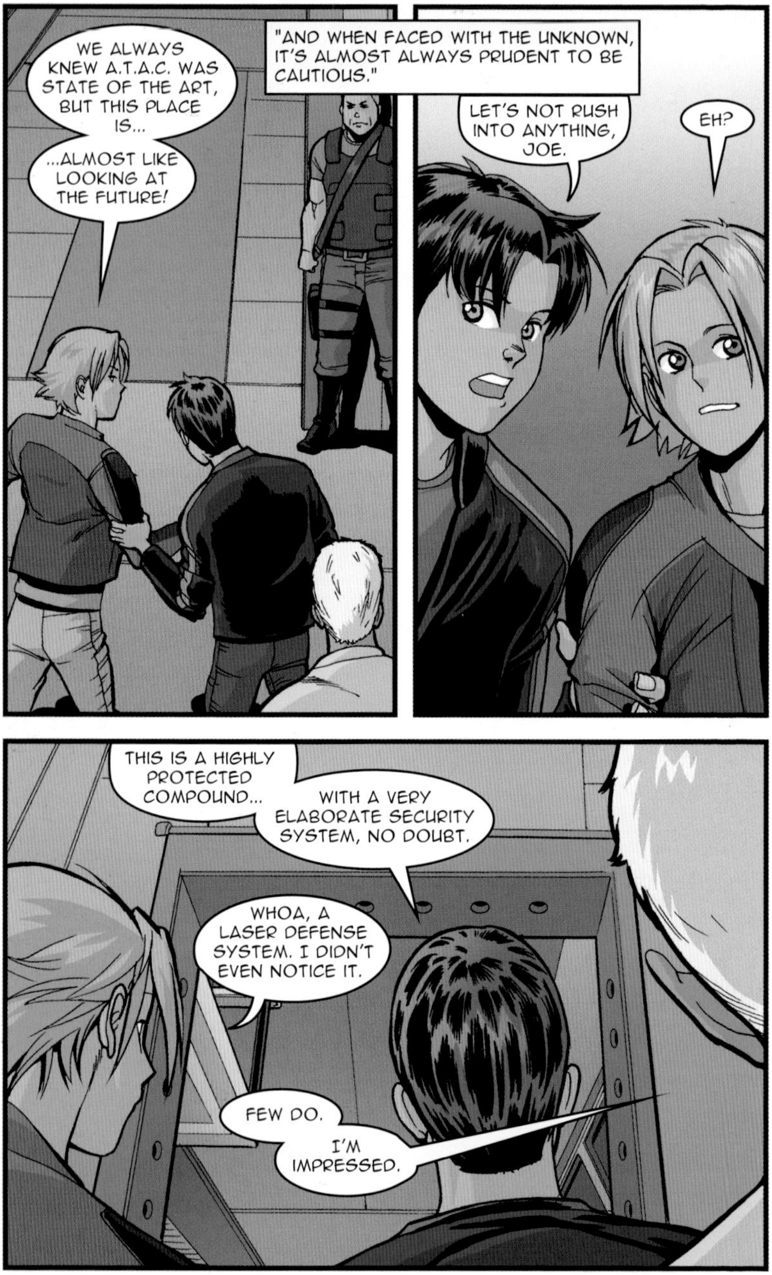
WE ALWAYS KNEW A.T.A.C. WAS STATE OF THE ART, BUT THIS PLACE IS...
...ALMOST LIKE LOOKING AT THE FUTURE!
"AND WHEN FACED WITH THE UNKNOWN, IT'S ALMOST ALWAYS PRUDENT TO BE CAUTIOUS."
LET'S NOT RUSH INTO ANYTHING, JOE.
EH?
THIS IS A HIGHLY PROTECTED COMPOUND...
WITH A VERY ELABORATE SECURITY SYSTEM, NO DOUBT.
WHOA, A LASER DEFENSE SYSTEM. I DIDN'T EVEN NOTICE IT.
FEW DO.
I'M IMPRESSED.

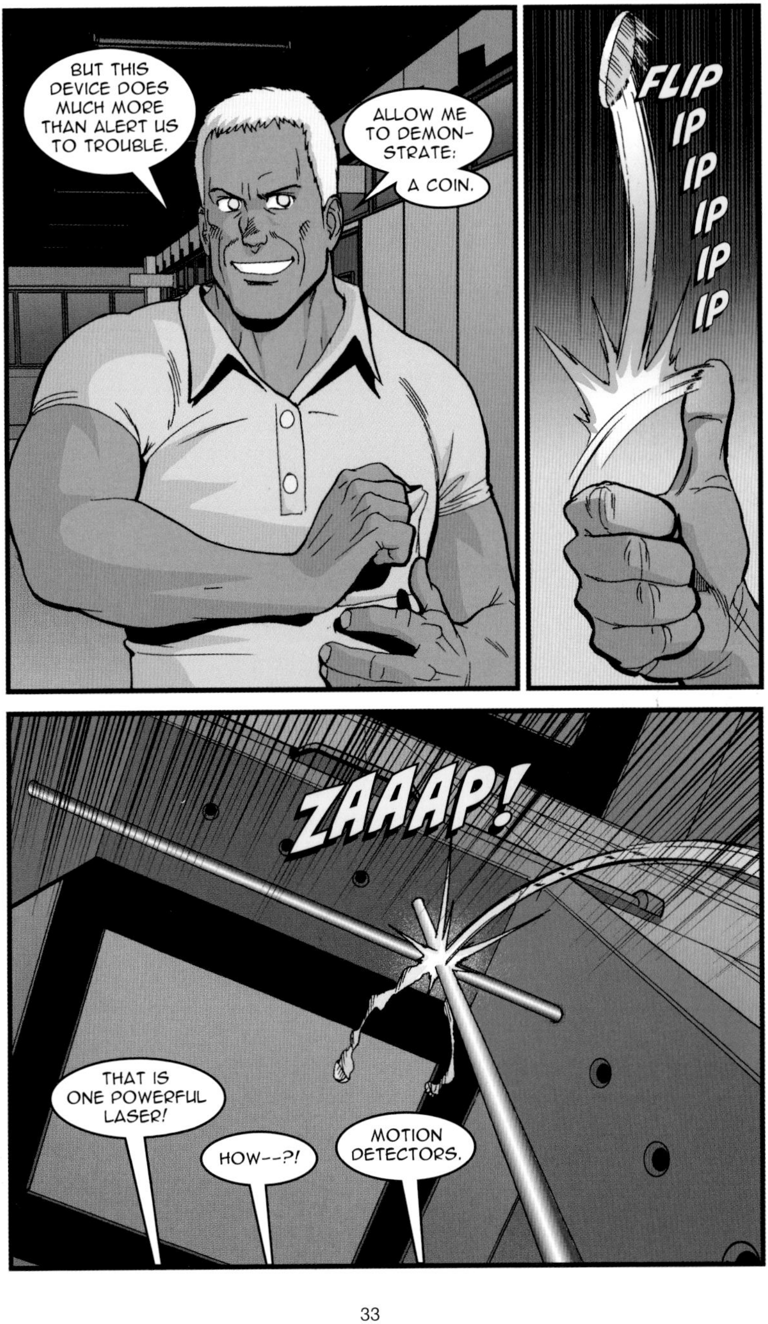
BUT THIS DEVICE DOES MUCH MORE THAN ALERT US TO TROUBLE.
ALLOW ME TO DEMON-STRATE:
A COIN.
FLIP IP IP IP IP IP
ZAAAP!
THAT IS ONE POWERFUL LASER!
HOW--?!
MOTION DETECTORS.

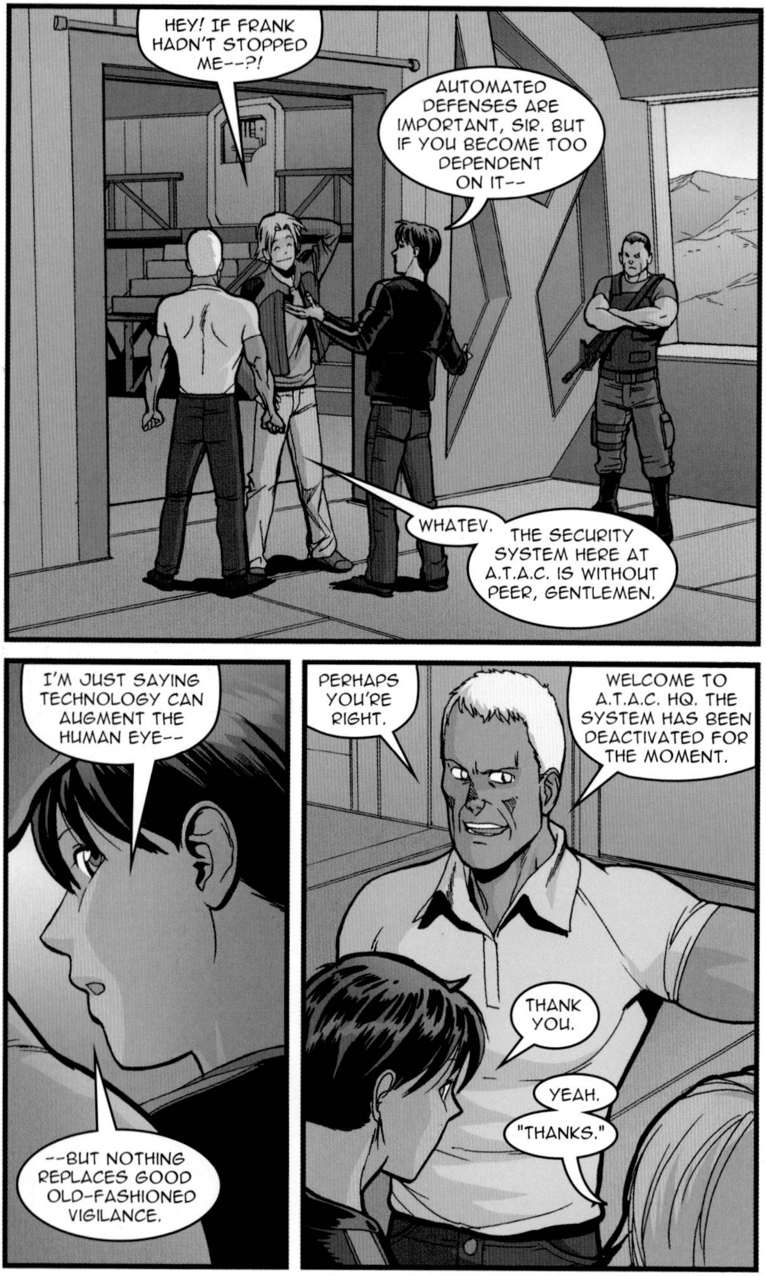
HEY! IF FRANK HADN'T STOPPED ME--?!
AUTOMATED DEFENSES ARE IMPORTANT, SIR. BUT IF YOU BECOME TOO DEPENDENT ON IT--
WHATEV.
THE SECURITY SYSTEM HERE AT A.T.A.C. IS WITHOUT PEER, GENTLEMEN.
I'M JUST SAYING TECHNOLOGY CAN AUGMENT THE HUMAN EYE--
--BUT NOTHING REPLACES GOOD OLD-FASHIONED VIGILANCE.
PERHAPS YOU'RE RIGHT.
WELCOME TO A.T.A.C. HQ. THE SYSTEM HAS BEEN DEACTIVATED FOR THE MOMENT.
THANK YOU.
YEAH.
"THANKS."

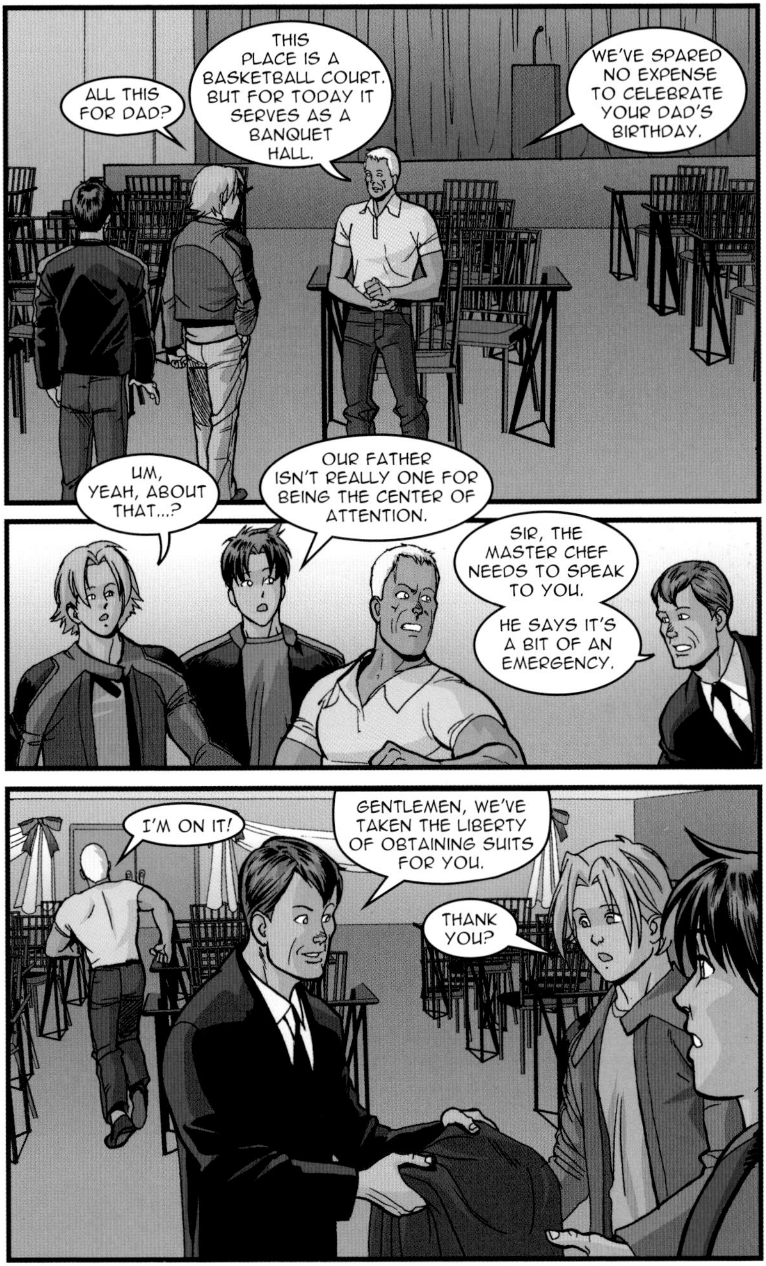
ALL THIS FOR DAD?
THIS PLACE IS A BASKETBALL COURT. BUT FOR TODAY IT SERVES AS A BANQUET HALL.
WE'VE SPARED NO EXPENSE TO CELEBRATE YOUR DAD'S BIRTHDAY.
UM, YEAH, ABOUT THAT...?
OUR FATHER ISN'T REALLY ONE FOR BEING THE CENTER OF ATTENTION.
SIR, THE MASTER CHEF NEEDS TO SPEAK TO YOU.
HE SAYS IT'S A BIT OF AN EMERGENCY.
I'M ON IT!
GENTLEMEN, WE'VE TAKEN THE LIBERTY OF OBTAINING SUITS FOR YOU.
THANK YOU?

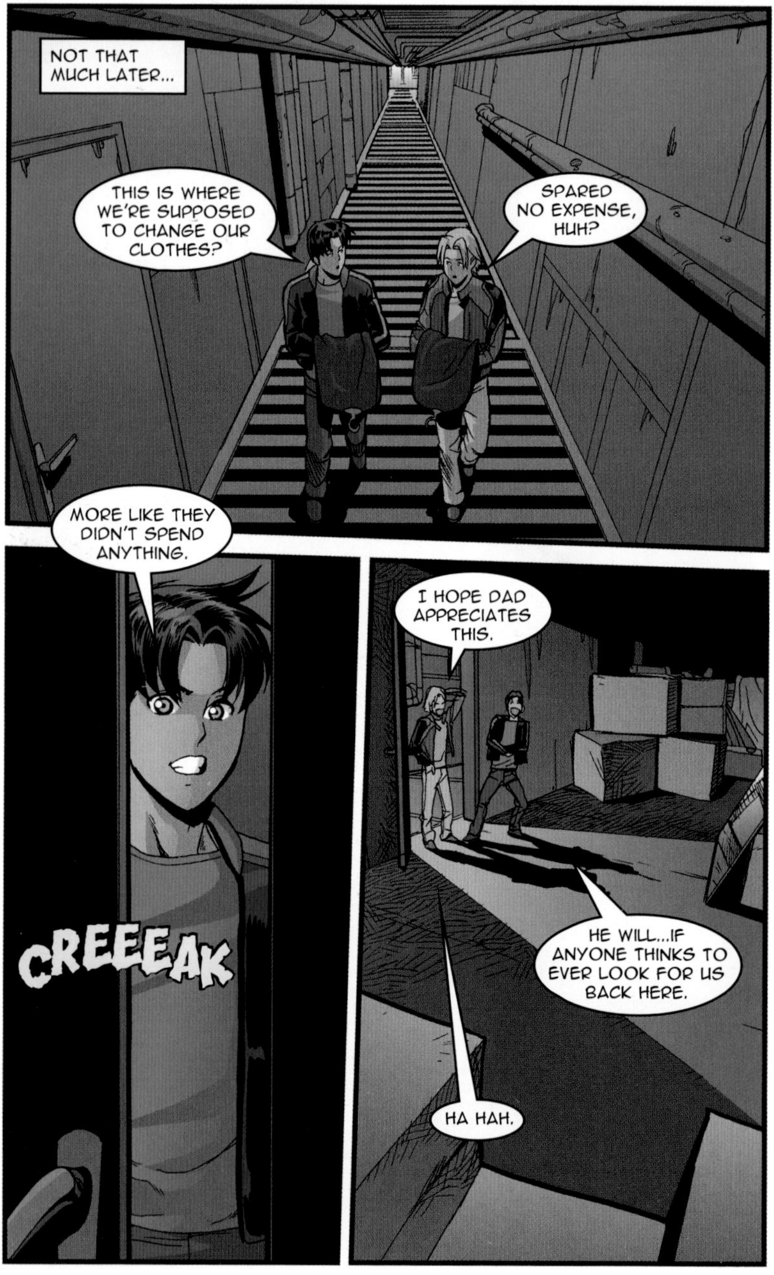
NOT THAT MUCH LATER...
THIS IS WHERE WE'RE SUPPOSED TO CHANGE OUR CLOTHES?
SPARED NO EXPENSE, HUH?
MORE LIKE THEY DIDN'T SPEND ANYTHING.
CREEEAK
I HOPE DAD APPRECIATES THIS.
HE WILL...IF ANYONE THINKS TO EVER LOOK FOR US BACK HERE.
HA HAH.

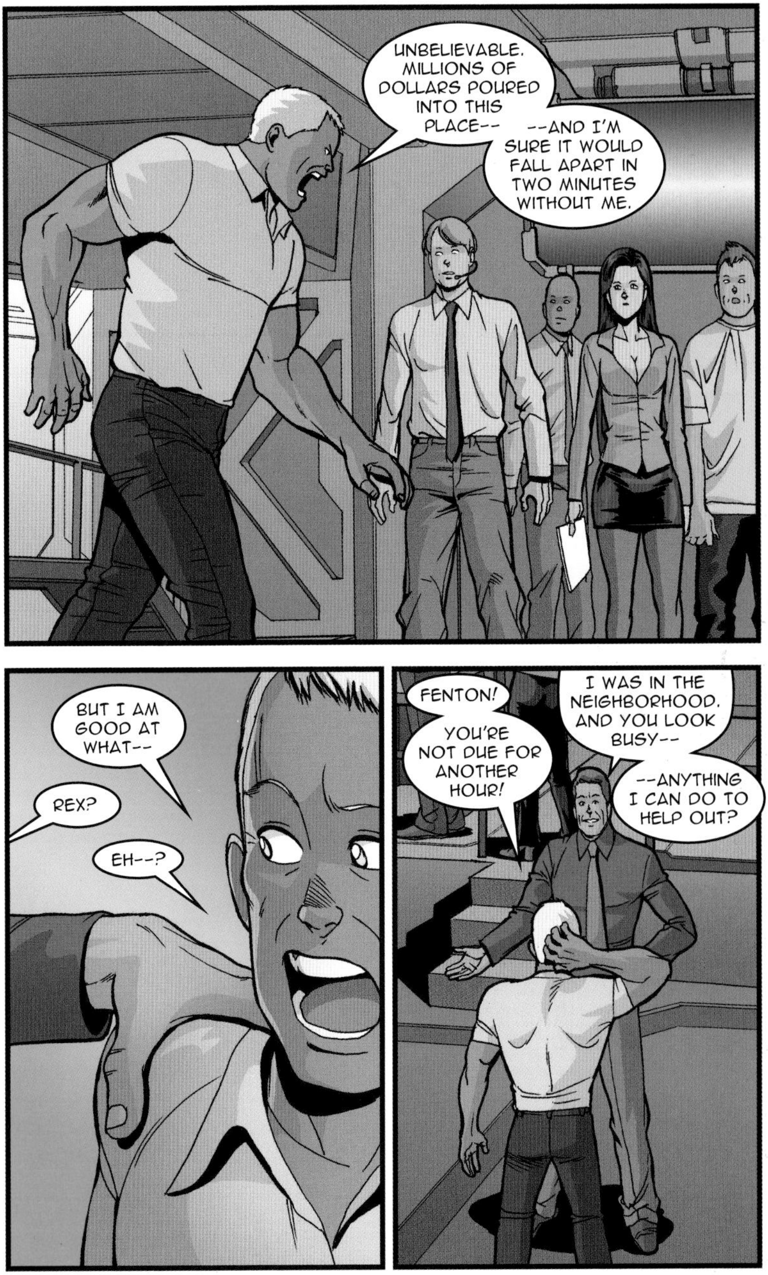
UNBELIEVABLE. MILLIONS OF DOLLARS POURED INTO THIS PLACE--
--AND I'M SURE IT WOULD FALL APART IN TWO MINUTES WITHOUT ME.
BUT I AM GOOD AT WHAT--
REX?
EH--?
FENTON!
YOU'RE NOT DUE FOR ANOTHER HOUR!
I WAS IN THE NEIGHBORHOOD. AND YOU LOOK BUSY--
--ANYTHING I CAN DO TO HELP OUT?

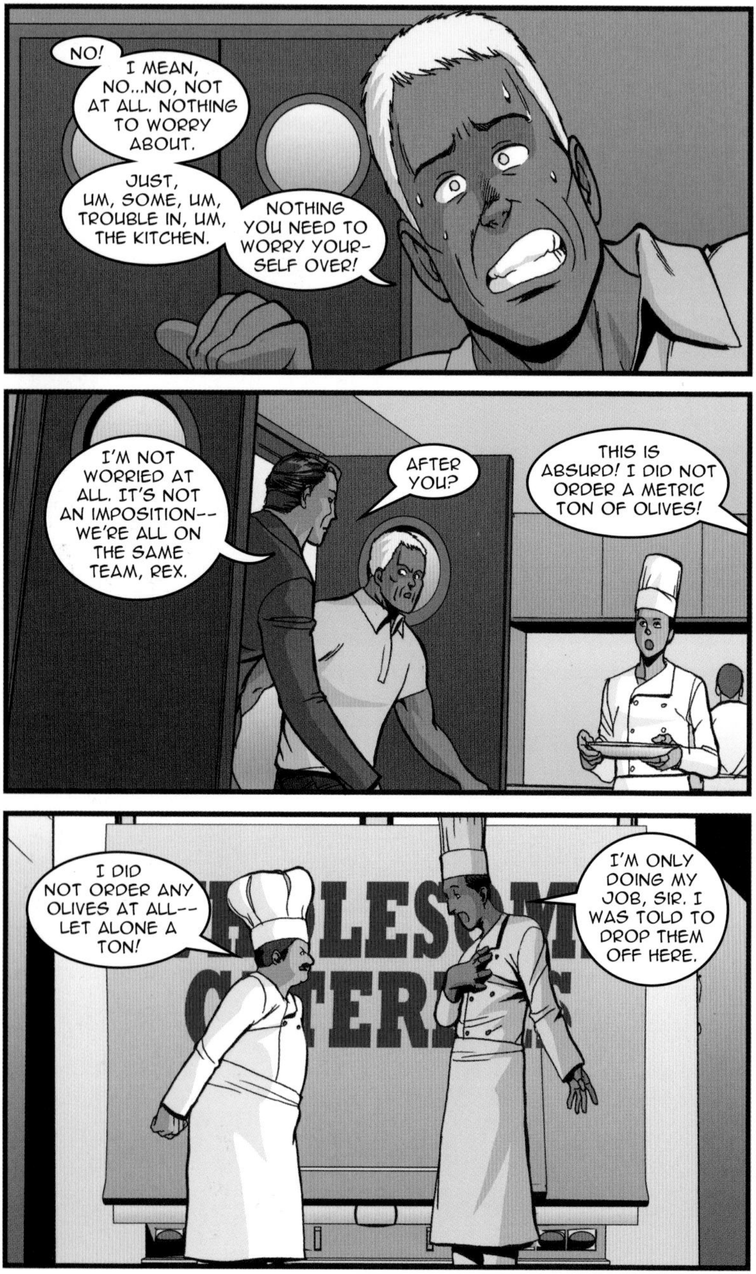
NO!
I MEAN, NO...NO, NOT AT ALL. NOTHING TO WORRY ABOUT.
JUST, UM, SOME, UM, TROUBLE IN, UM, THE KITCHEN.
NOTHING YOU NEED TO WORRY YOURSELF OVER!
I'M NOT WORRIED AT ALL. IT'S NOT AN IMPOSITION--WE'RE ALL ON THE SAME TEAM, REX.
AFTER YOU?
THIS IS ABSURD! I DID NOT ORDER A METRIC TON OF OLIVES!
I DID NOT ORDER ANY OLIVES AT ALL--LET ALONE A TON!
I'M ONLY DOING MY JOB, SIR. I WAS TOLD TO DROP THEM OFF HERE.

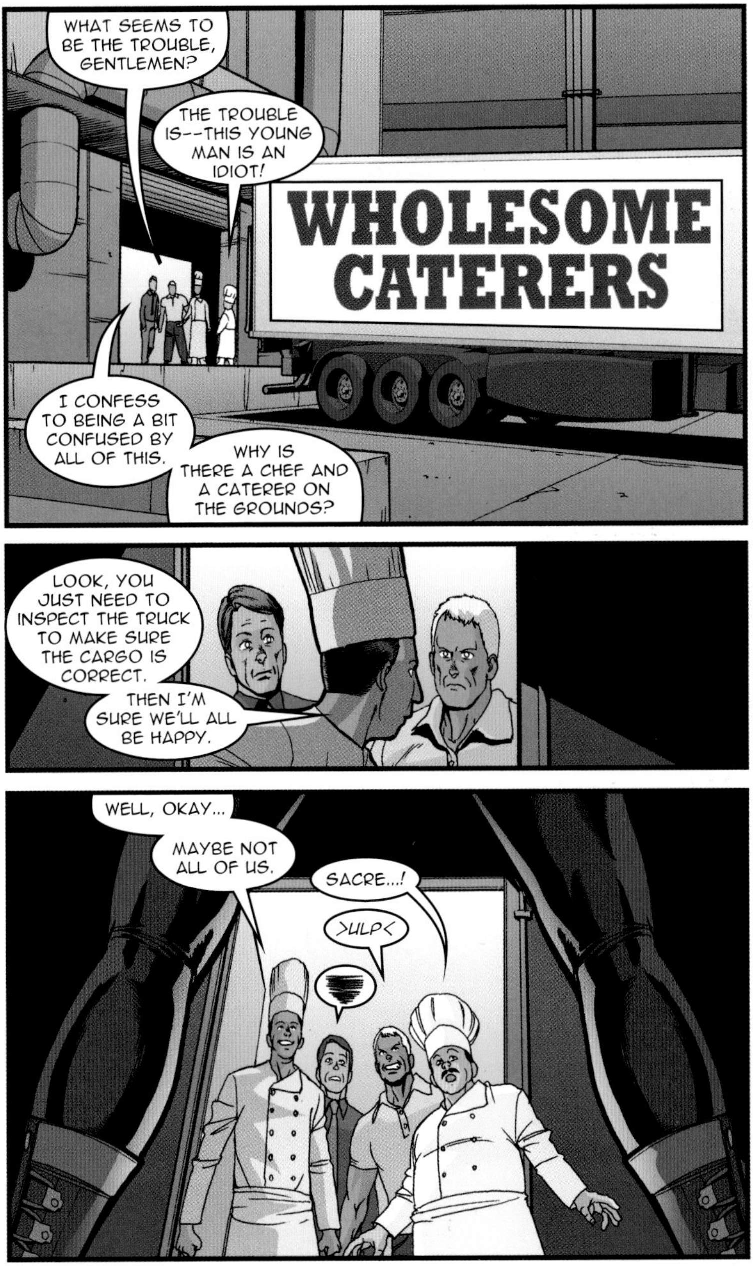
WHAT SEEMS TO BE THE TROUBLE, GENTLEMEN?
THE TROUBLE IS--THIS YOUNG MAN IS AN IDIOT!
WHOLESOME CATERERS
I CONFESS TO BEING A BIT CONFUSED BY ALL OF THIS.
WHY IS THERE A CHEF AND A CATERER ON THE GROUNDS?
LOOK, YOU JUST NEED TO INSPECT THE TRUCK TO MAKE SURE THE CARGO IS CORRECT.
THEN I'M SURE WE'LL ALL BE HAPPY.
WELL, OKAY...
MAYBE NOT ALL OF US.
SACRE...!
>ULP<

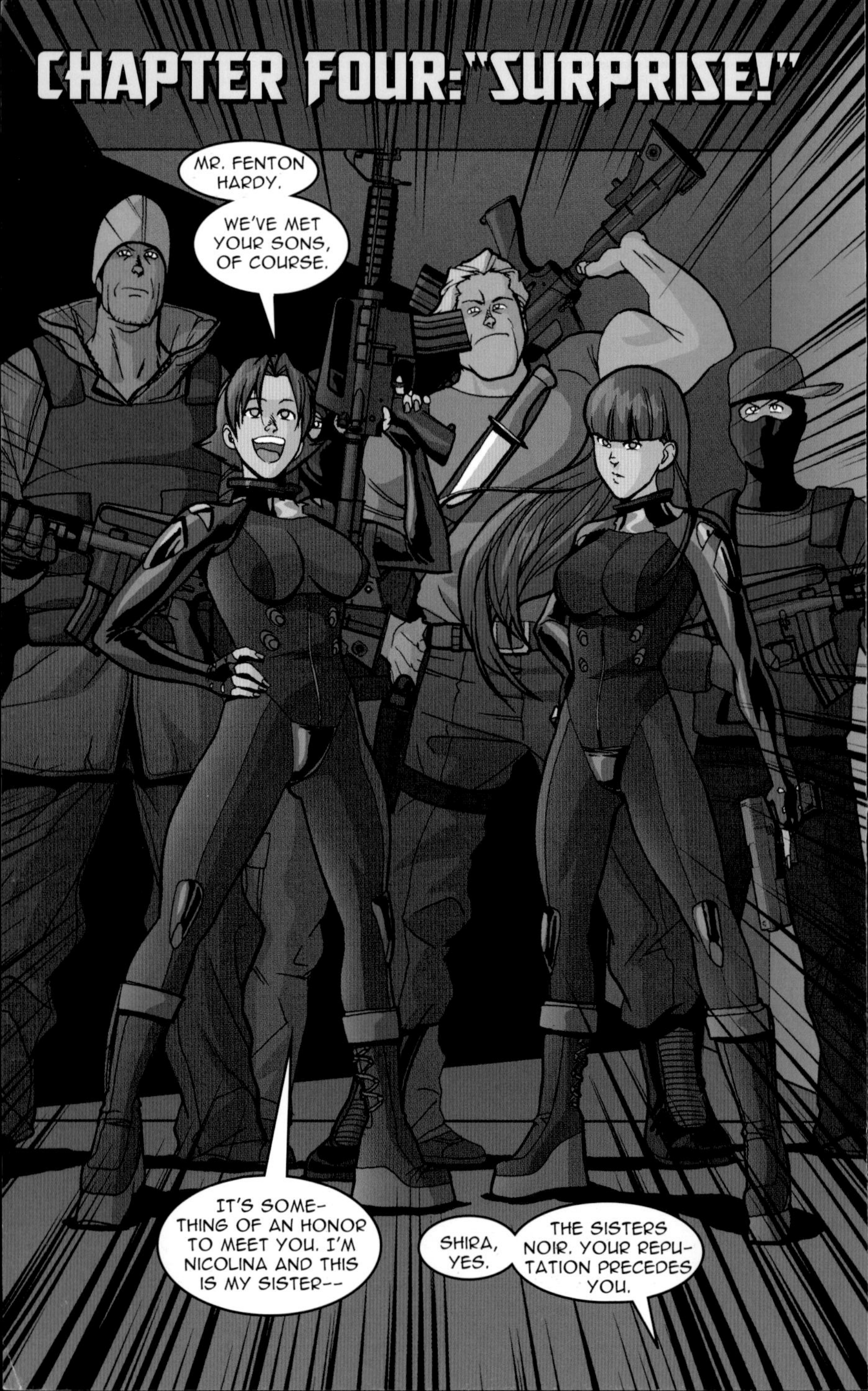
CHAPTER FOUR: "SURPRISE!"
MR. FENTON HARDY.
WE'VE MET YOUR SONS, OF COURSE.
IT'S SOMETHING OF AN HONOR TO MEET YOU. I'M NICOLINA AND THIS IS MY SISTER--
SHIRA, YES.
THE SISTERS NOIR. YOUR REPUTATION PRECEDES YOU.

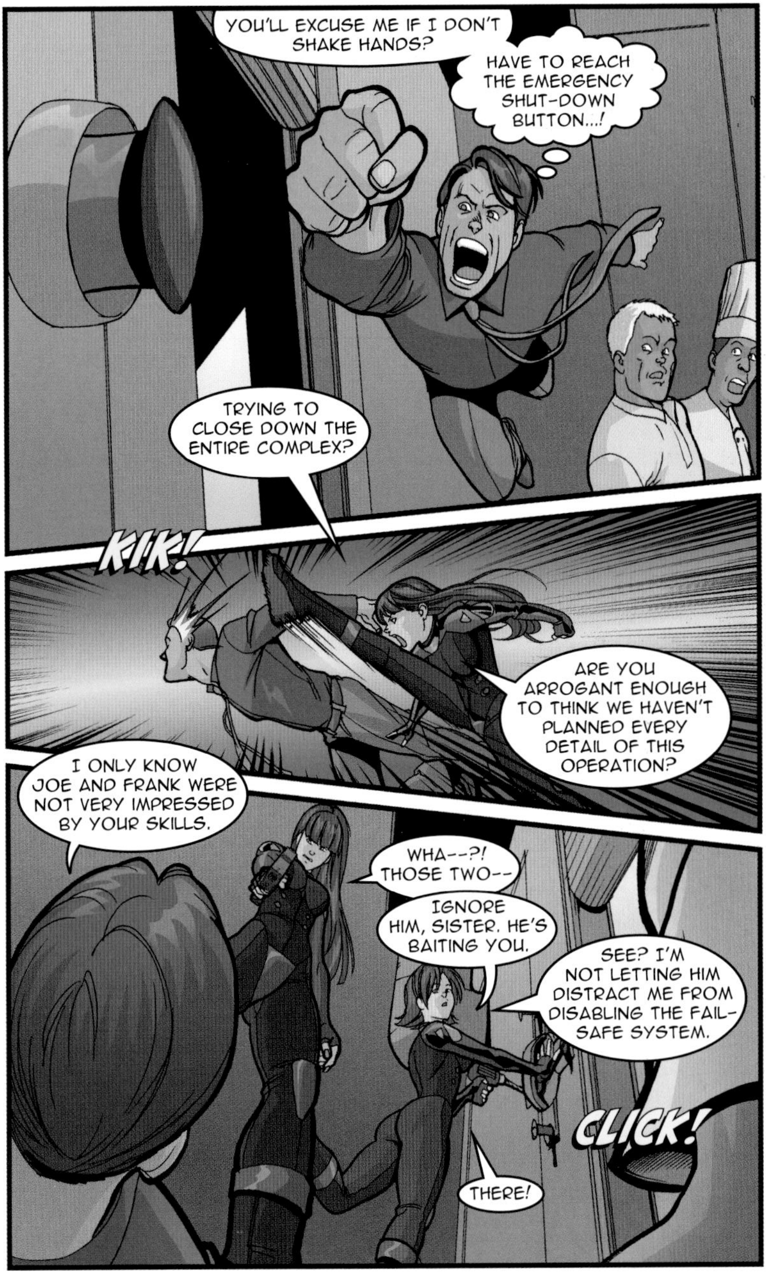
YOU'LL EXCUSE ME IF I DON'T SHAKE HANDS?
HAVE TO REACH THE EMERGENCY SHUT-DOWN BUTTON...!
TRYING TO CLOSE DOWN THE ENTIRE COMPLEX?
KIK!
ARE YOU ARROGANT ENOUGH TO THINK WE HAVEN'T PLANNED EVERY DETAIL OF THIS OPERATION?
I ONLY KNOW JOE AND FRANK WERE NOT VERY IMPRESSED BY YOUR SKILLS.
WHA--?! THOSE TWO--
IGNORE HIM, SISTER. HE'S BAITING YOU.
SEE? I'M NOT LETTING HIM DISTRACT ME FROM DISABLING THE FAIL-SAFE SYSTEM.
CLICK!
THERE!

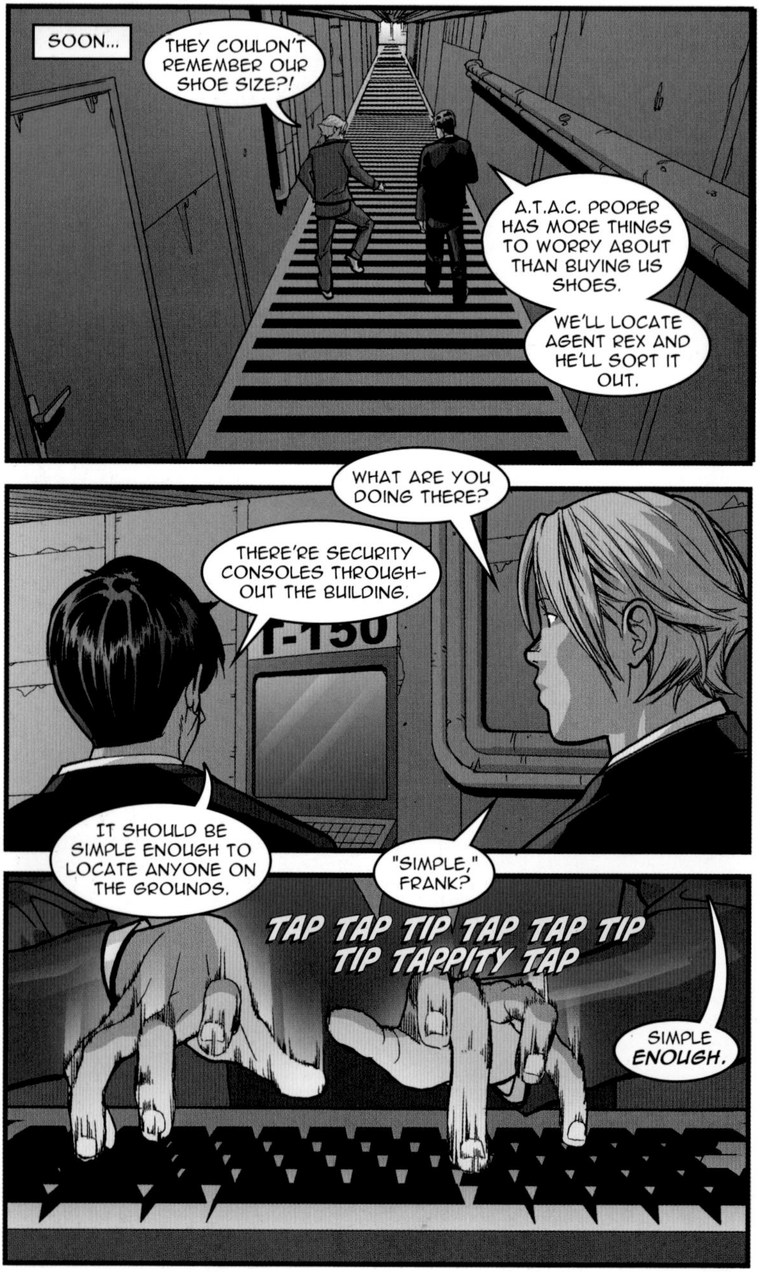
SOON...
THEY COULDN'T REMEMBER OUR SHOE SIZE?!
A.T.A.C. PROPER HAS MORE THINGS TO WORRY ABOUT THAN BUYING US SHOES.
WE'LL LOCATE AGENT REX AND HE'LL SORT IT OUT.
WHAT ARE YOU DOING THERE?
THERE'RE SECURITY CONSOLES THROUGH-OUT THE BUILDING.
T-150
IT SHOULD BE SIMPLE ENOUGH TO LOCATE ANYONE ON THE GROUNDS.
"SIMPLE," FRANK?
TAP TAP TIP TAP TAP TIP TIP TAPPITY TAP
SIMPLE ENOUGH.

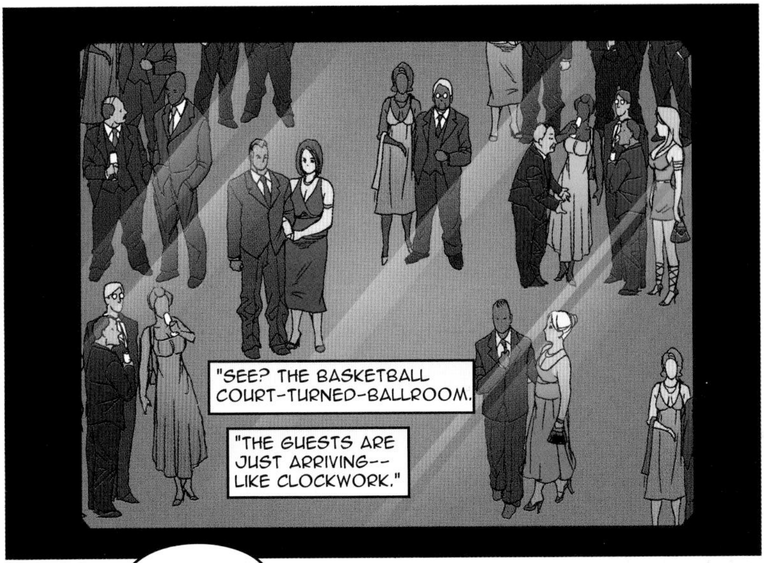
"SEE? THE BASKETBALL COURT-TURNED-BALLROOM.
"THE GUESTS ARE JUST ARRIVING--LIKE CLOCKWORK."

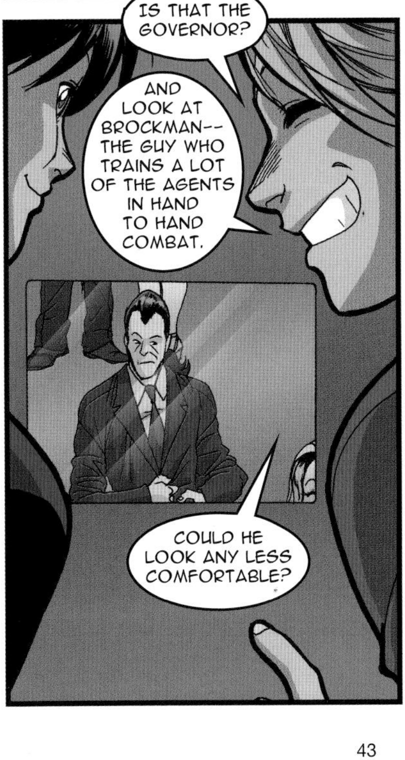
IS THAT THE GOVERNOR?
AND LOOK AT BROCKMAN--THE GUY WHO TRAINS A LOT OF THE AGENTS IN HAND TO HAND COMBAT.
COULD HE LOOK ANY LESS COMFORTABLE?

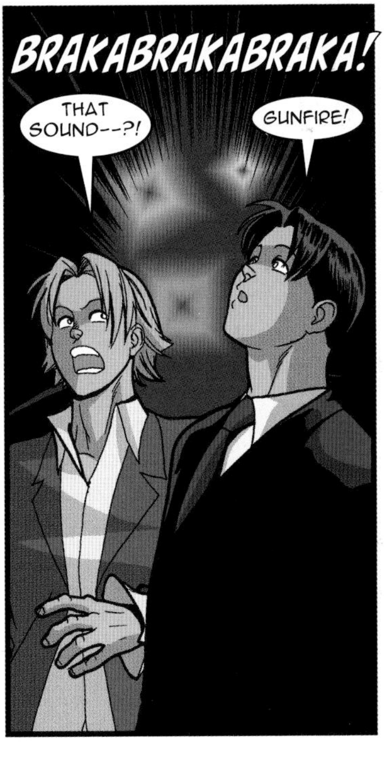
BRAKABRAKABRAKA!
THAT SOUND--?!
GUNFIRE!

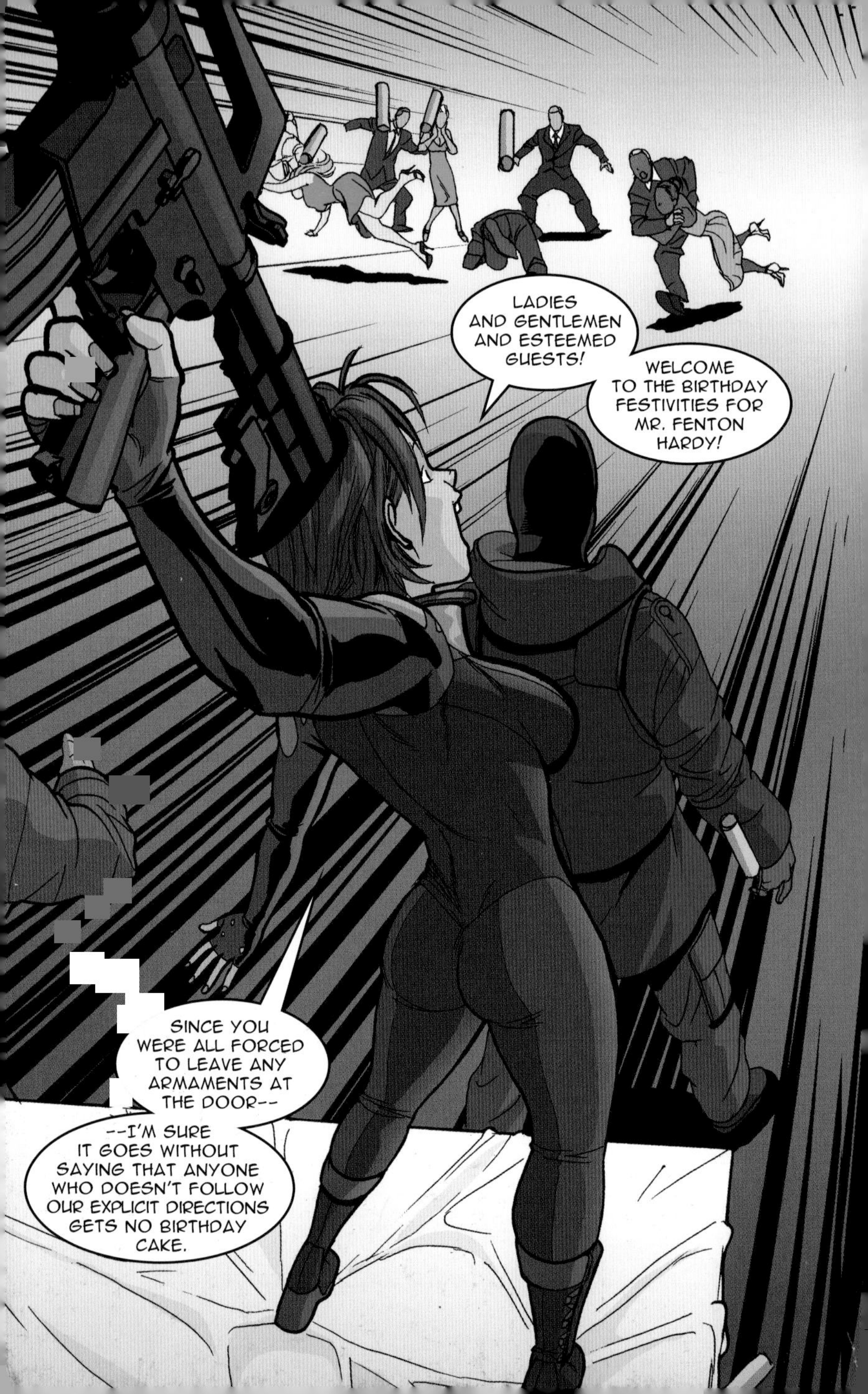
LADIES AND GENTLEMEN AND ESTEEMED GUESTS!
WELCOME TO THE BIRTHDAY FESTIVITIES FOR MR. FENTON HARDY!
SINCE YOU WERE ALL FORCED TO LEAVE ANY ARMAMENTS AT THE DOOR--
--I'M SURE IT GOES WITHOUT SAYING THAT ANYONE WHO DOESN'T FOLLOW OUR EXPLICIT DIRECTIONS GETS NO BIRTHDAY CAKE.

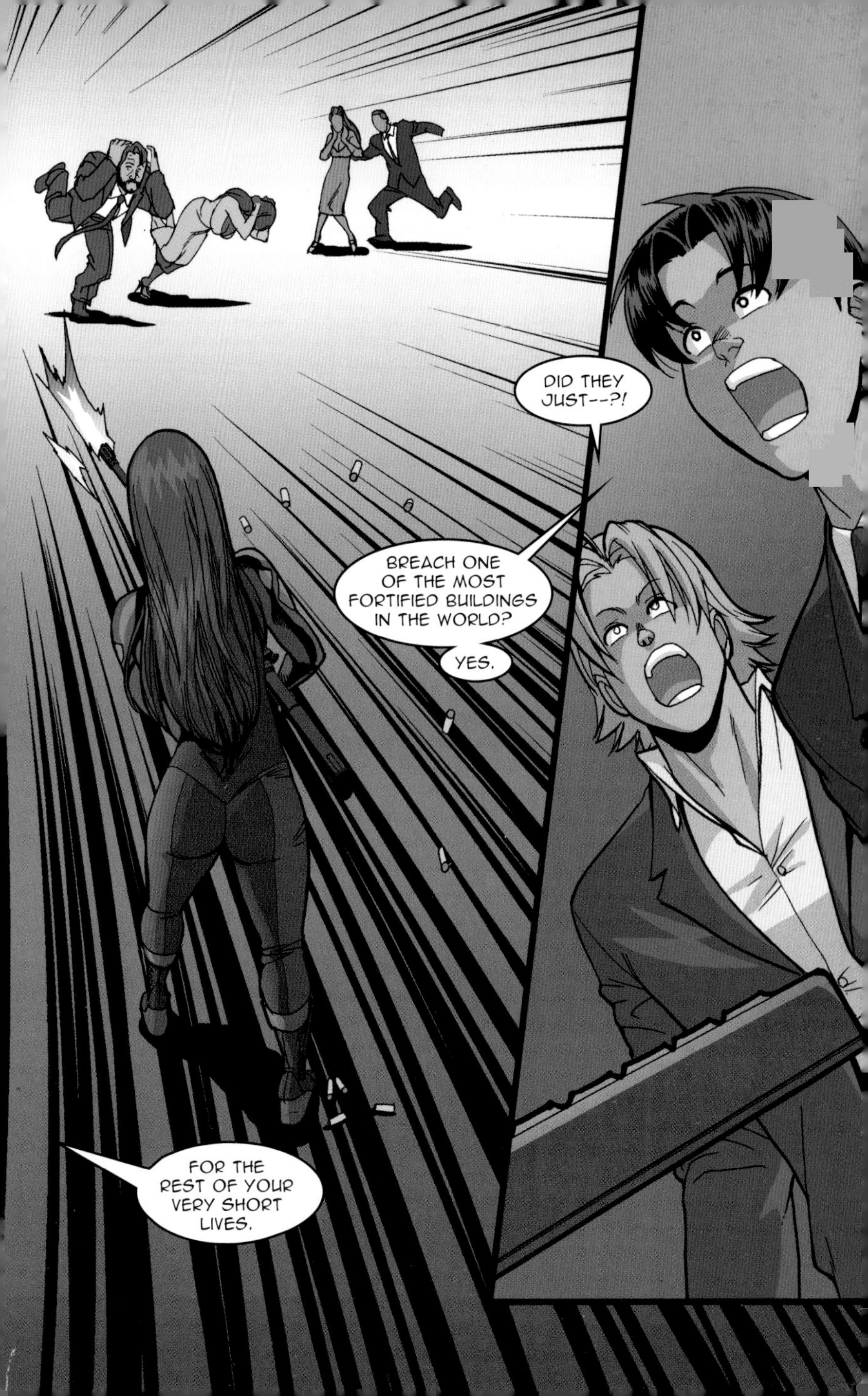
DID THEY JUST--?!
BREACH ONE OF THE MOST FORTIFIED BUILDINGS IN THE WORLD?
YES.
FOR THE REST OF YOUR VERY SHORT LIVES.

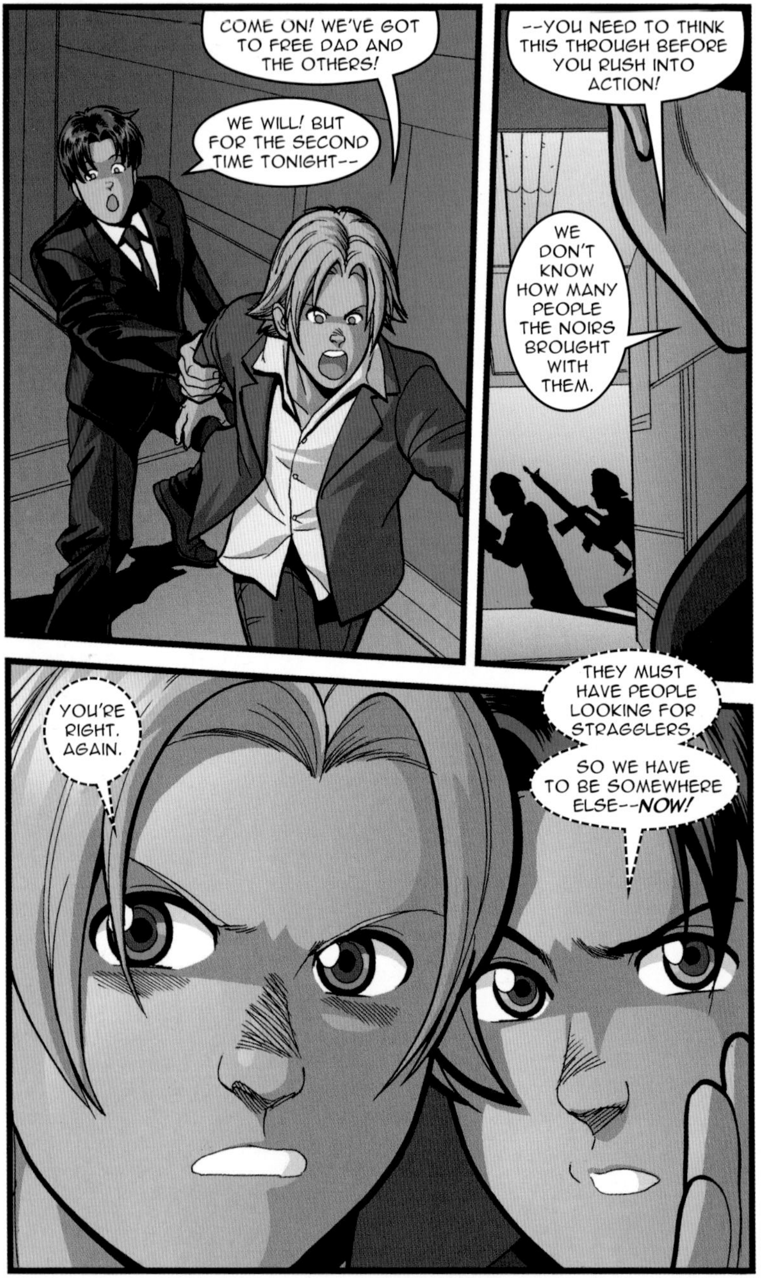
COME ON! WE'VE GOT TO FREE DAD AND THE OTHERS!
WE WILL! BUT FOR THE SECOND TIME TONIGHT--
--YOU NEED TO THINK THIS THROUGH BEFORE YOU RUSH INTO ACTION!
WE DON'T KNOW HOW MANY PEOPLE THE NOIRS BROUGHT WITH THEM.
YOU'RE RIGHT. AGAIN.
THEY MUST HAVE PEOPLE LOOKING FOR STRAGGLERS.
SO WE HAVE TO BE SOMEWHERE ELSE--*NOW!*

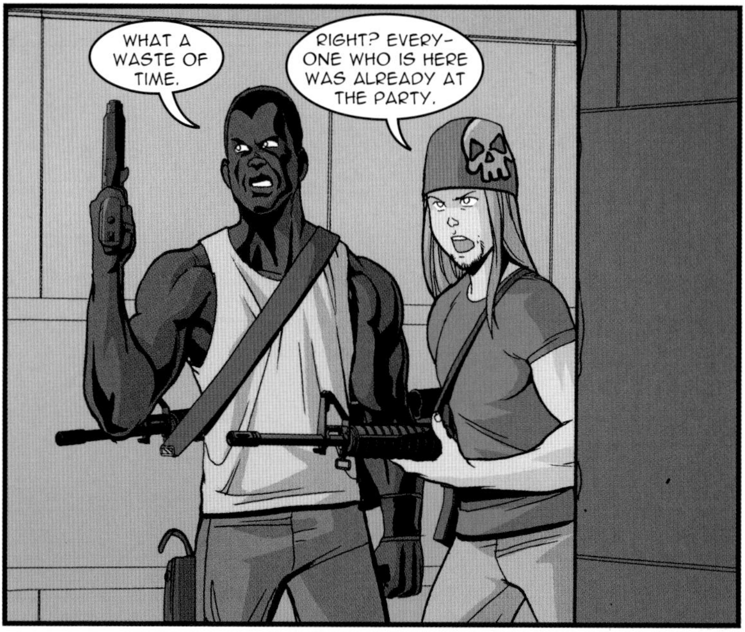
WHAT A WASTE OF TIME.
RIGHT? EVERY-ONE WHO IS HERE WAS ALREADY AT THE PARTY.

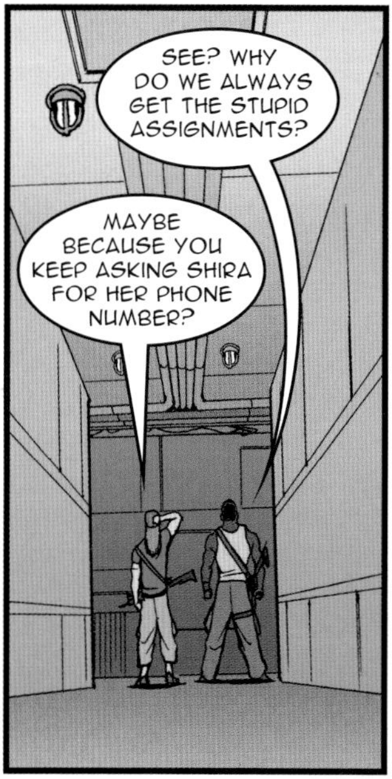
SEE? WHY DO WE ALWAYS GET THE STUPID ASSIGNMENTS?
MAYBE BECAUSE YOU KEEP ASKING SHIRA FOR HER PHONE NUMBER?

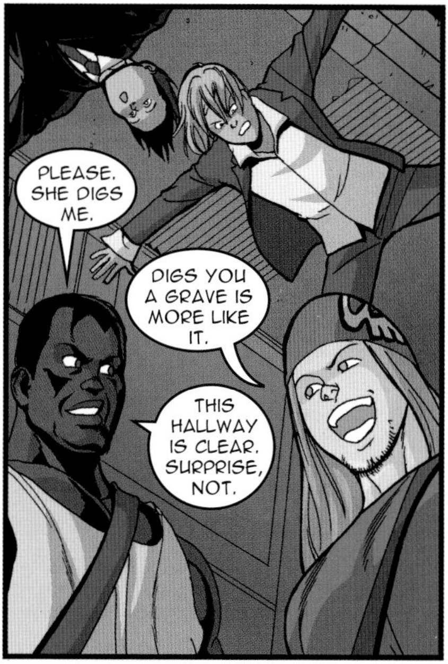
PLEASE. SHE DIGS ME.
DIGS YOU A GRAVE IS MORE LIKE IT.
THIS HALLWAY IS CLEAR. SURPRISE, NOT.

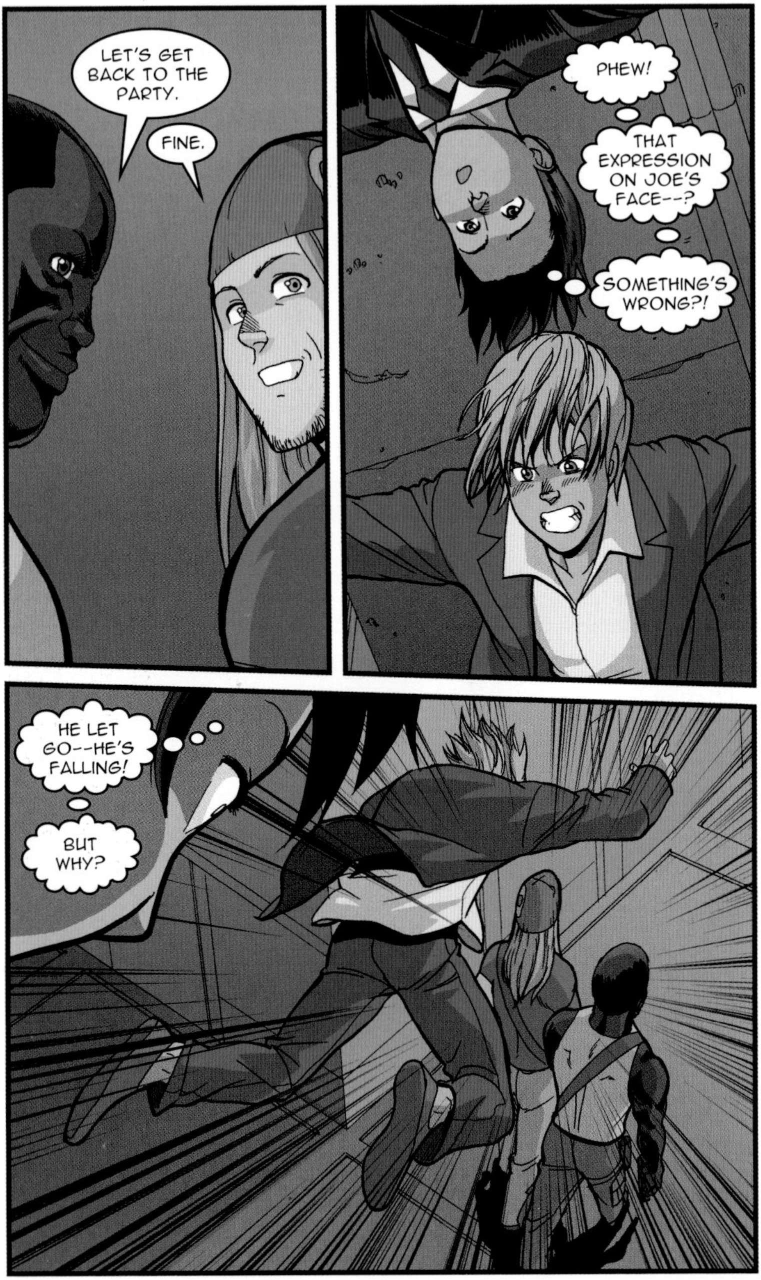
LET'S GET BACK TO THE PARTY.
FINE.
PHEW!
THAT EXPRESSION ON JOE'S FACE--?
SOMETHING'S WRONG?!
HE LET GO--HE'S FALLING!
BUT WHY?

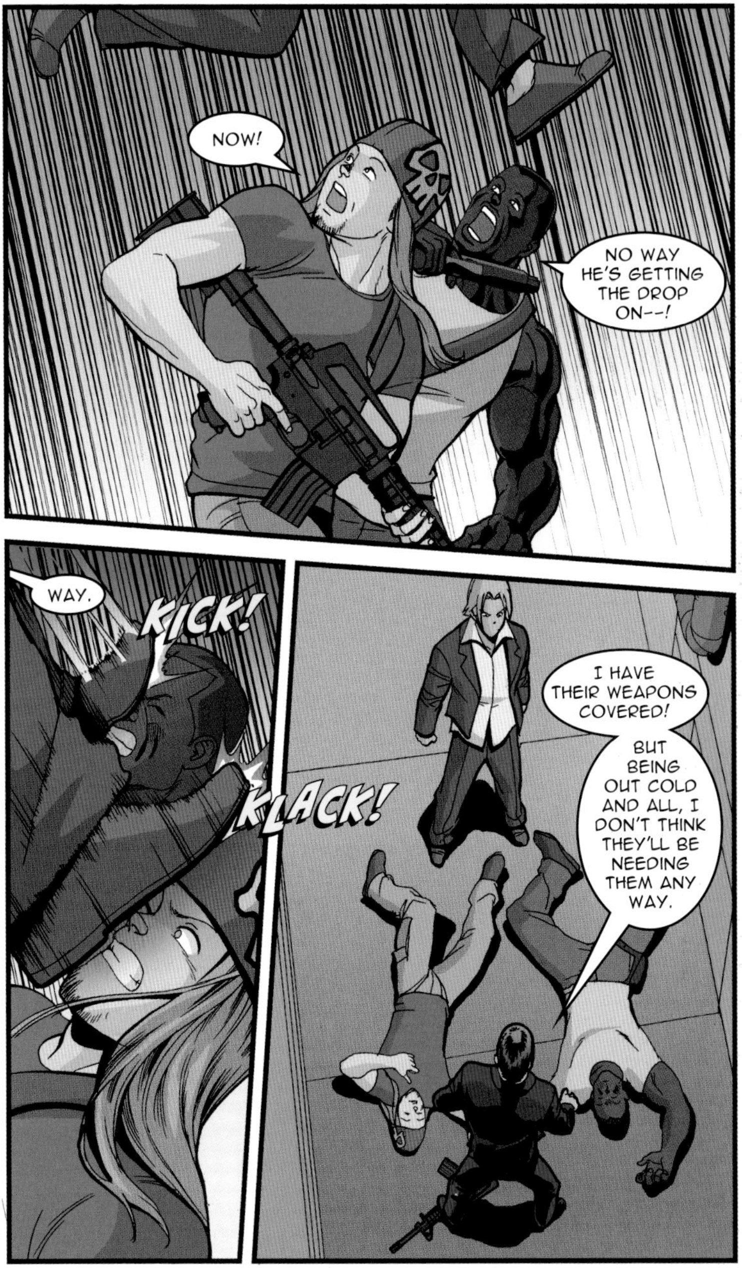
NOW!
NO WAY HE'S GETTING THE DROP ON--!
WAY.
KICK!
KLACK!
I HAVE THEIR WEAPONS COVERED!
BUT BEING OUT COLD AND ALL, I DON'T THINK THEY'LL BE NEEDING THEM ANY WAY.

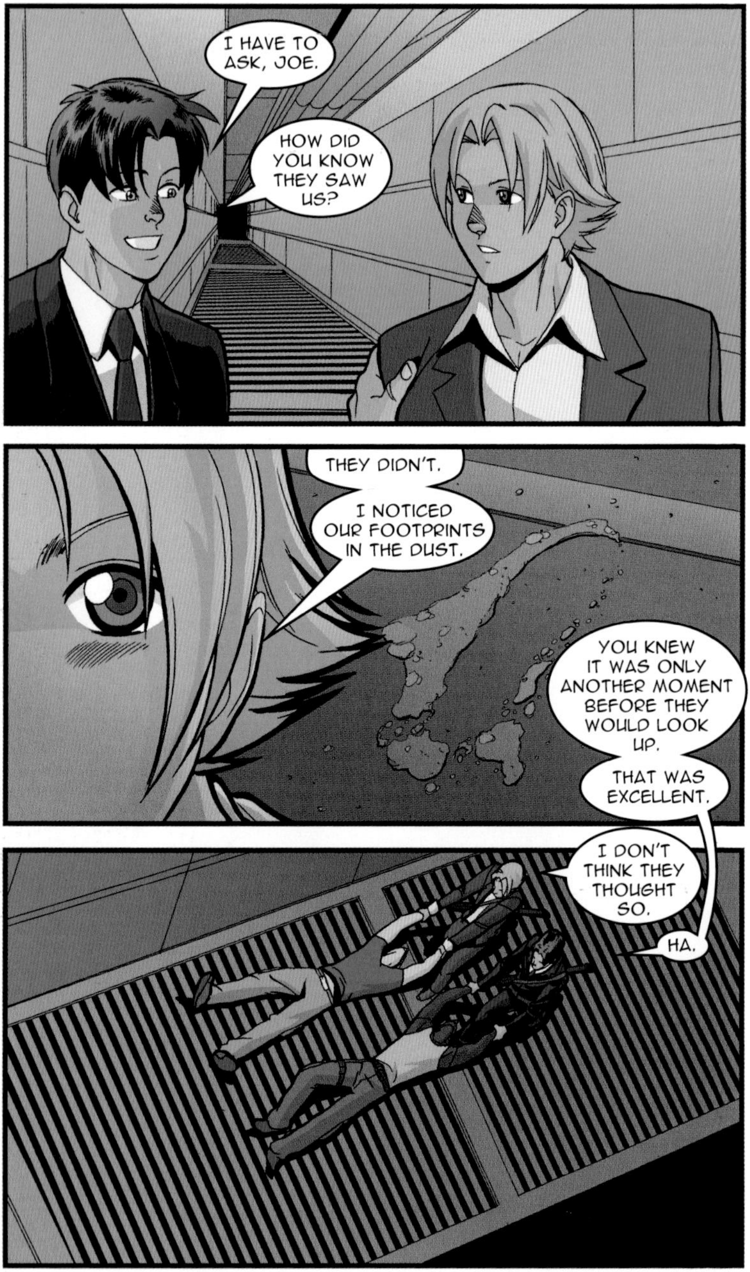
I HAVE TO ASK, JOE.
HOW DID YOU KNOW THEY SAW US?
THEY DIDN'T.
I NOTICED OUR FOOTPRINTS IN THE DUST.
YOU KNEW IT WAS ONLY ANOTHER MOMENT BEFORE THEY WOULD LOOK UP.
THAT WAS EXCELLENT.
I DON'T THINK THEY THOUGHT SO.
HA.

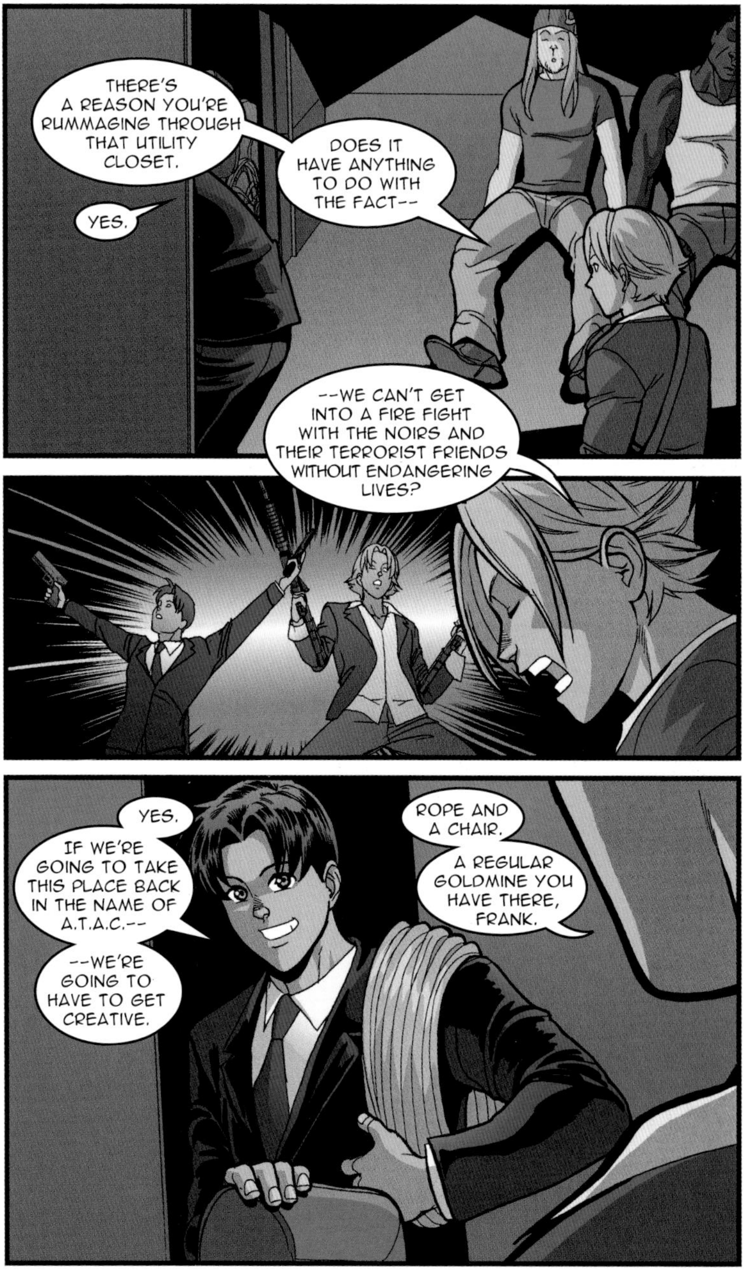
THERE'S A REASON YOU'RE RUMMAGING THROUGH THAT UTILITY CLOSET.
YES.
DOES IT HAVE ANYTHING TO DO WITH THE FACT--
--WE CAN'T GET INTO A FIRE FIGHT WITH THE NOIRS AND THEIR TERRORIST FRIENDS WITHOUT ENDANGERING LIVES?
YES.
IF WE'RE GOING TO TAKE THIS PLACE BACK IN THE NAME OF A.T.A.C.--
--WE'RE GOING TO HAVE TO GET CREATIVE.
ROPE AND A CHAIR.
A REGULAR GOLDMINE YOU HAVE THERE, FRANK.

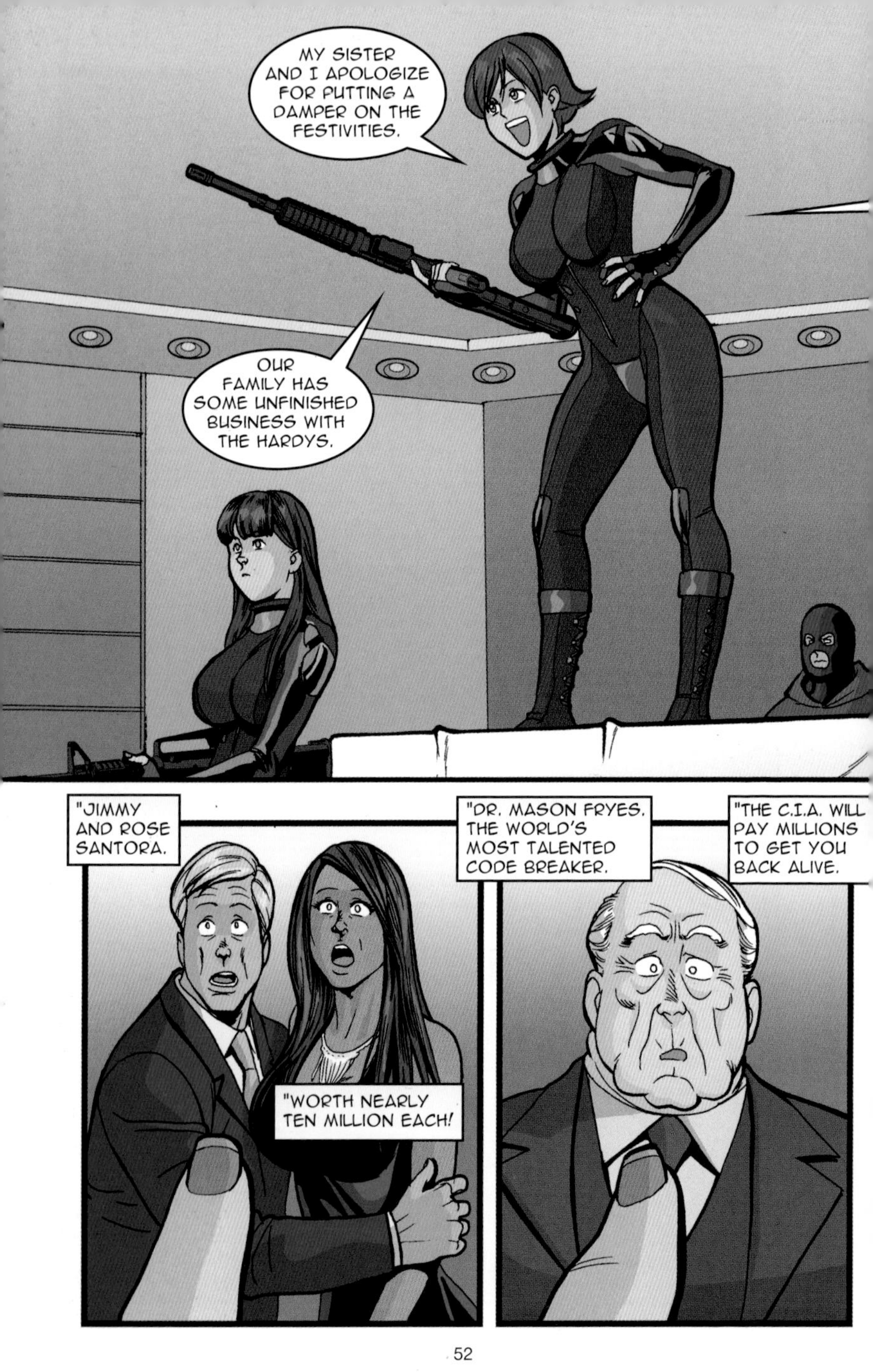
MY SISTER AND I APOLOGIZE FOR PUTTING A DAMPER ON THE FESTIVITIES.
OUR FAMILY HAS SOME UNFINISHED BUSINESS WITH THE HARDYS.
"JIMMY AND ROSE SANTORA.
"WORTH NEARLY TEN MILLION EACH!
"DR. MASON FRYES. THE WORLD'S MOST TALENTED CODE BREAKER.
"THE C.I.A. WILL PAY MILLIONS TO GET YOU BACK ALIVE.

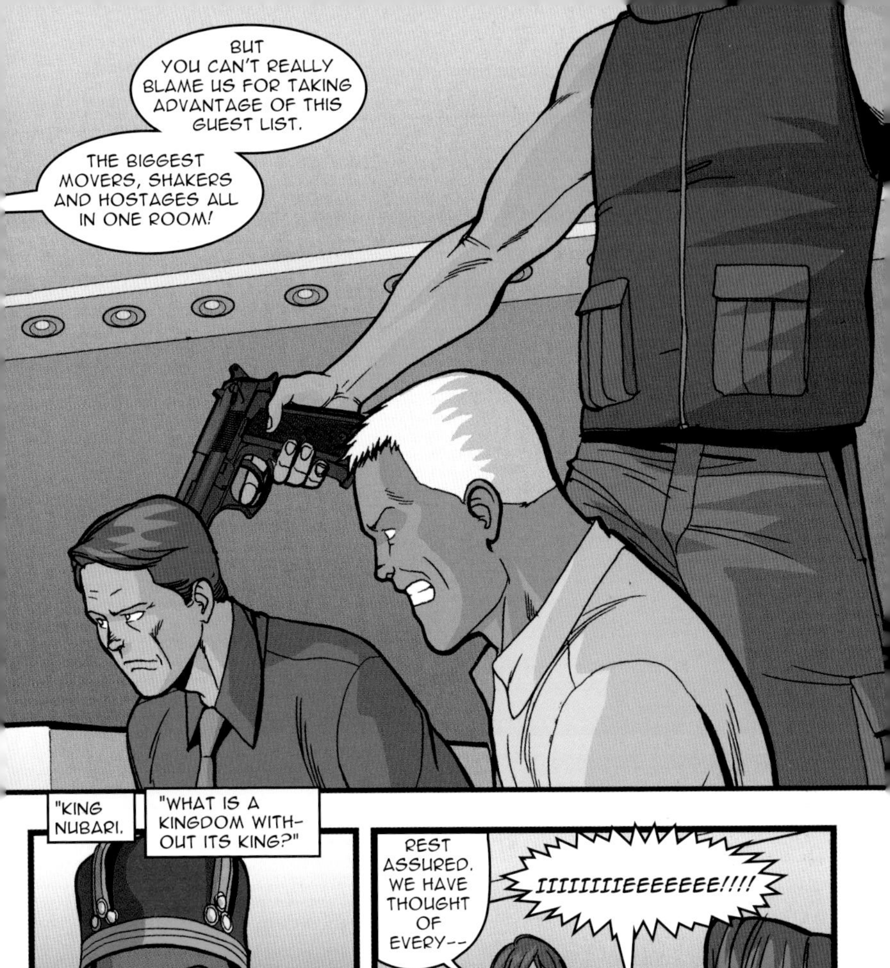
BUT YOU CAN'T REALLY BLAME US FOR TAKING ADVANTAGE OF THIS GUEST LIST.
THE BIGGEST MOVERS, SHAKERS AND HOSTAGES ALL IN ONE ROOM!

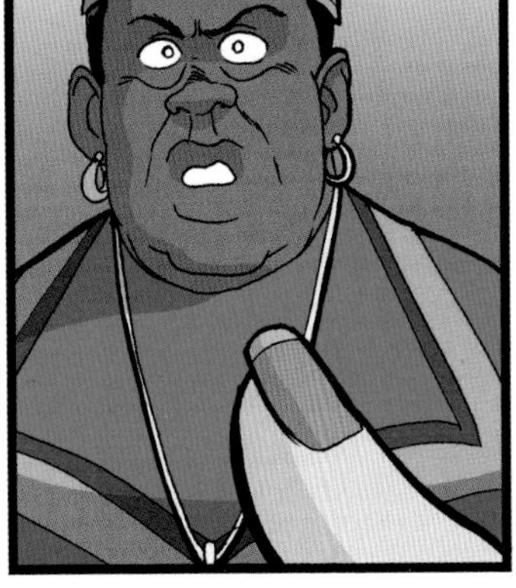
"KING NUBARI.
"WHAT IS A KINGDOM WITH-OUT ITS KING?"

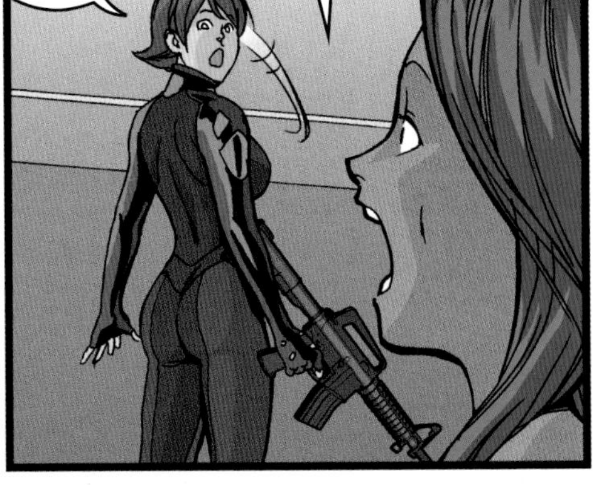
REST ASSURED. WE HAVE THOUGHT OF EVERY--
IIIIIIIIEEEEEEE!!!!

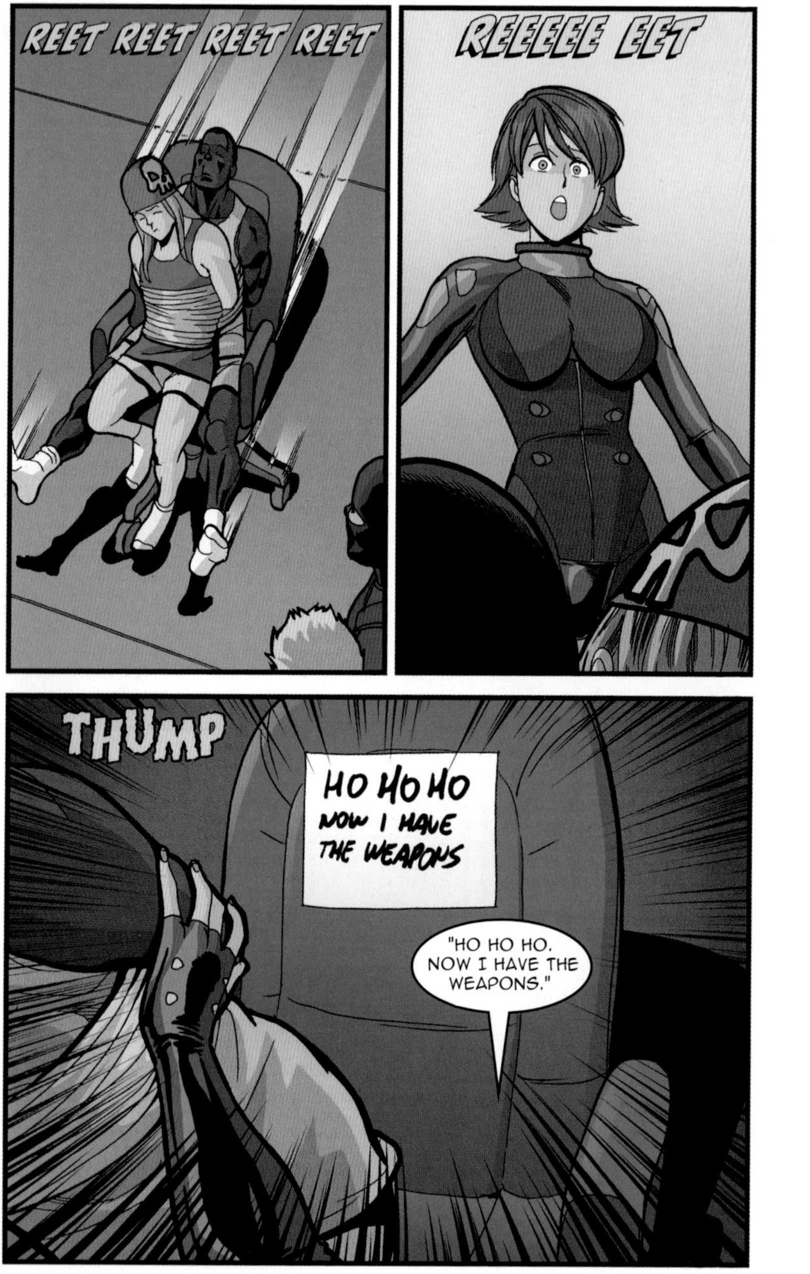
REET REET REET REET
REEEEE EET
THUMP
HO HO HO
NOW I HAVE
THE WEAPONS
"HO HO HO.
NOW I HAVE THE
WEAPONS."

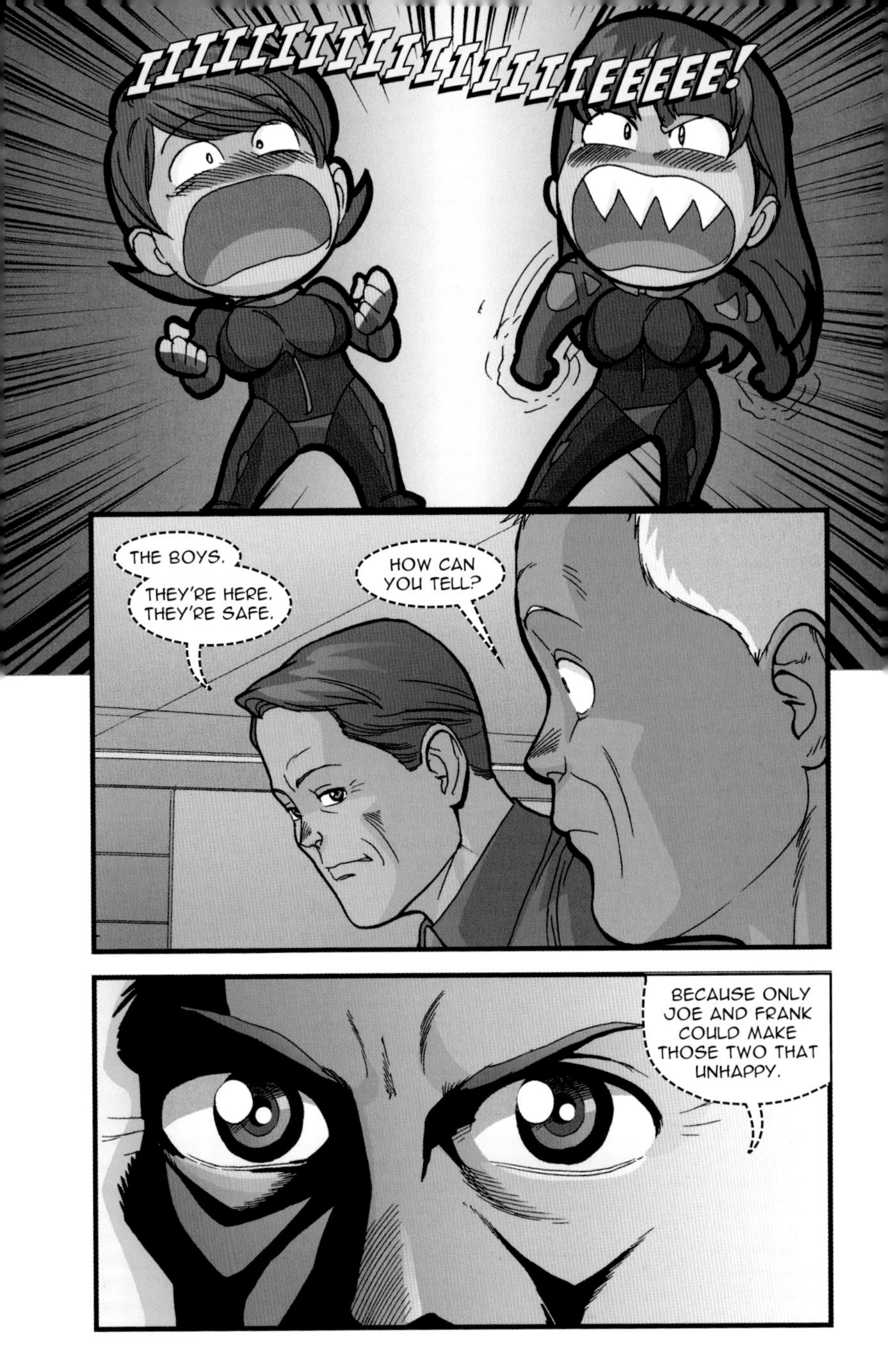
IIIIIIIIIIIIIIIIIIIEEEEEE!
THE BOYS.
THEY'RE HERE. THEY'RE SAFE.
HOW CAN YOU TELL?
BECAUSE ONLY JOE AND FRANK COULD MAKE THOSE TWO THAT UNHAPPY.

"HO HO HO?"

I SAW IT IN A MOVIE. LET'S GO.

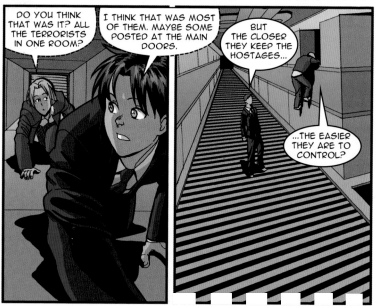

DO YOU THINK THAT WAS IT? ALL THE TERRORISTS IN ONE ROOM?

I THINK THAT WAS MOST OF THEM. MAYBE SOME POSTED AT THE MAIN DOORS.

BUT THE CLOSER THEY KEEP THE HOSTAGES...

...THE EASIER THEY ARE TO CONTROL?

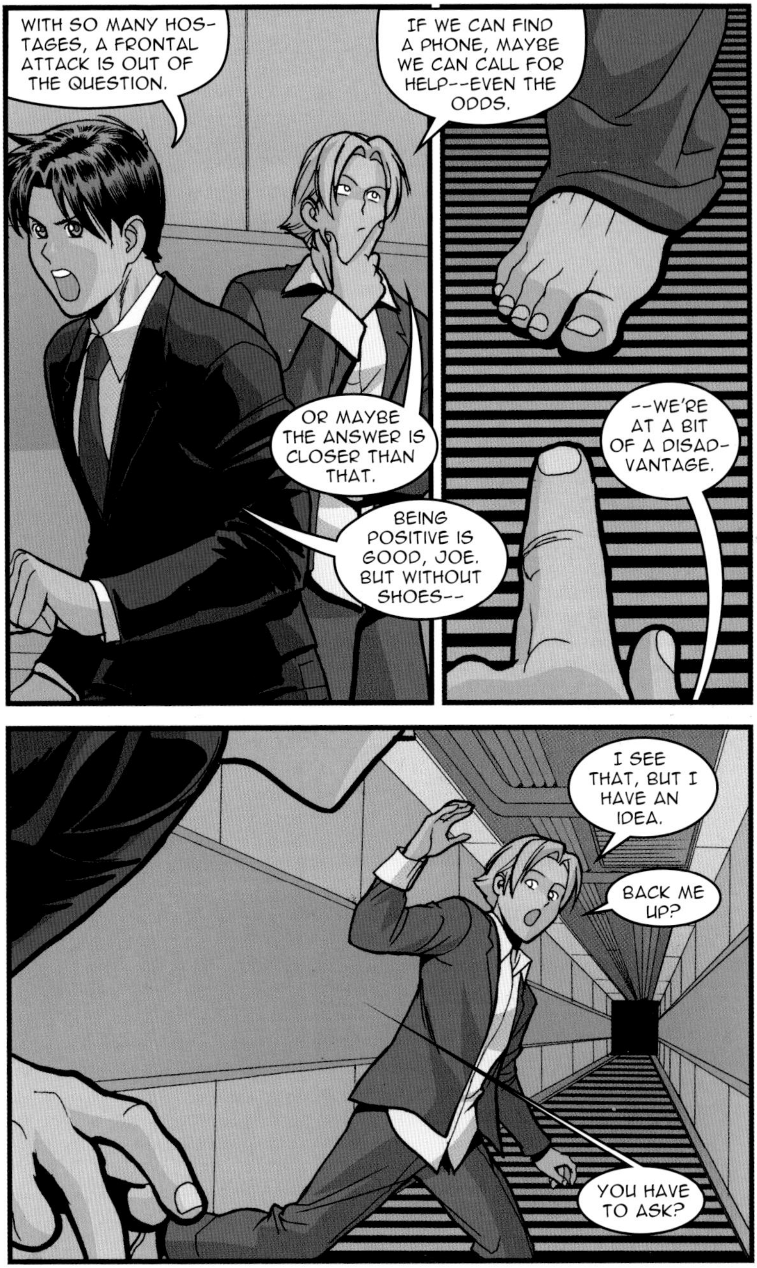
WITH SO MANY HOSTAGES, A FRONTAL ATTACK IS OUT OF THE QUESTION.
IF WE CAN FIND A PHONE, MAYBE WE CAN CALL FOR HELP--EVEN THE ODDS.
OR MAYBE THE ANSWER IS CLOSER THAN THAT.
BEING POSITIVE IS GOOD, JOE. BUT WITHOUT SHOES--
--WE'RE AT A BIT OF A DISADVANTAGE.
I SEE THAT, BUT I HAVE AN IDEA.
BACK ME UP?
YOU HAVE TO ASK?

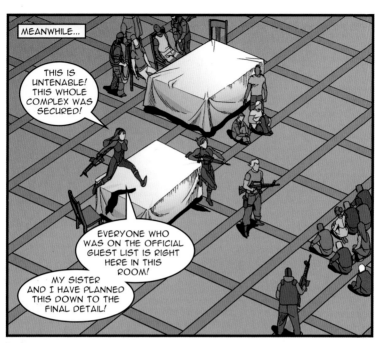

MEANWHILE...

THIS IS UNTENABLE! THIS WHOLE COMPLEX WAS SECURED!

EVERYONE WHO WAS ON THE OFFICIAL GUEST LIST IS RIGHT HERE IN THIS ROOM!

MY SISTER AND I HAVE PLANNED THIS DOWN TO THE FINAL DETAIL!

WHICH MEANS IF THIS OPERATION FAILS--IT IS YOUR FAULT! GOT IT?!

NOW GO FIND THAT INTRUDER!

NICOLINA IS IN HIGH DUNGEON. BUT SHIRA SEEMS A LITTLE.... DISTRACTED.

HMMM.

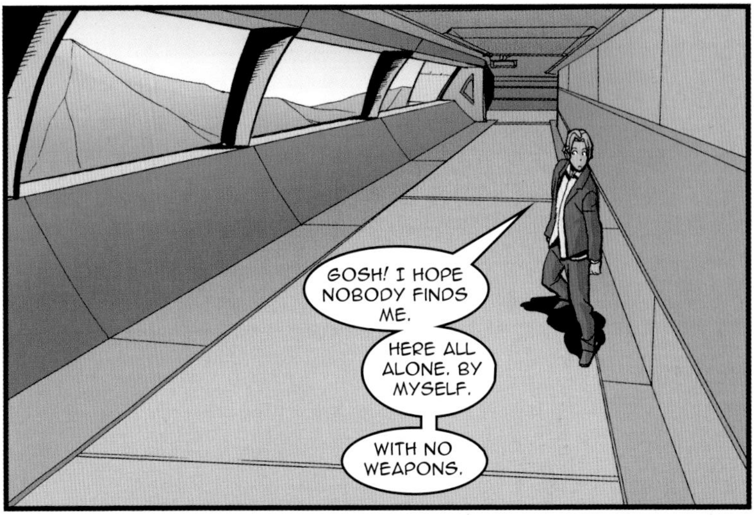
GOSH! I HOPE NOBODY FINDS ME.
HERE ALL ALONE. BY MYSELF.
WITH NO WEAPONS.

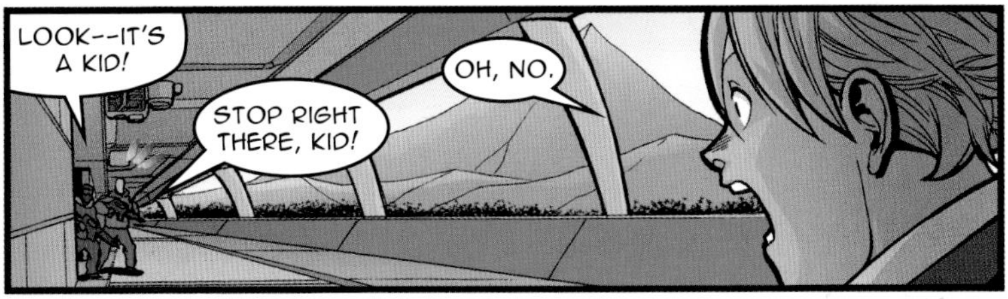
LOOK--IT'S A KID!
STOP RIGHT THERE, KID!
OH, NO.

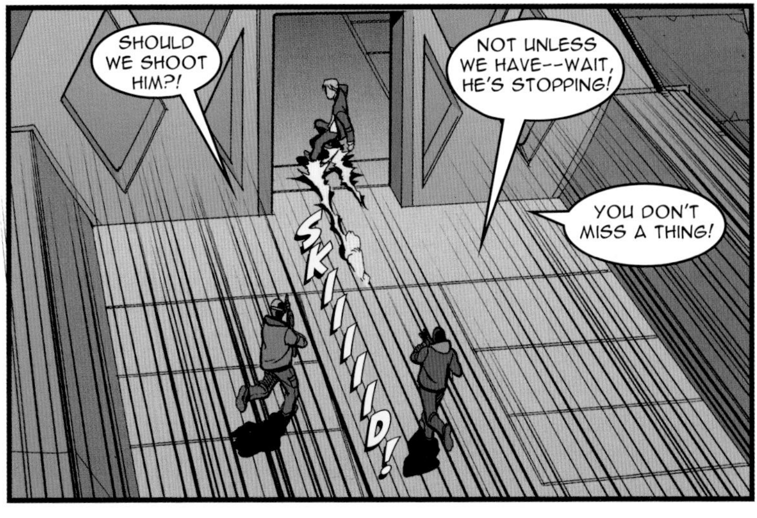
SHOULD WE SHOOT HIM?!
NOT UNLESS WE HAVE--WAIT, HE'S STOPPING!
YOU DON'T MISS A THING!
SKIIIIID!

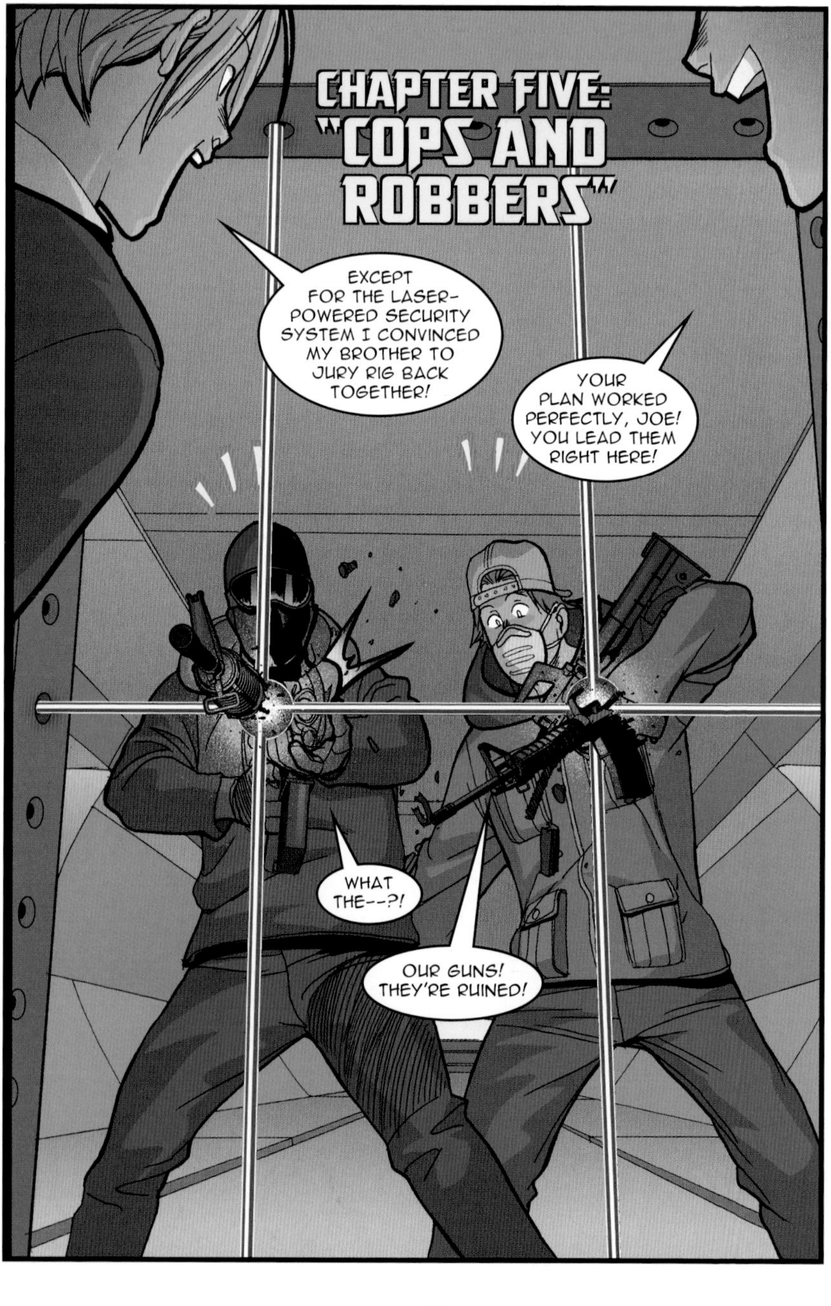

CHAPTER FIVE: "COPS AND ROBBERS"
EXCEPT FOR THE LASER-POWERED SECURITY SYSTEM I CONVINCED MY BROTHER TO JURY RIG BACK TOGETHER!
YOUR PLAN WORKED PERFECTLY, JOE! YOU LEAD THEM RIGHT HERE!
WHAT THE--?!
OUR GUNS! THEY'RE RUINED!

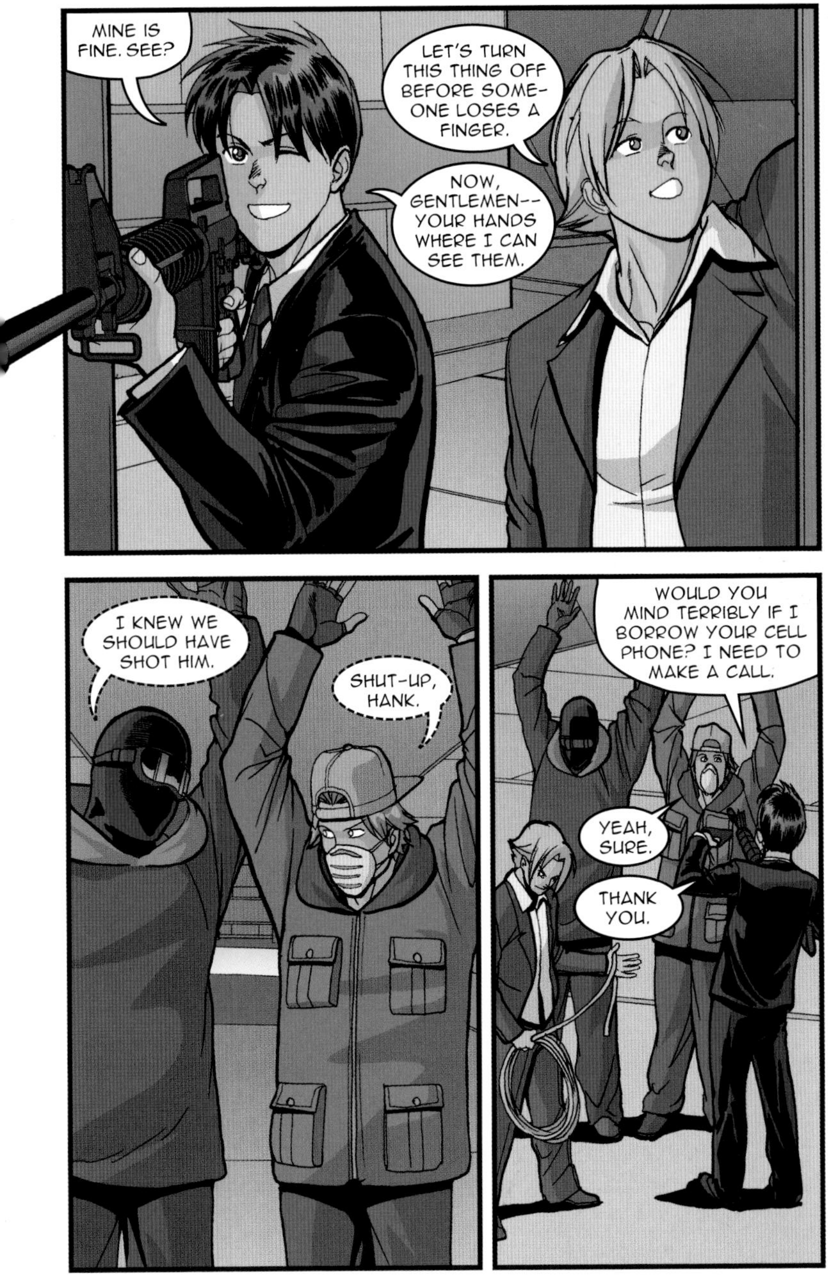
MINE IS FINE. SEE?
LET'S TURN THIS THING OFF BEFORE SOME-ONE LOSES A FINGER.
NOW, GENTLEMEN-- YOUR HANDS WHERE I CAN SEE THEM.
I KNEW WE SHOULD HAVE SHOT HIM.
SHUT-UP, HANK.
WOULD YOU MIND TERRIBLY IF I BORROW YOUR CELL PHONE? I NEED TO MAKE A CALL.
YEAH, SURE.
THANK YOU.

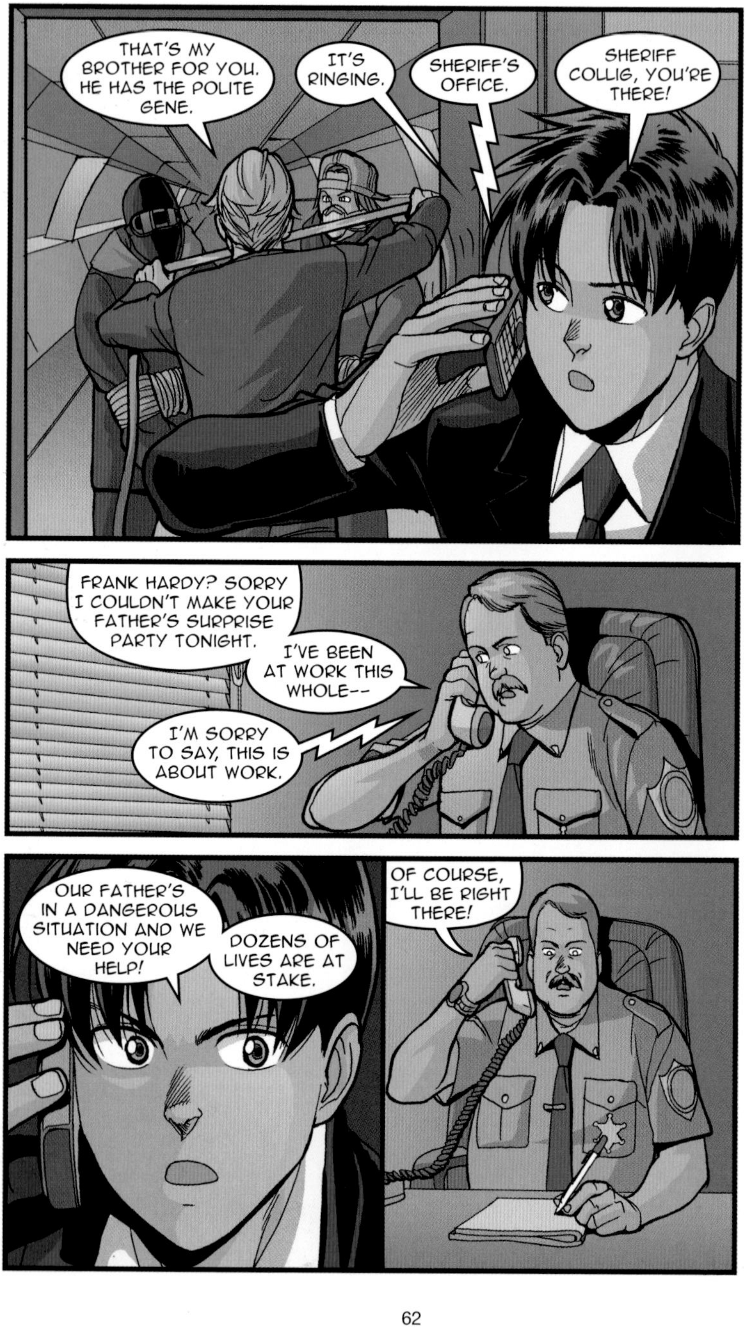
THAT'S MY BROTHER FOR YOU. HE HAS THE POLITE GENE.
IT'S RINGING.
SHERIFF'S OFFICE.
SHERIFF COLLIG, YOU'RE THERE!
FRANK HARDY? SORRY I COULDN'T MAKE YOUR FATHER'S SURPRISE PARTY TONIGHT.
I'VE BEEN AT WORK THIS WHOLE--
I'M SORRY TO SAY, THIS IS ABOUT WORK.
OUR FATHER'S IN A DANGEROUS SITUATION AND WE NEED YOUR HELP!
DOZENS OF LIVES ARE AT STAKE.
OF COURSE, I'LL BE RIGHT THERE!

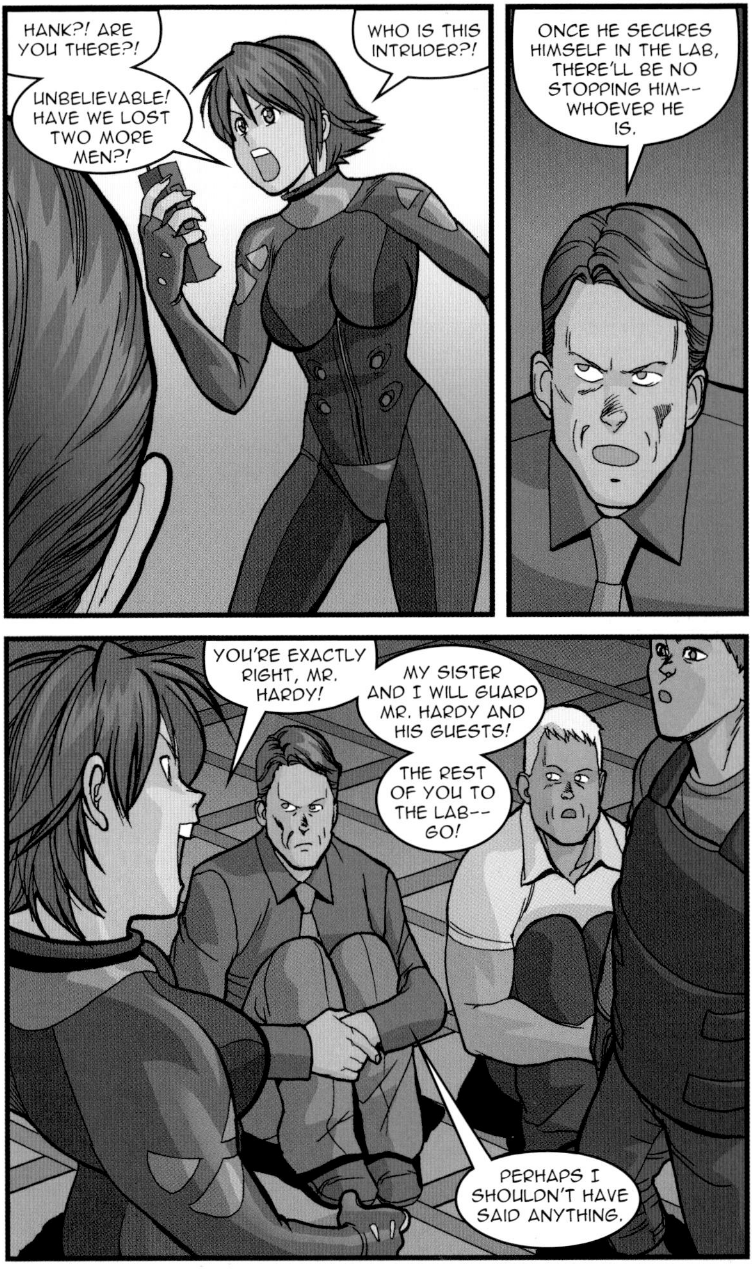
HANK?! ARE YOU THERE?!
UNBELIEVABLE! HAVE WE LOST TWO MORE MEN?!
WHO IS THIS INTRUDER?!
ONCE HE SECURES HIMSELF IN THE LAB, THERE'LL BE NO STOPPING HIM-- WHOEVER HE IS.
YOU'RE EXACTLY RIGHT, MR. HARDY!
MY SISTER AND I WILL GUARD MR. HARDY AND HIS GUESTS!
THE REST OF YOU TO THE LAB-- GO!
PERHAPS I SHOULDN'T HAVE SAID ANYTHING.

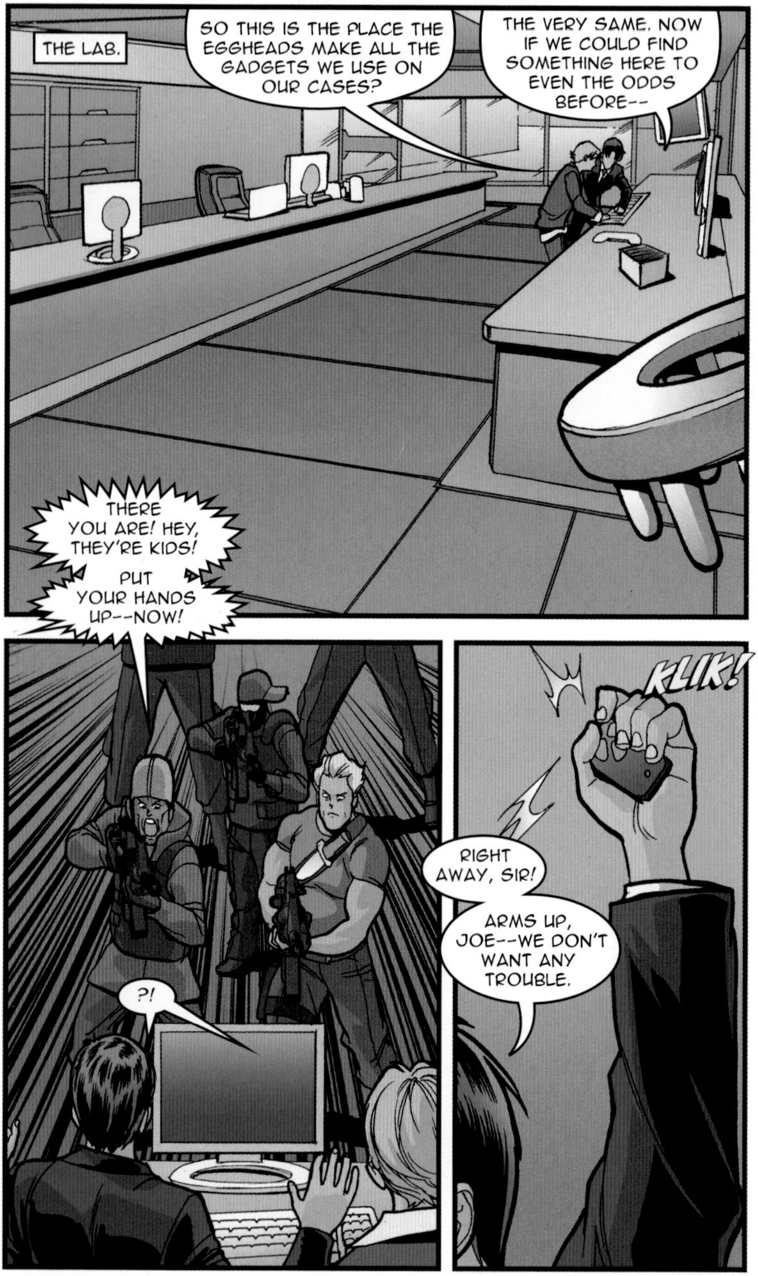
THE LAB.
SO THIS IS THE PLACE THE EGGHEADS MAKE ALL THE GADGETS WE USE ON OUR CASES?
THE VERY SAME. NOW IF WE COULD FIND SOMETHING HERE TO EVEN THE ODDS BEFORE--
THERE YOU ARE! HEY, THEY'RE KIDS!
PUT YOUR HANDS UP--NOW!
?!
KLIK!
RIGHT AWAY, SIR!
ARMS UP, JOE--WE DON'T WANT ANY TROUBLE.

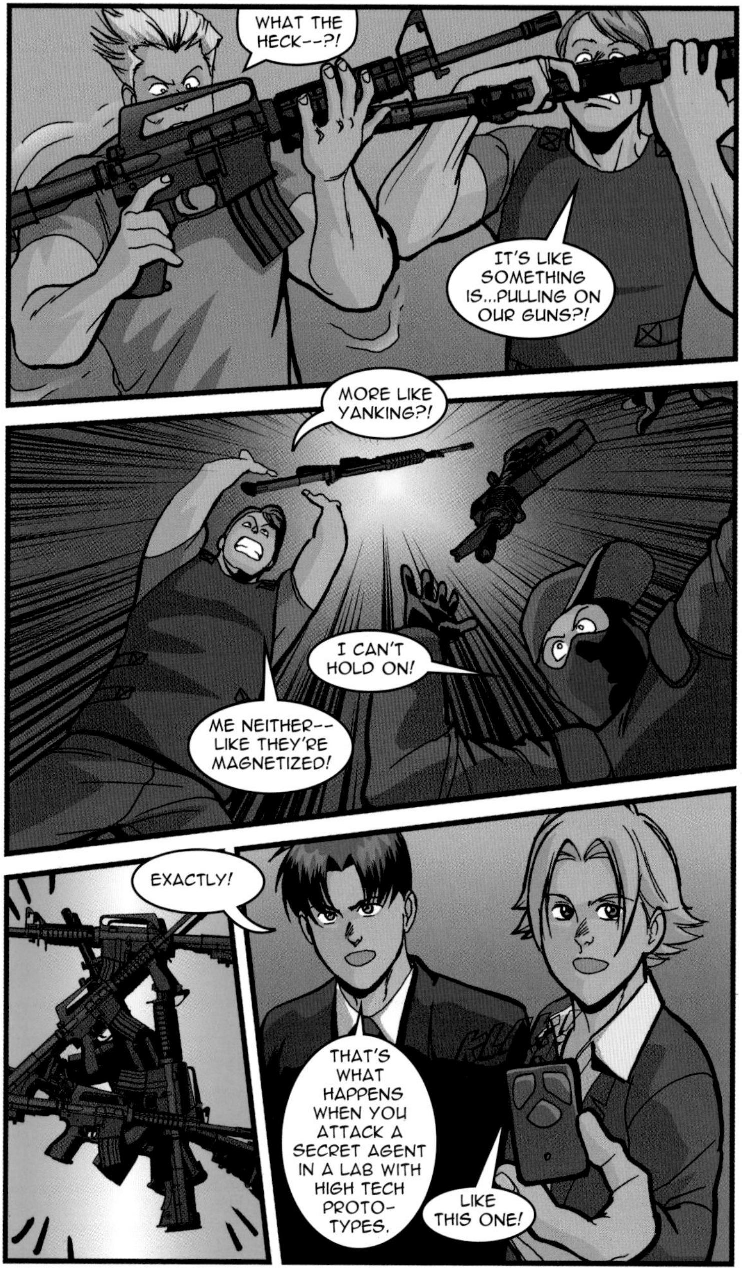
WHAT THE HECK--?!
IT'S LIKE SOMETHING IS...PULLING ON OUR GUNS?!
MORE LIKE YANKING?!
I CAN'T HOLD ON!
ME NEITHER--LIKE THEY'RE MAGNETIZED!
EXACTLY!
THAT'S WHAT HAPPENS WHEN YOU ATTACK A SECRET AGENT IN A LAB WITH HIGH TECH PROTO-TYPES.
LIKE THIS ONE!

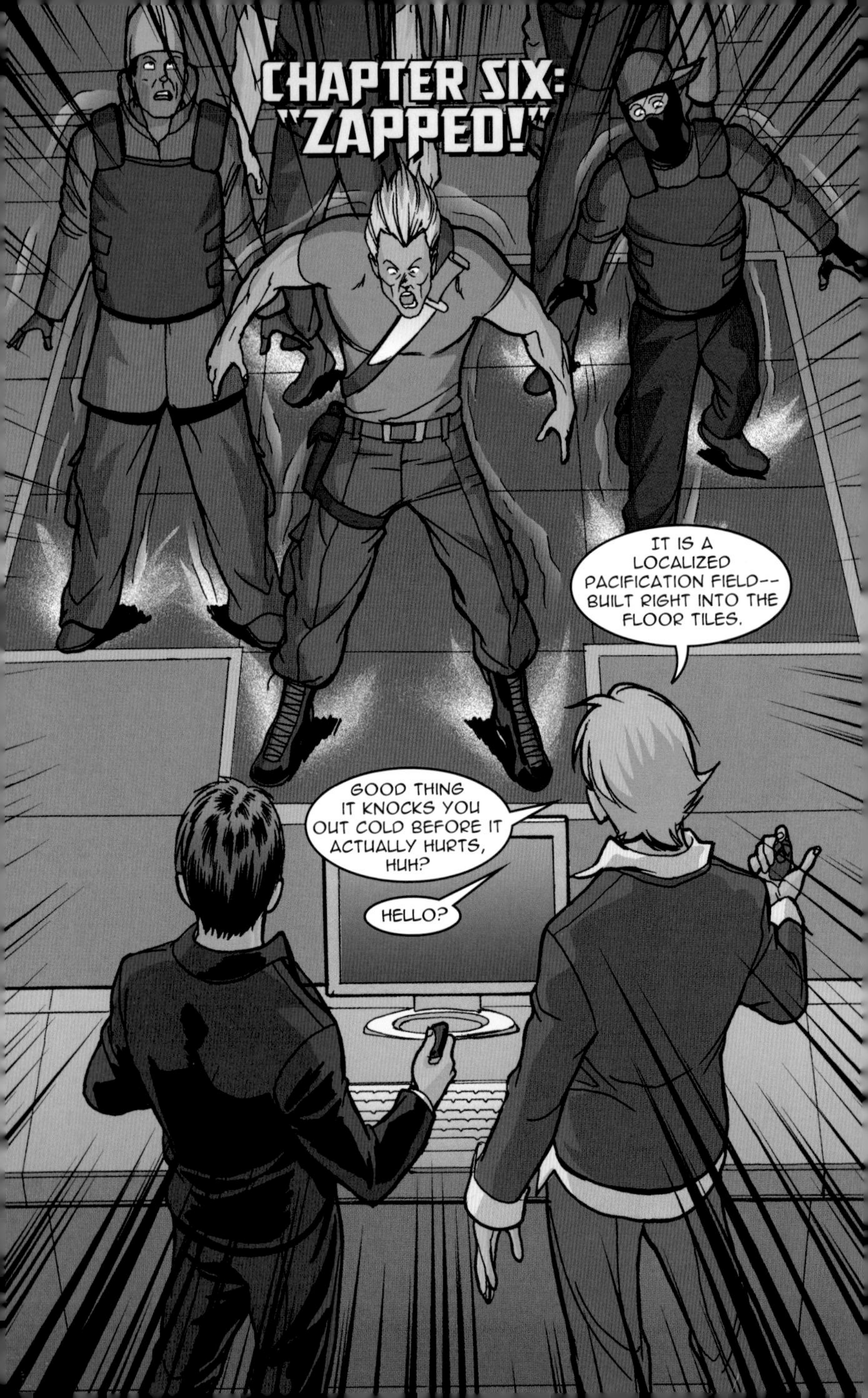
CHAPTER SIX:
"ZAPPED!"
IT IS A LOCALIZED PACIFICATION FIELD-- BUILT RIGHT INTO THE FLOOR TILES.
GOOD THING IT KNOCKS YOU OUT COLD BEFORE IT ACTUALLY HURTS, HUH?
HELLO?

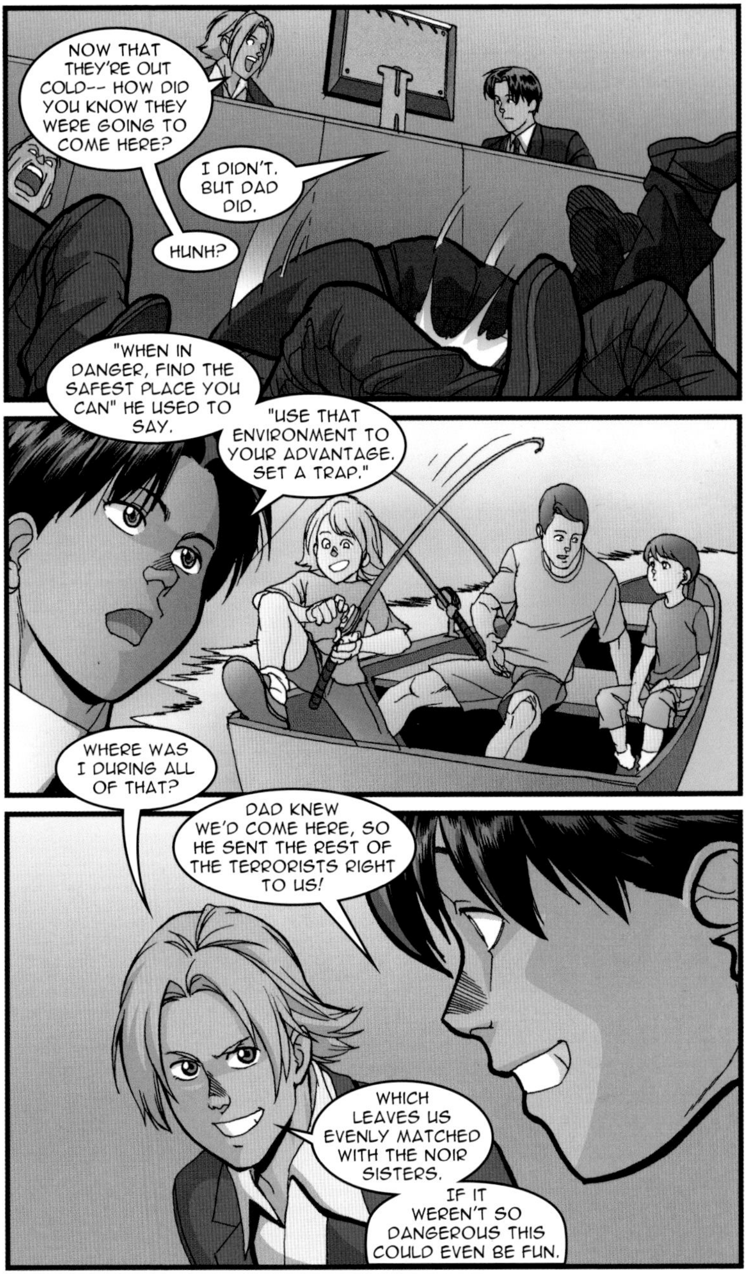
NOW THAT THEY'RE OUT COLD-- HOW DID YOU KNOW THEY WERE GOING TO COME HERE?
I DIDN'T. BUT DAD DID.
HUNH?
"WHEN IN DANGER, FIND THE SAFEST PLACE YOU CAN" HE USED TO SAY.
"USE THAT ENVIRONMENT TO YOUR ADVANTAGE. SET A TRAP."
WHERE WAS I DURING ALL OF THAT?
DAD KNEW WE'D COME HERE, SO HE SENT THE REST OF THE TERRORISTS RIGHT TO US!
WHICH LEAVES US EVENLY MATCHED WITH THE NOIR SISTERS.
IF IT WEREN'T SO DANGEROUS THIS COULD EVEN BE FUN.

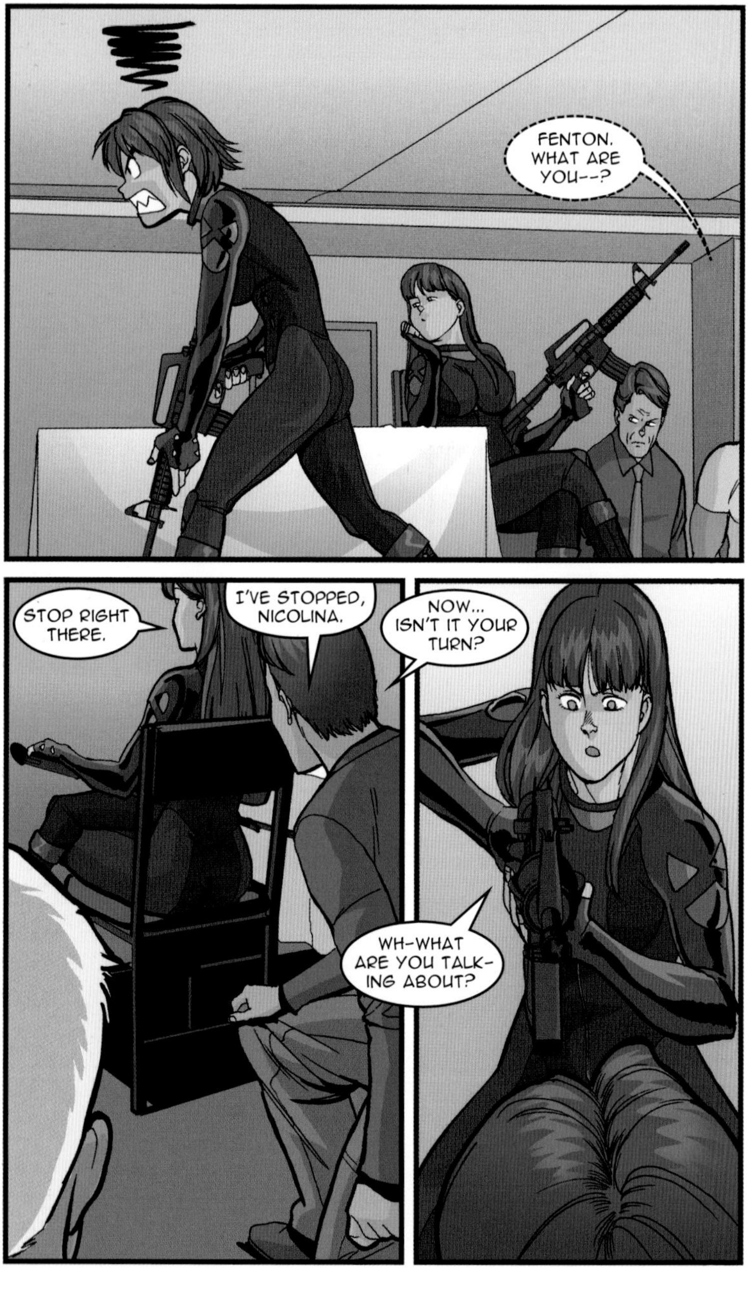
FENTON. WHAT ARE YOU--?
STOP RIGHT THERE.
I'VE STOPPED, NICOLINA.
NOW... ISN'T IT YOUR TURN?
WH-WHAT ARE YOU TALK-ING ABOUT?

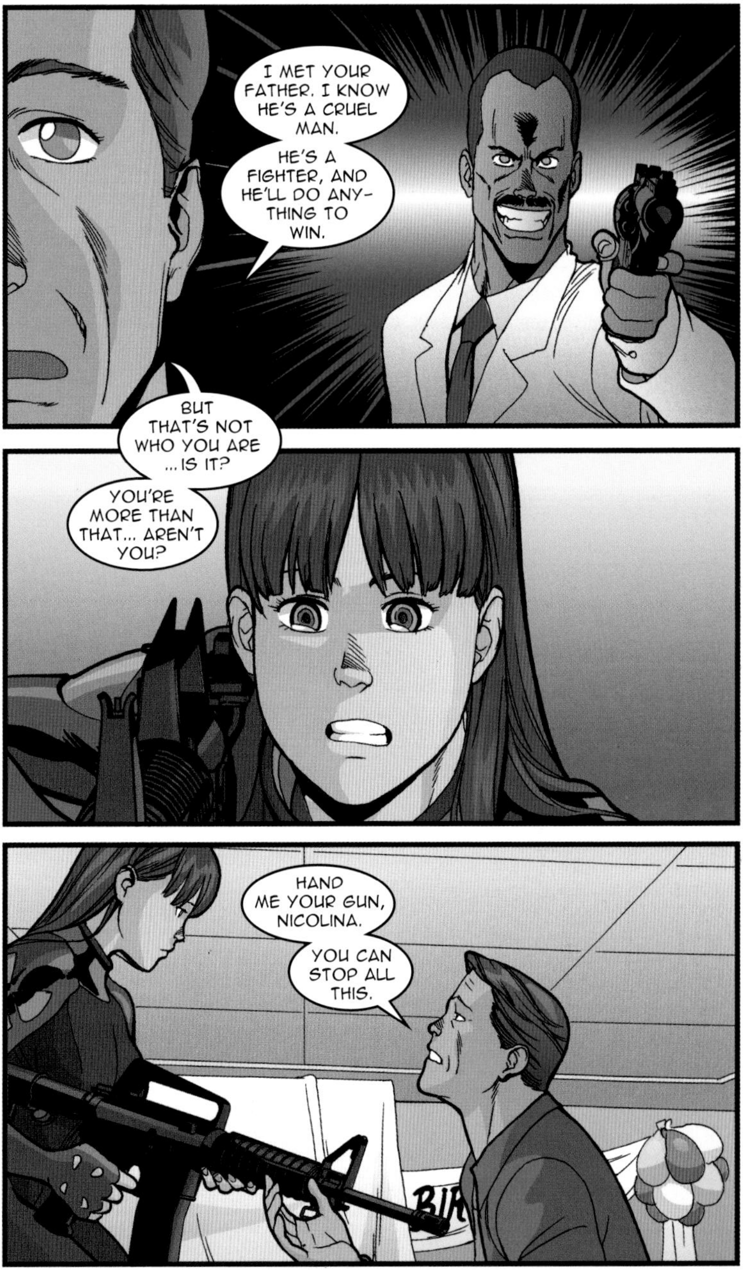
I MET YOUR FATHER. I KNOW HE'S A CRUEL MAN.
HE'S A FIGHTER, AND HE'LL DO ANY-THING TO WIN.
BUT THAT'S NOT WHO YOU ARE ...IS IT?
YOU'RE MORE THAN THAT... AREN'T YOU?
HAND ME YOUR GUN, NICOLINA.
YOU CAN STOP ALL THIS.

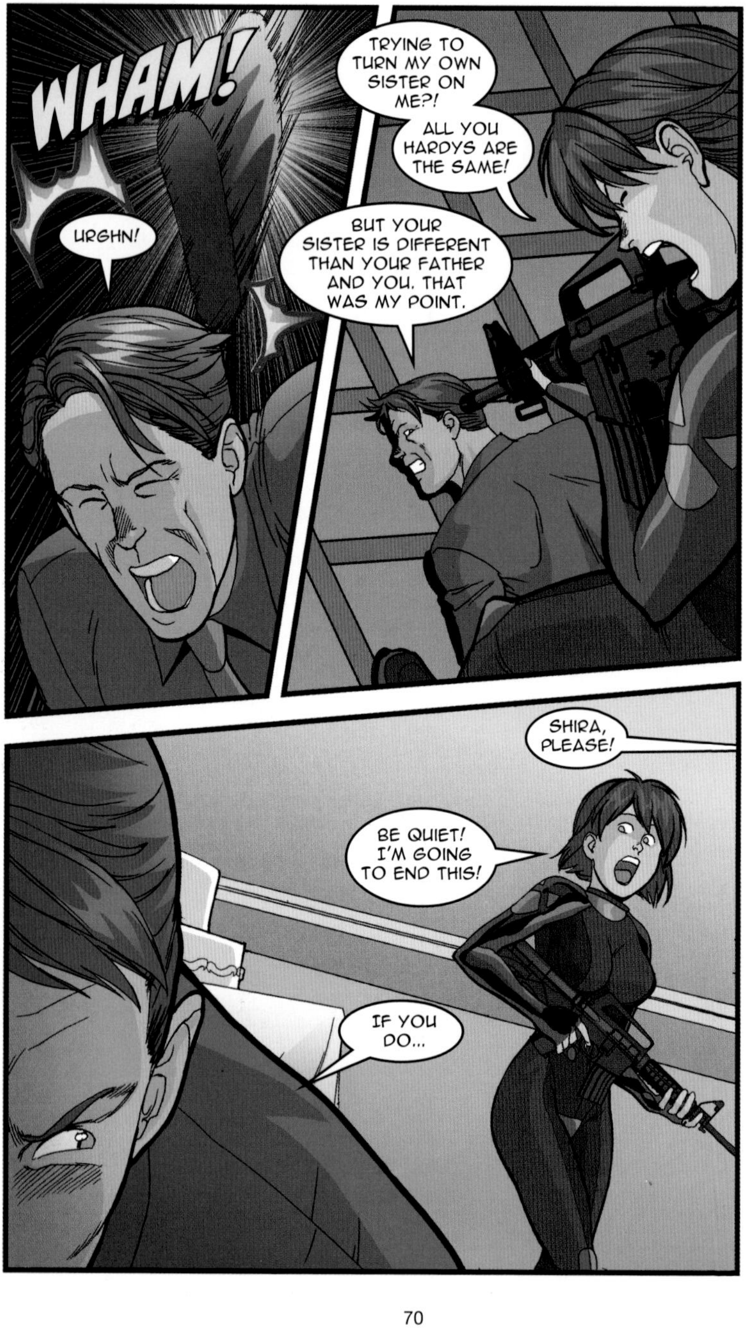
WHAM!
URGHN!
TRYING TO TURN MY OWN SISTER ON ME?!
ALL YOU HARDYS ARE THE SAME!
BUT YOUR SISTER IS DIFFERENT THAN YOUR FATHER AND YOU. THAT WAS MY POINT.
SHIRA, PLEASE!
BE QUIET! I'M GOING TO END THIS!
IF YOU DO...

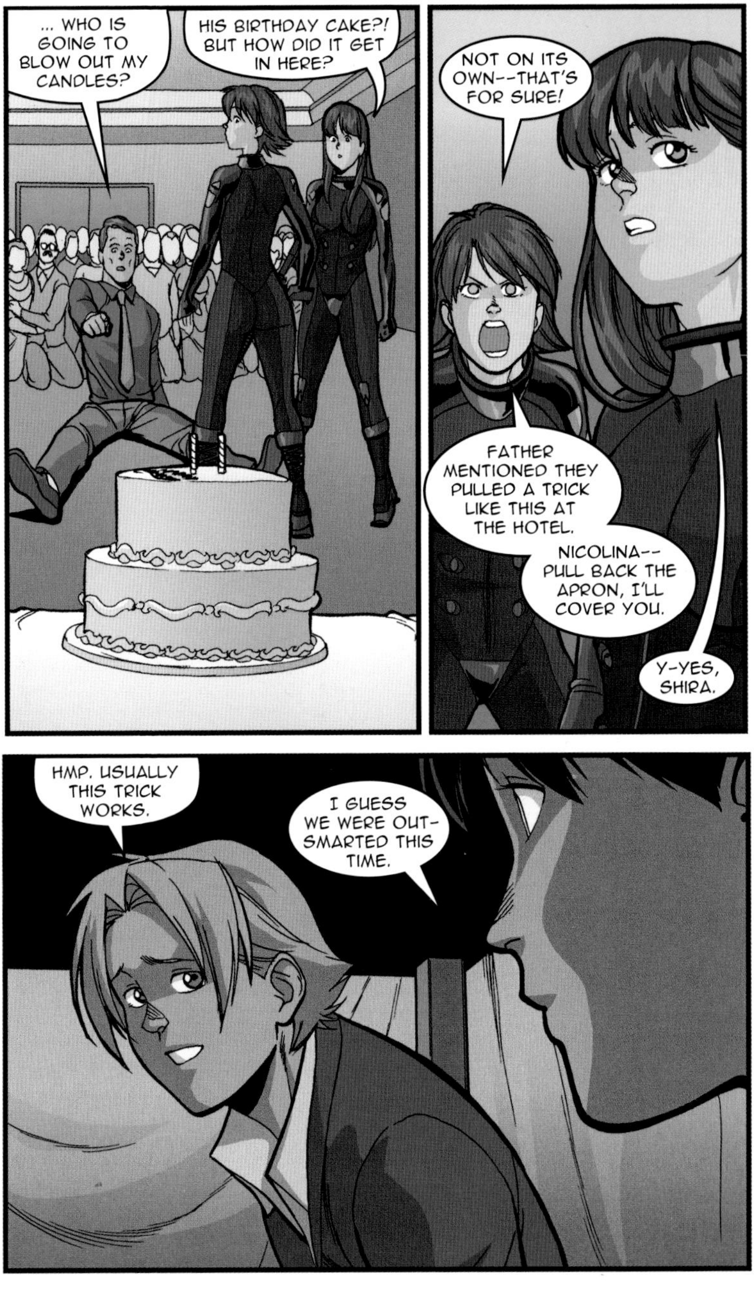
... WHO IS GOING TO BLOW OUT MY CANDLES?
HIS BIRTHDAY CAKE?! BUT HOW DID IT GET IN HERE?
NOT ON ITS OWN--THAT'S FOR SURE!
FATHER MENTIONED THEY PULLED A TRICK LIKE THIS AT THE HOTEL.
NICOLINA-- PULL BACK THE APRON, I'LL COVER YOU.
Y-YES, SHIRA.
HMP. USUALLY THIS TRICK WORKS.
I GUESS WE WERE OUT-SMARTED THIS TIME.

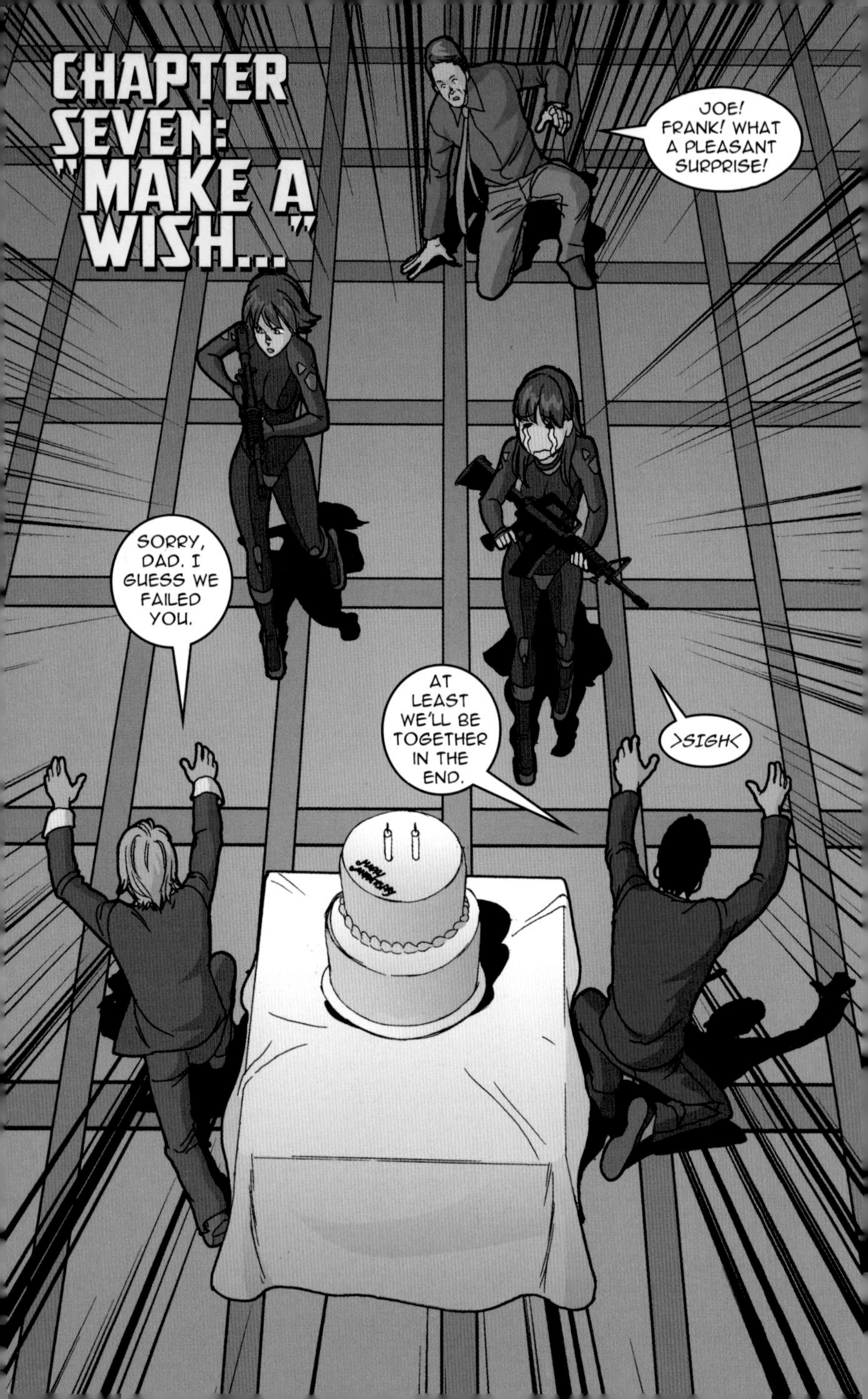
CHAPTER SEVEN: "MAKE A WISH..."
JOE! FRANK! WHAT A PLEASANT SURPRISE!
SORRY, DAD. I GUESS WE FAILED YOU.
AT LEAST WE'LL BE TOGETHER IN THE END.
>SIGH<

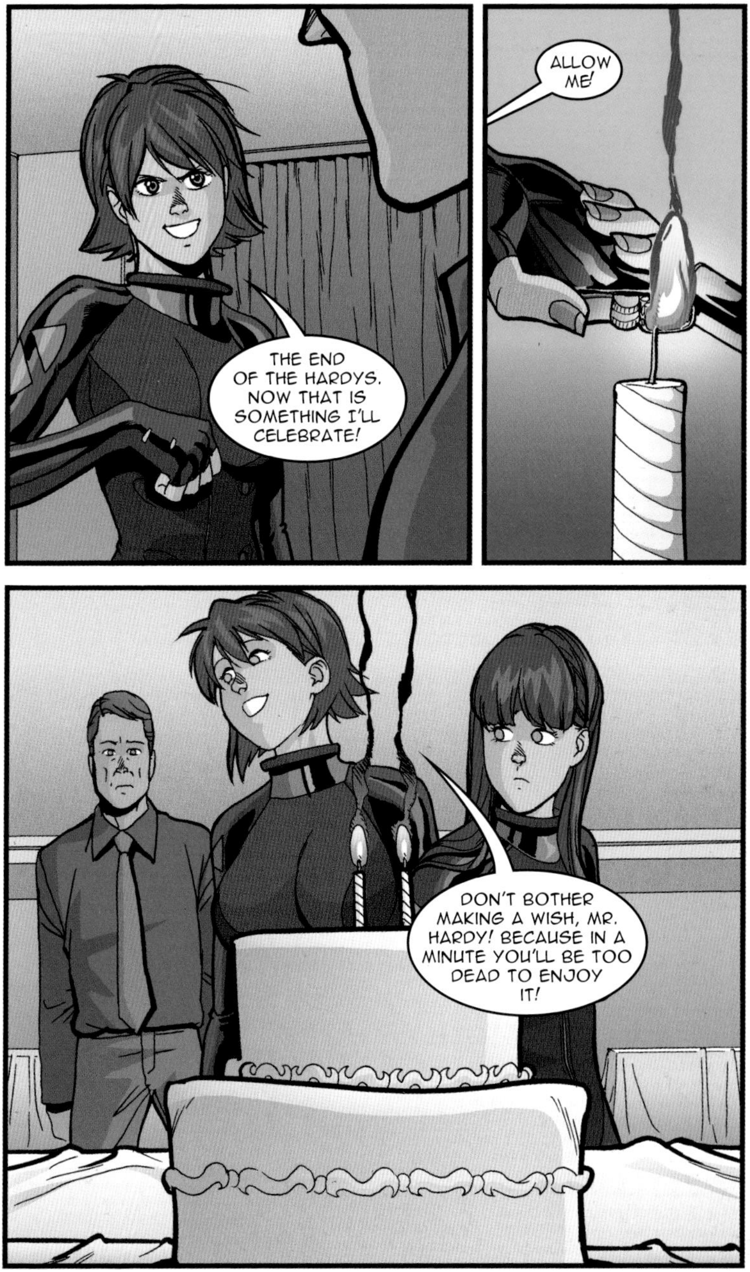
THE END OF THE HARDYS. NOW THAT IS SOMETHING I'LL CELEBRATE!
ALLOW ME!
DON'T BOTHER MAKING A WISH, MR. HARDY! BECAUSE IN A MINUTE YOU'LL BE TOO DEAD TO ENJOY IT!

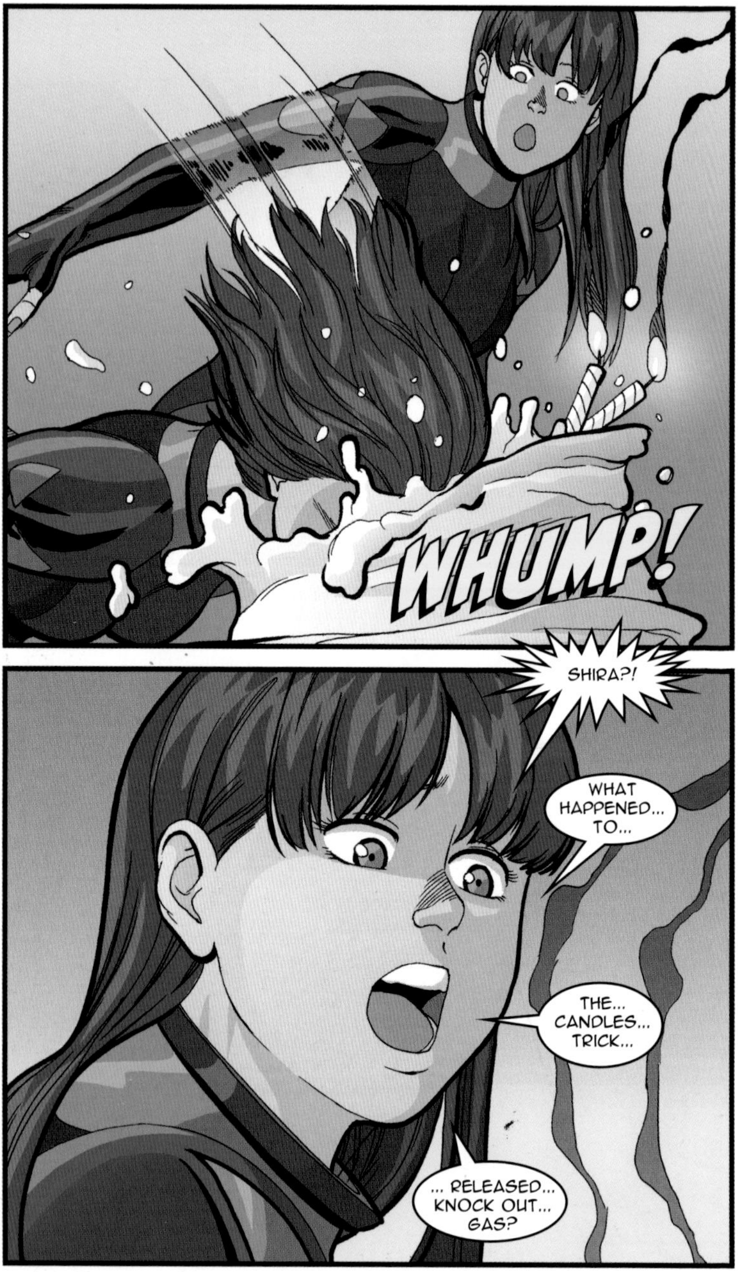
WHUMP!
SHIRA?!
WHAT HAPPENED... TO...
THE... CANDLES... TRICK...
... RELEASED... KNOCK OUT... GAS?

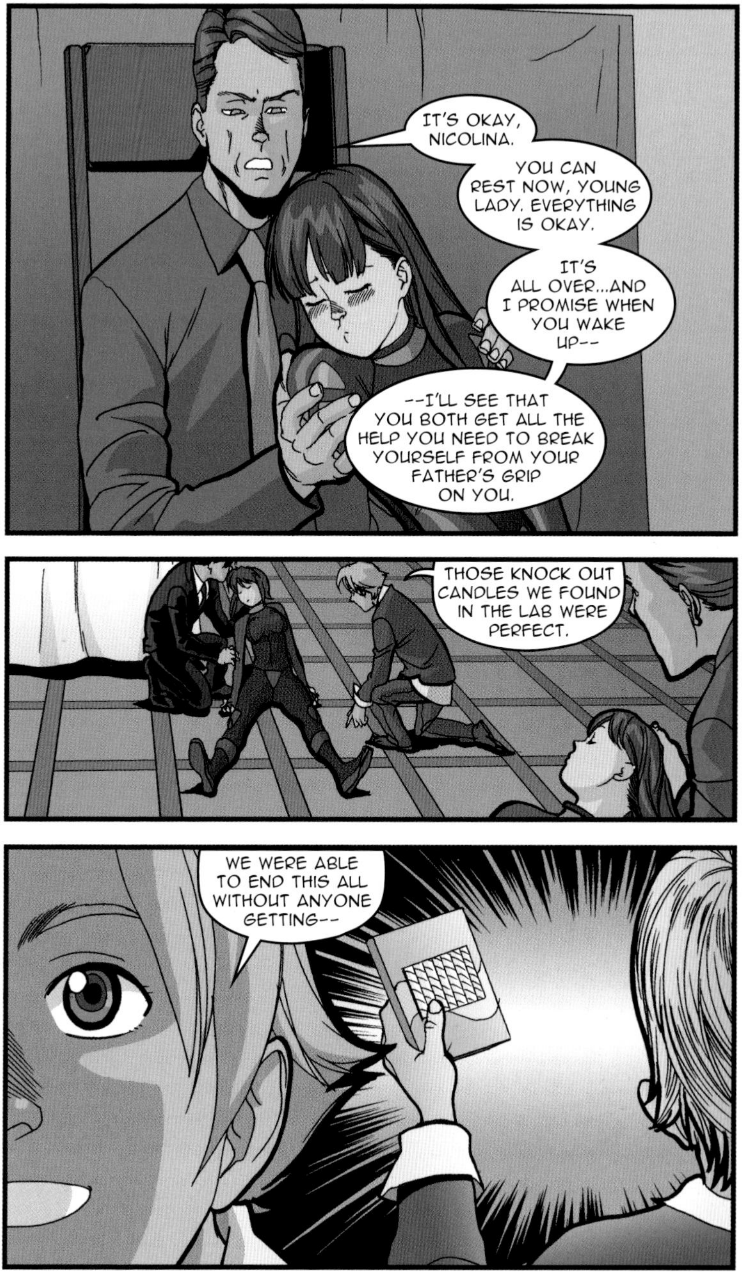
IT'S OKAY, NICOLINA.
YOU CAN REST NOW, YOUNG LADY. EVERYTHING IS OKAY.
IT'S ALL OVER...AND I PROMISE WHEN YOU WAKE UP--
--I'LL SEE THAT YOU BOTH GET ALL THE HELP YOU NEED TO BREAK YOURSELF FROM YOUR FATHER'S GRIP ON YOU.
THOSE KNOCK OUT CANDLES WE FOUND IN THE LAB WERE PERFECT.
WE WERE ABLE TO END THIS ALL WITHOUT ANYONE GETTING--

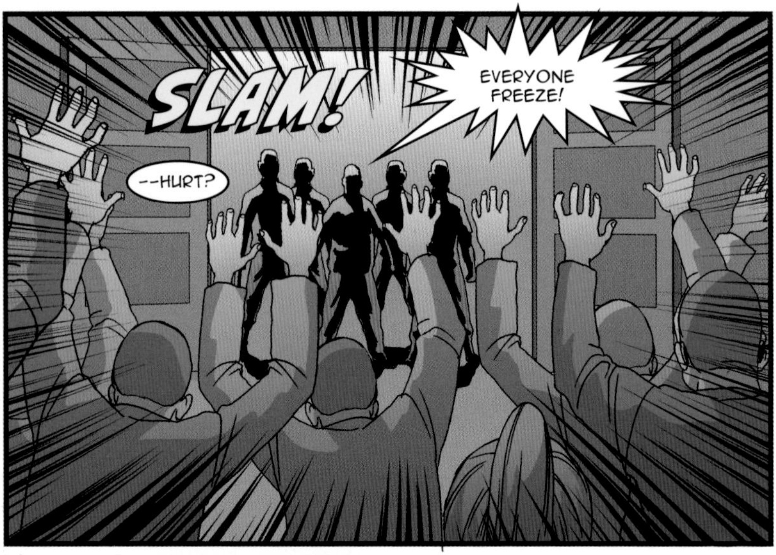
SLAM!
EVERYONE FREEZE!
--HURT?

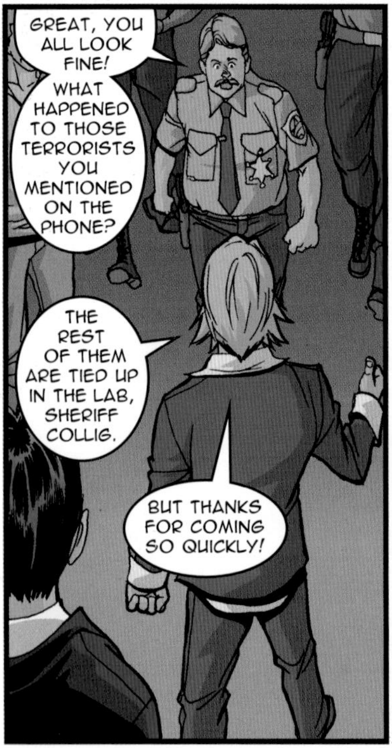
GREAT, YOU ALL LOOK FINE!
WHAT HAPPENED TO THOSE TERRORISTS YOU MENTIONED ON THE PHONE?
THE REST OF THEM ARE TIED UP IN THE LAB, SHERIFF COLLIG.
BUT THANKS FOR COMING SO QUICKLY!

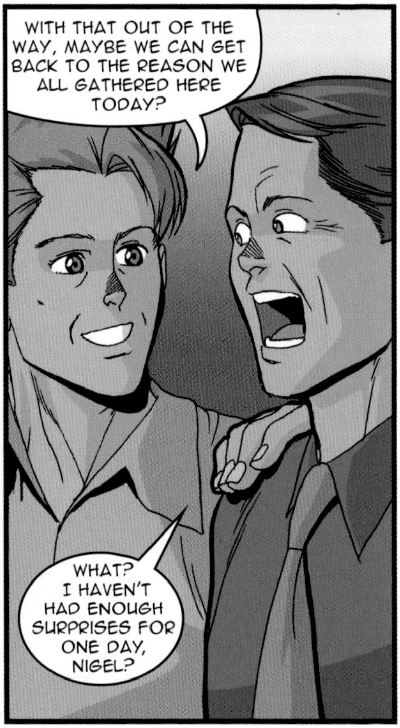
WITH THAT OUT OF THE WAY, MAYBE WE CAN GET BACK TO THE REASON WE ALL GATHERED HERE TODAY?
WHAT? I HAVEN'T HAD ENOUGH SURPRISES FOR ONE DAY, NIGEL?

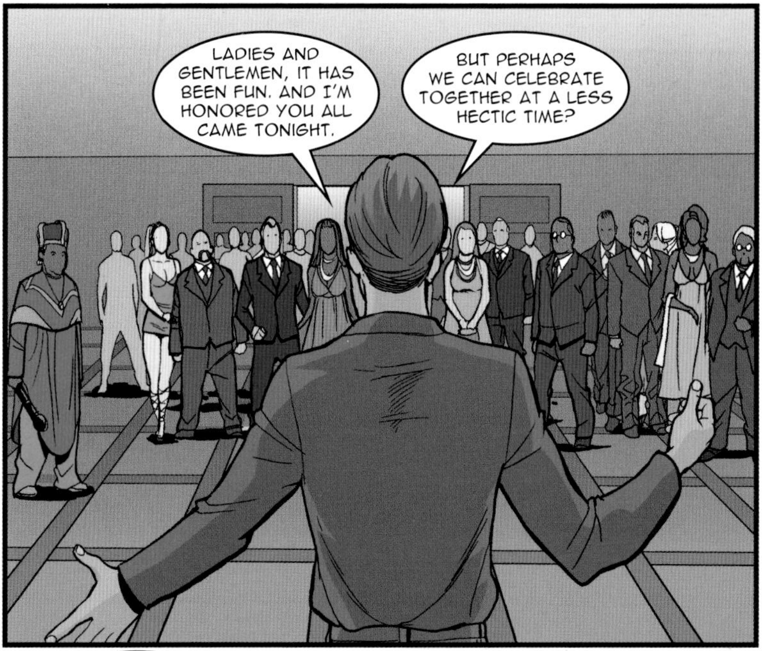
LADIES AND GENTLEMEN, IT HAS BEEN FUN. AND I'M HONORED YOU ALL CAME TONIGHT.
BUT PERHAPS WE CAN CELEBRATE TOGETHER AT A LESS HECTIC TIME?

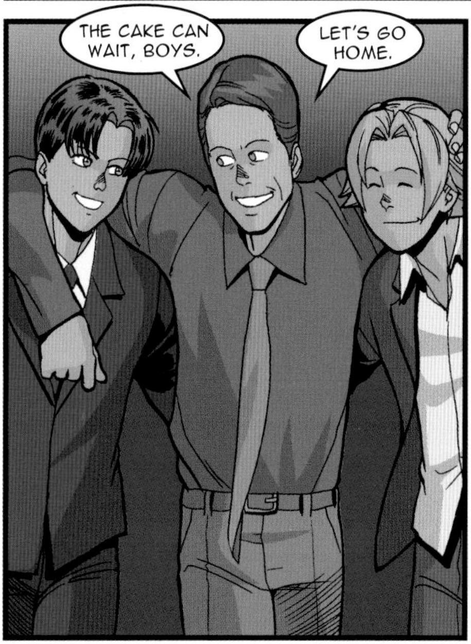
THE CAKE CAN WAIT, BOYS.
LET'S GO HOME.

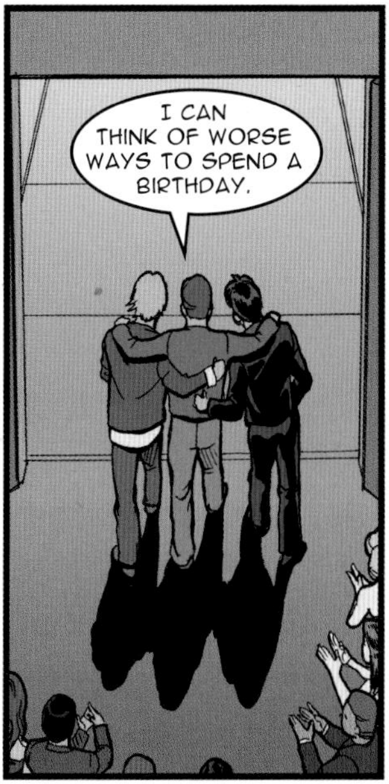
I CAN THINK OF WORSE WAYS TO SPEND A BIRTHDAY.

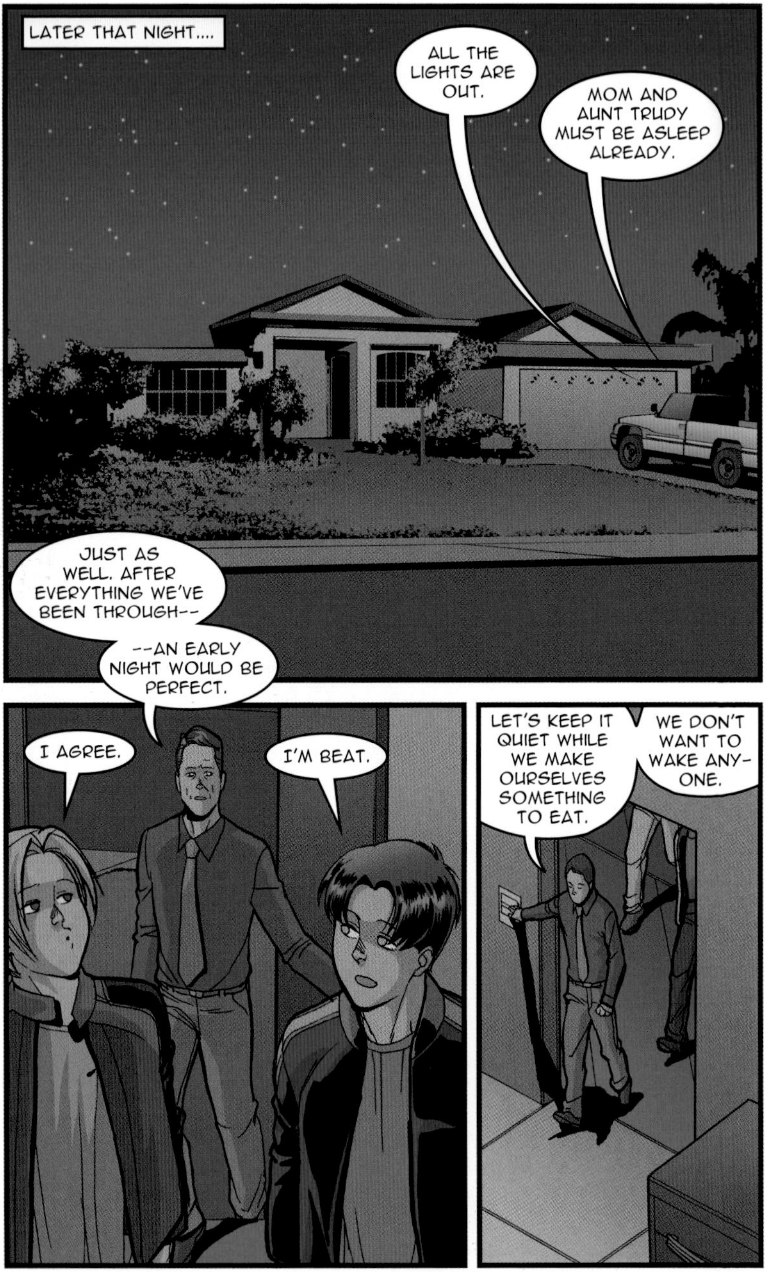
LATER THAT NIGHT....
ALL THE LIGHTS ARE OUT.
MOM AND AUNT TRUDY MUST BE ASLEEP ALREADY.
JUST AS WELL. AFTER EVERYTHING WE'VE BEEN THROUGH--
--AN EARLY NIGHT WOULD BE PERFECT.
I AGREE.
I'M BEAT.
LET'S KEEP IT QUIET WHILE WE MAKE OURSELVES SOMETHING TO EAT.
WE DON'T WANT TO WAKE ANY-ONE.

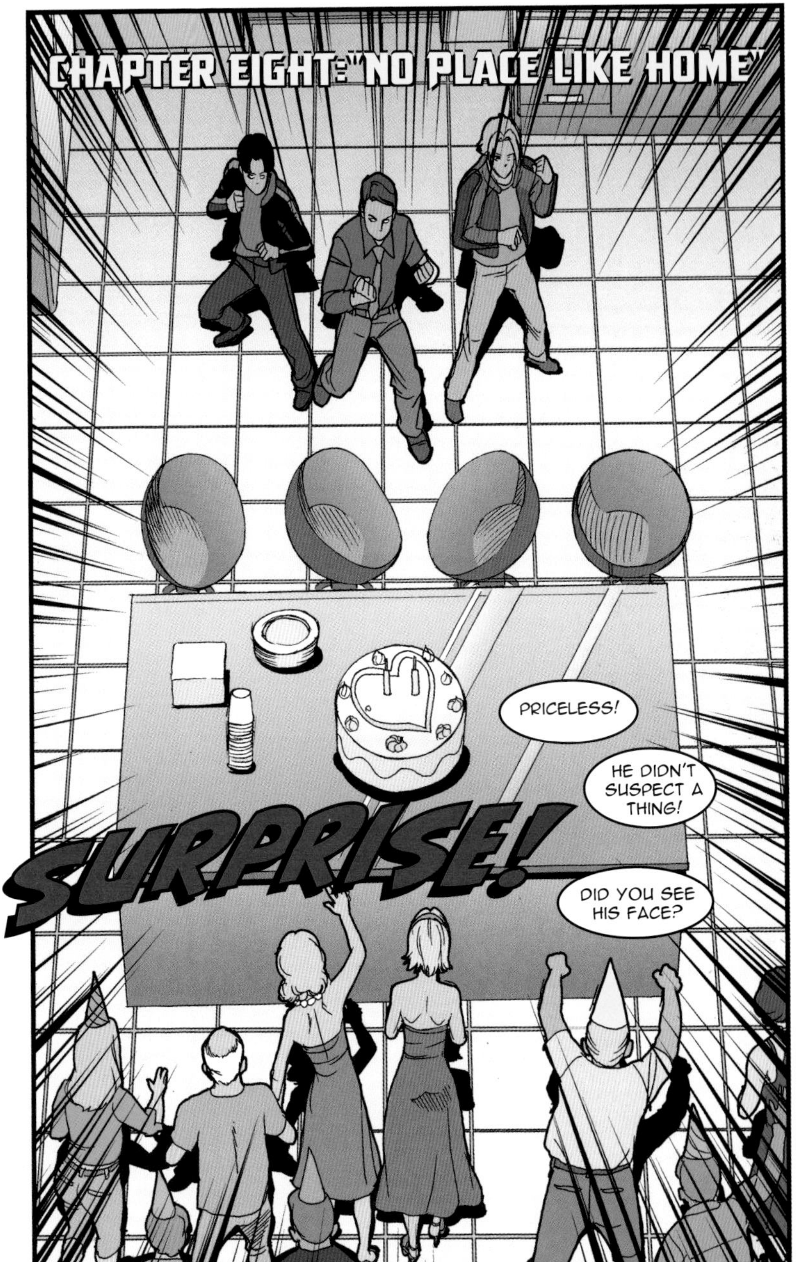
CHAPTER EIGHT: "NO PLACE LIKE HOME"
SURPRISE!
PRICELESS!
HE DIDN'T SUSPECT A THING!
DID YOU SEE HIS FACE?

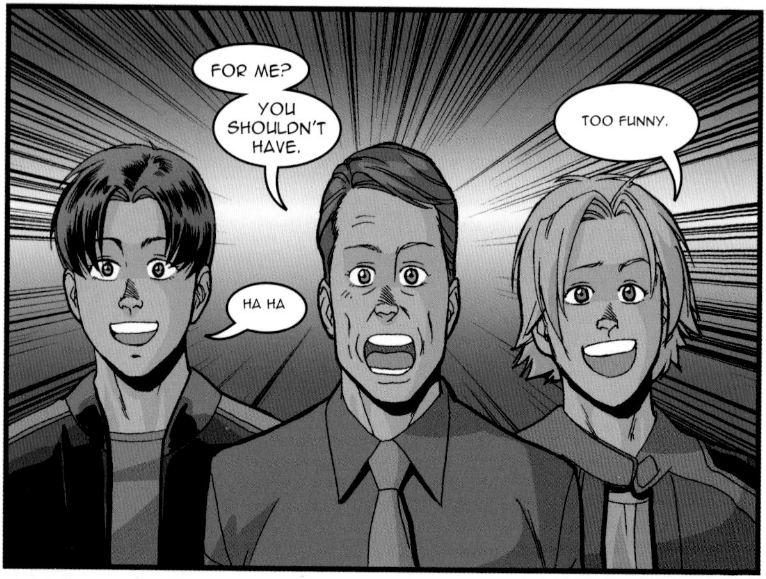
FOR ME?
YOU SHOULDN'T HAVE.
TOO FUNNY.
HA HA
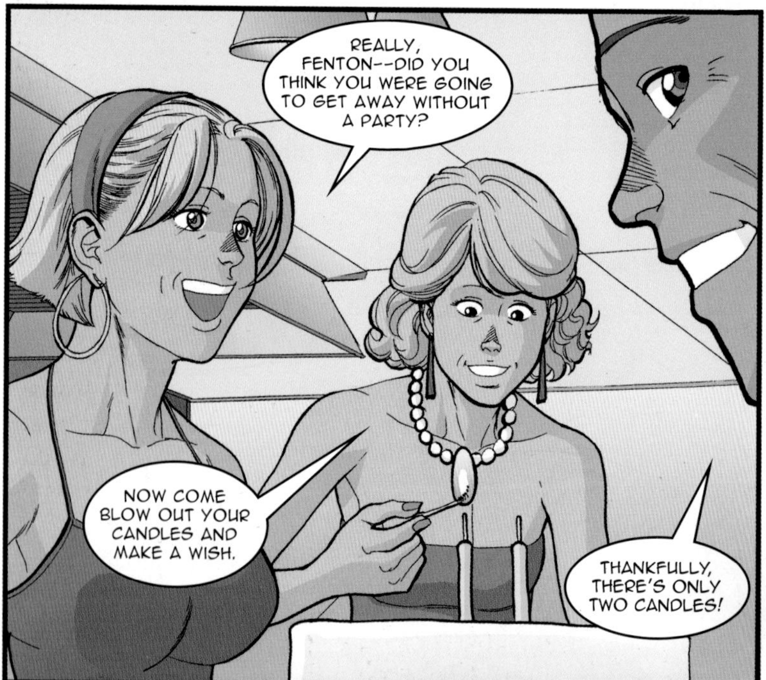
REALLY, FENTON--DID YOU THINK YOU WERE GOING TO GET AWAY WITHOUT A PARTY?
NOW COME BLOW OUT YOUR CANDLES AND MAKE A WISH.
THANKFULLY, THERE'S ONLY TWO CANDLES!

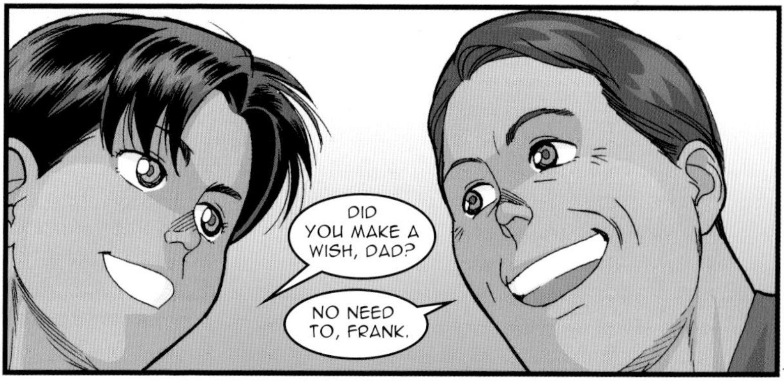
DID YOU MAKE A WISH, DAD?
NO NEED TO, FRANK.

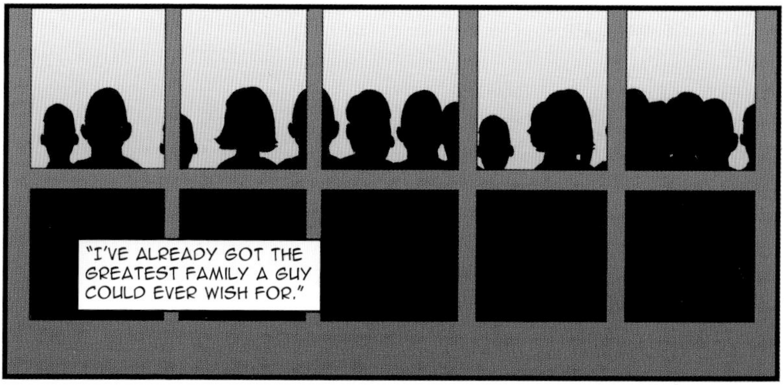
"I'VE ALREADY GOT THE GREATEST FAMILY A GUY COULD EVER WISH FOR."

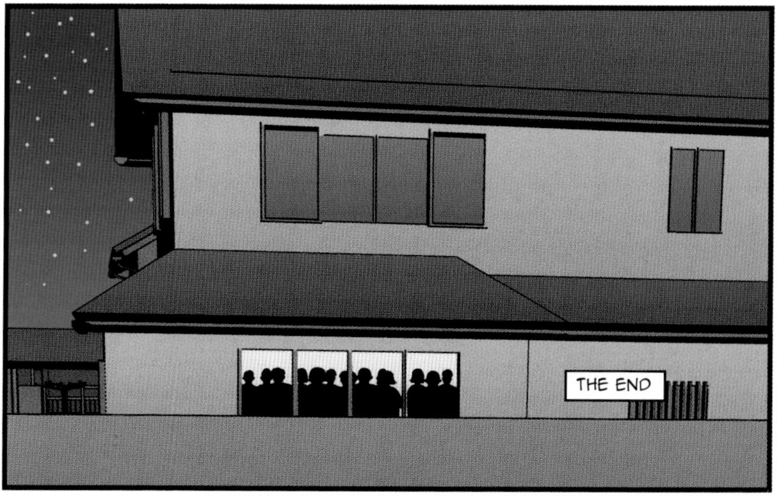
THE END

THE HARDY BOYS GRAPHIC NOVELS FROM PAPERCUTZ

#1 "The Ocean of Osyria"

#2 "Identity Theft"

#3 "Mad House"

#4 "Malled"

#5 "Sea You, Sea Me!"

#6 "Hyde & Shriek"

#7 "The Opposite Numbers"

#8 "Board To Death"

#9 "To Die Or Not To Die?"

#10 "A Hardy Day's Night"

#11 "Abracadeath"

#12 "Dude Ranch O' Death!"

#13 "The Deadliest Stunt"

#14 "Haley Danelle's Top Eight!"

#15 "Live Free, Die Hardy!"

#16 "Shhhhhh!"

#17 "Word Up!"

#18 "D.A.N.G.E.R Spells the Hangman"

#19 "Chaos at 30,000 Feet"

#20 "Deadly Strategy"

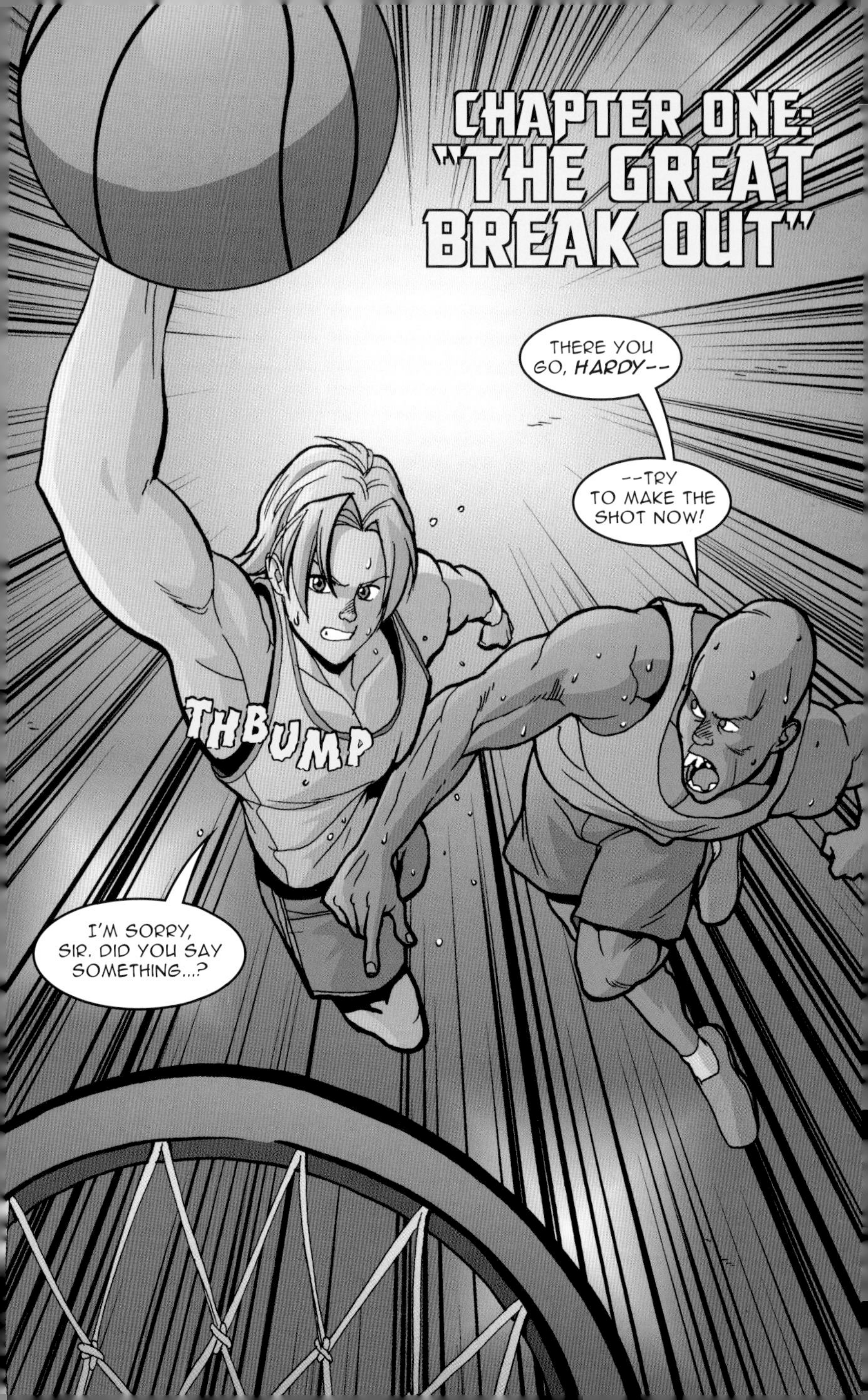

CHAPTER ONE:
"THE GREAT BREAK OUT"
THERE YOU GO, HARDY--
--TRY TO MAKE THE SHOT NOW!
THBUMP
I'M SORRY, SIR. DID YOU SAY SOMETHING...?

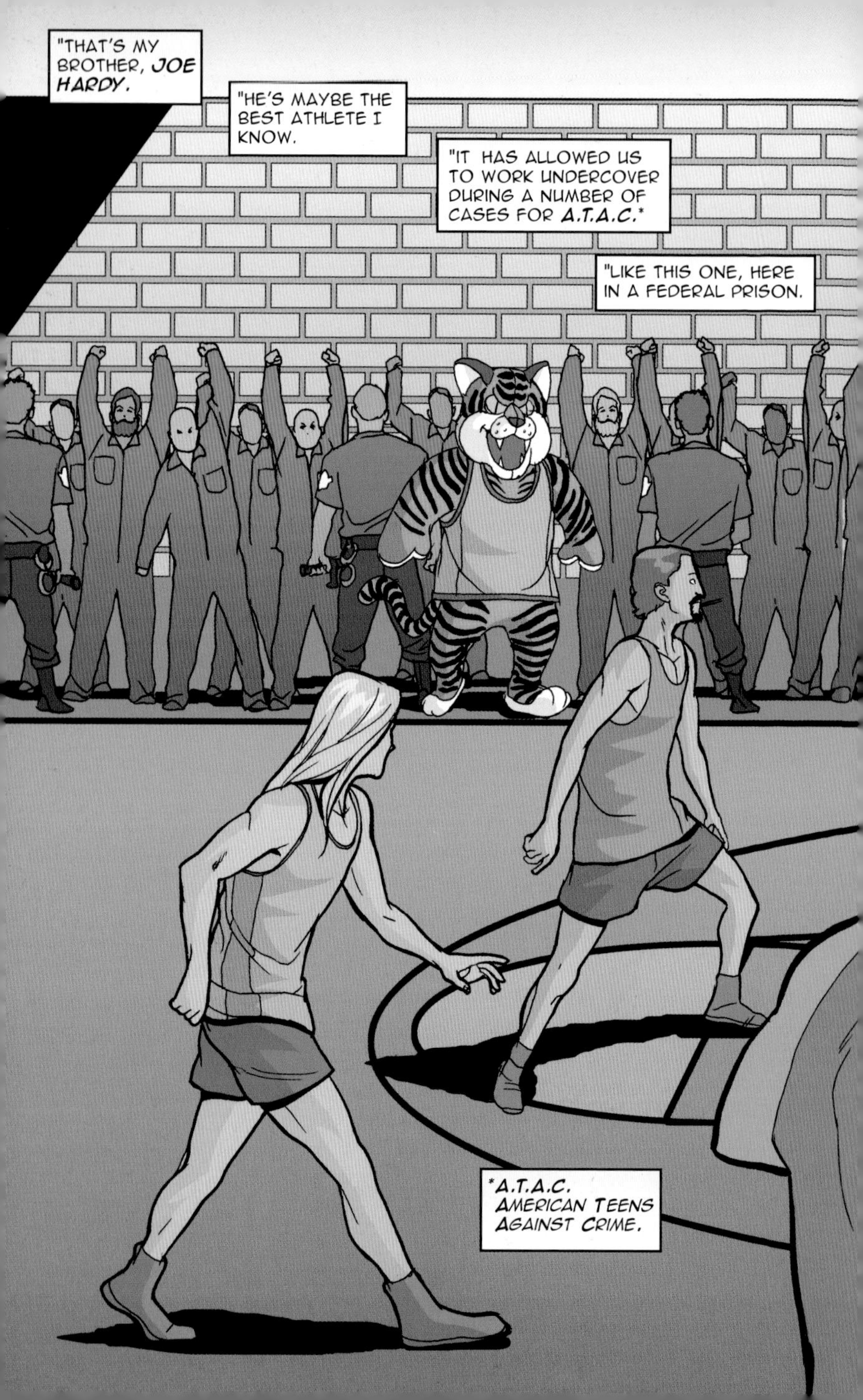
"THAT'S MY BROTHER, JOE HARDY.
"HE'S MAYBE THE BEST ATHLETE I KNOW.
"IT HAS ALLOWED US TO WORK UNDERCOVER DURING A NUMBER OF CASES FOR A.T.A.C.*
"LIKE THIS ONE, HERE IN A FEDERAL PRISON.
*A.T.A.C. AMERICAN TEENS AGAINST CRIME.

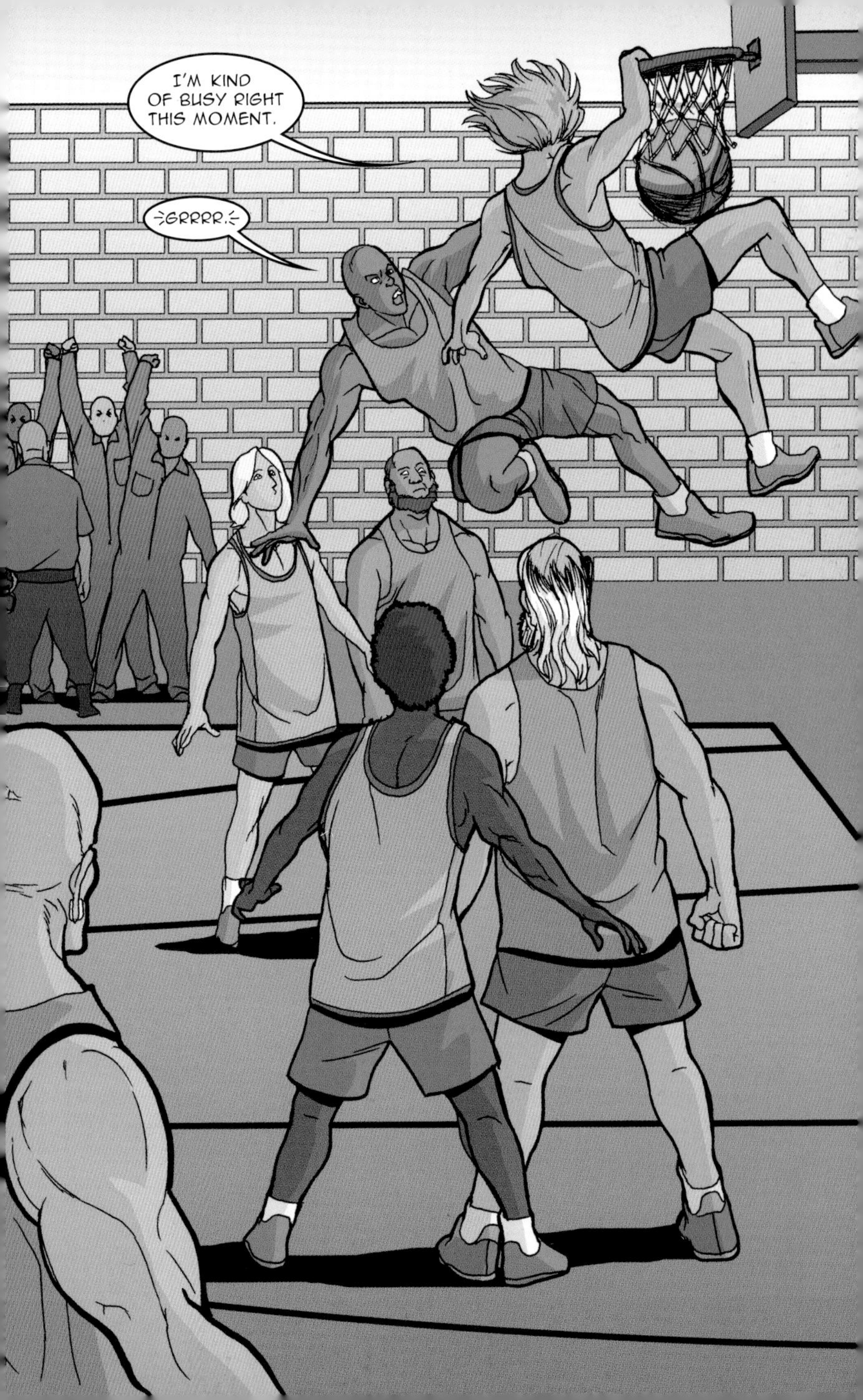
I'M KIND OF BUSY RIGHT THIS MOMENT.
GRRRR.

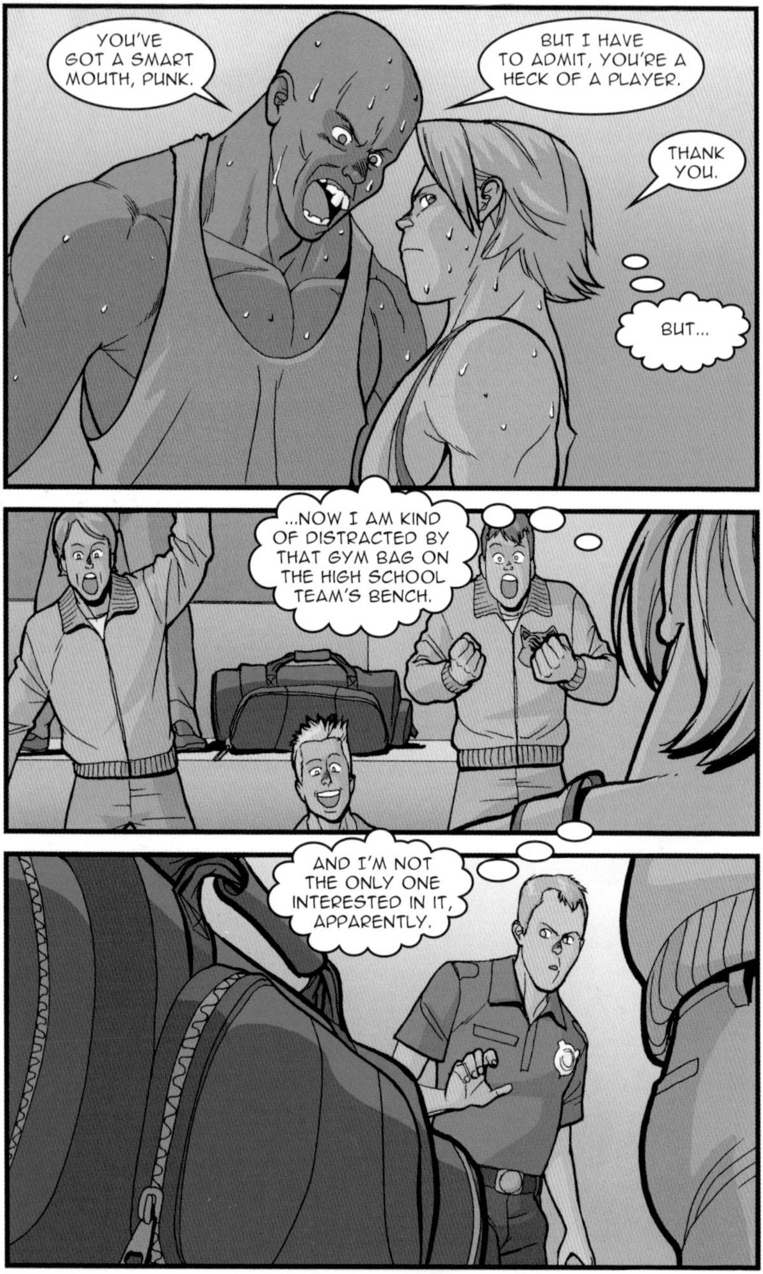
YOU'VE GOT A SMART MOUTH, PUNK.
BUT I HAVE TO ADMIT, YOU'RE A HECK OF A PLAYER.
THANK YOU.
BUT...
...NOW I AM KIND OF DISTRACTED BY THAT GYM BAG ON THE HIGH SCHOOL TEAM'S BENCH.
AND I'M NOT THE ONLY ONE INTERESTED IN IT, APPARENTLY.

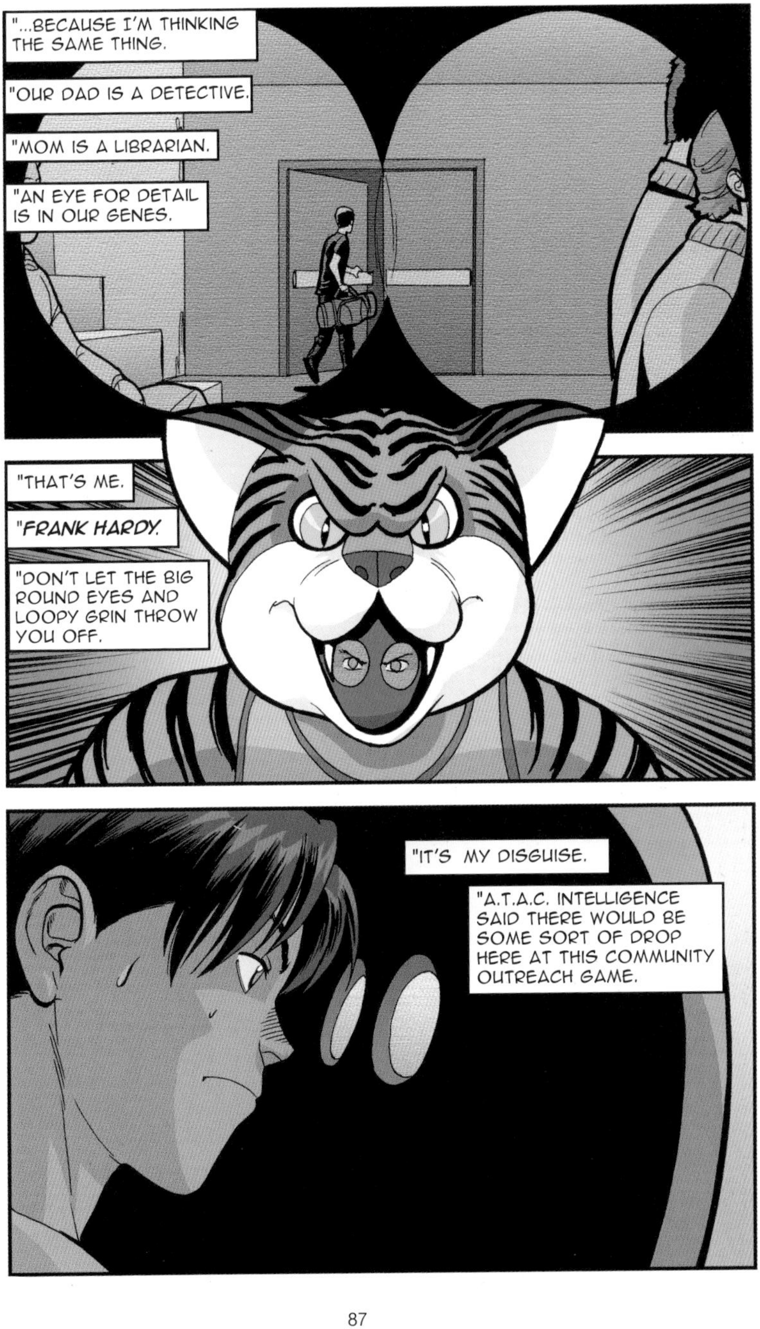
"...BECAUSE I'M THINKING THE SAME THING.
"OUR DAD IS A DETECTIVE.
"MOM IS A LIBRARIAN.
"AN EYE FOR DETAIL IS IN OUR GENES.
"THAT'S ME.
"*FRANK HARDY.*
"DON'T LET THE BIG ROUND EYES AND LOOPY GRIN THROW YOU OFF.
"IT'S MY DISGUISE.
"A.T.A.C. INTELLIGENCE SAID THERE WOULD BE SOME SORT OF DROP HERE AT THIS COMMUNITY OUTREACH GAME.

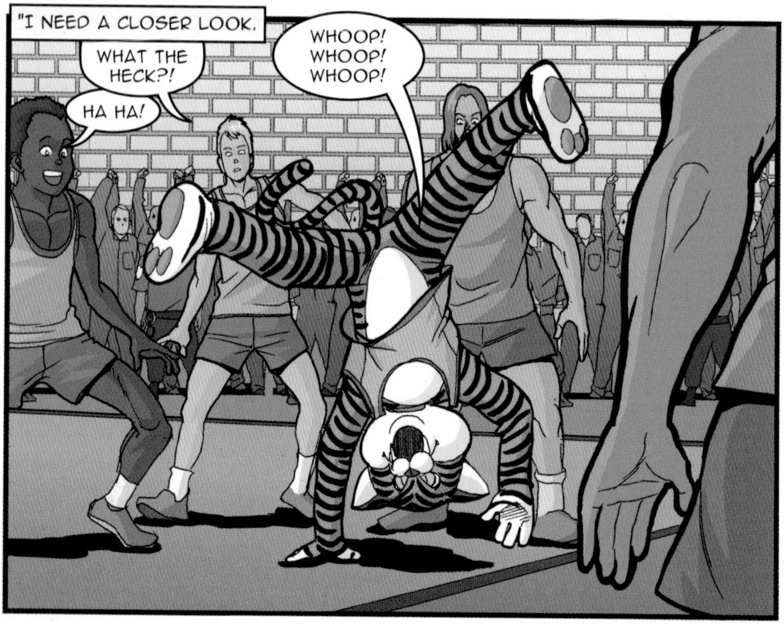
"I NEED A CLOSER LOOK.
WHAT THE HECK?!
HA HA!
WHOOP! WHOOP! WHOOP!

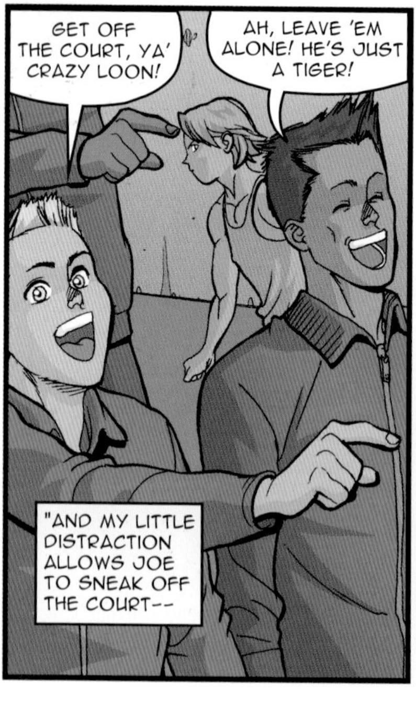
GET OFF THE COURT, YA' CRAZY LOON!
AH, LEAVE 'EM ALONE! HE'S JUST A TIGER!
"AND MY LITTLE DISTRACTION ALLOWS JOE TO SNEAK OFF THE COURT--

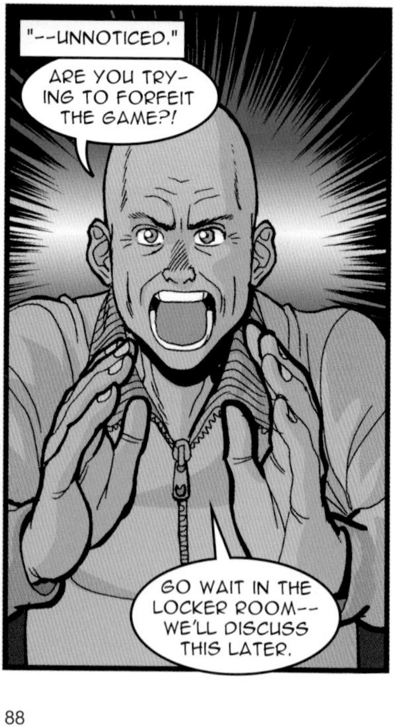
"--UNNOTICED."
ARE YOU TRY-ING TO FORFEIT THE GAME?!
GO WAIT IN THE LOCKER ROOM-- WE'LL DISCUSS THIS LATER.

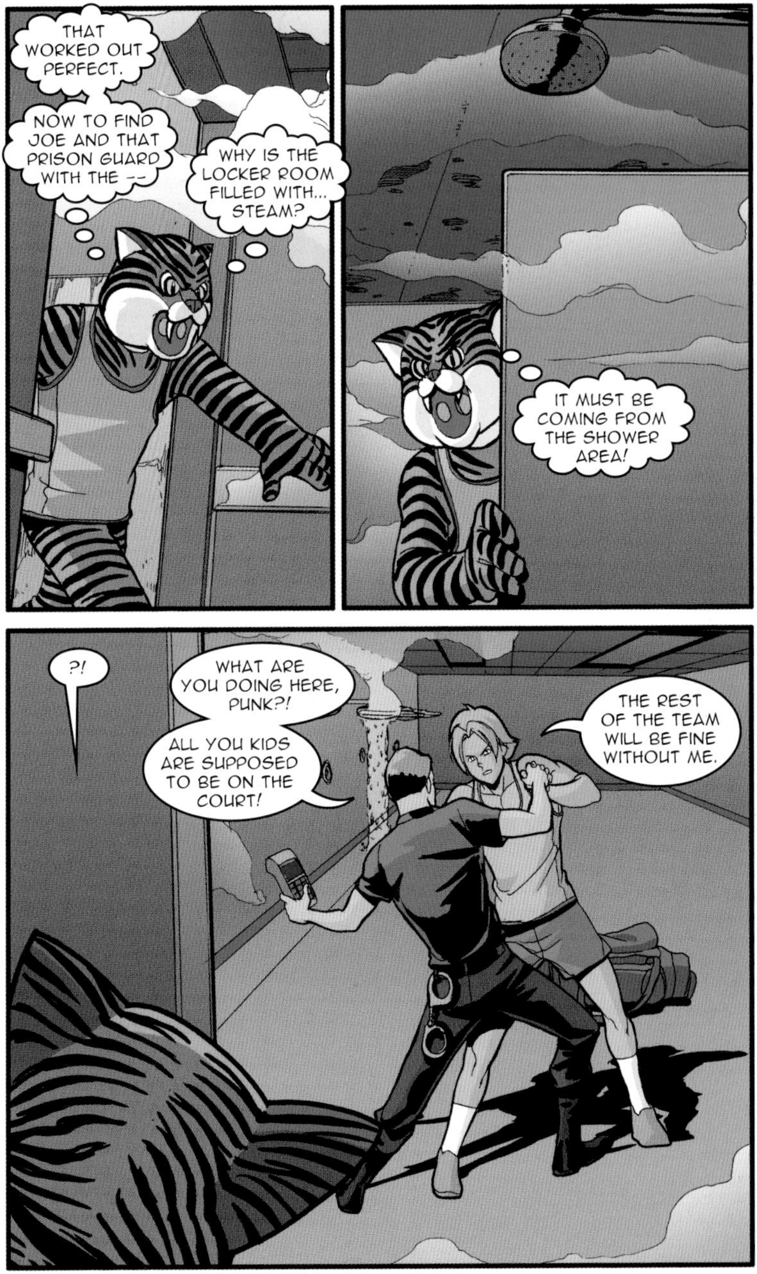
THAT WORKED OUT PERFECT.
NOW TO FIND JOE AND THAT PRISON GUARD WITH THE --
WHY IS THE LOCKER ROOM FILLED WITH... STEAM?
IT MUST BE COMING FROM THE SHOWER AREA!
?!
WHAT ARE YOU DOING HERE, PUNK?!
ALL YOU KIDS ARE SUPPOSED TO BE ON THE COURT!
THE REST OF THE TEAM WILL BE FINE WITHOUT ME.

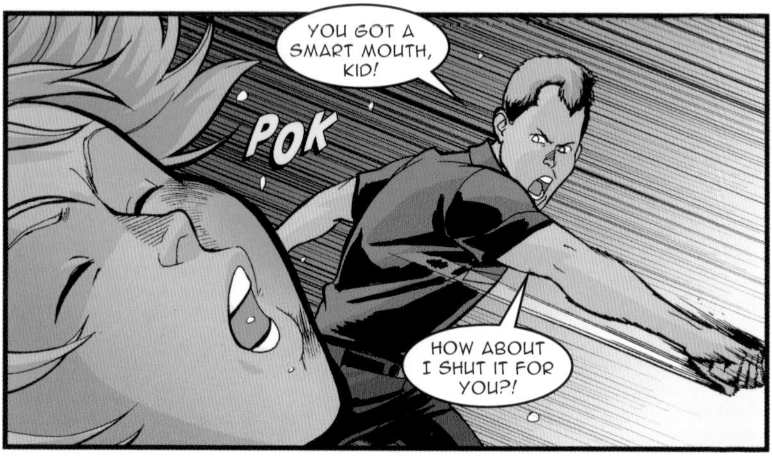
YOU GOT A SMART MOUTH, KID!
POK
HOW ABOUT I SHUT IT FOR YOU?!

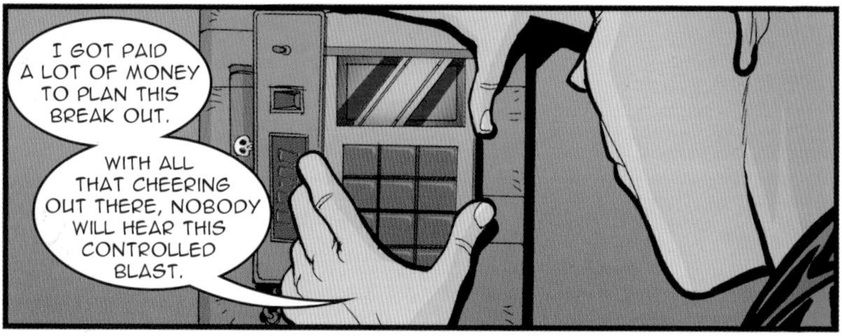
I GOT PAID A LOT OF MONEY TO PLAN THIS BREAK OUT.
WITH ALL THAT CHEERING OUT THERE, NOBODY WILL HEAR THIS CONTROLLED BLAST.

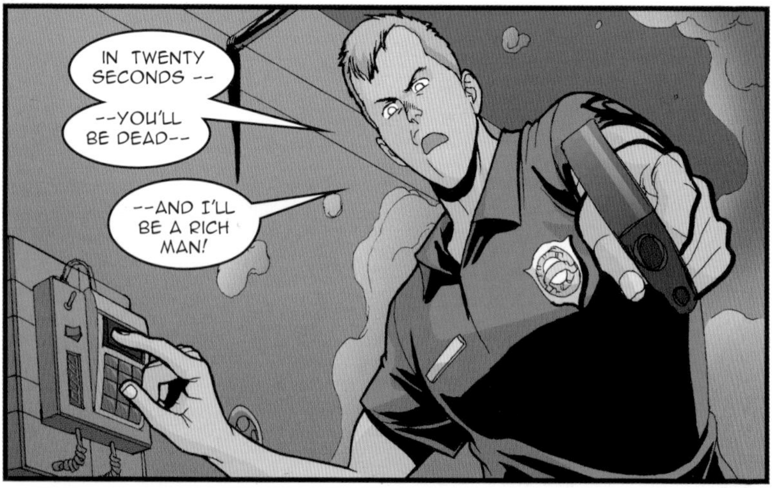
IN TWENTY SECONDS --
--YOU'LL BE DEAD--
--AND I'LL BE A RICH MAN!

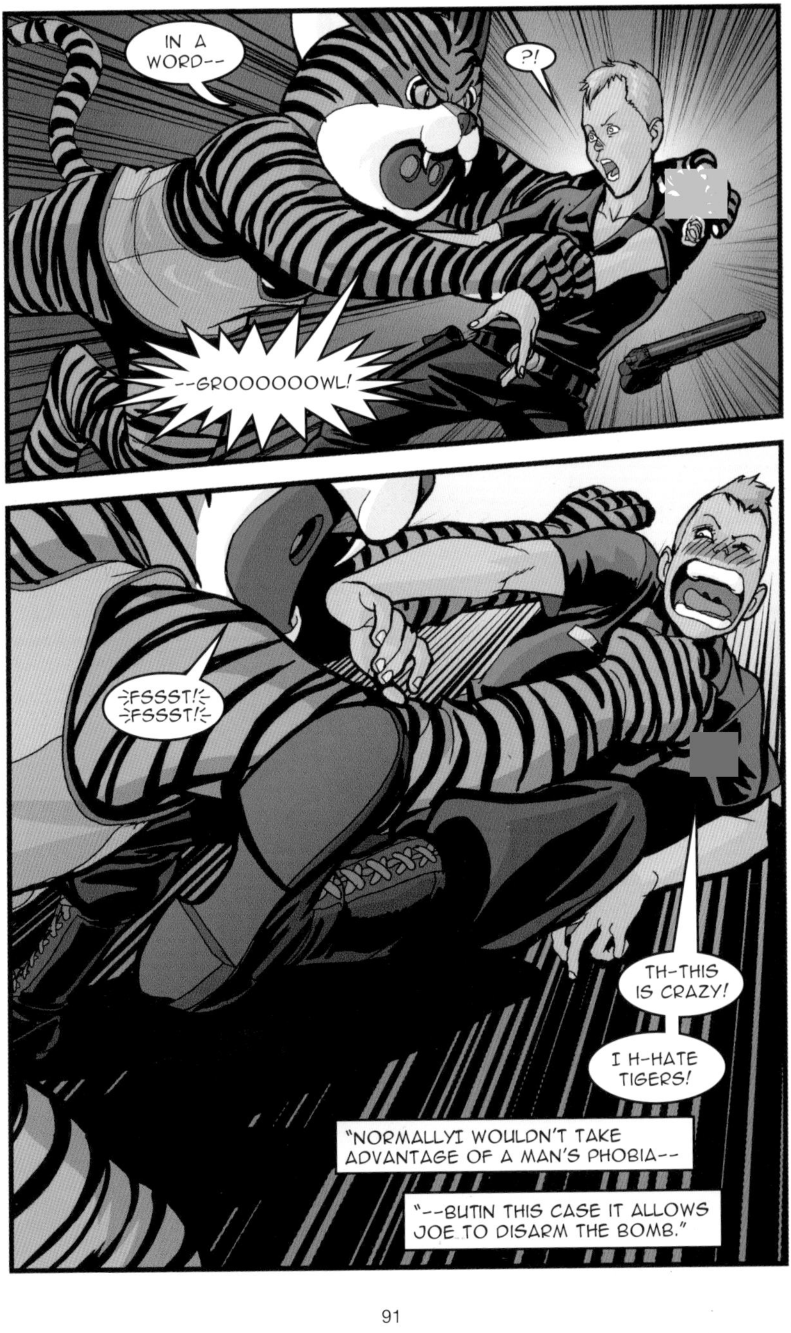
IN A WORD--
?!
--GROOOOOOOWL!
FSSST! FSSST!
TH-THIS IS CRAZY!
I H-HATE TIGERS!
"NORMALLYI WOULDN'T TAKE ADVANTAGE OF A MAN'S PHOBIA--
"--BUTIN THIS CASE IT ALLOWS JOE TO DISARM THE BOMB."

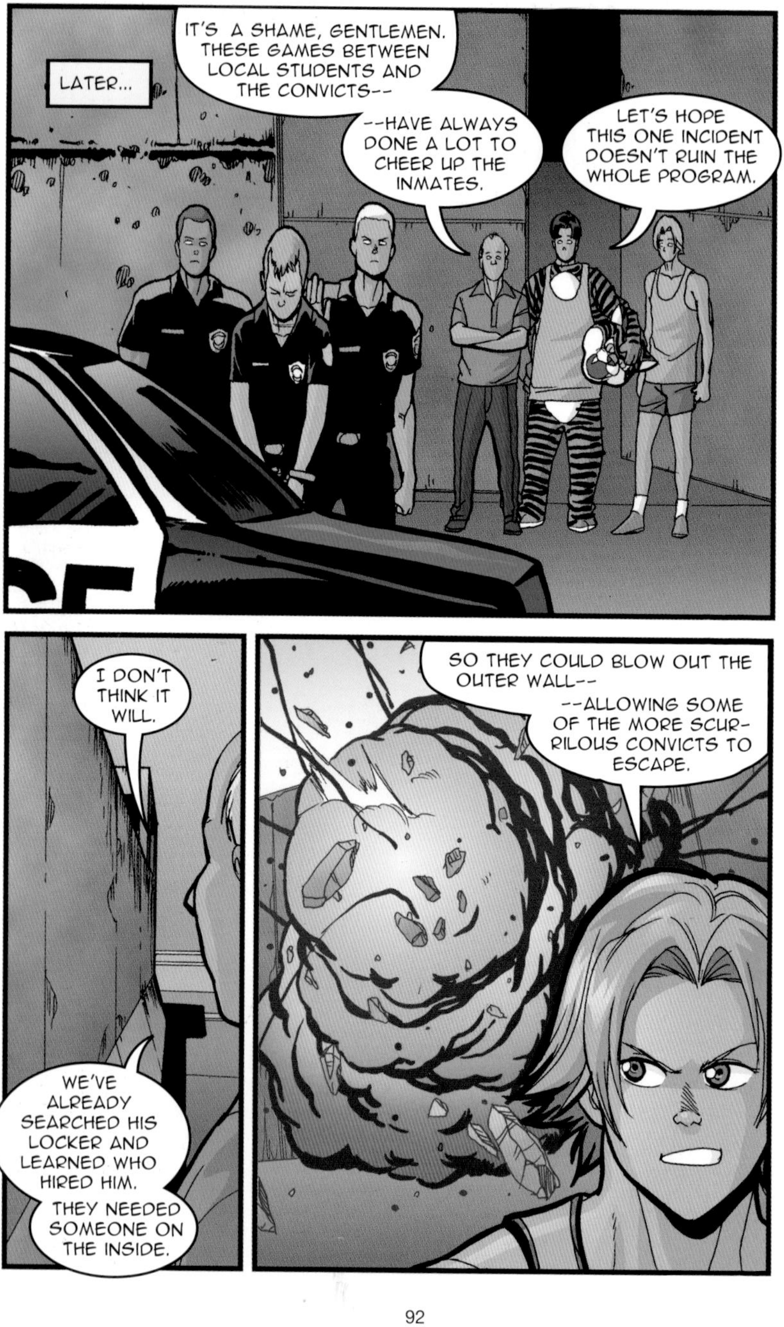
LATER...
IT'S A SHAME, GENTLEMEN. THESE GAMES BETWEEN LOCAL STUDENTS AND THE CONVICTS--
--HAVE ALWAYS DONE A LOT TO CHEER UP THE INMATES.
LET'S HOPE THIS ONE INCIDENT DOESN'T RUIN THE WHOLE PROGRAM.
I DON'T THINK IT WILL.
WE'VE ALREADY SEARCHED HIS LOCKER AND LEARNED WHO HIRED HIM.
THEY NEEDED SOMEONE ON THE INSIDE.
SO THEY COULD BLOW OUT THE OUTER WALL--
--ALLOWING SOME OF THE MORE SCUR-RILOUS CONVICTS TO ESCAPE.

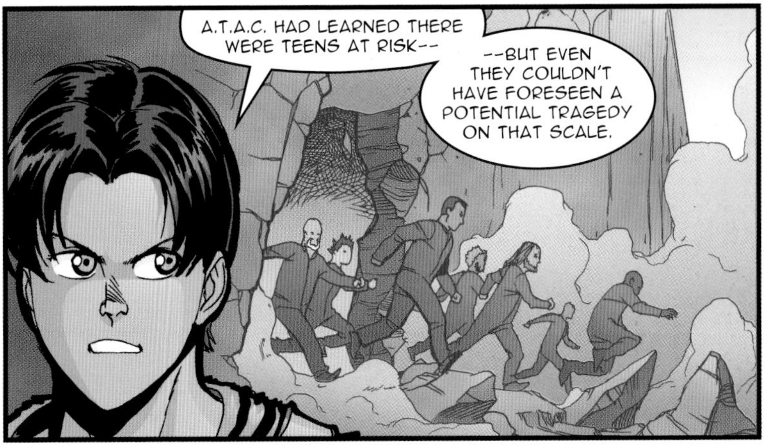
A.T.A.C. HAD LEARNED THERE WERE TEENS AT RISK--
--BUT EVEN THEY COULDN'T HAVE FORESEEN A POTENTIAL TRAGEDY ON THAT SCALE.

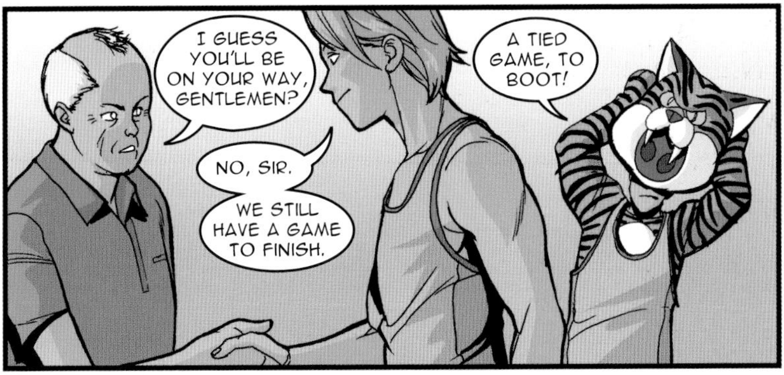
I GUESS YOU'LL BE ON YOUR WAY, GENTLEMEN?
NO, SIR.
WE STILL HAVE A GAME TO FINISH.
A TIED GAME, TO BOOT!

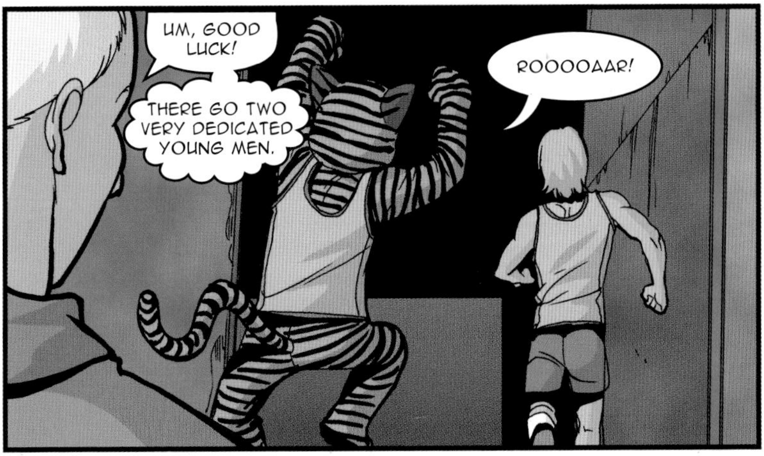
UM, GOOD LUCK!
THERE GO TWO VERY DEDICATED YOUNG MEN.
ROOOOAAR!

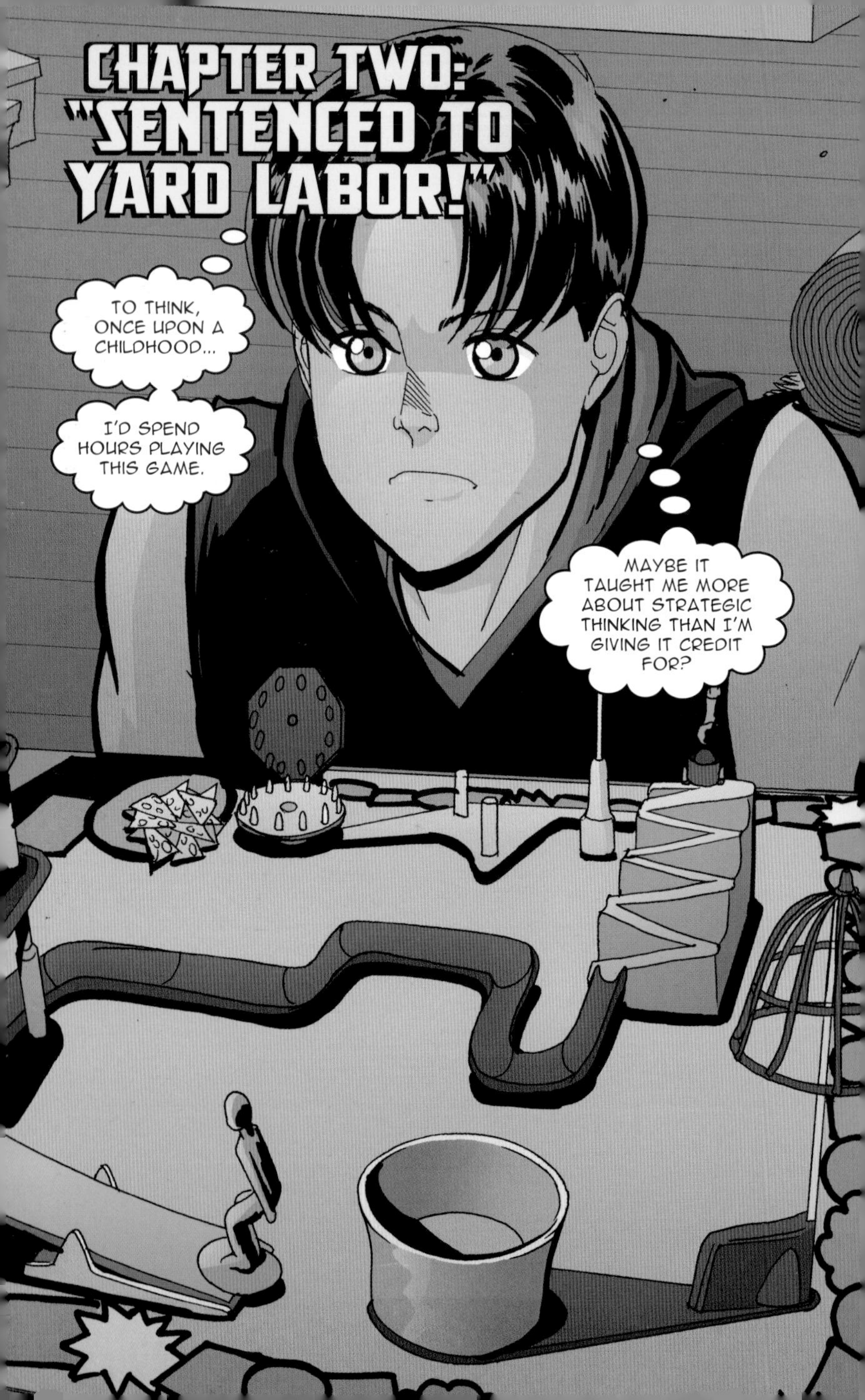
CHAPTER TWO: "SENTENCED TO YARD LABOR!"
TO THINK, ONCE UPON A CHILDHOOD...
I'D SPEND HOURS PLAYING THIS GAME.
MAYBE IT TAUGHT ME MORE ABOUT STRATEGIC THINKING THAN I'M GIVING IT CREDIT FOR?

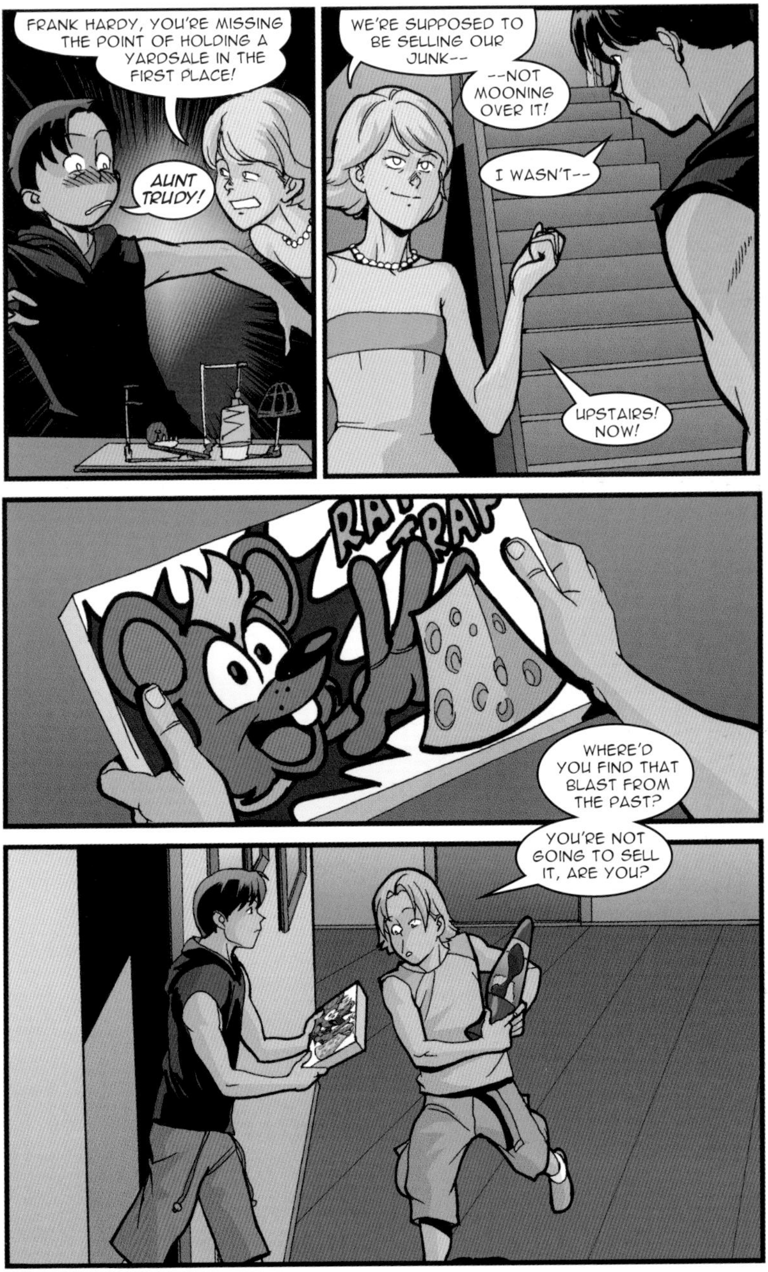
FRANK HARDY, YOU'RE MISSING THE POINT OF HOLDING A YARDSALE IN THE FIRST PLACE!
AUNT TRUDY!
WE'RE SUPPOSED TO BE SELLING OUR JUNK--
--NOT MOONING OVER IT!
I WASN'T--
UPSTAIRS! NOW!
WHERE'D YOU FIND THAT BLAST FROM THE PAST?
YOU'RE NOT GOING TO SELL IT, ARE YOU?

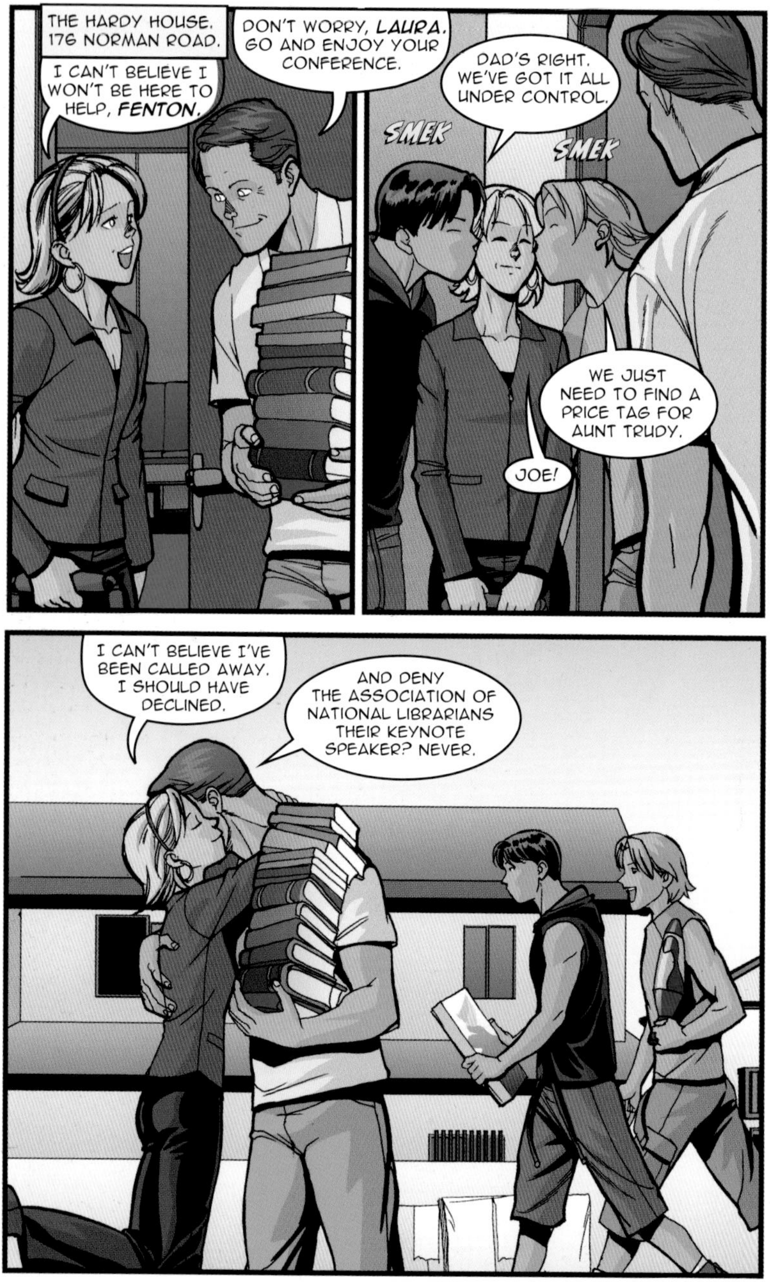
THE HARDY HOUSE. 176 NORMAN ROAD.
I CAN'T BELIEVE I WON'T BE HERE TO HELP, FENTON.
DON'T WORRY, LAURA. GO AND ENJOY YOUR CONFERENCE.
SMEK
DAD'S RIGHT. WE'VE GOT IT ALL UNDER CONTROL.
SMEK
WE JUST NEED TO FIND A PRICE TAG FOR AUNT TRUDY.
JOE!
I CAN'T BELIEVE I'VE BEEN CALLED AWAY. I SHOULD HAVE DECLINED.
AND DENY THE ASSOCIATION OF NATIONAL LIBRARIANS THEIR KEYNOTE SPEAKER? NEVER.

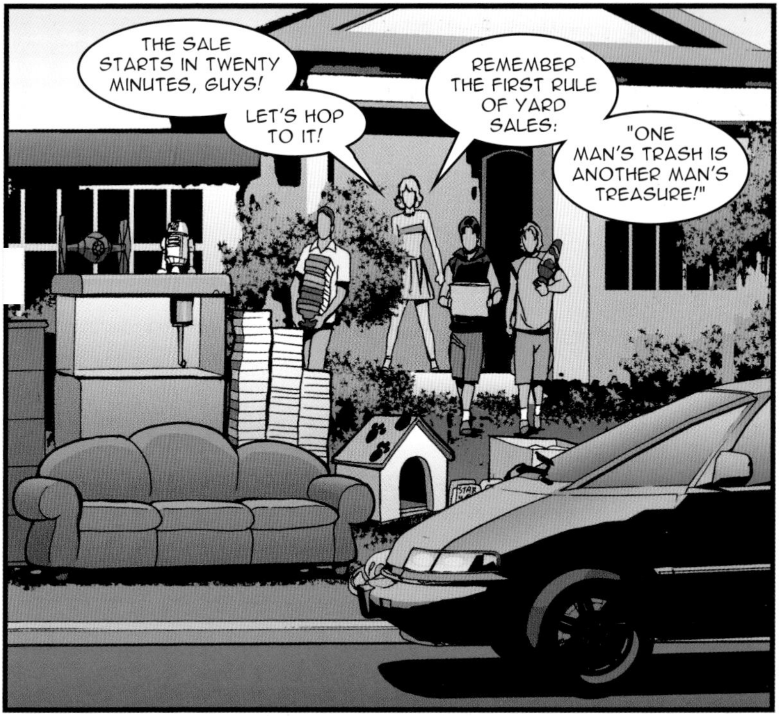
THE SALE STARTS IN TWENTY MINUTES, GUYS!
LET'S HOP TO IT!
REMEMBER THE FIRST RULE OF YARD SALES:
"ONE MAN'S TRASH IS ANOTHER MAN'S TREASURE!"

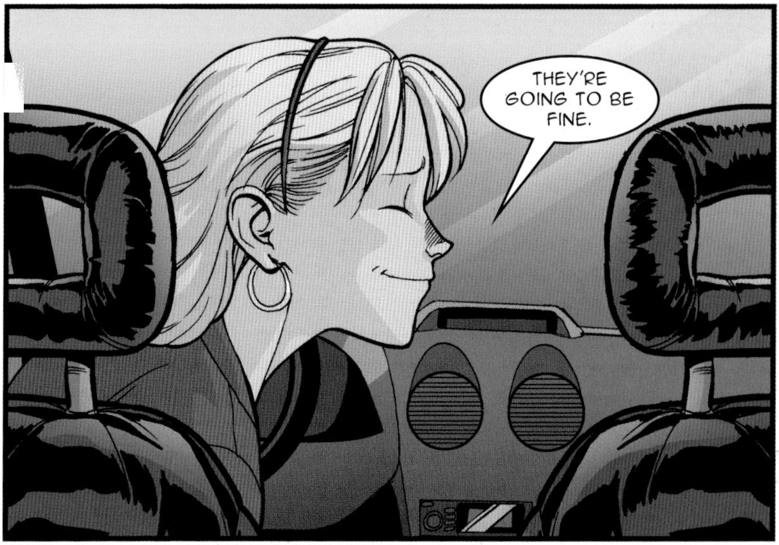
THEY'RE GOING TO BE FINE.

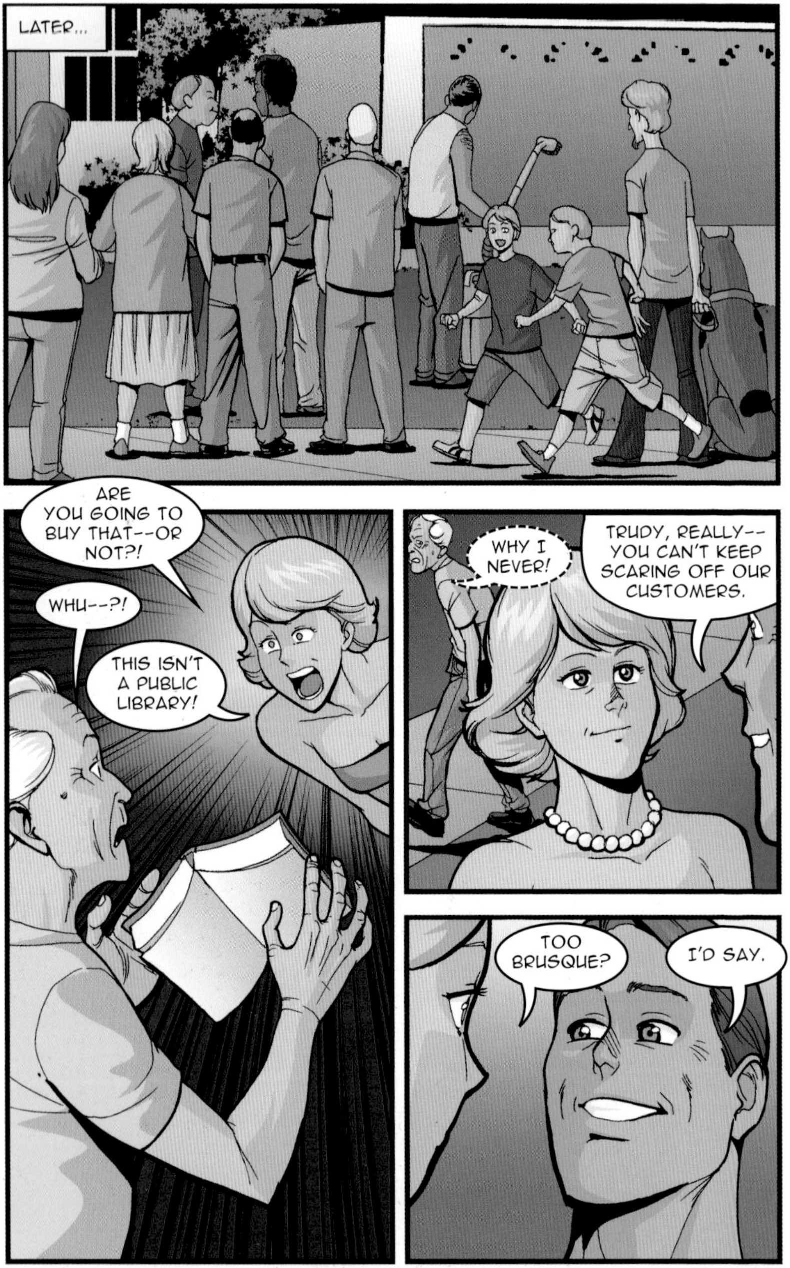
LATER...
ARE YOU GOING TO BUY THAT--OR NOT?!
WHU--?!
THIS ISN'T A PUBLIC LIBRARY!
WHY I NEVER!
TRUDY, REALLY--YOU CAN'T KEEP SCARING OFF OUR CUSTOMERS.
TOO BRUSQUE?
I'D SAY.

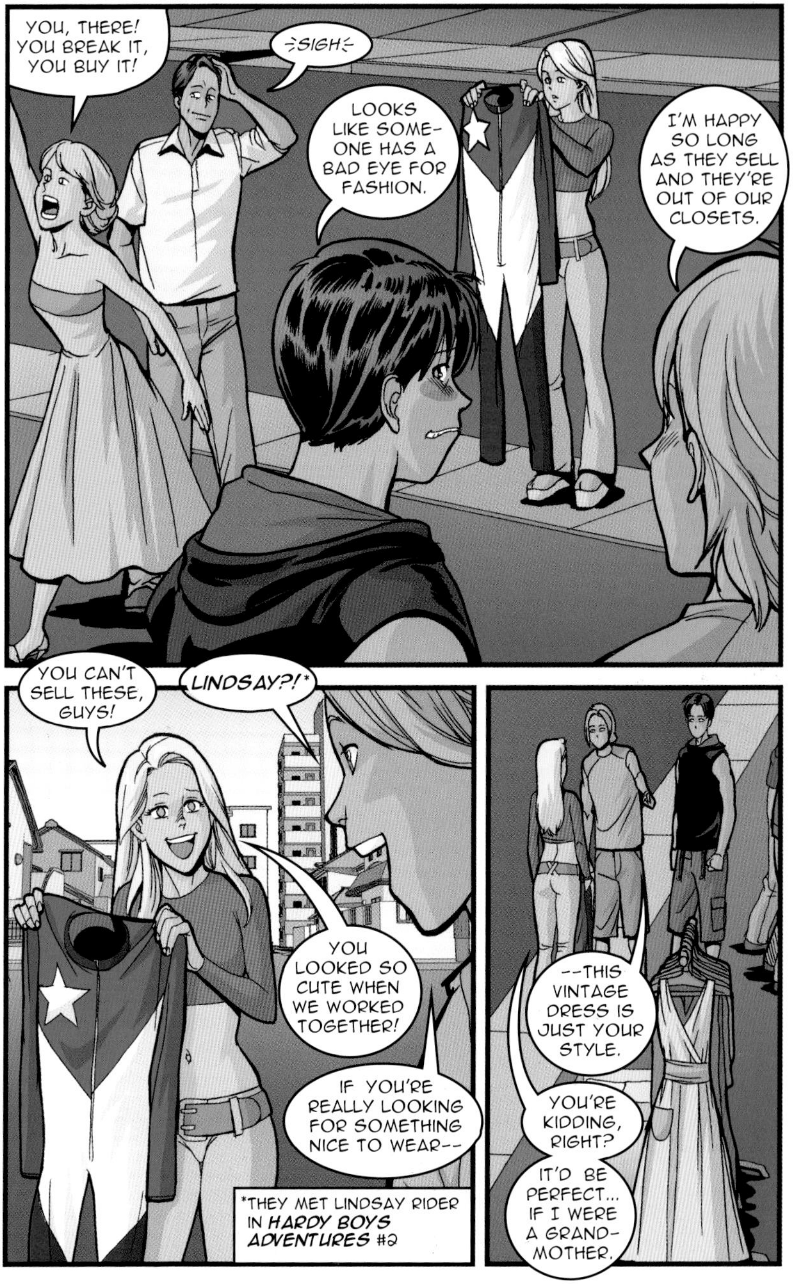
YOU, THERE! YOU BREAK IT, YOU BUY IT!
SIGH
LOOKS LIKE SOME-ONE HAS A BAD EYE FOR FASHION.
I'M HAPPY SO LONG AS THEY SELL AND THEY'RE OUT OF OUR CLOSETS.
YOU CAN'T SELL THESE, GUYS!
LINDSAY?!*
YOU LOOKED SO CUTE WHEN WE WORKED TOGETHER!
IF YOU'RE REALLY LOOKING FOR SOMETHING NICE TO WEAR--
*THEY MET LINDSAY RIDER IN HARDY BOYS ADVENTURES #2
--THIS VINTAGE DRESS IS JUST YOUR STYLE.
YOU'RE KIDDING, RIGHT?
IT'D BE PERFECT... IF I WERE A GRAND-MOTHER.

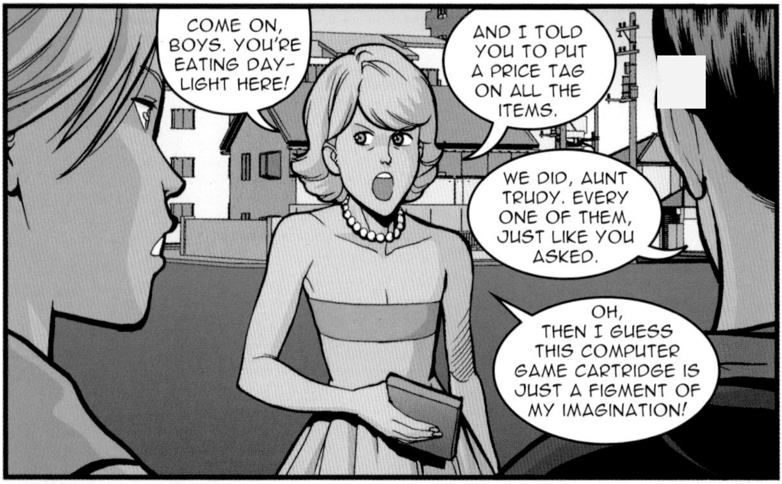
COME ON, BOYS. YOU'RE EATING DAY-LIGHT HERE!
AND I TOLD YOU TO PUT A PRICE TAG ON ALL THE ITEMS.
WE DID, AUNT TRUDY. EVERY ONE OF THEM, JUST LIKE YOU ASKED.
OH, THEN I GUESS THIS COMPUTER GAME CARTRIDGE IS JUST A FIGMENT OF MY IMAGINATION!

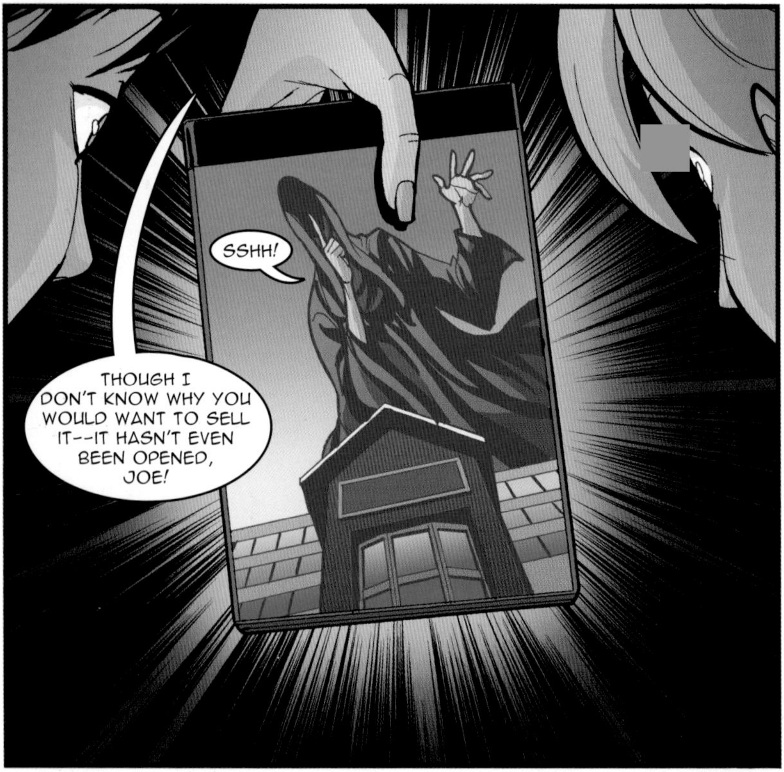
SSHH!
THOUGH I DON'T KNOW WHY YOU WOULD WANT TO SELL IT--IT HASN'T EVEN BEEN OPENED, JOE!

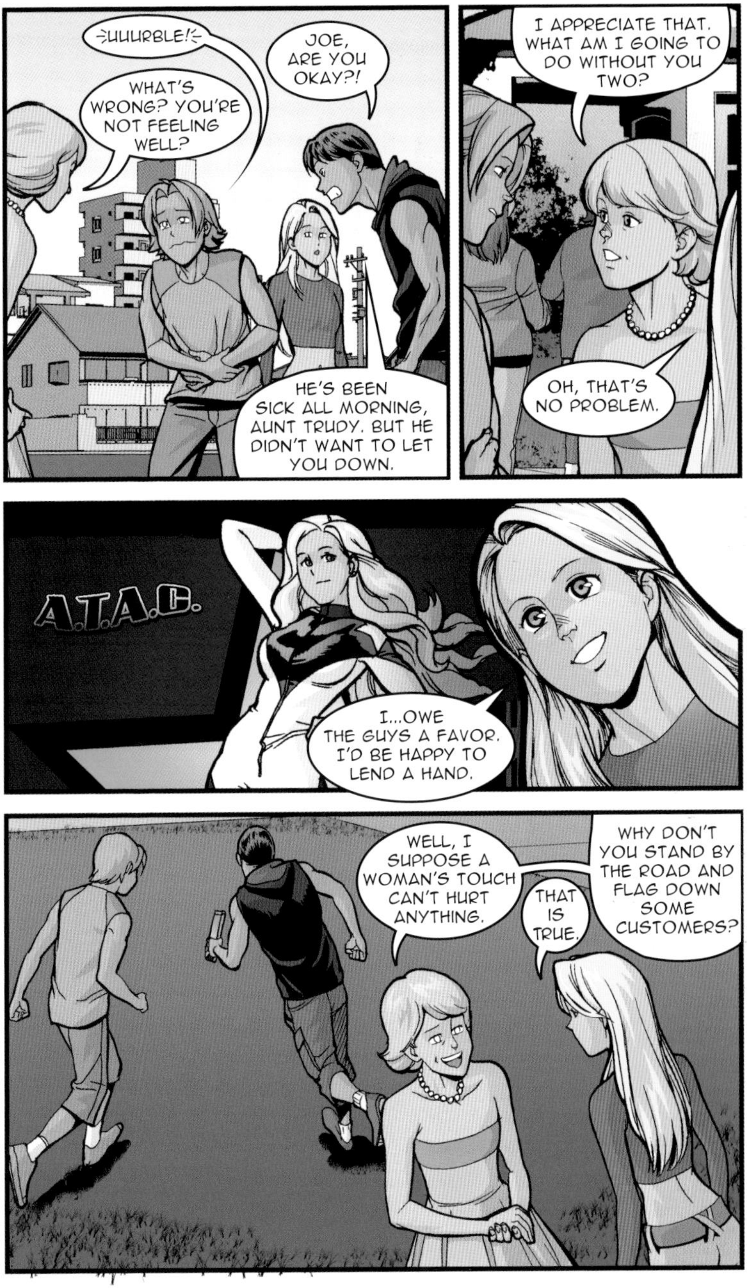

UUURBLE!
WHAT'S WRONG? YOU'RE NOT FEELING WELL?
JOE, ARE YOU OKAY?!
HE'S BEEN SICK ALL MORNING, AUNT TRUDY. BUT HE DIDN'T WANT TO LET YOU DOWN.
I APPRECIATE THAT. WHAT AM I GOING TO DO WITHOUT YOU TWO?
OH, THAT'S NO PROBLEM.
A.T.A.C.
I...OWE THE GUYS A FAVOR. I'D BE HAPPY TO LEND A HAND.
WELL, I SUPPOSE A WOMAN'S TOUCH CAN'T HURT ANYTHING.
THAT IS TRUE.
WHY DON'T YOU STAND BY THE ROAD AND FLAG DOWN SOME CUSTOMERS?

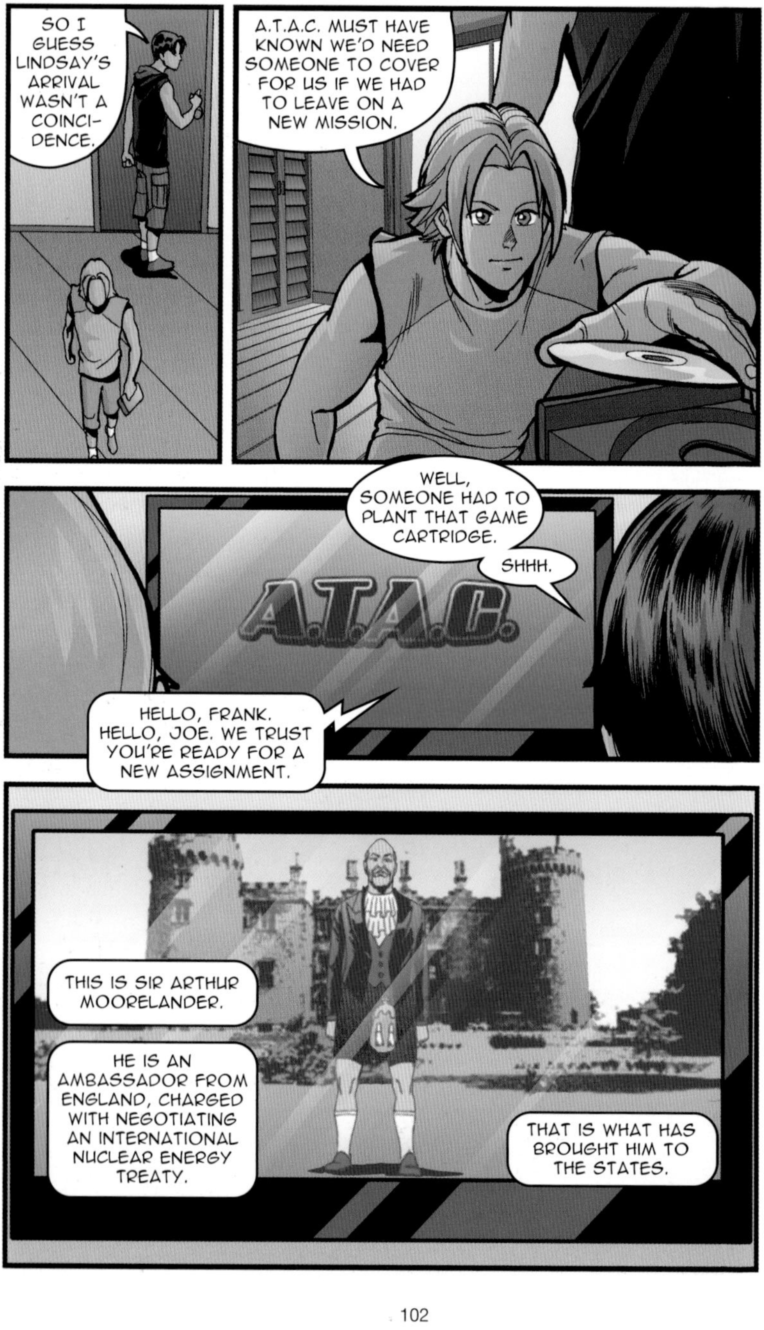
SO I GUESS LINDSAY'S ARRIVAL WASN'T A COINCIDENCE.
A.T.A.C. MUST HAVE KNOWN WE'D NEED SOMEONE TO COVER FOR US IF WE HAD TO LEAVE ON A NEW MISSION.
WELL, SOMEONE HAD TO PLANT THAT GAME CARTRIDGE.
SHHH.
A.T.A.C.
HELLO, FRANK. HELLO, JOE. WE TRUST YOU'RE READY FOR A NEW ASSIGNMENT.
THIS IS SIR ARTHUR MOORELANDER.
HE IS AN AMBASSADOR FROM ENGLAND, CHARGED WITH NEGOTIATING AN INTERNATIONAL NUCLEAR ENERGY TREATY.
THAT IS WHAT HAS BROUGHT HIM TO THE STATES.

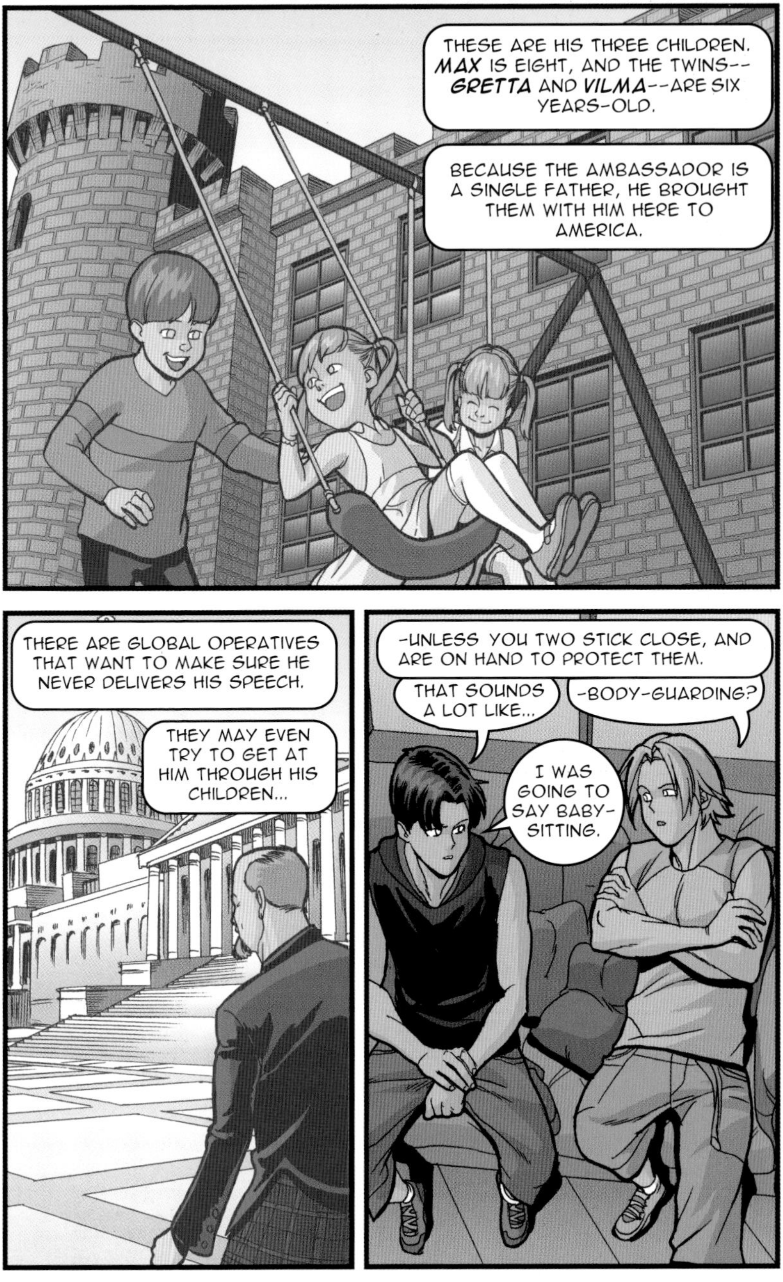
THESE ARE HIS THREE CHILDREN. MAX IS EIGHT, AND THE TWINS--GRETTA AND VILMA--ARE SIX YEARS-OLD.
BECAUSE THE AMBASSADOR IS A SINGLE FATHER, HE BROUGHT THEM WITH HIM HERE TO AMERICA.
THERE ARE GLOBAL OPERATIVES THAT WANT TO MAKE SURE HE NEVER DELIVERS HIS SPEECH.
THEY MAY EVEN TRY TO GET AT HIM THROUGH HIS CHILDREN...
-UNLESS YOU TWO STICK CLOSE, AND ARE ON HAND TO PROTECT THEM.
THAT SOUNDS A LOT LIKE...
-BODY-GUARDING?
I WAS GOING TO SAY BABY-SITTING.

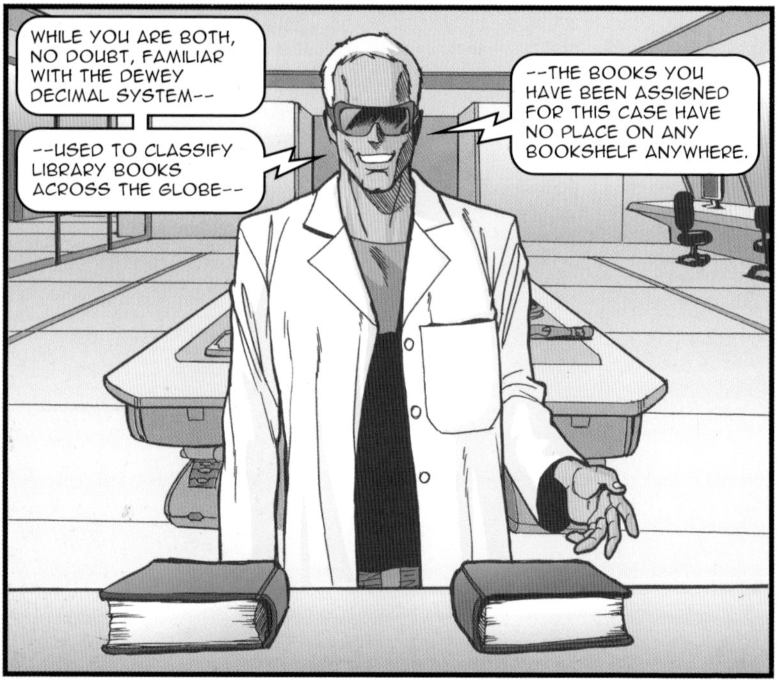
WHILE YOU ARE BOTH, NO DOUBT, FAMILIAR WITH THE DEWEY DECIMAL SYSTEM--
--USED TO CLASSIFY LIBRARY BOOKS ACROSS THE GLOBE--
--THE BOOKS YOU HAVE BEEN ASSIGNED FOR THIS CASE HAVE NO PLACE ON ANY BOOKSHELF ANYWHERE.

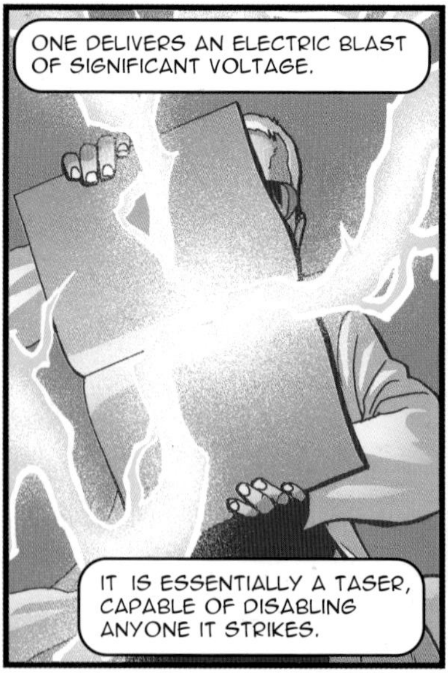
ONE DELIVERS AN ELECTRIC BLAST OF SIGNIFICANT VOLTAGE.
IT IS ESSENTIALLY A TASER, CAPABLE OF DISABLING ANYONE IT STRIKES.

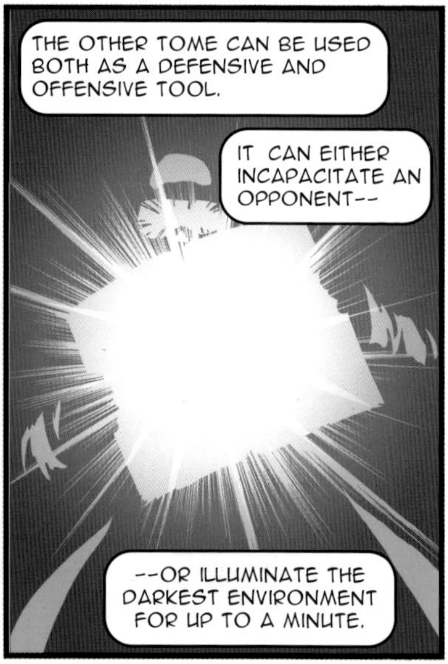
THE OTHER TOME CAN BE USED BOTH AS A DEFENSIVE AND OFFENSIVE TOOL.
IT CAN EITHER INCAPACITATE AN OPPONENT--
--OR ILLUMINATE THE DARKEST ENVIRONMENT FOR UP TO A MINUTE.

THAT IS ONE BRIGHT LIGHT.
WHO COMES UP WITH THESE DEVICES?
I DON'T KNOW--BUT A JOB AS AN A.T.A.C. TECH AFTER GRADUATING FROM COLLEGE?
I CAN THINK OF WORSE JOBS.
GOOD LUCK, GENTLEMEN.
A.T.A.C.
A YOUNG FAMILY--AND THE FATE OF SEVERAL COUNTRIES--DEPEND ON YOU.
FRANK?
JOE.
DO YOU THINK IT IS STRANGE THAT I'D RATHER GO OFF ON AN ASSIGNMENT WHERE WE'RE RISKING OUR LIVES--
--THAN GO BACK TO AUNT TRUDY'S YARD SALE?
HM.

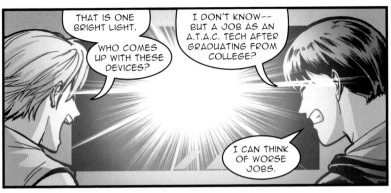

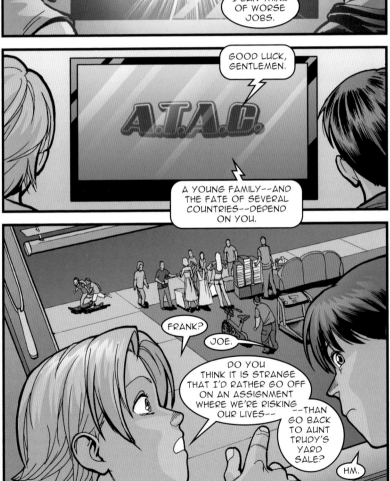

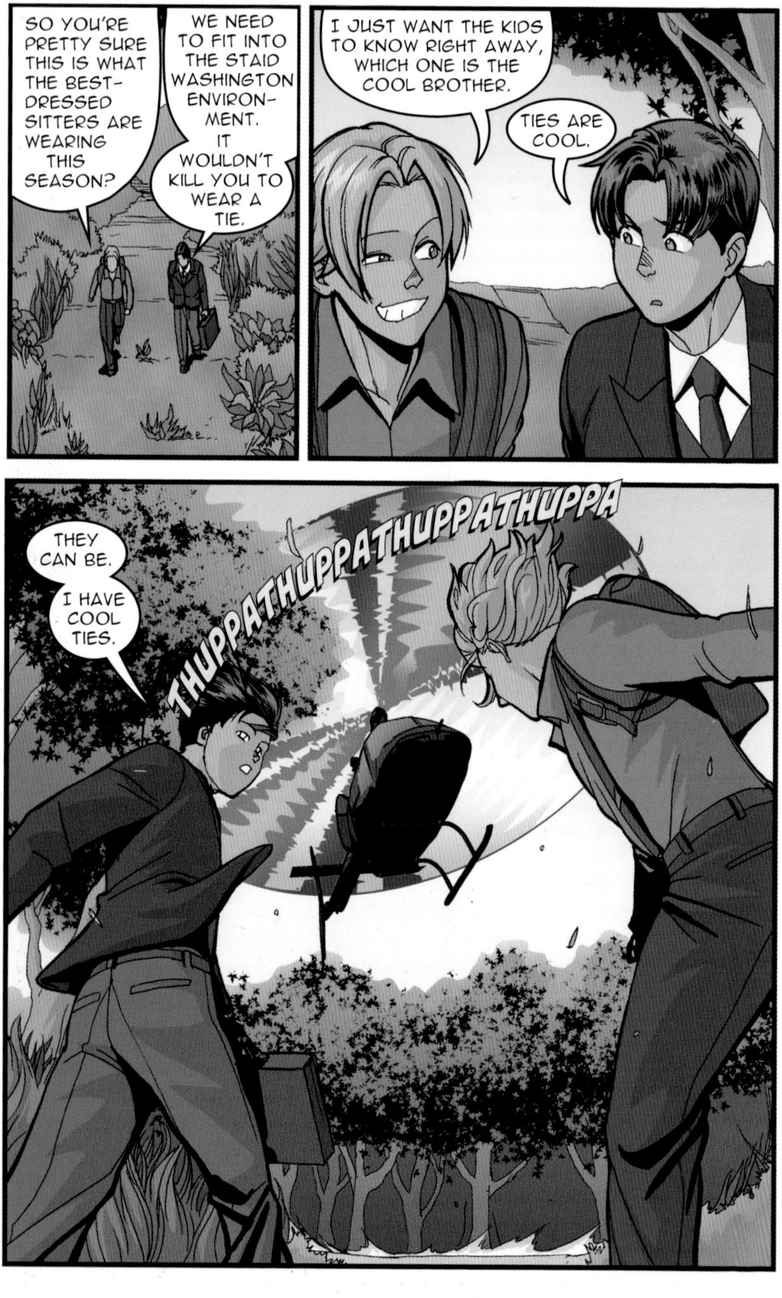
SO YOU'RE PRETTY SURE THIS IS WHAT THE BEST-DRESSED SITTERS ARE WEARING THIS SEASON?
WE NEED TO FIT INTO THE STAID WASHINGTON ENVIRONMENT.
IT WOULDN'T KILL YOU TO WEAR A TIE.
I JUST WANT THE KIDS TO KNOW RIGHT AWAY, WHICH ONE IS THE COOL BROTHER.
TIES ARE COOL.
THEY CAN BE.
I HAVE COOL TIES.
THUPPATHUPPATHUPPATHUPPA

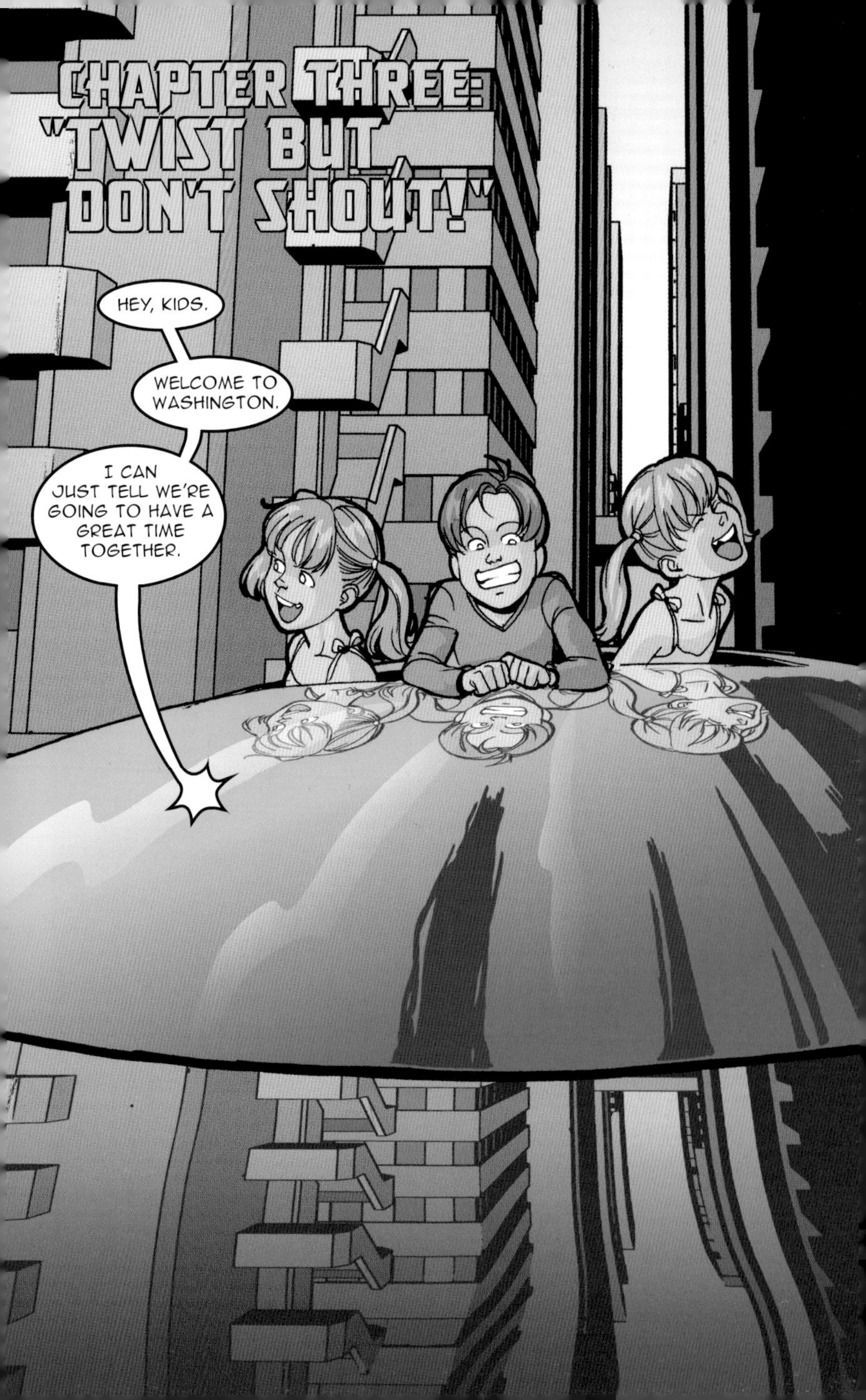
CHAPTER THREE:
"TWIST BUT, DON'T SHOUT!"
HEY, KIDS.
WELCOME TO WASHINGTON.
I CAN JUST TELL WE'RE GOING TO HAVE A GREAT TIME TOGETHER.

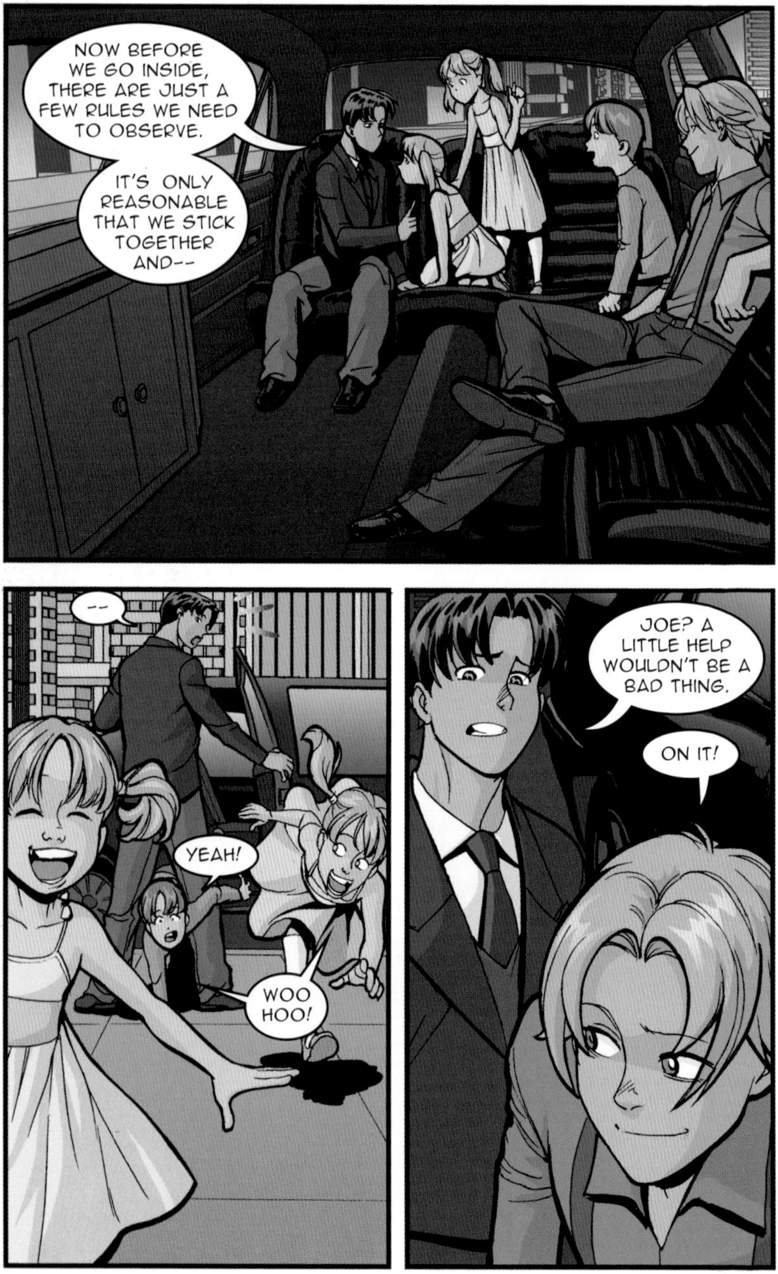
NOW BEFORE WE GO INSIDE, THERE ARE JUST A FEW RULES WE NEED TO OBSERVE.
IT'S ONLY REASONABLE THAT WE STICK TOGETHER AND--
--
YEAH!
WOO HOO!
JOE? A LITTLE HELP WOULDN'T BE A BAD THING.
ON IT!

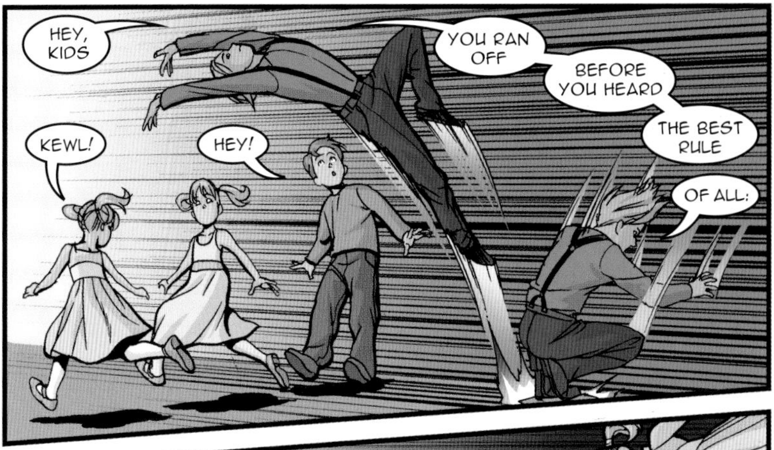
HEY, KIDS
YOU RAN OFF
BEFORE YOU HEARD
THE BEST RULE
OF ALL:
KEWL!
HEY!

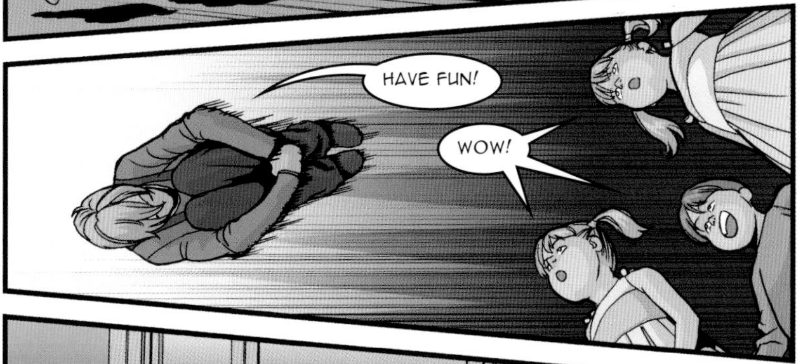
HAVE FUN!
WOW!

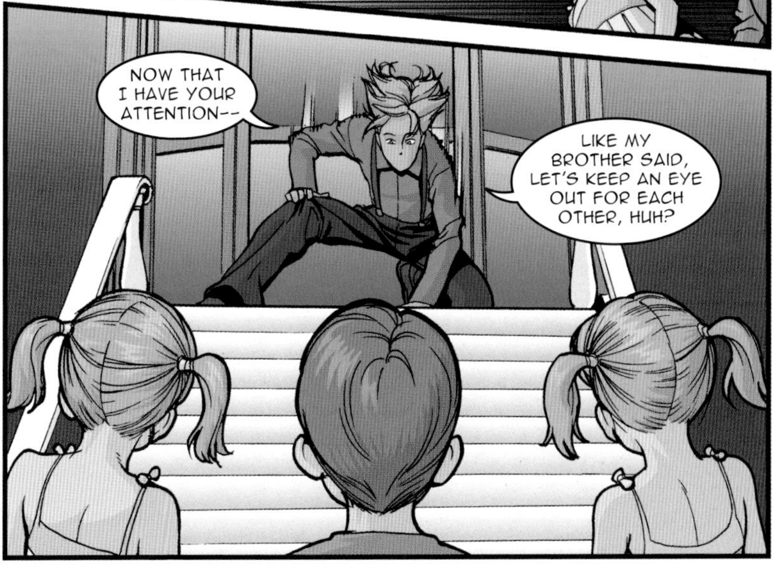
NOW THAT I HAVE YOUR ATTENTION--
LIKE MY BROTHER SAID, LET'S KEEP AN EYE OUT FOR EACH OTHER, HUH?

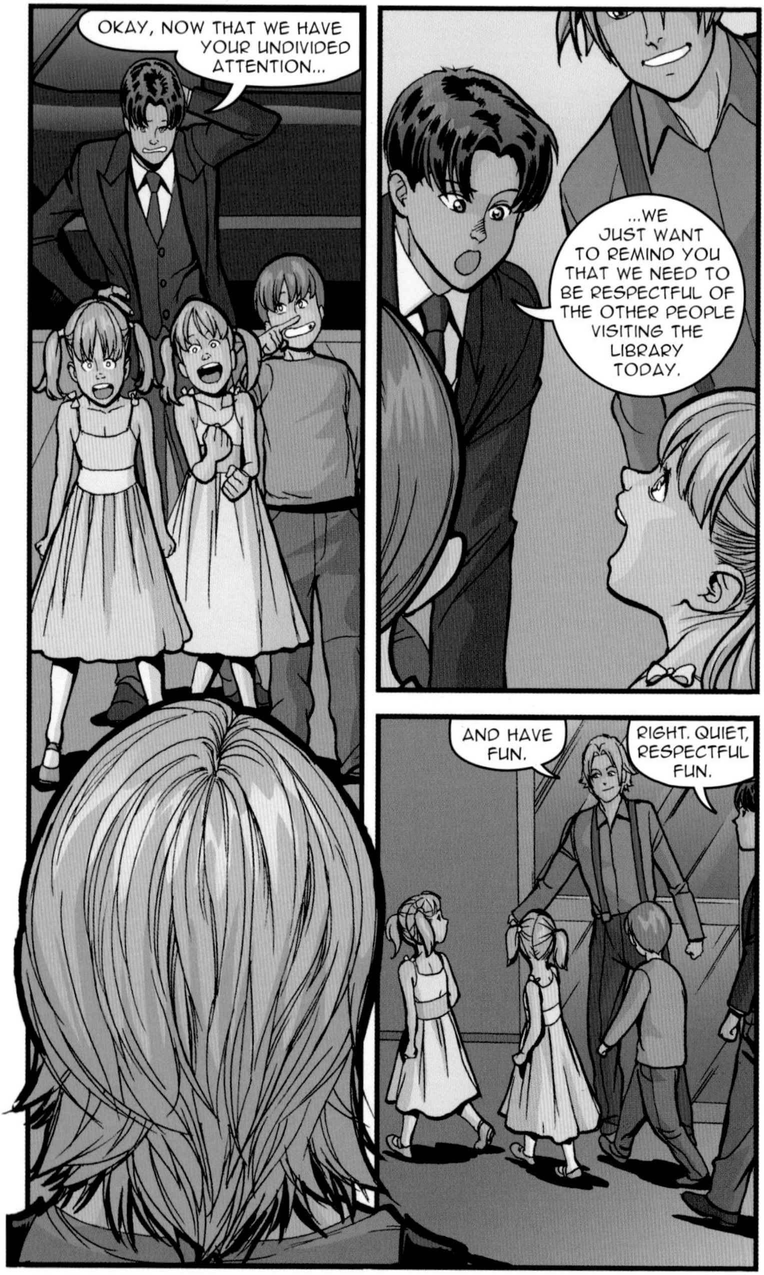
OKAY, NOW THAT WE HAVE YOUR UNDIVIDED ATTENTION...
...WE JUST WANT TO REMIND YOU THAT WE NEED TO BE RESPECTFUL OF THE OTHER PEOPLE VISITING THE LIBRARY TODAY.
AND HAVE FUN.
RIGHT. QUIET, RESPECTFUL FUN.

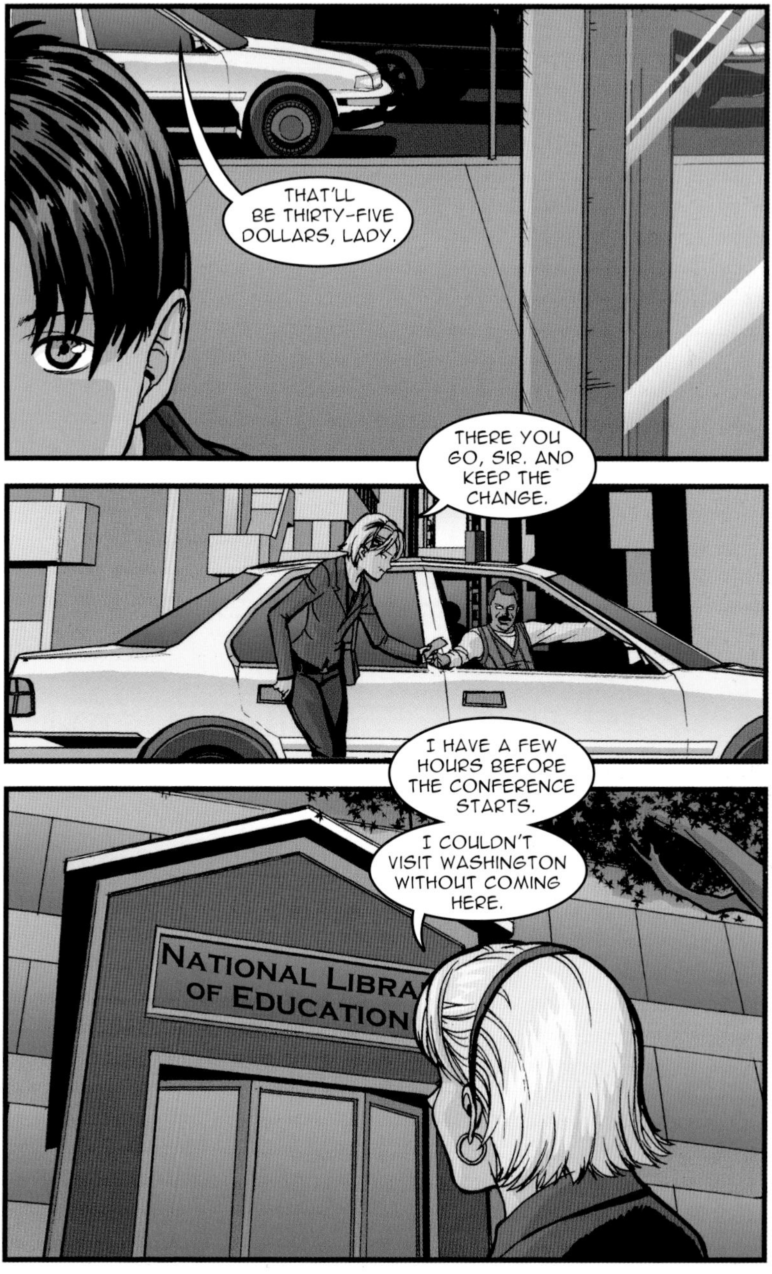
THAT'LL BE THIRTY-FIVE DOLLARS, LADY.
THERE YOU GO, SIR. AND KEEP THE CHANGE.
I HAVE A FEW HOURS BEFORE THE CONFERENCE STARTS.
I COULDN'T VISIT WASHINGTON WITHOUT COMING HERE.
NATIONAL LIBRA OF EDUCATION

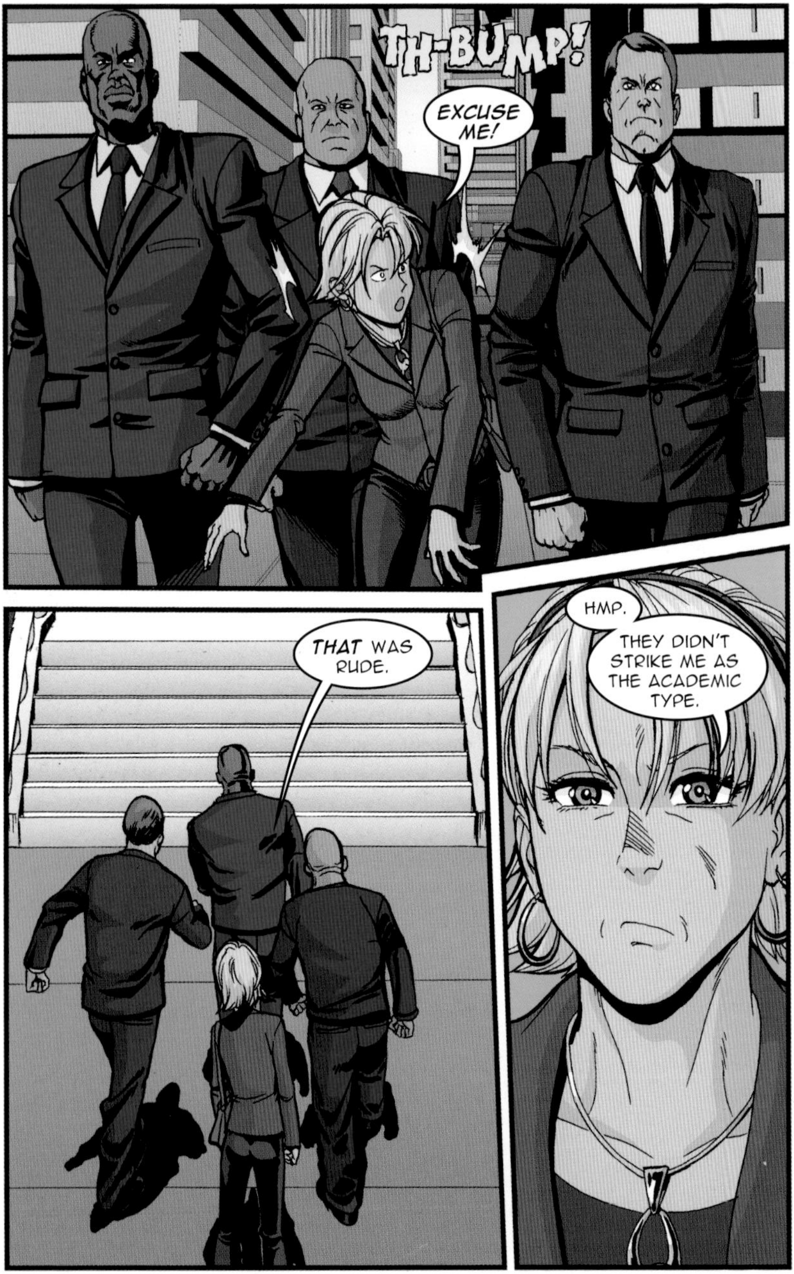
TH-BUMP!
EXCUSE ME!
THAT WAS RUDE.
HMP.
THEY DIDN'T STRIKE ME AS THE ACADEMIC TYPE.

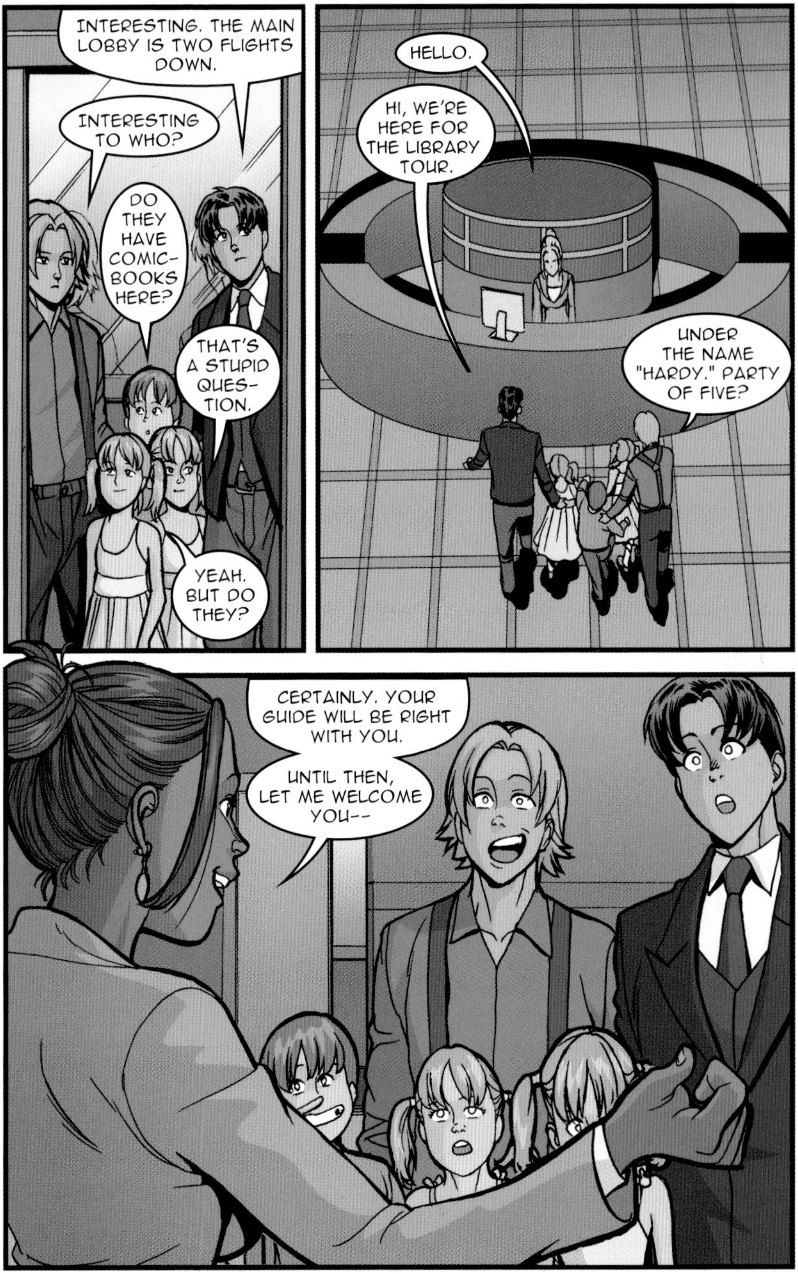
INTERESTING. THE MAIN LOBBY IS TWO FLIGHTS DOWN.
INTERESTING TO WHO?
DO THEY HAVE COMIC-BOOKS HERE?
THAT'S A STUPID QUES-TION.
YEAH. BUT DO THEY?
HELLO.
HI, WE'RE HERE FOR THE LIBRARY TOUR.
UNDER THE NAME "HARDY." PARTY OF FIVE?
CERTAINLY. YOUR GUIDE WILL BE RIGHT WITH YOU.
UNTIL THEN, LET ME WELCOME YOU--

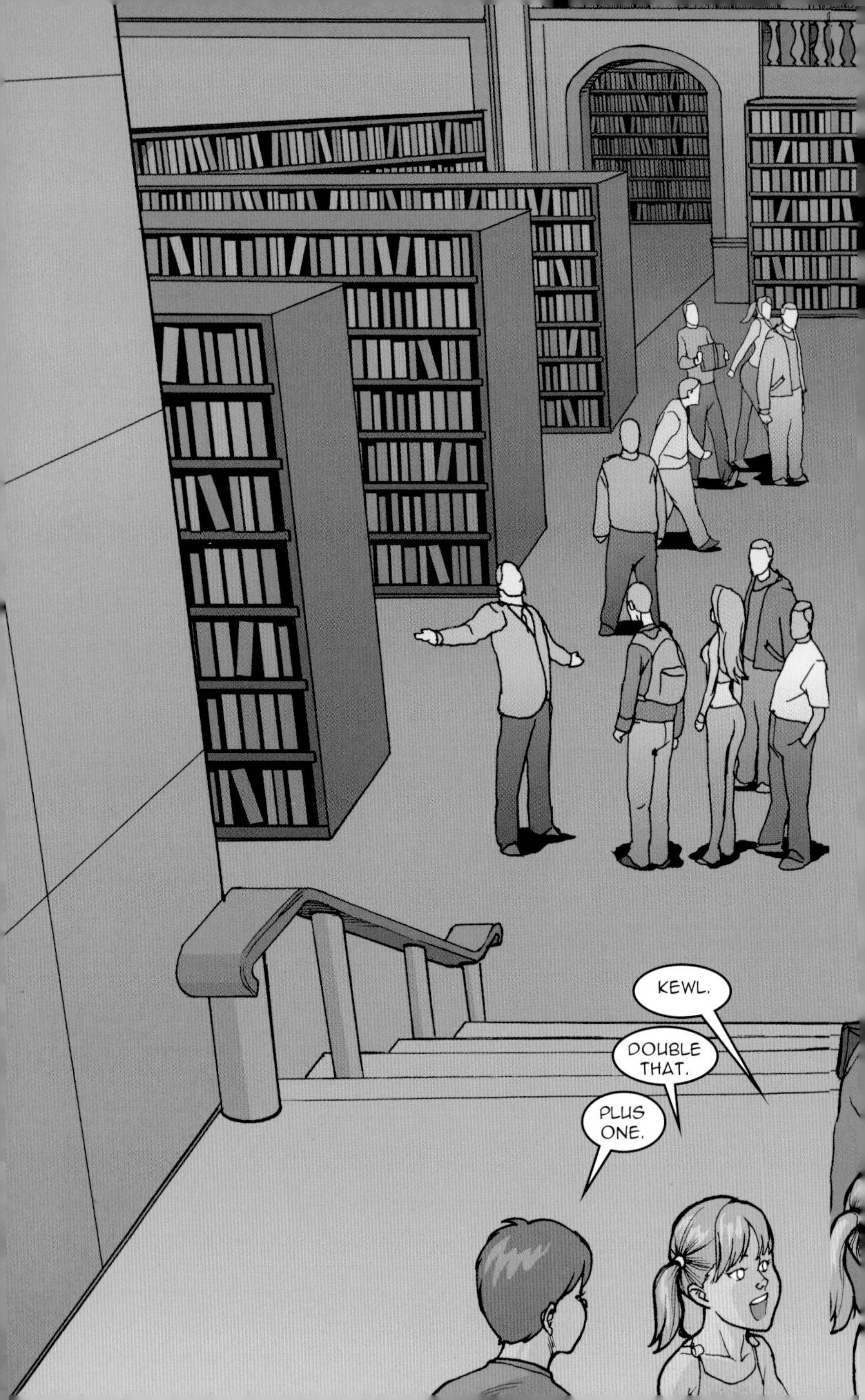
KEWL.
DOUBLE THAT.
PLUS ONE.

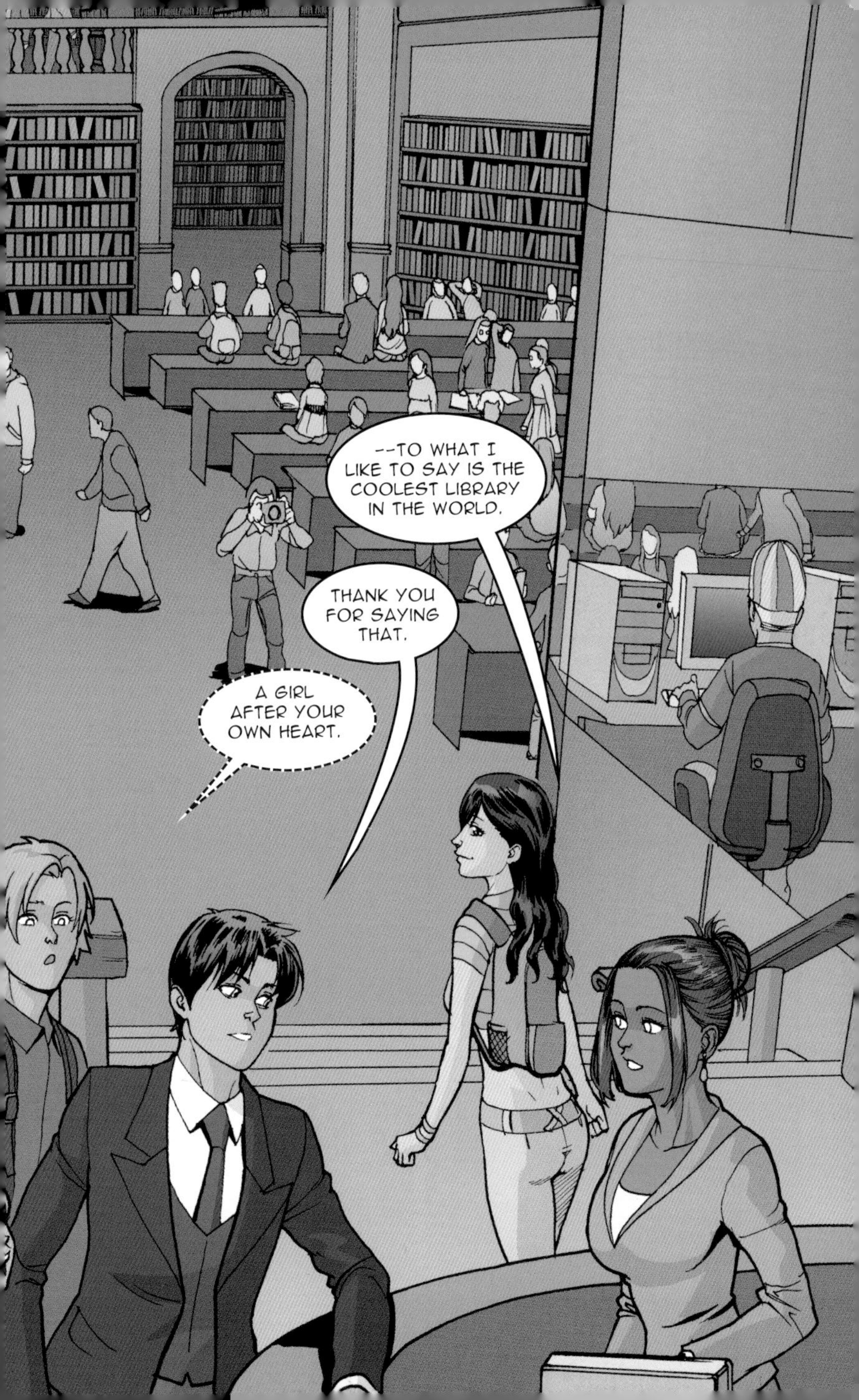
--TO WHAT I LIKE TO SAY IS THE COOLEST LIBRARY IN THE WORLD.
THANK YOU FOR SAYING THAT.
A GIRL AFTER YOUR OWN HEART.

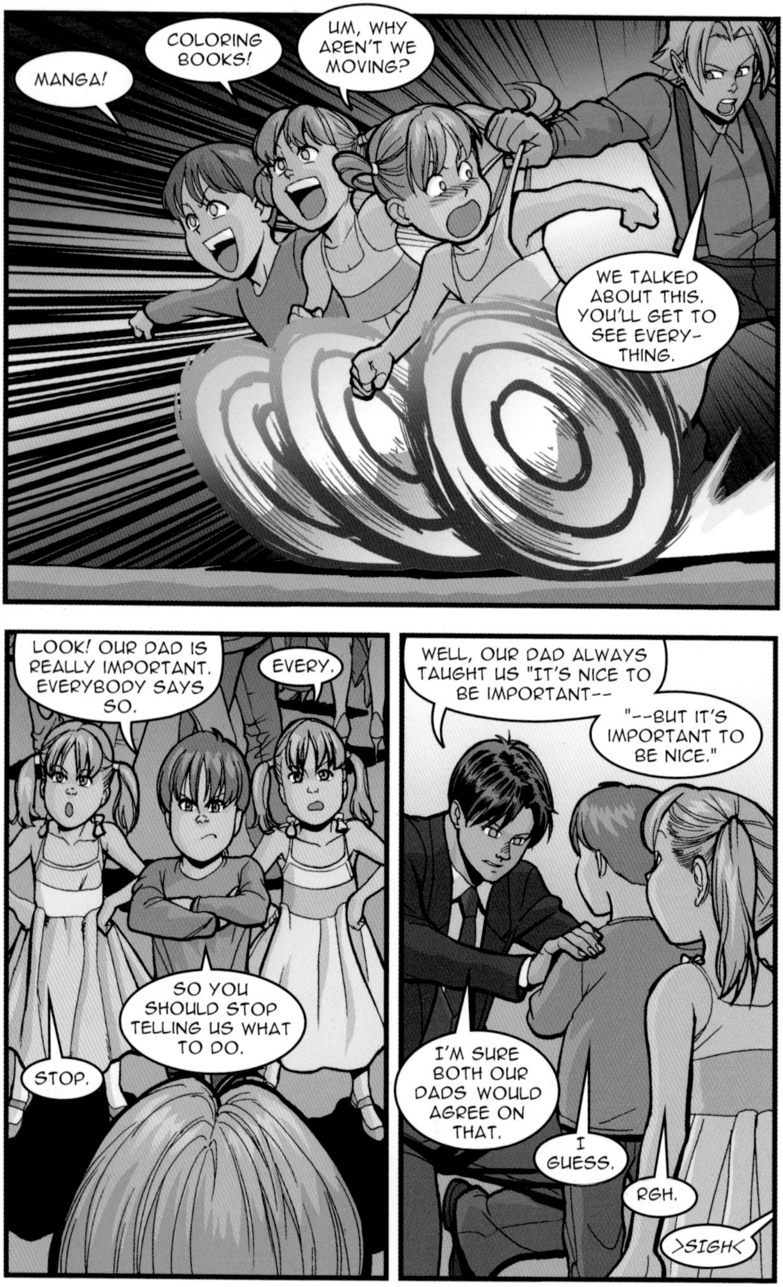

MANGA!
COLORING BOOKS!
UM, WHY AREN'T WE MOVING?
WE TALKED ABOUT THIS. YOU'LL GET TO SEE EVERY-THING.
LOOK! OUR DAD IS REALLY IMPORTANT. EVERYBODY SAYS SO.
EVERY.
SO YOU SHOULD STOP TELLING US WHAT TO DO.
STOP.
WELL, OUR DAD ALWAYS TAUGHT US "IT'S NICE TO BE IMPORTANT--
"--BUT IT'S IMPORTANT TO BE NICE."
I'M SURE BOTH OUR DADS WOULD AGREE ON THAT.
I GUESS.
RGH.
>SIGH<

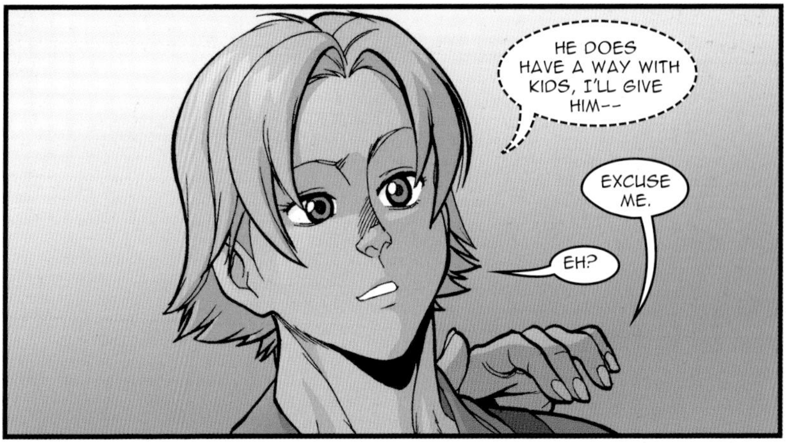
HE DOES HAVE A WAY WITH KIDS, I'LL GIVE HIM--
EXCUSE ME.
EH?

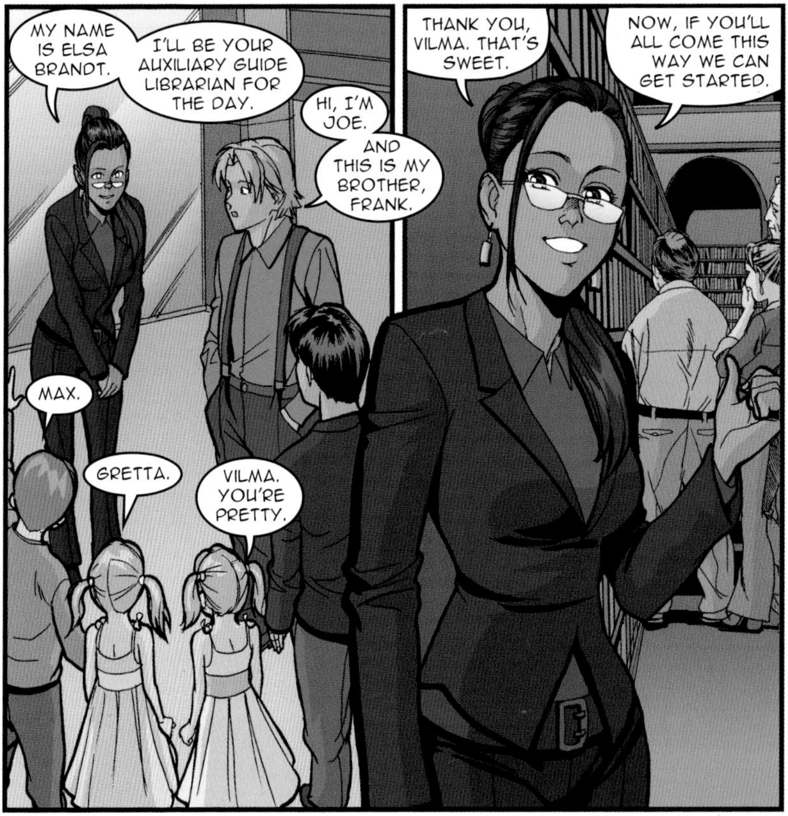
MY NAME IS ELSA BRANDT.
I'LL BE YOUR AUXILIARY GUIDE LIBRARIAN FOR THE DAY.
HI, I'M JOE.
AND THIS IS MY BROTHER, FRANK.
MAX.
GRETTA.
VILMA. YOU'RE PRETTY.
THANK YOU, VILMA. THAT'S SWEET.
NOW, IF YOU'LL ALL COME THIS WAY WE CAN GET STARTED.

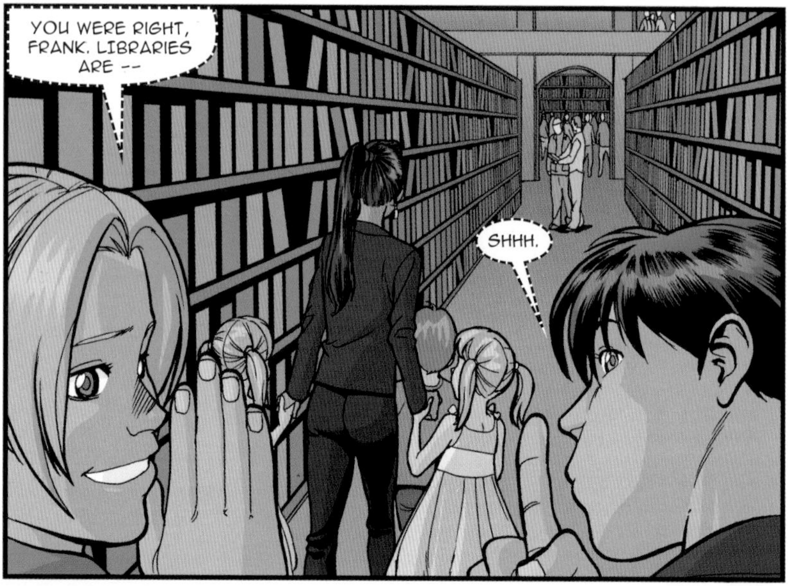
YOU WERE RIGHT, FRANK. LIBRARIES ARE --
SHHH.

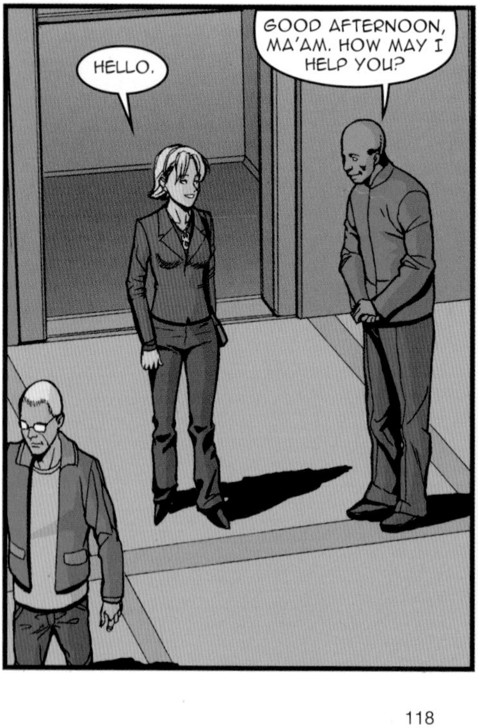
HELLO.
GOOD AFTERNOON, MA'AM. HOW MAY I HELP YOU?

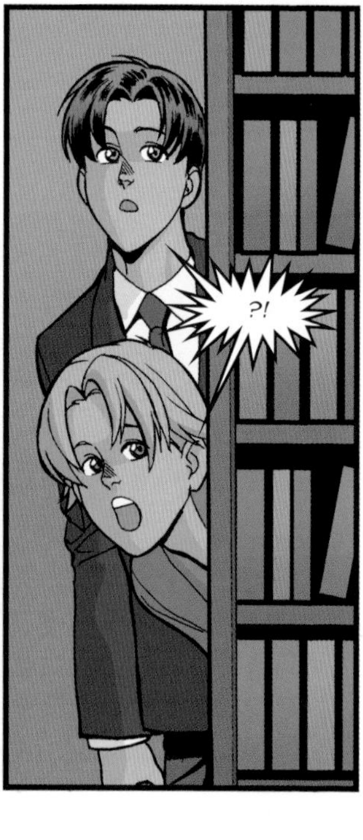
?!

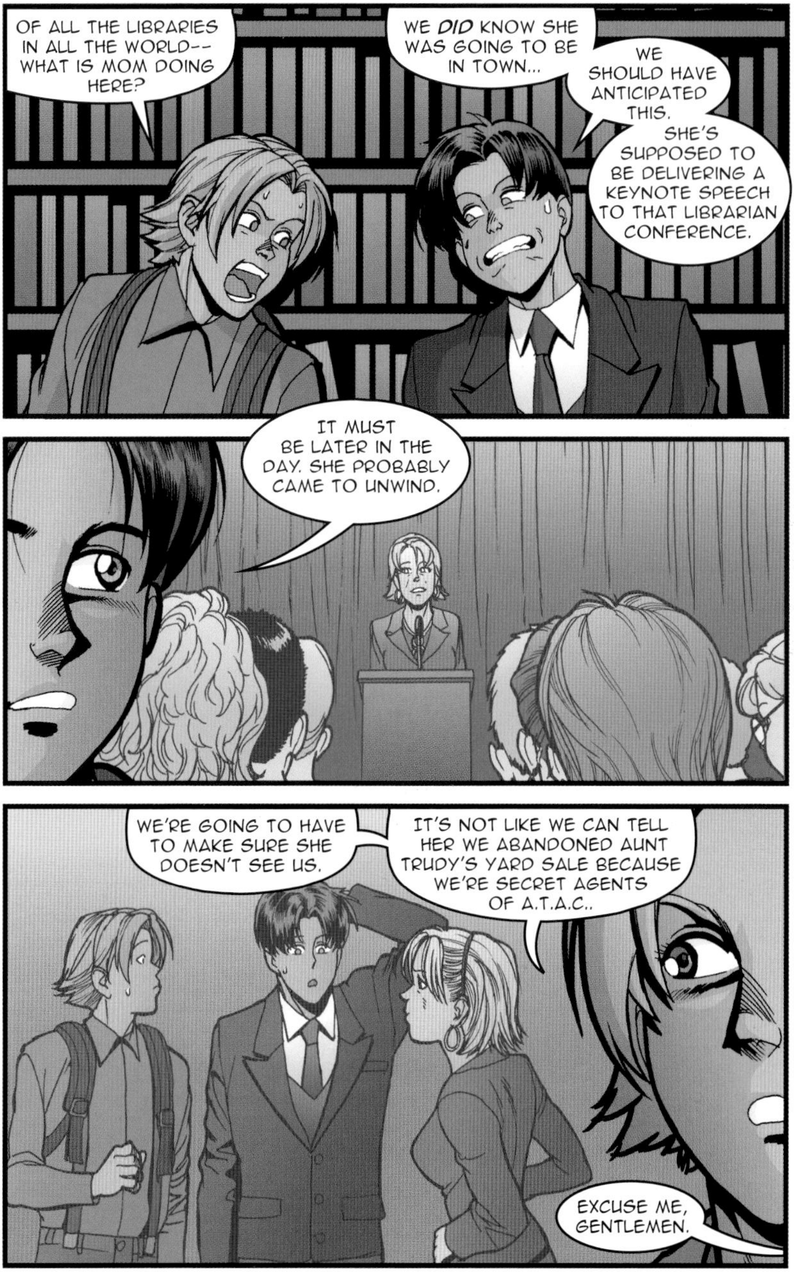
OF ALL THE LIBRARIES IN ALL THE WORLD-- WHAT IS MOM DOING HERE?
WE *DID* KNOW SHE WAS GOING TO BE IN TOWN...
WE SHOULD HAVE ANTICIPATED THIS.
SHE'S SUPPOSED TO BE DELIVERING A KEYNOTE SPEECH TO THAT LIBRARIAN CONFERENCE.
IT MUST BE LATER IN THE DAY. SHE PROBABLY CAME TO UNWIND.
WE'RE GOING TO HAVE TO MAKE SURE SHE DOESN'T SEE US.
IT'S NOT LIKE WE CAN TELL HER WE ABANDONED AUNT TRUDY'S YARD SALE BECAUSE WE'RE SECRET AGENTS OF A.T.A.C..
EXCUSE ME, GENTLEMEN.

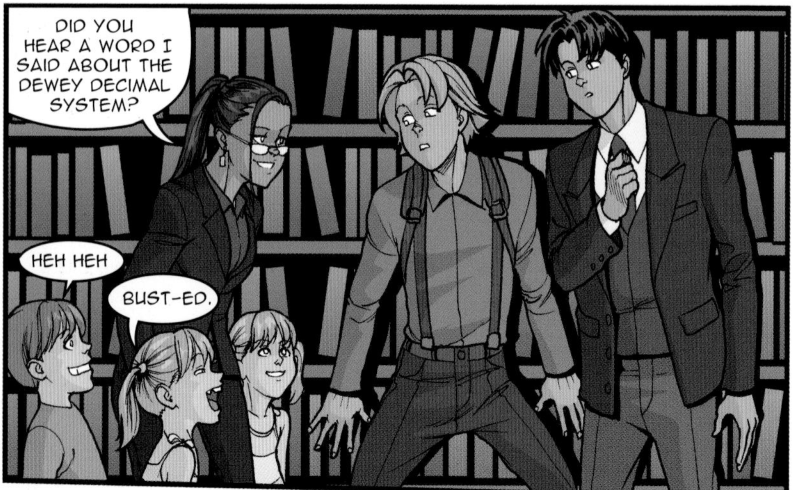
DID YOU HEAR A WORD I SAID ABOUT THE DEWEY DECIMAL SYSTEM?
HEH HEH
BUST-ED.

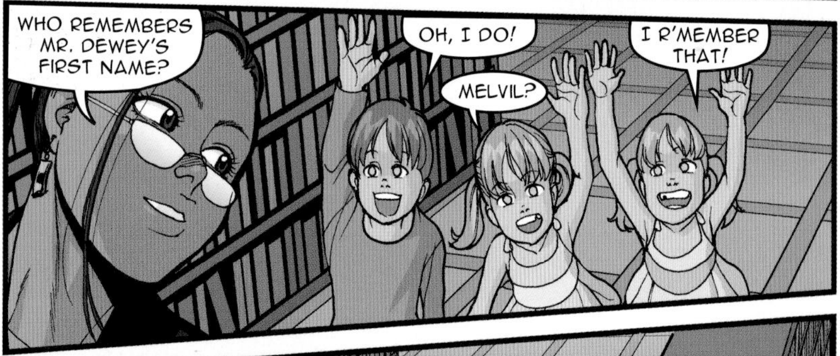
WHO REMEMBERS MR. DEWEY'S FIRST NAME?
OH, I DO!
MELVIL?
I R'MEMBER THAT!

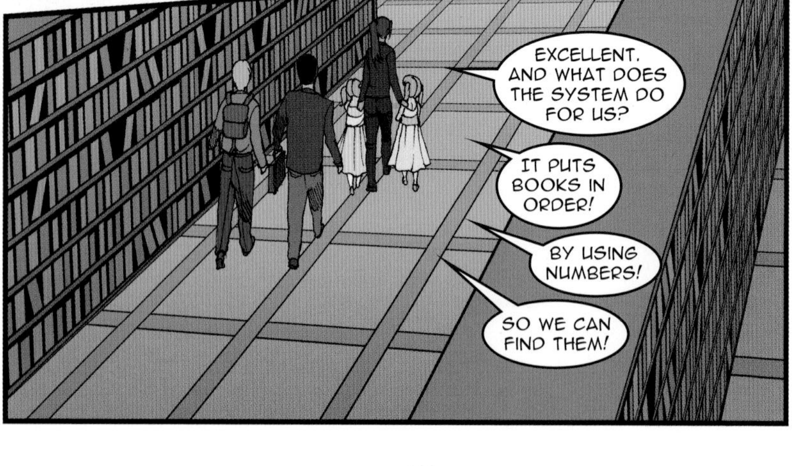
EXCELLENT. AND WHAT DOES THE SYSTEM DO FOR US?
IT PUTS BOOKS IN ORDER!
BY USING NUMBERS!
SO WE CAN FIND THEM!

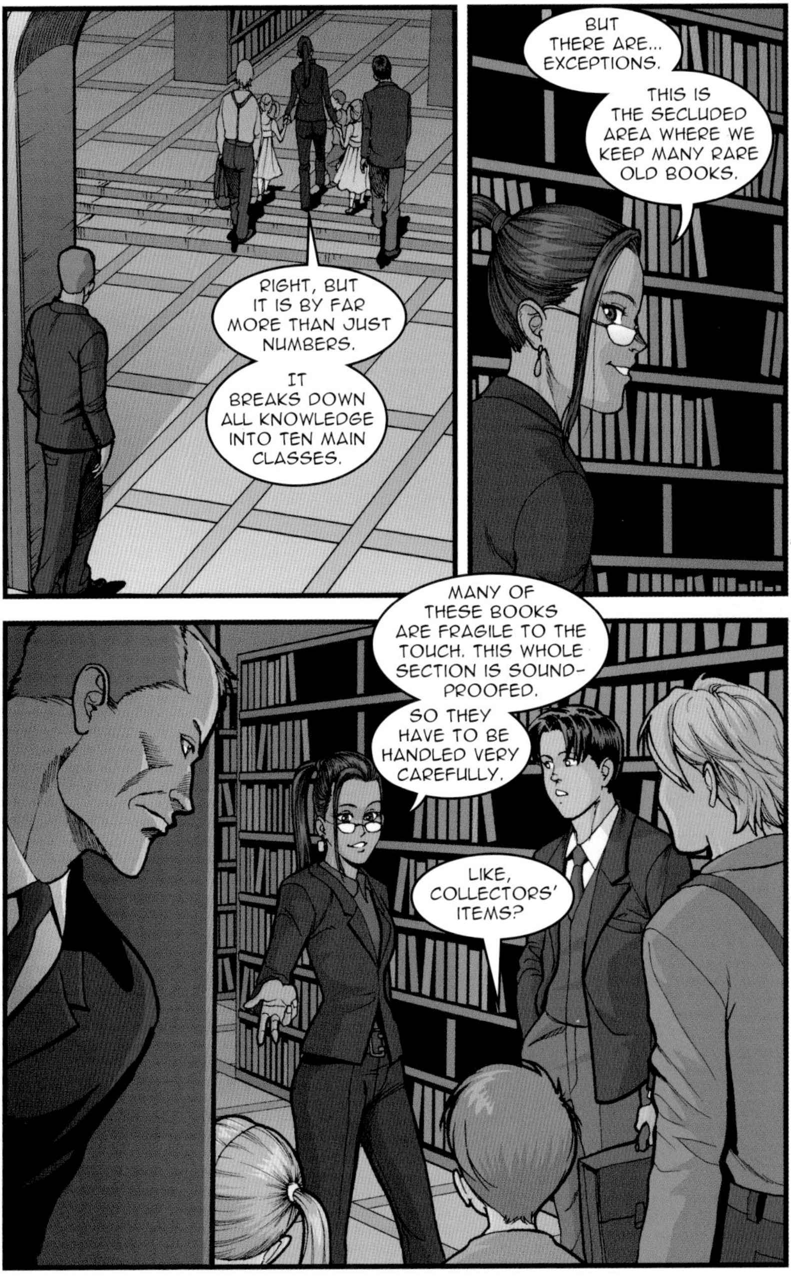
RIGHT, BUT IT IS BY FAR MORE THAN JUST NUMBERS.
IT BREAKS DOWN ALL KNOWLEDGE INTO TEN MAIN CLASSES.
BUT THERE ARE... EXCEPTIONS.
THIS IS THE SECLUDED AREA WHERE WE KEEP MANY RARE OLD BOOKS.
MANY OF THESE BOOKS ARE FRAGILE TO THE TOUCH. THIS WHOLE SECTION IS SOUND-PROOFED.
SO THEY HAVE TO BE HANDLED VERY CAREFULLY.
LIKE, COLLECTORS' ITEMS?

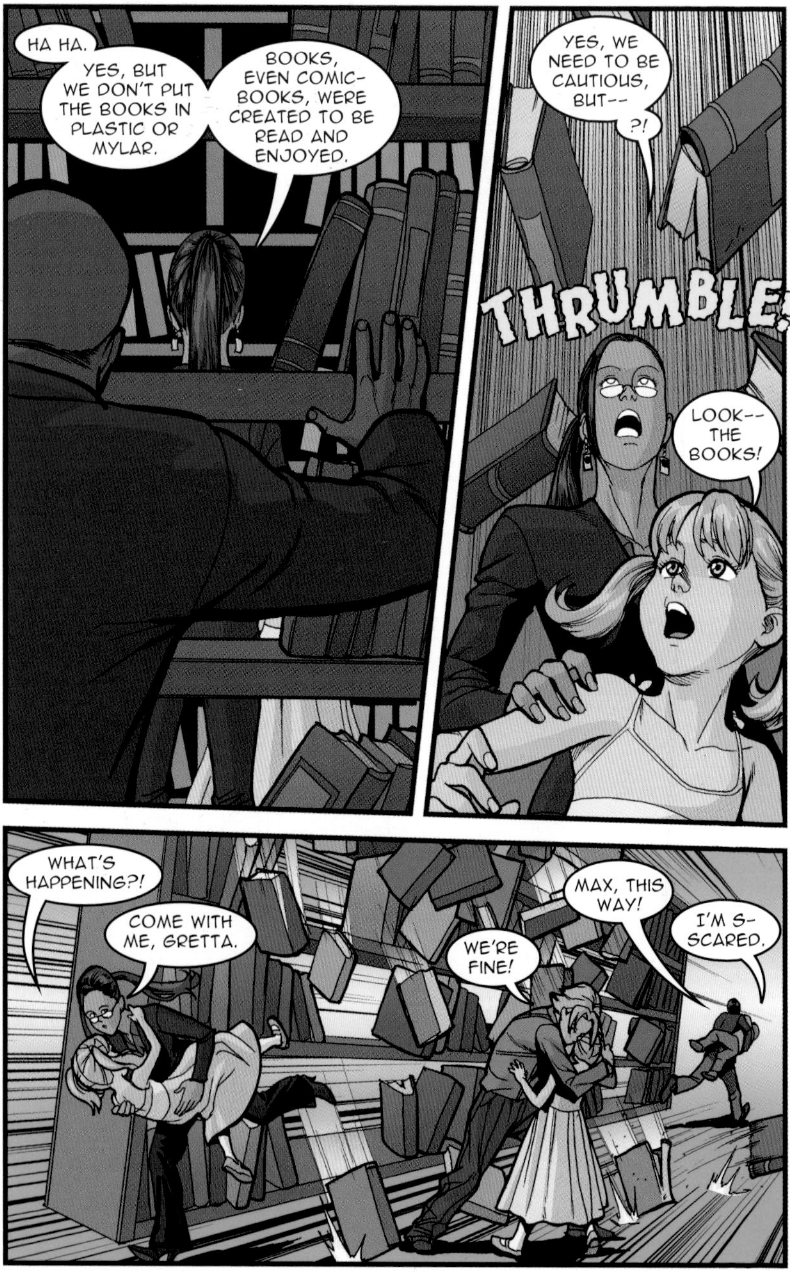
HA HA.
YES, BUT WE DON'T PUT THE BOOKS IN PLASTIC OR MYLAR.
BOOKS, EVEN COMIC-BOOKS, WERE CREATED TO BE READ AND ENJOYED.
YES, WE NEED TO BE CAUTIOUS, BUT--
?!
THRUMBLE!
LOOK-- THE BOOKS!
WHAT'S HAPPENING?!
COME WITH ME, GRETTA.
WE'RE FINE!
MAX, THIS WAY!
I'M S-SCARED.

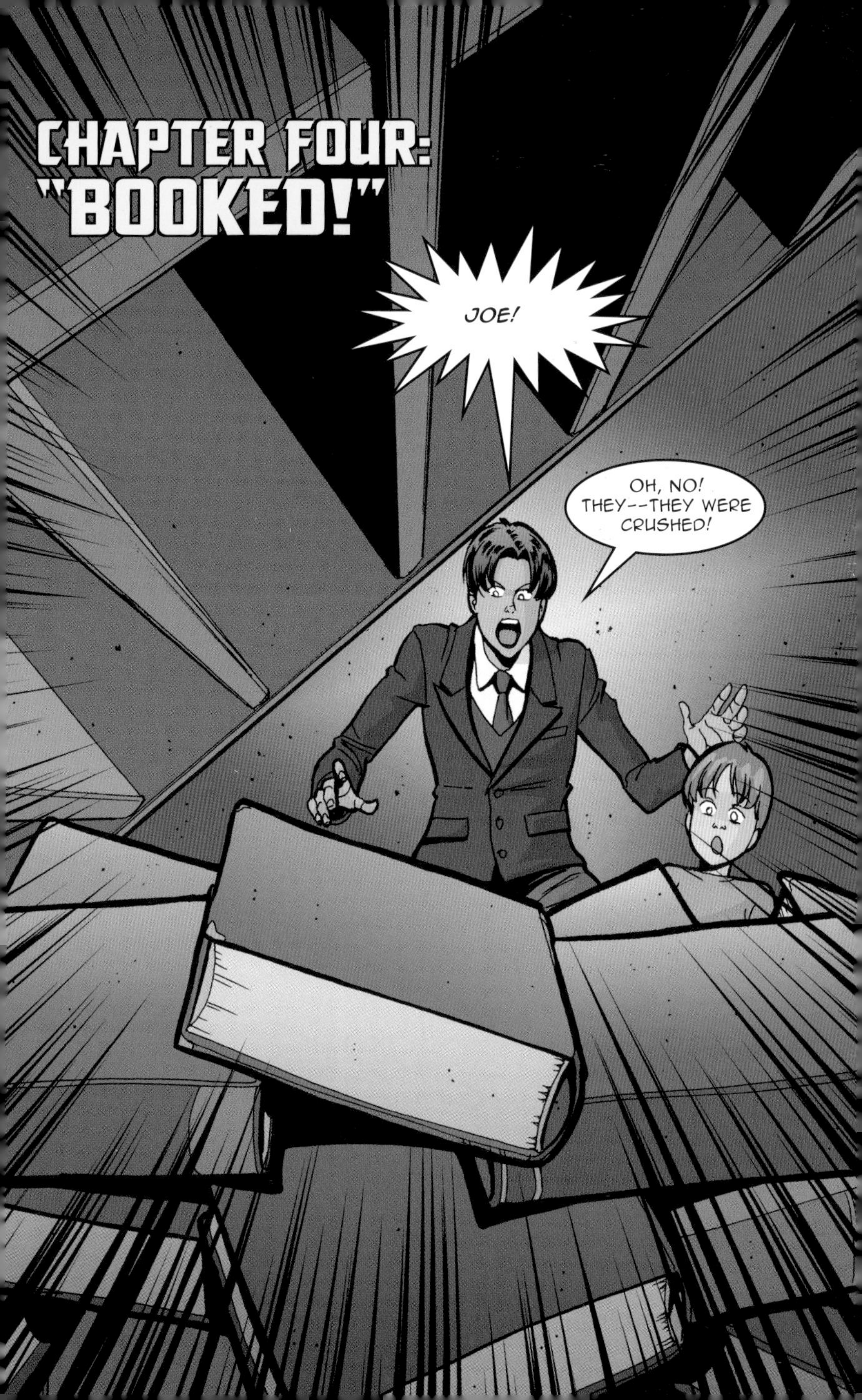
CHAPTER FOUR:
"BOOKED!"
JOE!
OH, NO! THEY--THEY WERE CRUSHED!

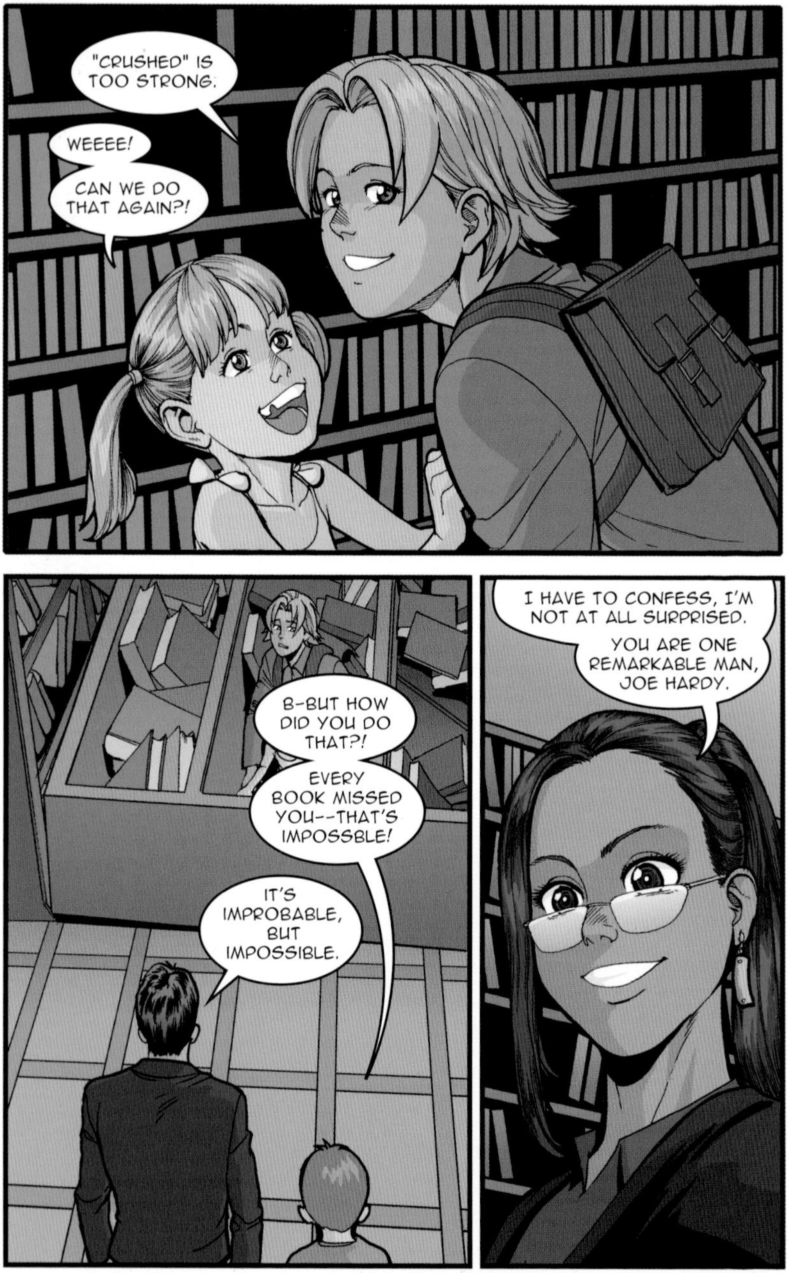

"CRUSHED" IS TOO STRONG.
WEEEE!
CAN WE DO THAT AGAIN?!
B-BUT HOW DID YOU DO THAT?!
EVERY BOOK MISSED YOU--THAT'S IMPOSSBLE!
IT'S IMPROBABLE, BUT IMPOSSIBLE.
I HAVE TO CONFESS, I'M NOT AT ALL SURPRISED.
YOU ARE ONE REMARKABLE MAN, JOE HARDY.

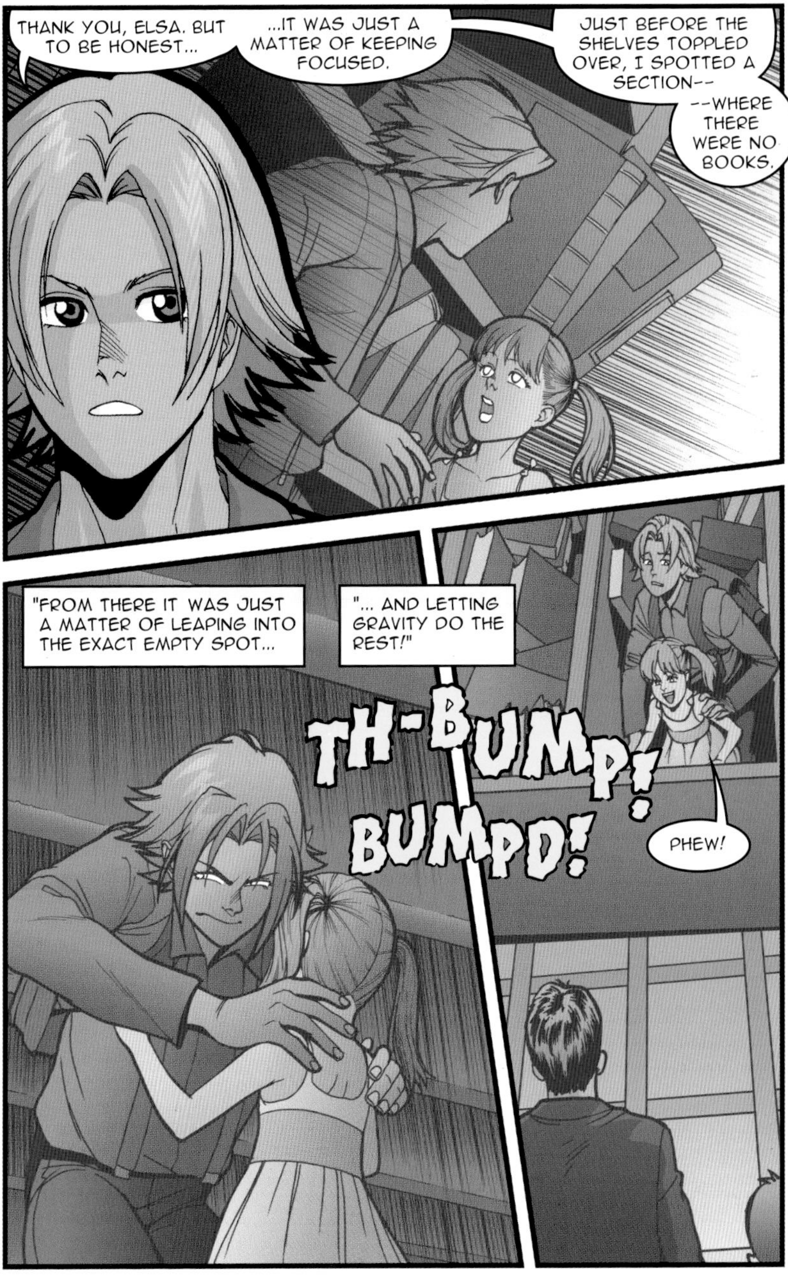
THANK YOU, ELSA. BUT TO BE HONEST...
...IT WAS JUST A MATTER OF KEEPING FOCUSED.
JUST BEFORE THE SHELVES TOPPLED OVER, I SPOTTED A SECTION--
--WHERE THERE WERE NO BOOKS.
"FROM THERE IT WAS JUST A MATTER OF LEAPING INTO THE EXACT EMPTY SPOT...
"... AND LETTING GRAVITY DO THE REST!"
TH-BUMP!
BUMPD!
PHEW!

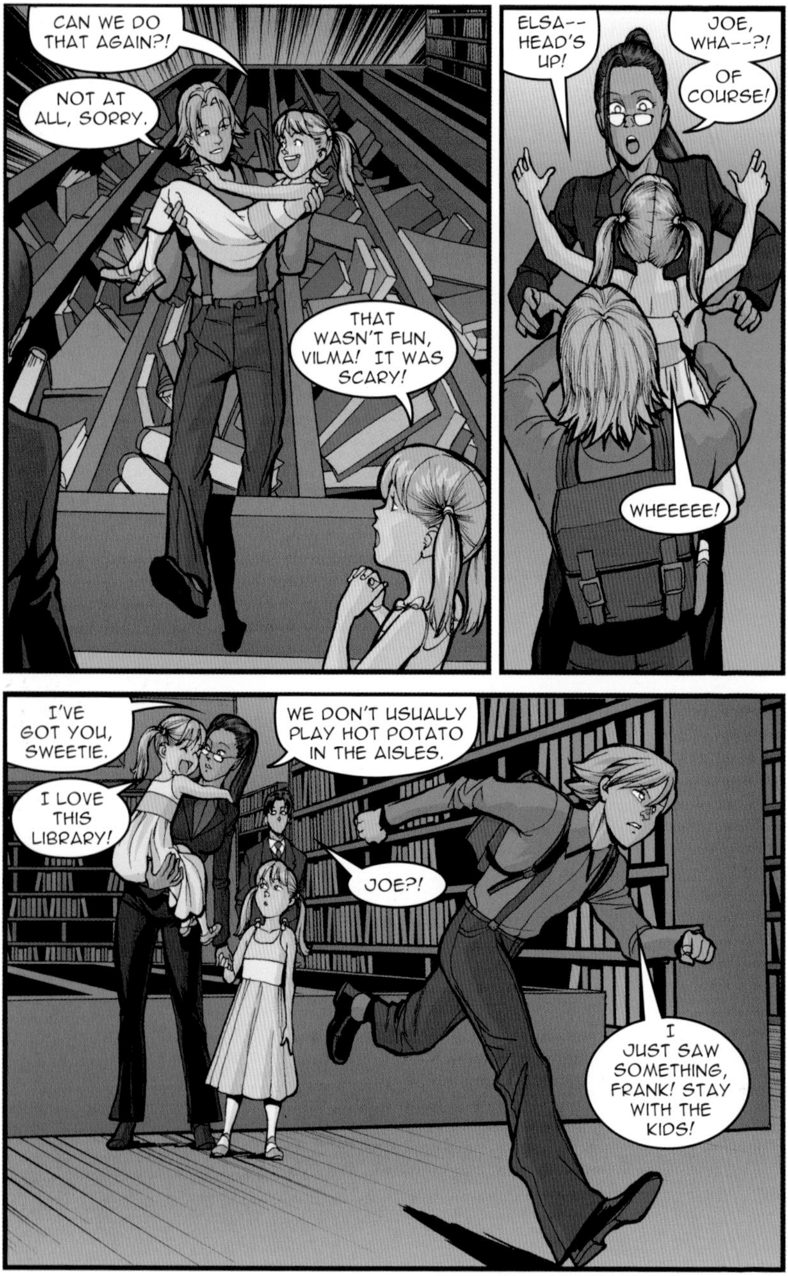
CAN WE DO THAT AGAIN?!
NOT AT ALL, SORRY.
THAT WASN'T FUN, VILMA! IT WAS SCARY!
ELSA-- HEAD'S UP!
JOE, WHA--?!
OF COURSE!
WHEEEEE!
I'VE GOT YOU, SWEETIE.
I LOVE THIS LIBRARY!
WE DON'T USUALLY PLAY HOT POTATO IN THE AISLES.
JOE?!
I JUST SAW SOMETHING, FRANK! STAY WITH THE KIDS!

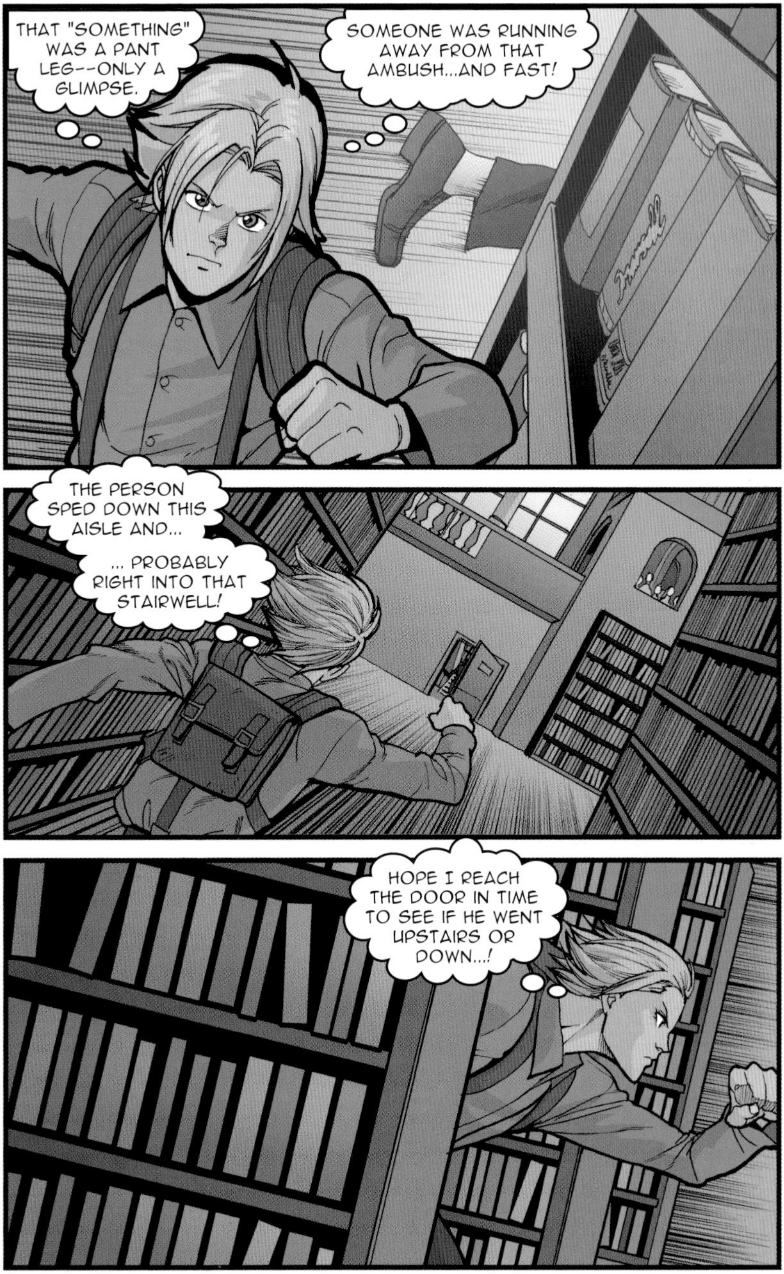

THAT "SOMETHING" WAS A PANT LEG--ONLY A GLIMPSE.
SOMEONE WAS RUNNING AWAY FROM THAT AMBUSH...AND FAST!
THE PERSON SPED DOWN THIS AISLE AND...
... PROBABLY RIGHT INTO THAT STAIRWELL!
HOPE I REACH THE DOOR IN TIME TO SEE IF HE WENT UPSTAIRS OR DOWN...!

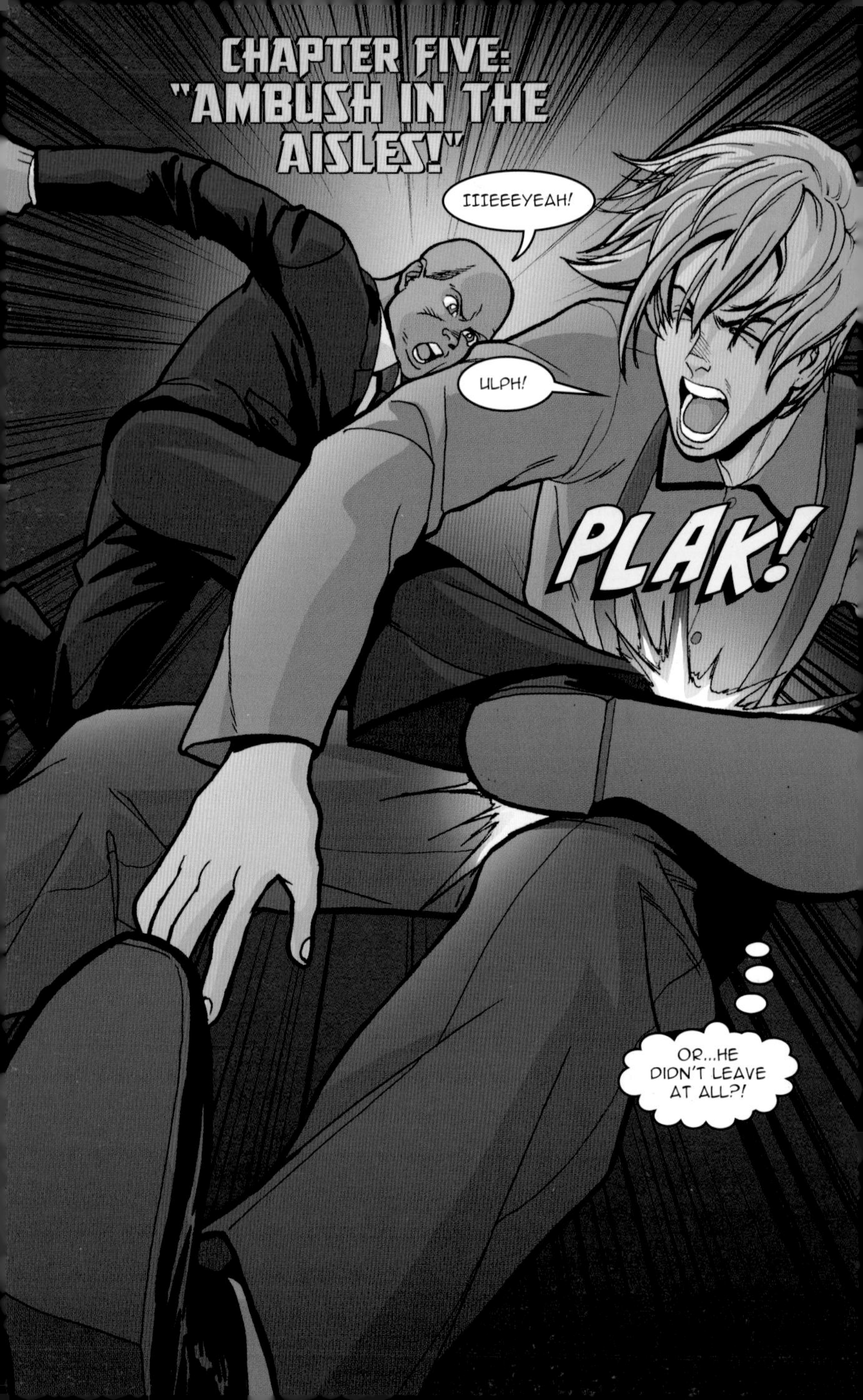
CHAPTER FIVE:
"AMBUSH IN THE AISLES!"
IIIEEEYEAH!
ULPH!
PLAK!
OR...HE DIDN'T LEAVE AT ALL?!

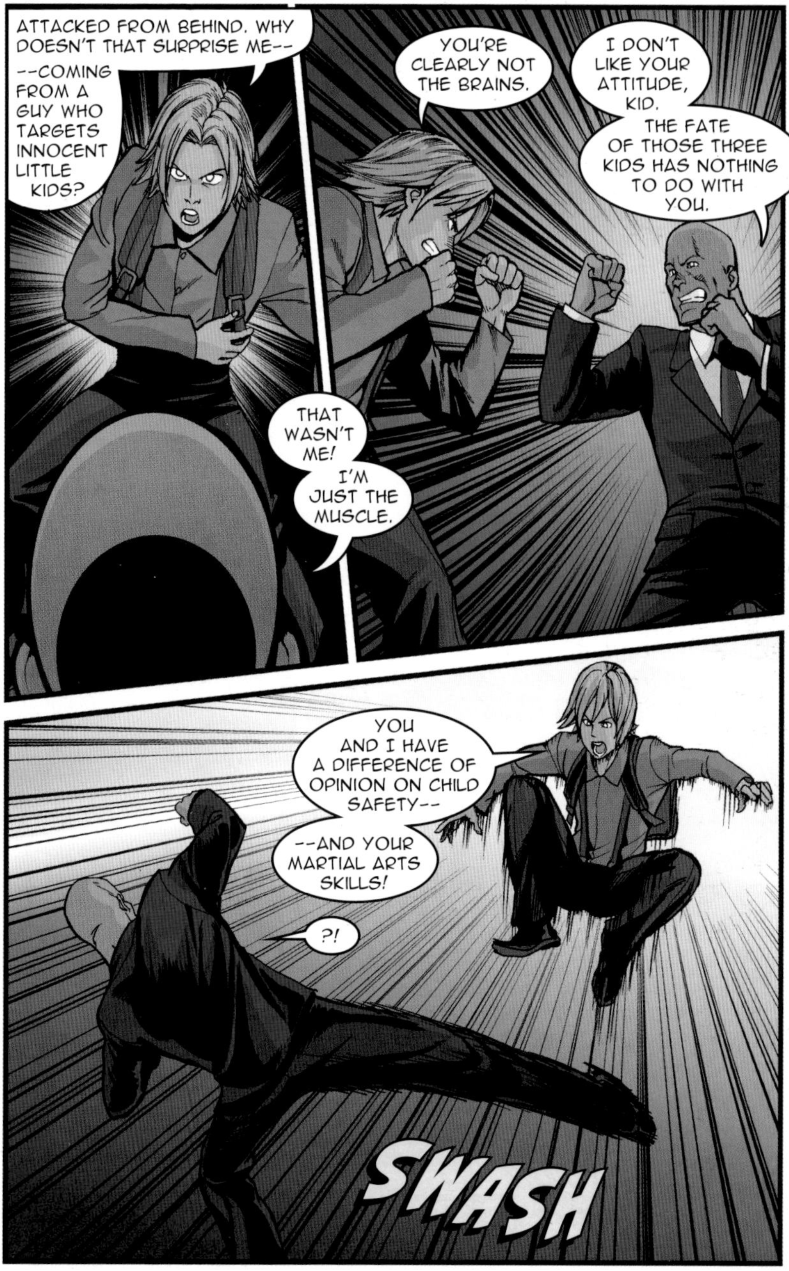
ATTACKED FROM BEHIND. WHY DOESN'T THAT SURPRISE ME--
--COMING FROM A GUY WHO TARGETS INNOCENT LITTLE KIDS?
YOU'RE CLEARLY NOT THE BRAINS.
I DON'T LIKE YOUR ATTITUDE, KID.
THE FATE OF THOSE THREE KIDS HAS NOTHING TO DO WITH YOU.
THAT WASN'T ME!
I'M JUST THE MUSCLE.
YOU AND I HAVE A DIFFERENCE OF OPINION ON CHILD SAFETY--
--AND YOUR MARTIAL ARTS SKILLS!
?!
SWASH

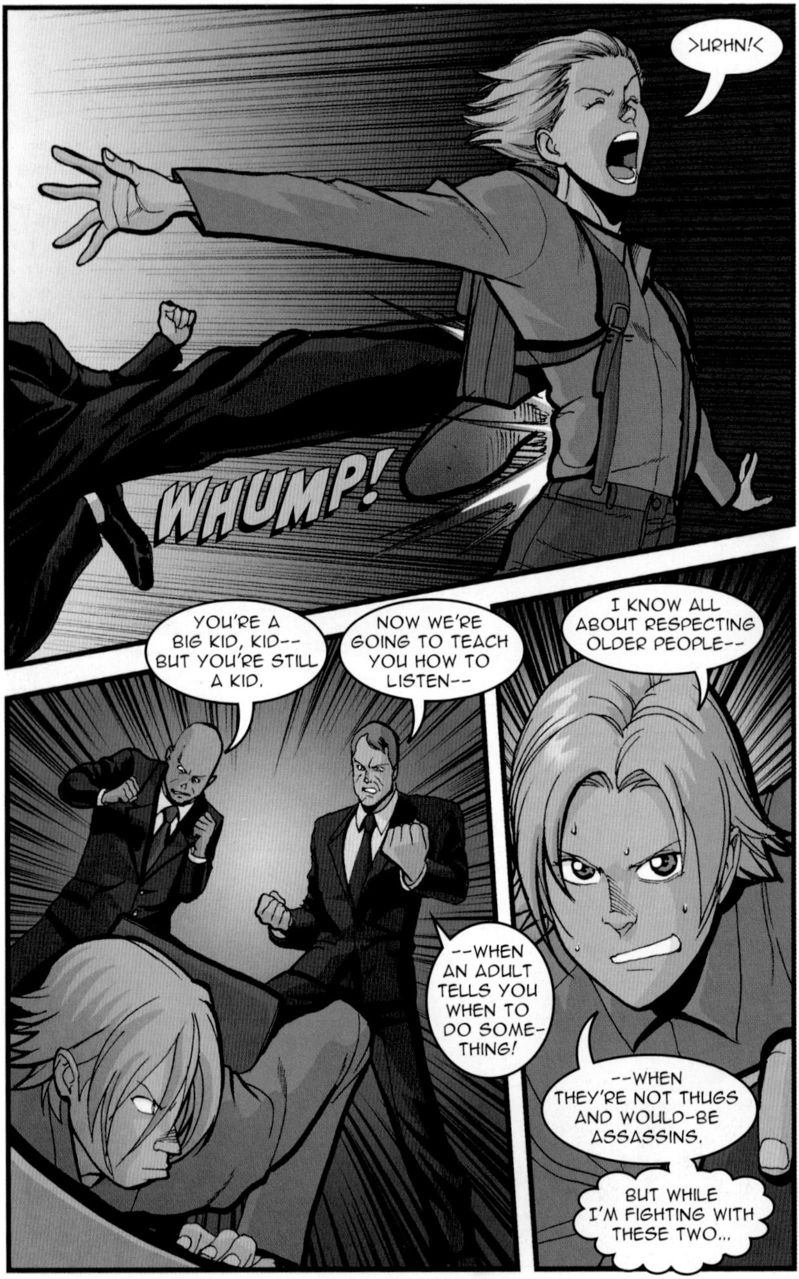
>URHN!<
WHUMP!
YOU'RE A BIG KID, KID-- BUT YOU'RE STILL A KID.
NOW WE'RE GOING TO TEACH YOU HOW TO LISTEN--
--WHEN AN ADULT TELLS YOU WHEN TO DO SOME-THING!
I KNOW ALL ABOUT RESPECTING OLDER PEOPLE--
--WHEN THEY'RE NOT THUGS AND WOULD-BE ASSASSINS.
BUT WHILE I'M FIGHTING WITH THESE TWO...

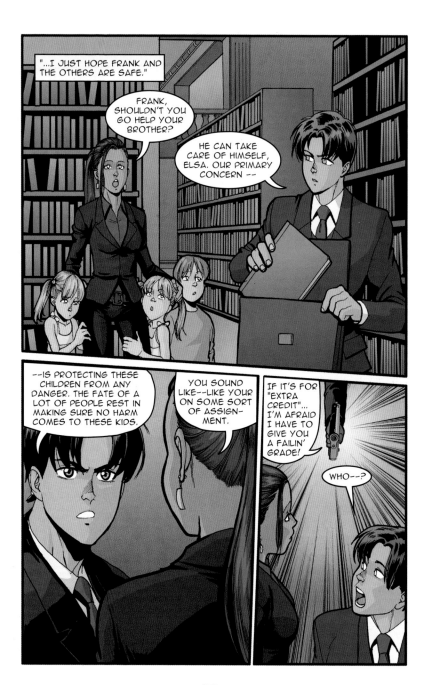

"...I JUST HOPE FRANK AND THE OTHERS ARE SAFE."

FRANK, SHOULDN'T YOU GO HELP YOUR BROTHER?

HE CAN TAKE CARE OF HIMSELF, ELSA. OUR PRIMARY CONCERN --

--IS PROTECTING THESE CHILDREN FROM ANY DANGER. THE FATE OF A LOT OF PEOPLE REST IN MAKING SURE NO HARM COMES TO THESE KIDS.

YOU SOUND LIKE--LIKE YOUR ON SOME SORT OF ASSIGN-MENT.

IF IT'S FOR "EXTRA CREDIT"... I'M AFRAID I HAVE TO GIVE YOU A FAILIN' GRADE!

WHO--?

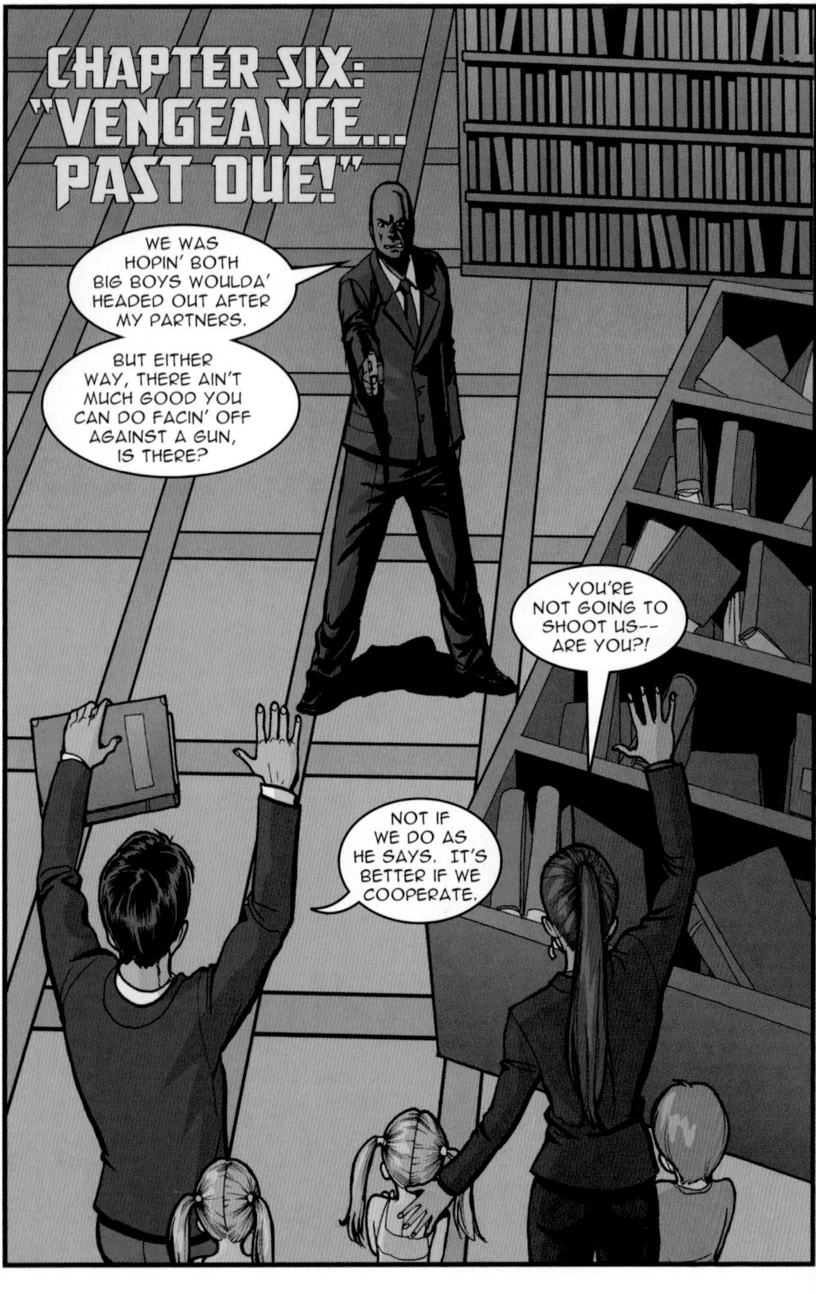
CHAPTER SIX: "VENGEANCE... PAST DUE!"
WE WAS HOPIN' BOTH BIG BOYS WOULDA' HEADED OUT AFTER MY PARTNERS.
BUT EITHER WAY, THERE AIN'T MUCH GOOD YOU CAN DO FACIN' OFF AGAINST A GUN, IS THERE?
YOU'RE NOT GOING TO SHOOT US-- ARE YOU?!
NOT IF WE DO AS HE SAYS. IT'S BETTER IF WE COOPERATE.

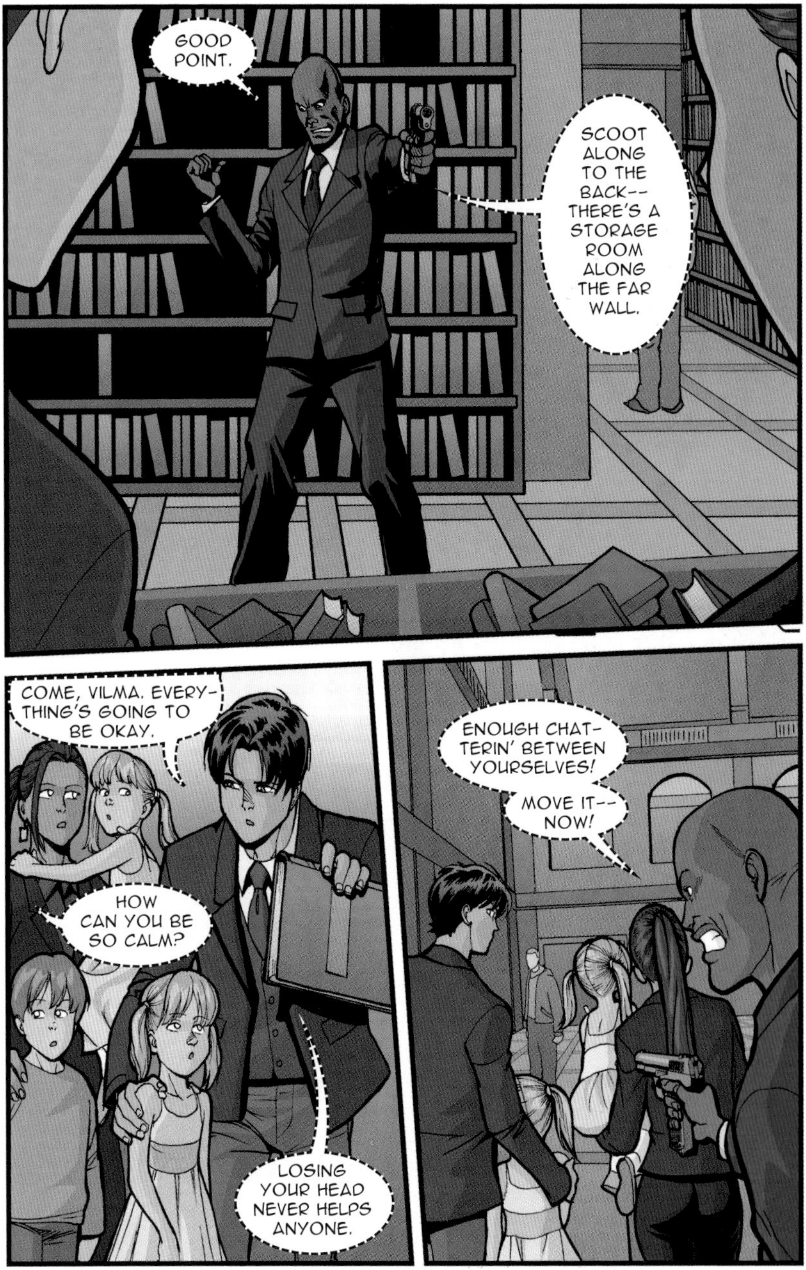
GOOD POINT.
SCOOT ALONG TO THE BACK-- THERE'S A STORAGE ROOM ALONG THE FAR WALL.
COME, VILMA. EVERY-THING'S GOING TO BE OKAY.
HOW CAN YOU BE SO CALM?
LOSING YOUR HEAD NEVER HELPS ANYONE.
ENOUGH CHAT-TERIN' BETWEEN YOURSELVES!
MOVE IT-- NOW!

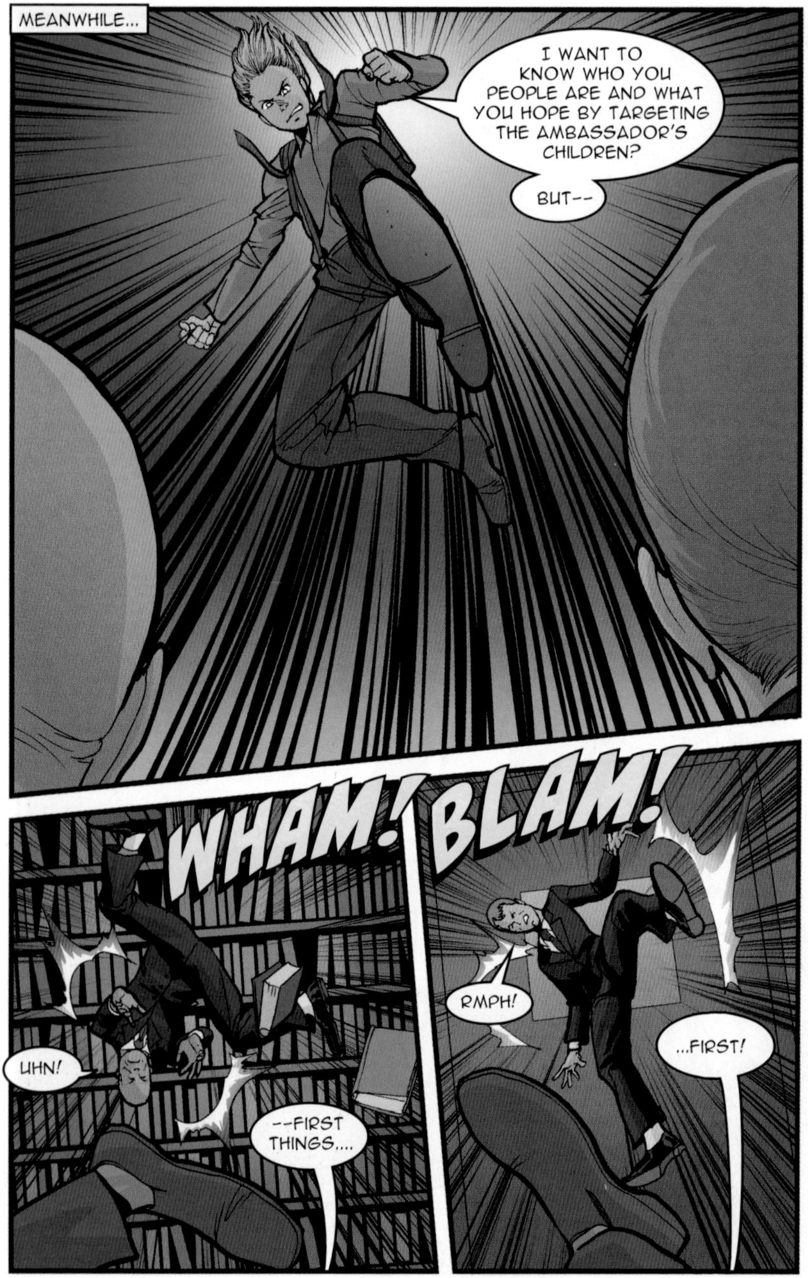
MEANWHILE...
I WANT TO KNOW WHO YOU PEOPLE ARE AND WHAT YOU HOPE BY TARGETING THE AMBASSADOR'S CHILDREN?
BUT--
WHAM!
UHN!
--FIRST THINGS....
BLAM!
RMPH!
...FIRST!

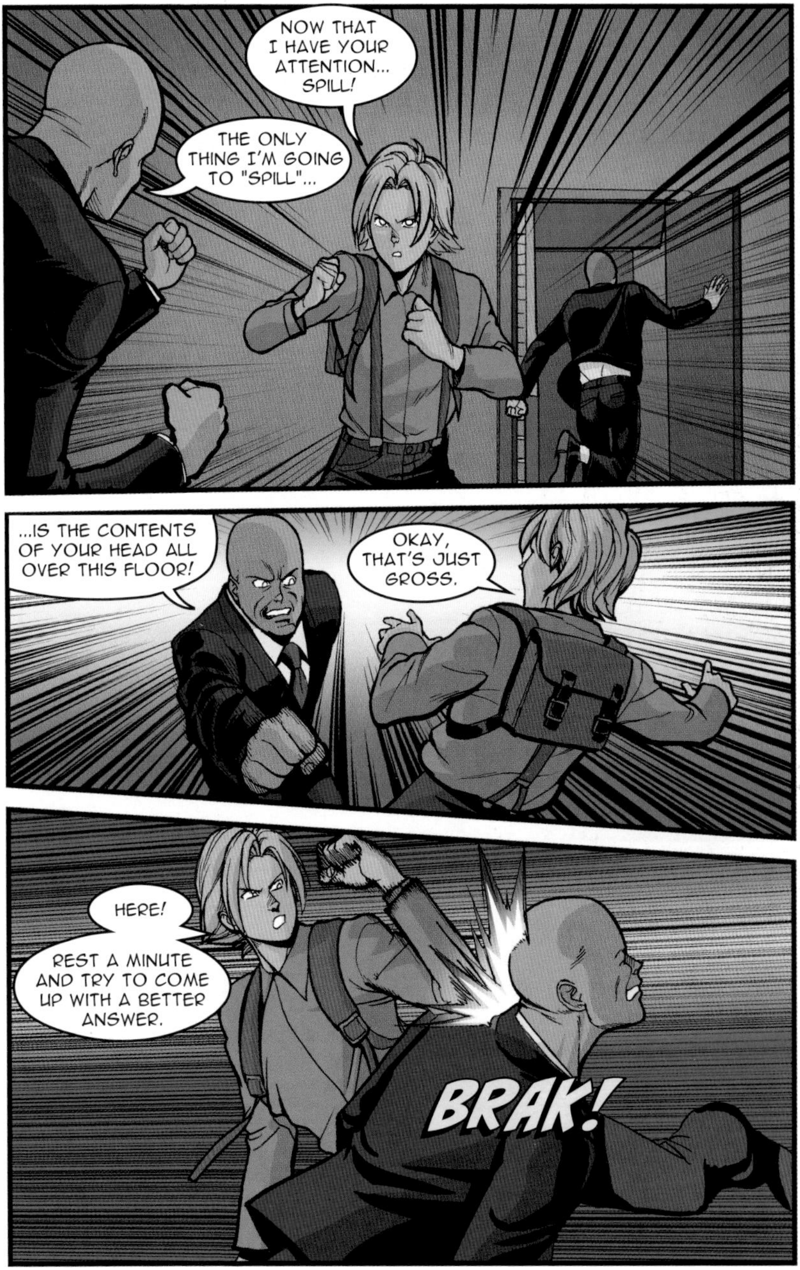
NOW THAT I HAVE YOUR ATTENTION... SPILL!
THE ONLY THING I'M GOING TO "SPILL"...
...IS THE CONTENTS OF YOUR HEAD ALL OVER THIS FLOOR!
OKAY, THAT'S JUST GROSS.
HERE!
REST A MINUTE AND TRY TO COME UP WITH A BETTER ANSWER.
BRAK!

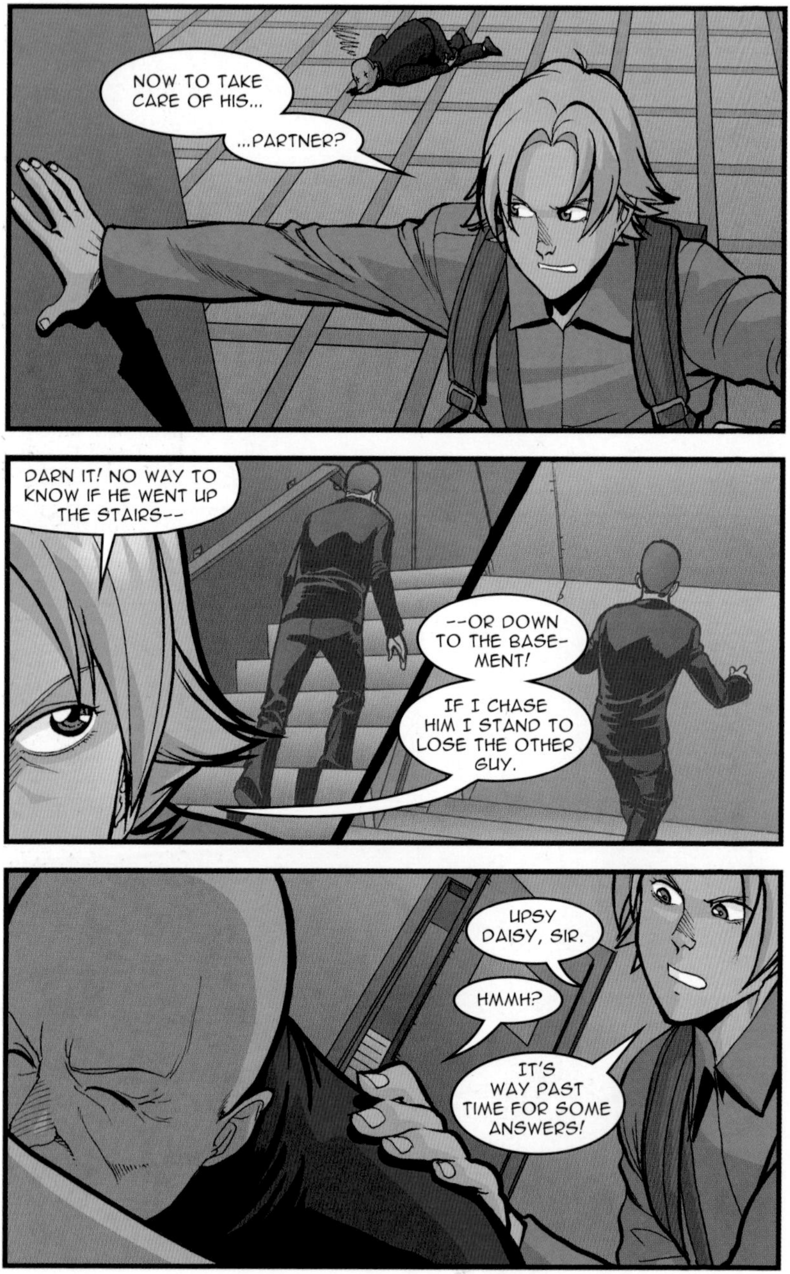
NOW TO TAKE CARE OF HIS...
...PARTNER?
DARN IT! NO WAY TO KNOW IF HE WENT UP THE STAIRS--
--OR DOWN TO THE BASE-MENT!
IF I CHASE HIM I STAND TO LOSE THE OTHER GUY.
UPSY DAISY, SIR.
HMMH?
IT'S WAY PAST TIME FOR SOME ANSWERS!

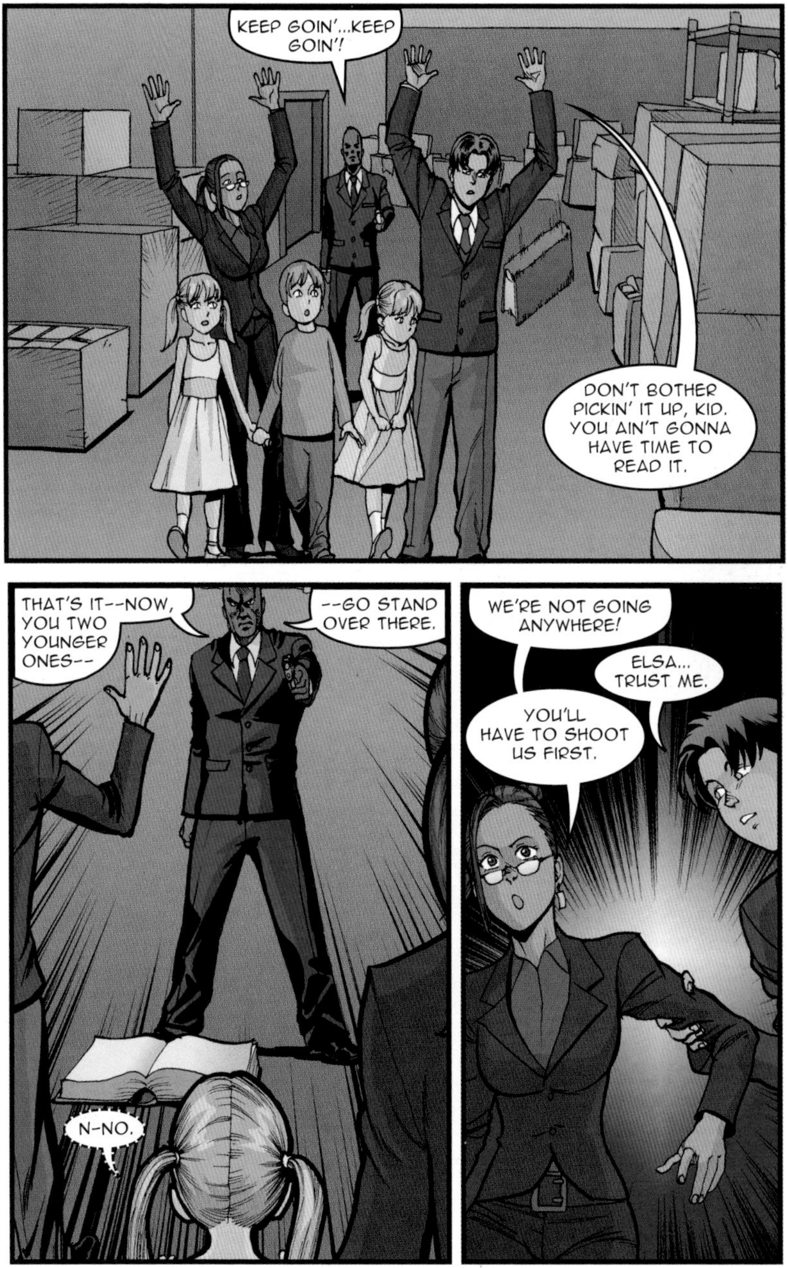
KEEP GOIN'...KEEP GOIN'!
DON'T BOTHER PICKIN' IT UP, KID. YOU AIN'T GONNA HAVE TIME TO READ IT.
THAT'S IT--NOW, YOU TWO YOUNGER ONES--
--GO STAND OVER THERE.
N-NO.
WE'RE NOT GOING ANYWHERE!
YOU'LL HAVE TO SHOOT US FIRST.
ELSA... TRUST ME.

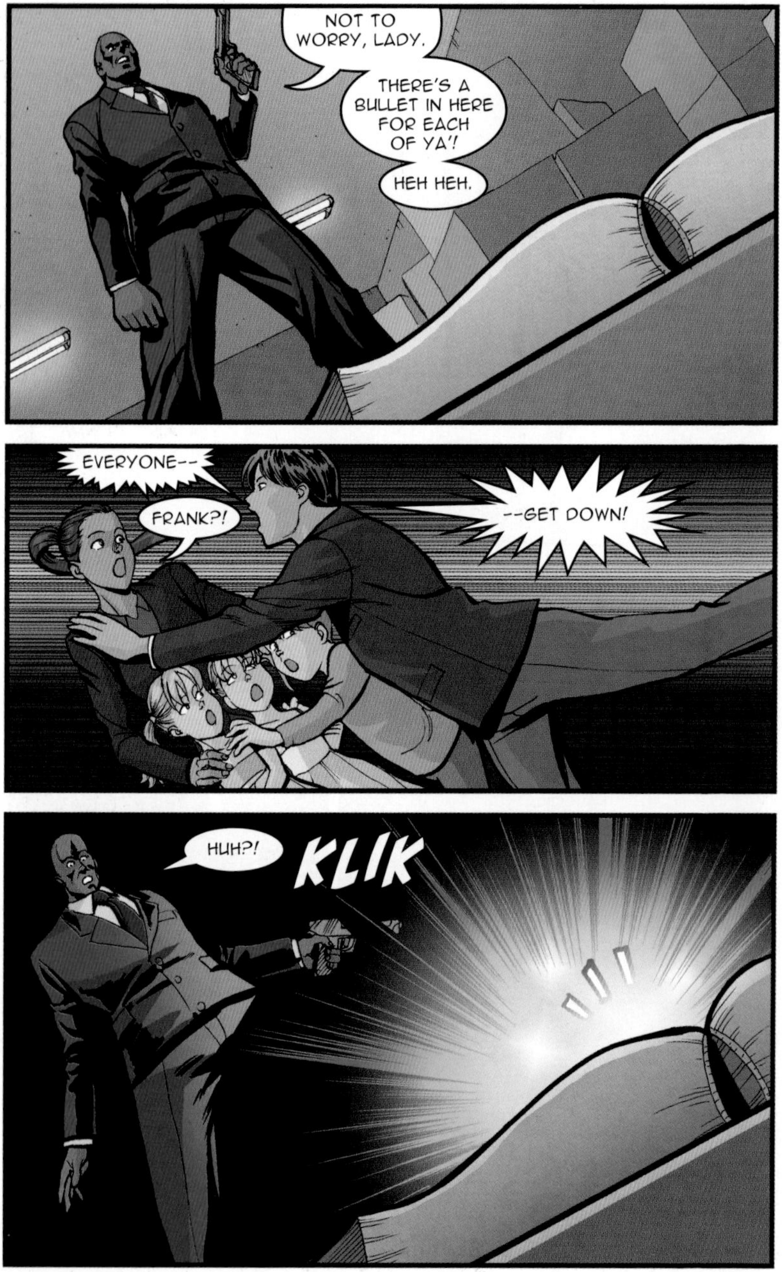
NOT TO WORRY, LADY.
THERE'S A BULLET IN HERE FOR EACH OF YA'!
HEH HEH.
EVERYONE--
FRANK?!
--GET DOWN!
HUH?!
KLIK

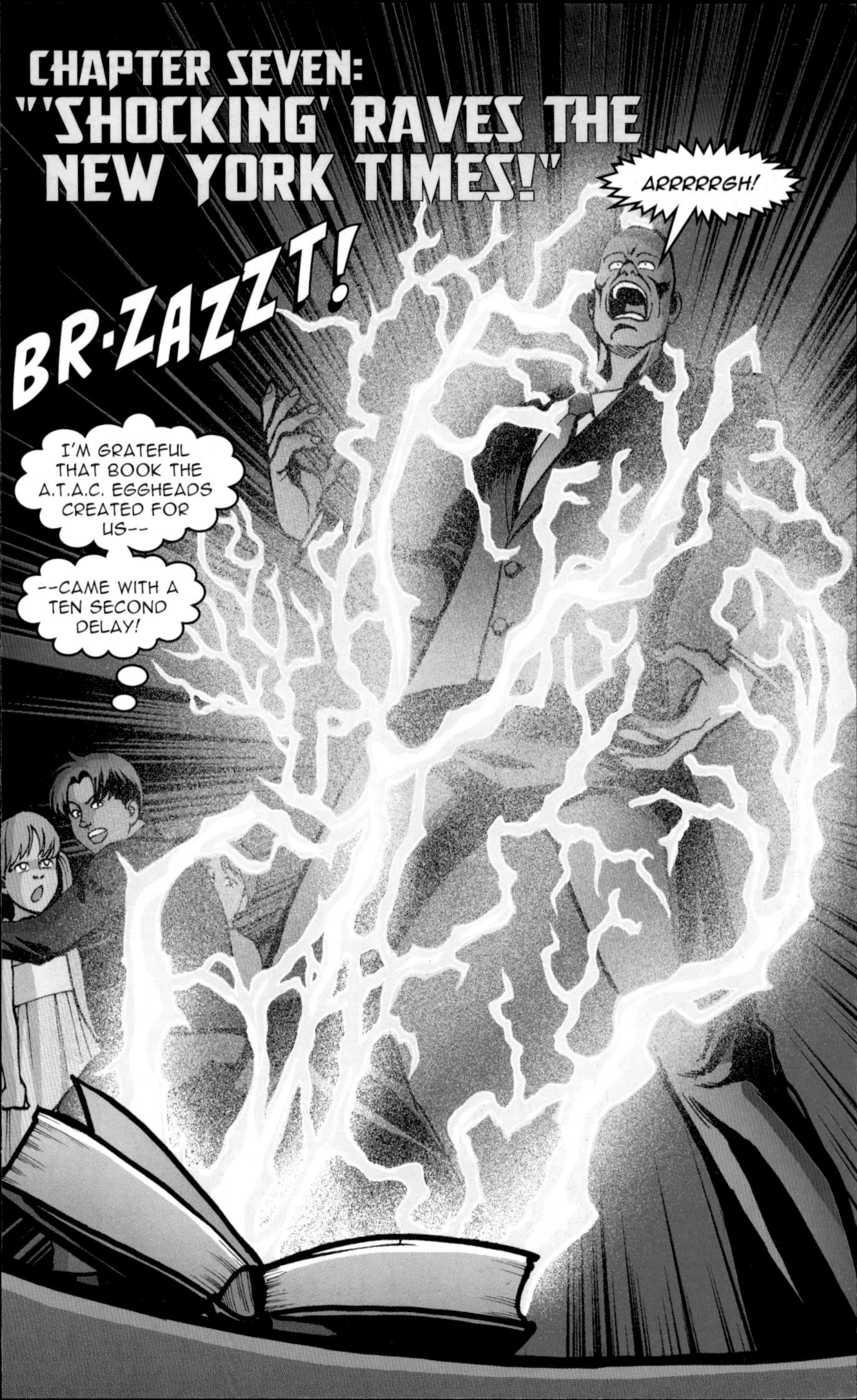
CHAPTER SEVEN:
"'SHOCKING' RAVES THE NEW YORK TIMES!"
ARRRRRGH!
BR-ZAZZT!
I'M GRATEFUL THAT BOOK THE A.T.A.C. EGGHEADS CREATED FOR US--
--CAME WITH A TEN SECOND DELAY!

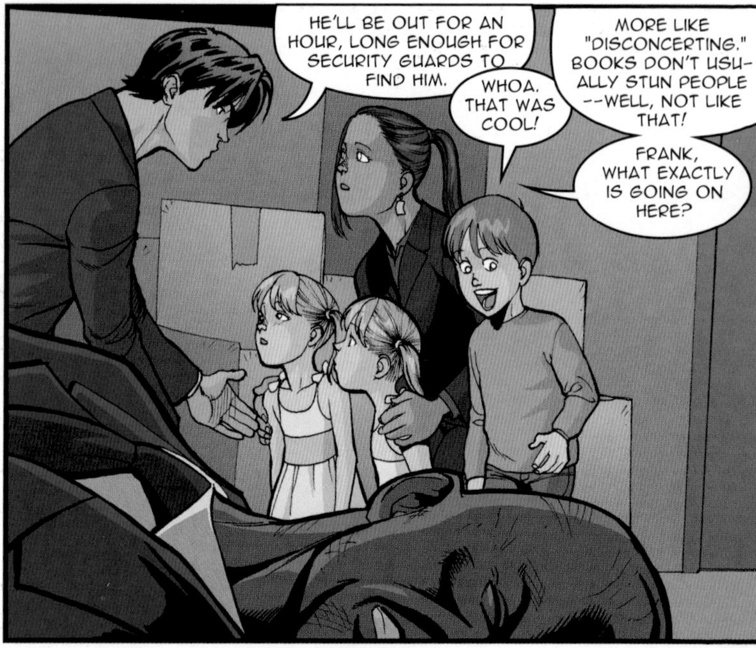
HE'LL BE OUT FOR AN HOUR, LONG ENOUGH FOR SECURITY GUARDS TO FIND HIM.
WHOA. THAT WAS COOL!
MORE LIKE "DISCONCERTING." BOOKS DON'T USU-ALLY STUN PEOPLE --WELL, NOT LIKE THAT!
FRANK, WHAT EXACTLY IS GOING ON HERE?

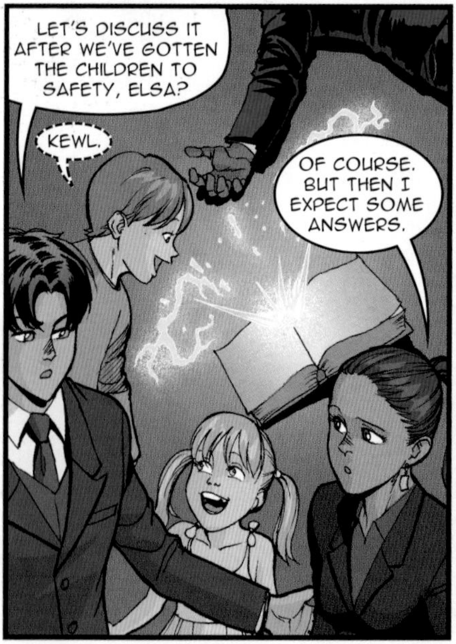
LET'S DISCUSS IT AFTER WE'VE GOTTEN THE CHILDREN TO SAFETY, ELSA?
KEWL.
OF COURSE. BUT THEN I EXPECT SOME ANSWERS.

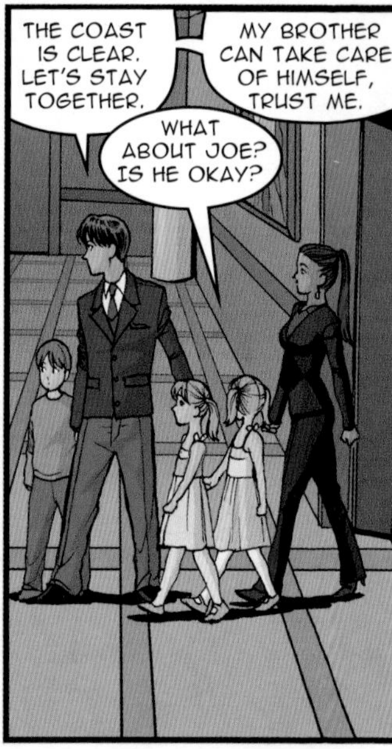
THE COAST IS CLEAR. LET'S STAY TOGETHER.
WHAT ABOUT JOE? IS HE OKAY?
MY BROTHER CAN TAKE CARE OF HIMSELF, TRUST ME.

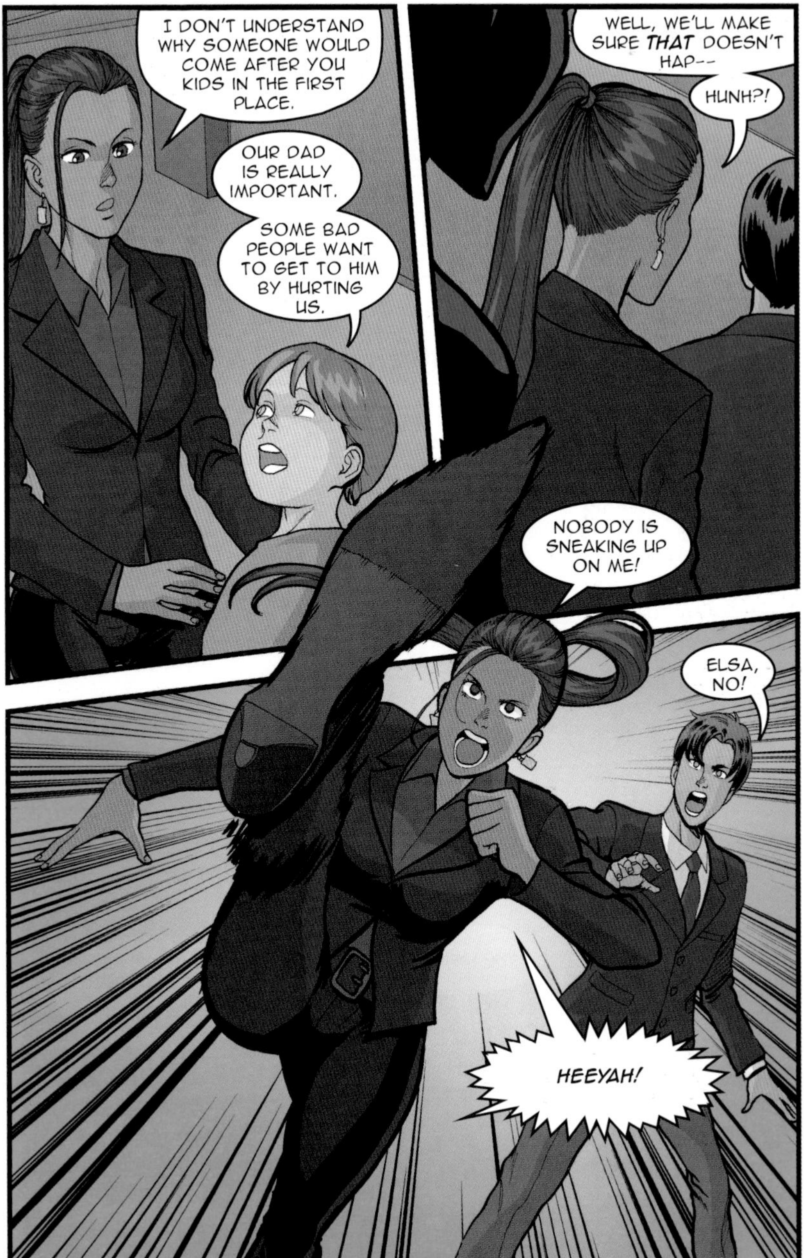
I DON'T UNDERSTAND WHY SOMEONE WOULD COME AFTER YOU KIDS IN THE FIRST PLACE.
OUR DAD IS REALLY IMPORTANT.
SOME BAD PEOPLE WANT TO GET TO HIM BY HURTING US.
WELL, WE'LL MAKE SURE *THAT* DOESN'T HAP--
HUNH?!
NOBODY IS SNEAKING UP ON ME!
ELSA, NO!
HEEYAH!

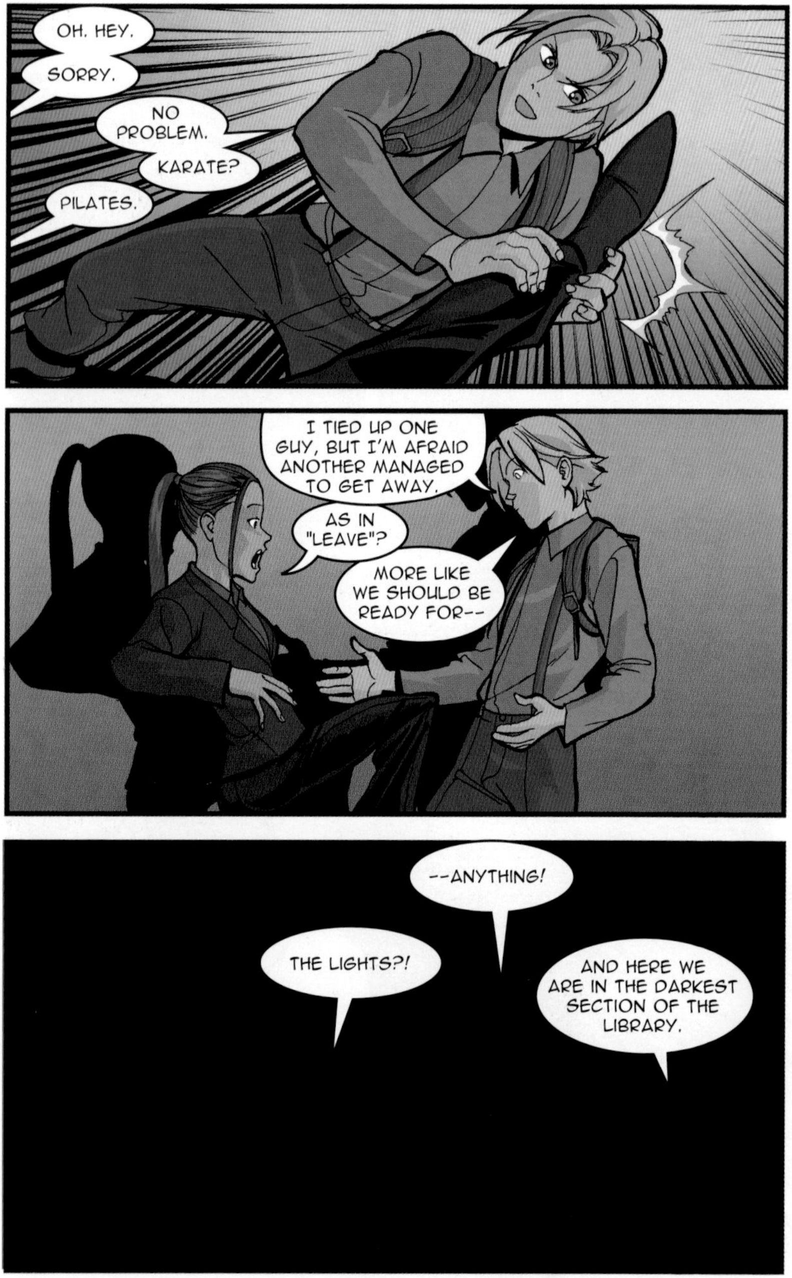
OH. HEY.
SORRY.
NO PROBLEM.
KARATE?
PILATES.
I TIED UP ONE GUY, BUT I'M AFRAID ANOTHER MANAGED TO GET AWAY.
AS IN "LEAVE"?
MORE LIKE WE SHOULD BE READY FOR--
--ANYTHING!
THE LIGHTS?!
AND HERE WE ARE IN THE DARKEST SECTION OF THE LIBRARY.

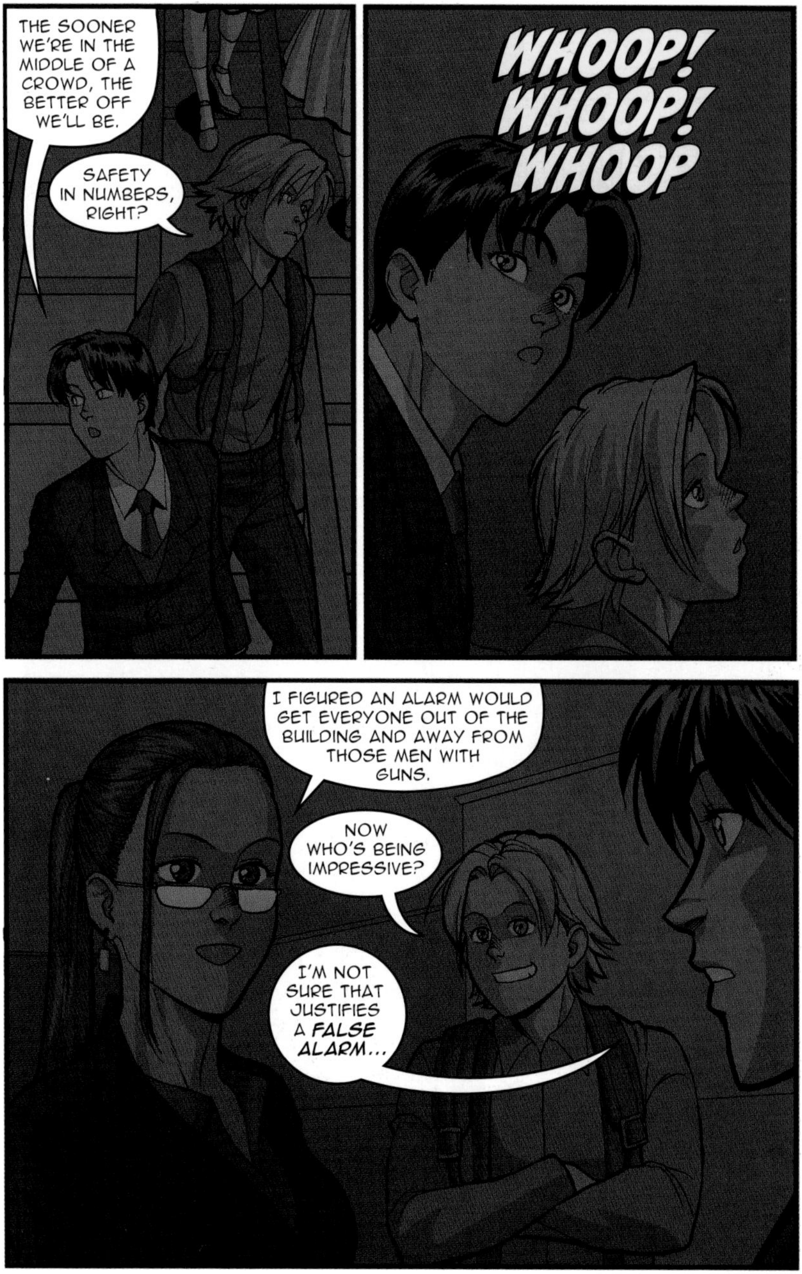
THE SOONER WE'RE IN THE MIDDLE OF A CROWD, THE BETTER OFF WE'LL BE.
SAFETY IN NUMBERS, RIGHT?
WHOOP! WHOOP! WHOOP
I FIGURED AN ALARM WOULD GET EVERYONE OUT OF THE BUILDING AND AWAY FROM THOSE MEN WITH GUNS.
NOW WHO'S BEING IMPRESSIVE?
I'M NOT SURE THAT JUSTIFIES A *FALSE ALARM*...

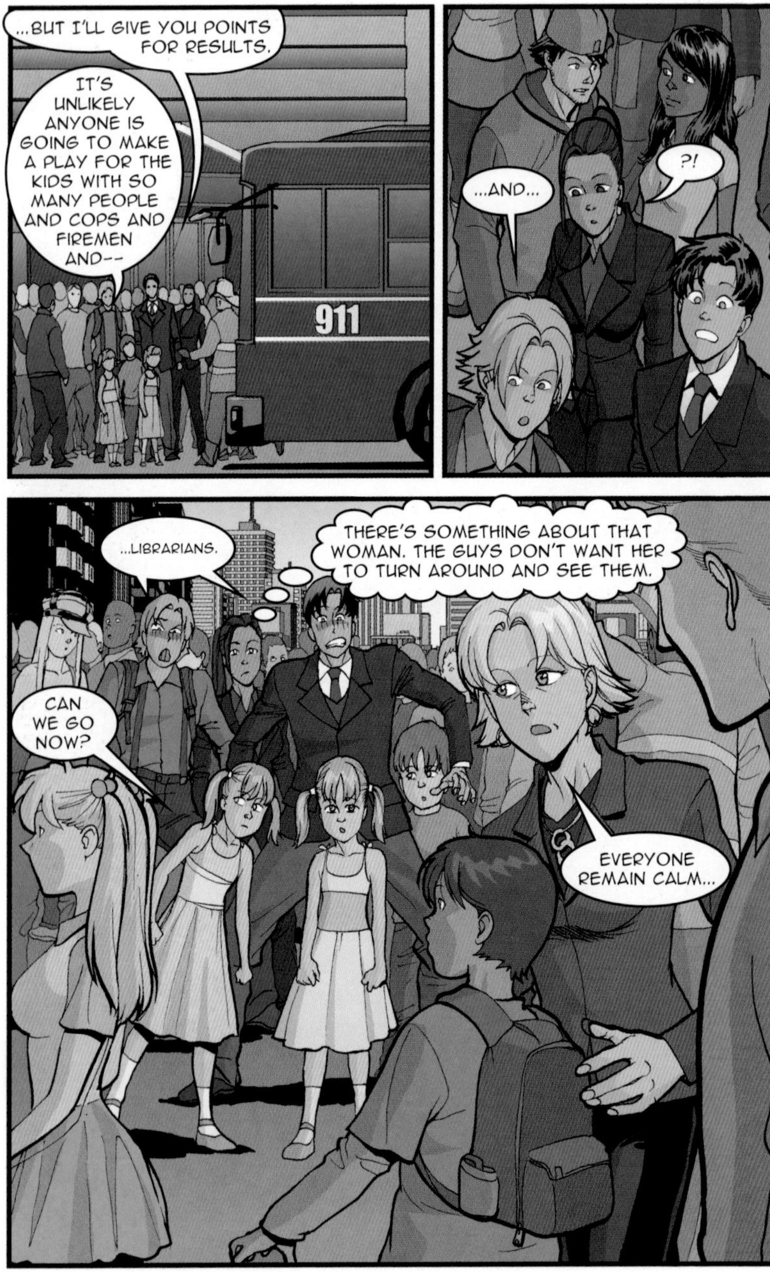
...BUT I'LL GIVE YOU POINTS FOR RESULTS.
IT'S UNLIKELY ANYONE IS GOING TO MAKE A PLAY FOR THE KIDS WITH SO MANY PEOPLE AND COPS AND FIREMEN AND--
911
...AND...
?!
...LIBRARIANS.
THERE'S SOMETHING ABOUT THAT WOMAN. THE GUYS DON'T WANT HER TO TURN AROUND AND SEE THEM.
CAN WE GO NOW?
EVERYONE REMAIN CALM...

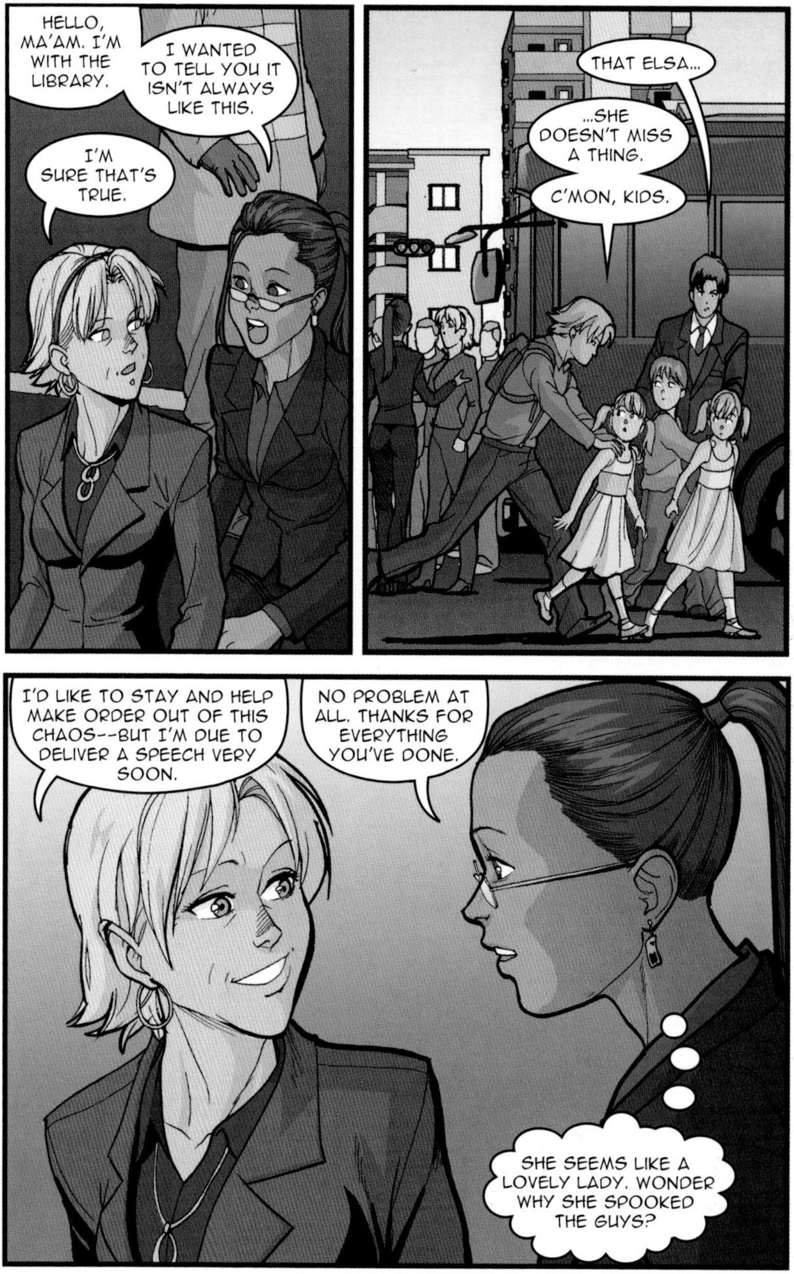
HELLO, MA'AM. I'M WITH THE LIBRARY.
I WANTED TO TELL YOU IT ISN'T ALWAYS LIKE THIS.
I'M SURE THAT'S TRUE.
THAT ELSA...
...SHE DOESN'T MISS A THING.
C'MON, KIDS.
I'D LIKE TO STAY AND HELP MAKE ORDER OUT OF THIS CHAOS--BUT I'M DUE TO DELIVER A SPEECH VERY SOON.
NO PROBLEM AT ALL. THANKS FOR EVERYTHING YOU'VE DONE.
SHE SEEMS LIKE A LOVELY LADY. WONDER WHY SHE SPOOKED THE GUYS?

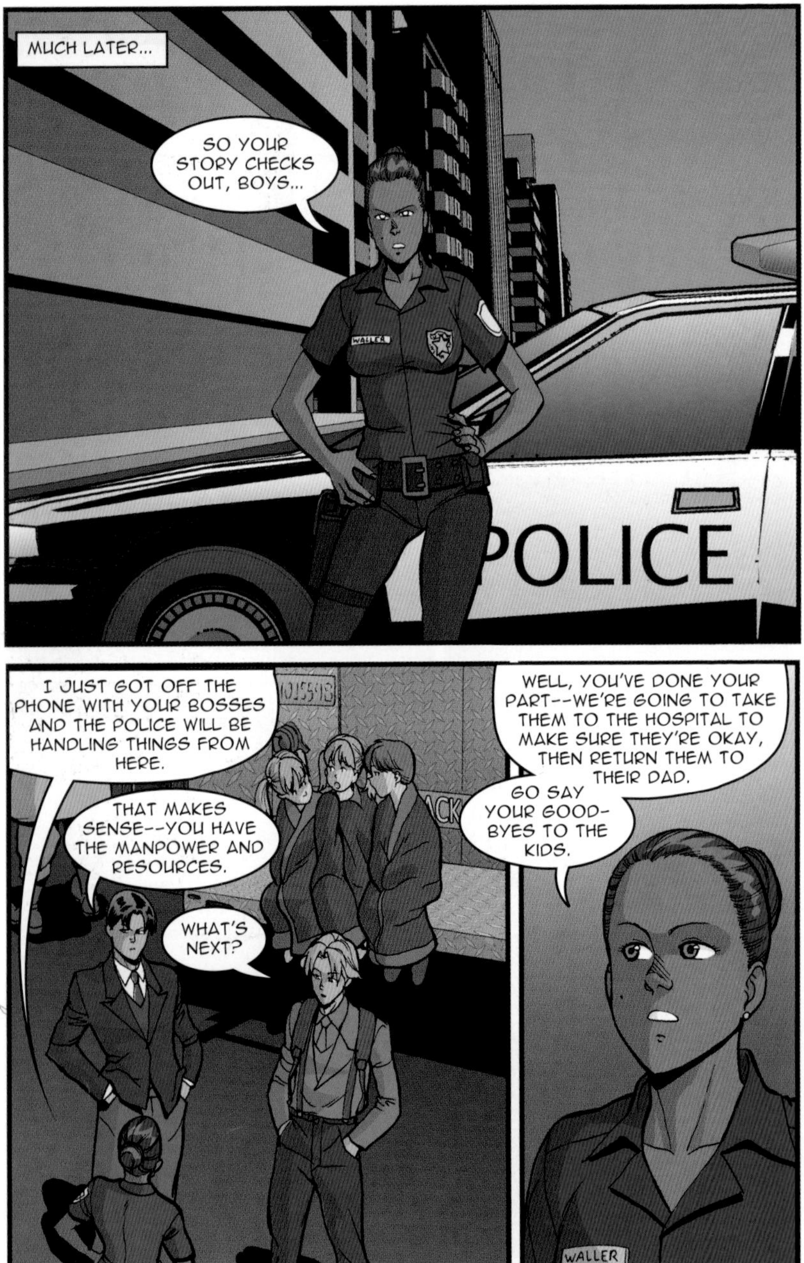
MUCH LATER...
SO YOUR STORY CHECKS OUT, BOYS...
WALLER
POLICE
I JUST GOT OFF THE PHONE WITH YOUR BOSSES AND THE POLICE WILL BE HANDLING THINGS FROM HERE.
THAT MAKES SENSE--YOU HAVE THE MANPOWER AND RESOURCES.
WHAT'S NEXT?
WELL, YOU'VE DONE YOUR PART--WE'RE GOING TO TAKE THEM TO THE HOSPITAL TO MAKE SURE THEY'RE OKAY, THEN RETURN THEM TO THEIR DAD.
GO SAY YOUR GOOD-BYES TO THE KIDS.
WALLER

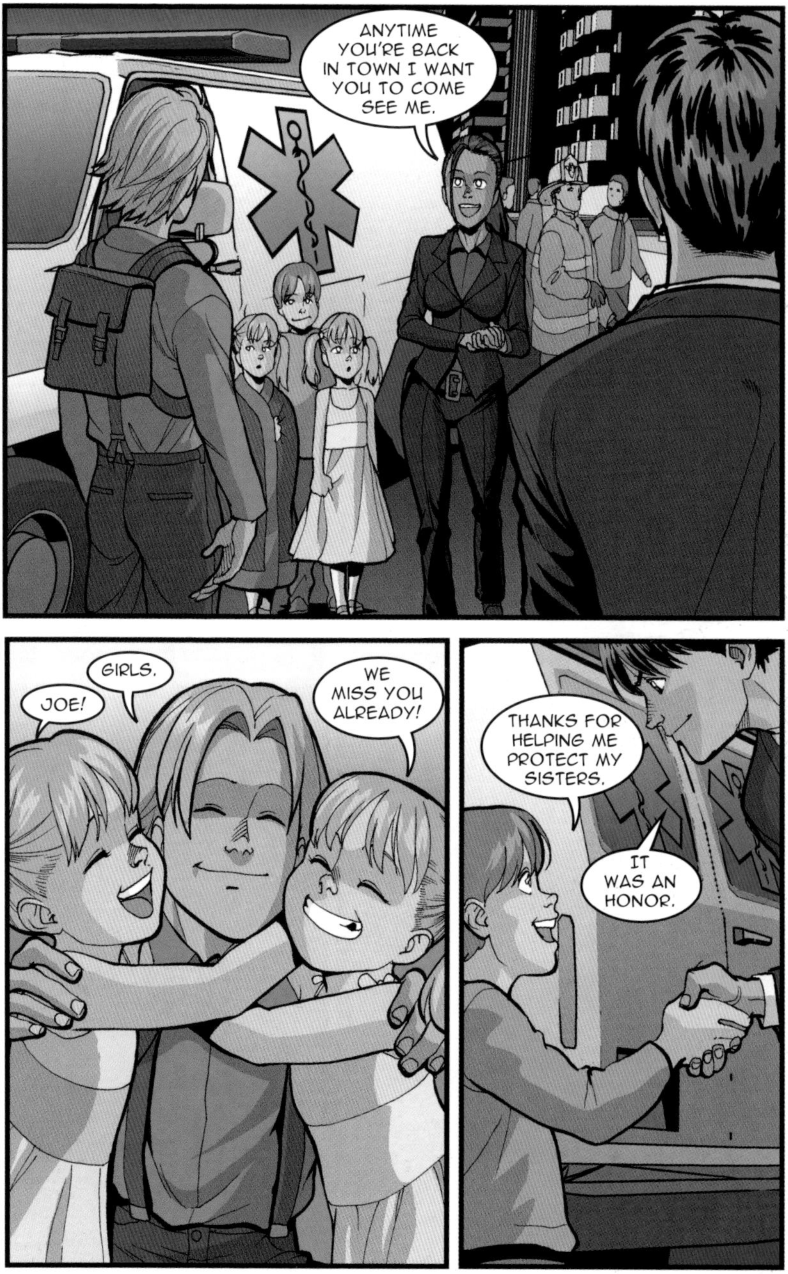
ANYTIME YOU'RE BACK IN TOWN I WANT YOU TO COME SEE ME.
JOE!
GIRLS.
WE MISS YOU ALREADY!
THANKS FOR HELPING ME PROTECT MY SISTERS.
IT WAS AN HONOR.

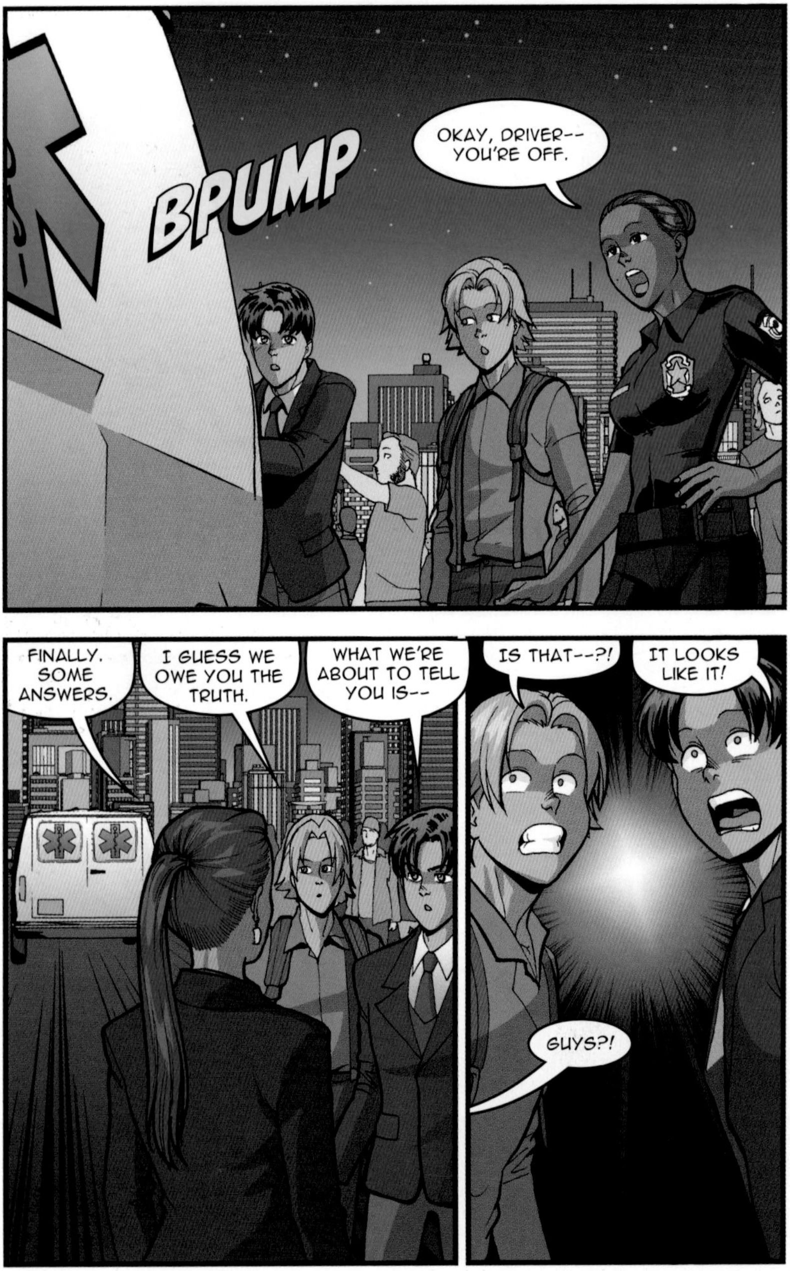
BPUMP
OKAY, DRIVER-- YOU'RE OFF.
FINALLY. SOME ANSWERS.
I GUESS WE OWE YOU THE TRUTH.
WHAT WE'RE ABOUT TO TELL YOU IS--
IS THAT--?!
IT LOOKS LIKE IT!
GUYS?!

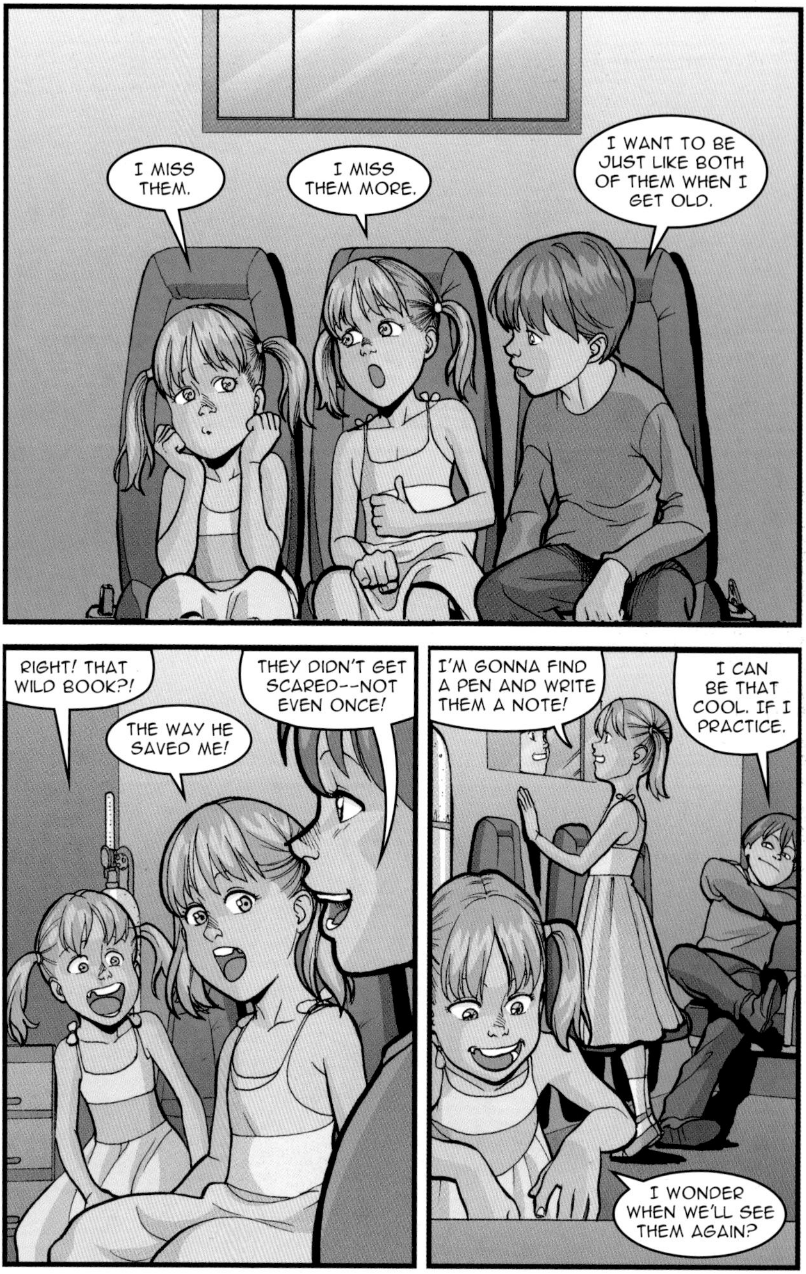
I MISS THEM.
I MISS THEM MORE.
I WANT TO BE JUST LIKE BOTH OF THEM WHEN I GET OLD.
RIGHT! THAT WILD BOOK?!
THE WAY HE SAVED ME!
THEY DIDN'T GET SCARED--NOT EVEN ONCE!
I'M GONNA FIND A PEN AND WRITE THEM A NOTE!
I CAN BE THAT COOL. IF I PRACTICE.
I WONDER WHEN WE'LL SEE THEM AGAIN?

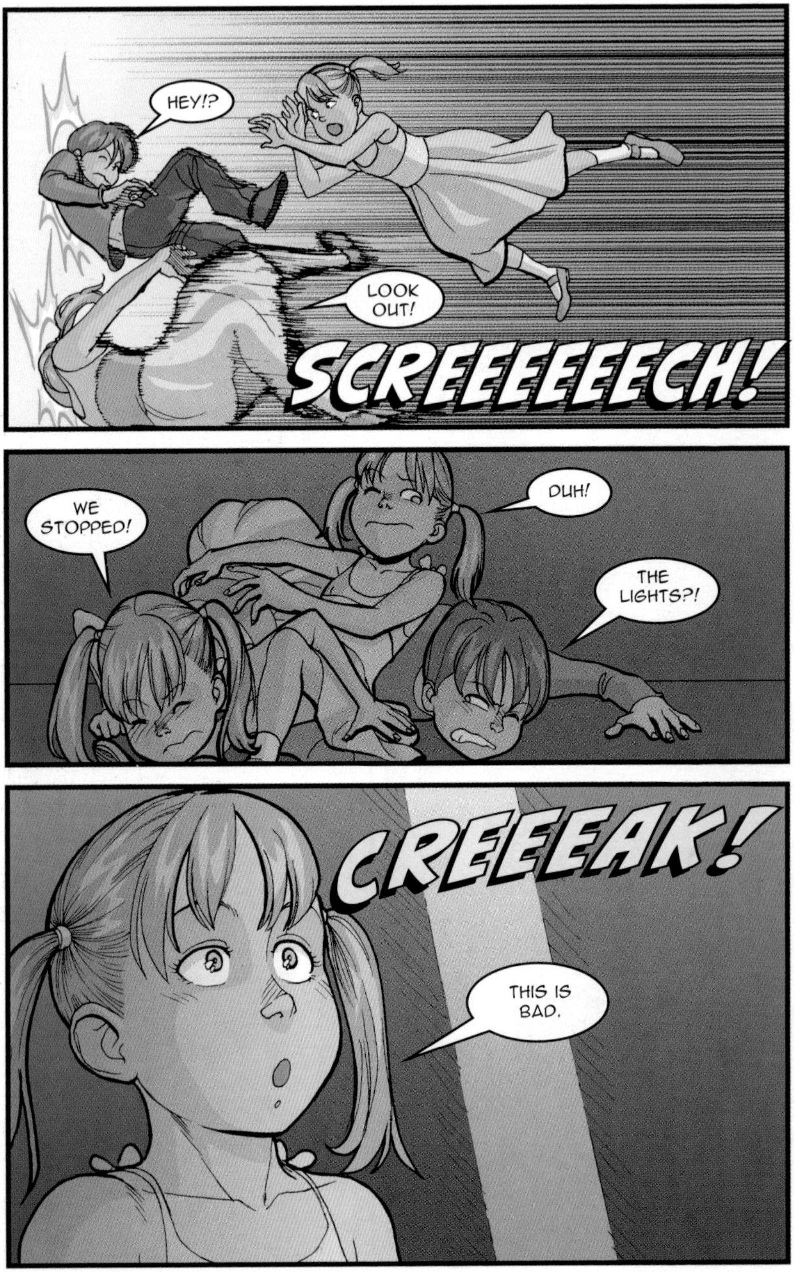
HEY!?
LOOK OUT!
SCREEEEEEECH!
WE STOPPED!
DUH!
THE LIGHTS?!
CREEEAK!
THIS IS BAD.

CHAPTER EIGHT: "A GOOD BOOK ALWAYS ILLUMINATES!"

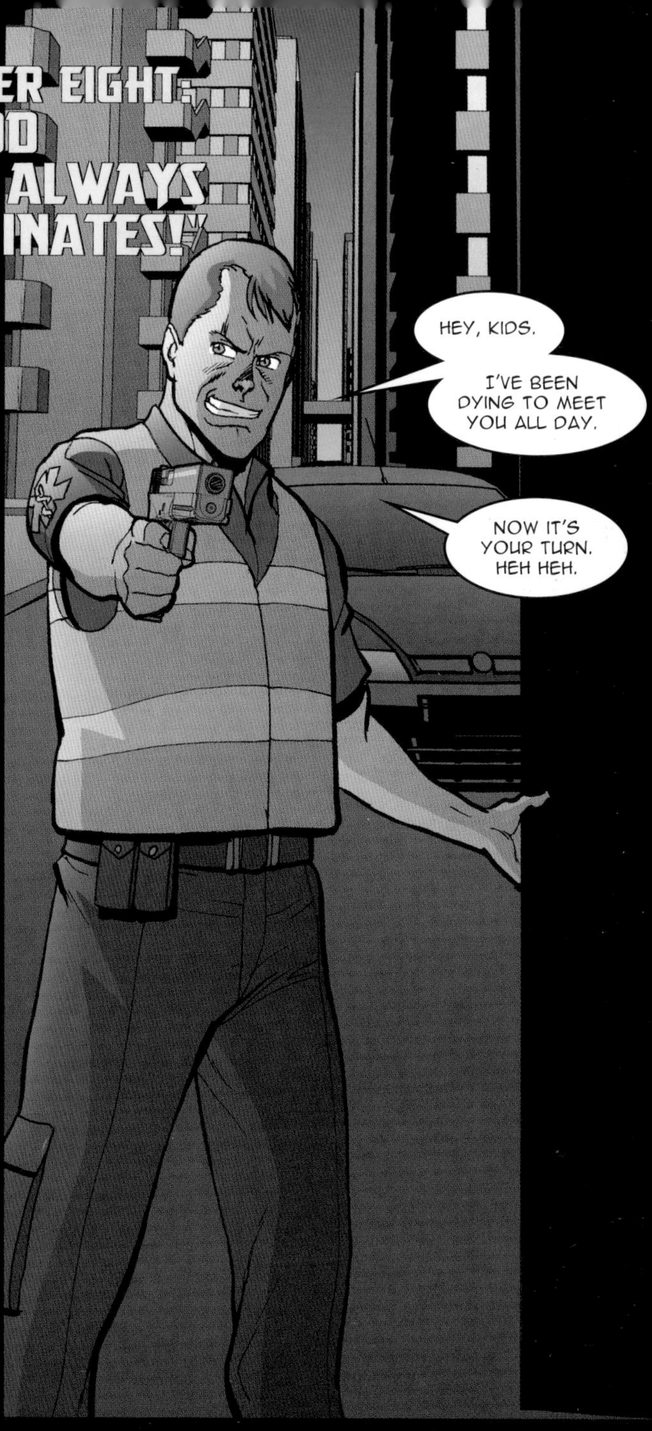
HEY, KIDS.
I'VE BEEN DYING TO MEET YOU ALL DAY.
NOW IT'S YOUR TURN. HEH HEH.

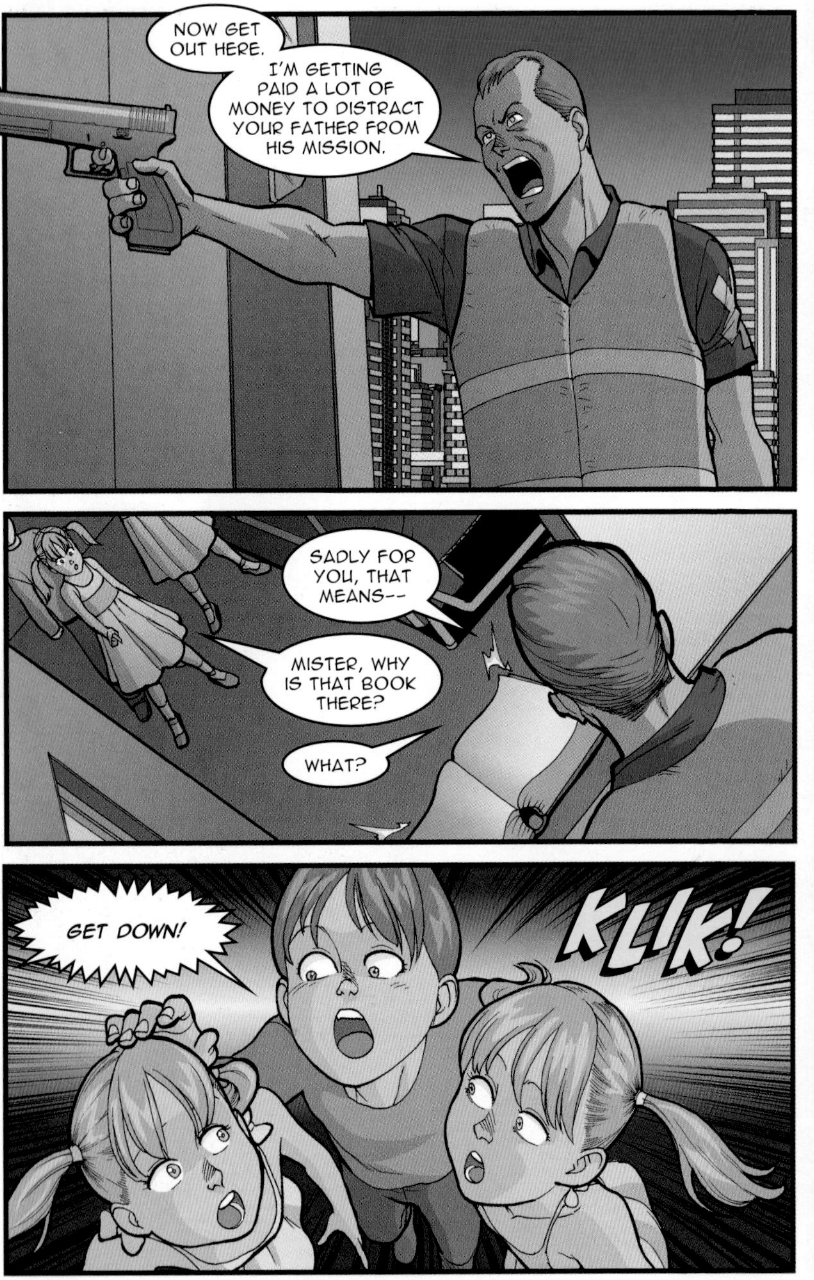
NOW GET OUT HERE.
I'M GETTING PAID A LOT OF MONEY TO DISTRACT YOUR FATHER FROM HIS MISSION.
SADLY FOR YOU, THAT MEANS--
MISTER, WHY IS THAT BOOK THERE?
WHAT?
GET DOWN!
KLIK!

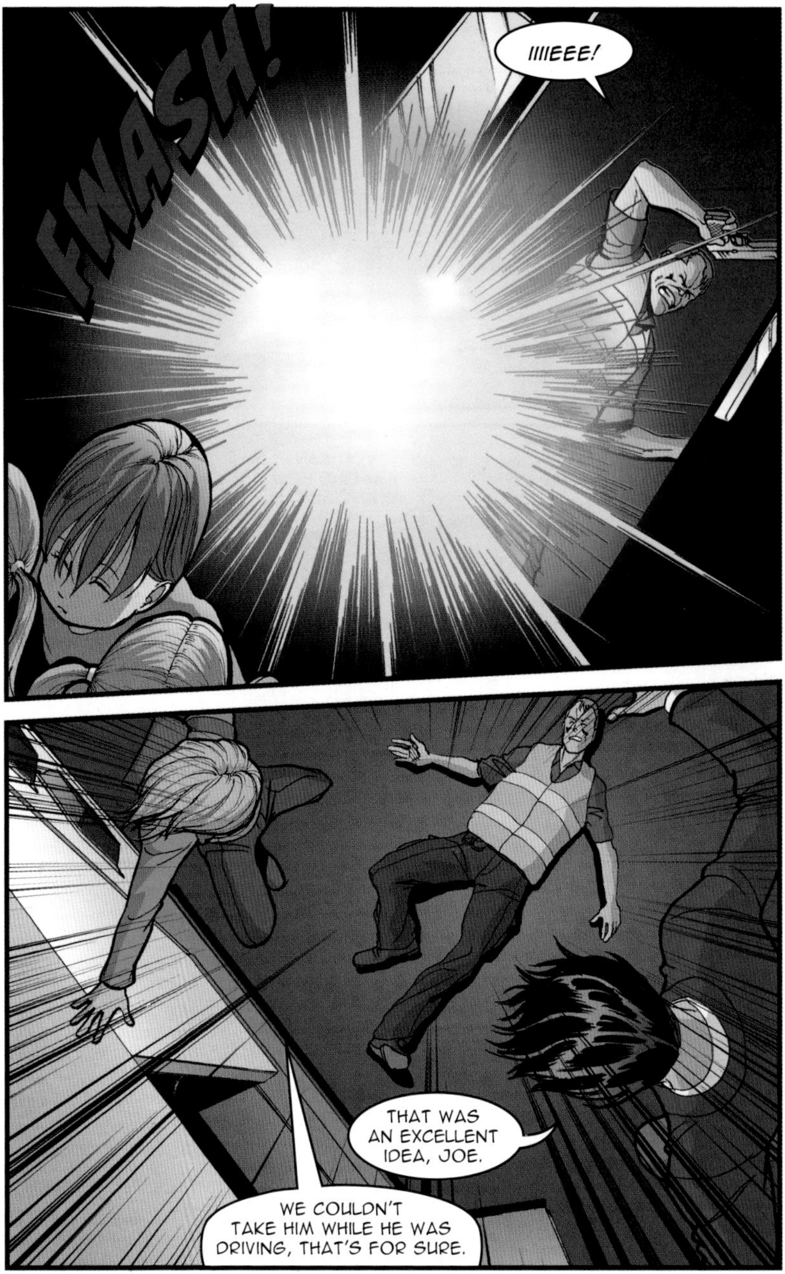
FWASH!
IIIIEEE!
THAT WAS AN EXCELLENT IDEA, JOE.
WE COULDN'T TAKE HIM WHILE HE WAS DRIVING, THAT'S FOR SURE.

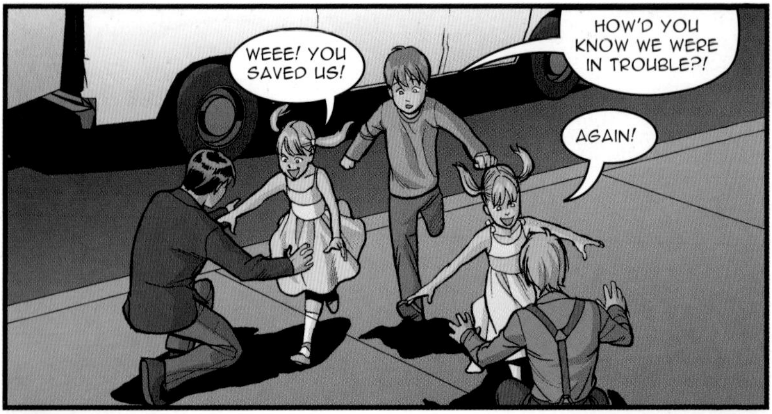
WEEE! YOU SAVED US!
HOW'D YOU KNOW WE WERE IN TROUBLE?!
AGAIN!

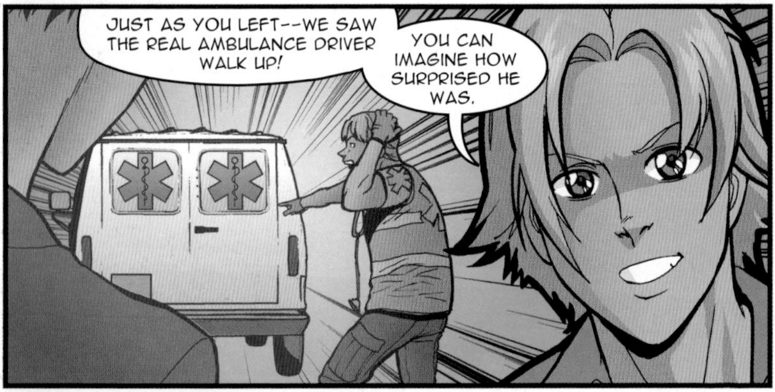
JUST AS YOU LEFT--WE SAW THE REAL AMBULANCE DRIVER WALK UP!
YOU CAN IMAGINE HOW SURPRISED HE WAS.

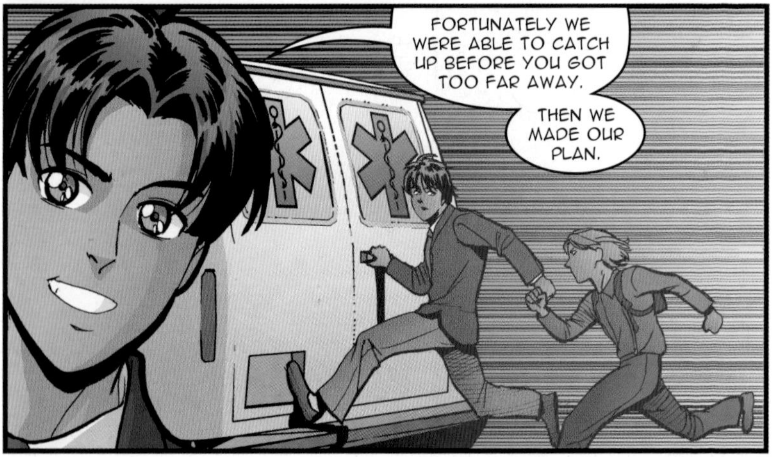
FORTUNATELY WE WERE ABLE TO CATCH UP BEFORE YOU GOT TOO FAR AWAY.
THEN WE MADE OUR PLAN.

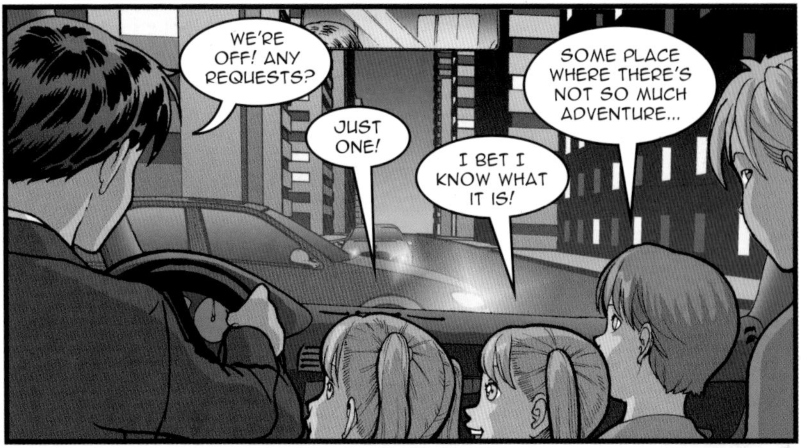
WE'RE OFF! ANY REQUESTS?
JUST ONE!
SOME PLACE WHERE THERE'S NOT SO MUCH ADVENTURE...
I BET I KNOW WHAT IT IS!

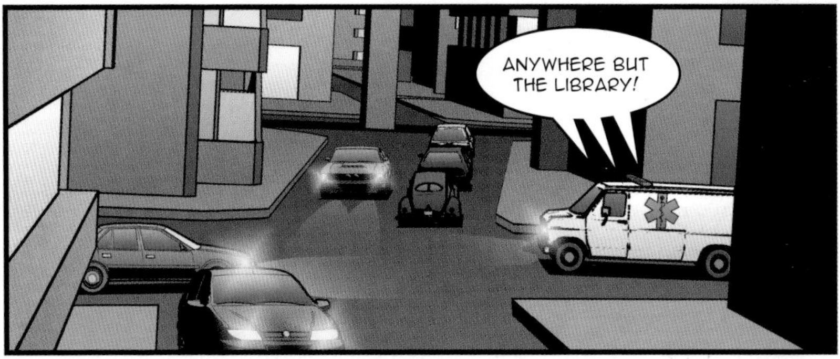
ANYWHERE BUT THE LIBRARY!

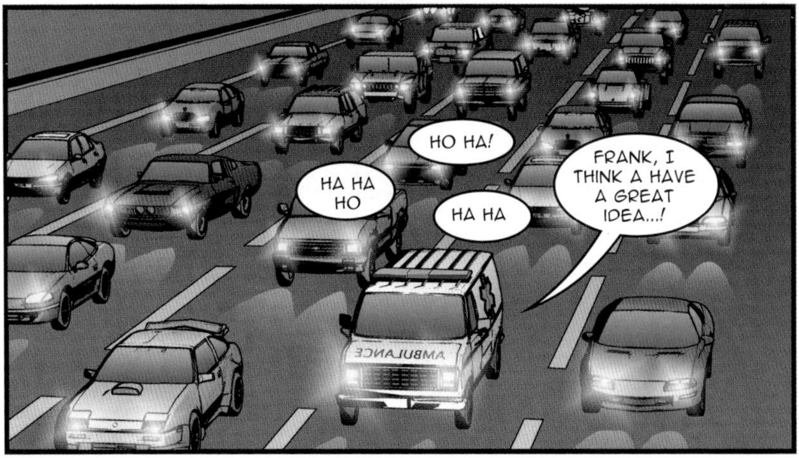
HO HA!
HA HA HO
HA HA
FRANK, I THINK A HAVE A GREAT IDEA...!
AMBULANCE

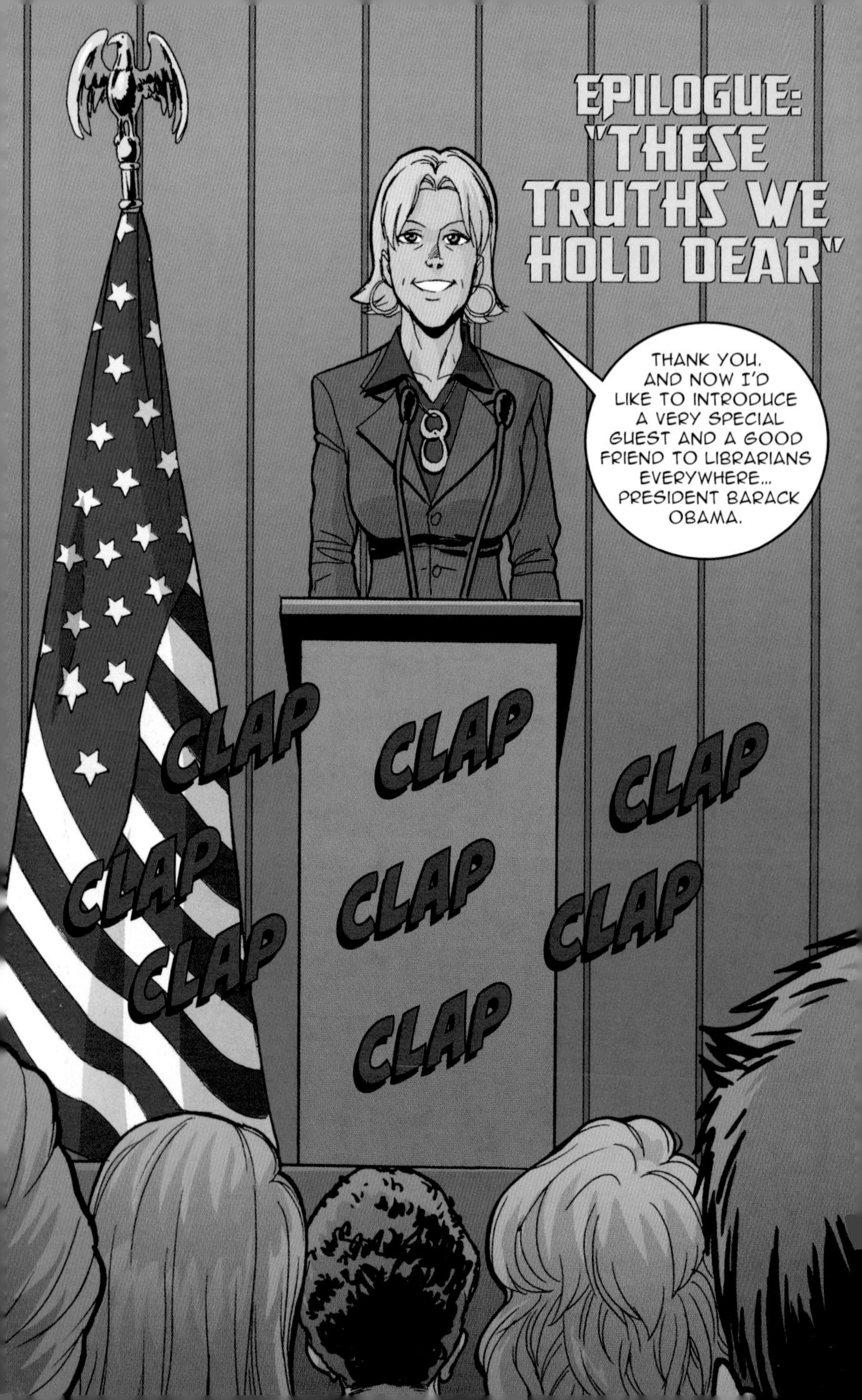
EPILOGUE: "THESE TRUTHS WE HOLD DEAR"
THANK YOU. AND NOW I'D LIKE TO INTRODUCE A VERY SPECIAL GUEST AND A GOOD FRIEND TO LIBRARIANS EVERYWHERE... PRESIDENT BARACK OBAMA.
CLAP
CLAP
CLAP
CLAP
CLAP
CLAP
CLAP
CLAP

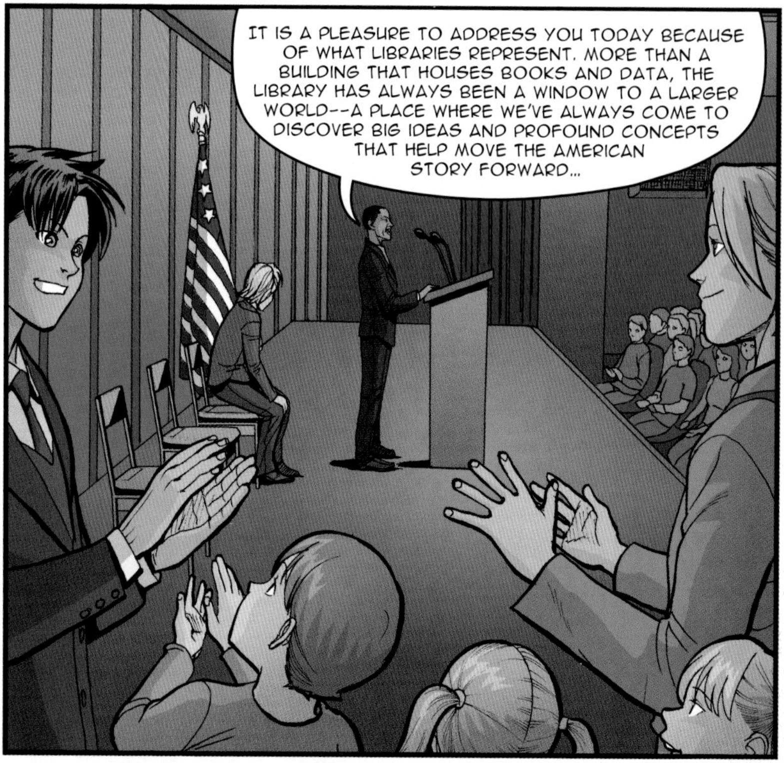
IT IS A PLEASURE TO ADDRESS YOU TODAY BECAUSE OF WHAT LIBRARIES REPRESENT. MORE THAN A BUILDING THAT HOUSES BOOKS AND DATA, THE LIBRARY HAS ALWAYS BEEN A WINDOW TO A LARGER WORLD--A PLACE WHERE WE'VE ALWAYS COME TO DISCOVER BIG IDEAS AND PROFOUND CONCEPTS THAT HELP MOVE THE AMERICAN STORY FORWARD...

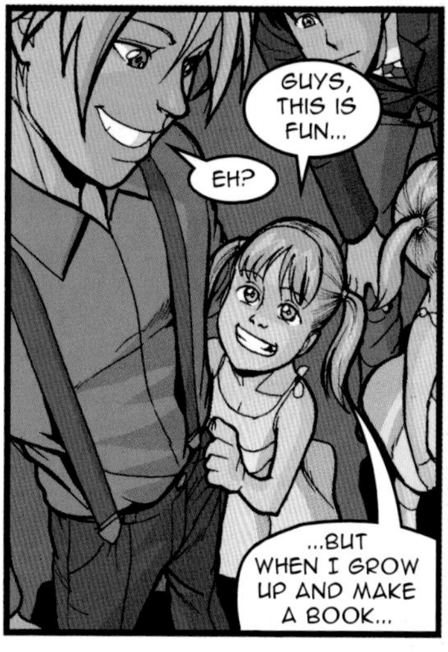
GUYS, THIS IS FUN...
EH?
...BUT WHEN I GROW UP AND MAKE A BOOK...

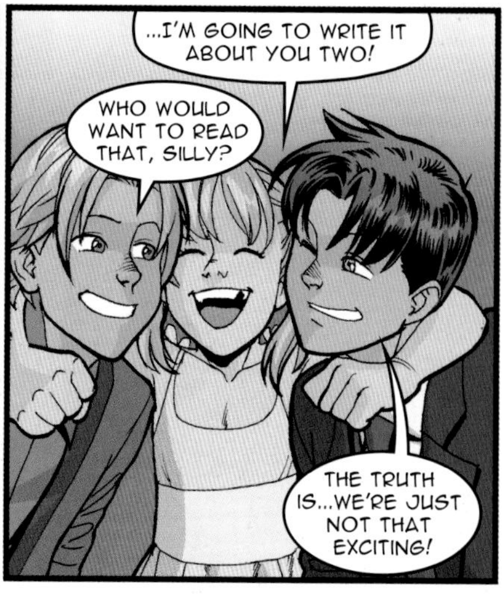
...I'M GOING TO WRITE IT ABOUT YOU TWO!
WHO WOULD WANT TO READ THAT, SILLY?
THE TRUTH IS...WE'RE JUST NOT THAT EXCITING!

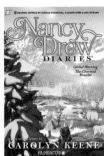

CHAPTER ONE:
"OH MY STARS AND GARTERS!"

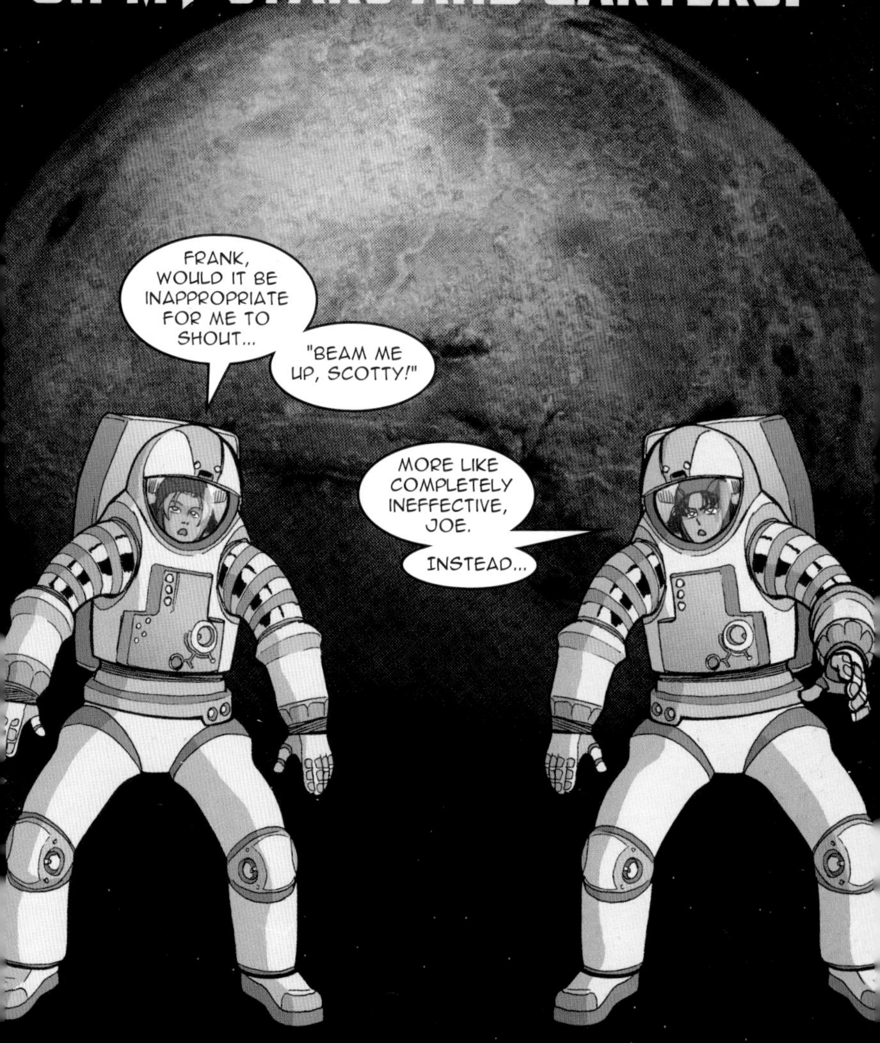

FRANK, WOULD IT BE INAPPROPRIATE FOR ME TO SHOUT...
"BEAM ME UP, SCOTTY!"
MORE LIKE COMPLETELY INEFFECTIVE, JOE.
INSTEAD...

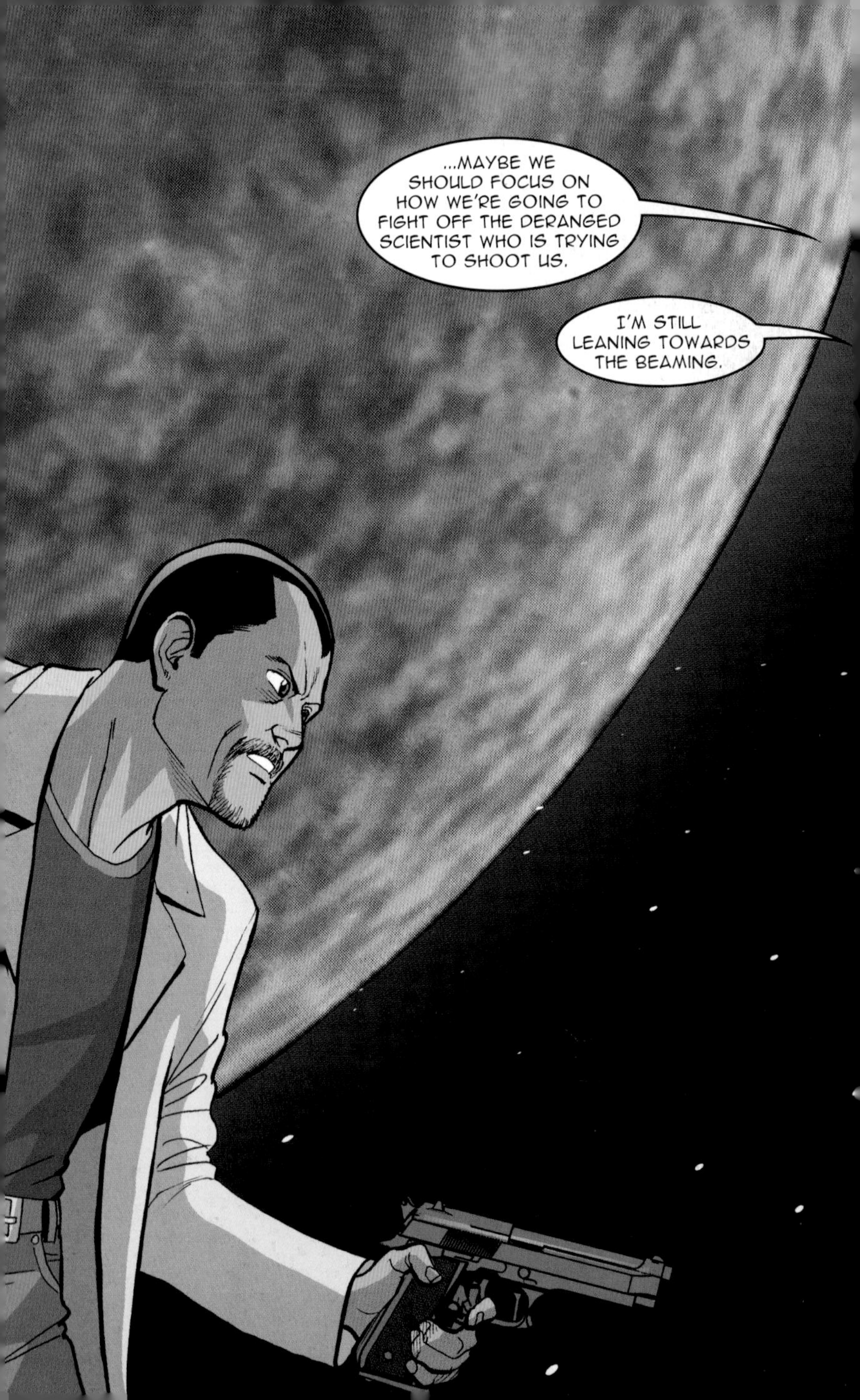
...MAYBE WE SHOULD FOCUS ON HOW WE'RE GOING TO FIGHT OFF THE DERANGED SCIENTIST WHO IS TRYING TO SHOOT US.
I'M STILL LEANING TOWARDS THE BEAMING.

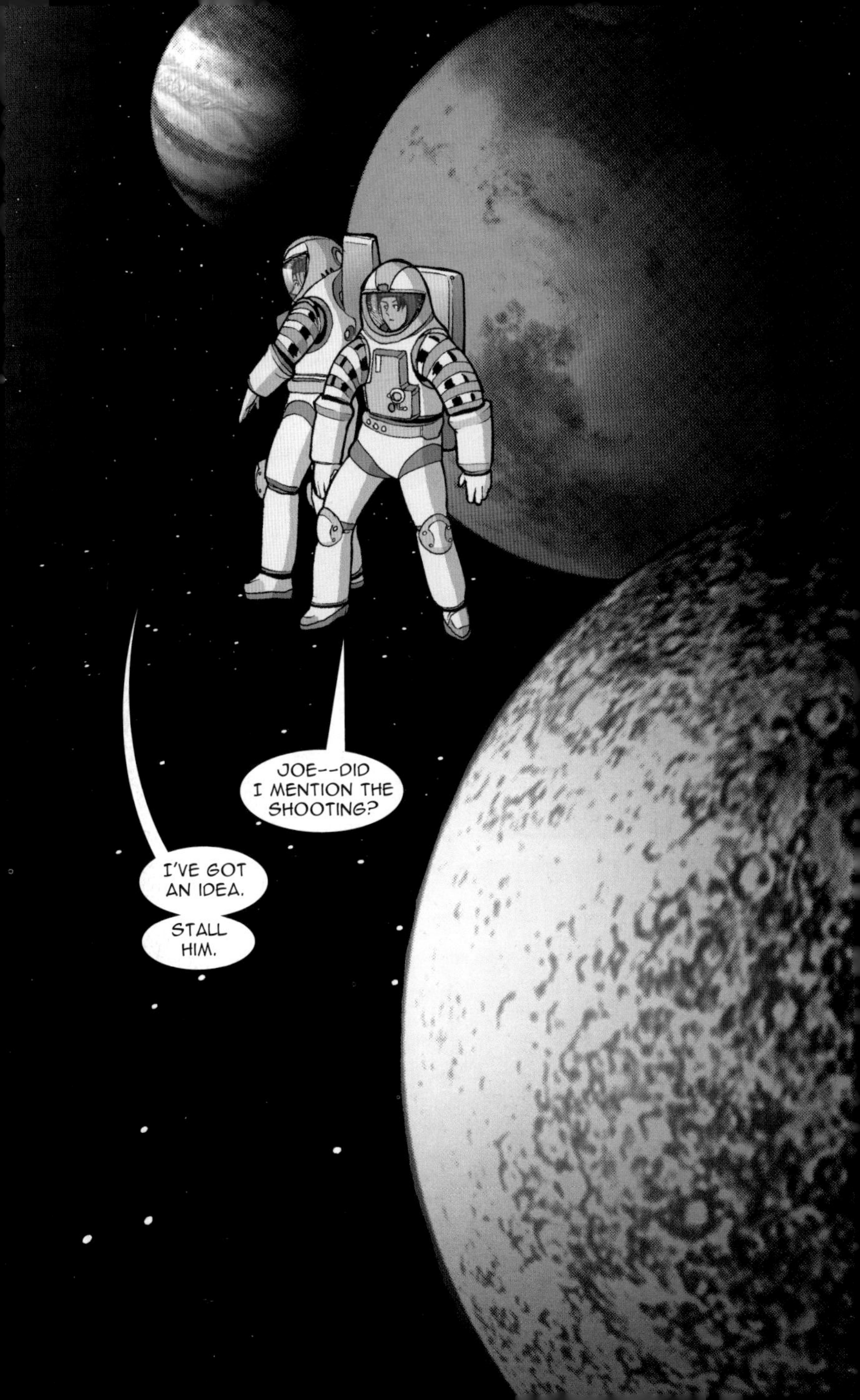
JOE--DID I MENTION THE SHOOTING?
I'VE GOT AN IDEA.
STALL HIM.

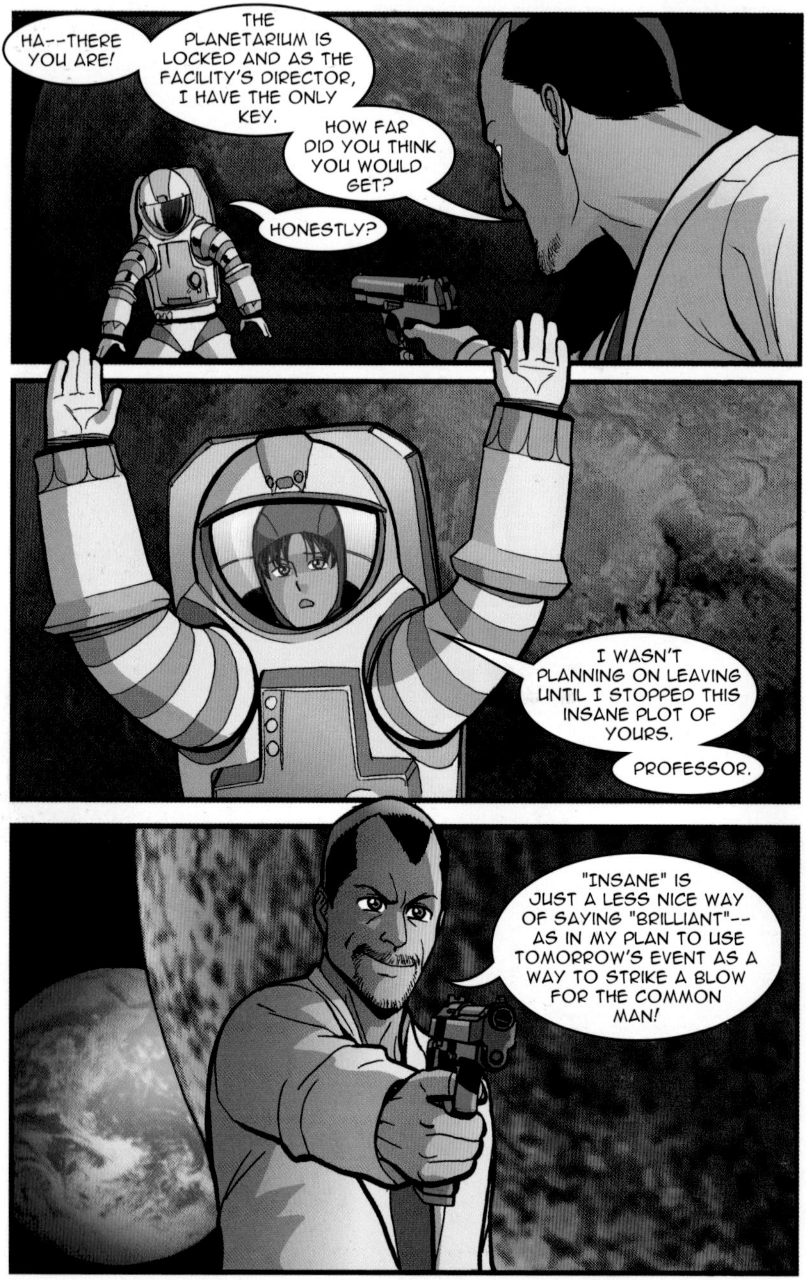
HA--THERE YOU ARE!
THE PLANETARIUM IS LOCKED AND AS THE FACILITY'S DIRECTOR, I HAVE THE ONLY KEY.
HOW FAR DID YOU THINK YOU WOULD GET?
HONESTLY?
I WASN'T PLANNING ON LEAVING UNTIL I STOPPED THIS INSANE PLOT OF YOURS.
PROFESSOR.
"INSANE" IS JUST A LESS NICE WAY OF SAYING "BRILLIANT"-- AS IN MY PLAN TO USE TOMORROW'S EVENT AS A WAY TO STRIKE A BLOW FOR THE COMMON MAN!

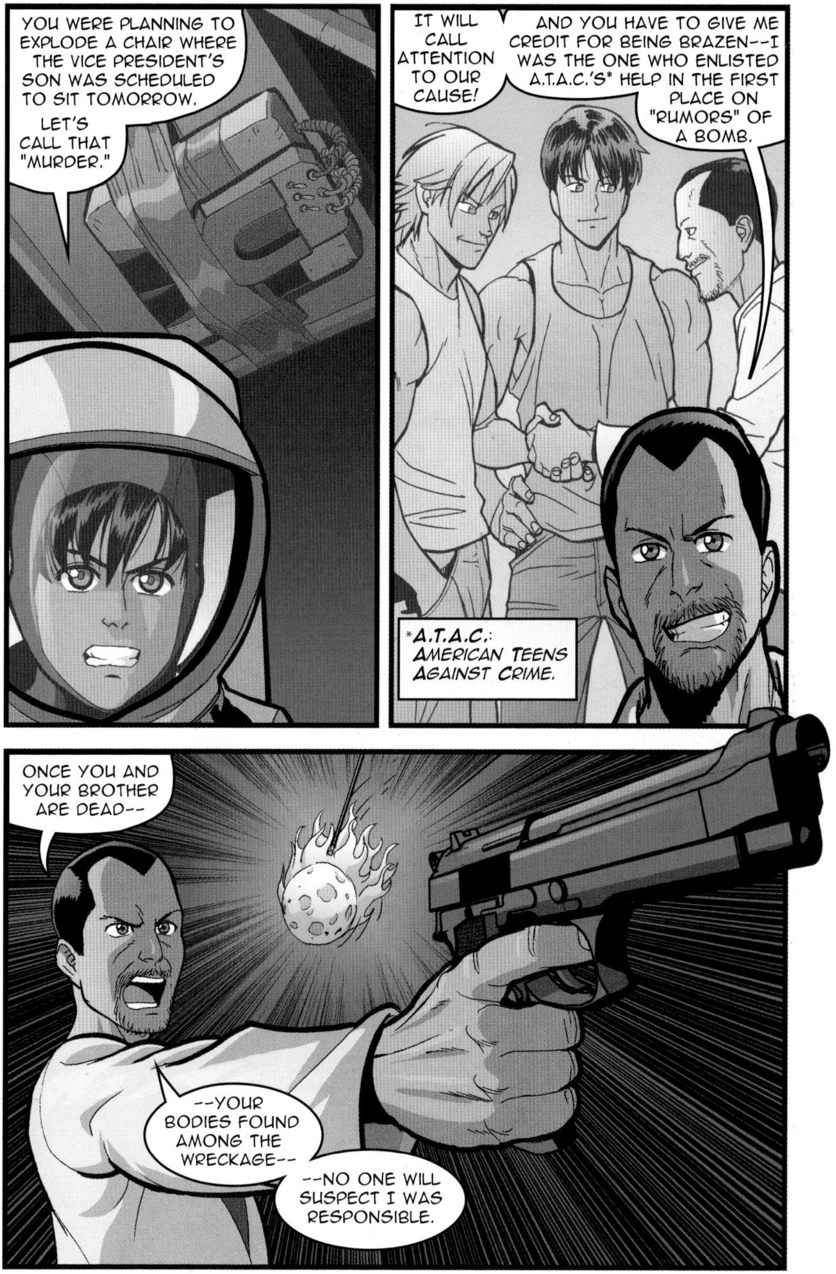
YOU WERE PLANNING TO EXPLODE A CHAIR WHERE THE VICE PRESIDENT'S SON WAS SCHEDULED TO SIT TOMORROW.
LET'S CALL THAT "MURDER."
IT WILL CALL ATTENTION TO OUR CAUSE!
AND YOU HAVE TO GIVE ME CREDIT FOR BEING BRAZEN--I WAS THE ONE WHO ENLISTED A.T.A.C.'S* HELP IN THE FIRST PLACE ON "RUMORS" OF A BOMB.
*A.T.A.C.: AMERICAN TEENS AGAINST CRIME.
ONCE YOU AND YOUR BROTHER ARE DEAD--
--YOUR BODIES FOUND AMONG THE WRECKAGE--
--NO ONE WILL SUSPECT I WAS RESPONSIBLE.

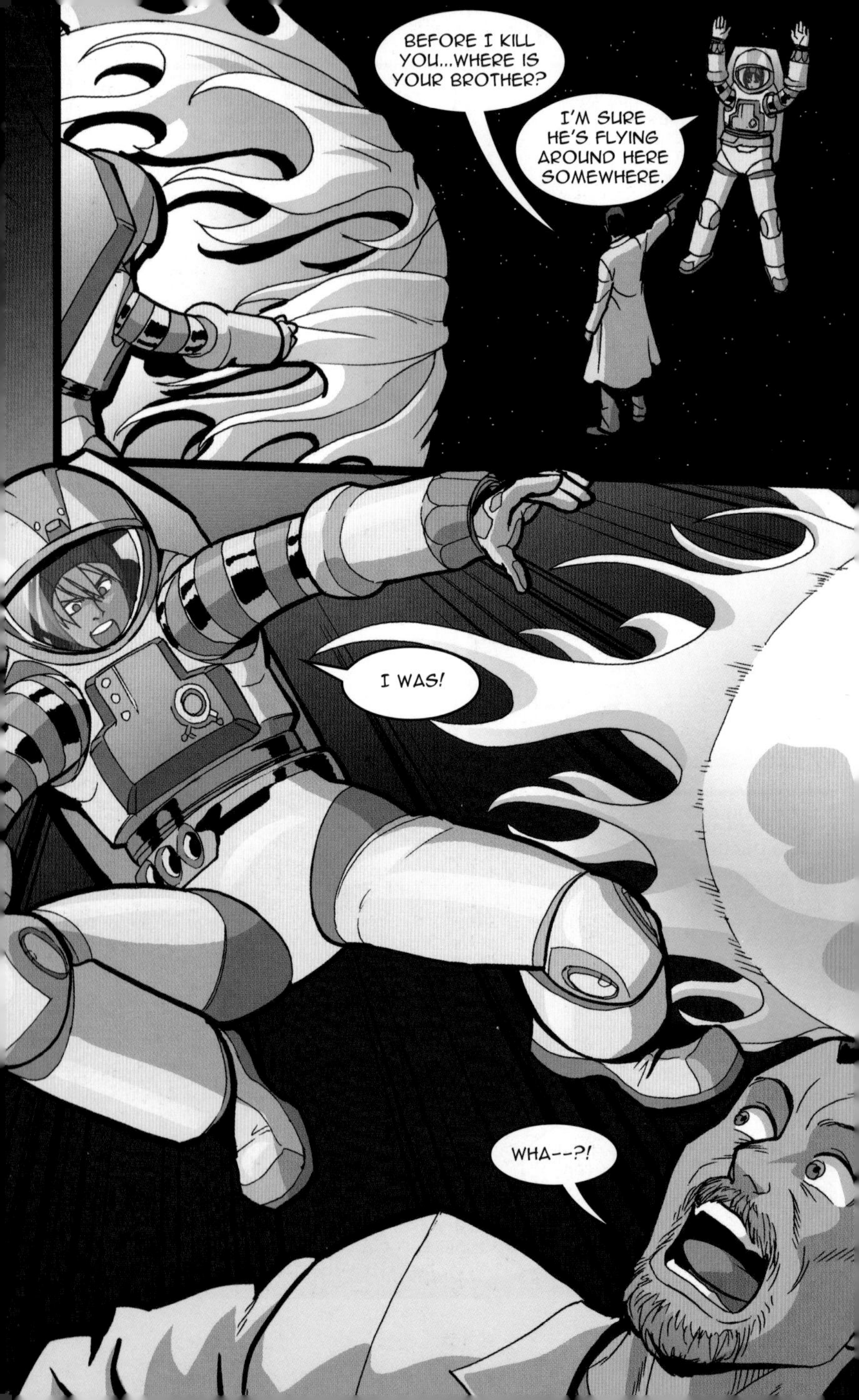
BEFORE I KILL YOU...WHERE IS YOUR BROTHER?
I'M SURE HE'S FLYING AROUND HERE SOMEWHERE.
I WAS!
WHA--?!

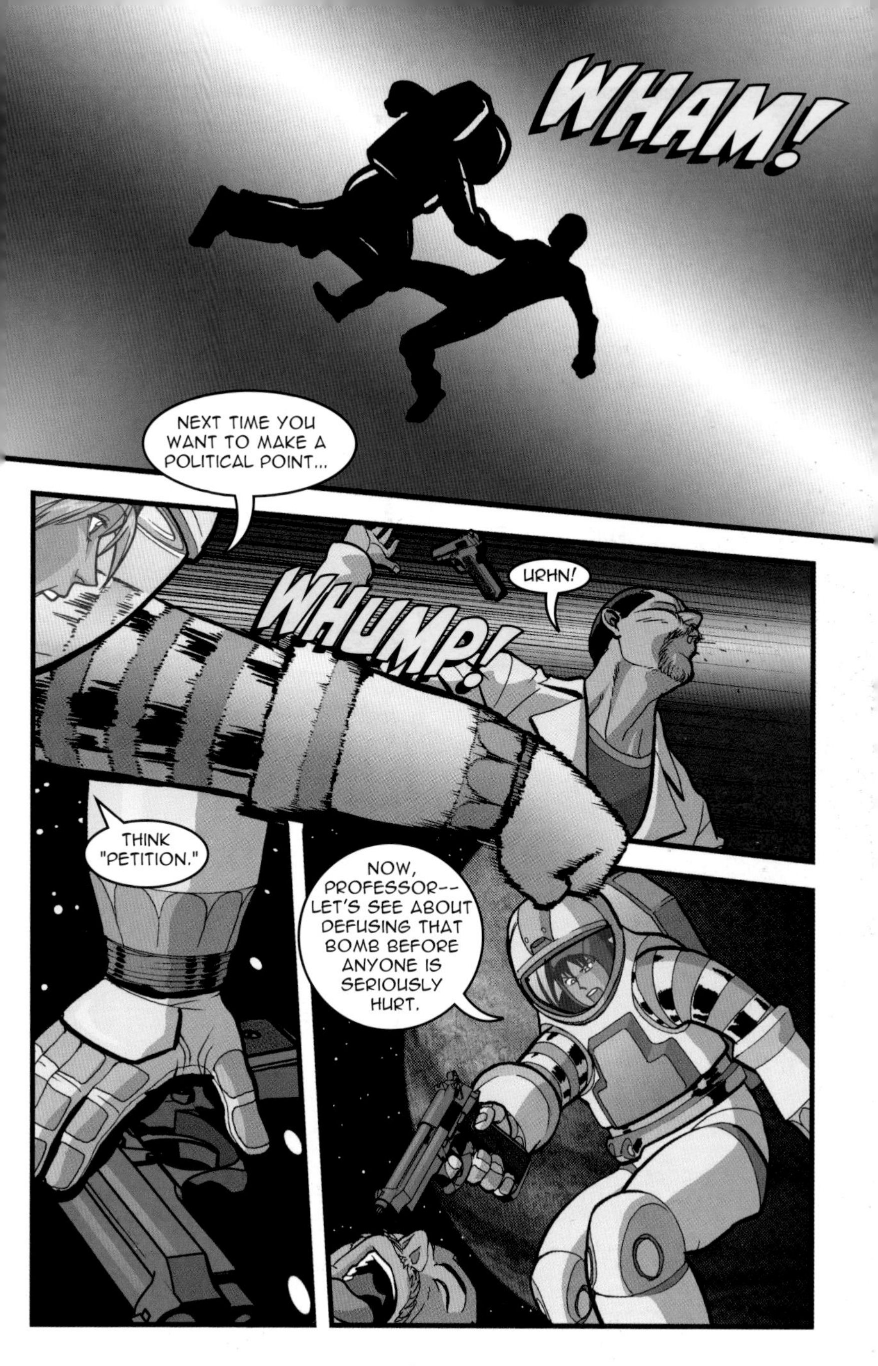
WHAM!
NEXT TIME YOU WANT TO MAKE A POLITICAL POINT...
WHUMP!
URHN!
THINK "PETITION."
NOW, PROFESSOR-- LET'S SEE ABOUT DEFUSING THAT BOMB BEFORE ANYONE IS SERIOUSLY HURT.

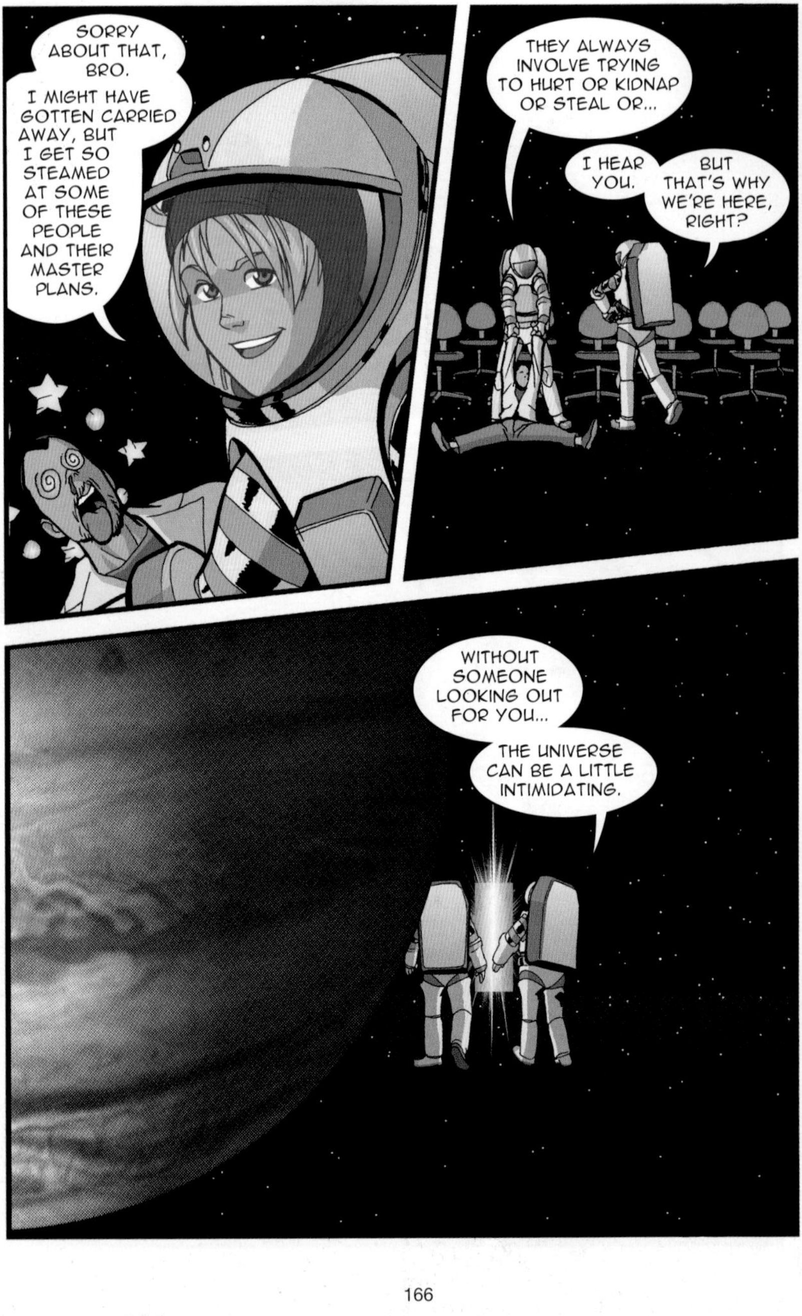
SORRY ABOUT THAT, BRO.
I MIGHT HAVE GOTTEN CARRIED AWAY, BUT I GET SO STEAMED AT SOME OF THESE PEOPLE AND THEIR MASTER PLANS.
THEY ALWAYS INVOLVE TRYING TO HURT OR KIDNAP OR STEAL OR...
I HEAR YOU.
BUT THAT'S WHY WE'RE HERE, RIGHT?
WITHOUT SOMEONE LOOKING OUT FOR YOU...
THE UNIVERSE CAN BE A LITTLE INTIMIDATING.

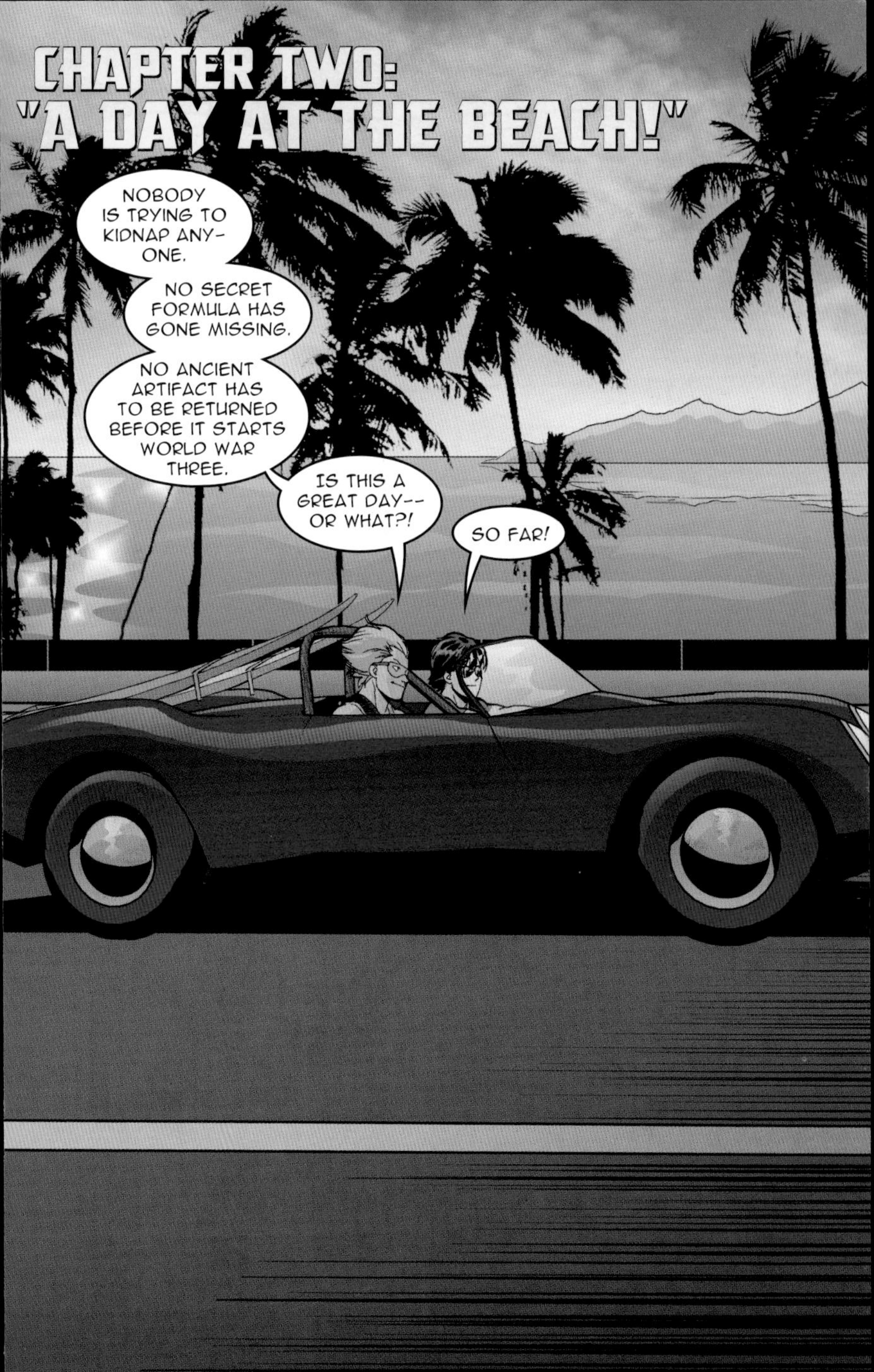
CHAPTER TWO:
"A DAY AT THE BEACH!"
NOBODY IS TRYING TO KIDNAP ANY-ONE.
NO SECRET FORMULA HAS GONE MISSING.
NO ANCIENT ARTIFACT HAS TO BE RETURNED BEFORE IT STARTS WORLD WAR THREE.
IS THIS A GREAT DAY-- OR WHAT?!
SO FAR!

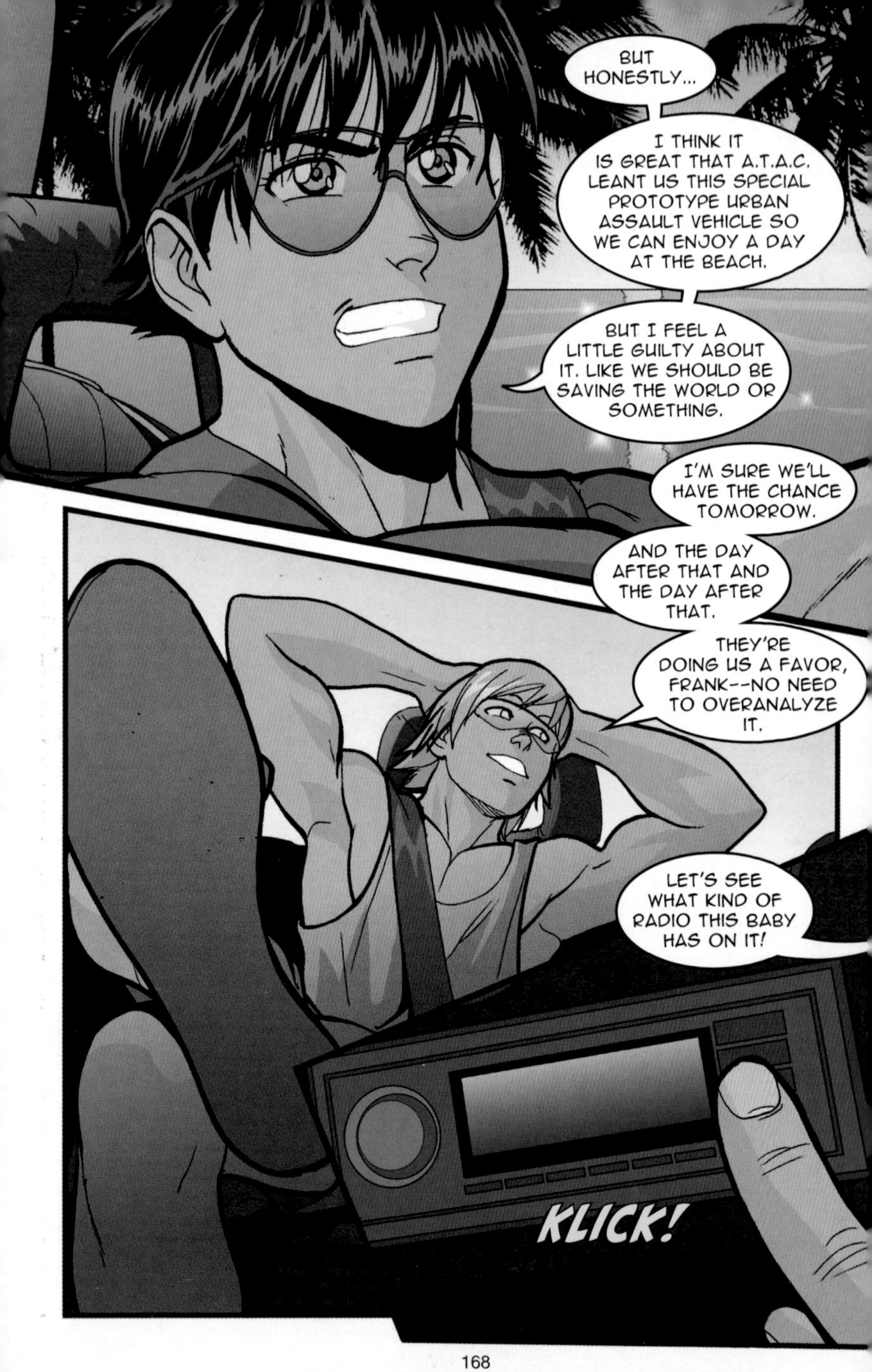

BUT HONESTLY...
I THINK IT IS GREAT THAT A.T.A.C. LEANT US THIS SPECIAL PROTOTYPE URBAN ASSAULT VEHICLE SO WE CAN ENJOY A DAY AT THE BEACH.
BUT I FEEL A LITTLE GUILTY ABOUT IT. LIKE WE SHOULD BE SAVING THE WORLD OR SOMETHING.
I'M SURE WE'LL HAVE THE CHANCE TOMORROW.
AND THE DAY AFTER THAT AND THE DAY AFTER THAT.
THEY'RE DOING US A FAVOR, FRANK--NO NEED TO OVERANALYZE IT.
LET'S SEE WHAT KIND OF RADIO THIS BABY HAS ON IT!
KLICK!

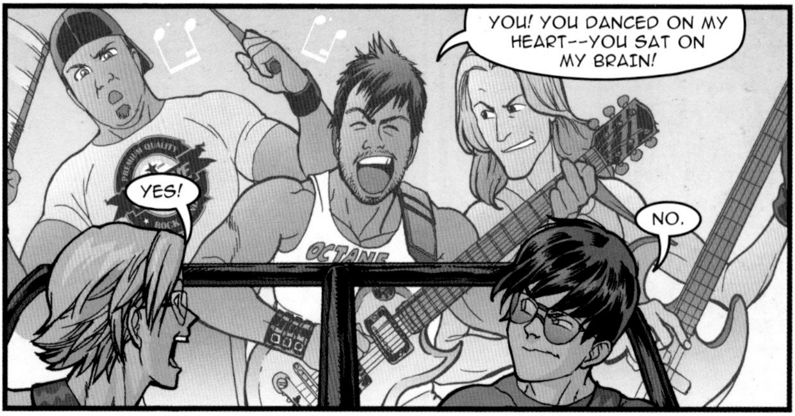
YOU! YOU DANCED ON MY HEART--YOU SAT ON MY BRAIN!
YES!
NO.

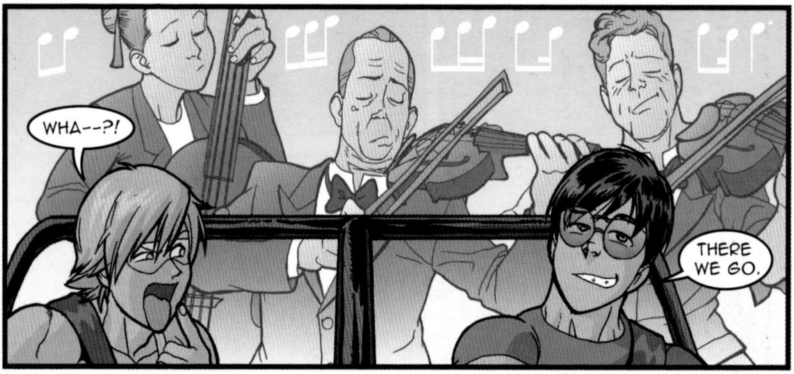
WHA--?!
THERE WE GO.

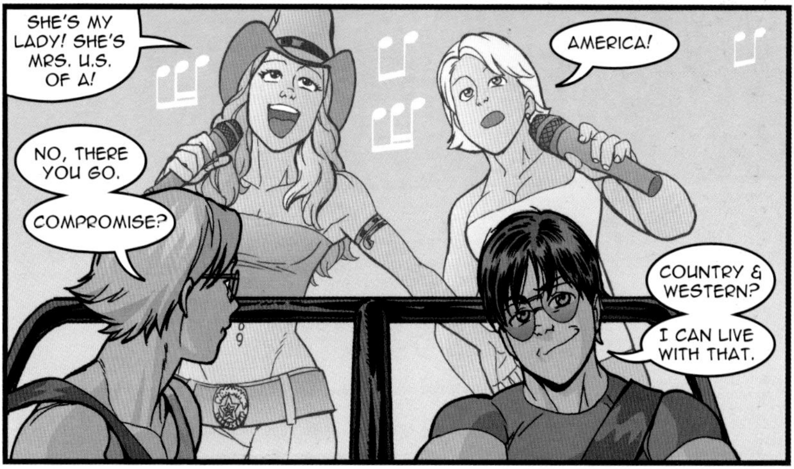
SHE'S MY LADY! SHE'S MRS. U.S. OF A!
AMERICA!
NO, THERE YOU GO.
COMPROMISE?
COUNTRY & WESTERN?
I CAN LIVE WITH THAT.

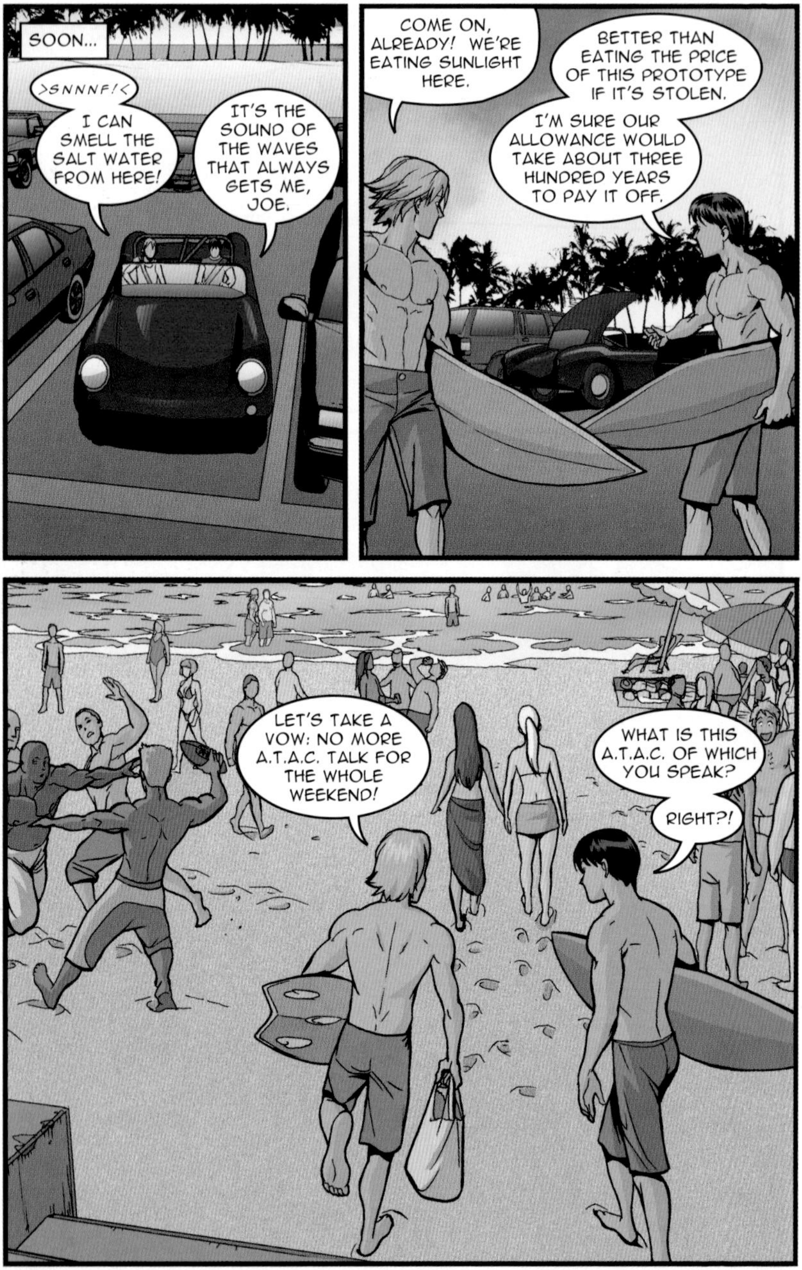
SOON...
>SNNNF!<
I CAN SMELL THE SALT WATER FROM HERE!
IT'S THE SOUND OF THE WAVES THAT ALWAYS GETS ME, JOE.
COME ON, ALREADY! WE'RE EATING SUNLIGHT HERE.
BETTER THAN EATING THE PRICE OF THIS PROTOTYPE IF IT'S STOLEN.
I'M SURE OUR ALLOWANCE WOULD TAKE ABOUT THREE HUNDRED YEARS TO PAY IT OFF.
LET'S TAKE A VOW: NO MORE A.T.A.C. TALK FOR THE WHOLE WEEKEND!
WHAT IS THIS A.T.A.C. OF WHICH YOU SPEAK?
RIGHT?!

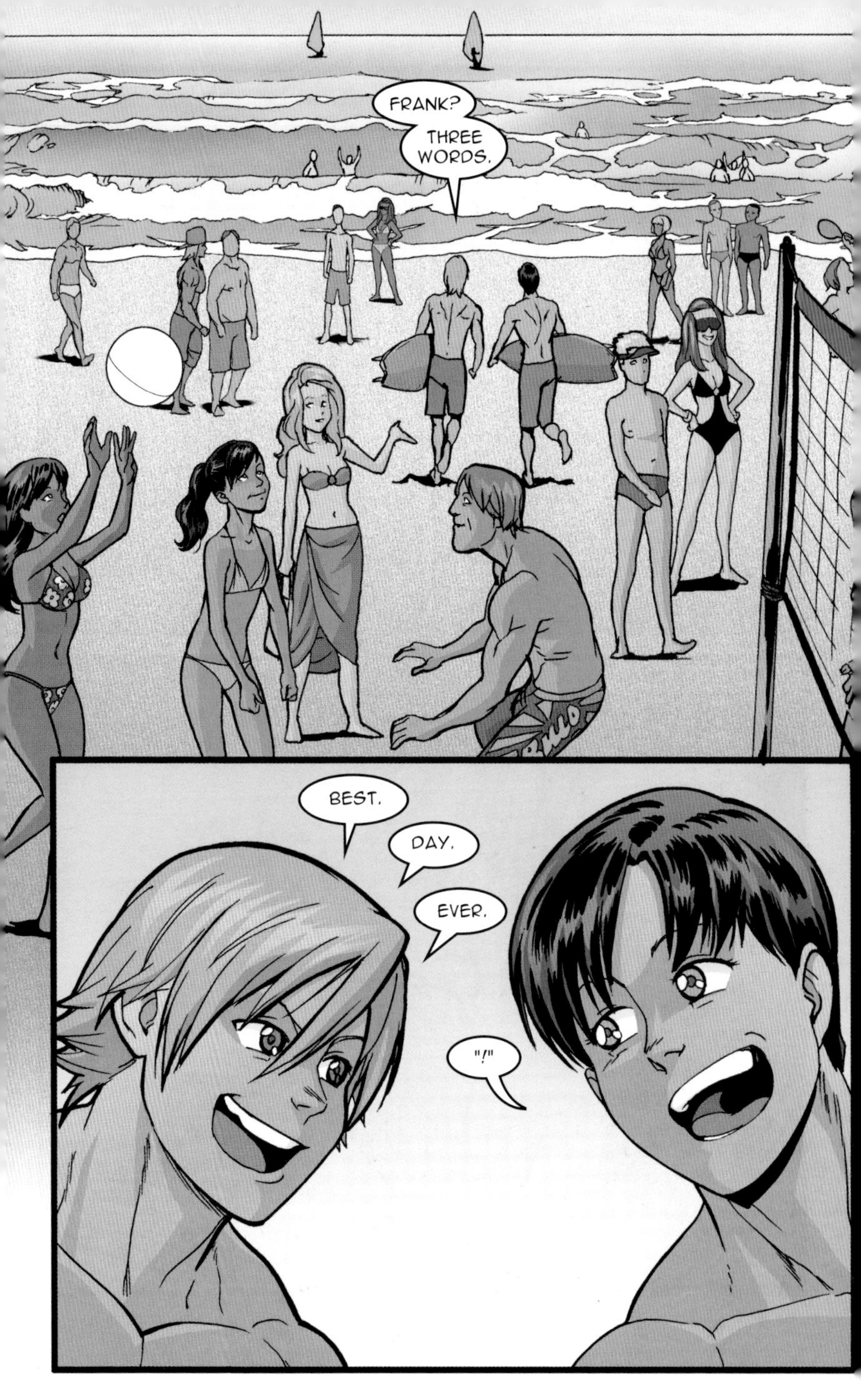
FRANK?
THREE WORDS.
BEST.
DAY.
EVER.
"!"

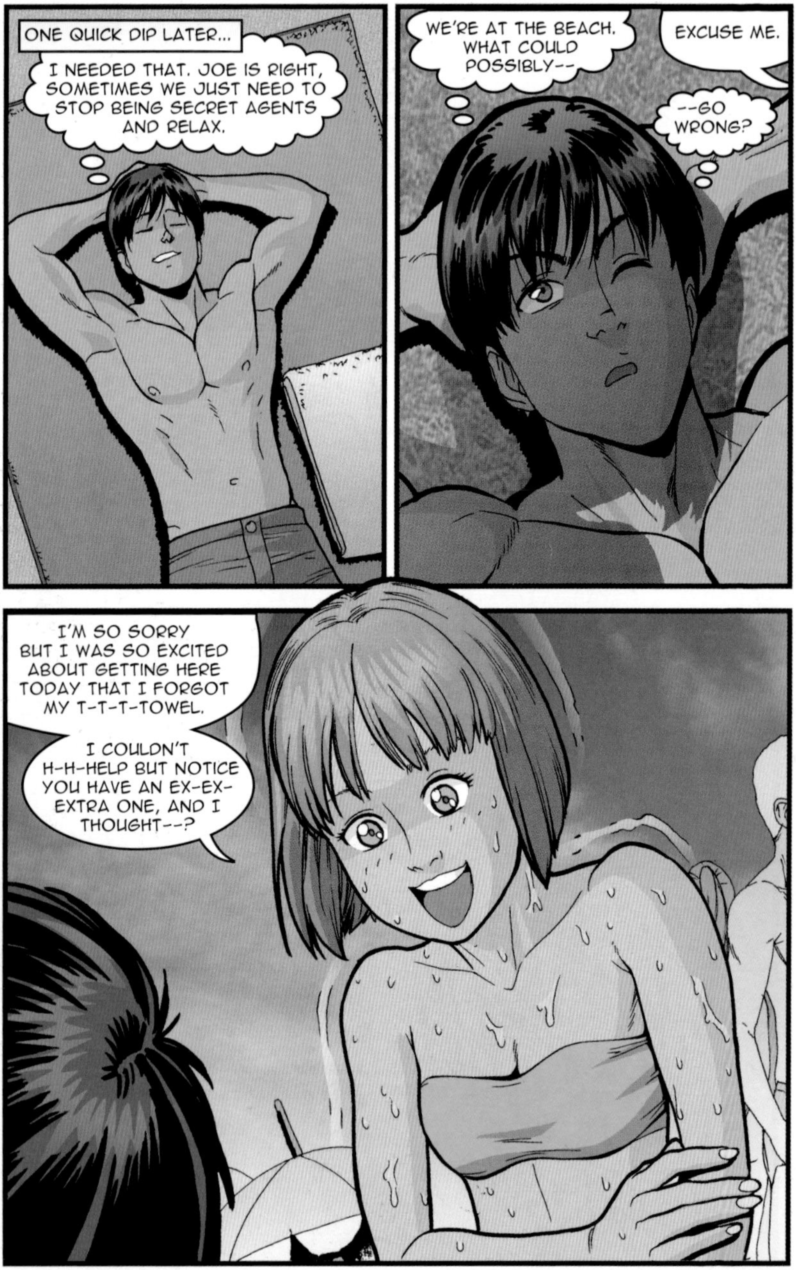
ONE QUICK DIP LATER...
I NEEDED THAT. JOE IS RIGHT, SOMETIMES WE JUST NEED TO STOP BEING SECRET AGENTS AND RELAX.
WE'RE AT THE BEACH. WHAT COULD POSSIBLY--
EXCUSE ME.
--GO WRONG?
I'M SO SORRY BUT I WAS SO EXCITED ABOUT GETTING HERE TODAY THAT I FORGOT MY T-T-T-TOWEL.
I COULDN'T H-H-HELP BUT NOTICE YOU HAVE AN EX-EX-EXTRA ONE, AND I THOUGHT--?

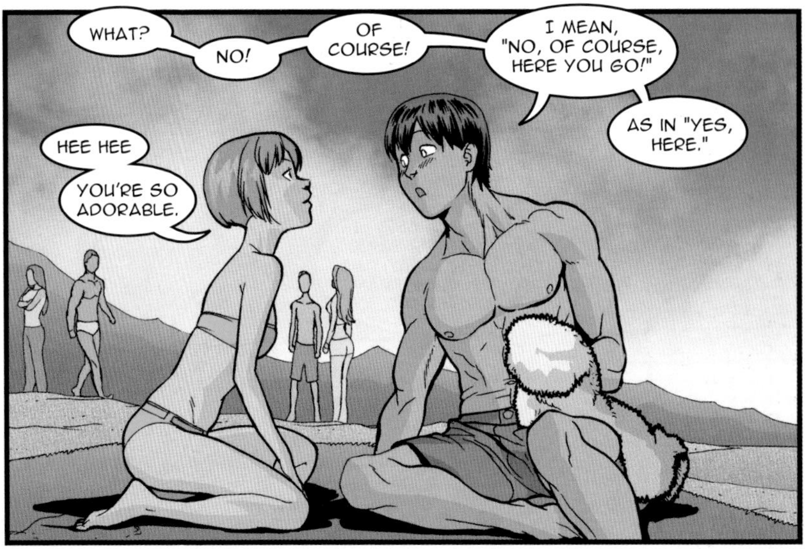
WHAT?
NO!
OF COURSE!
I MEAN, "NO, OF COURSE, HERE YOU GO!"
AS IN "YES, HERE."
HEE HEE
YOU'RE SO ADORABLE.

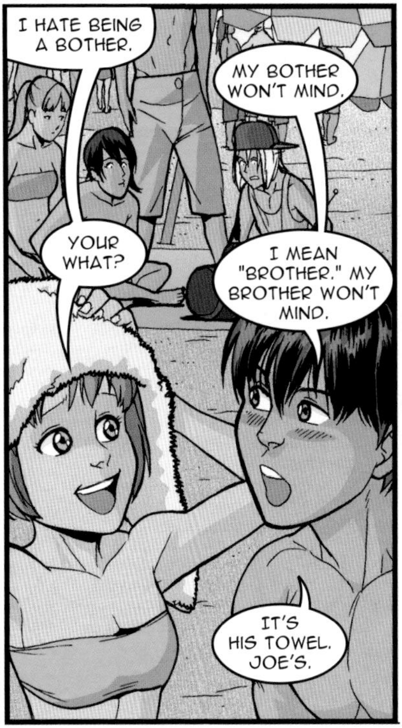
I HATE BEING A BOTHER.
MY BOTHER WON'T MIND.
YOUR WHAT?
I MEAN "BROTHER." MY BROTHER WON'T MIND.
IT'S HIS TOWEL. JOE'S.

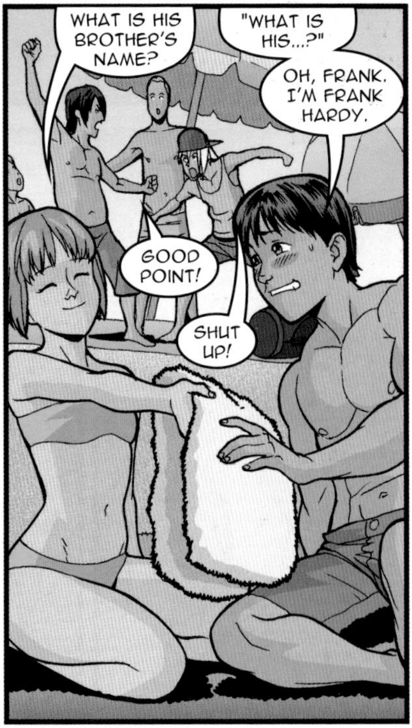
WHAT IS HIS BROTHER'S NAME?
"WHAT IS HIS...?"
OH, FRANK. I'M FRANK HARDY.
GOOD POINT!
SHUT UP!

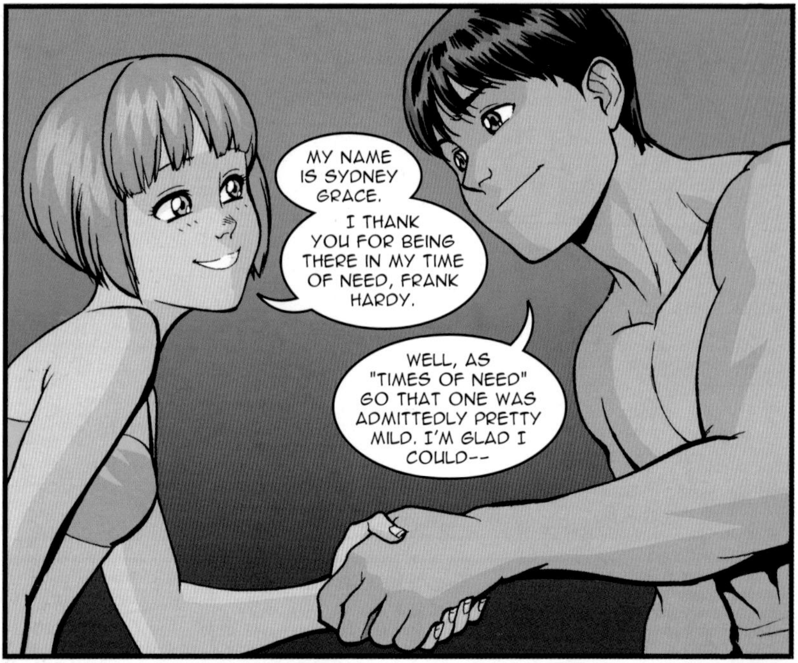
MY NAME IS SYDNEY GRACE.
I THANK YOU FOR BEING THERE IN MY TIME OF NEED, FRANK HARDY.
WELL, AS "TIMES OF NEED" GO THAT ONE WAS ADMITTEDLY PRETTY MILD. I'M GLAD I COULD--

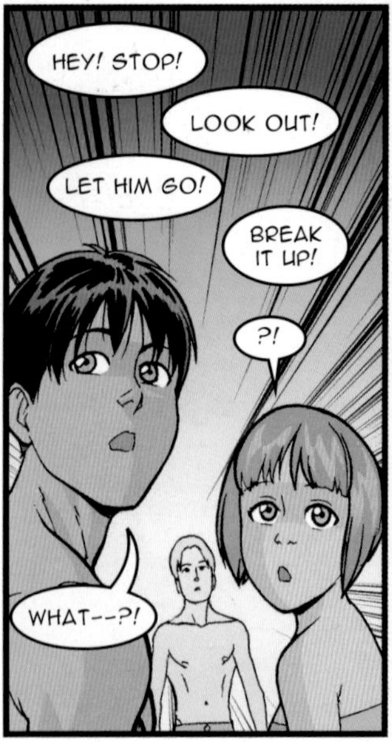
HEY! STOP!
LOOK OUT!
LET HIM GO!
BREAK IT UP!
?!
WHAT--?!

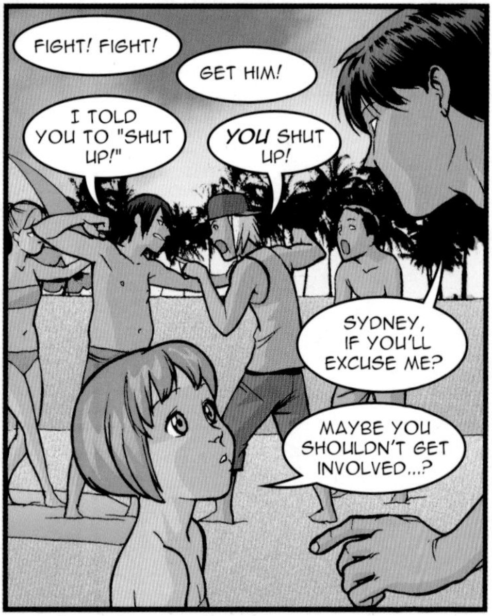
FIGHT! FIGHT!
GET HIM!
I TOLD YOU TO "SHUT UP!"
YOU SHUT UP!
SYDNEY, IF YOU'LL EXCUSE ME?
MAYBE YOU SHOULDN'T GET INVOLVED...?

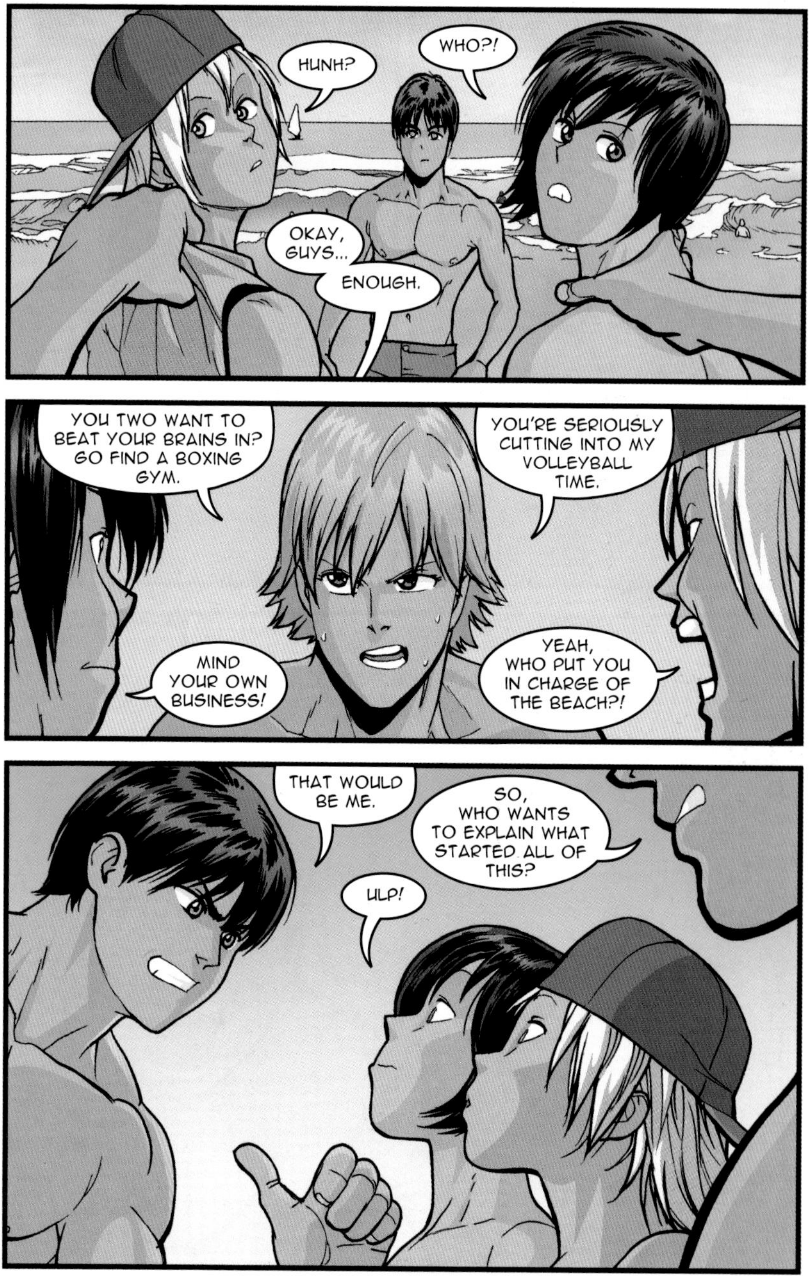
HUNH?
WHO?!
OKAY, GUYS...
ENOUGH.
YOU TWO WANT TO BEAT YOUR BRAINS IN? GO FIND A BOXING GYM.
YOU'RE SERIOUSLY CUTTING INTO MY VOLLEYBALL TIME.
MIND YOUR OWN BUSINESS!
YEAH, WHO PUT YOU IN CHARGE OF THE BEACH?!
THAT WOULD BE ME.
SO, WHO WANTS TO EXPLAIN WHAT STARTED ALL OF THIS?
ULP!

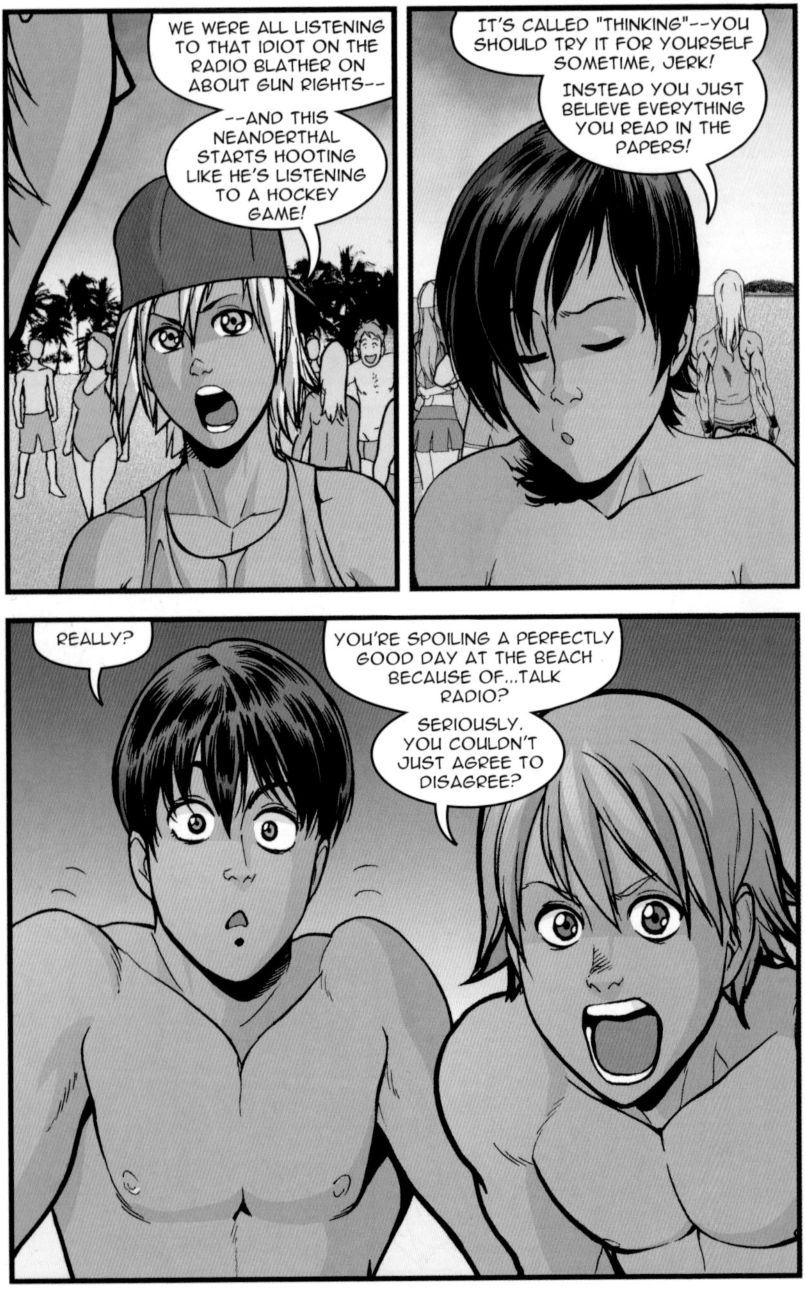
WE WERE ALL LISTENING TO THAT IDIOT ON THE RADIO BLATHER ON ABOUT GUN RIGHTS--
--AND THIS NEANDERTHAL STARTS HOOTING LIKE HE'S LISTENING TO A HOCKEY GAME!
IT'S CALLED "THINKING"--YOU SHOULD TRY IT FOR YOURSELF SOMETIME, JERK!
INSTEAD YOU JUST BELIEVE EVERYTHING YOU READ IN THE PAPERS!
REALLY?
YOU'RE SPOILING A PERFECTLY GOOD DAY AT THE BEACH BECAUSE OF...TALK RADIO?
SERIOUSLY. YOU COULDN'T JUST AGREE TO DISAGREE?

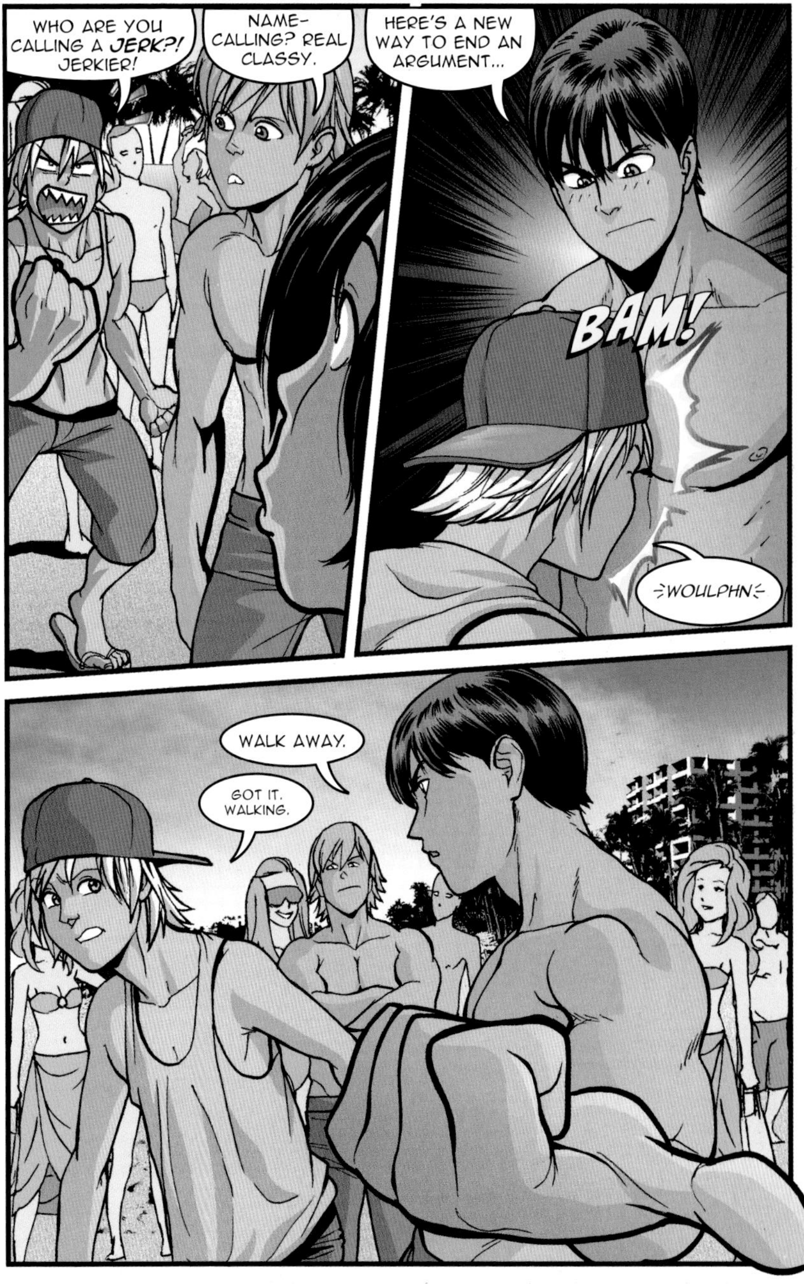
WHO ARE YOU CALLING A JERK?! JERKIER!
NAME-CALLING? REAL CLASSY.
HERE'S A NEW WAY TO END AN ARGUMENT...
BAM!
WOULPHN
WALK AWAY.
GOT IT. WALKING.

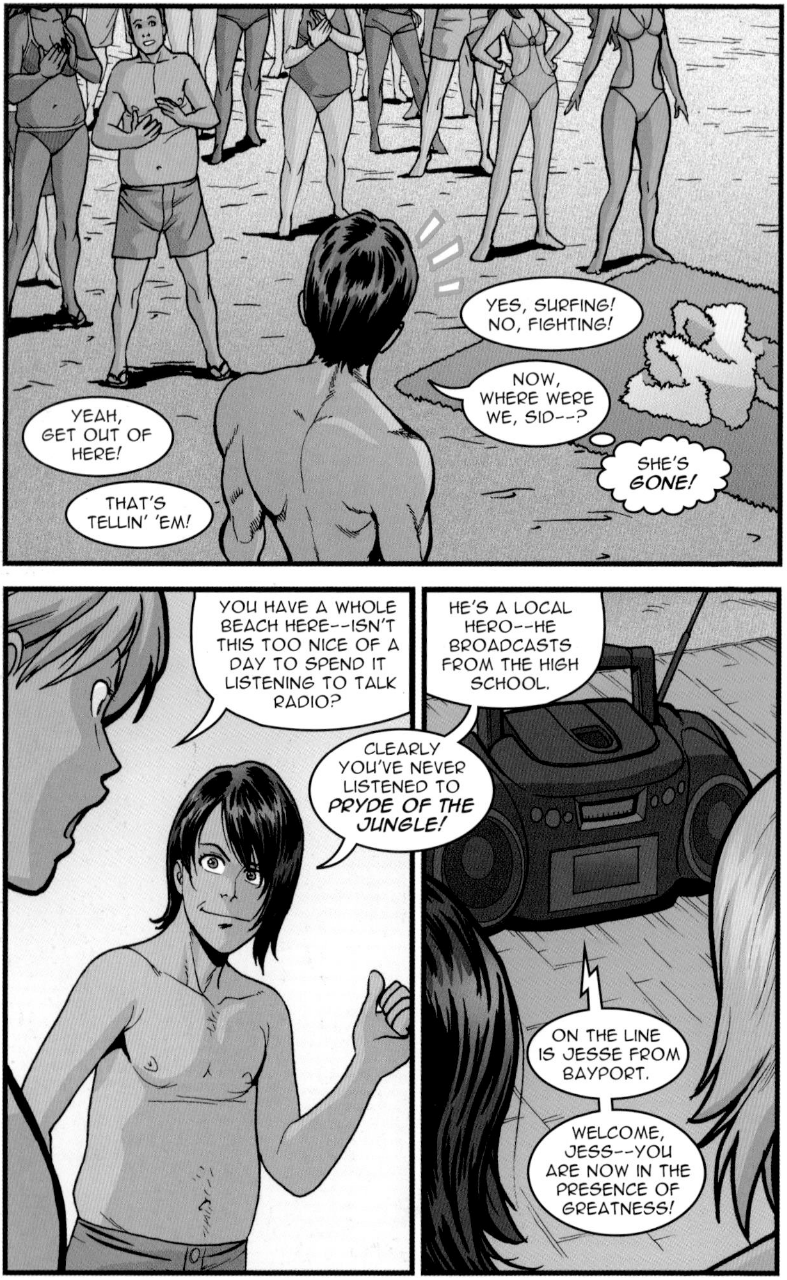
YES, SURFING! NO, FIGHTING!
NOW, WHERE WERE WE, SID--?
SHE'S GONE!
YEAH, GET OUT OF HERE!
THAT'S TELLIN' 'EM!
YOU HAVE A WHOLE BEACH HERE--ISN'T THIS TOO NICE OF A DAY TO SPEND IT LISTENING TO TALK RADIO?
CLEARLY YOU'VE NEVER LISTENED TO PRYDE OF THE JUNGLE!
HE'S A LOCAL HERO--HE BROADCASTS FROM THE HIGH SCHOOL.
ON THE LINE IS JESSE FROM BAYPORT.
WELCOME, JESS--YOU ARE NOW IN THE PRESENCE OF GREATNESS!

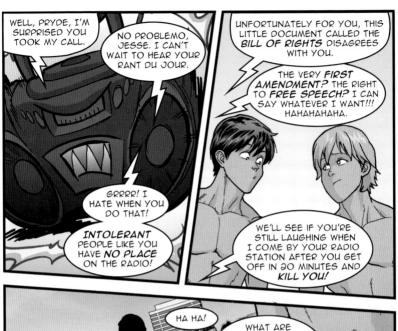

WELL, PRYDE, I'M SURPRISED YOU TOOK MY CALL.

NO PROBLEMO, JESSE. I CAN'T WAIT TO HEAR YOUR RANT DU JOUR.

UNFORTUNATELY FOR YOU, THIS LITTLE DOCUMENT CALLED THE *BILL OF RIGHTS* DISAGREES WITH YOU.

THE VERY *FIRST AMENDMENT?* THE RIGHT TO *FREE SPEECH?* I CAN SAY WHATEVER I WANT!!! HAHAHAHAHA.

GRRRR! I HATE WHEN YOU DO THAT!

INTOLERANT PEOPLE LIKE YOU HAVE *NO PLACE* ON THE RADIO!

WE'LL SEE IF YOU'RE STILL LAUGHING WHEN I COME BY YOUR RADIO STATION AFTER YOU GET OFF IN 20 MINUTES AND *KILL YOU!*

HA HA!

WHAT ARE YOU GOING TO DO, JESSE--*TOLERATE* ME TO DEATH?! LOSER!

HE'S SO FUNNY!

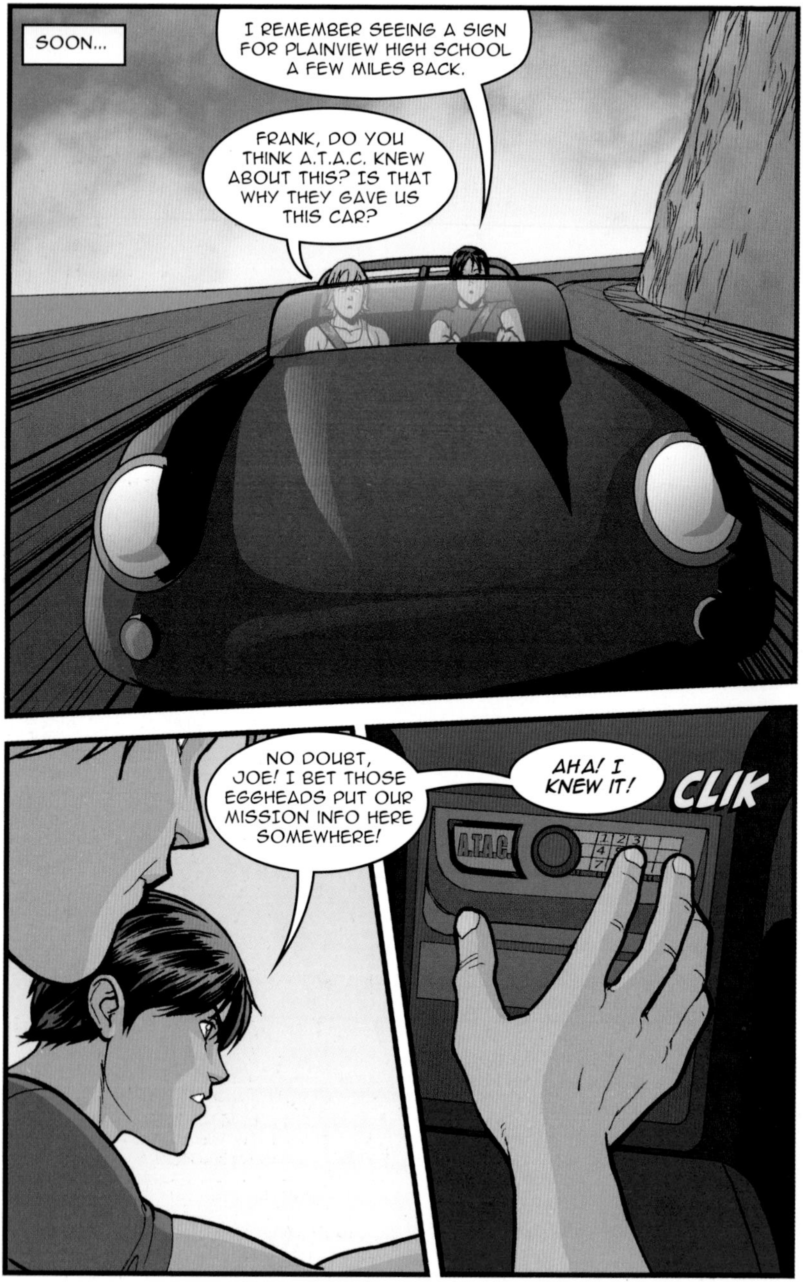
SOON...
I REMEMBER SEEING A SIGN FOR PLAINVIEW HIGH SCHOOL A FEW MILES BACK.
FRANK, DO YOU THINK A.T.A.C. KNEW ABOUT THIS? IS THAT WHY THEY GAVE US THIS CAR?
NO DOUBT, JOE! I BET THOSE EGGHEADS PUT OUR MISSION INFO HERE SOMEWHERE!
AHA! I KNEW IT!
CLIK
A.T.A.C.

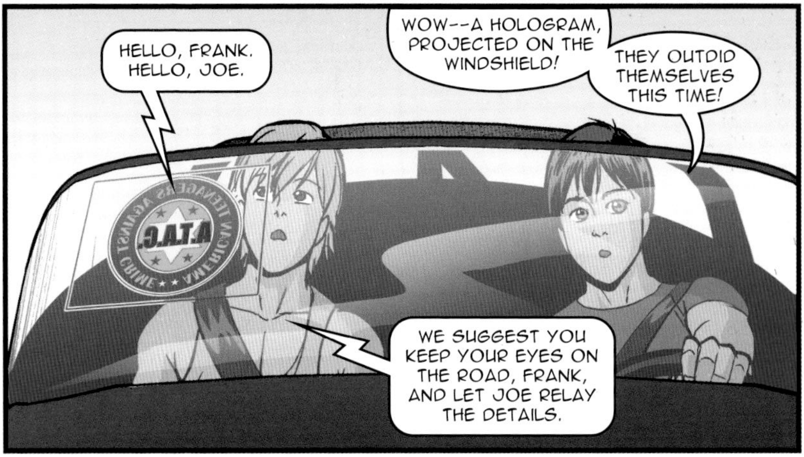
HELLO, FRANK. HELLO, JOE.
WOW--A HOLOGRAM, PROJECTED ON THE WINDSHIELD!
THEY OUTDID THEMSELVES THIS TIME!
A.T.A.C.
AMERICAN TEENAGERS AGAINST CRIME
WE SUGGEST YOU KEEP YOUR EYES ON THE ROAD, FRANK, AND LET JOE RELAY THE DETAILS.

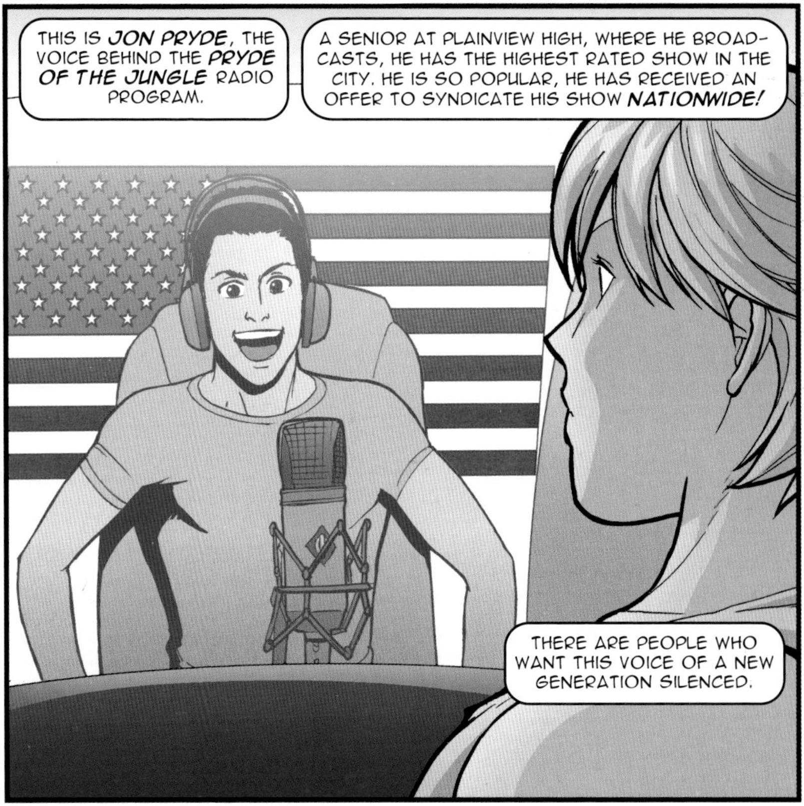
THIS IS ***JON PRYDE***, THE VOICE BEHIND THE ***PRYDE OF THE JUNGLE*** RADIO PROGRAM.
A SENIOR AT PLAINVIEW HIGH, WHERE HE BROADCASTS, HE HAS THE HIGHEST RATED SHOW IN THE CITY. HE IS SO POPULAR, HE HAS RECEIVED AN OFFER TO SYNDICATE HIS SHOW ***NATIONWIDE!***
THERE ARE PEOPLE WHO WANT THIS VOICE OF A NEW GENERATION SILENCED.

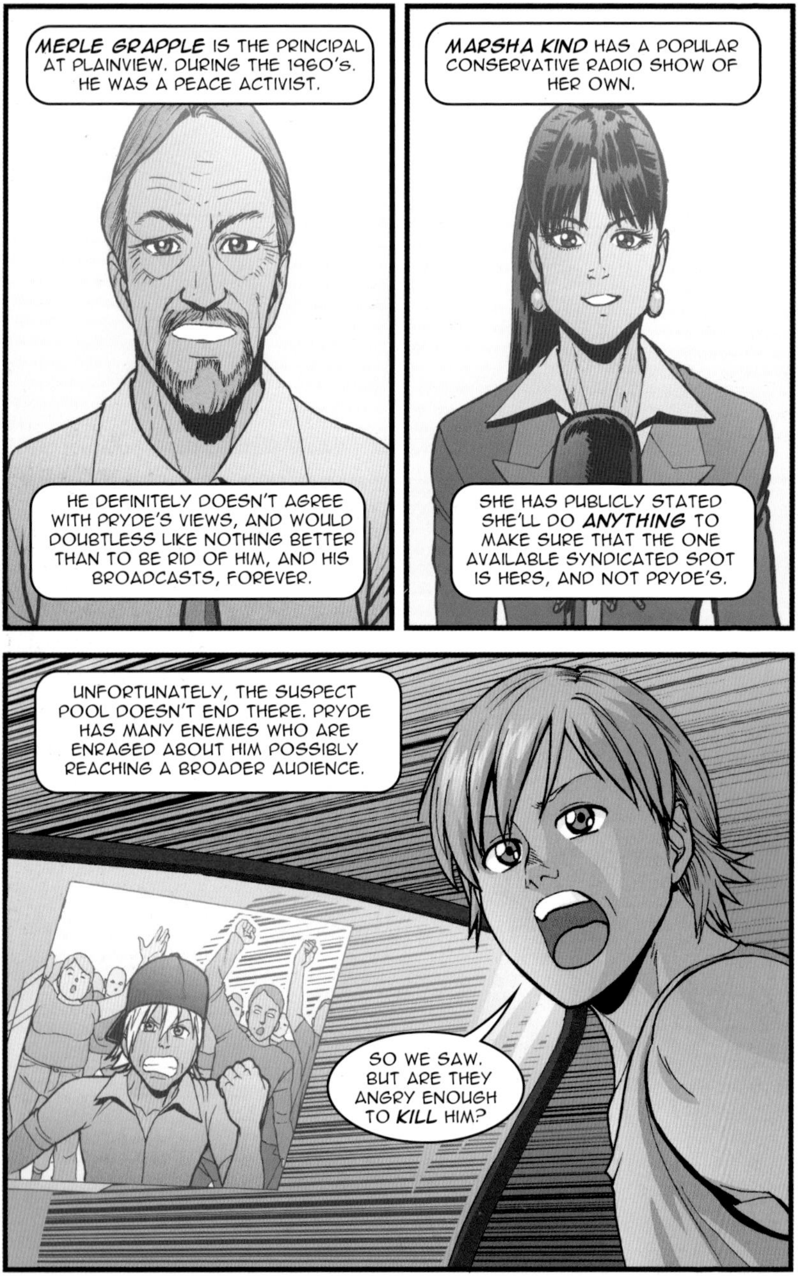
MERLE GRAPPLE IS THE PRINCIPAL AT PLAINVIEW. DURING THE 1960'S. HE WAS A PEACE ACTIVIST.
HE DEFINITELY DOESN'T AGREE WITH PRYDE'S VIEWS, AND WOULD DOUBTLESS LIKE NOTHING BETTER THAN TO BE RID OF HIM, AND HIS BROADCASTS, FOREVER.
MARSHA KIND HAS A POPULAR CONSERVATIVE RADIO SHOW OF HER OWN.
SHE HAS PUBLICLY STATED SHE'LL DO ANYTHING TO MAKE SURE THAT THE ONE AVAILABLE SYNDICATED SPOT IS HERS, AND NOT PRYDE'S.
UNFORTUNATELY, THE SUSPECT POOL DOESN'T END THERE. PRYDE HAS MANY ENEMIES WHO ARE ENRAGED ABOUT HIM POSSIBLY REACHING A BROADER AUDIENCE.
SO WE SAW. BUT ARE THEY ANGRY ENOUGH TO KILL HIM?

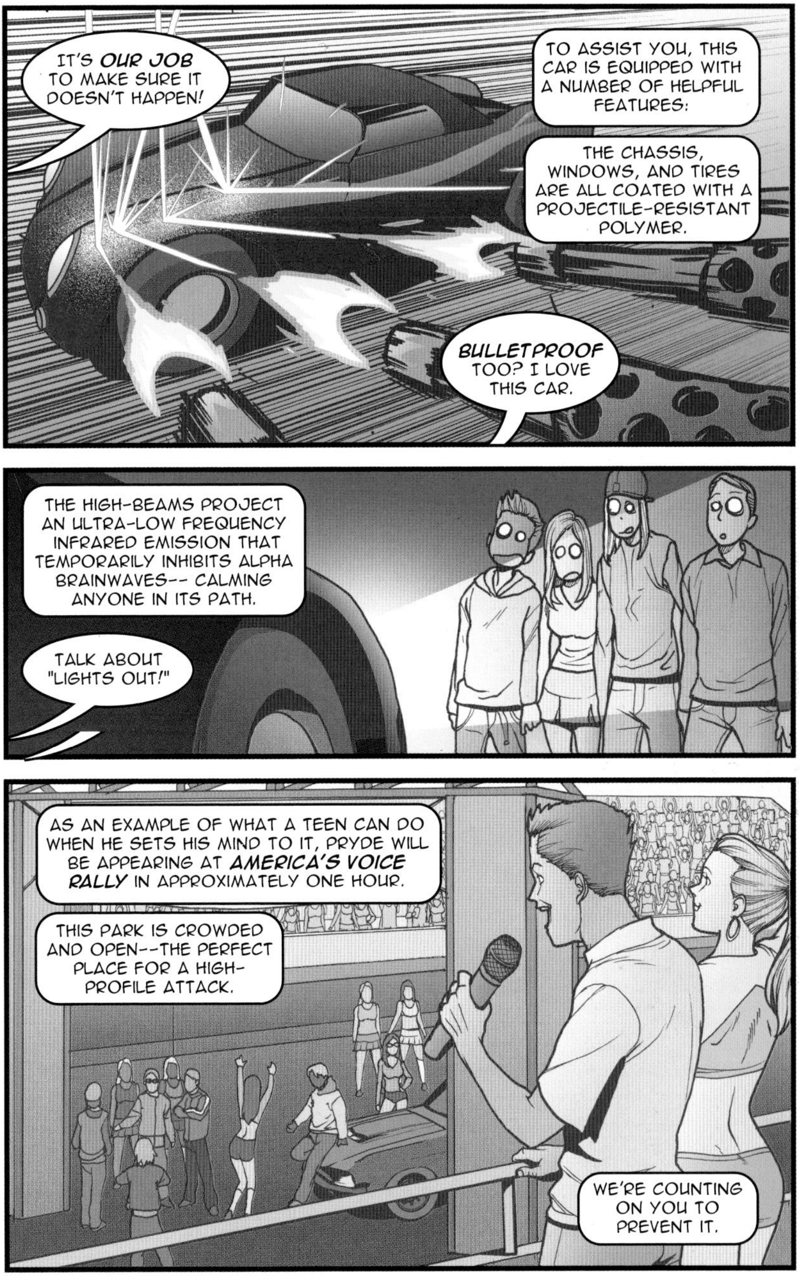
IT'S OUR JOB TO MAKE SURE IT DOESN'T HAPPEN!
TO ASSIST YOU, THIS CAR IS EQUIPPED WITH A NUMBER OF HELPFUL FEATURES:
THE CHASSIS, WINDOWS, AND TIRES ARE ALL COATED WITH A PROJECTILE-RESISTANT POLYMER.
BULLETPROOF TOO? I LOVE THIS CAR.
THE HIGH-BEAMS PROJECT AN ULTRA-LOW FREQUENCY INFRARED EMISSION THAT TEMPORARILY INHIBITS ALPHA BRAINWAVES-- CALMING ANYONE IN ITS PATH.
TALK ABOUT "LIGHTS OUT!"
AS AN EXAMPLE OF WHAT A TEEN CAN DO WHEN HE SETS HIS MIND TO IT, PRYDE WILL BE APPEARING AT AMERICA'S VOICE RALLY IN APPROXIMATELY ONE HOUR.
THIS PARK IS CROWDED AND OPEN--THE PERFECT PLACE FOR A HIGH-PROFILE ATTACK.
WE'RE COUNTING ON YOU TO PREVENT IT.

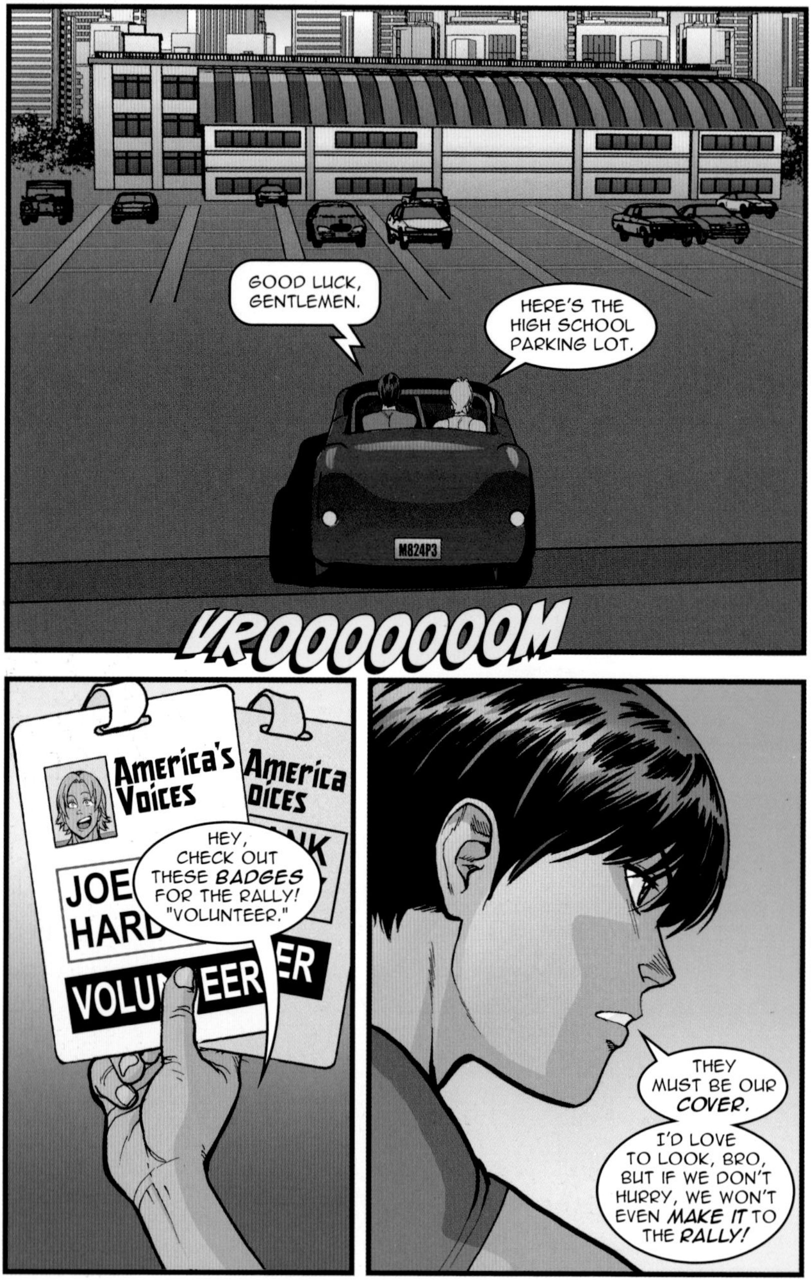
GOOD LUCK, GENTLEMEN.
HERE'S THE HIGH SCHOOL PARKING LOT.
M824P3
VROOOOOOOM
America's Voices
HEY, CHECK OUT THESE *BADGES* FOR THE RALLY! "VOLUNTEER."
THEY MUST BE OUR *COVER.*
I'D LOVE TO LOOK, BRO, BUT IF WE DON'T HURRY, WE WON'T EVEN *MAKE IT* TO THE *RALLY!*

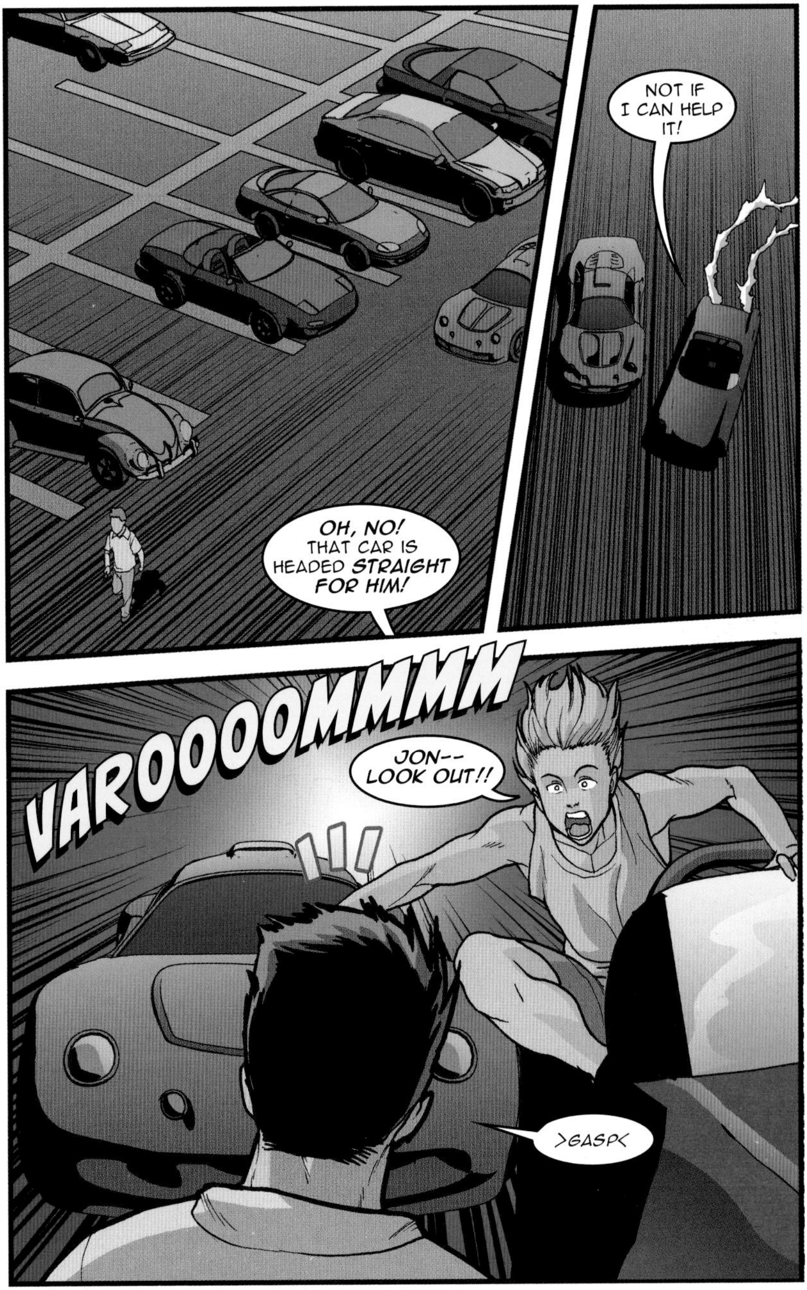
OH, NO! THAT CAR IS HEADED STRAIGHT FOR HIM!
NOT IF I CAN HELP IT!
VAROOOOMMMM
JON-- LOOK OUT!!
>GASP<

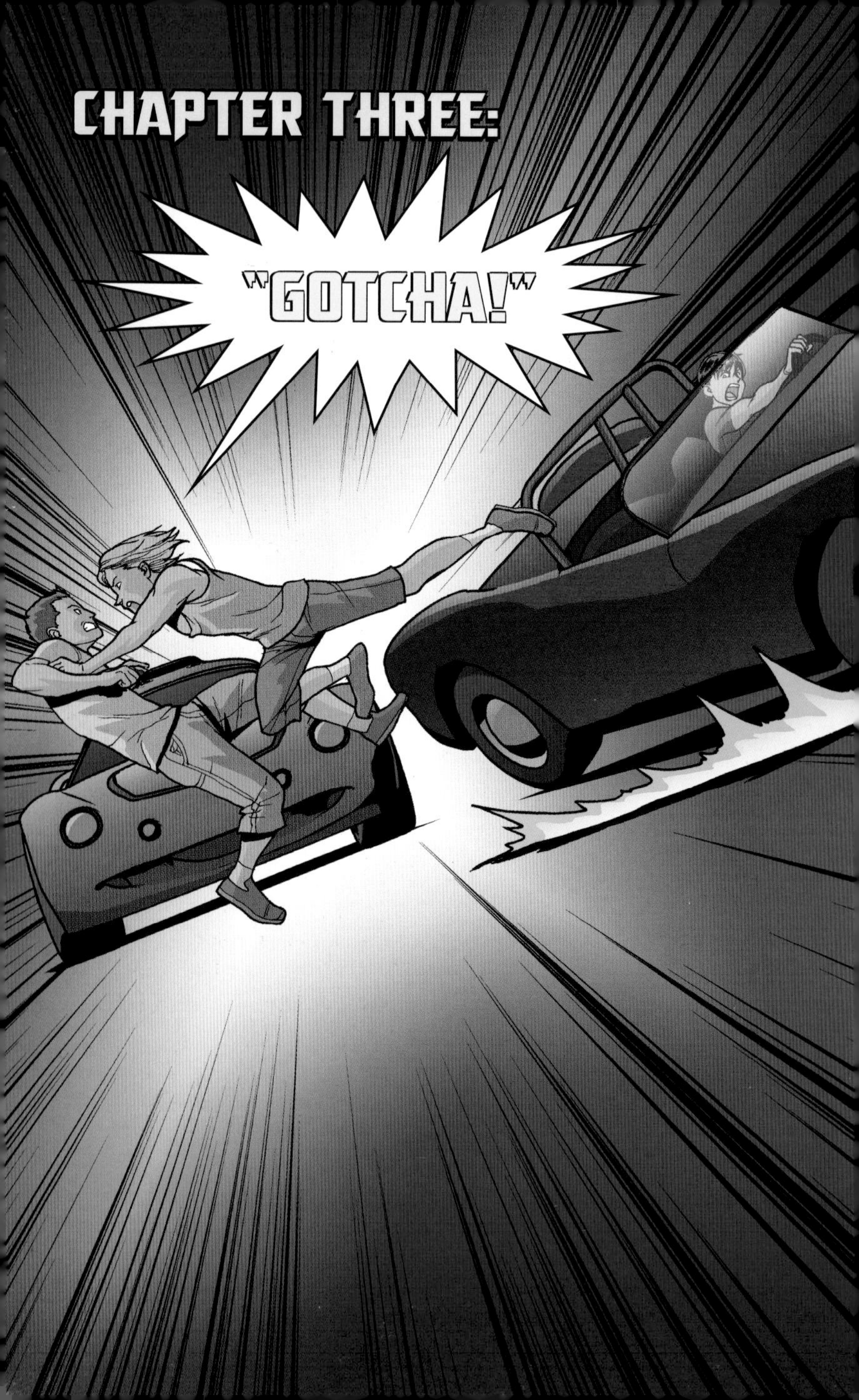
CHAPTER THREE:
"GOTCHA!"

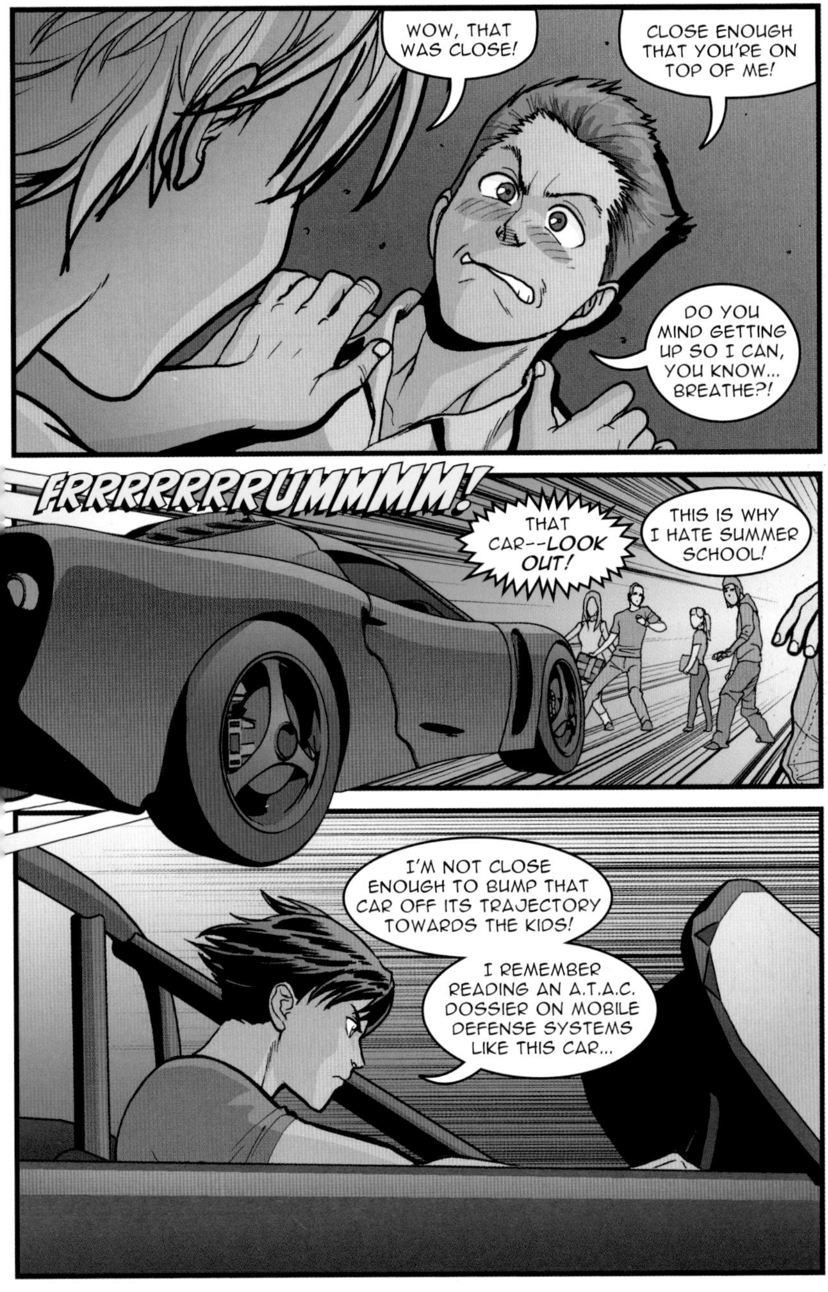
WOW, THAT WAS CLOSE!
CLOSE ENOUGH THAT YOU'RE ON TOP OF ME!
DO YOU MIND GETTING UP SO I CAN, YOU KNOW... BREATHE?!
FRRRRRRRUMMMMM!
THAT CAR--LOOK OUT!
THIS IS WHY I HATE SUMMER SCHOOL!
I'M NOT CLOSE ENOUGH TO BUMP THAT CAR OFF ITS TRAJECTORY TOWARDS THE KIDS!
I REMEMBER READING AN A.T.A.C. DOSSIER ON MOBILE DEFENSE SYSTEMS LIKE THIS CAR...

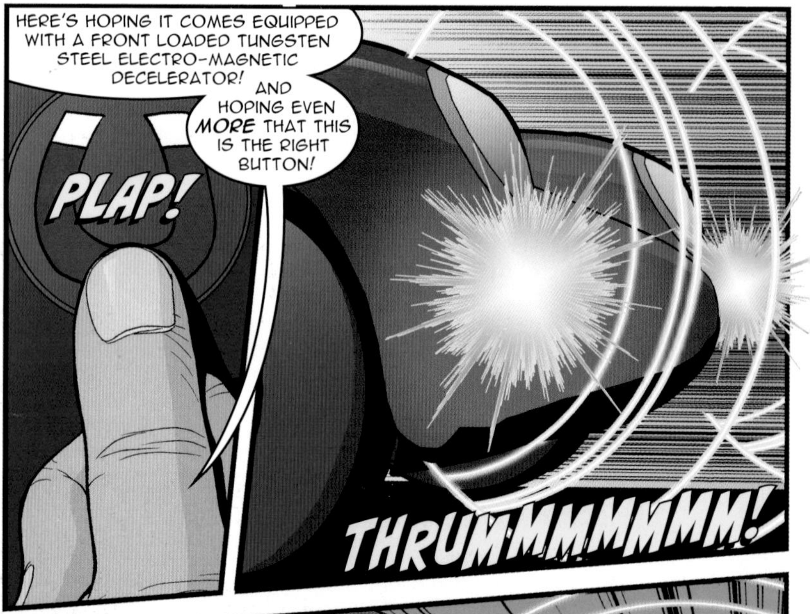
HERE'S HOPING IT COMES EQUIPPED WITH A FRONT LOADED TUNGSTEN STEEL ELECTRO-MAGNETIC DECELERATOR!
AND HOPING EVEN MORE THAT THIS IS THE RIGHT BUTTON!
PLAP!
THRUMMMMMMM!

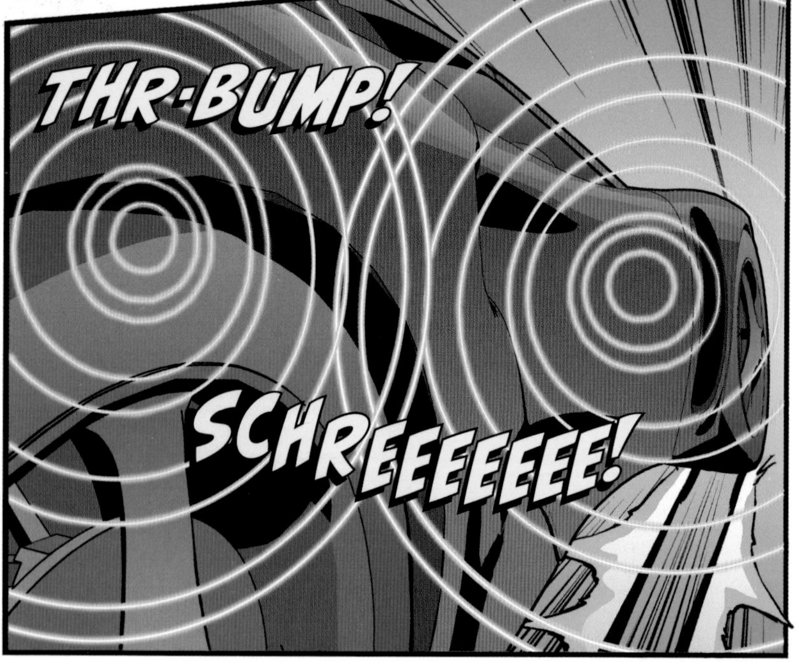
THR-BUMP!
SCHREEEEEEE!

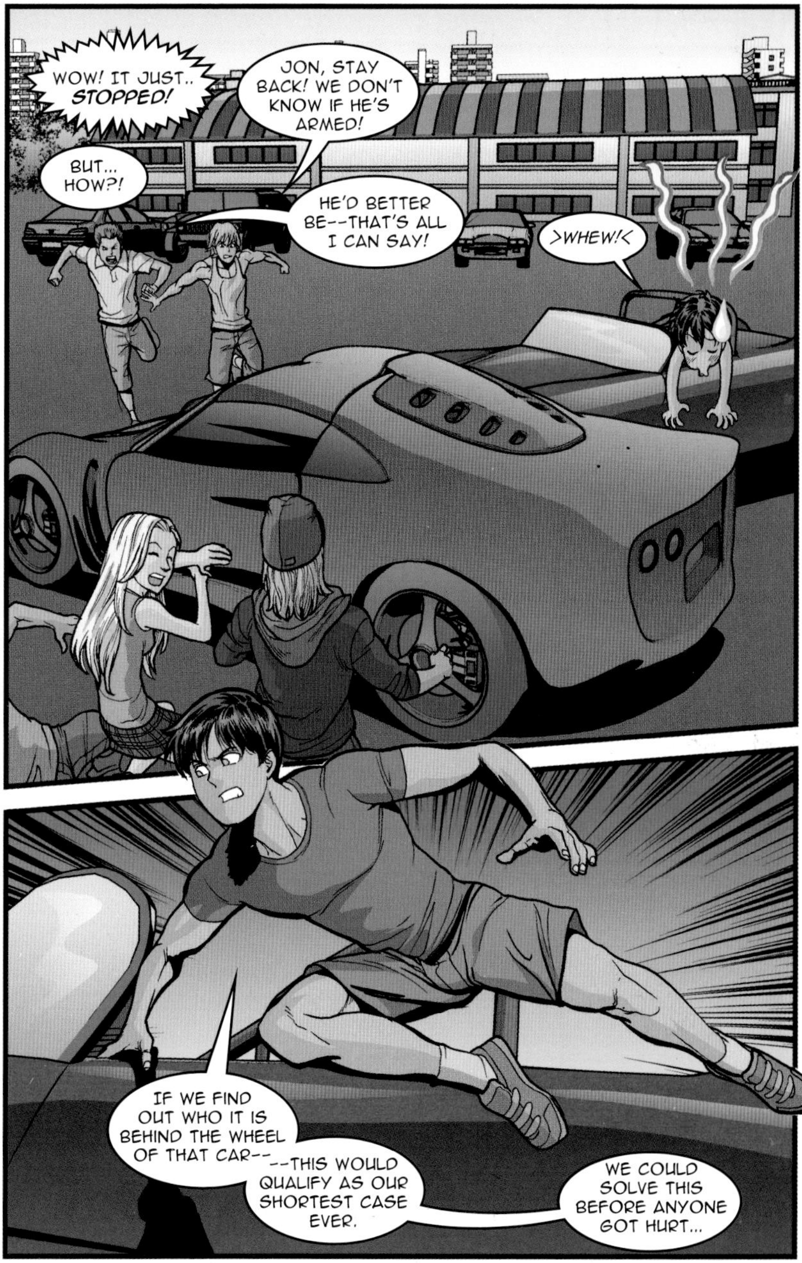
WOW! IT JUST.. STOPPED!
JON, STAY BACK! WE DON'T KNOW IF HE'S ARMED!
BUT... HOW?!
HE'D BETTER BE--THAT'S ALL I CAN SAY!
>WHEW!<
IF WE FIND OUT WHO IT IS BEHIND THE WHEEL OF THAT CAR--
--THIS WOULD QUALIFY AS OUR SHORTEST CASE EVER.
WE COULD SOLVE THIS BEFORE ANYONE GOT HURT...

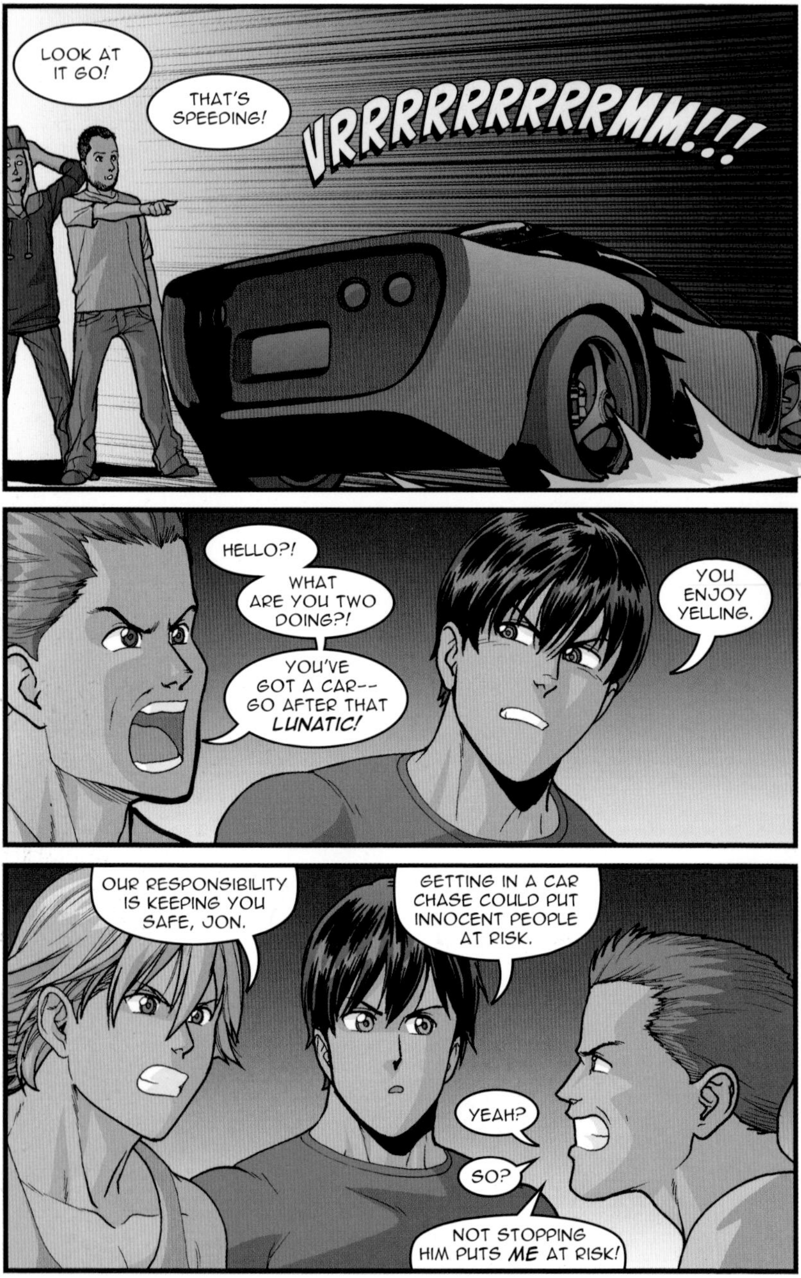
LOOK AT IT GO!
THAT'S SPEEDING!
VRRRRRRRRRMM!!!
HELLO?!
WHAT ARE YOU TWO DOING?!
YOU'VE GOT A CAR--GO AFTER THAT LUNATIC!
YOU ENJOY YELLING.
OUR RESPONSIBILITY IS KEEPING YOU SAFE, JON.
GETTING IN A CAR CHASE COULD PUT INNOCENT PEOPLE AT RISK.
YEAH?
SO?
NOT STOPPING HIM PUTS ME AT RISK!

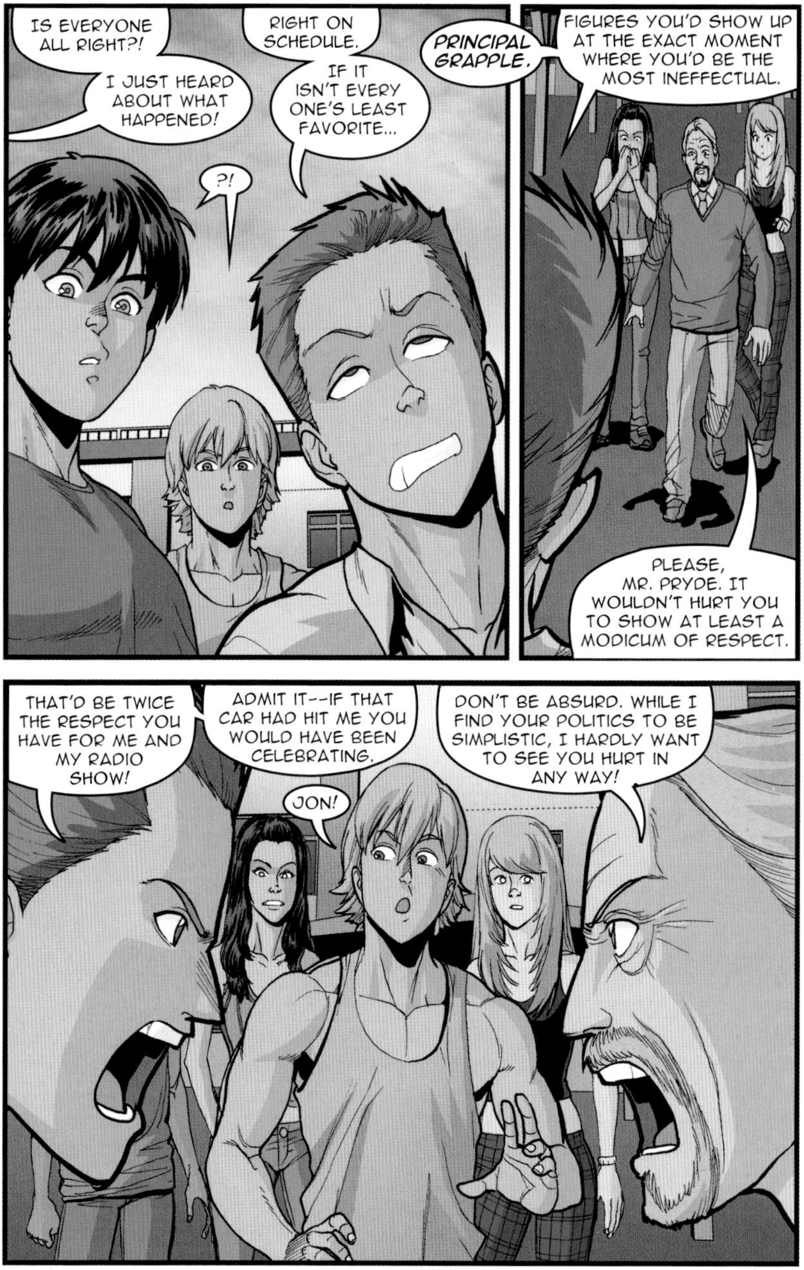
IS EVERYONE ALL RIGHT?!
I JUST HEARD ABOUT WHAT HAPPENED!
RIGHT ON SCHEDULE.
IF IT ISN'T EVERY ONE'S LEAST FAVORITE...
?!
PRINCIPAL GRAPPLE.
FIGURES YOU'D SHOW UP AT THE EXACT MOMENT WHERE YOU'D BE THE MOST INEFFECTUAL.
PLEASE, MR. PRYDE. IT WOULDN'T HURT YOU TO SHOW AT LEAST A MODICUM OF RESPECT.
THAT'D BE TWICE THE RESPECT YOU HAVE FOR ME AND MY RADIO SHOW!
ADMIT IT--IF THAT CAR HAD HIT ME YOU WOULD HAVE BEEN CELEBRATING.
JON!
DON'T BE ABSURD. WHILE I FIND YOUR POLITICS TO BE SIMPLISTIC, I HARDLY WANT TO SEE YOU HURT IN ANY WAY!

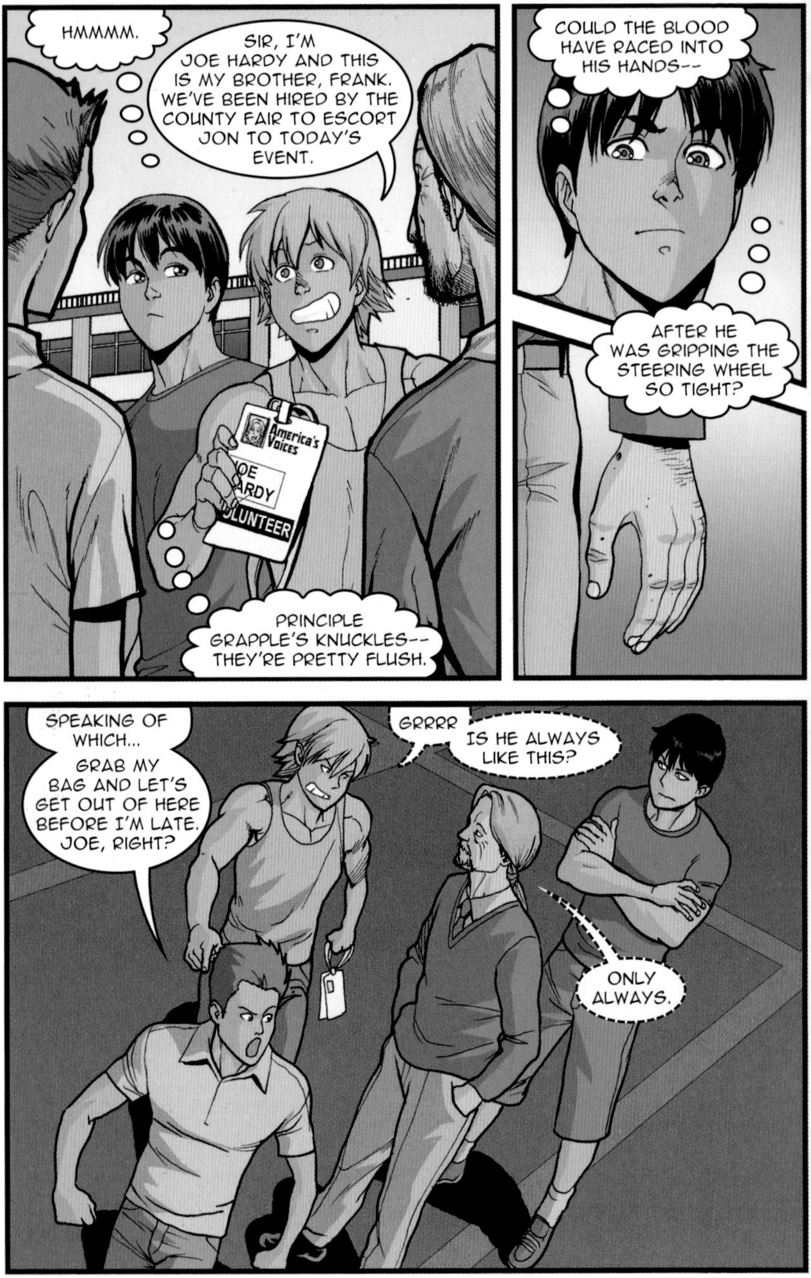
HMMMM.
SIR, I'M JOE HARDY AND THIS IS MY BROTHER, FRANK. WE'VE BEEN HIRED BY THE COUNTY FAIR TO ESCORT JON TO TODAY'S EVENT.
America's Voices
JOE HARDY
VOLUNTEER
PRINCIPLE GRAPPLE'S KNUCKLES-- THEY'RE PRETTY FLUSH.
COULD THE BLOOD HAVE RACED INTO HIS HANDS--
AFTER HE WAS GRIPPING THE STEERING WHEEL SO TIGHT?
SPEAKING OF WHICH...
GRAB MY BAG AND LET'S GET OUT OF HERE BEFORE I'M LATE. JOE, RIGHT?
GRRRR
IS HE ALWAYS LIKE THIS?
ONLY ALWAYS.

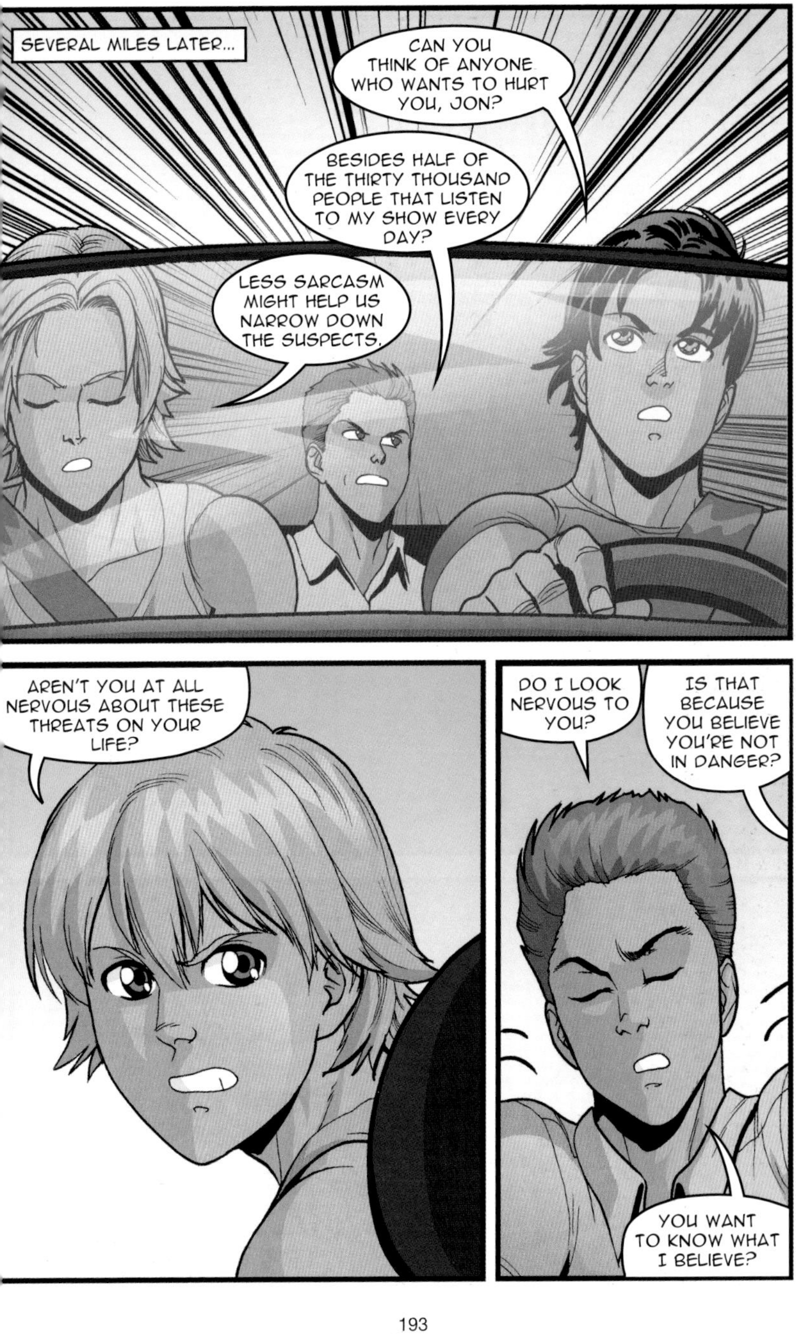
SEVERAL MILES LATER...
CAN YOU THINK OF ANYONE WHO WANTS TO HURT YOU, JON?
BESIDES HALF OF THE THIRTY THOUSAND PEOPLE THAT LISTEN TO MY SHOW EVERY DAY?
LESS SARCASM MIGHT HELP US NARROW DOWN THE SUSPECTS.
AREN'T YOU AT ALL NERVOUS ABOUT THESE THREATS ON YOUR LIFE?
DO I LOOK NERVOUS TO YOU?
IS THAT BECAUSE YOU BELIEVE YOU'RE NOT IN DANGER?
YOU WANT TO KNOW WHAT I BELIEVE?

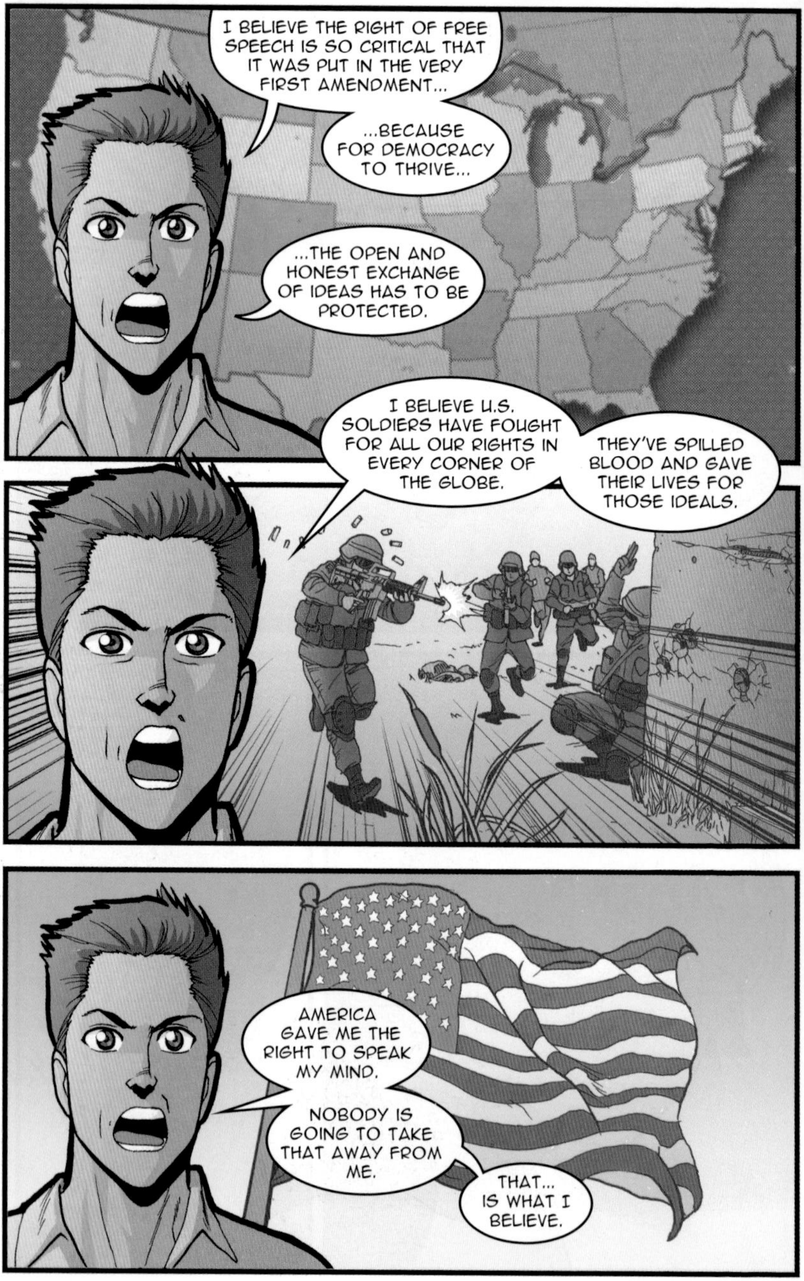
I BELIEVE THE RIGHT OF FREE SPEECH IS SO CRITICAL THAT IT WAS PUT IN THE VERY FIRST AMENDMENT...
...BECAUSE FOR DEMOCRACY TO THRIVE...
...THE OPEN AND HONEST EXCHANGE OF IDEAS HAS TO BE PROTECTED.
I BELIEVE U.S. SOLDIERS HAVE FOUGHT FOR ALL OUR RIGHTS IN EVERY CORNER OF THE GLOBE.
THEY'VE SPILLED BLOOD AND GAVE THEIR LIVES FOR THOSE IDEALS.
AMERICA GAVE ME THE RIGHT TO SPEAK MY MIND.
NOBODY IS GOING TO TAKE THAT AWAY FROM ME.
THAT... IS WHAT I BELIEVE.

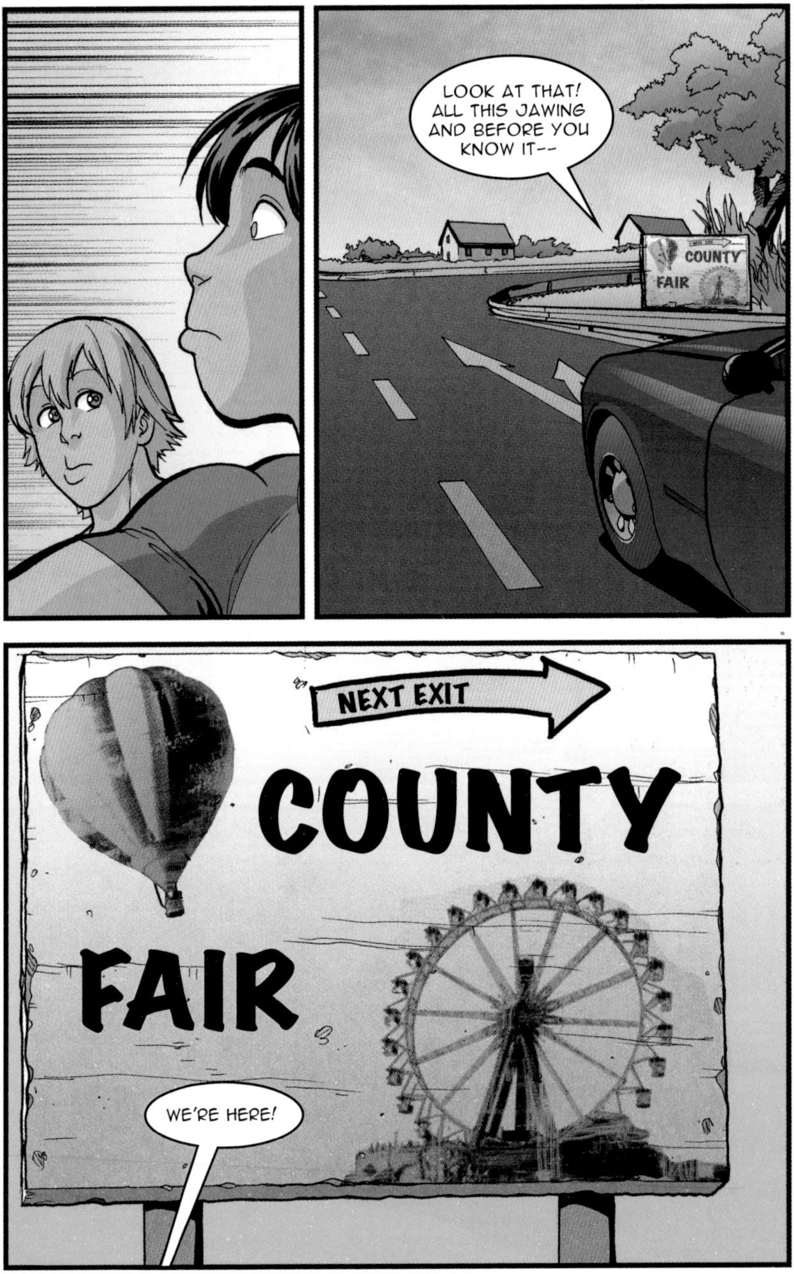
LOOK AT THAT! ALL THIS JAWING AND BEFORE YOU KNOW IT--
COUNTY
FAIR
NEXT EXIT
COUNTY
FAIR
WE'RE HERE!

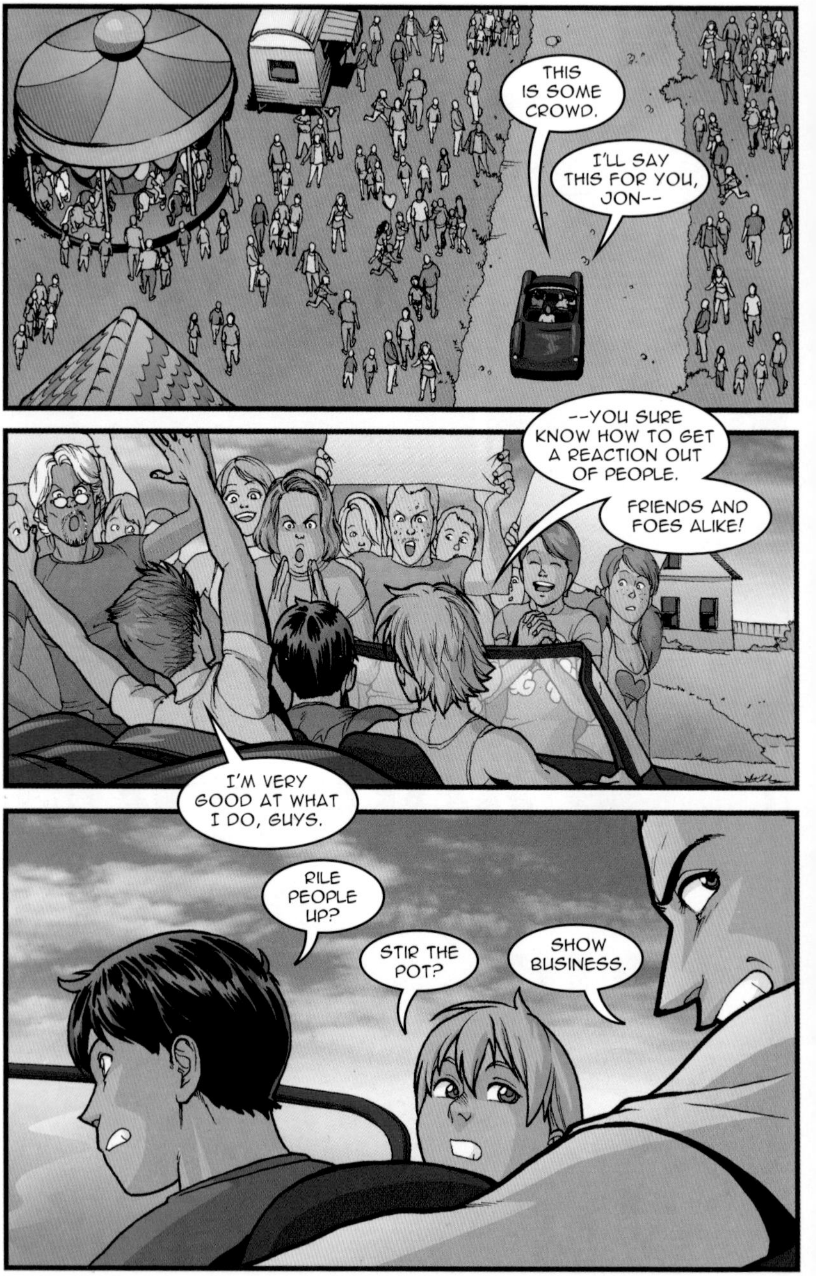
THIS IS SOME CROWD.
I'LL SAY THIS FOR YOU, JON--
--YOU SURE KNOW HOW TO GET A REACTION OUT OF PEOPLE.
FRIENDS AND FOES ALIKE!
I'M VERY GOOD AT WHAT I DO, GUYS.
RILE PEOPLE UP?
STIR THE POT?
SHOW BUSINESS.

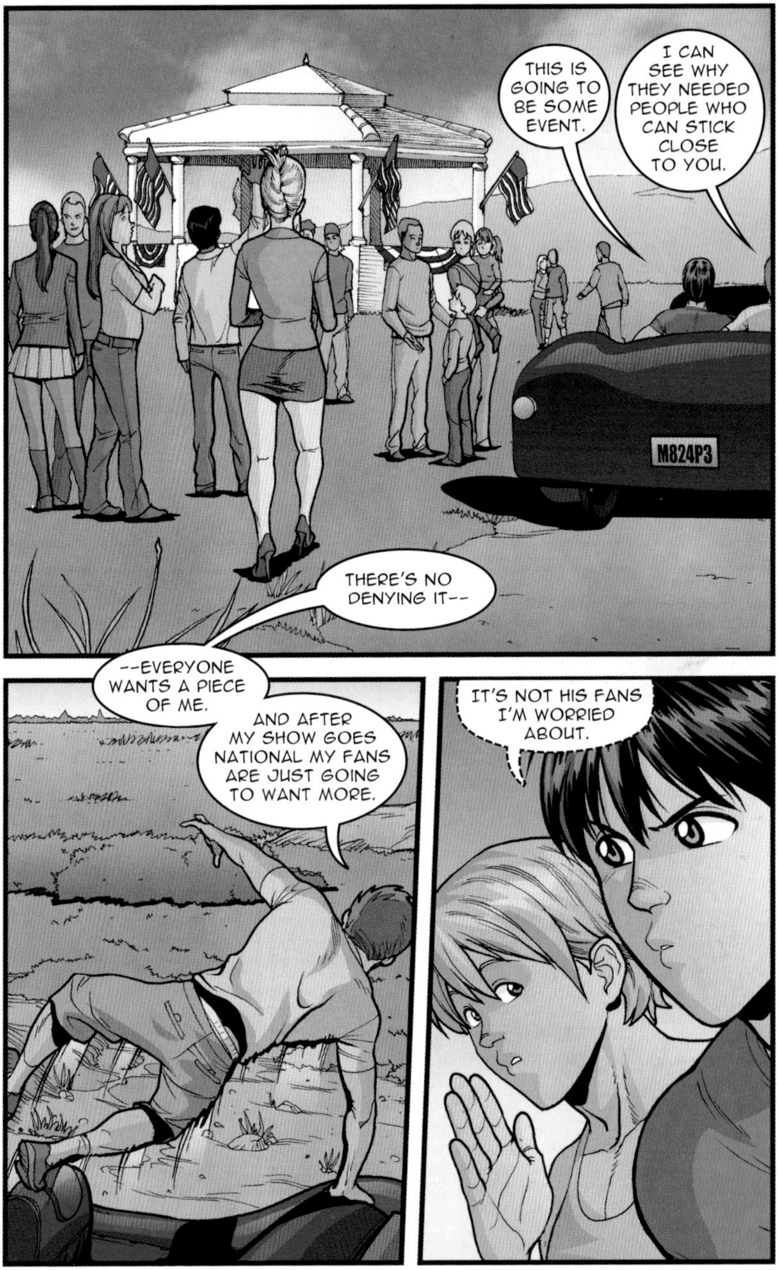
THIS IS GOING TO BE SOME EVENT.
I CAN SEE WHY THEY NEEDED PEOPLE WHO CAN STICK CLOSE TO YOU.
M824P3
THERE'S NO DENYING IT--
--EVERYONE WANTS A PIECE OF ME.
AND AFTER MY SHOW GOES NATIONAL MY FANS ARE JUST GOING TO WANT MORE.
IT'S NOT HIS FANS I'M WORRIED ABOUT.

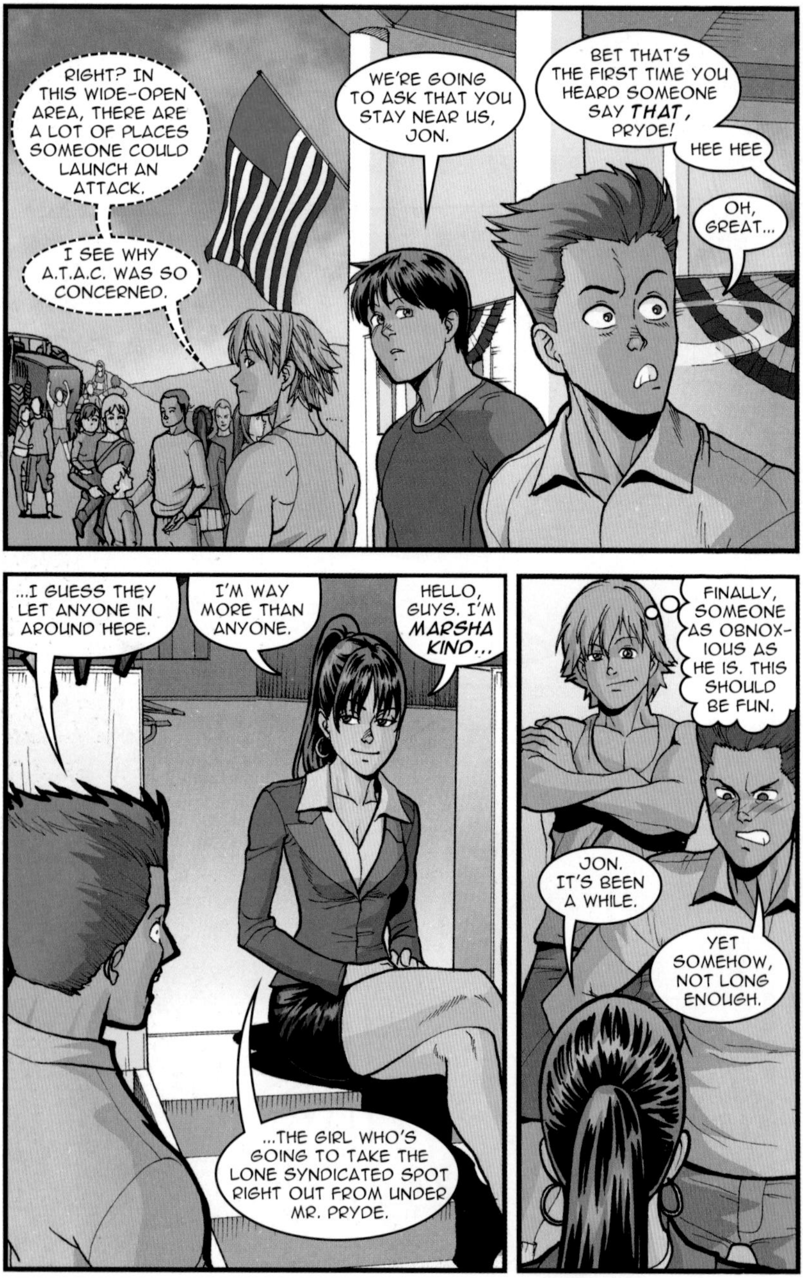
RIGHT? IN THIS WIDE-OPEN AREA, THERE ARE A LOT OF PLACES SOMEONE COULD LAUNCH AN ATTACK.
I SEE WHY A.T.A.C. WAS SO CONCERNED.
WE'RE GOING TO ASK THAT YOU STAY NEAR US, JON.
BET THAT'S THE FIRST TIME YOU HEARD SOMEONE SAY THAT, PRYDE!
HEE HEE
OH, GREAT...
...I GUESS THEY LET ANYONE IN AROUND HERE.
I'M WAY MORE THAN ANYONE.
HELLO, GUYS. I'M MARSHA KIND...
...THE GIRL WHO'S GOING TO TAKE THE LONE SYNDICATED SPOT RIGHT OUT FROM UNDER MR. PRYDE.
FINALLY, SOMEONE AS OBNOXIOUS AS HE IS. THIS SHOULD BE FUN.
JON. IT'S BEEN A WHILE.
YET SOMEHOW, NOT LONG ENOUGH.

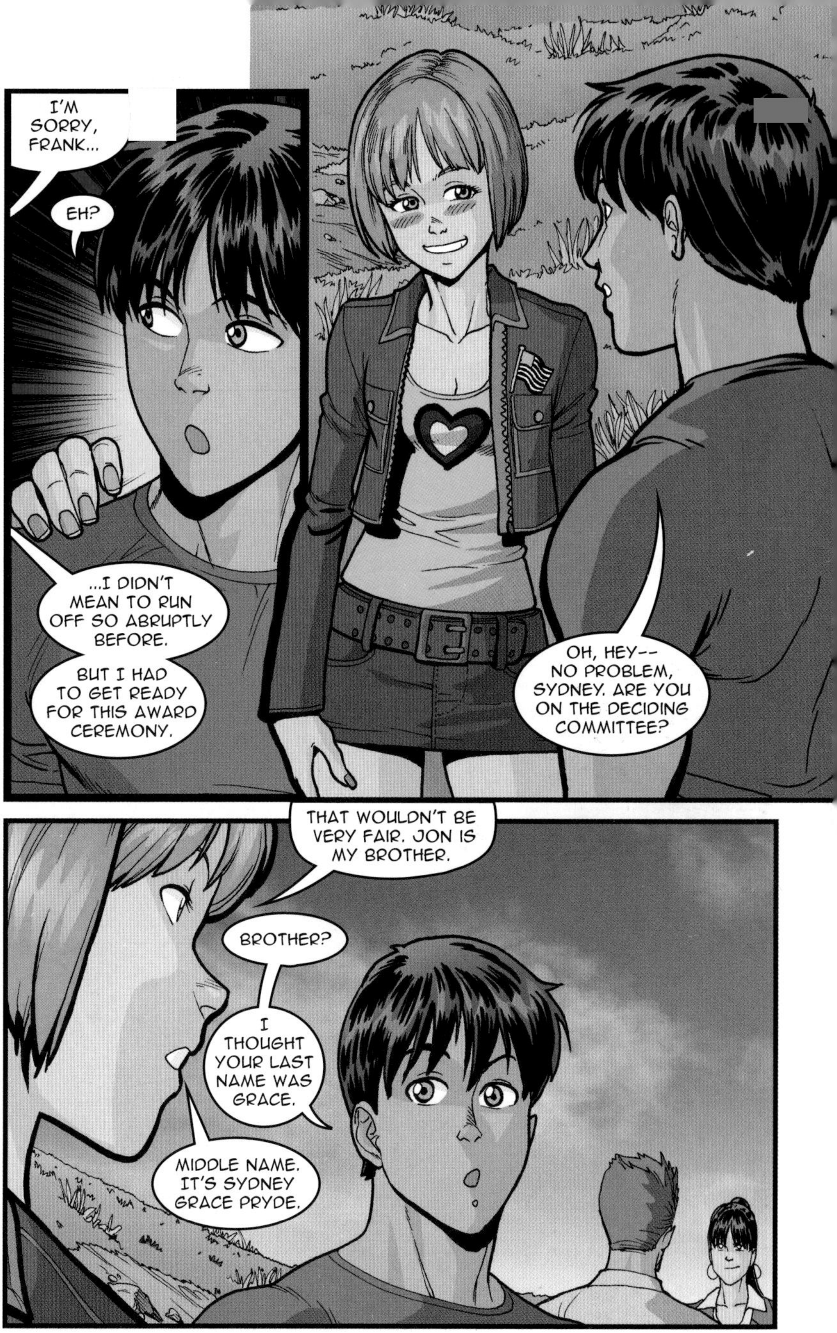
I'M SORRY, FRANK...
EH?
...I DIDN'T MEAN TO RUN OFF SO ABRUPTLY BEFORE.
BUT I HAD TO GET READY FOR THIS AWARD CEREMONY.
OH, HEY-- NO PROBLEM, SYDNEY. ARE YOU ON THE DECIDING COMMITTEE?
THAT WOULDN'T BE VERY FAIR. JON IS MY BROTHER.
BROTHER?
I THOUGHT YOUR LAST NAME WAS GRACE.
MIDDLE NAME. IT'S SYDNEY GRACE PRYDE.

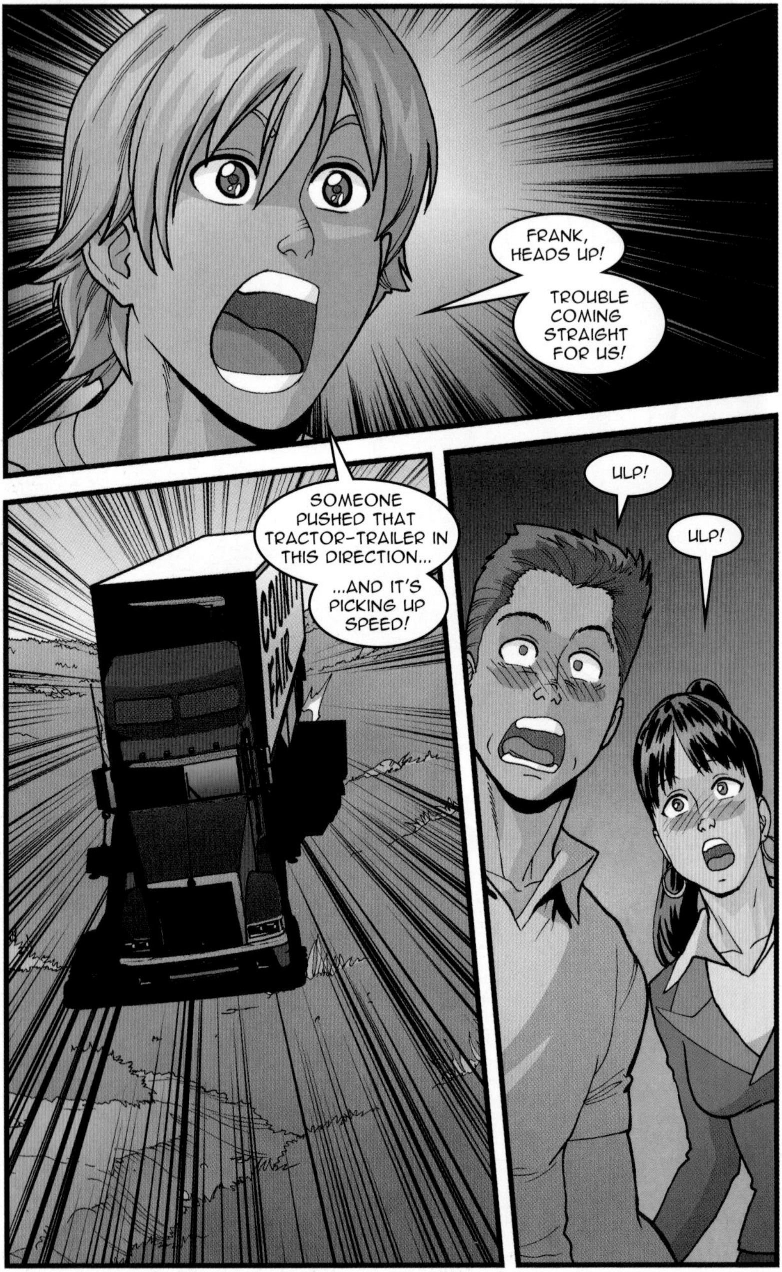
FRANK, HEADS UP!
TROUBLE COMING STRAIGHT FOR US!
SOMEONE PUSHED THAT TRACTOR-TRAILER IN THIS DIRECTION...
...AND IT'S PICKING UP SPEED!
COUNTY FAIR
ULP!
ULP!

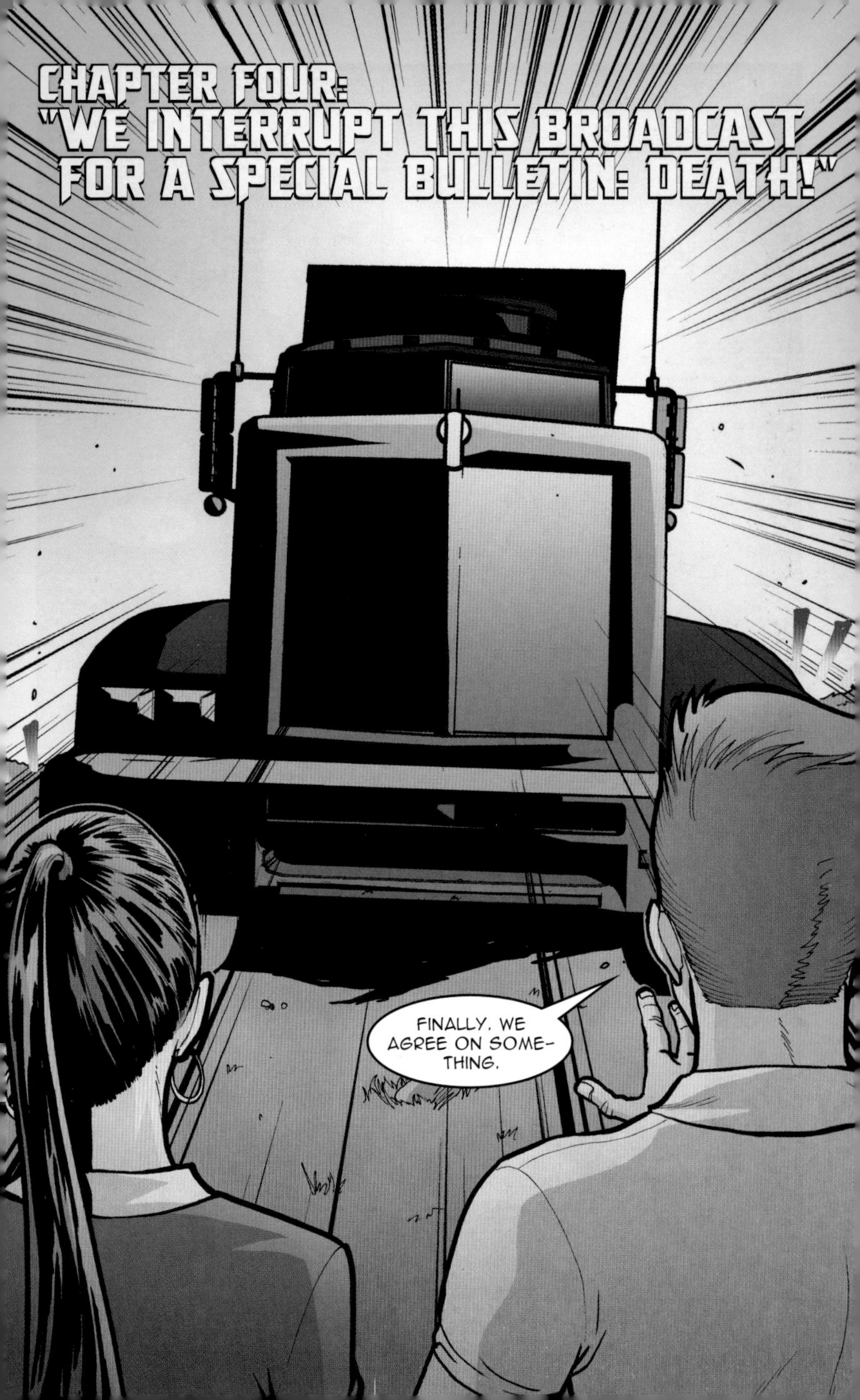
CHAPTER FOUR:
"WE INTERRUPT THIS BROADCAST FOR A SPECIAL BULLETIN: DEATH!"
FINALLY. WE AGREE ON SOMETHING.

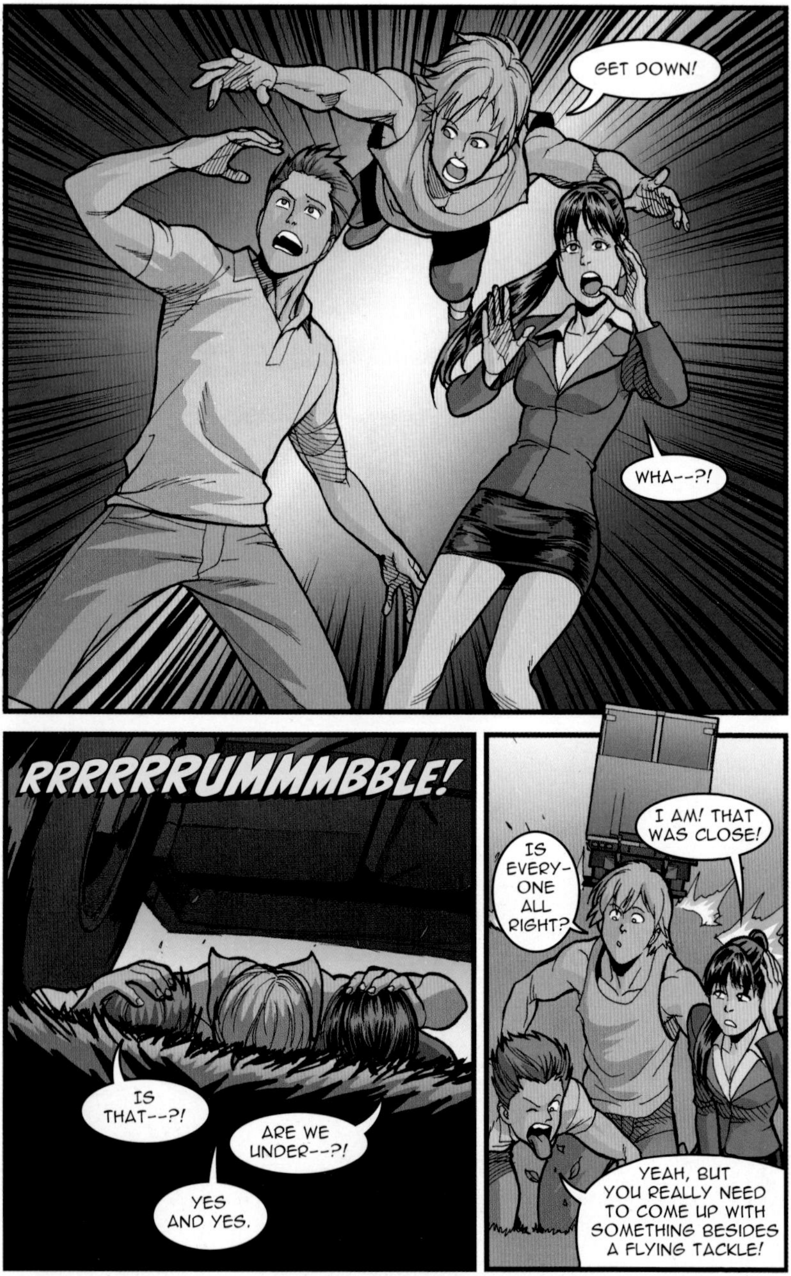
GET DOWN!
WHA--?!
RRRRRRUMMMMBBLE!
IS THAT--?!
ARE WE UNDER--?!
YES AND YES.
IS EVERY-ONE ALL RIGHT?
I AM! THAT WAS CLOSE!
YEAH, BUT YOU REALLY NEED TO COME UP WITH SOMETHING BESIDES A FLYING TACKLE!

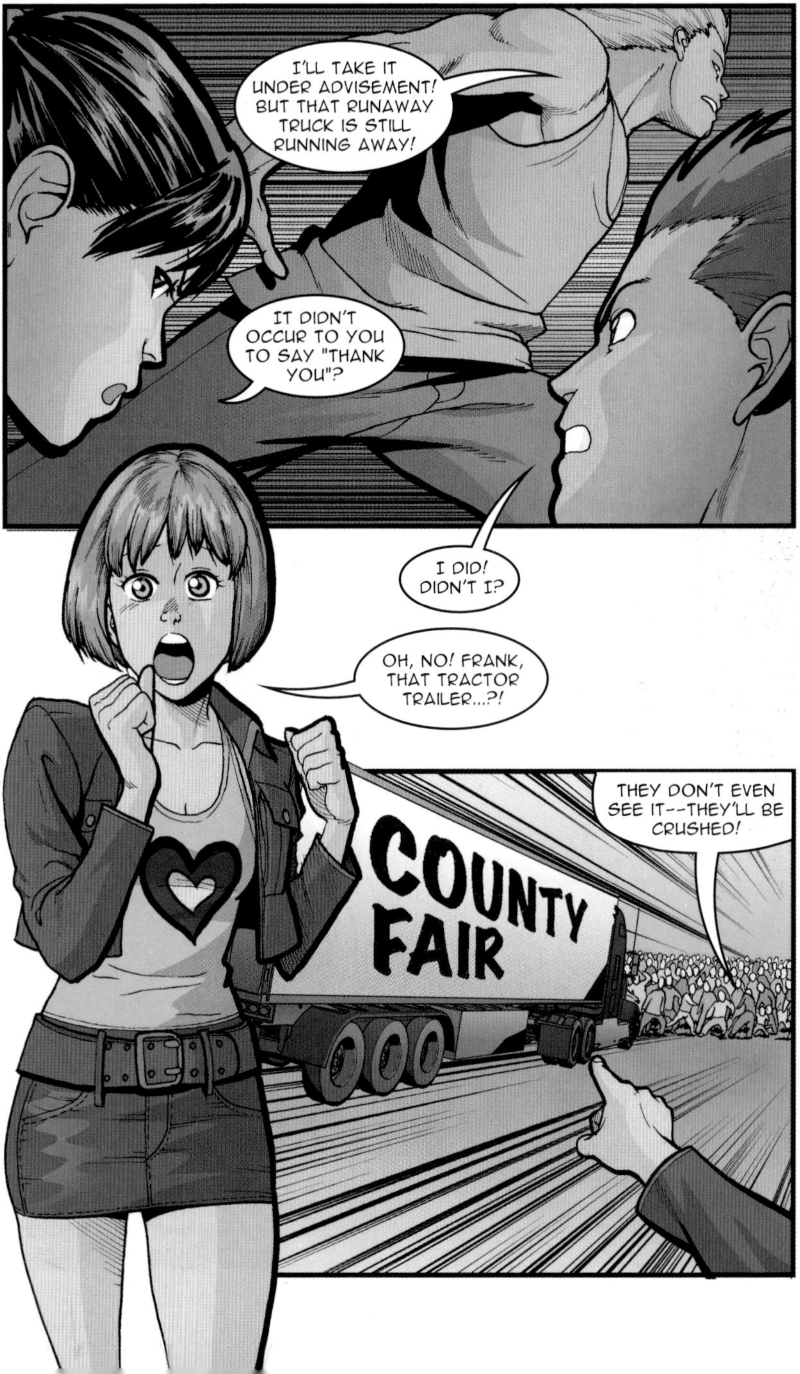
I'LL TAKE IT UNDER ADVISEMENT! BUT THAT RUNAWAY TRUCK IS STILL RUNNING AWAY!
IT DIDN'T OCCUR TO YOU TO SAY "THANK YOU"?
I DID! DIDN'T I?
OH, NO! FRANK, THAT TRACTOR TRAILER...?!
THEY DON'T EVEN SEE IT--THEY'LL BE CRUSHED!
COUNTY FAIR

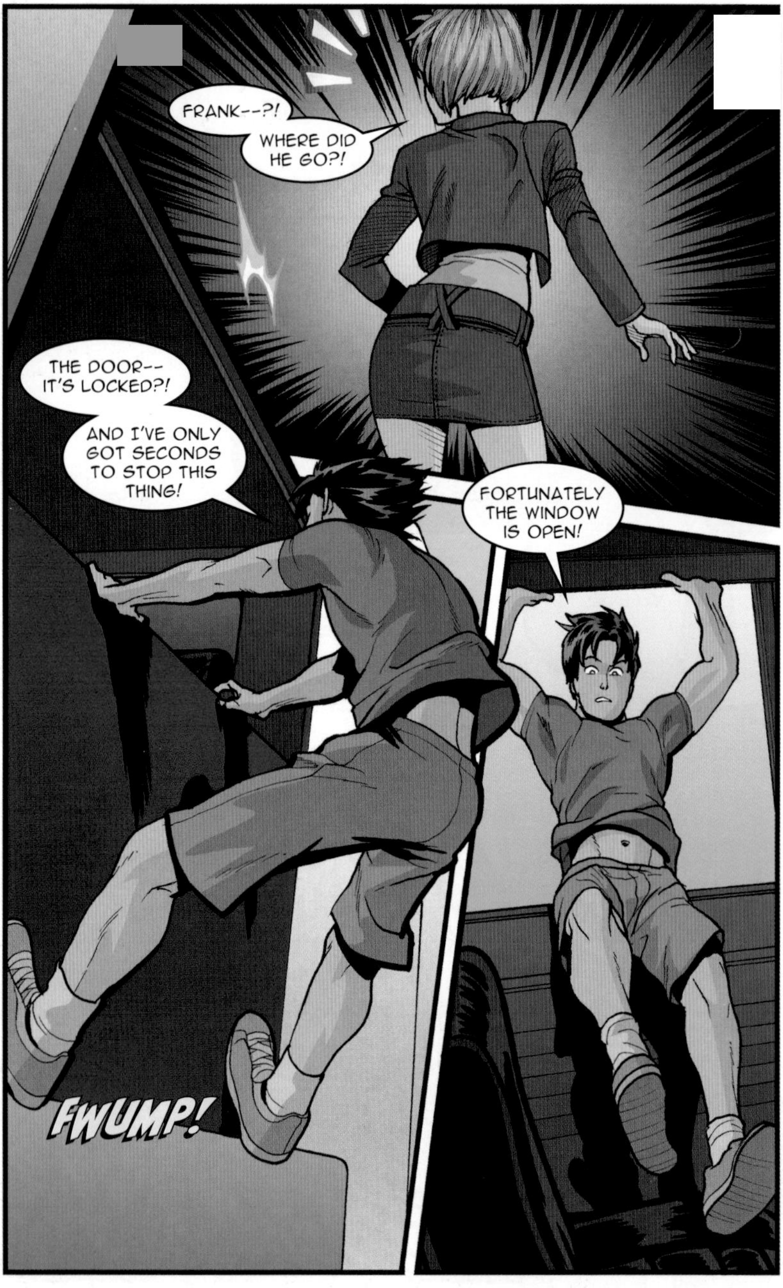
FRANK--?!
WHERE DID HE GO?!
THE DOOR-- IT'S LOCKED?!
AND I'VE ONLY GOT SECONDS TO STOP THIS THING!
FORTUNATELY THE WINDOW IS OPEN!
FWUMP!

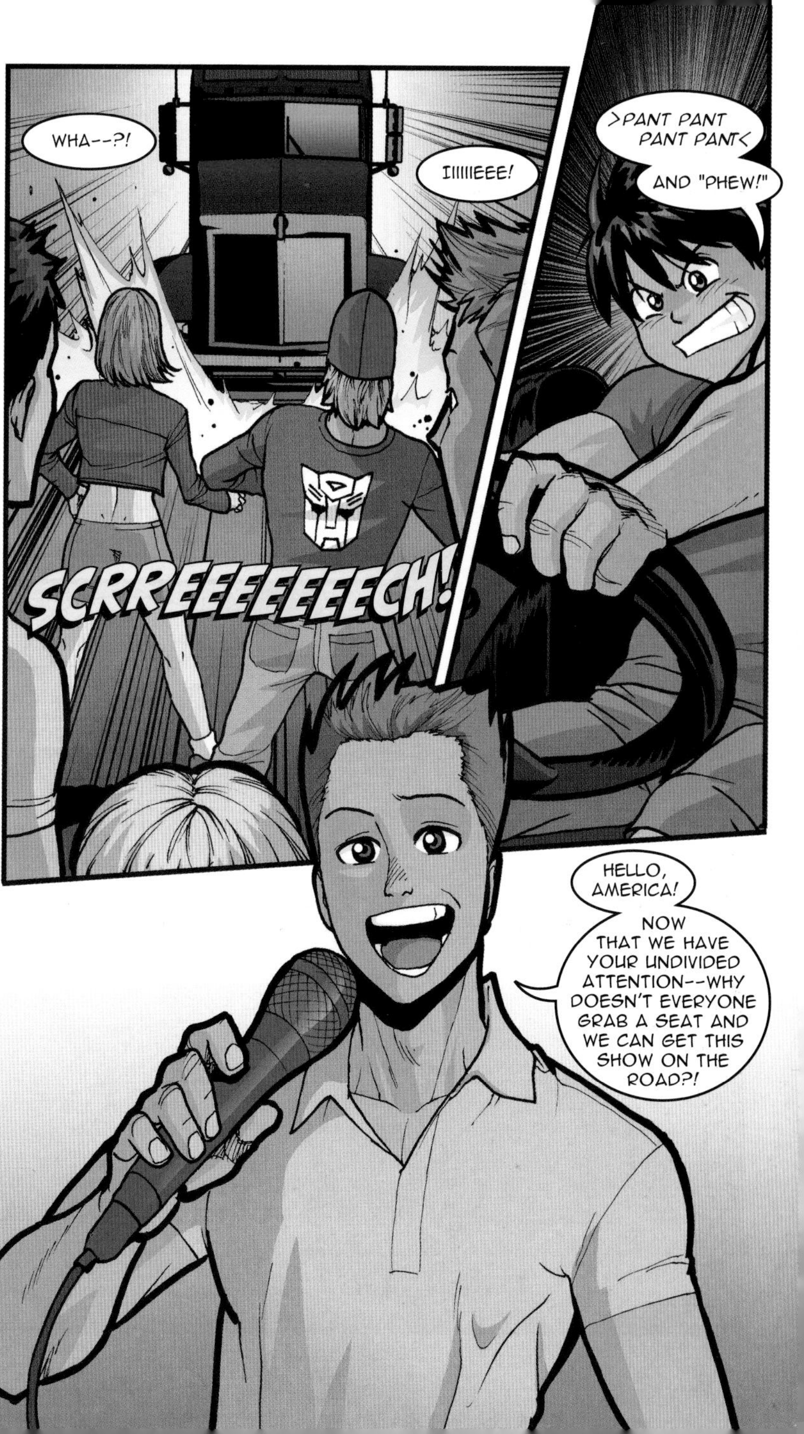
WHA--?!
IIIIIEEE!
SCRREEEEEEEEECH!
>PANT PANT PANT PANT<
AND "PHEW!"
HELLO, AMERICA!
NOW THAT WE HAVE YOUR UNDIVIDED ATTENTION--WHY DOESN'T EVERYONE GRAB A SEAT AND WE CAN GET THIS SHOW ON THE ROAD?!

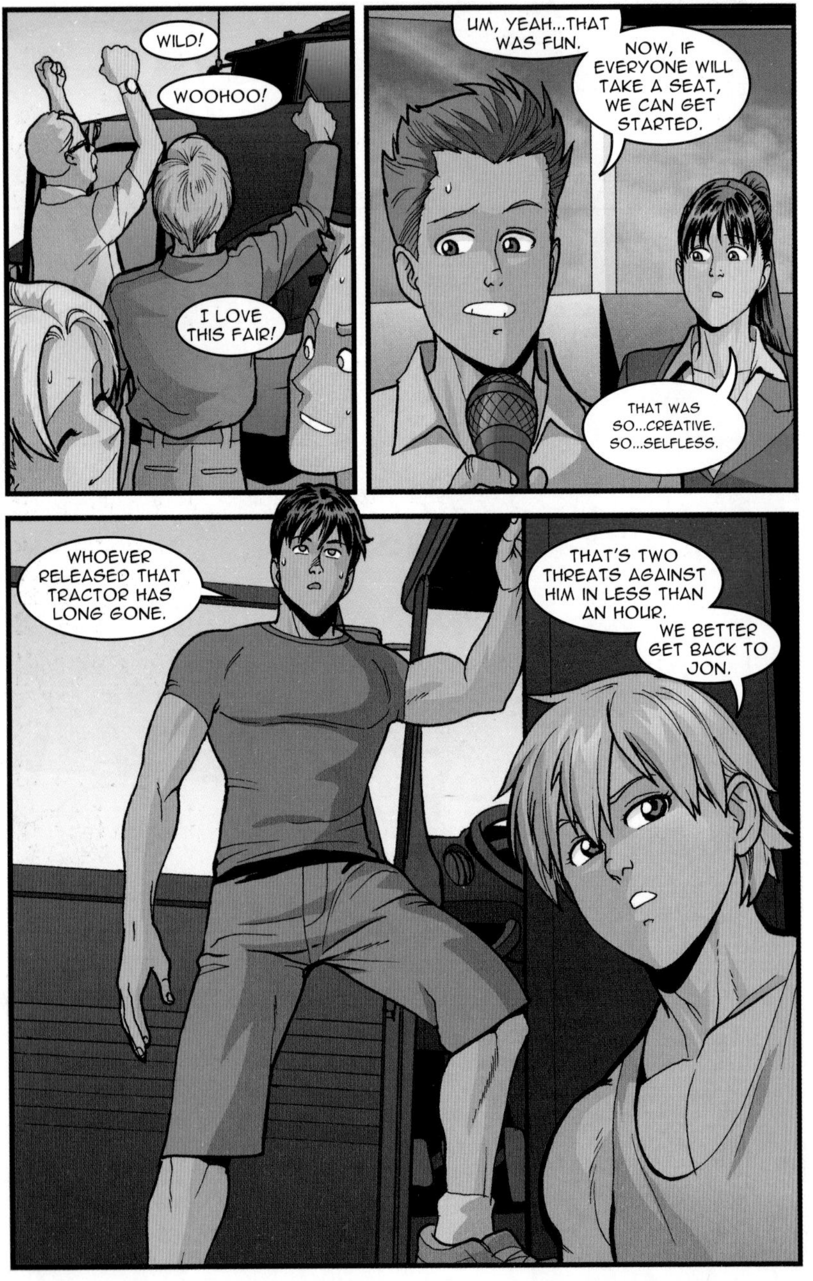
WILD!
WOOHOO!
I LOVE THIS FAIR!
UM, YEAH...THAT WAS FUN.
NOW, IF EVERYONE WILL TAKE A SEAT, WE CAN GET STARTED.
THAT WAS SO...CREATIVE. SO...SELFLESS.
WHOEVER RELEASED THAT TRACTOR HAS LONG GONE.
THAT'S TWO THREATS AGAINST HIM IN LESS THAN AN HOUR.
WE BETTER GET BACK TO JON.

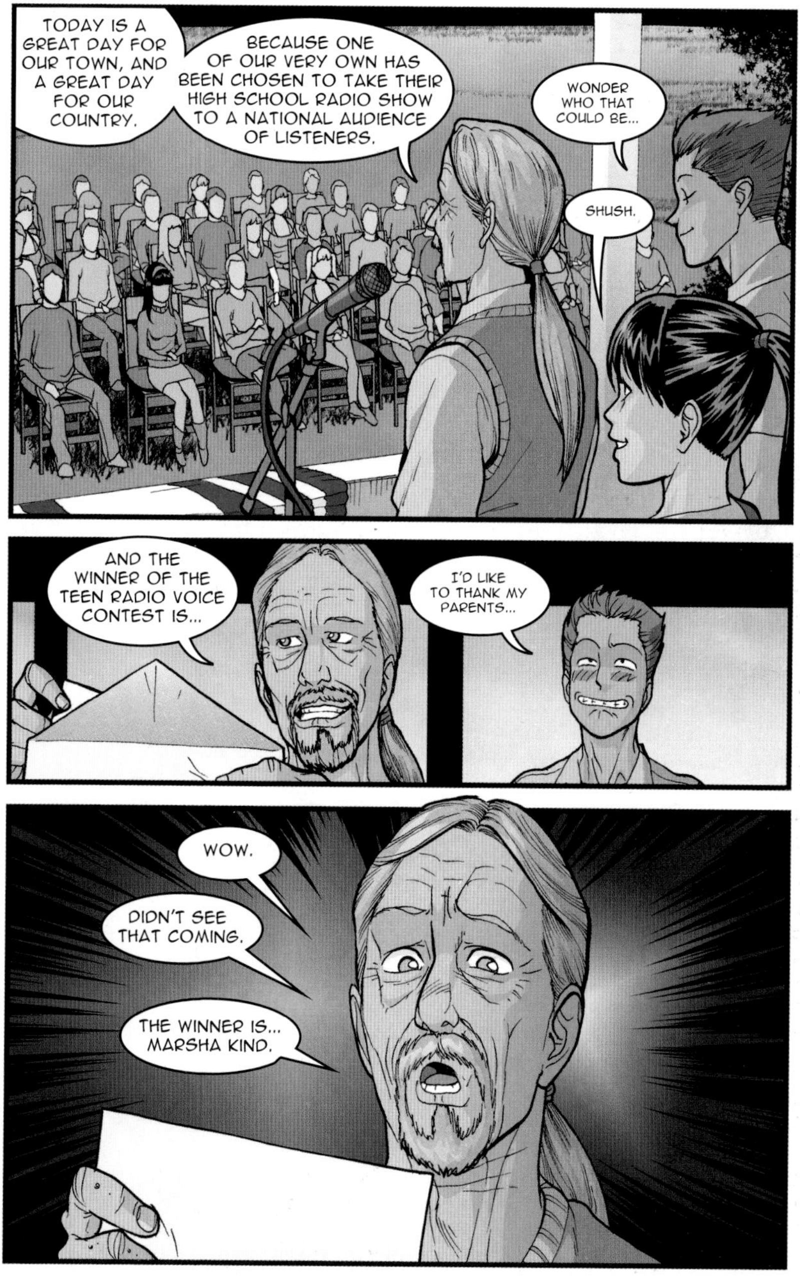
TODAY IS A GREAT DAY FOR OUR TOWN, AND A GREAT DAY FOR OUR COUNTRY.
BECAUSE ONE OF OUR VERY OWN HAS BEEN CHOSEN TO TAKE THEIR HIGH SCHOOL RADIO SHOW TO A NATIONAL AUDIENCE OF LISTENERS.
WONDER WHO THAT COULD BE...
SHUSH.
AND THE WINNER OF THE TEEN RADIO VOICE CONTEST IS...
I'D LIKE TO THANK MY PARENTS...
WOW.
DIDN'T SEE THAT COMING.
THE WINNER IS... MARSHA KIND.

CHAPTER FIVE: "NOOOOOOOOOO!!"

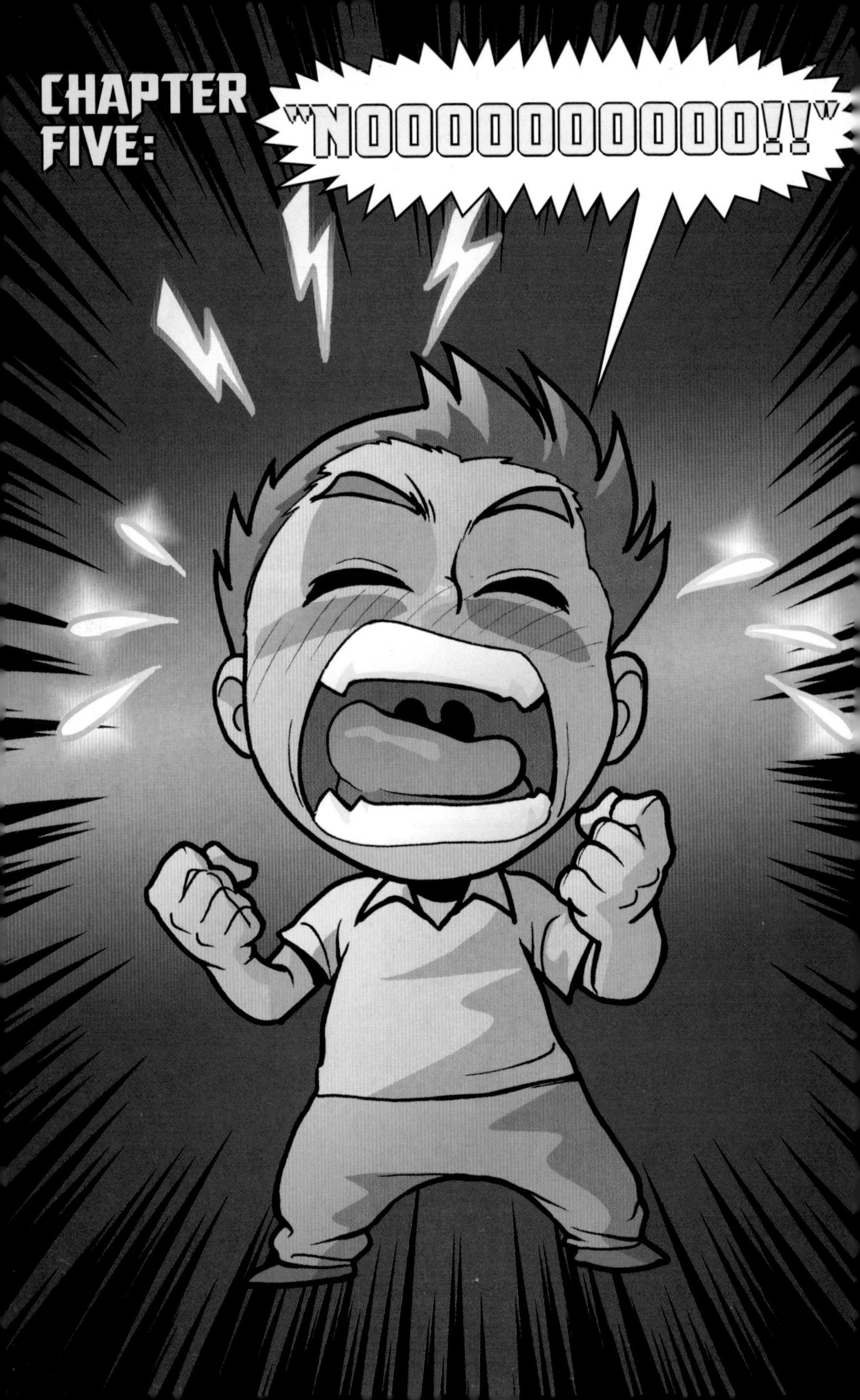
"NOOOOOOOOOO!!"

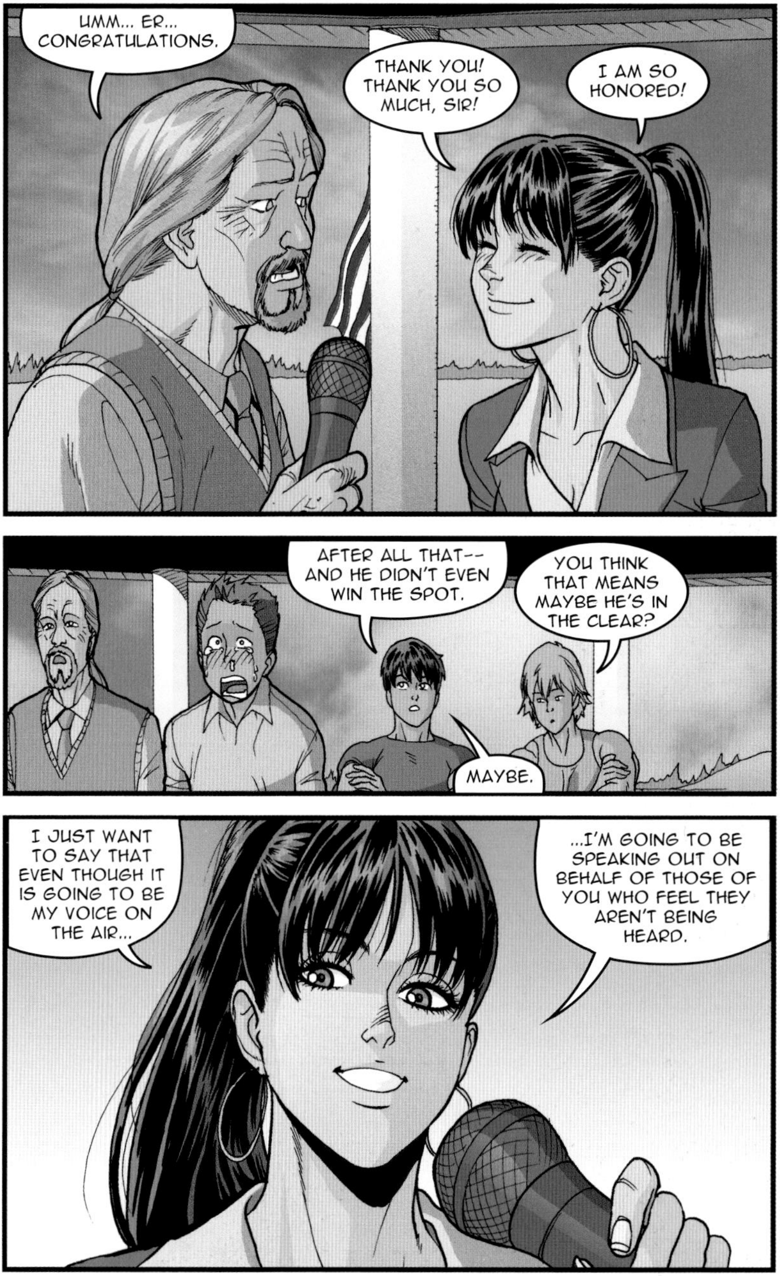
UMM... ER... CONGRATULATIONS.
THANK YOU! THANK YOU SO MUCH, SIR!
I AM SO HONORED!
AFTER ALL THAT-- AND HE DIDN'T EVEN WIN THE SPOT.
YOU THINK THAT MEANS MAYBE HE'S IN THE CLEAR?
MAYBE.
I JUST WANT TO SAY THAT EVEN THOUGH IT IS GOING TO BE MY VOICE ON THE AIR...
...I'M GOING TO BE SPEAKING OUT ON BEHALF OF THOSE OF YOU WHO FEEL THEY AREN'T BEING HEARD.

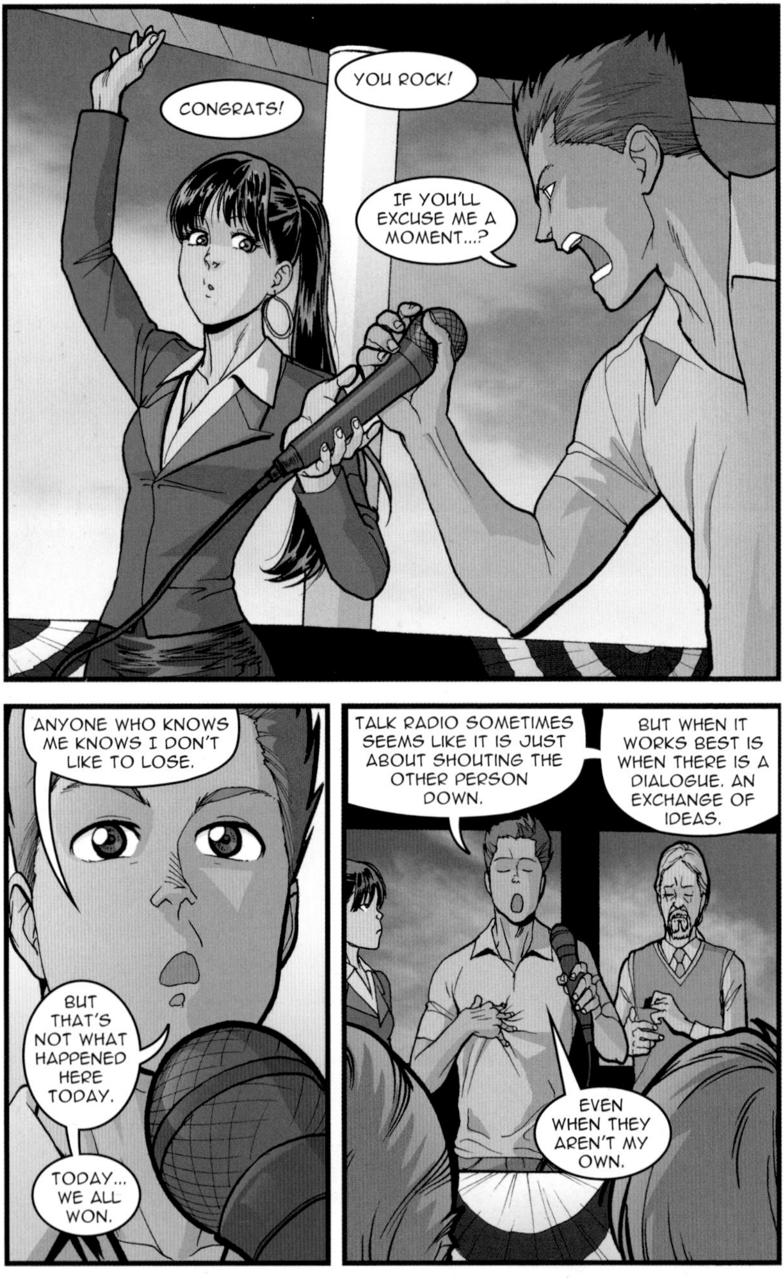
CONGRATS!
YOU ROCK!
IF YOU'LL EXCUSE ME A MOMENT...?
ANYONE WHO KNOWS ME KNOWS I DON'T LIKE TO LOSE.
BUT THAT'S NOT WHAT HAPPENED HERE TODAY.
TODAY... WE ALL WON.
TALK RADIO SOMETIMES SEEMS LIKE IT IS JUST ABOUT SHOUTING THE OTHER PERSON DOWN.
BUT WHEN IT WORKS BEST IS WHEN THERE IS A DIALOGUE. AN EXCHANGE OF IDEAS.
EVEN WHEN THEY AREN'T MY OWN.

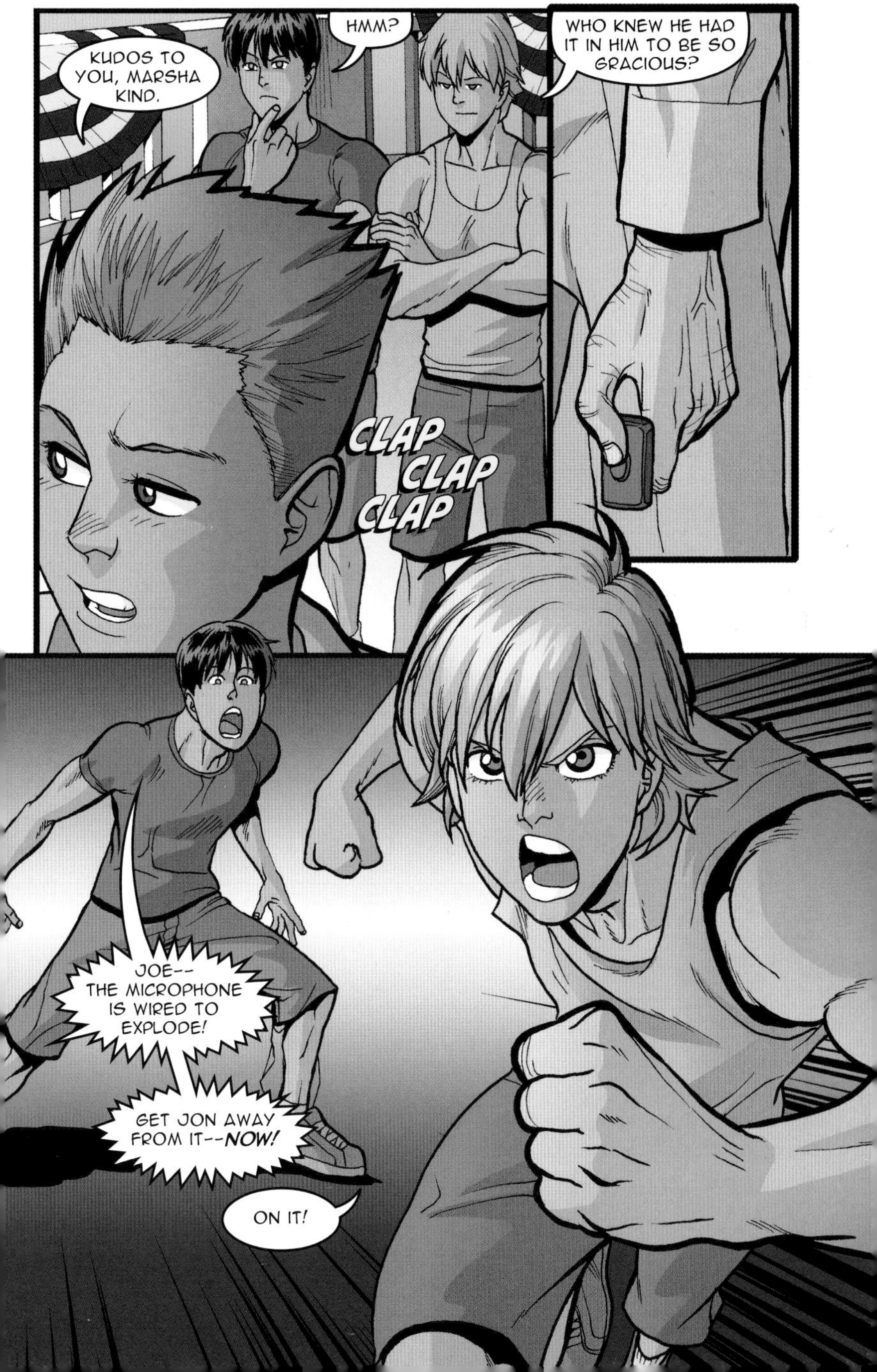
KUDOS TO YOU, MARSHA KIND.
HMM?
WHO KNEW HE HAD IT IN HIM TO BE SO GRACIOUS?
CLAP CLAP CLAP
JOE-- THE MICROPHONE IS WIRED TO EXPLODE!
GET JON AWAY FROM IT--NOW!
ON IT!

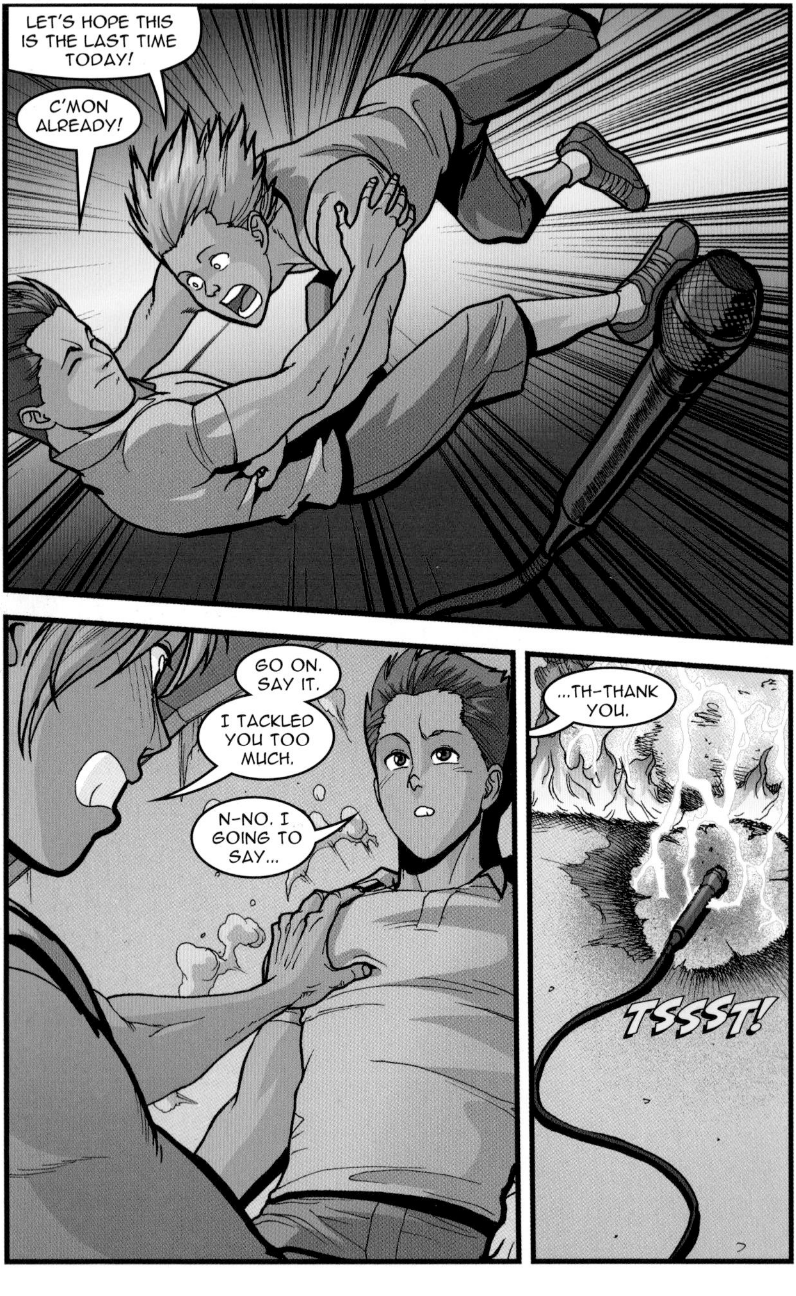
LET'S HOPE THIS IS THE LAST TIME TODAY!
C'MON ALREADY!
GO ON. SAY IT.
I TACKLED YOU TOO MUCH.
N-NO. I GOING TO SAY...
...TH-THANK YOU.
TSSST!

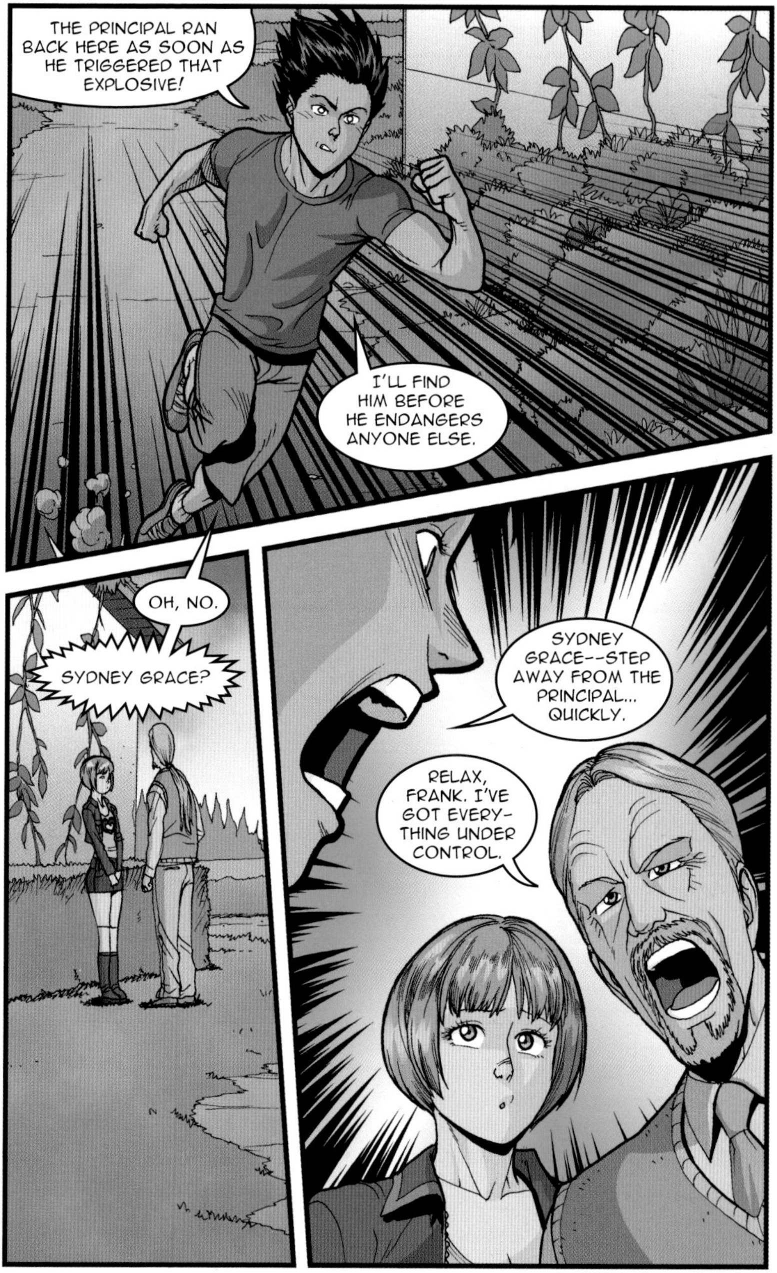
THE PRINCIPAL RAN BACK HERE AS SOON AS HE TRIGGERED THAT EXPLOSIVE!
I'LL FIND HIM BEFORE HE ENDANGERS ANYONE ELSE.
OH, NO.
SYDNEY GRACE?
SYDNEY GRACE--STEP AWAY FROM THE PRINCIPAL... QUICKLY.
RELAX, FRANK. I'VE GOT EVERY-THING UNDER CONTROL.

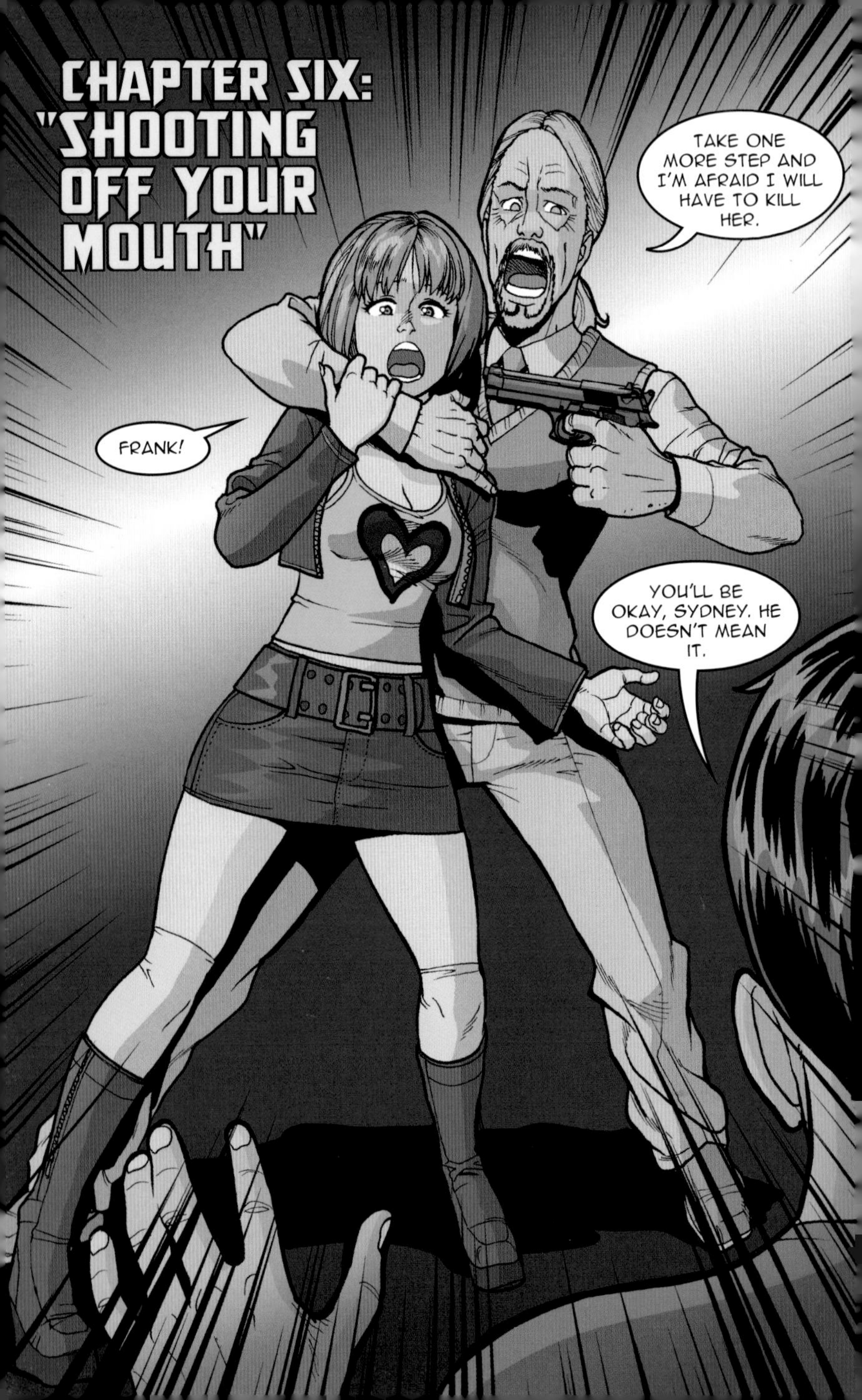
CHAPTER SIX:
"SHOOTING OFF YOUR MOUTH"
TAKE ONE MORE STEP AND I'M AFRAID I WILL HAVE TO KILL HER.
FRANK!
YOU'LL BE OKAY, SYDNEY. HE DOESN'T MEAN IT.

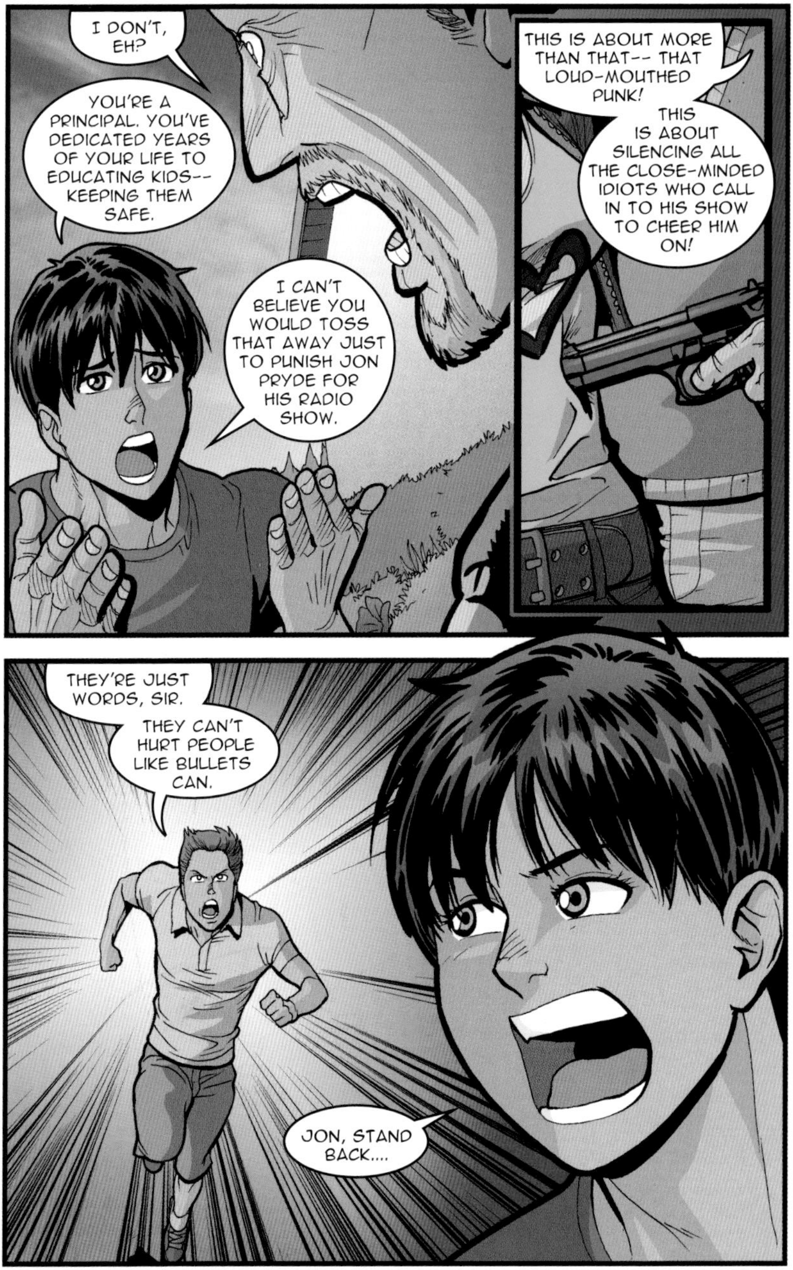

I DON'T, EH?
YOU'RE A PRINCIPAL. YOU'VE DEDICATED YEARS OF YOUR LIFE TO EDUCATING KIDS-- KEEPING THEM SAFE.
I CAN'T BELIEVE YOU WOULD TOSS THAT AWAY JUST TO PUNISH JON PRYDE FOR HIS RADIO SHOW.
THIS IS ABOUT MORE THAN THAT-- THAT LOUD-MOUTHED PUNK!
THIS IS ABOUT SILENCING ALL THE CLOSE-MINDED IDIOTS WHO CALL IN TO HIS SHOW TO CHEER HIM ON!
THEY'RE JUST WORDS, SIR.
THEY CAN'T HURT PEOPLE LIKE BULLETS CAN.
JON, STAND BACK....

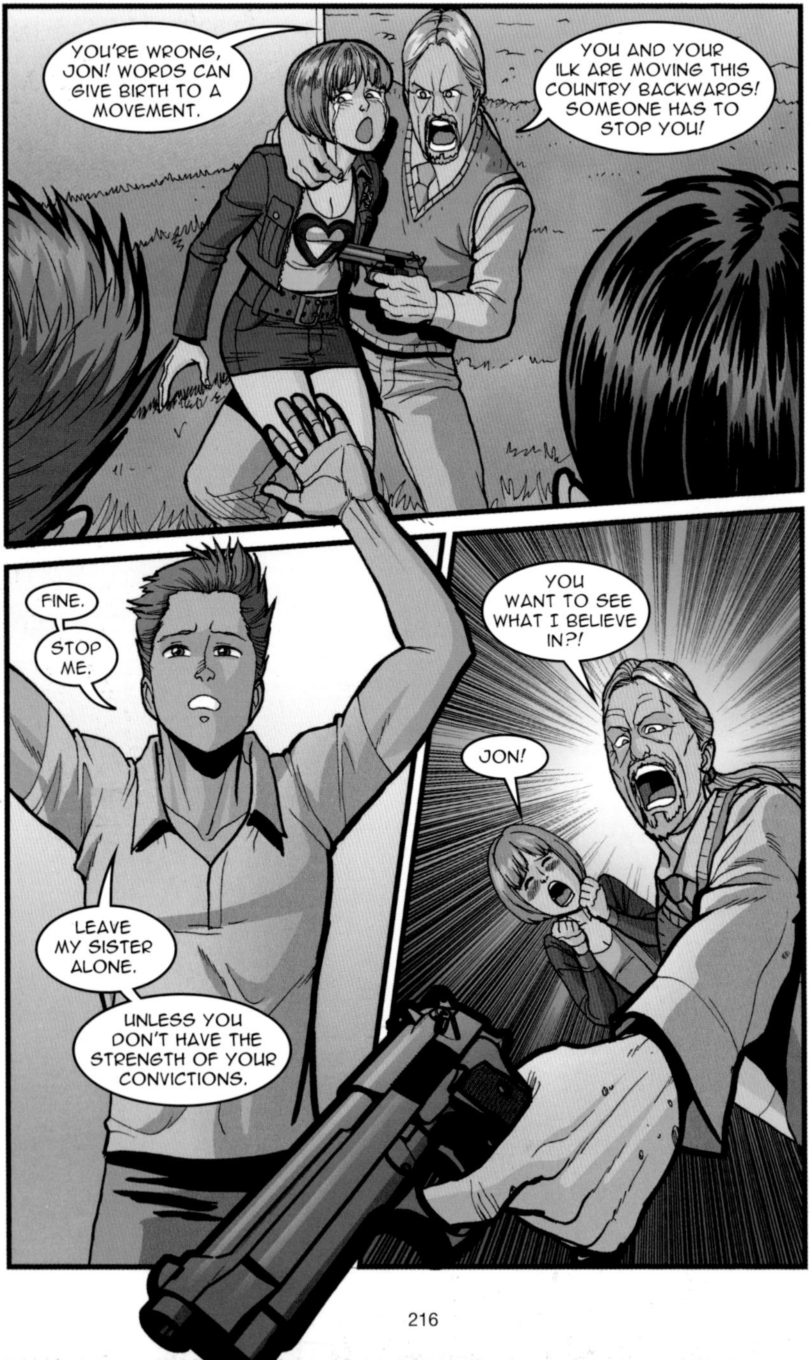
YOU'RE WRONG, JON! WORDS CAN GIVE BIRTH TO A MOVEMENT.
YOU AND YOUR ILK ARE MOVING THIS COUNTRY BACKWARDS! SOMEONE HAS TO STOP YOU!
FINE.
STOP ME.
LEAVE MY SISTER ALONE.
UNLESS YOU DON'T HAVE THE STRENGTH OF YOUR CONVICTIONS.
YOU WANT TO SEE WHAT I BELIEVE IN?!
JON!

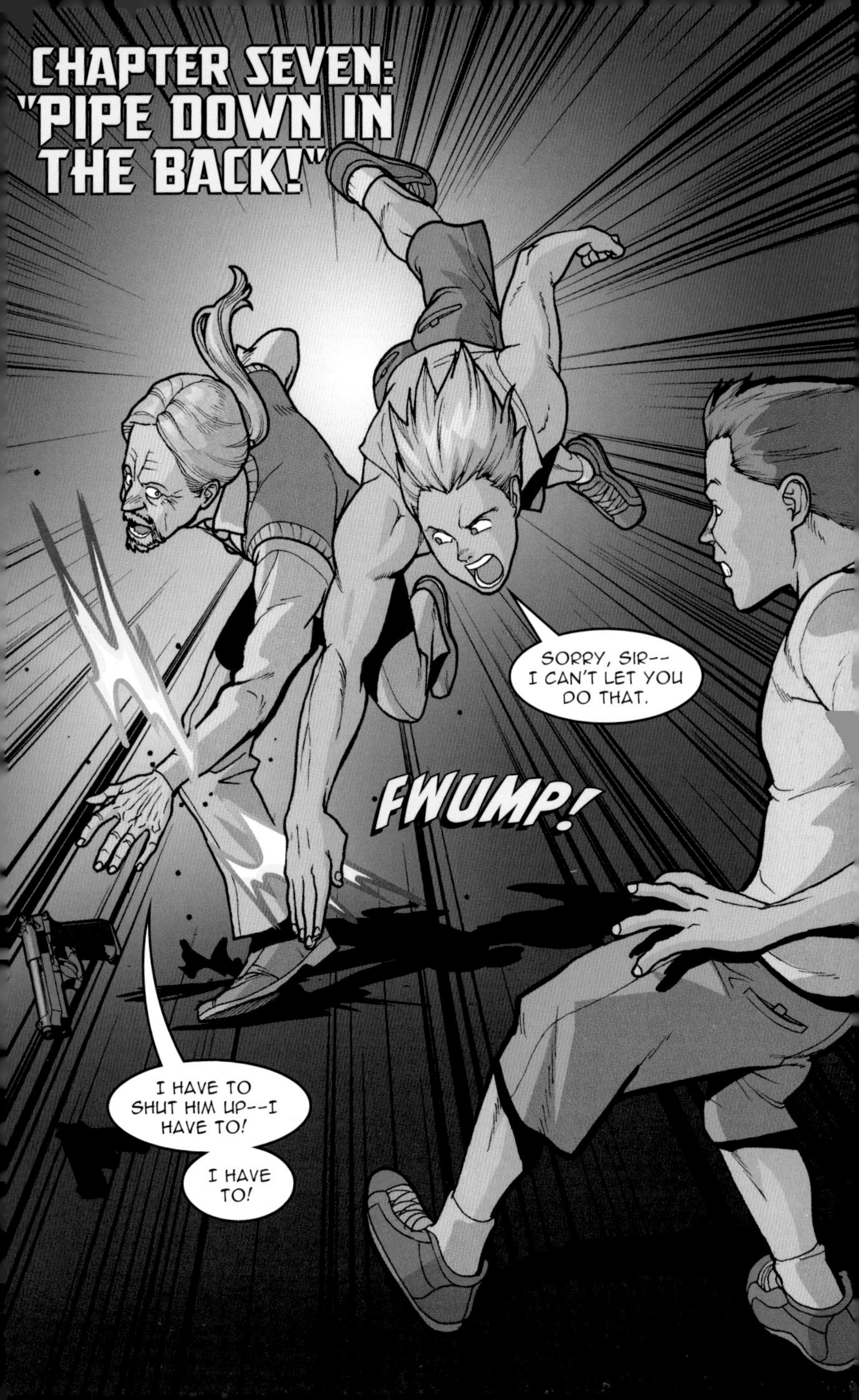
CHAPTER SEVEN: "PIPE DOWN IN THE BACK!"
SORRY, SIR-- I CAN'T LET YOU DO THAT.
FWUMP!
I HAVE TO SHUT HIM UP--I HAVE TO!
I HAVE TO!

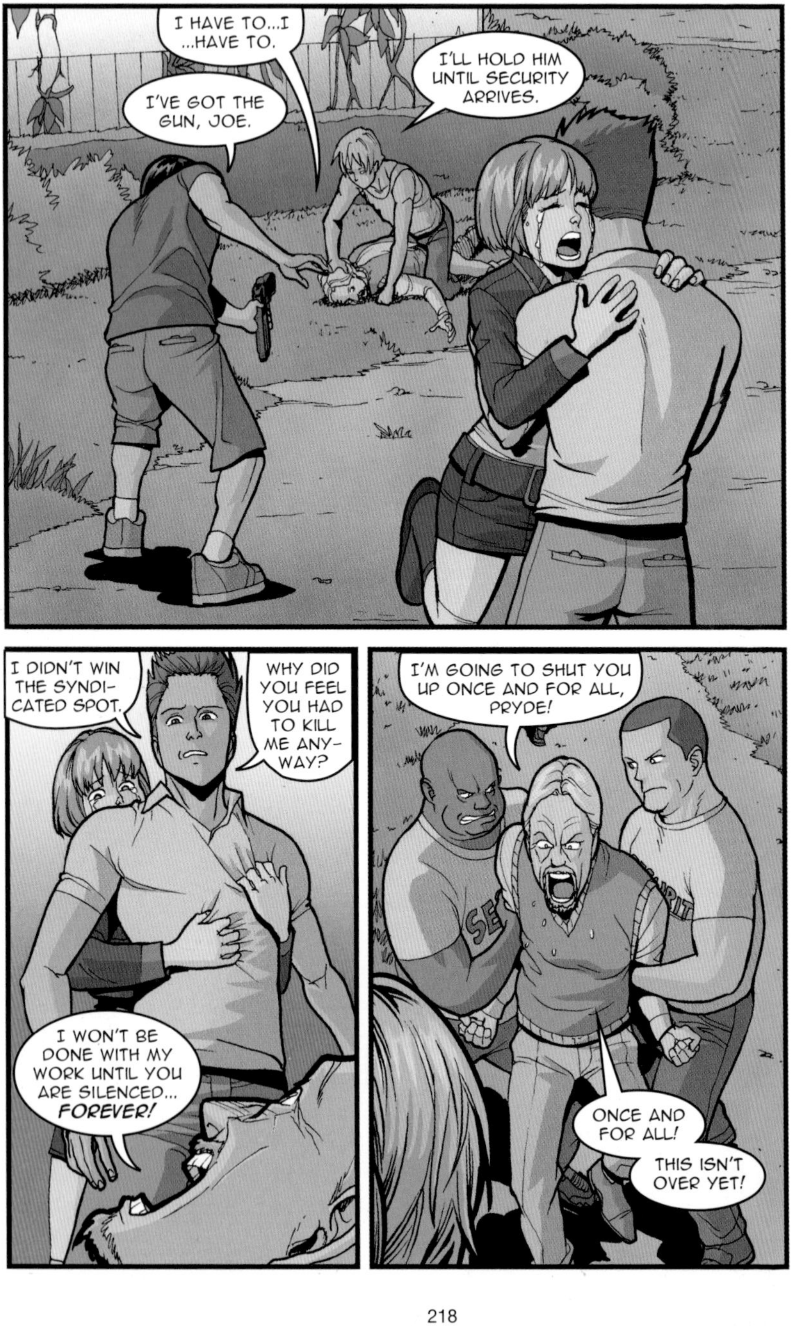
I'VE GOT THE GUN, JOE.
I HAVE TO...I ...HAVE TO.
I'LL HOLD HIM UNTIL SECURITY ARRIVES.
I DIDN'T WIN THE SYNDI-CATED SPOT.
WHY DID YOU FEEL YOU HAD TO KILL ME ANY-WAY?
I WON'T BE DONE WITH MY WORK UNTIL YOU ARE SILENCED... *FOREVER!*
I'M GOING TO SHUT YOU UP ONCE AND FOR ALL, PRYDE!
ONCE AND FOR ALL!
THIS ISN'T OVER YET!

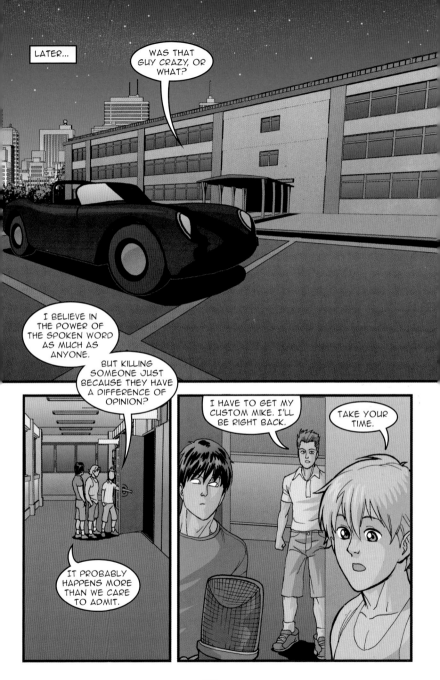

LATER...

WAS THAT GUY CRAZY, OR WHAT?

I BELIEVE IN THE POWER OF THE SPOKEN WORD AS MUCH AS ANYONE.

BUT KILLING SOMEONE JUST BECAUSE THEY HAVE A DIFFERENCE OF OPINION?

IT PROBABLY HAPPENS MORE THAN WE CARE TO ADMIT.

I HAVE TO GET MY CUSTOM MIKE. I'LL BE RIGHT BACK.

TAKE YOUR TIME.

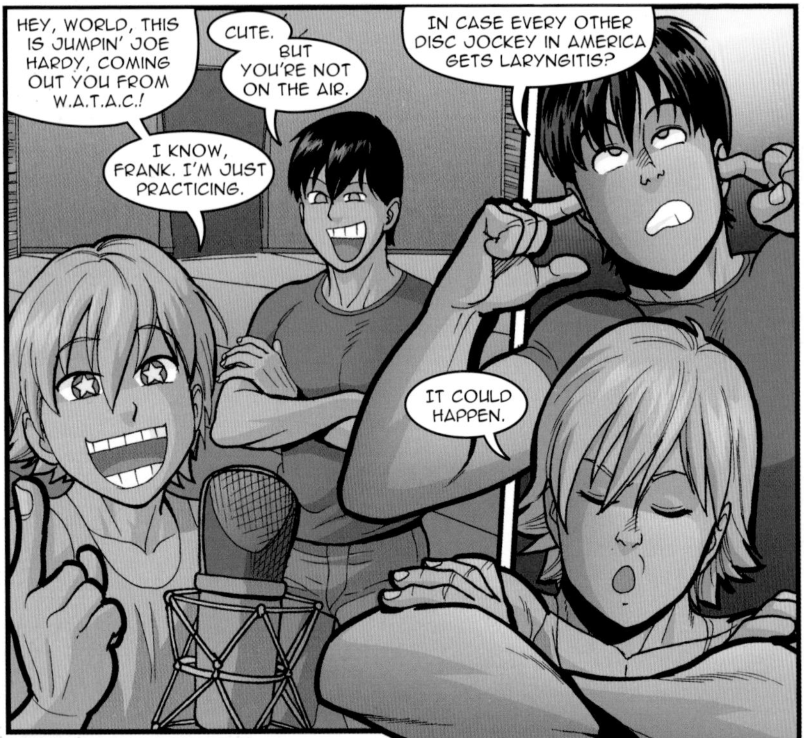
HEY, WORLD, THIS IS JUMPIN' JOE HARDY, COMING OUT YOU FROM W.A.T.A.C.!
CUTE.
BUT YOU'RE NOT ON THE AIR.
I KNOW, FRANK. I'M JUST PRACTICING.
IN CASE EVERY OTHER DISC JOCKEY IN AMERICA GETS LARYNGITIS?
IT COULD HAPPEN.

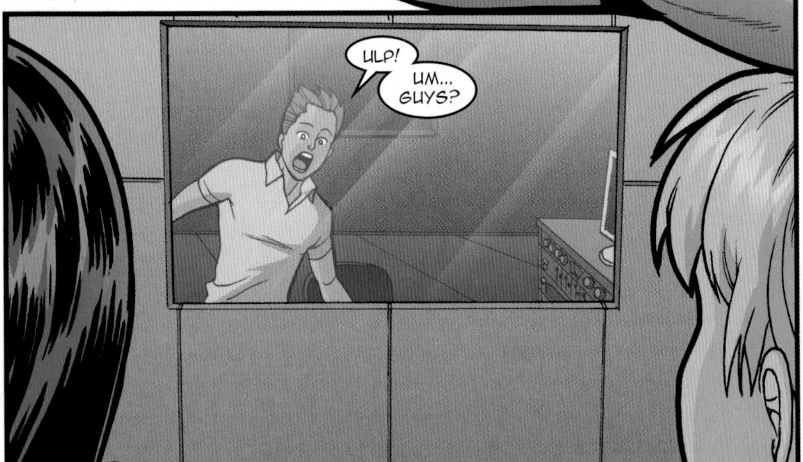
ULP!
UM... GUYS?

CHAPTER EIGHT: "EXPLODING IN RAGE!"

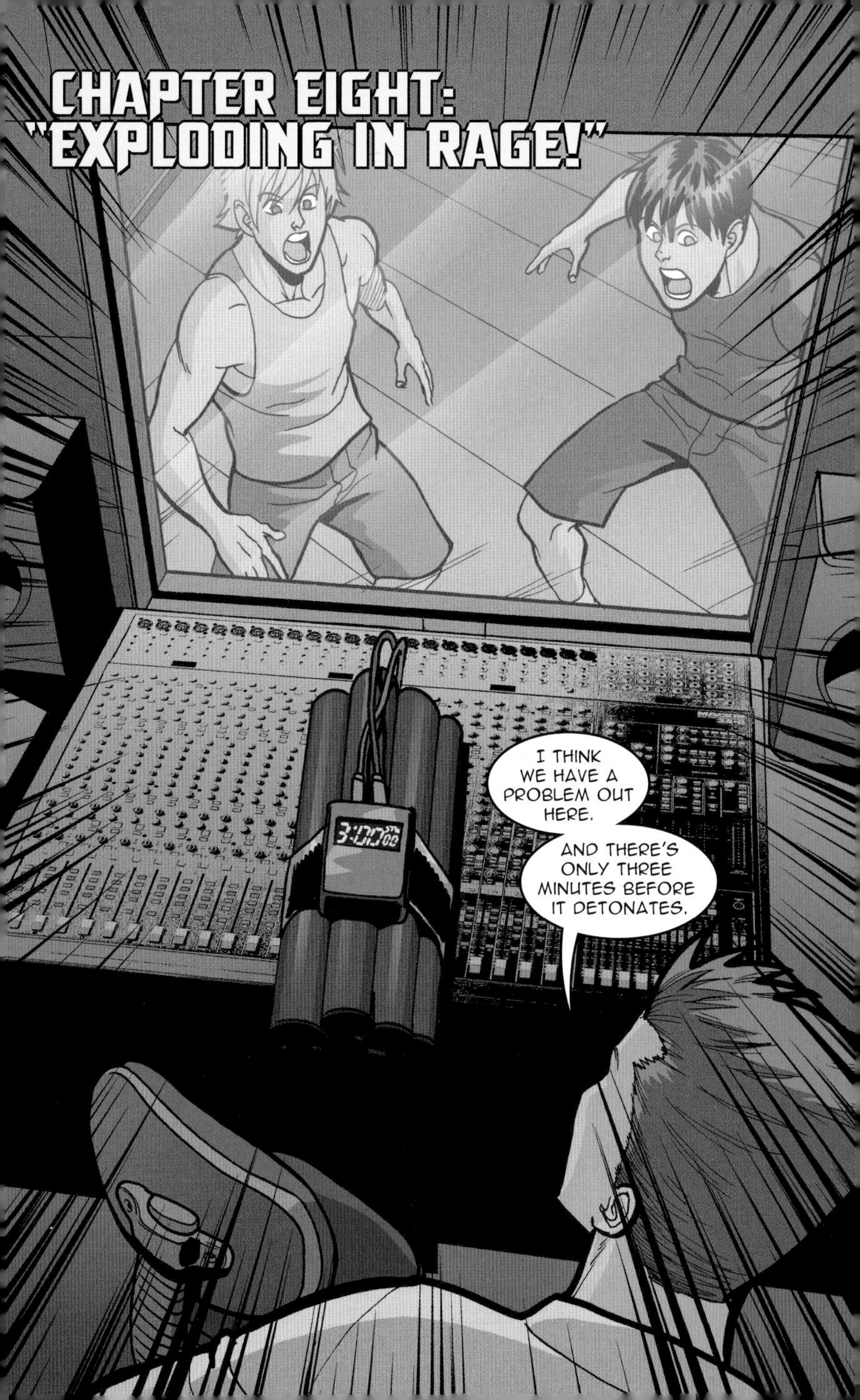
3:00 00
I THINK WE HAVE A PROBLEM OUT HERE.
AND THERE'S ONLY THREE MINUTES BEFORE IT DETONATES.

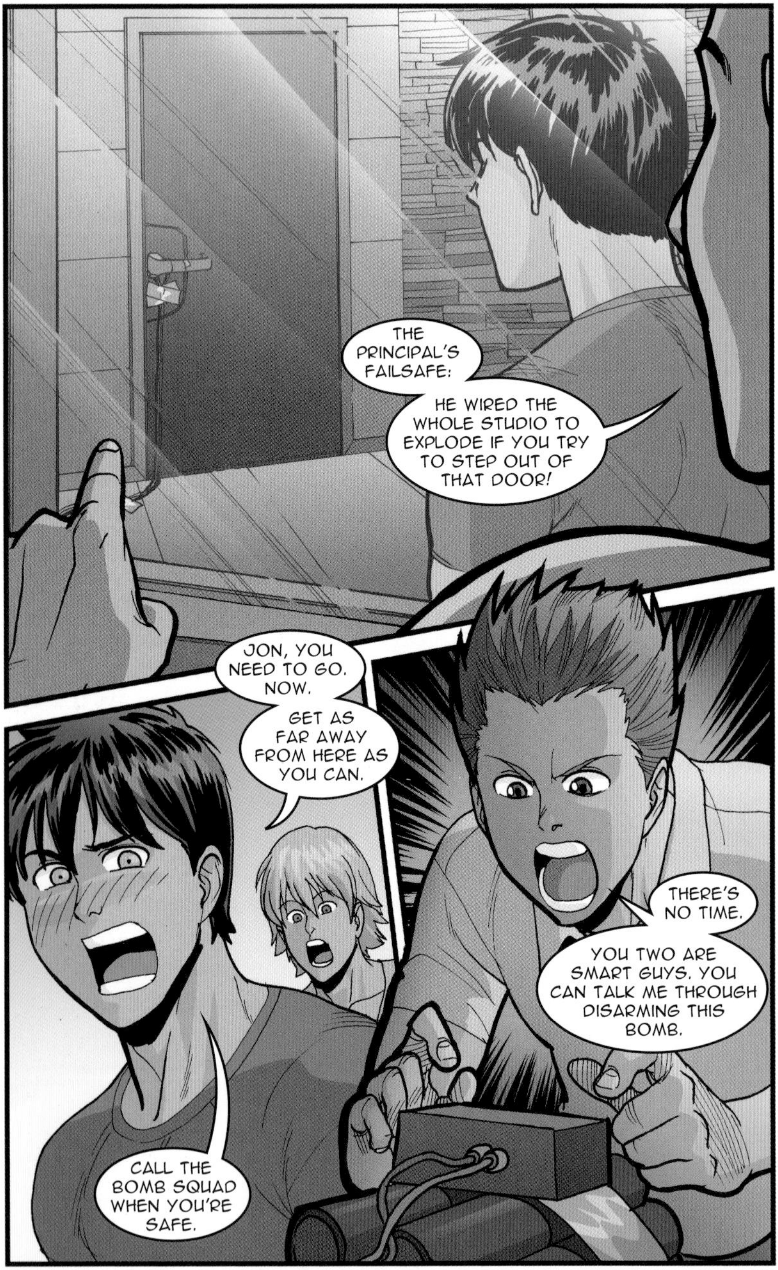
THE PRINCIPAL'S FAILSAFE:
HE WIRED THE WHOLE STUDIO TO EXPLODE IF YOU TRY TO STEP OUT OF THAT DOOR!
JON, YOU NEED TO GO. NOW.
GET AS FAR AWAY FROM HERE AS YOU CAN.
CALL THE BOMB SQUAD WHEN YOU'RE SAFE.
THERE'S NO TIME.
YOU TWO ARE SMART GUYS. YOU CAN TALK ME THROUGH DISARMING THIS BOMB.

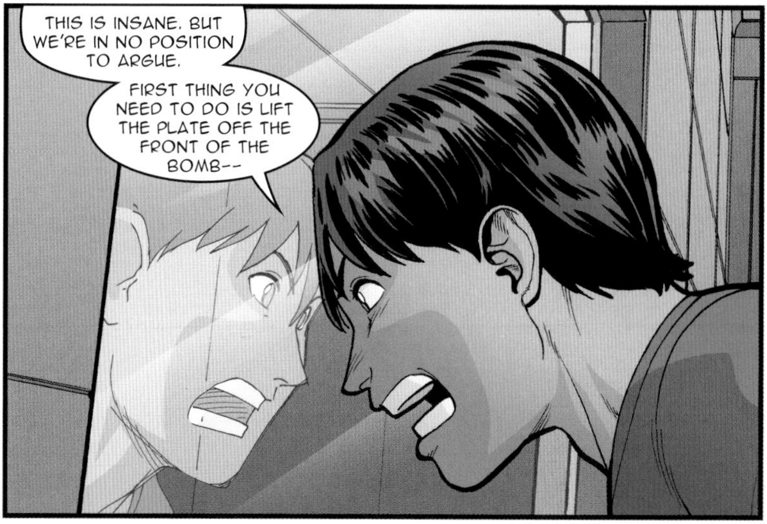
THIS IS INSANE. BUT WE'RE IN NO POSITION TO ARGUE.
FIRST THING YOU NEED TO DO IS LIFT THE PLATE OFF THE FRONT OF THE BOMB--

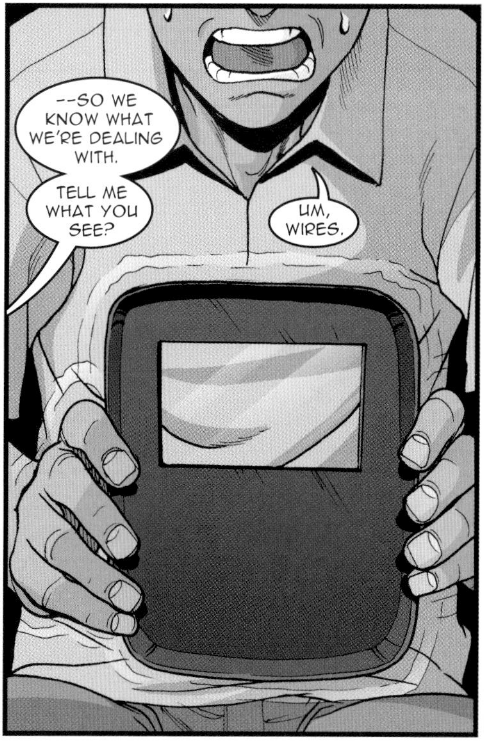
--SO WE KNOW WHAT WE'RE DEALING WITH.
TELL ME WHAT YOU SEE?
UM, WIRES.

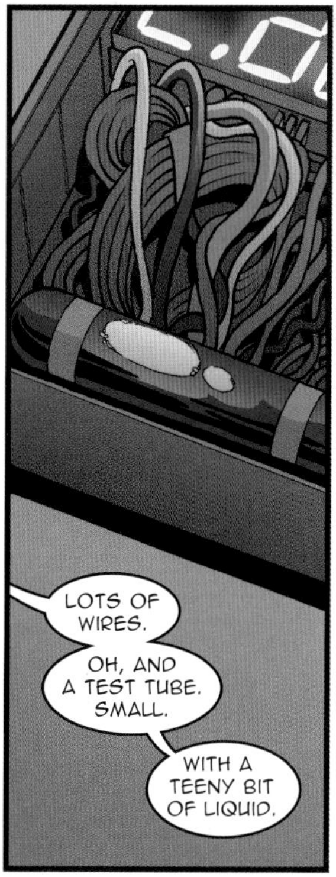
LOTS OF WIRES.
OH, AND A TEST TUBE. SMALL.
WITH A TEENY BIT OF LIQUID.

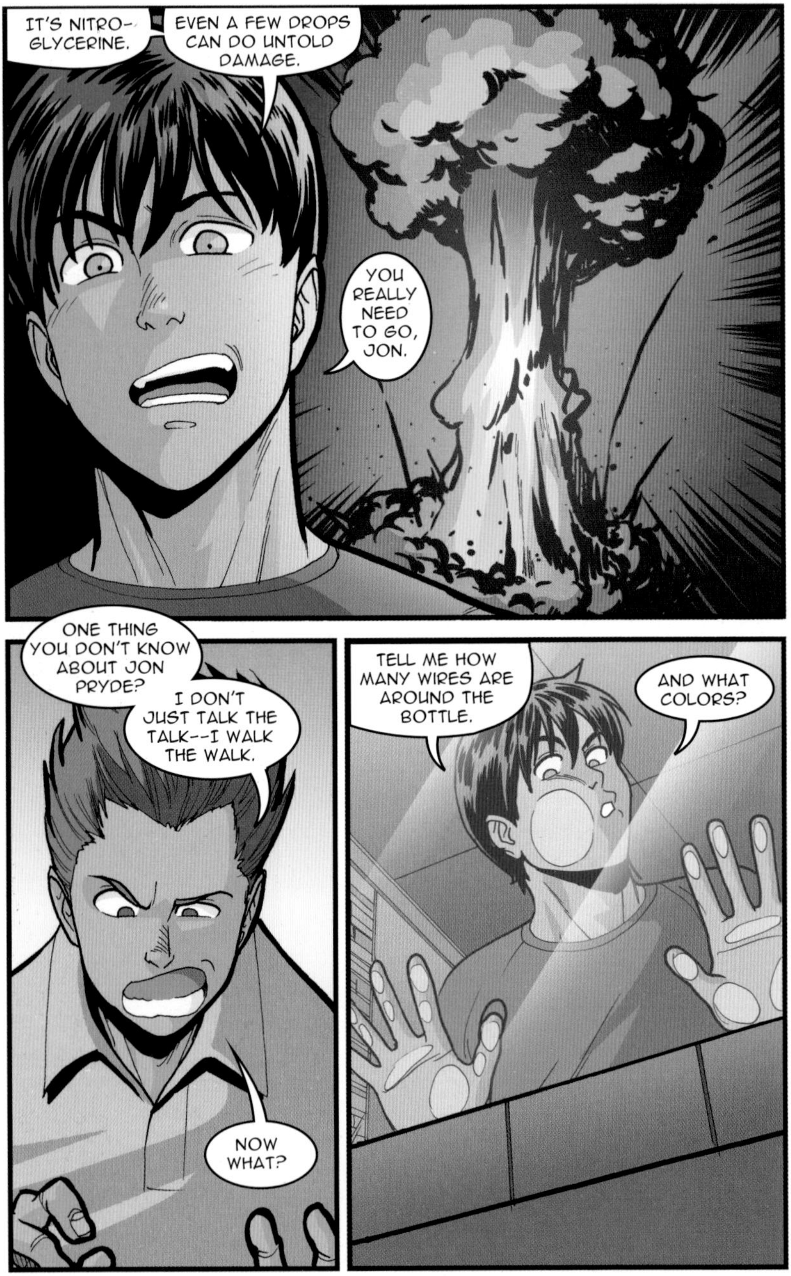

IT'S NITRO-GLYCERINE.
EVEN A FEW DROPS CAN DO UNTOLD DAMAGE.
YOU REALLY NEED TO GO, JON.
ONE THING YOU DON'T KNOW ABOUT JON PRYDE?
I DON'T JUST TALK THE TALK--I WALK THE WALK.
NOW WHAT?
TELL ME HOW MANY WIRES ARE AROUND THE BOTTLE.
AND WHAT COLORS?

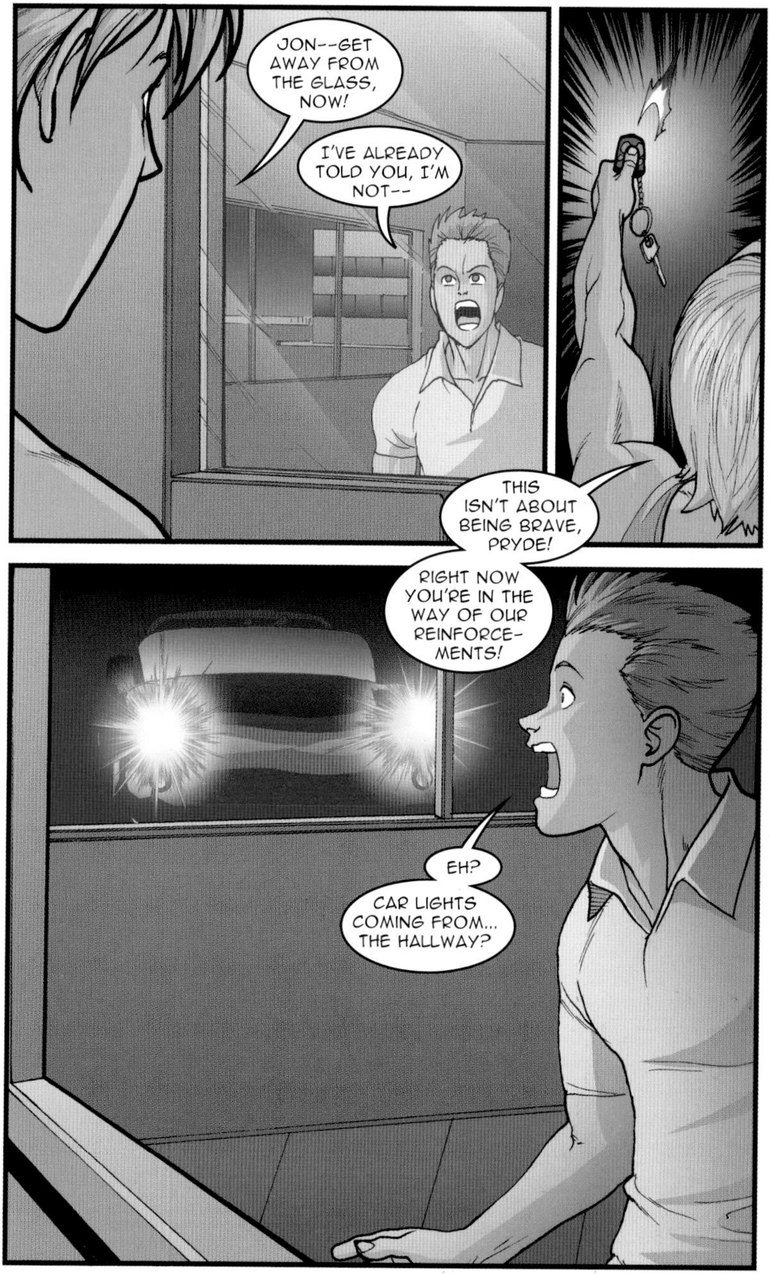
JON--GET AWAY FROM THE GLASS, NOW!
I'VE ALREADY TOLD YOU, I'M NOT--
THIS ISN'T ABOUT BEING BRAVE, PRYDE!
RIGHT NOW YOU'RE IN THE WAY OF OUR REINFORCE-MENTS!
EH?
CAR LIGHTS COMING FROM... THE HALLWAY?

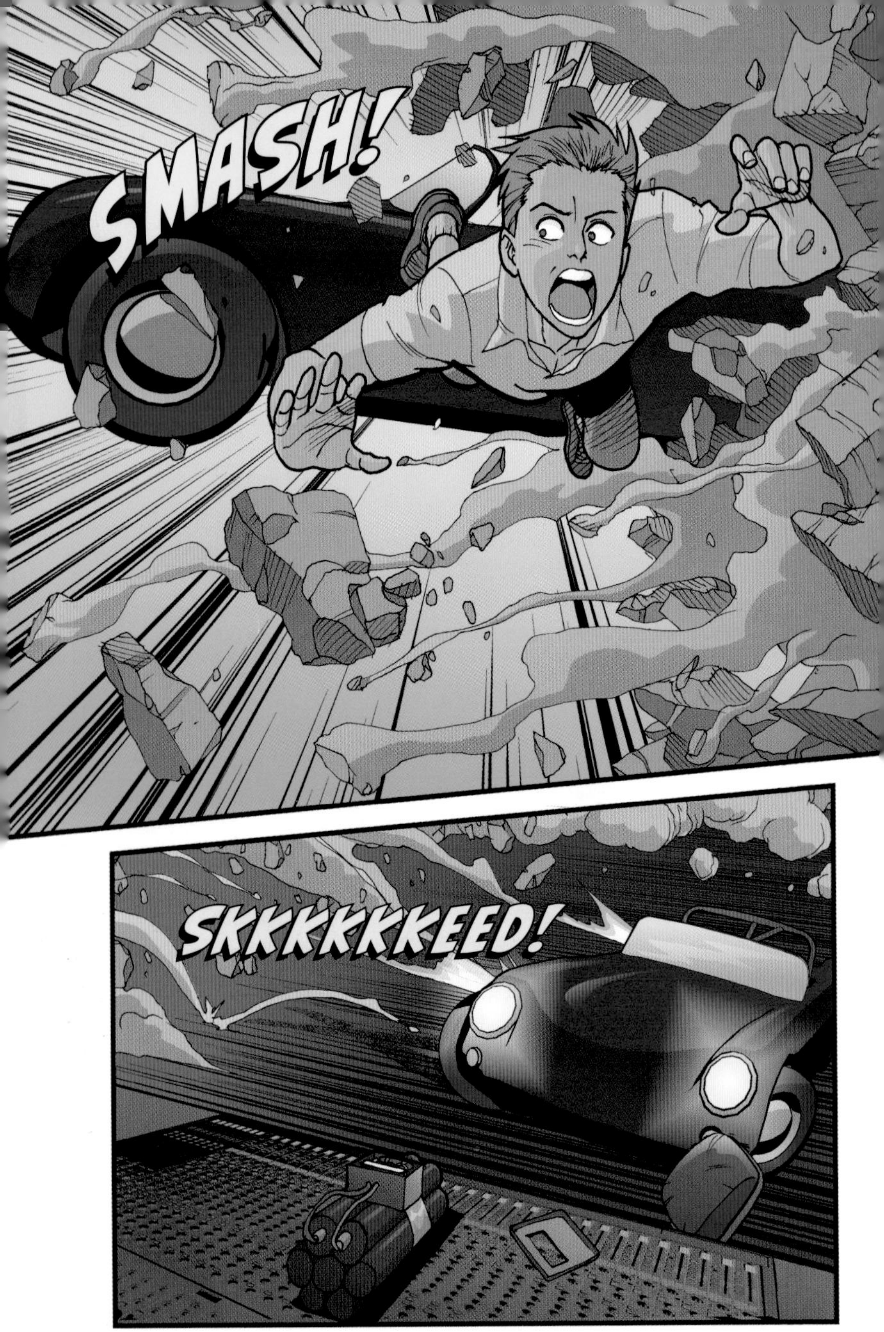
SMASH!
SKKKKKKEED!

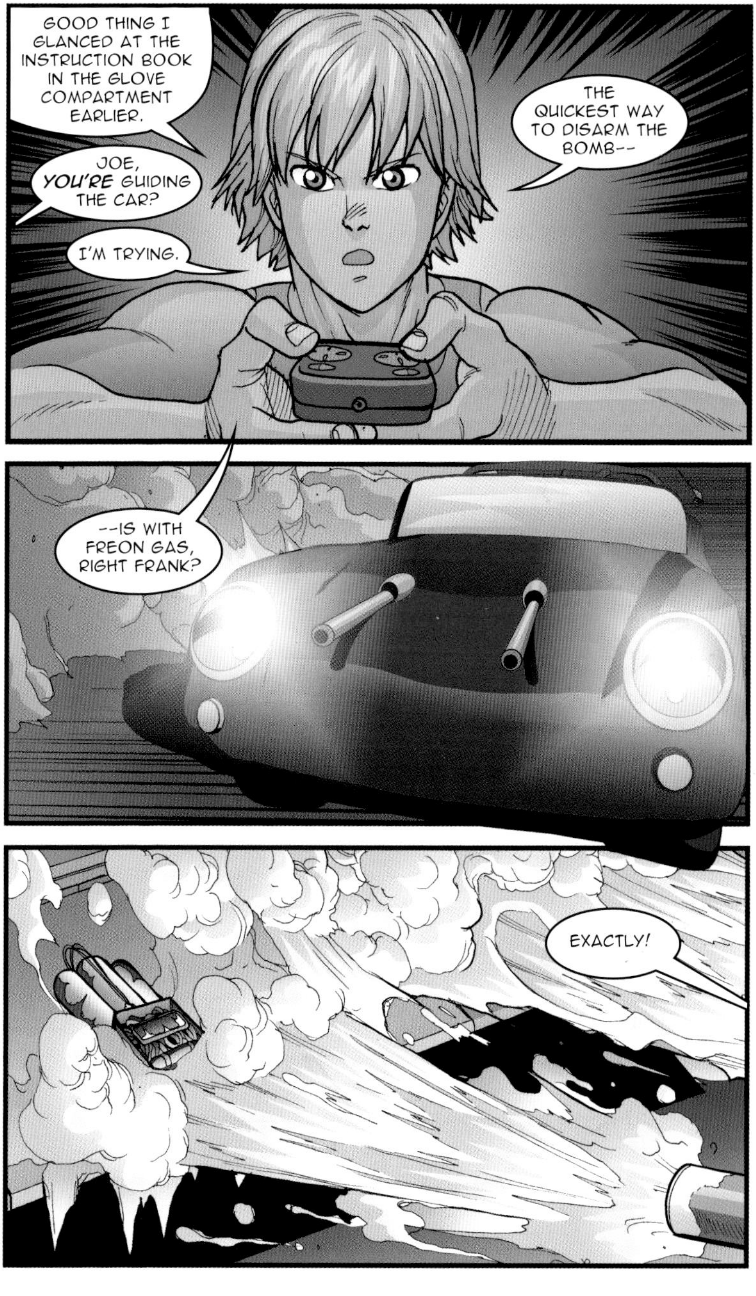
GOOD THING I GLANCED AT THE INSTRUCTION BOOK IN THE GLOVE COMPARTMENT EARLIER.
THE QUICKEST WAY TO DISARM THE BOMB--
JOE, YOU'RE GUIDING THE CAR?
I'M TRYING.
--IS WITH FREON GAS, RIGHT FRANK?
EXACTLY!

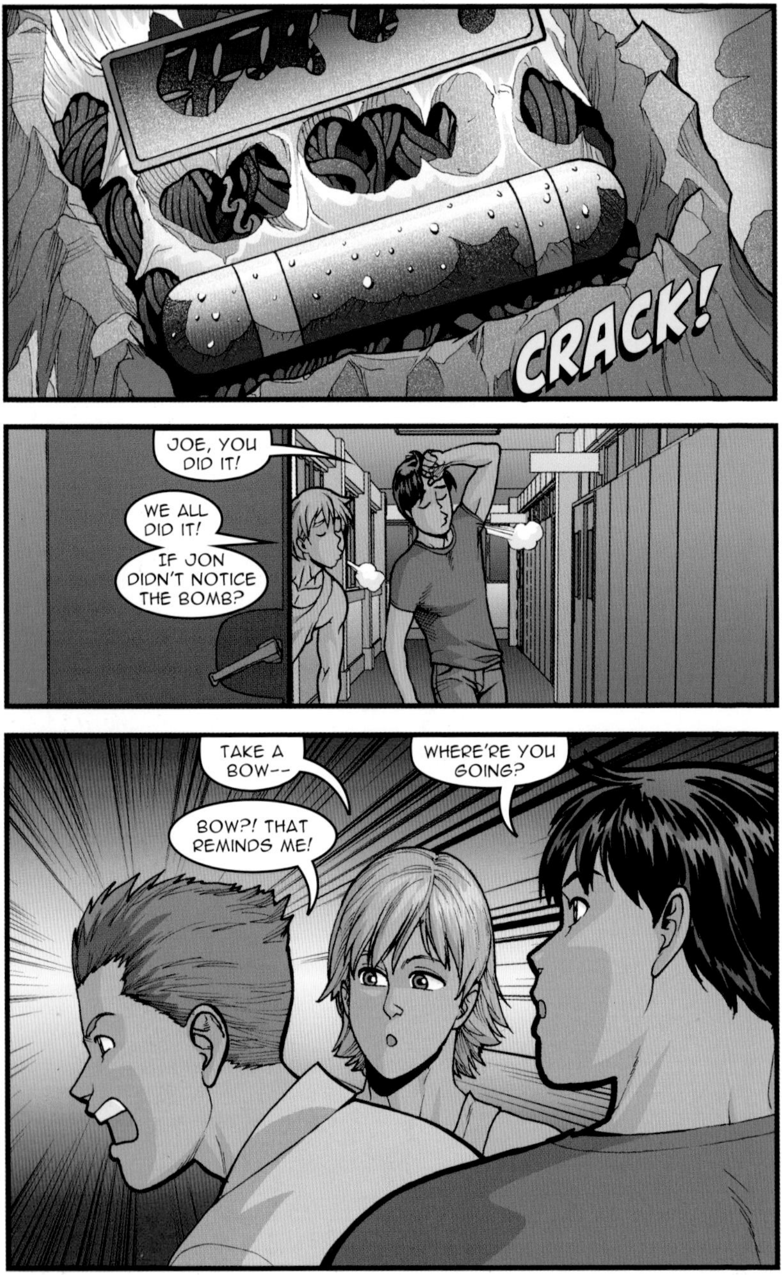
CRACK!
JOE, YOU DID IT!
WE ALL DID IT!
IF JON DIDN'T NOTICE THE BOMB?
TAKE A BOW--
WHERE'RE YOU GOING?
BOW?! THAT REMINDS ME!

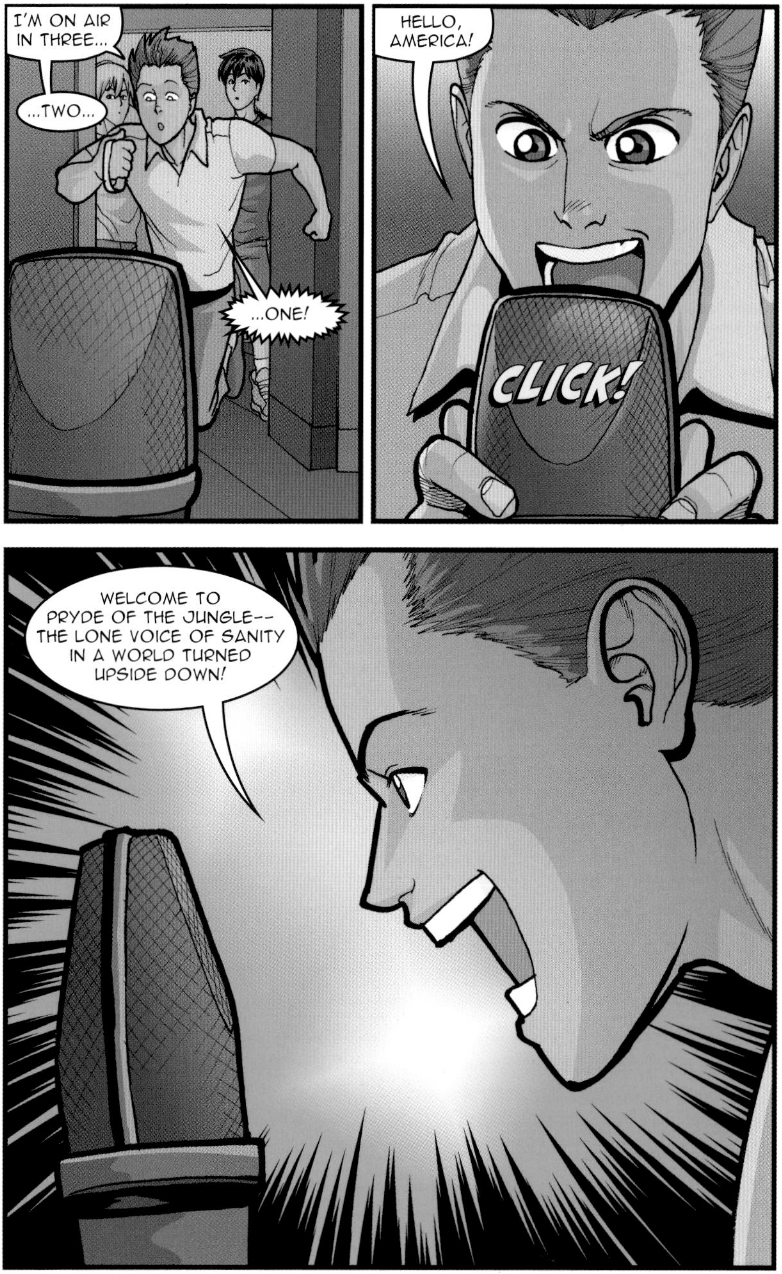
I'M ON AIR IN THREE...
...TWO...
...ONE!
HELLO, AMERICA!
CLICK!
WELCOME TO PRYDE OF THE JUNGLE-- THE LONE VOICE OF SANITY IN A WORLD TURNED UPSIDE DOWN!

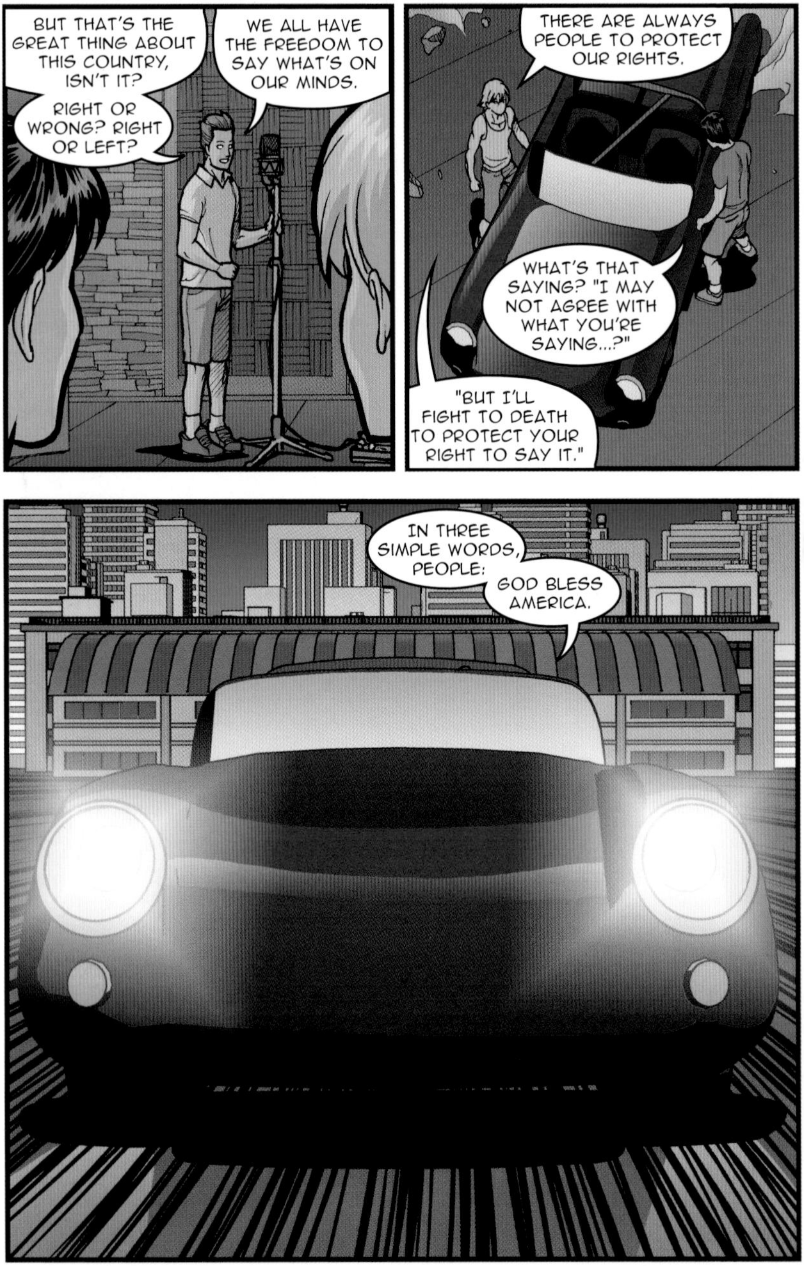
BUT THAT'S THE GREAT THING ABOUT THIS COUNTRY, ISN'T IT?
RIGHT OR WRONG? RIGHT OR LEFT?
WE ALL HAVE THE FREEDOM TO SAY WHAT'S ON OUR MINDS.
THERE ARE ALWAYS PEOPLE TO PROTECT OUR RIGHTS.
WHAT'S THAT SAYING? "I MAY NOT AGREE WITH WHAT YOU'RE SAYING...?"
"BUT I'LL FIGHT TO DEATH TO PROTECT YOUR RIGHT TO SAY IT."
IN THREE SIMPLE WORDS, PEOPLE:
GOD BLESS AMERICA.

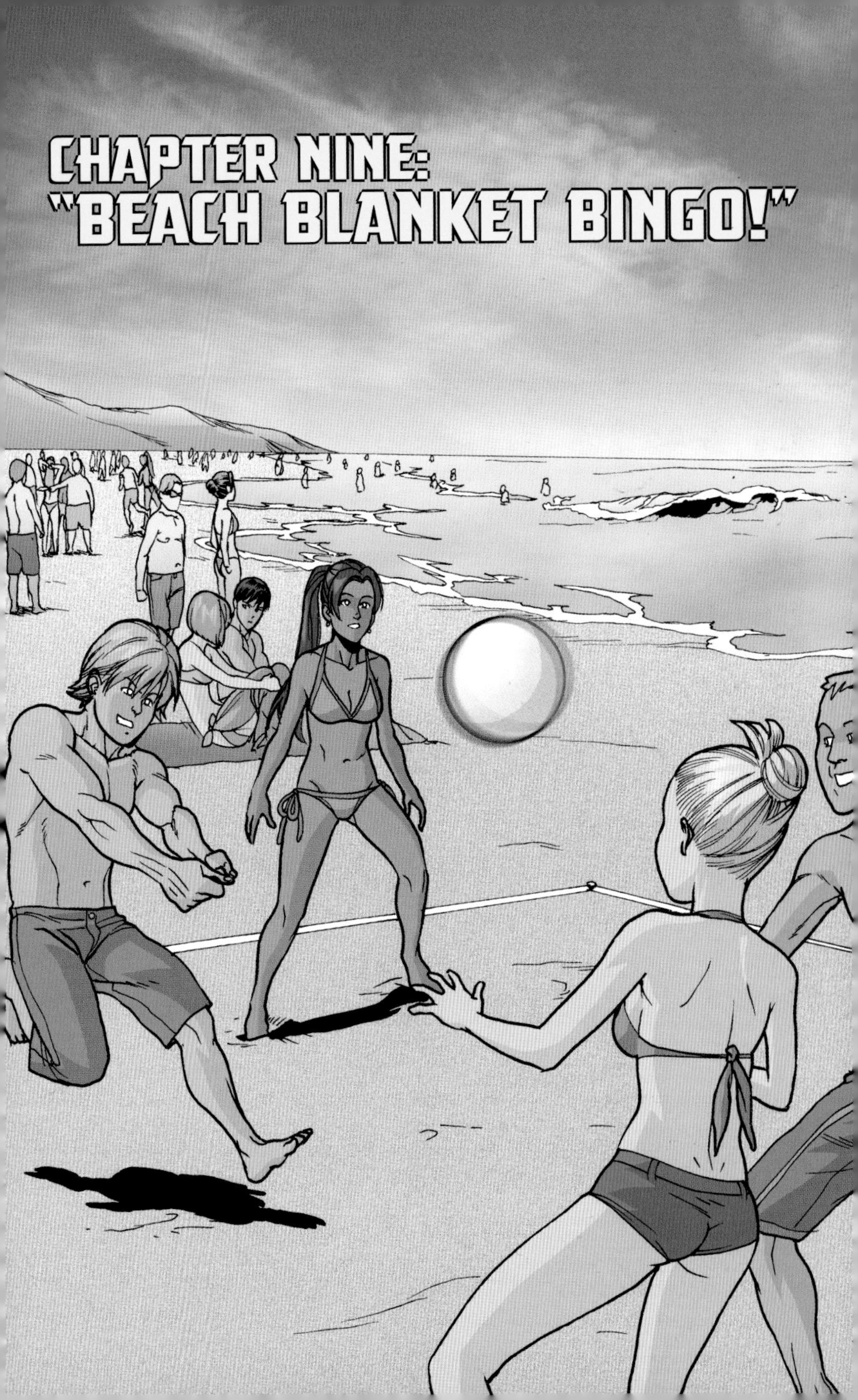
CHAPTER NINE:
"BEACH BLANKET BINGO!"

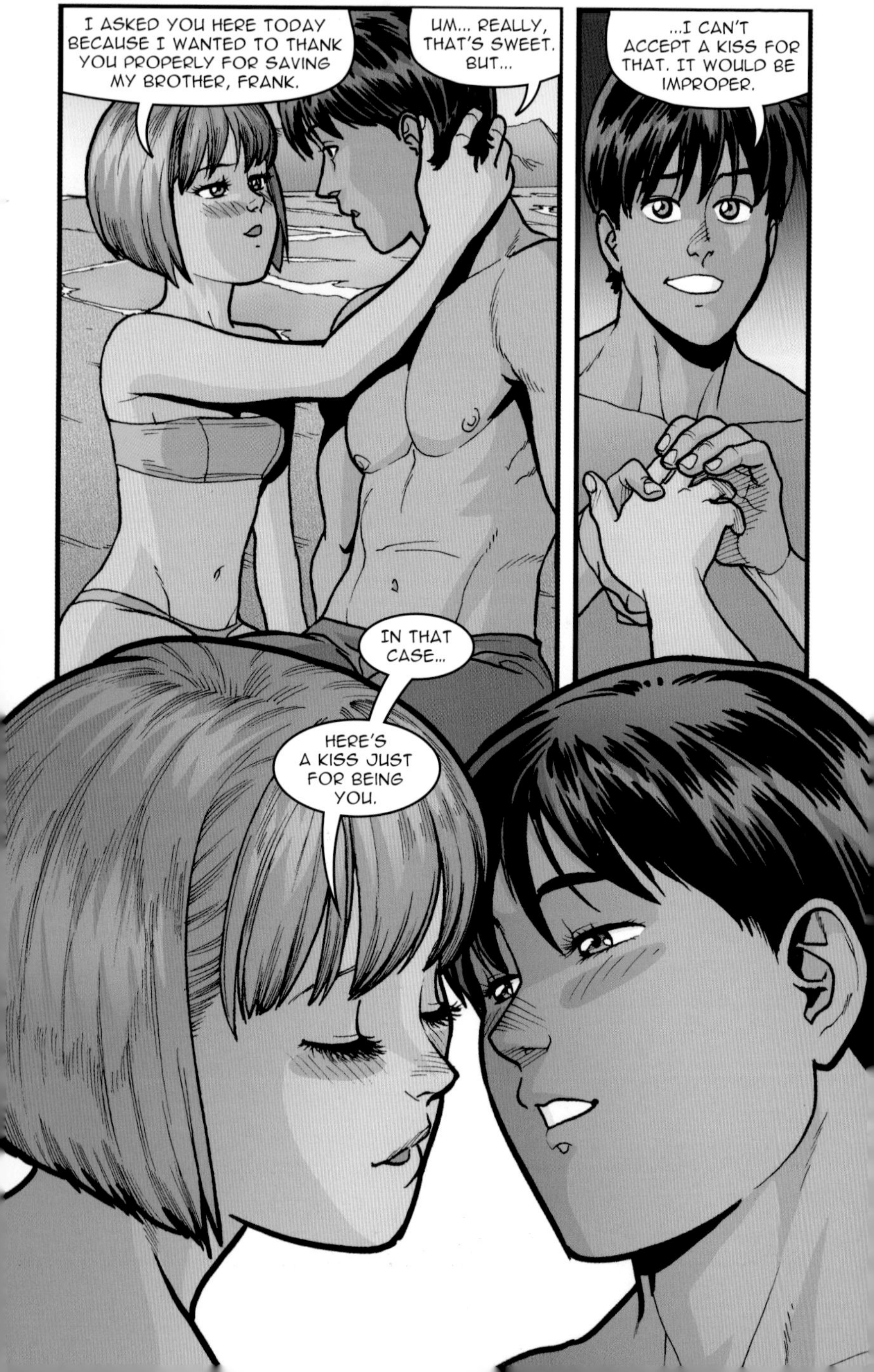
I ASKED YOU HERE TODAY BECAUSE I WANTED TO THANK YOU PROPERLY FOR SAVING MY BROTHER, FRANK.
UM... REALLY, THAT'S SWEET. BUT...
...I CAN'T ACCEPT A KISS FOR THAT. IT WOULD BE IMPROPER.
IN THAT CASE...
HERE'S A KISS JUST FOR BEING YOU.

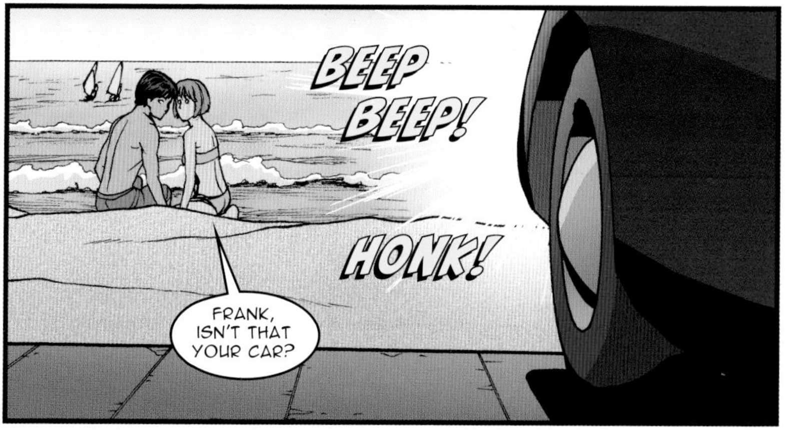
BEEP BEEP!
HONK!
FRANK, ISN'T THAT YOUR CAR?

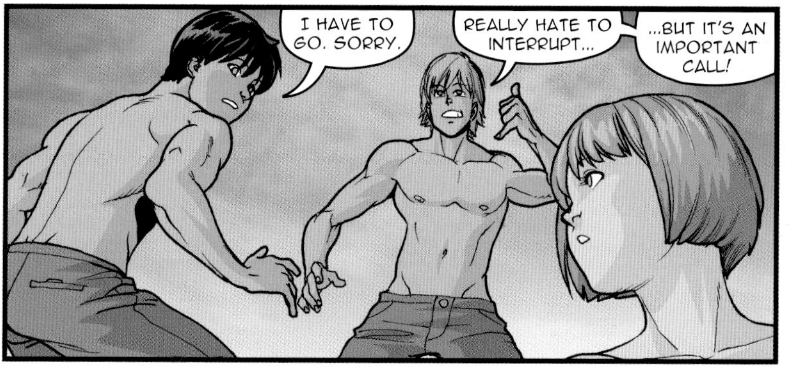
I HAVE TO GO. SORRY.
REALLY HATE TO INTERRUPT...
...BUT IT'S AN IMPORTANT CALL!

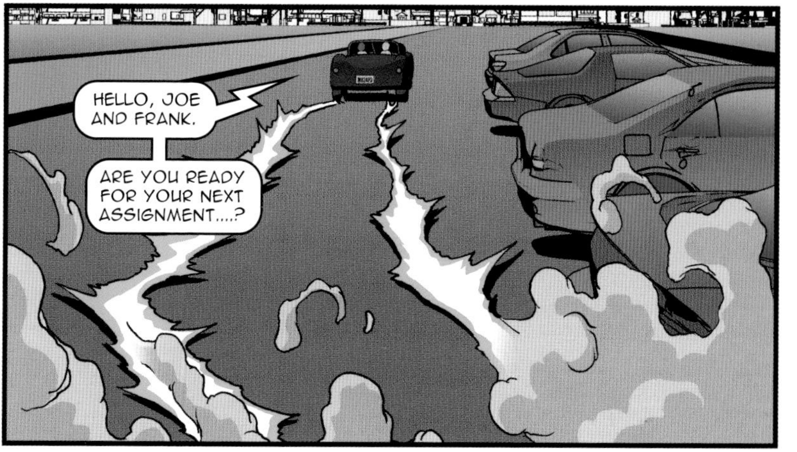
HELLO, JOE AND FRANK.
ARE YOU READY FOR YOUR NEXT ASSIGNMENT....?

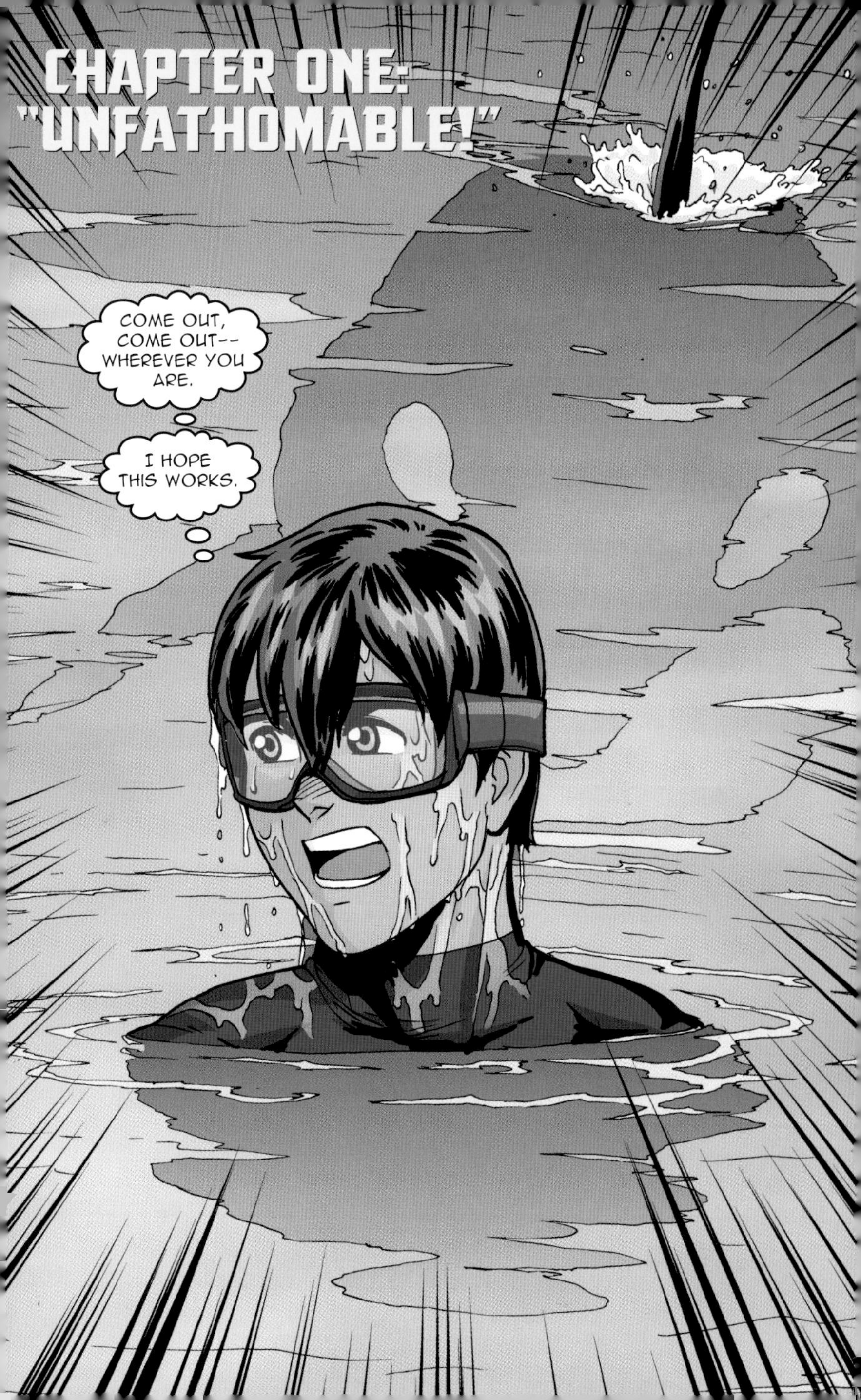
CHAPTER ONE:
"UNFATHOMABLE!"
COME OUT, COME OUT-- WHEREVER YOU ARE.
I HOPE THIS WORKS.

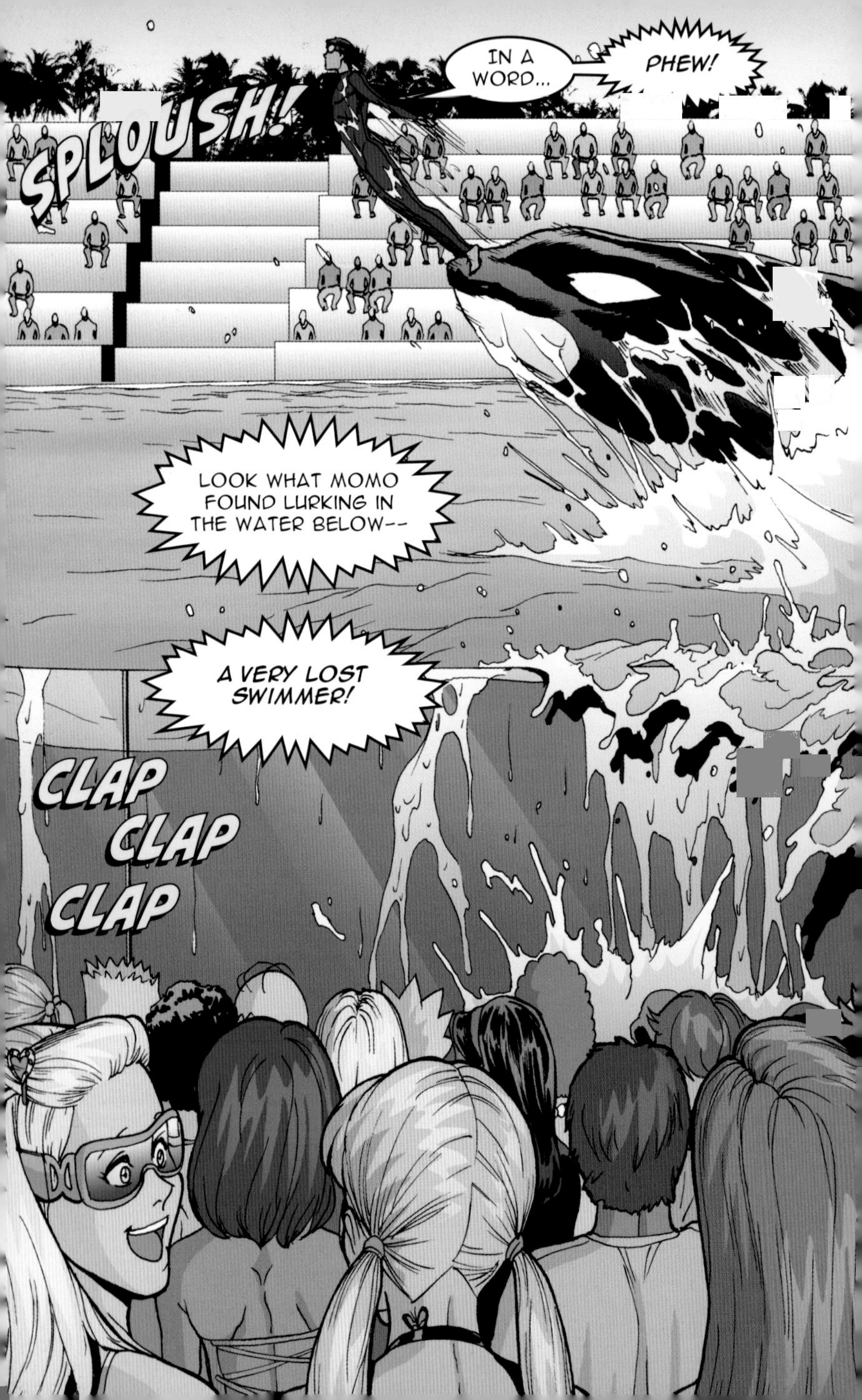
SPLOUSH!
IN A WORD...
PHEW!
LOOK WHAT MOMO FOUND LURKING IN THE WATER BELOW--
A VERY LOST SWIMMER!
CLAP
CLAP
CLAP

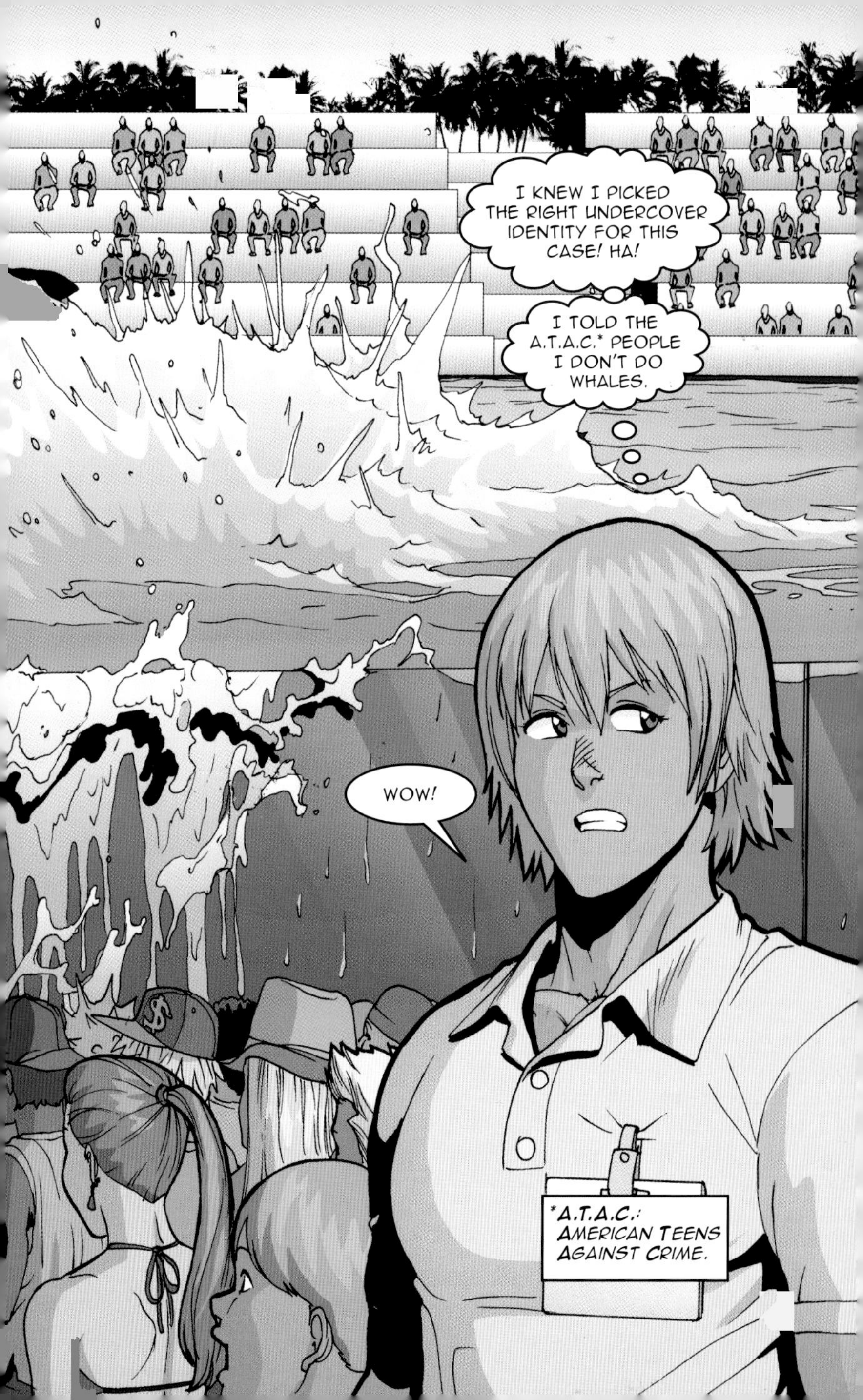
I KNEW I PICKED THE RIGHT UNDERCOVER IDENTITY FOR THIS CASE! HA!
I TOLD THE A.T.A.C.* PEOPLE I DON'T DO WHALES.
WOW!
*A.T.A.C.: AMERICAN TEENS AGAINST CRIME.

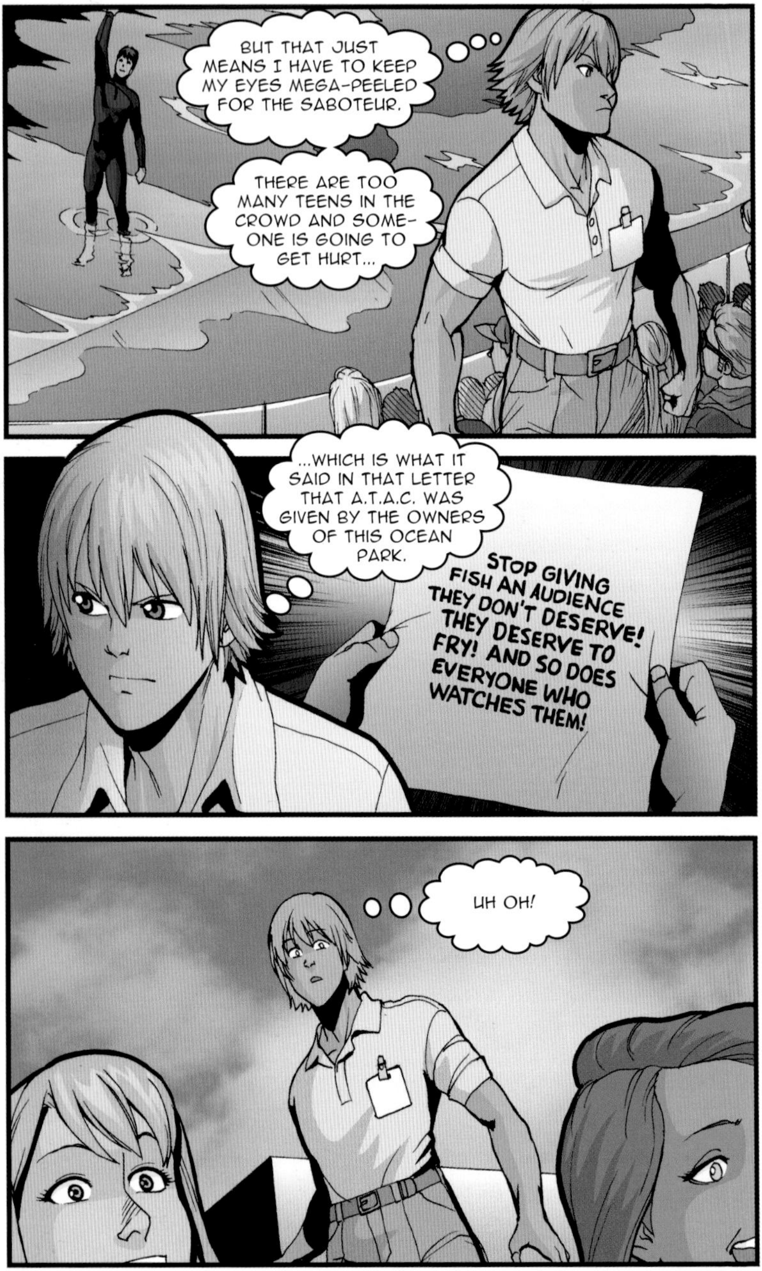
BUT THAT JUST MEANS I HAVE TO KEEP MY EYES MEGA-PEELED FOR THE SABOTEUR.
THERE ARE TOO MANY TEENS IN THE CROWD AND SOME-ONE IS GOING TO GET HURT...
...WHICH IS WHAT IT SAID IN THAT LETTER THAT A.T.A.C. WAS GIVEN BY THE OWNERS OF THIS OCEAN PARK.
STOP GIVING FISH AN AUDIENCE THEY DON'T DESERVE! THEY DESERVE TO FRY! AND SO DOES EVERYONE WHO WATCHES THEM!
UH OH!

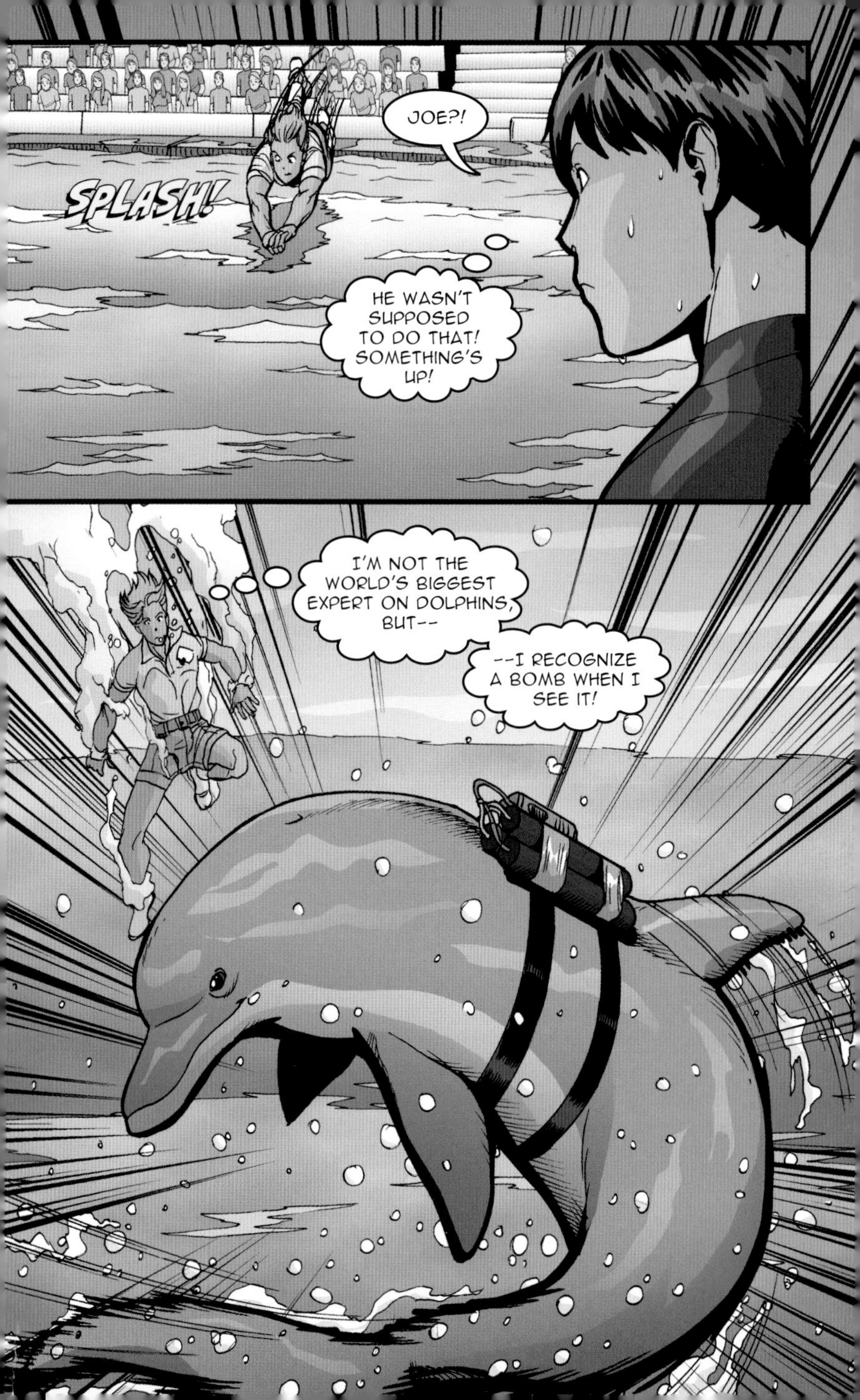

SPLASH!
JOE?!
HE WASN'T SUPPOSED TO DO THAT! SOMETHING'S UP!
I'M NOT THE WORLD'S BIGGEST EXPERT ON DOLPHINS, BUT--
--I RECOGNIZE A BOMB WHEN I SEE IT!

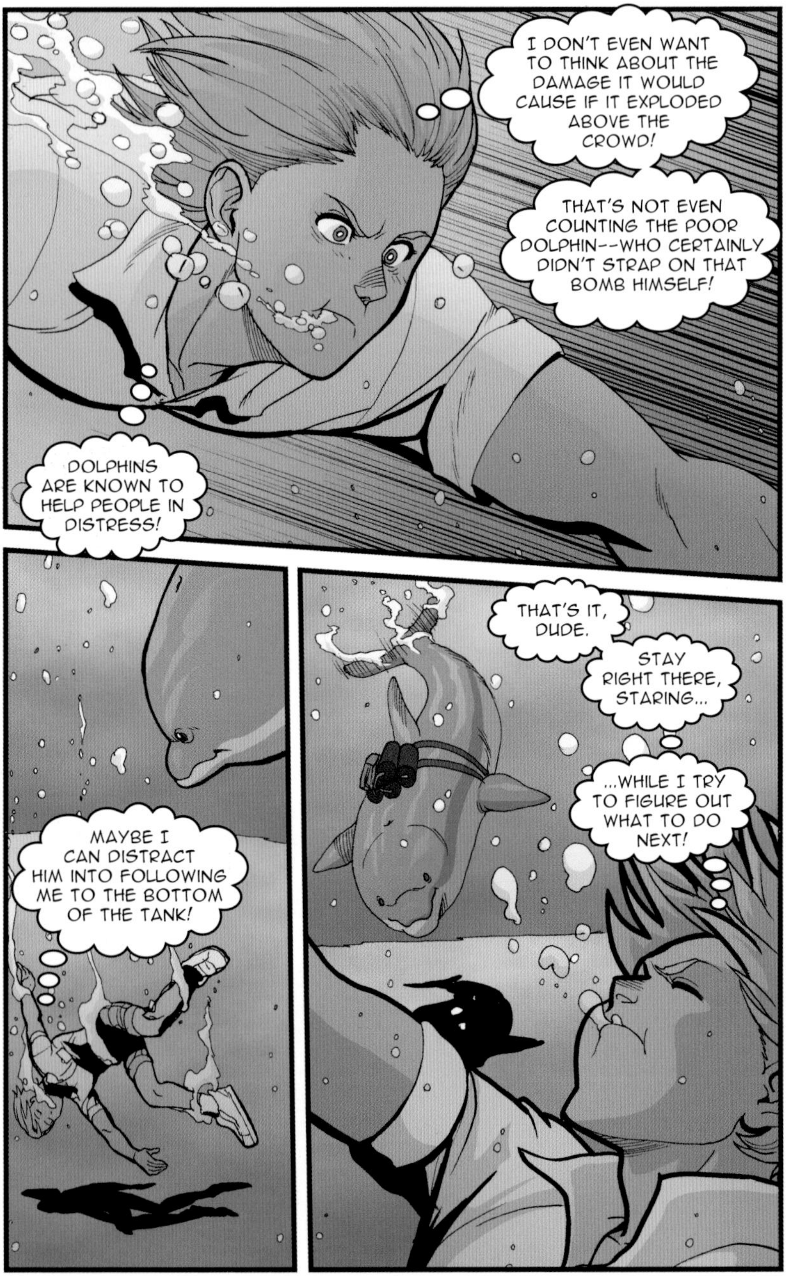
I DON'T EVEN WANT TO THINK ABOUT THE DAMAGE IT WOULD CAUSE IF IT EXPLODED ABOVE THE CROWD!
THAT'S NOT EVEN COUNTING THE POOR DOLPHIN--WHO CERTAINLY DIDN'T STRAP ON THAT BOMB HIMSELF!
DOLPHINS ARE KNOWN TO HELP PEOPLE IN DISTRESS!
MAYBE I CAN DISTRACT HIM INTO FOLLOWING ME TO THE BOTTOM OF THE TANK!
THAT'S IT, DUDE.
STAY RIGHT THERE, STARING...
...WHILE I TRY TO FIGURE OUT WHAT TO DO NEXT!

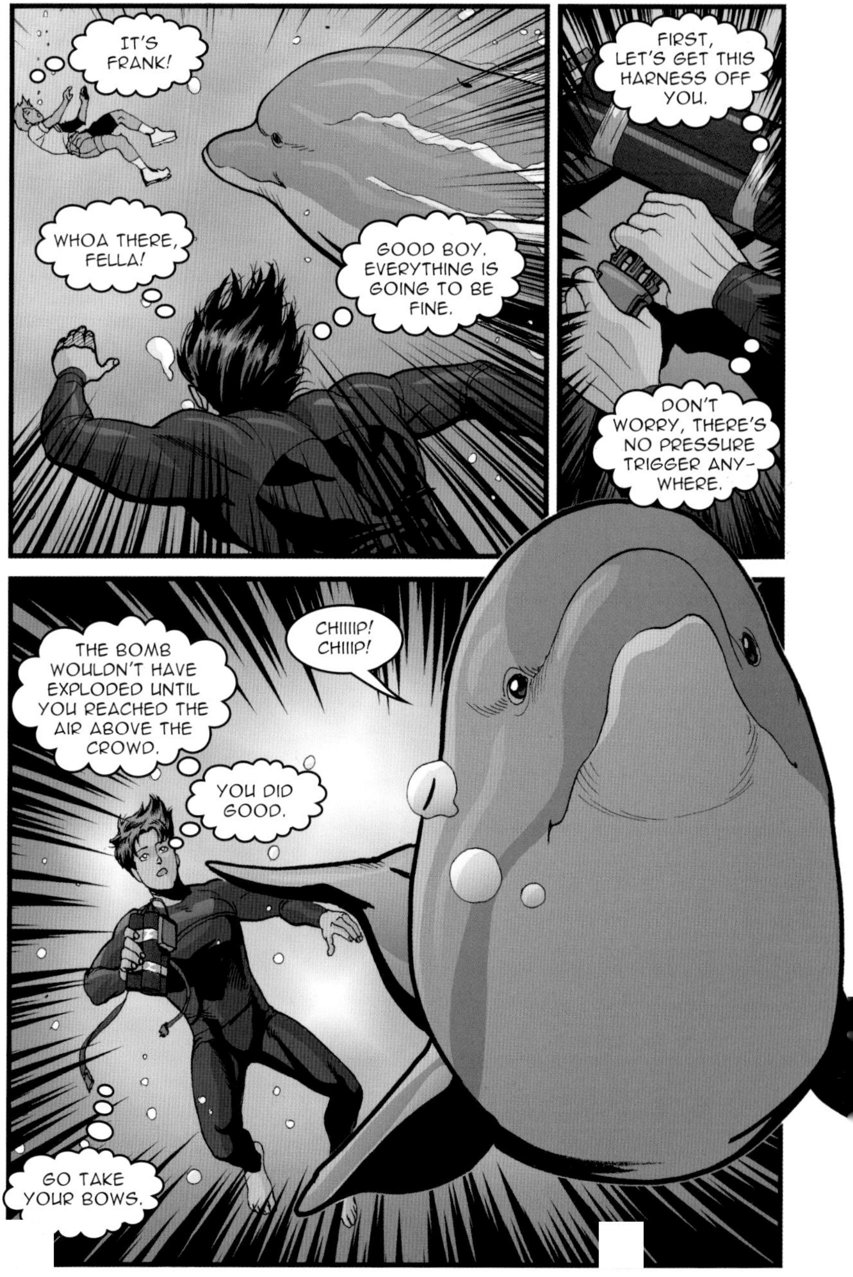
IT'S FRANK!
WHOA THERE, FELLA!
GOOD BOY. EVERYTHING IS GOING TO BE FINE.
FIRST, LET'S GET THIS HARNESS OFF YOU.
DON'T WORRY, THERE'S NO PRESSURE TRIGGER ANY-WHERE.
THE BOMB WOULDN'T HAVE EXPLODED UNTIL YOU REACHED THE AIR ABOVE THE CROWD.
CHIIIIP! CHIIIP!
YOU DID GOOD.
GO TAKE YOUR BOWS.

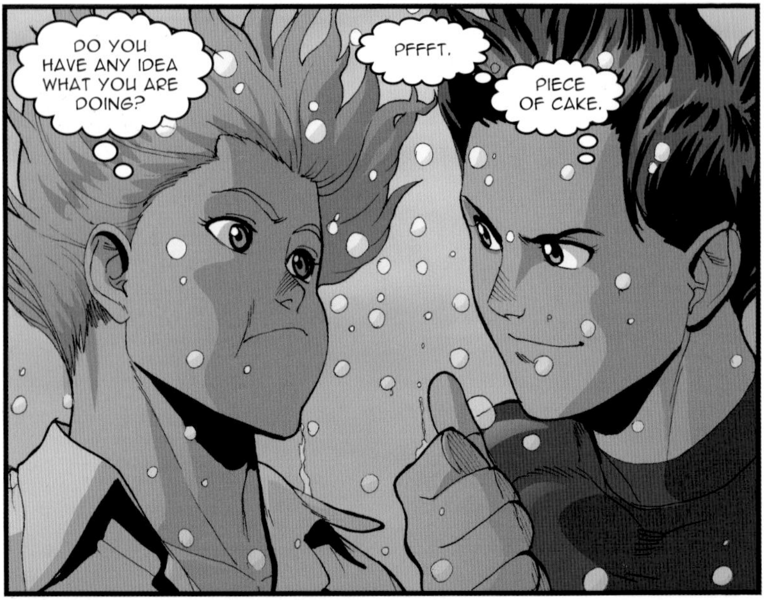
DO YOU HAVE ANY IDEA WHAT YOU ARE DOING?
PFFFT.
PIECE OF CAKE.

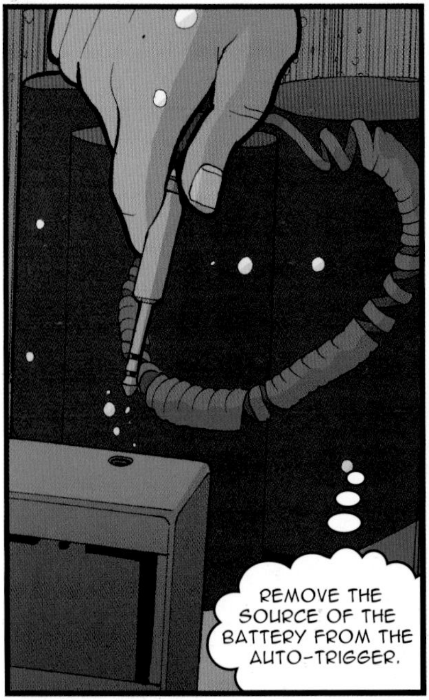
REMOVE THE SOURCE OF THE BATTERY FROM THE AUTO-TRIGGER.

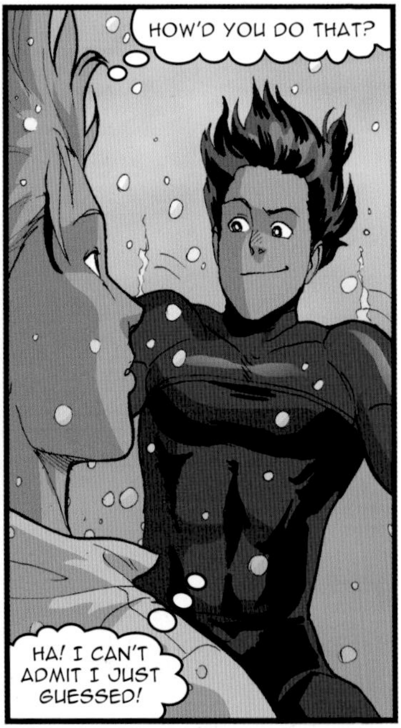
HOW'D YOU DO THAT?
HA! I CAN'T ADMIT I JUST GUESSED!

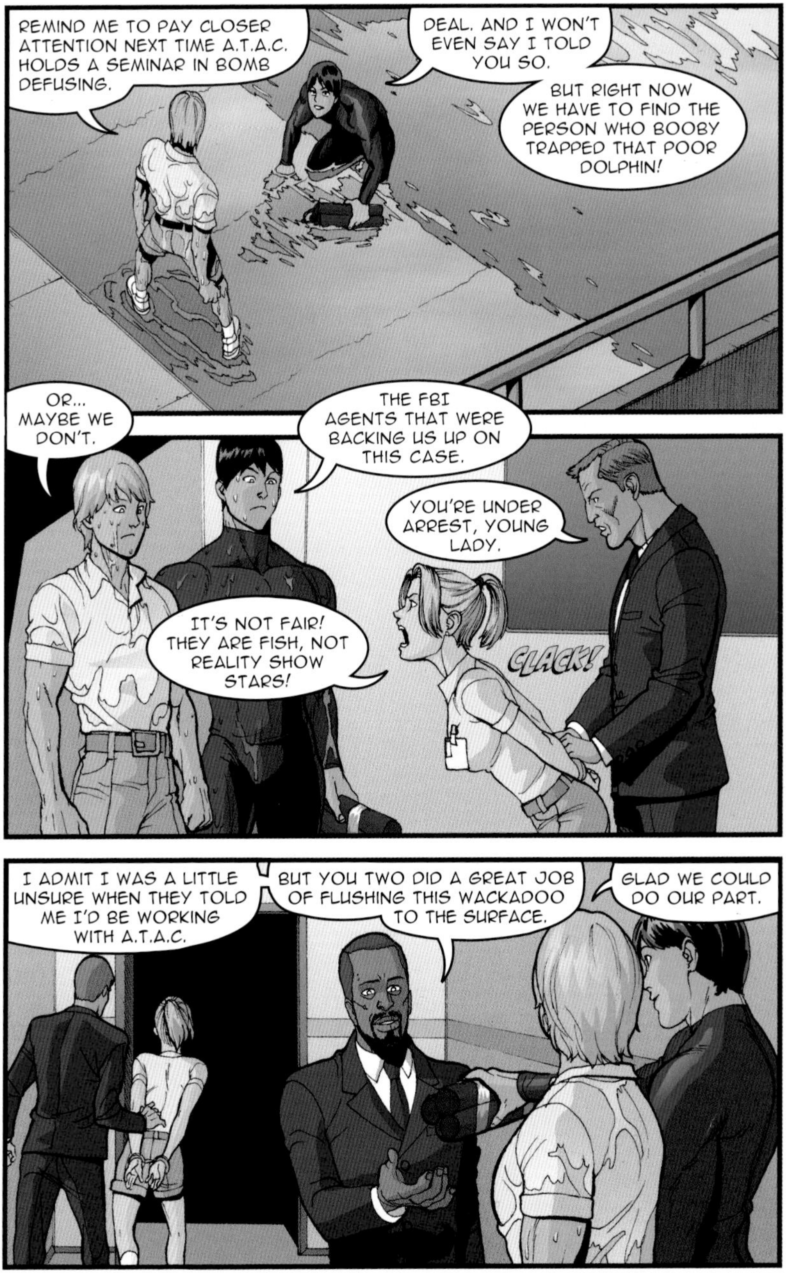
REMIND ME TO PAY CLOSER ATTENTION NEXT TIME A.T.A.C. HOLDS A SEMINAR IN BOMB DEFUSING.
DEAL. AND I WON'T EVEN SAY I TOLD YOU SO.
BUT RIGHT NOW WE HAVE TO FIND THE PERSON WHO BOOBY TRAPPED THAT POOR DOLPHIN!
OR... MAYBE WE DON'T.
THE FBI AGENTS THAT WERE BACKING US UP ON THIS CASE.
YOU'RE UNDER ARREST, YOUNG LADY.
IT'S NOT FAIR! THEY ARE FISH, NOT REALITY SHOW STARS!
CLACK!
I ADMIT I WAS A LITTLE UNSURE WHEN THEY TOLD ME I'D BE WORKING WITH A.T.A.C.
BUT YOU TWO DID A GREAT JOB OF FLUSHING THIS WACKADOO TO THE SURFACE.
GLAD WE COULD DO OUR PART.

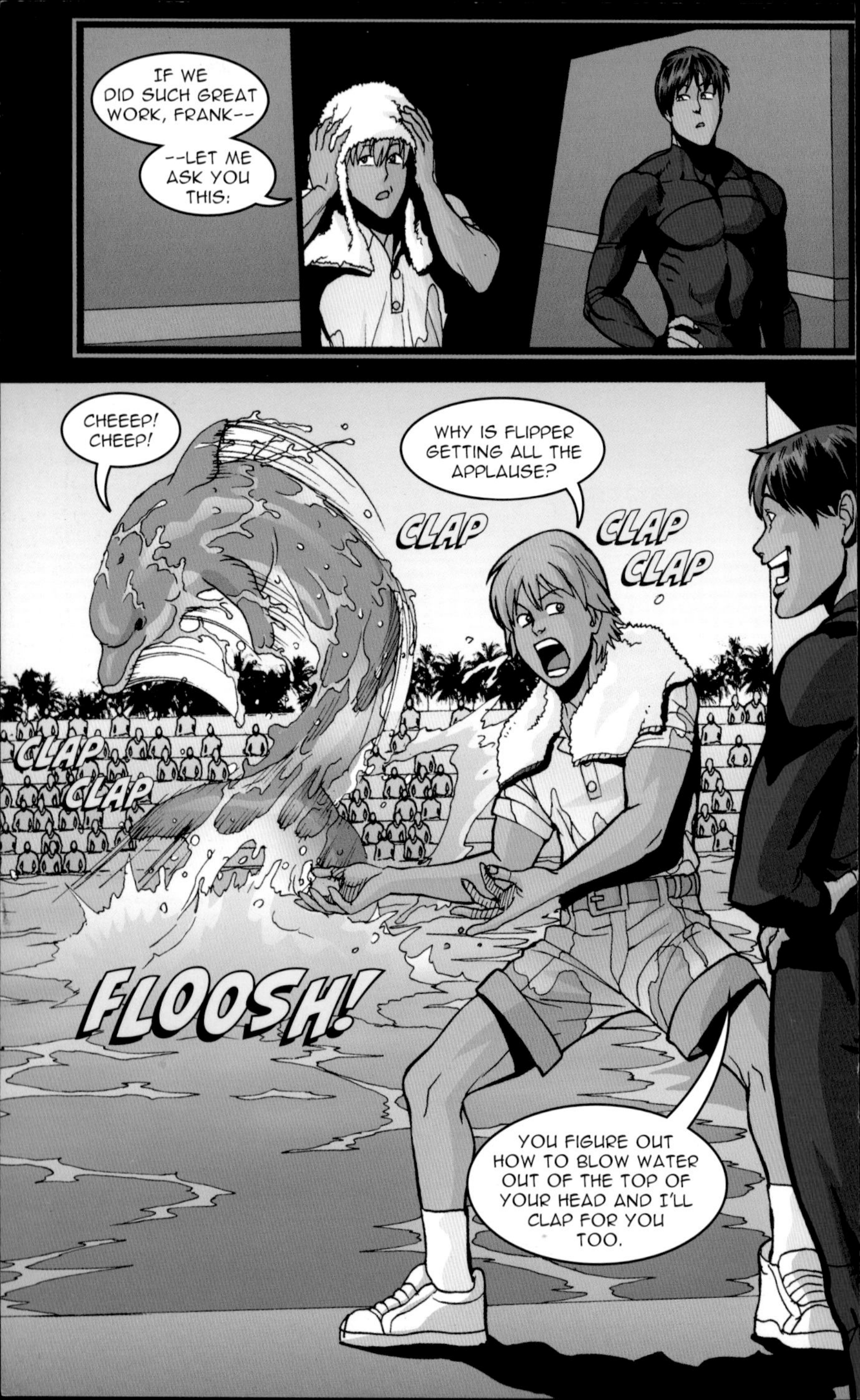
IF WE DID SUCH GREAT WORK, FRANK--
--LET ME ASK YOU THIS:
CHEEEP! CHEEP!
WHY IS FLIPPER GETTING ALL THE APPLAUSE?
CLAP
CLAP
CLAP
CLAP
CLAP
FLOOSH!
YOU FIGURE OUT HOW TO BLOW WATER OUT OF THE TOP OF YOUR HEAD AND I'LL CLAP FOR YOU TOO.

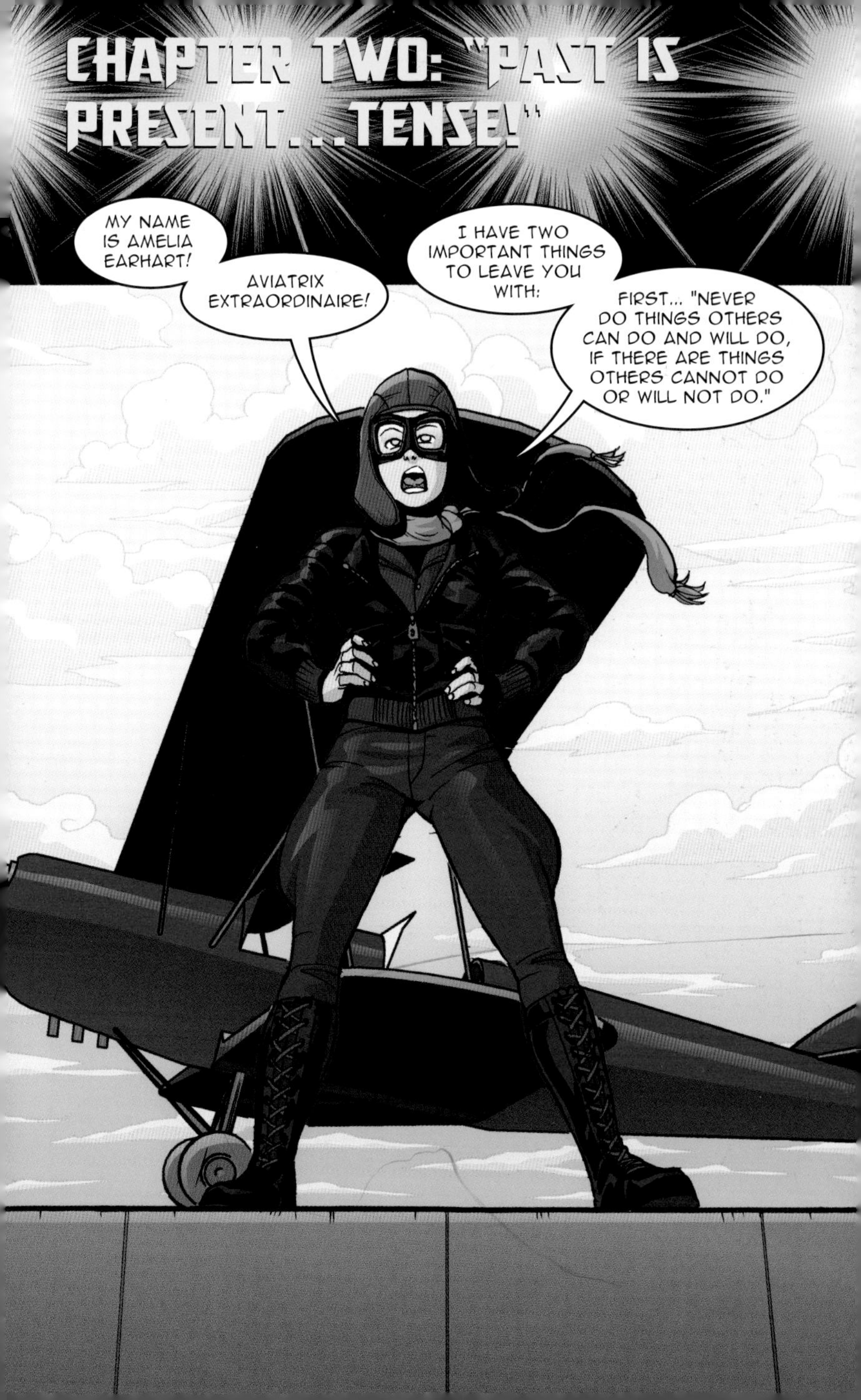
CHAPTER TWO: "PAST IS PRESENT...TENSE!"
MY NAME IS AMELIA EARHART!
AVIATRIX EXTRAORDINAIRE!
I HAVE TWO IMPORTANT THINGS TO LEAVE YOU WITH:
FIRST... "NEVER DO THINGS OTHERS CAN DO AND WILL DO, IF THERE ARE THINGS OTHERS CANNOT DO OR WILL NOT DO."

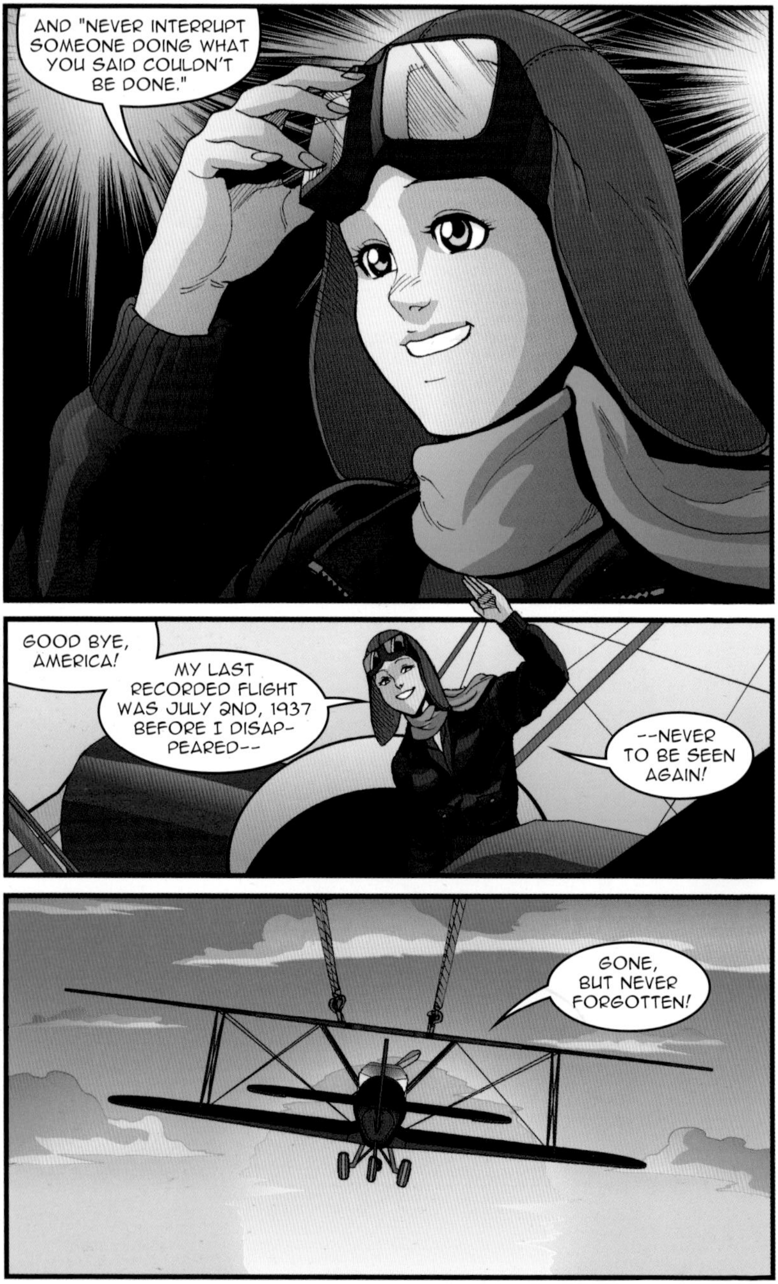
AND "NEVER INTERRUPT SOMEONE DOING WHAT YOU SAID COULDN'T BE DONE."
GOOD BYE, AMERICA!
MY LAST RECORDED FLIGHT WAS JULY 2ND, 1937 BEFORE I DISAP-PEARED--
--NEVER TO BE SEEN AGAIN!
GONE, BUT NEVER FORGOTTEN!

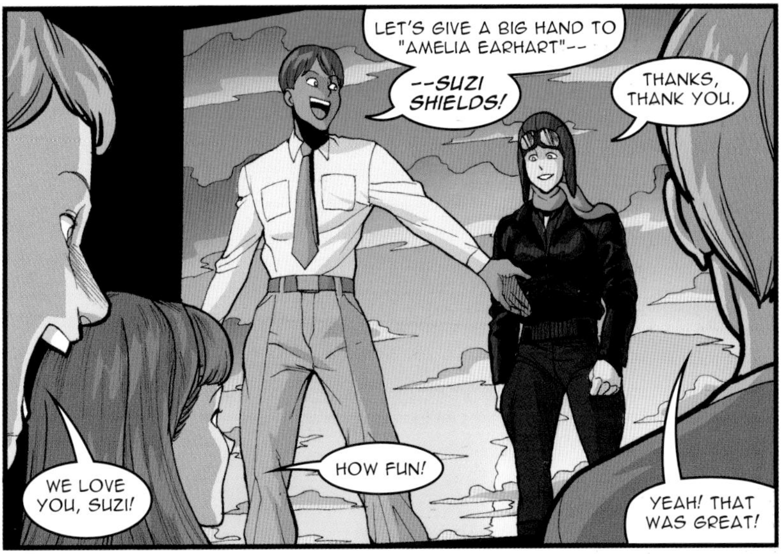
LET'S GIVE A BIG HAND TO "AMELIA EARHART"--
--SUZI SHIELDS!
THANKS, THANK YOU.
WE LOVE YOU, SUZI!
HOW FUN!
YEAH! THAT WAS GREAT!

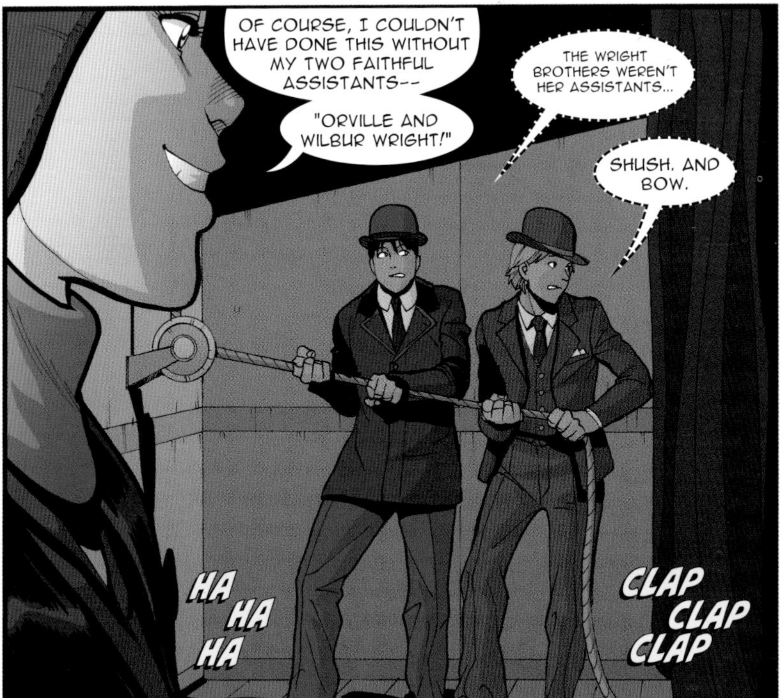
OF COURSE, I COULDN'T HAVE DONE THIS WITHOUT MY TWO FAITHFUL ASSISTANTS--
"ORVILLE AND WILBUR WRIGHT!"
THE WRIGHT BROTHERS WEREN'T HER ASSISTANTS...
SHUSH. AND BOW.
HA HA HA
CLAP CLAP CLAP

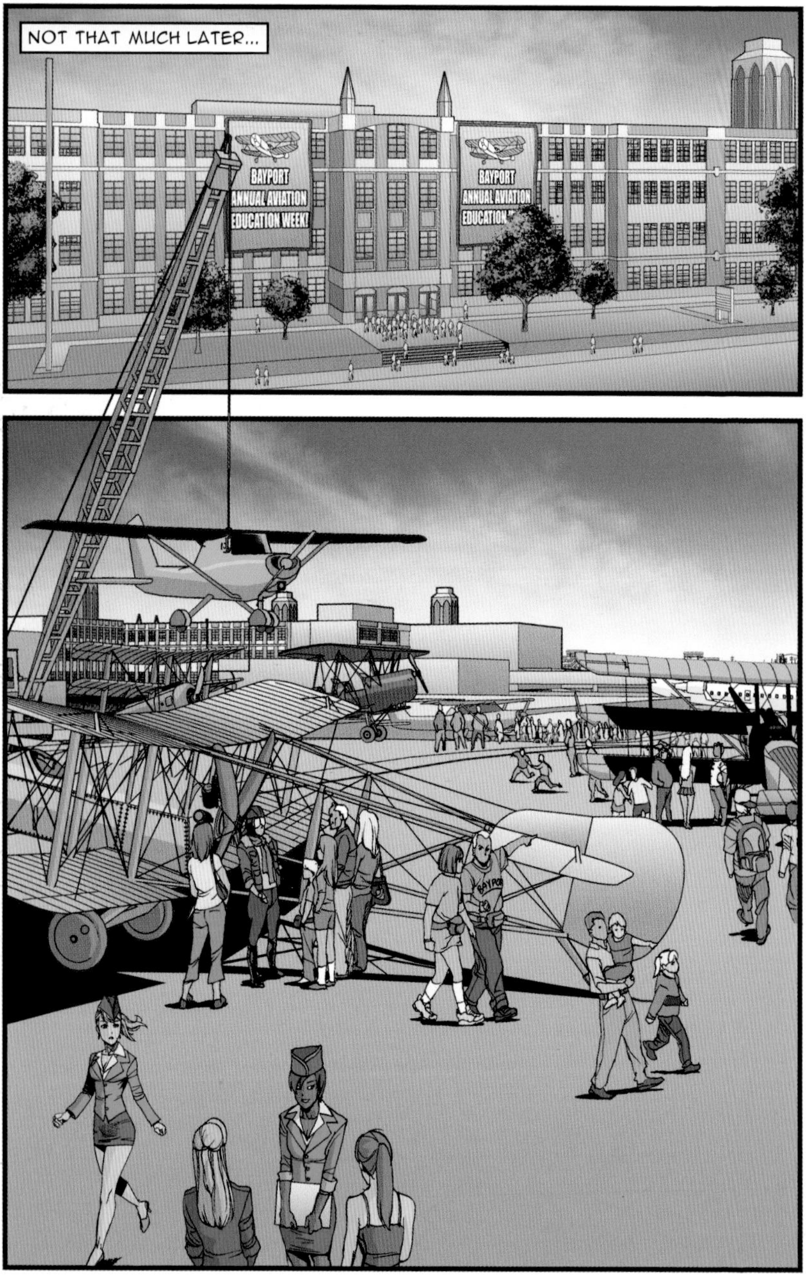
NOT THAT MUCH LATER...
BAYPORT ANNUAL AVIATION EDUCATION WEEK!
BAYPORT ANNUAL AVIATION EDUCATION
BAYPORT

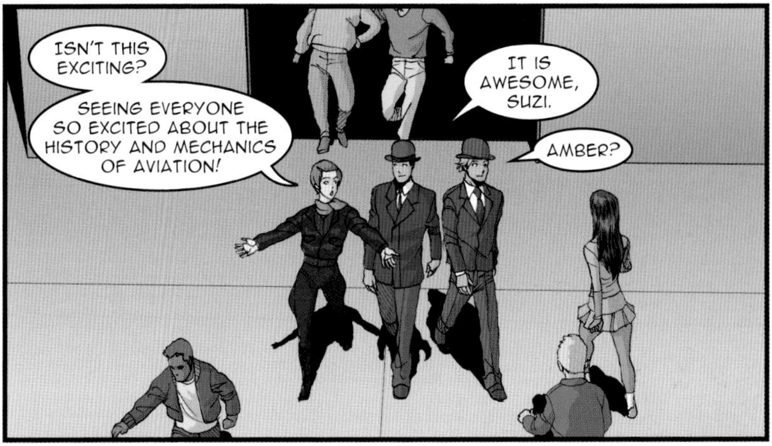
ISN'T THIS EXCITING?
SEEING EVERYONE SO EXCITED ABOUT THE HISTORY AND MECHANICS OF AVIATION!
IT IS AWESOME, SUZI.
AMBER?

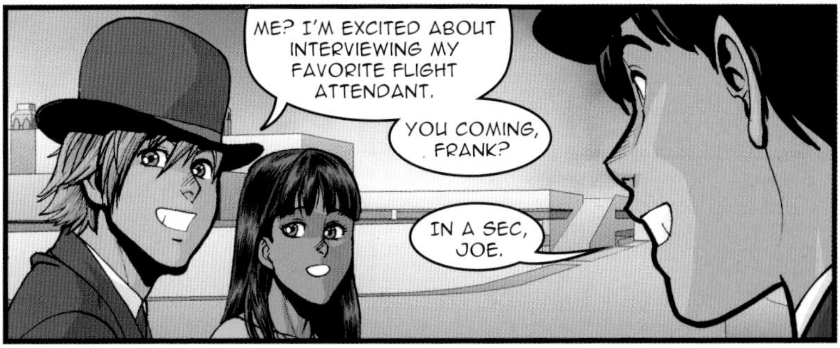
ME? I'M EXCITED ABOUT INTERVIEWING MY FAVORITE FLIGHT ATTENDANT.
YOU COMING, FRANK?
IN A SEC, JOE.

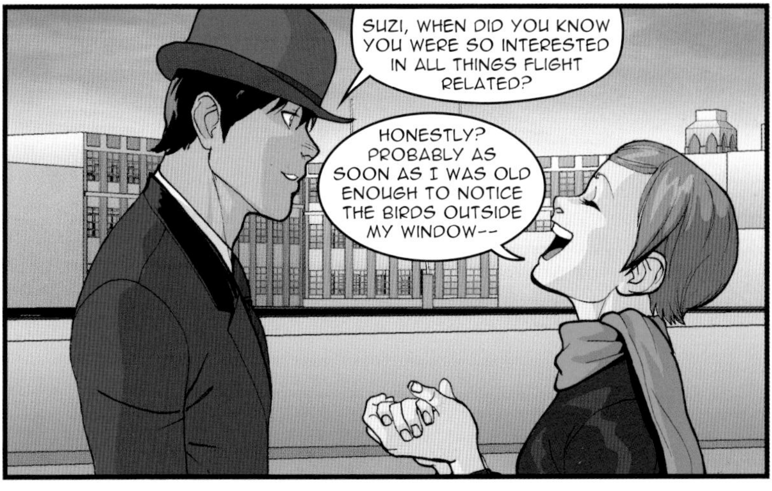
SUZI, WHEN DID YOU KNOW YOU WERE SO INTERESTED IN ALL THINGS FLIGHT RELATED?
HONESTLY? PROBABLY AS SOON AS I WAS OLD ENOUGH TO NOTICE THE BIRDS OUTSIDE MY WINDOW--

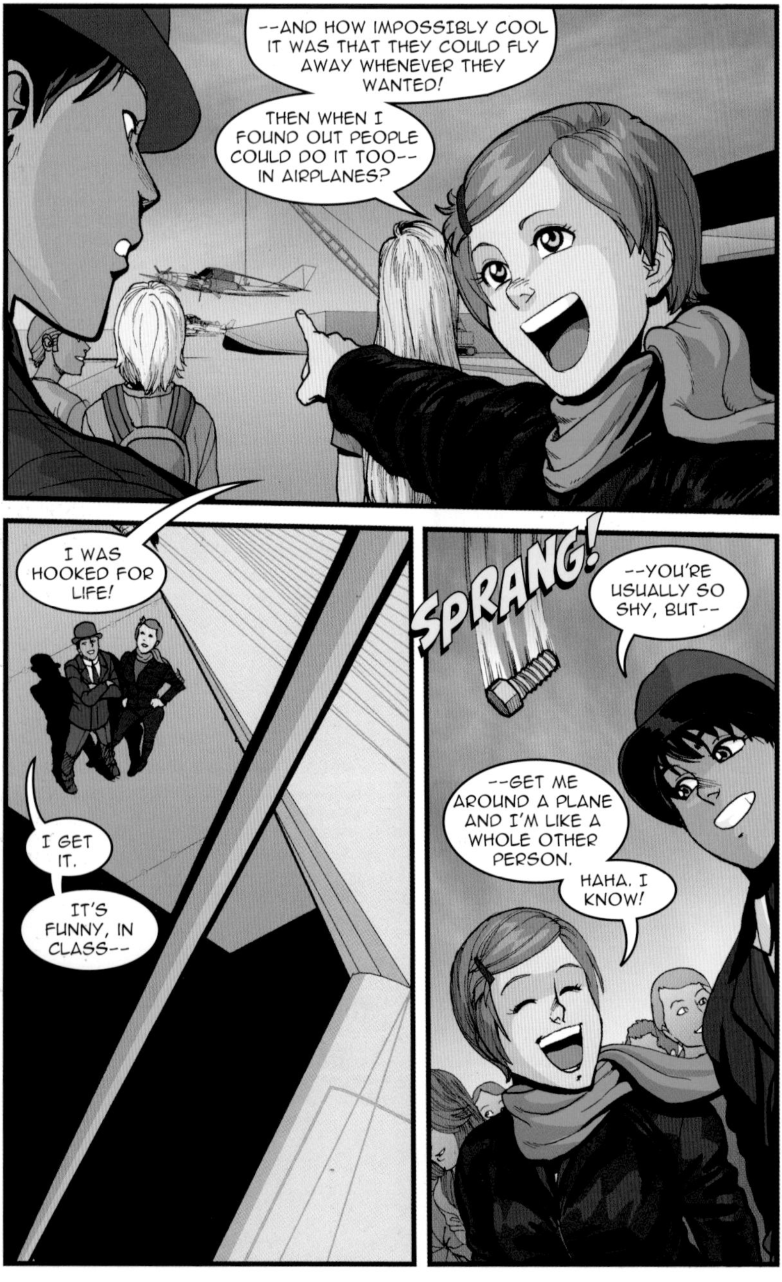
--AND HOW IMPOSSIBLY COOL IT WAS THAT THEY COULD FLY AWAY WHENEVER THEY WANTED!
THEN WHEN I FOUND OUT PEOPLE COULD DO IT TOO-- IN AIRPLANES?
I WAS HOOKED FOR LIFE!
I GET IT.
IT'S FUNNY, IN CLASS--
SPRANG!
--YOU'RE USUALLY SO SHY, BUT--
--GET ME AROUND A PLANE AND I'M LIKE A WHOLE OTHER PERSON.
HAHA. I KNOW!

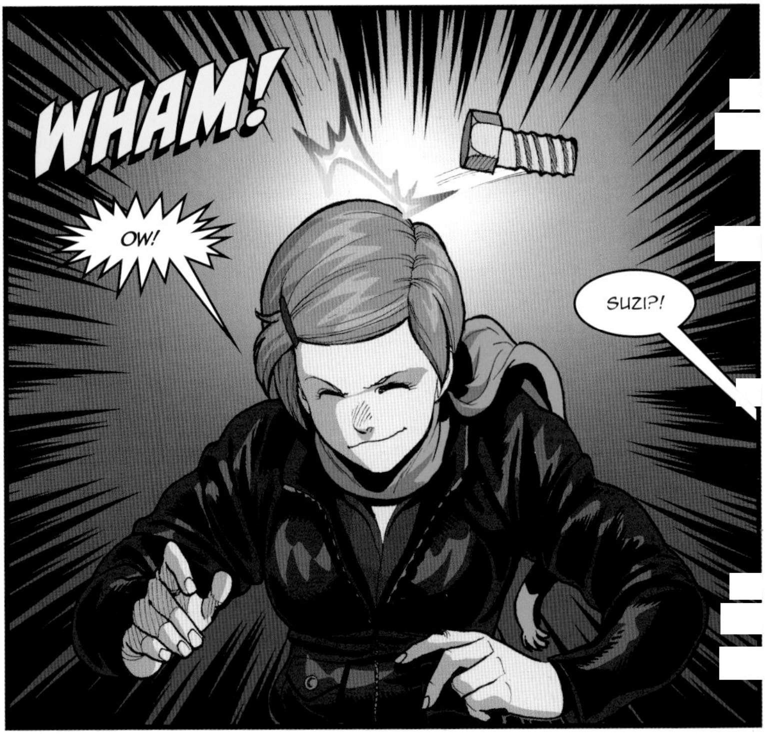
WHAM!
OW!
SUZI?!

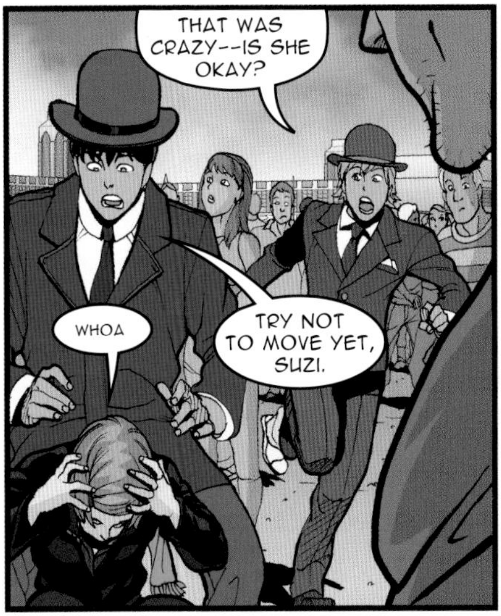
THAT WAS CRAZY--IS SHE OKAY?
WHOA
TRY NOT TO MOVE YET, SUZI.

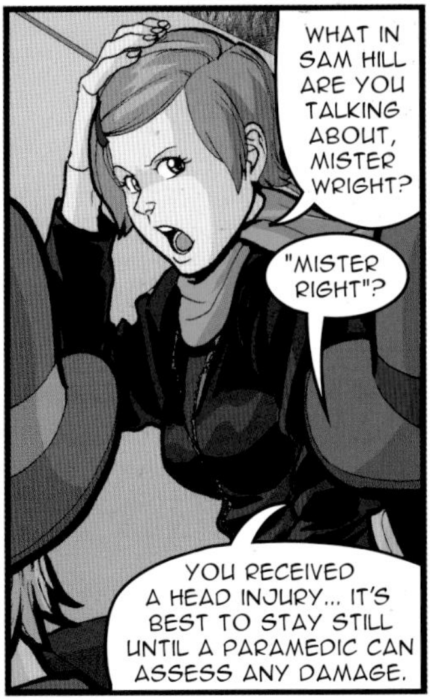
WHAT IN SAM HILL ARE YOU TALKING ABOUT, MISTER WRIGHT?
"MISTER RIGHT"?
YOU RECEIVED A HEAD INJURY... IT'S BEST TO STAY STILL UNTIL A PARAMEDIC CAN ASSESS ANY DAMAGE.

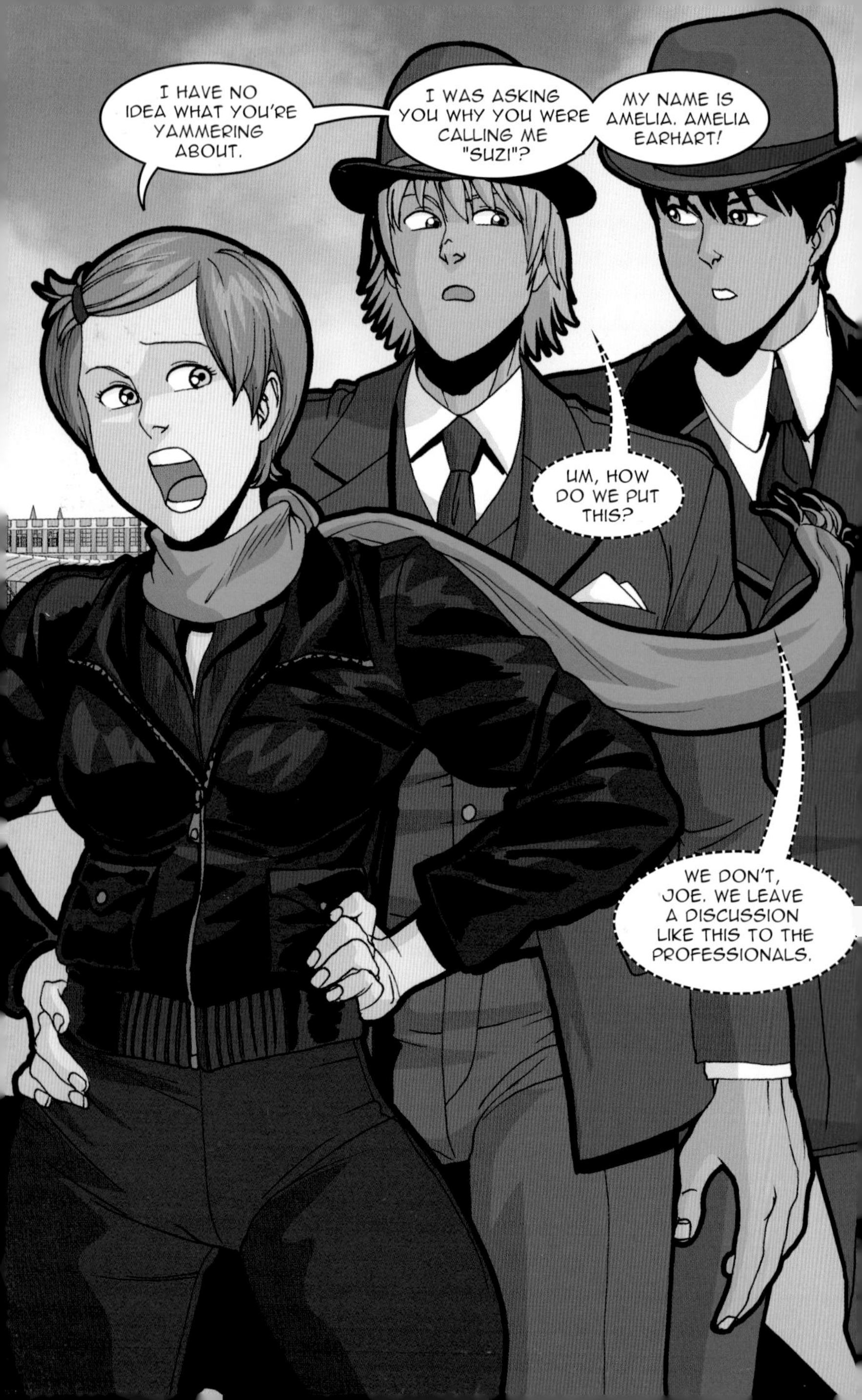
I HAVE NO IDEA WHAT YOU'RE YAMMERING ABOUT.
I WAS ASKING YOU WHY YOU WERE CALLING ME "SUZI"?
MY NAME IS AMELIA. AMELIA EARHART!
UM, HOW DO WE PUT THIS?
WE DON'T, JOE. WE LEAVE A DISCUSSION LIKE THIS TO THE PROFESSIONALS.

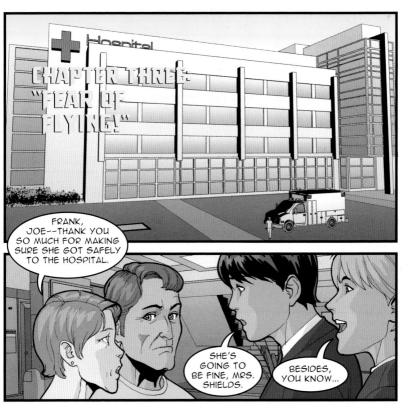

CHAPTER THREE: "FEAR OF FLYING!"

FRANK, JOE--THANK YOU SO MUCH FOR MAKING SURE SHE GOT SAFELY TO THE HOSPITAL.

SHE'S GOING TO BE FINE, MRS. SHIELDS.

BESIDES, YOU KNOW...

PHYSICALLY, SHE'S IN PERFECT CONDITION.

THERE WAS NO PERMANENT DAMAGE FROM THE BOLT--SO I AM CONFIDENT THAT WITH TIME AND PATIENCE--

--SHE'LL BE BACK TO HER OLD SELF IN NO TIME.

THANK YOU, DOCTOR.

THAT'S GOOD NEWS!

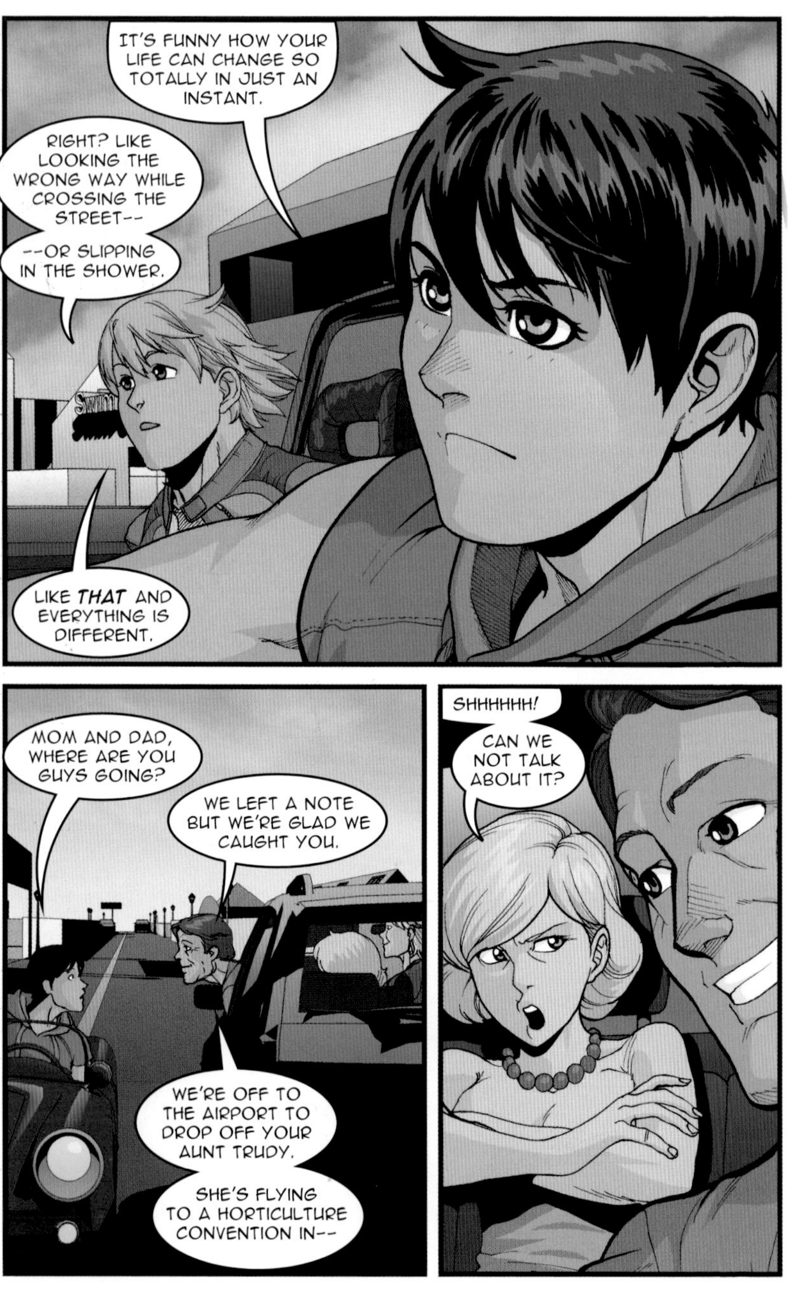
IT'S FUNNY HOW YOUR LIFE CAN CHANGE SO TOTALLY IN JUST AN INSTANT.
RIGHT? LIKE LOOKING THE WRONG WAY WHILE CROSSING THE STREET--
--OR SLIPPING IN THE SHOWER.
LIKE THAT AND EVERYTHING IS DIFFERENT.
MOM AND DAD, WHERE ARE YOU GUYS GOING?
WE LEFT A NOTE BUT WE'RE GLAD WE CAUGHT YOU.
WE'RE OFF TO THE AIRPORT TO DROP OFF YOUR AUNT TRUDY.
SHE'S FLYING TO A HORTICULTURE CONVENTION IN--
SHHHHHH!
CAN WE NOT TALK ABOUT IT?

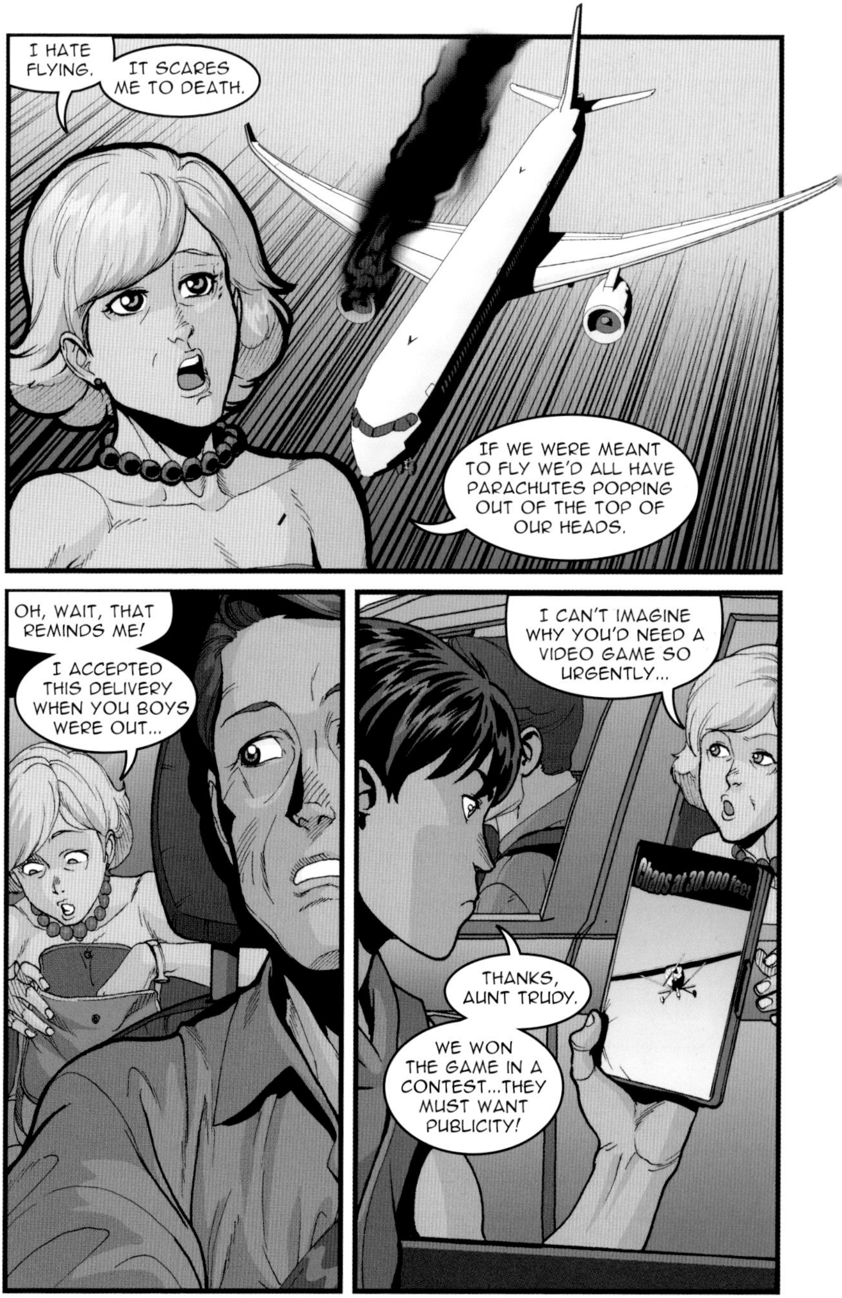
I HATE FLYING.
IT SCARES ME TO DEATH.
IF WE WERE MEANT TO FLY WE'D ALL HAVE PARACHUTES POPPING OUT OF THE TOP OF OUR HEADS.
OH, WAIT, THAT REMINDS ME!
I ACCEPTED THIS DELIVERY WHEN YOU BOYS WERE OUT...
I CAN'T IMAGINE WHY YOU'D NEED A VIDEO GAME SO URGENTLY...
Chaos at 30,000 feet
THANKS, AUNT TRUDY.
WE WON THE GAME IN A CONTEST...THEY MUST WANT PUBLICITY!

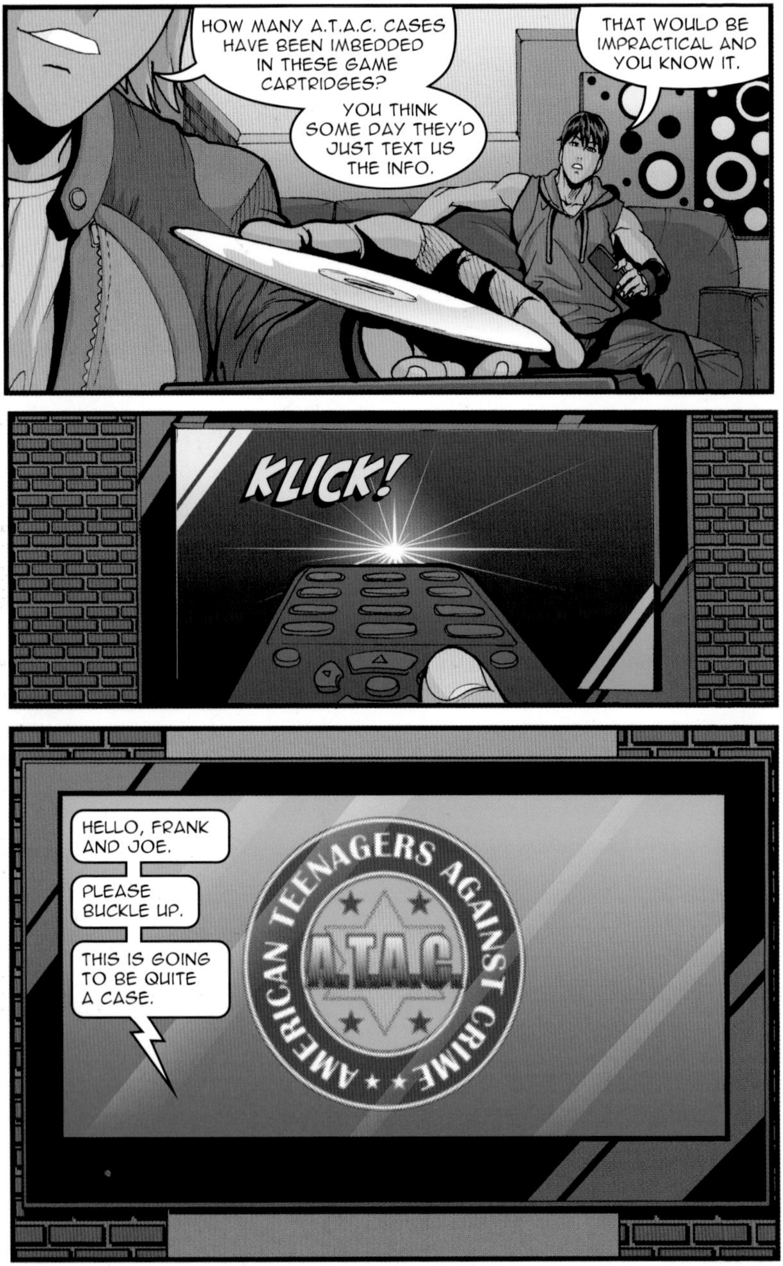
HOW MANY A.T.A.C. CASES HAVE BEEN IMBEDDED IN THESE GAME CARTRIDGES?
YOU THINK SOME DAY THEY'D JUST TEXT US THE INFO.
THAT WOULD BE IMPRACTICAL AND YOU KNOW IT.
KLICK!
HELLO, FRANK AND JOE.
PLEASE BUCKLE UP.
THIS IS GOING TO BE QUITE A CASE.
AMERICAN TEENAGERS AGAINST CRIME
A.T.A.C.

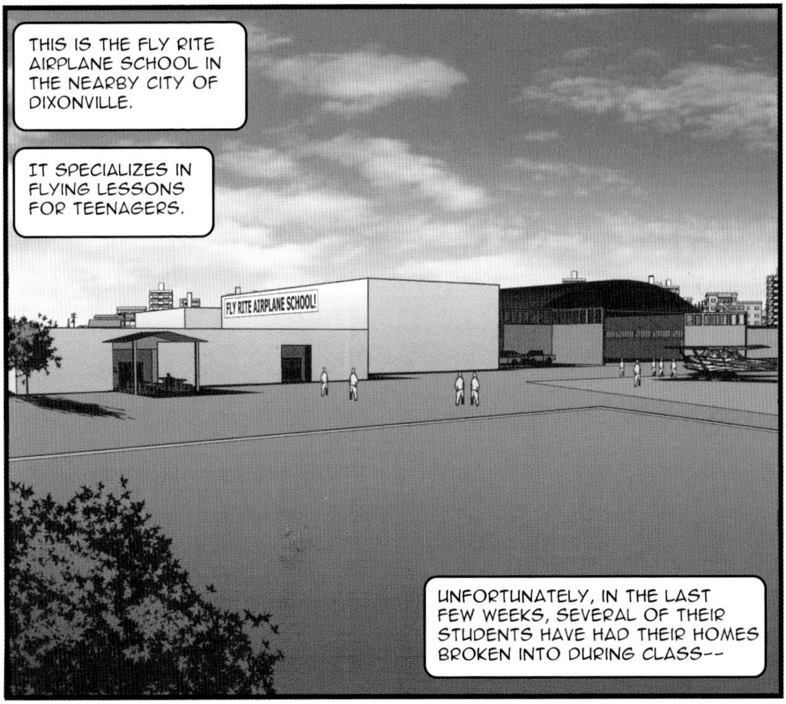
THIS IS THE FLY RITE AIRPLANE SCHOOL IN THE NEARBY CITY OF DIXONVILLE.
IT SPECIALIZES IN FLYING LESSONS FOR TEENAGERS.
FLY RITE AIRPLANE SCHOOL!
UNFORTUNATELY, IN THE LAST FEW WEEKS, SEVERAL OF THEIR STUDENTS HAVE HAD THEIR HOMES BROKEN INTO DURING CLASS--

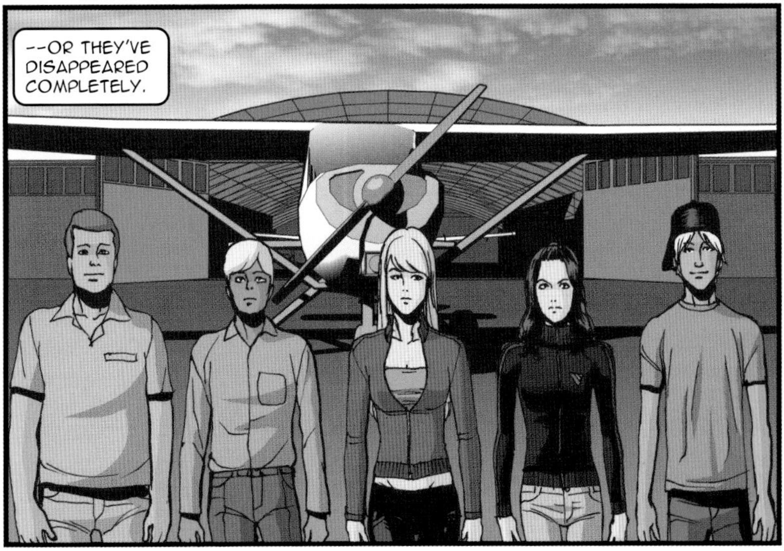
--OR THEY'VE DISAPPEARED COMPLETELY.

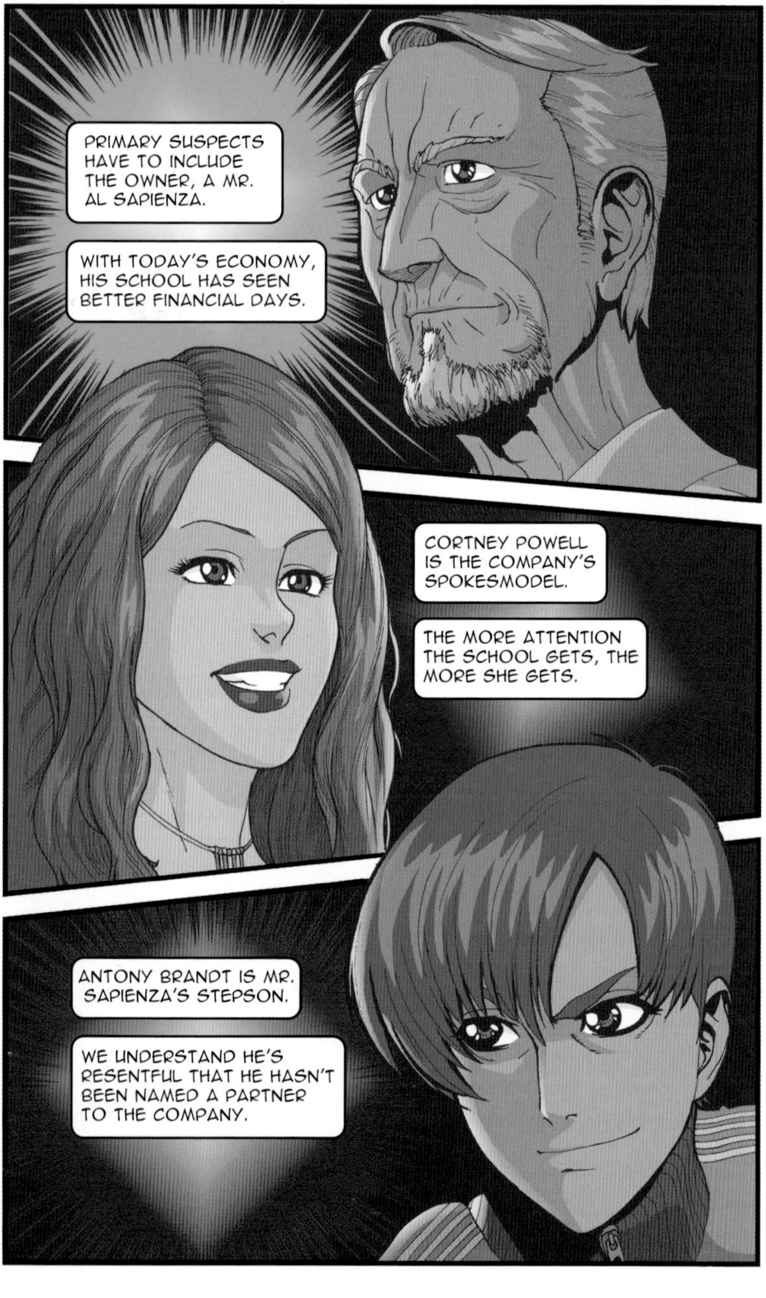
PRIMARY SUSPECTS HAVE TO INCLUDE THE OWNER, A MR. AL SAPIENZA.
WITH TODAY'S ECONOMY, HIS SCHOOL HAS SEEN BETTER FINANCIAL DAYS.
CORTNEY POWELL IS THE COMPANY'S SPOKESMODEL.
THE MORE ATTENTION THE SCHOOL GETS, THE MORE SHE GETS.
ANTONY BRANDT IS MR. SAPIENZA'S STEPSON.
WE UNDERSTAND HE'S RESENTFUL THAT HE HASN'T BEEN NAMED A PARTNER TO THE COMPANY.

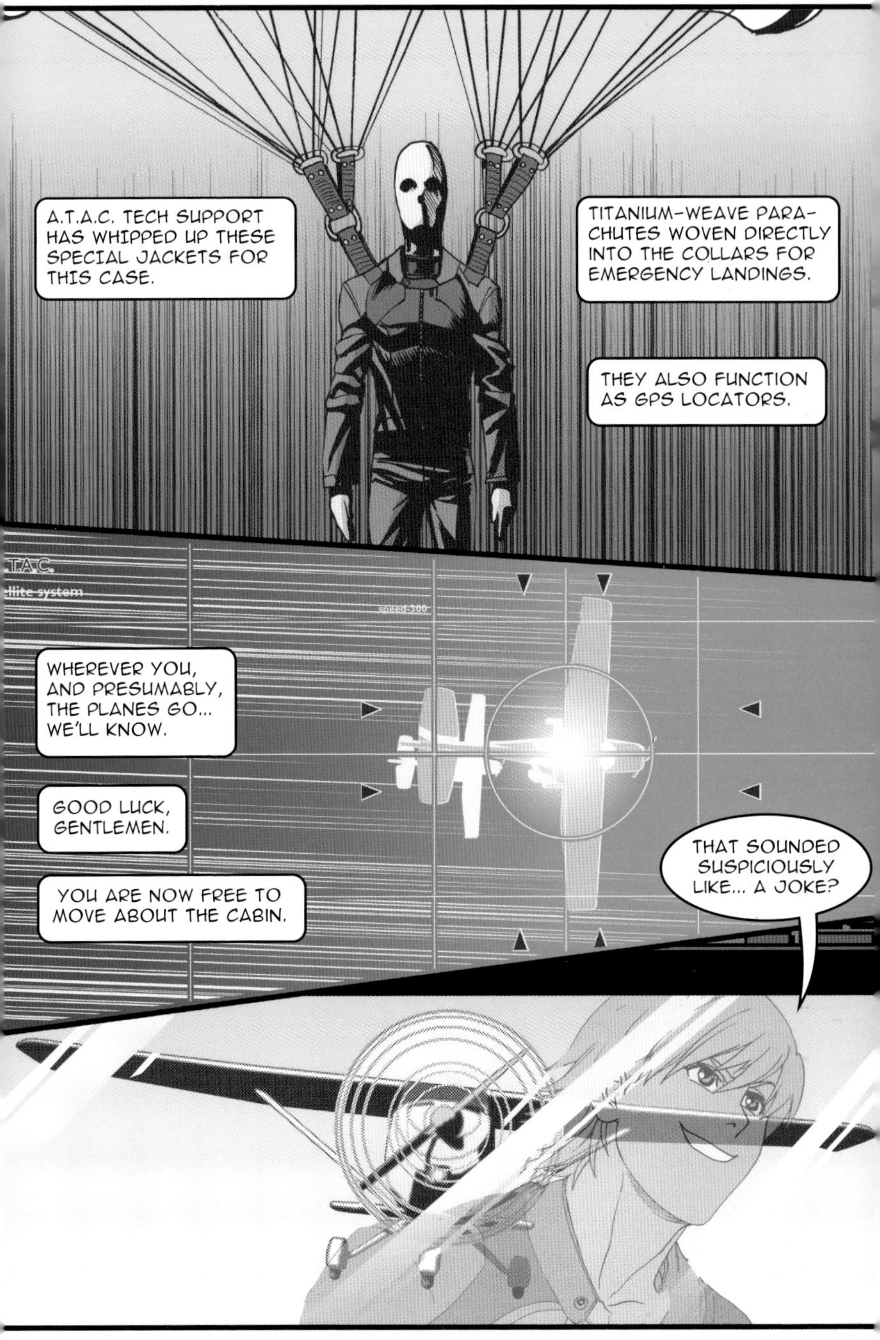
A.T.A.C. TECH SUPPORT HAS WHIPPED UP THESE SPECIAL JACKETS FOR THIS CASE.
TITANIUM-WEAVE PARACHUTES WOVEN DIRECTLY INTO THE COLLARS FOR EMERGENCY LANDINGS.
THEY ALSO FUNCTION AS GPS LOCATORS.
T.A.C.
llite system
speed-300
WHEREVER YOU, AND PRESUMABLY, THE PLANES GO... WE'LL KNOW.
GOOD LUCK, GENTLEMEN.
YOU ARE NOW FREE TO MOVE ABOUT THE CABIN.
THAT SOUNDED SUSPICIOUSLY LIKE... A JOKE?

CHAPTER FOUR: "DEATH BY NORTHWEST!"

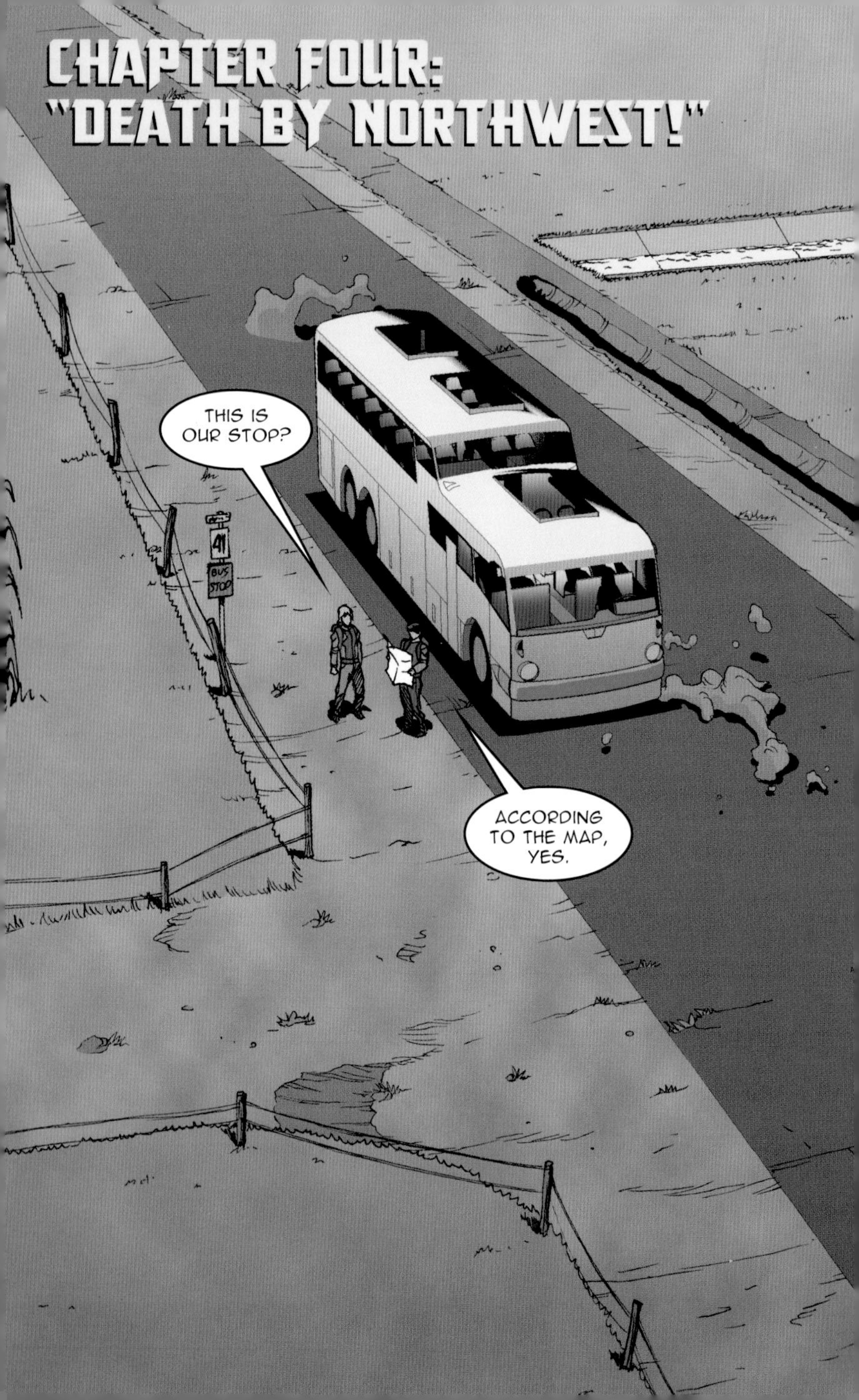

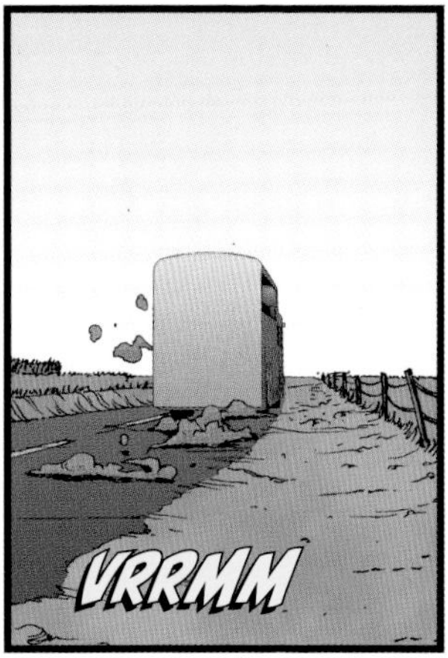
VRRMM

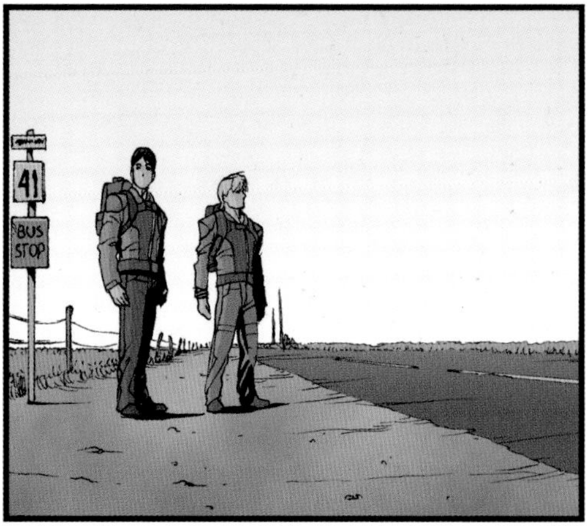
41
BUS STOP

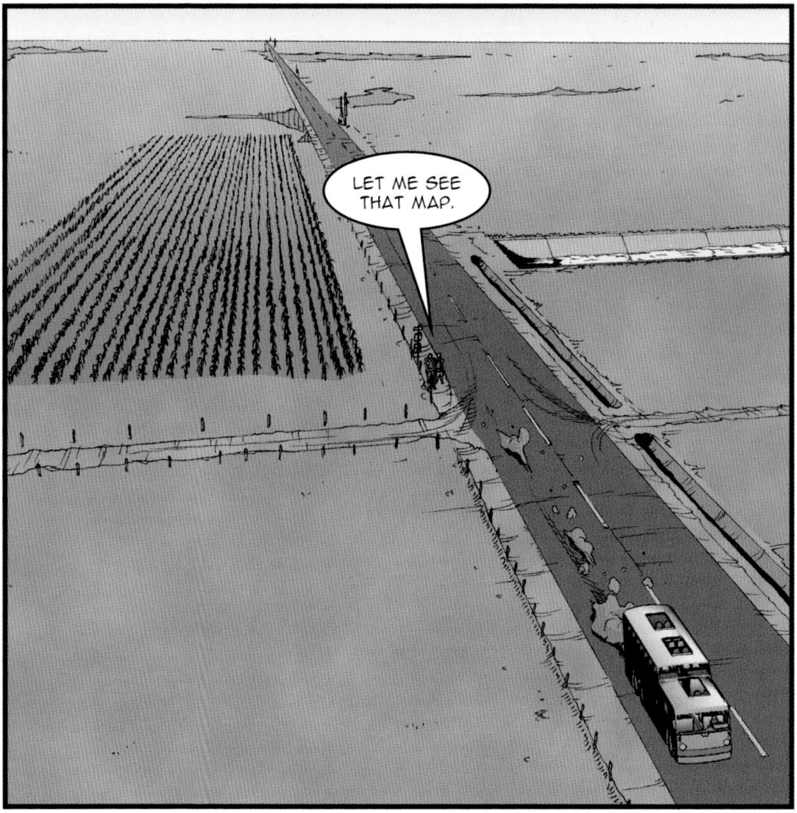
LET ME SEE THAT MAP.

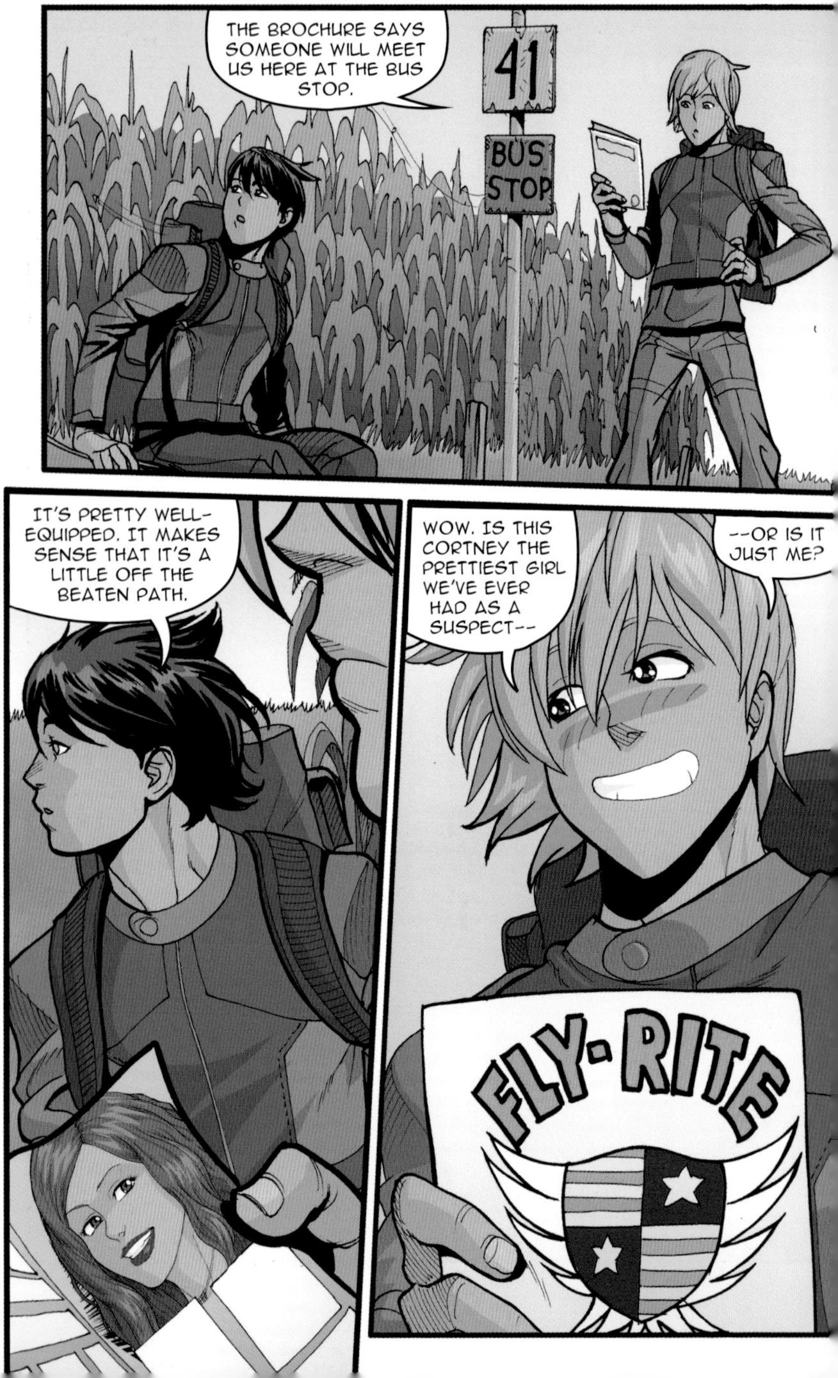
THE BROCHURE SAYS SOMEONE WILL MEET US HERE AT THE BUS STOP.
41
BUS STOP
IT'S PRETTY WELL-EQUIPPED. IT MAKES SENSE THAT IT'S A LITTLE OFF THE BEATEN PATH.
WOW. IS THIS CORTNEY THE PRETTIEST GIRL WE'VE EVER HAD AS A SUSPECT--
--OR IS IT JUST ME?
FLY-RITE

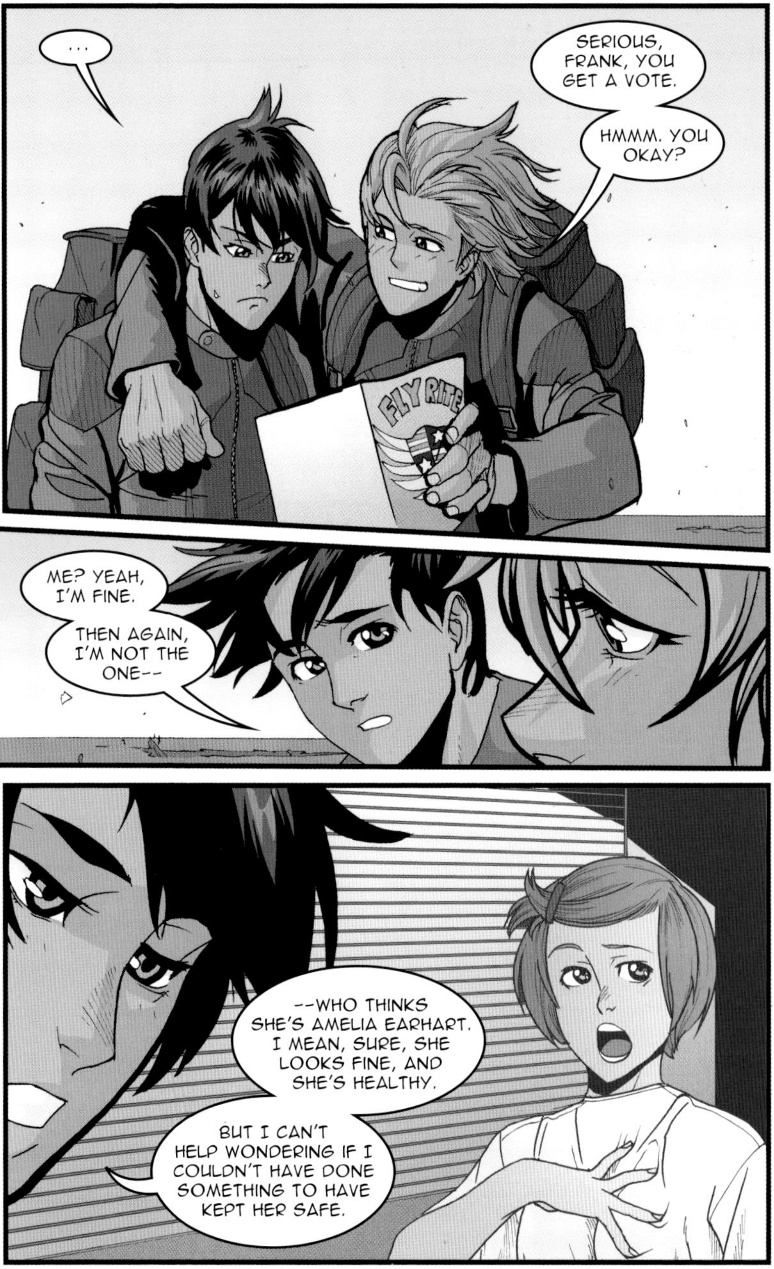
...
SERIOUS, FRANK, YOU GET A VOTE.
HMMM. YOU OKAY?
FLY RITE
ME? YEAH, I'M FINE.
THEN AGAIN, I'M NOT THE ONE--
--WHO THINKS SHE'S AMELIA EARHART. I MEAN, SURE, SHE LOOKS FINE, AND SHE'S HEALTHY.
BUT I CAN'T HELP WONDERING IF I COULDN'T HAVE DONE SOMETHING TO HAVE KEPT HER SAFE.

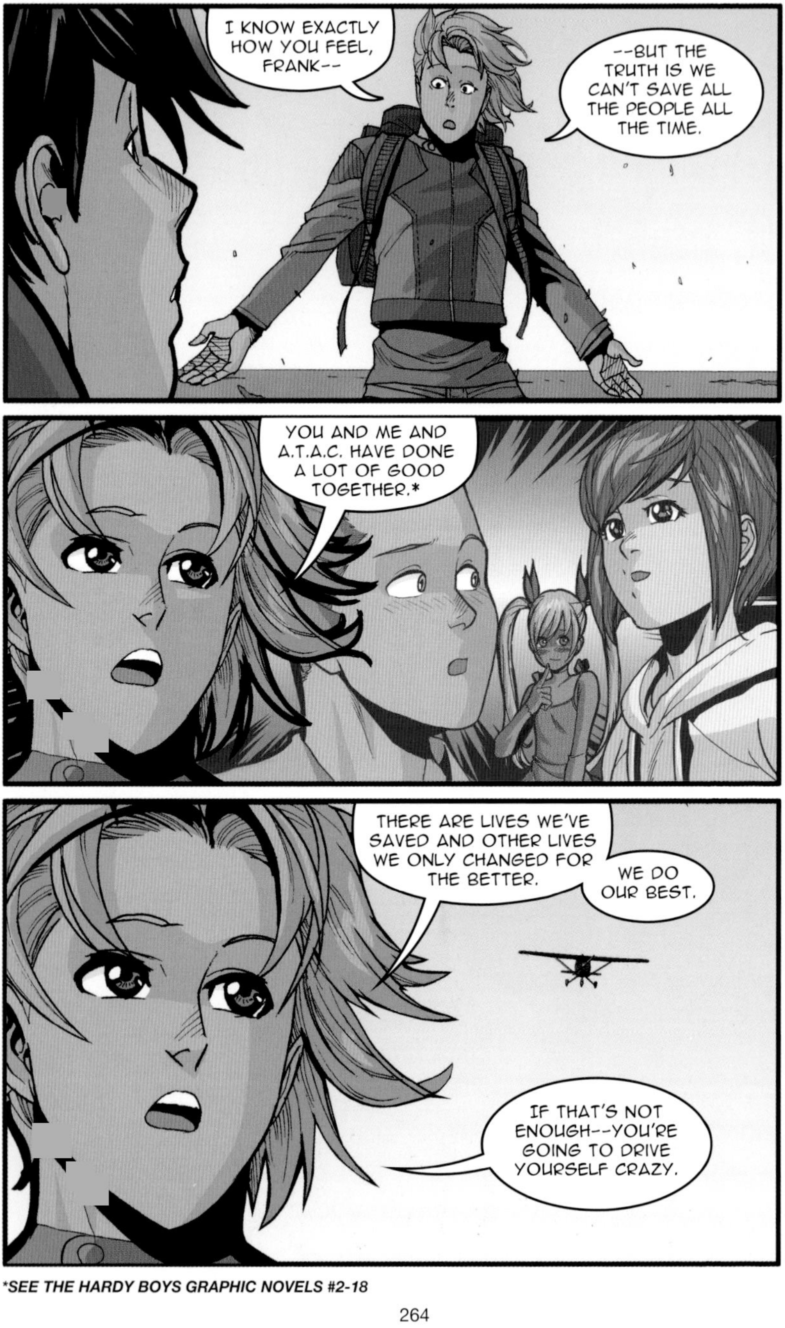
I KNOW EXACTLY HOW YOU FEEL, FRANK--
--BUT THE TRUTH IS WE CAN'T SAVE ALL THE PEOPLE ALL THE TIME.
YOU AND ME AND A.T.A.C. HAVE DONE A LOT OF GOOD TOGETHER.*
THERE ARE LIVES WE'VE SAVED AND OTHER LIVES WE ONLY CHANGED FOR THE BETTER.
WE DO OUR BEST.
IF THAT'S NOT ENOUGH--YOU'RE GOING TO DRIVE YOURSELF CRAZY.

SEE THE HARDY BOYS GRAPHIC NOVELS #2-18

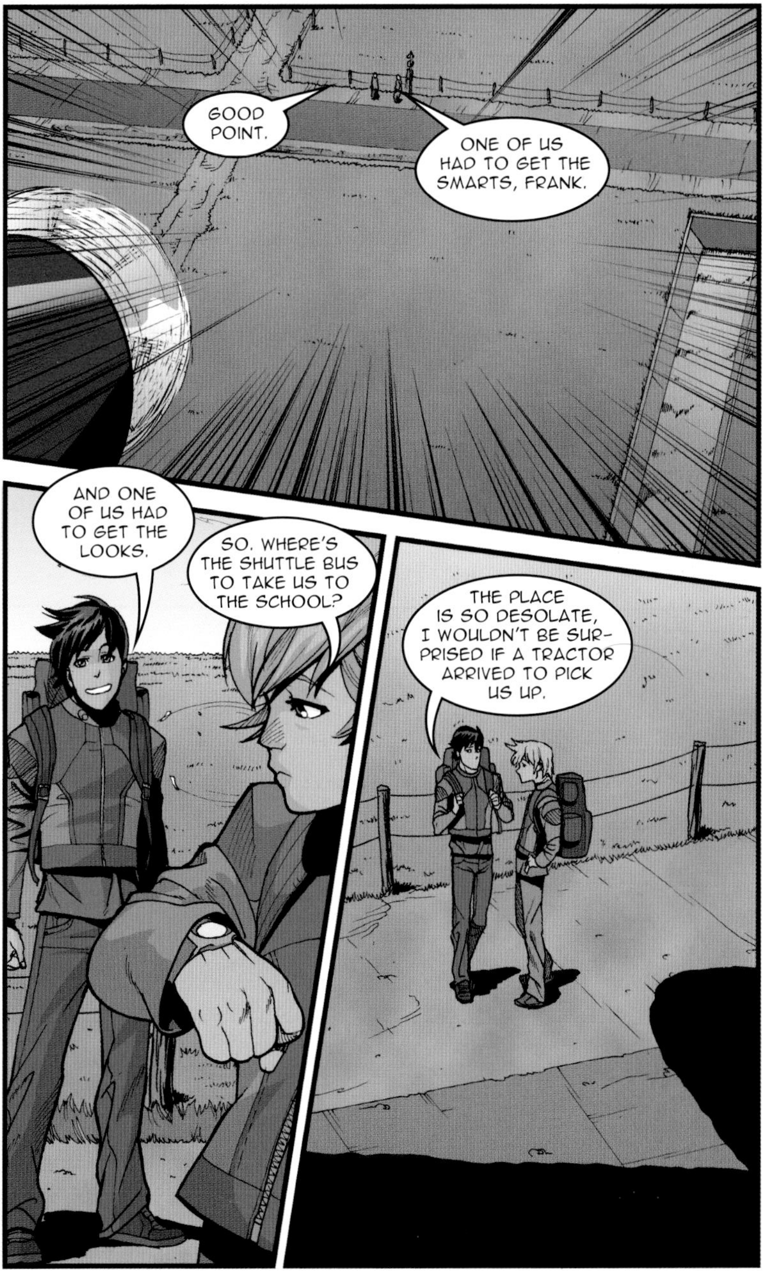
GOOD POINT.
ONE OF US HAD TO GET THE SMARTS, FRANK.
AND ONE OF US HAD TO GET THE LOOKS.
SO. WHERE'S THE SHUTTLE BUS TO TAKE US TO THE SCHOOL?
THE PLACE IS SO DESOLATE, I WOULDN'T BE SUR-PRISED IF A TRACTOR ARRIVED TO PICK US UP.

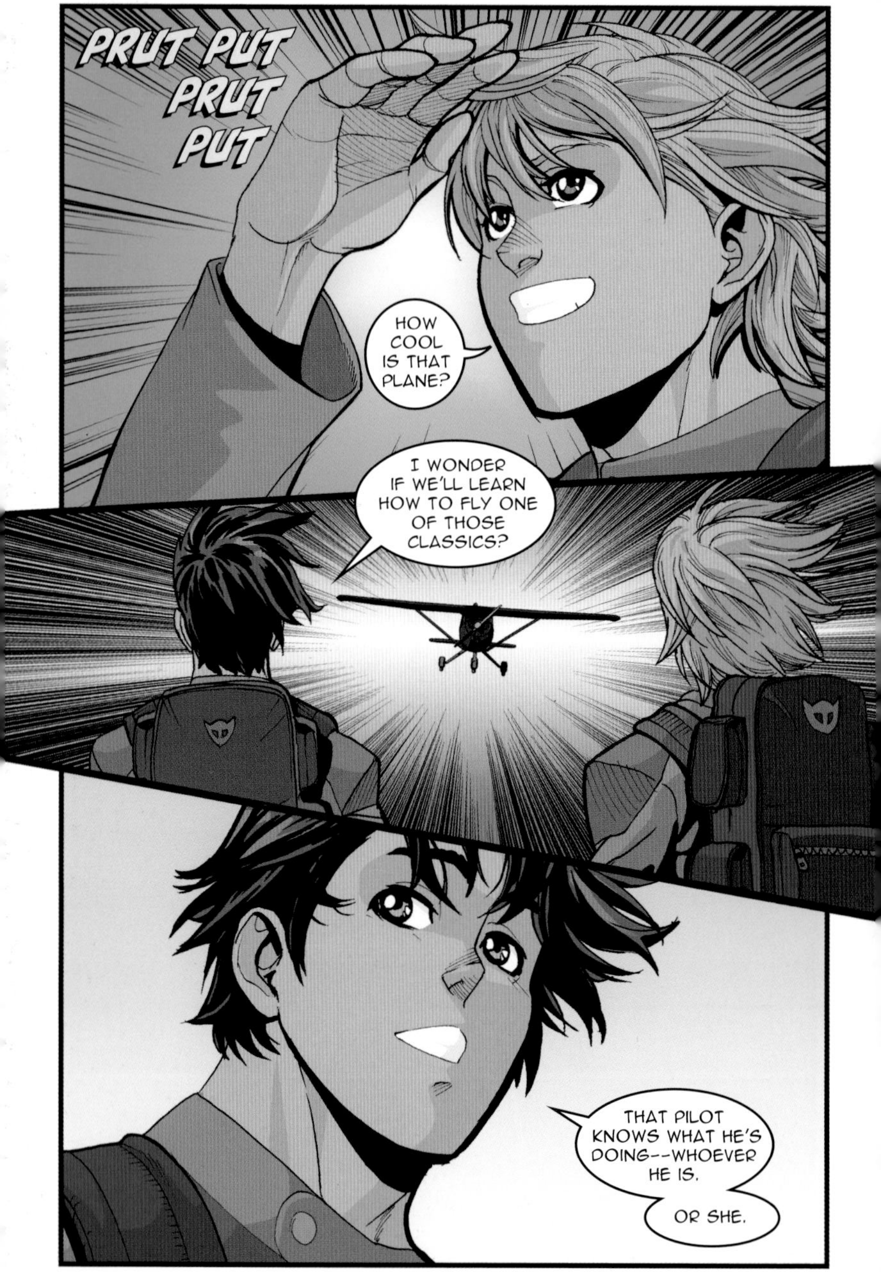
PRUT PUT PRUT PUT
HOW COOL IS THAT PLANE?
I WONDER IF WE'LL LEARN HOW TO FLY ONE OF THOSE CLASSICS?
THAT PILOT KNOWS WHAT HE'S DOING--WHOEVER HE IS.
OR SHE.

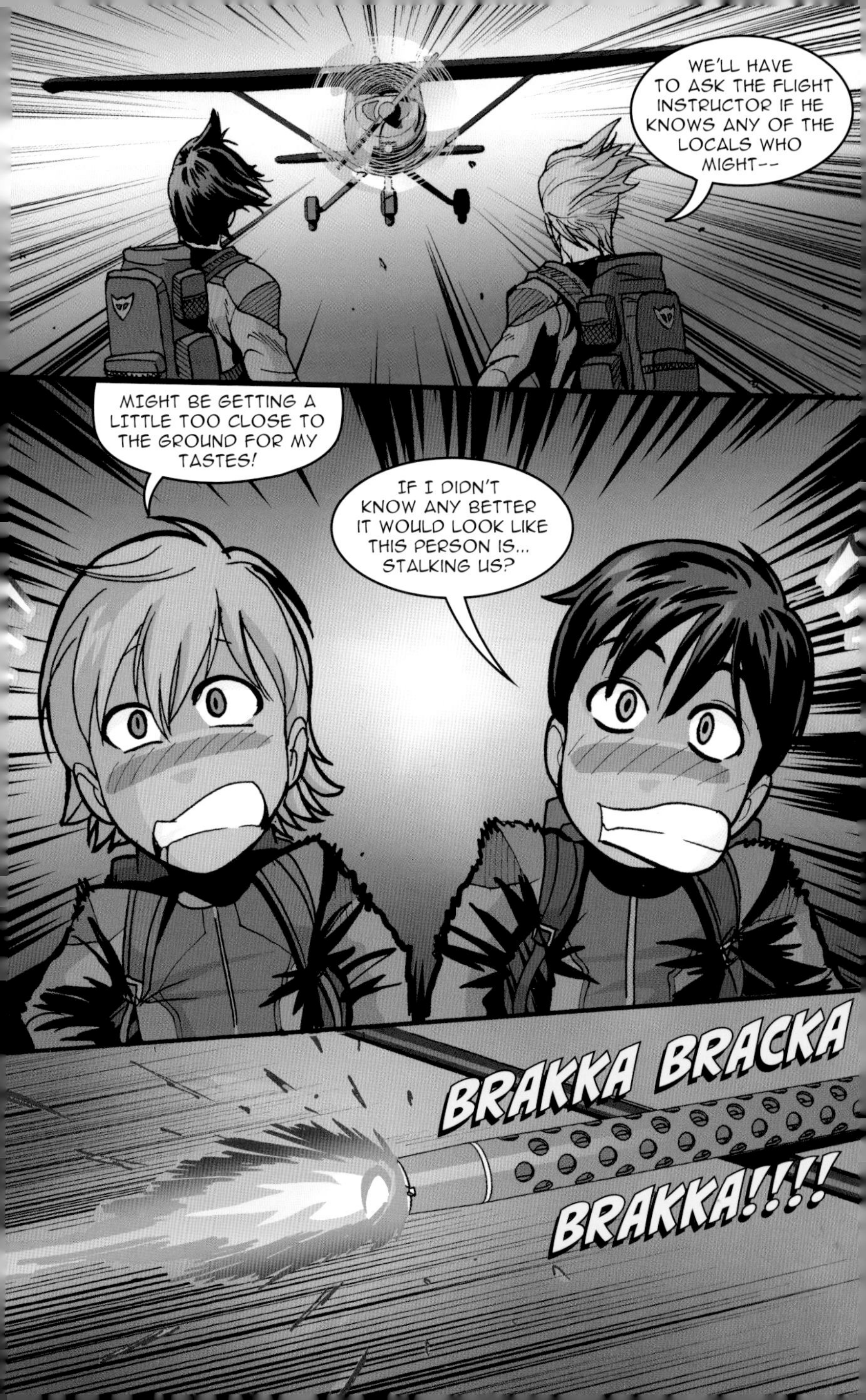
WE'LL HAVE TO ASK THE FLIGHT INSTRUCTOR IF HE KNOWS ANY OF THE LOCALS WHO MIGHT--
MIGHT BE GETTING A LITTLE TOO CLOSE TO THE GROUND FOR MY TASTES!
IF I DIDN'T KNOW ANY BETTER IT WOULD LOOK LIKE THIS PERSON IS... STALKING US?
BRAKKA BRACKA
BRAKKA!!!!

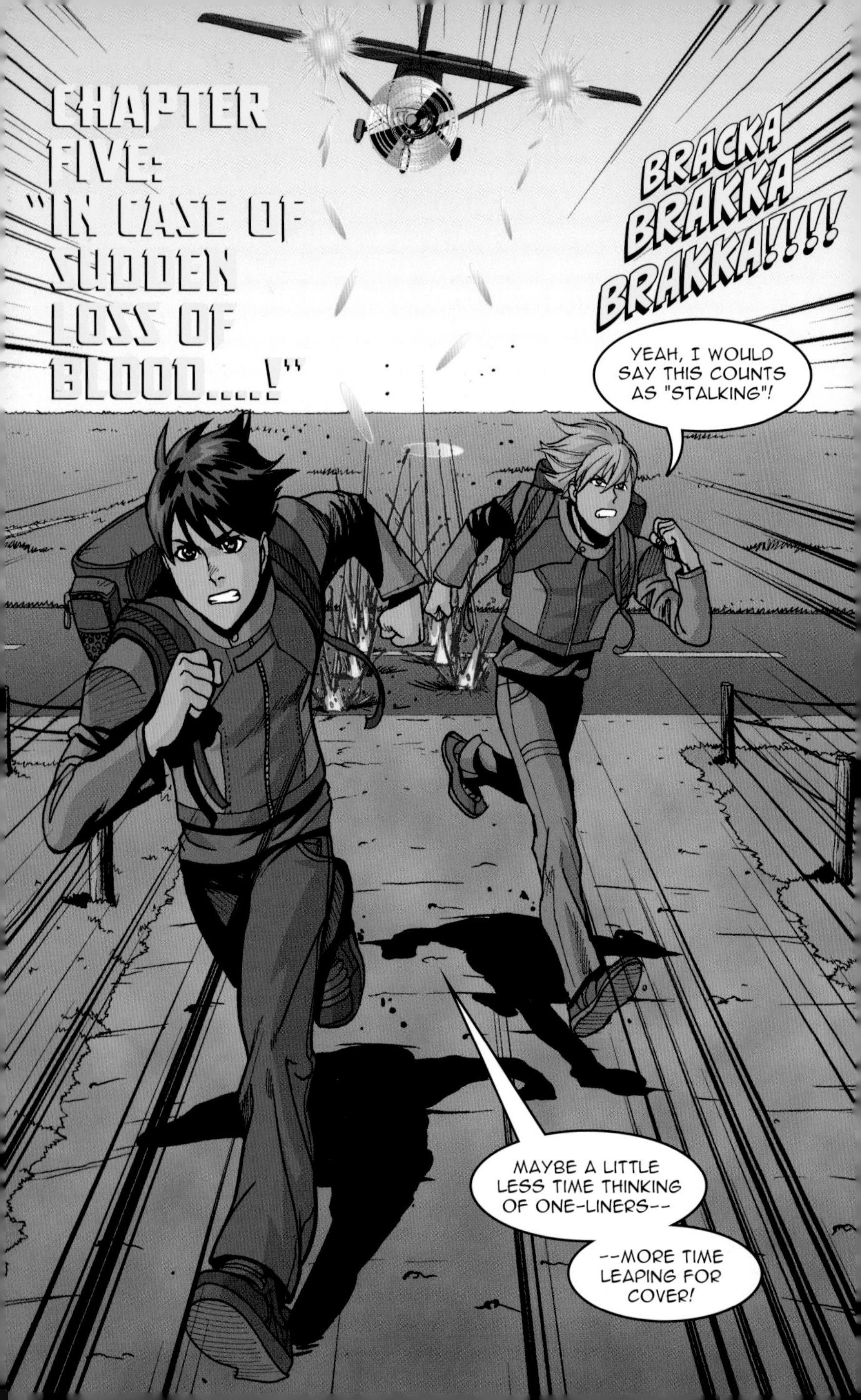
CHAPTER FIVE: "IN CASE OF SUDDEN LOSS OF BLOOD....!"
BRACKA BRAKKA BRAKKA!!!!
YEAH, I WOULD SAY THIS COUNTS AS "STALKING"!
MAYBE A LITTLE LESS TIME THINKING OF ONE-LINERS--
--MORE TIME LEAPING FOR COVER!

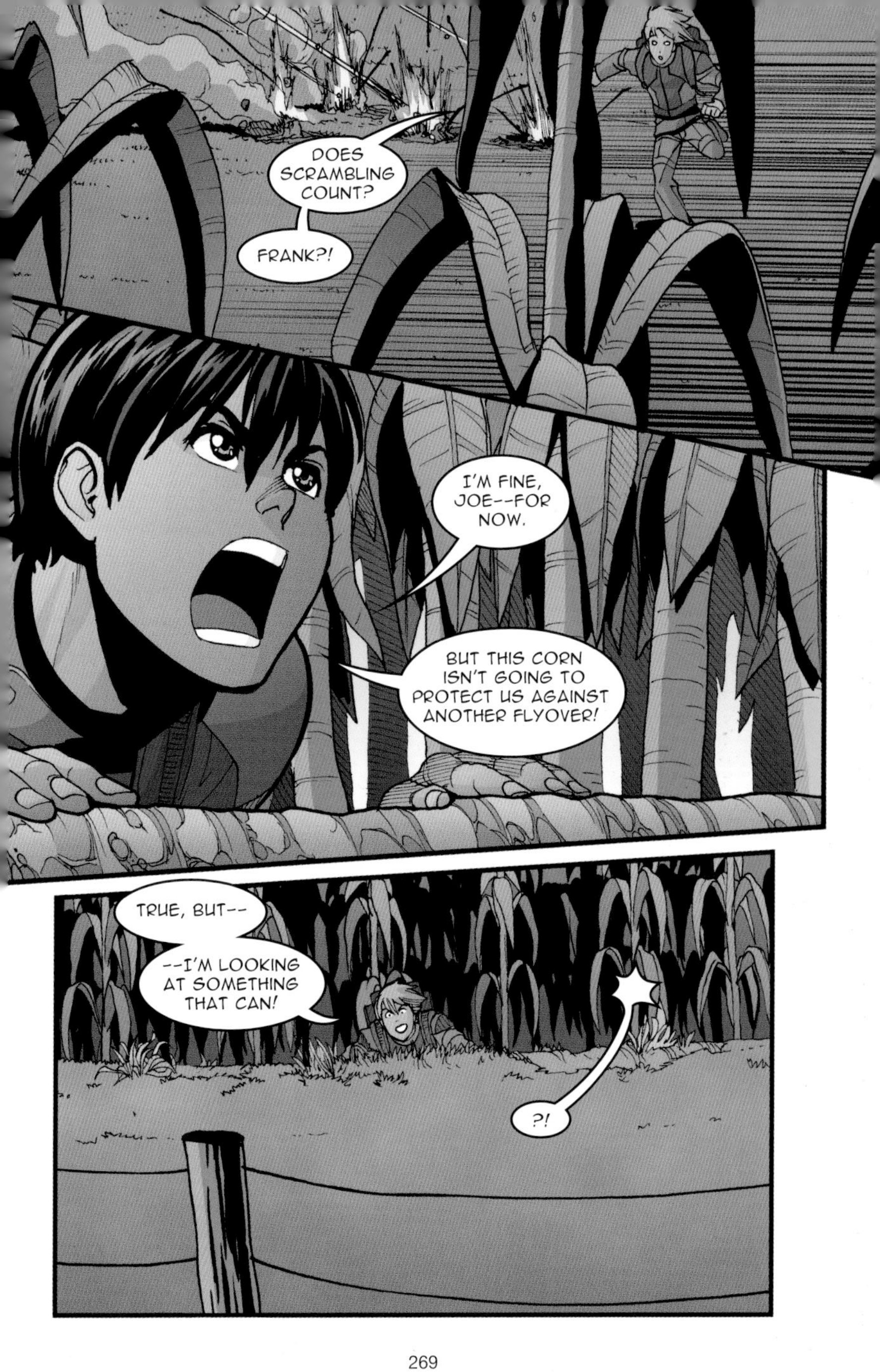
DOES SCRAMBLING COUNT?
FRANK?!
I'M FINE, JOE--FOR NOW.
BUT THIS CORN ISN'T GOING TO PROTECT US AGAINST ANOTHER FLYOVER!
TRUE, BUT--
--I'M LOOKING AT SOMETHING THAT CAN!
?!

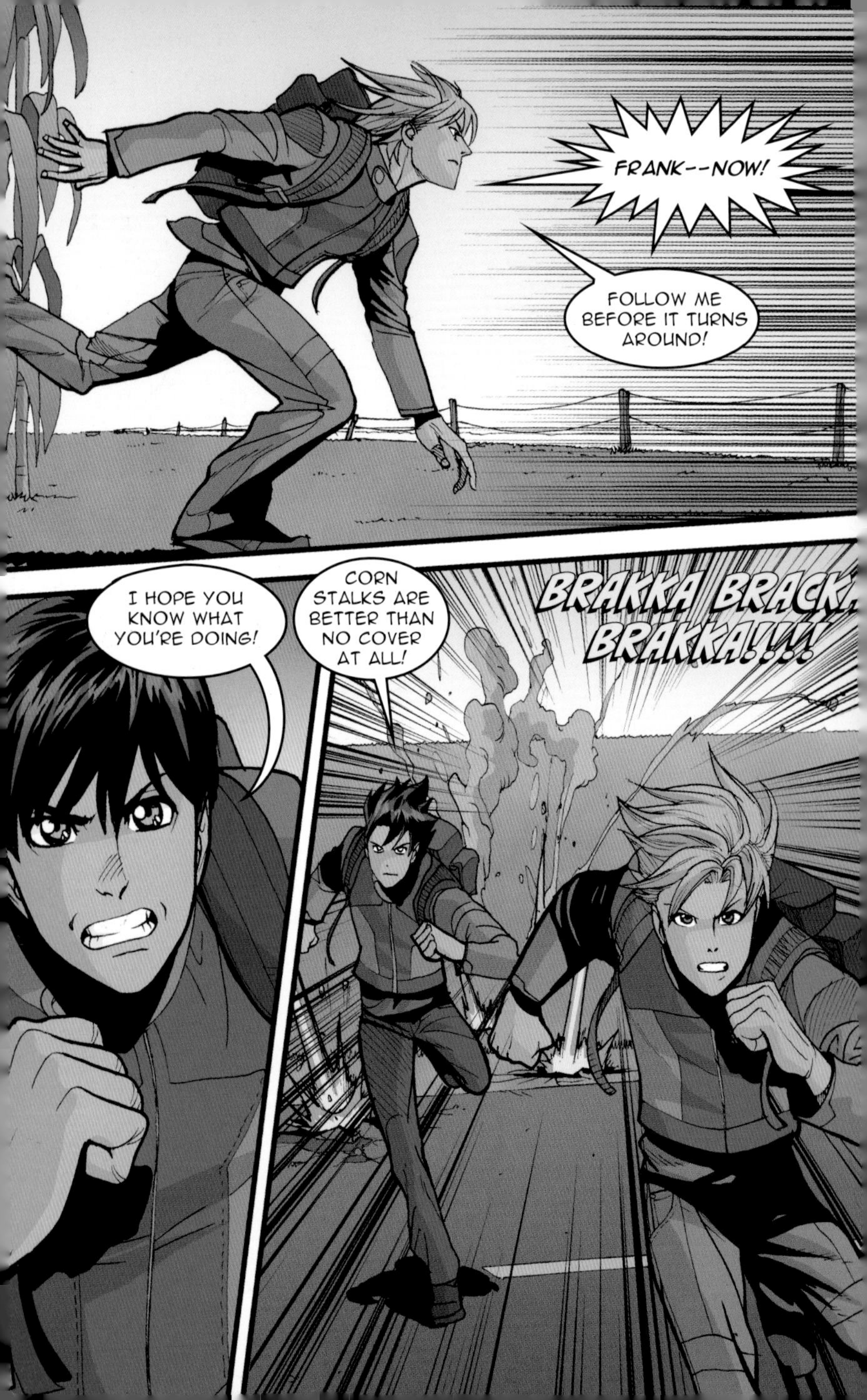
FRANK--NOW!
FOLLOW ME BEFORE IT TURNS AROUND!
I HOPE YOU KNOW WHAT YOU'RE DOING!
CORN STALKS ARE BETTER THAN NO COVER AT ALL!
BRAKKA BRACK, BRAKKA!!!!

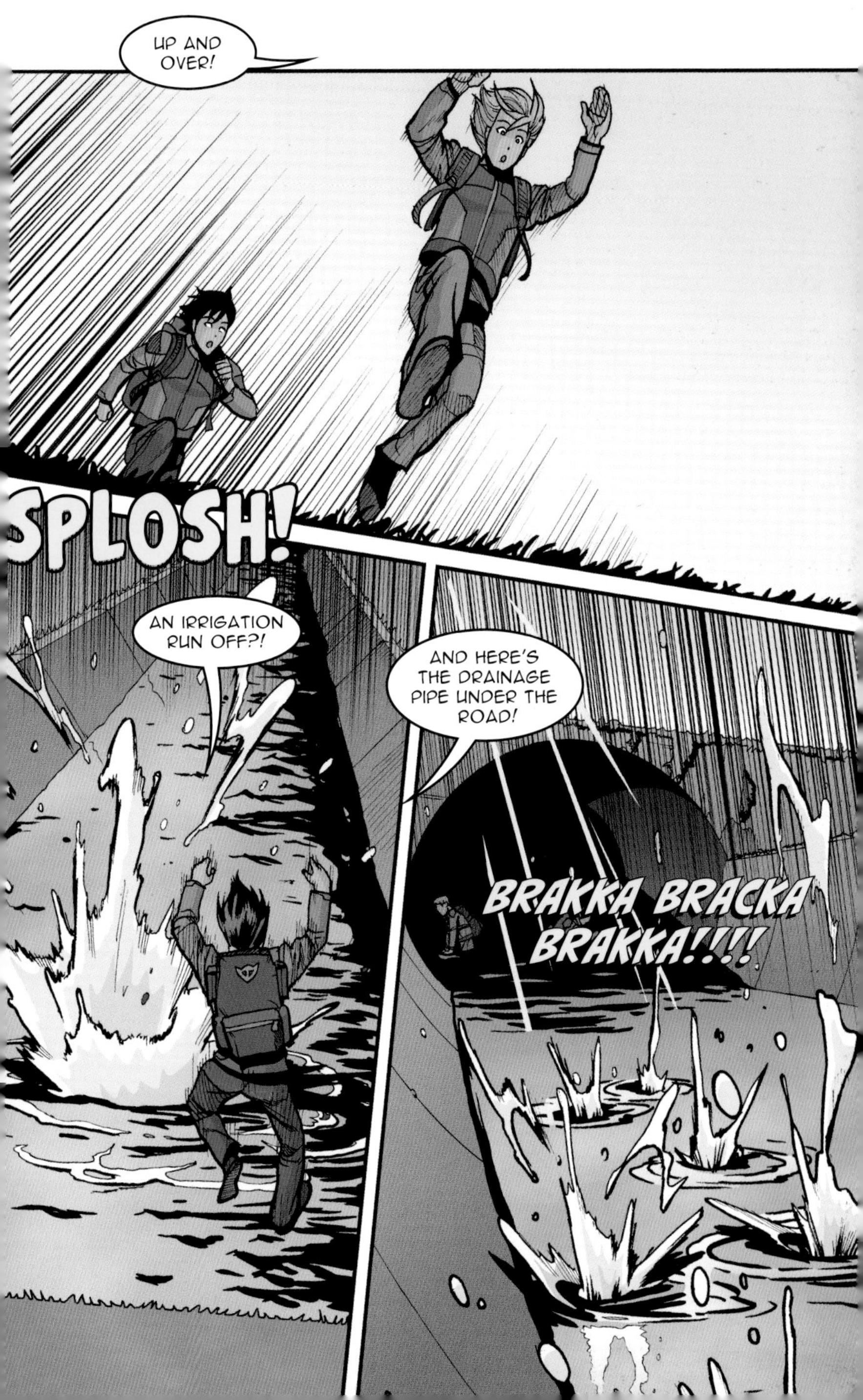
UP AND OVER!
SPLOSH!
AN IRRIGATION RUN OFF?!
AND HERE'S THE DRAINAGE PIPE UNDER THE ROAD!
BRAKKA BRACKA BRAKKA!!!!

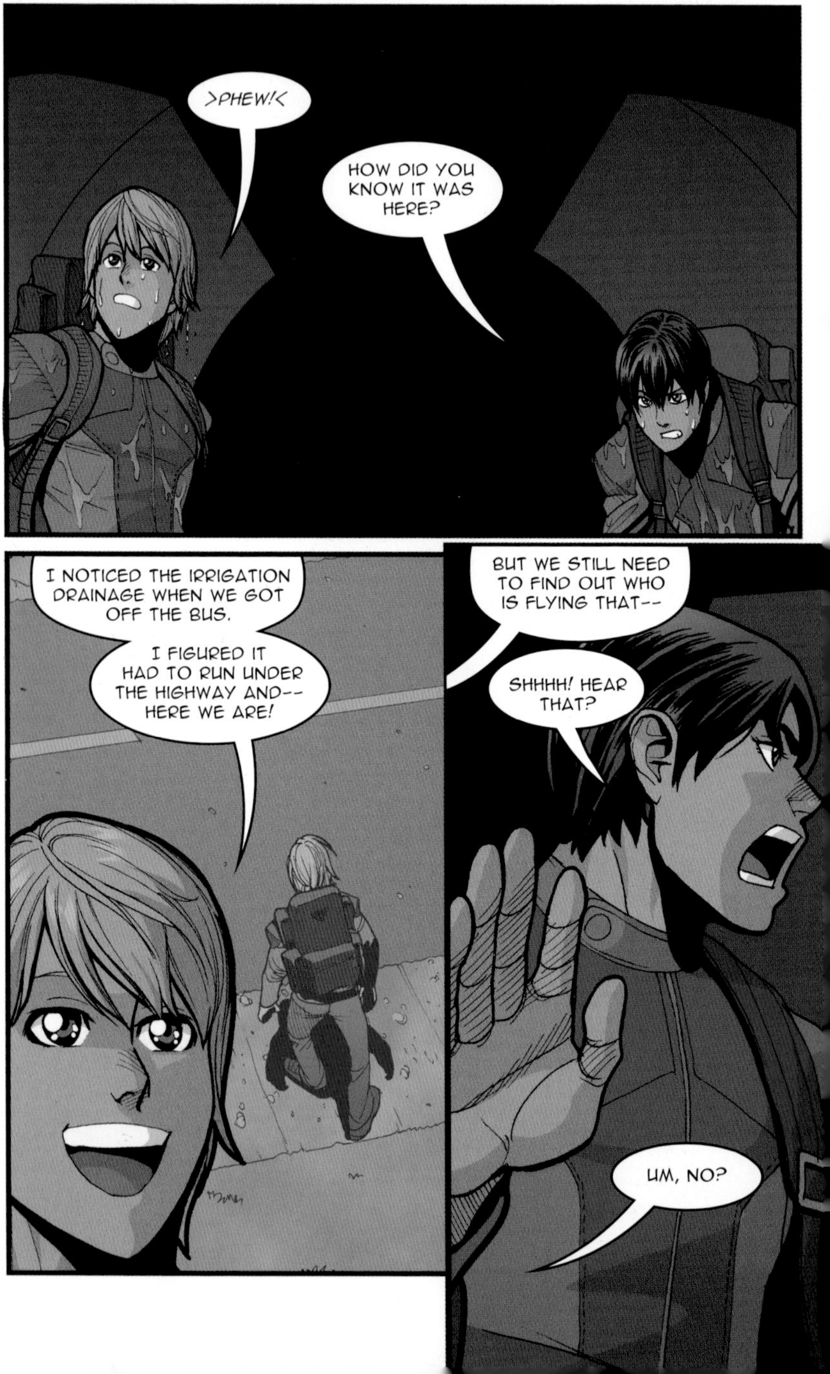
>PHEW!<
HOW DID YOU KNOW IT WAS HERE?
I NOTICED THE IRRIGATION DRAINAGE WHEN WE GOT OFF THE BUS.
I FIGURED IT HAD TO RUN UNDER THE HIGHWAY AND-- HERE WE ARE!
BUT WE STILL NEED TO FIND OUT WHO IS FLYING THAT--
SHHHH! HEAR THAT?
UM, NO?

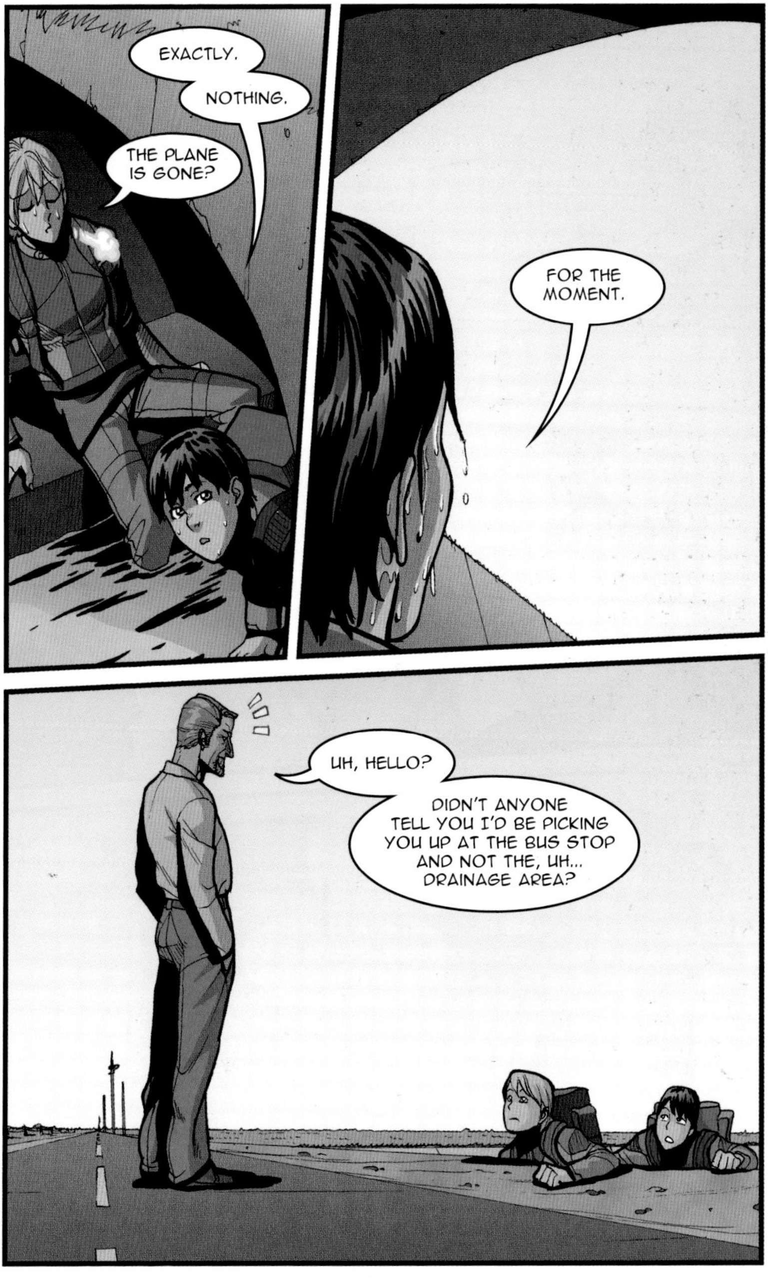
EXACTLY.
NOTHING.
THE PLANE IS GONE?
FOR THE MOMENT.
UH, HELLO?
DIDN'T ANYONE TELL YOU I'D BE PICKING YOU UP AT THE BUS STOP AND NOT THE, UH... DRAINAGE AREA?

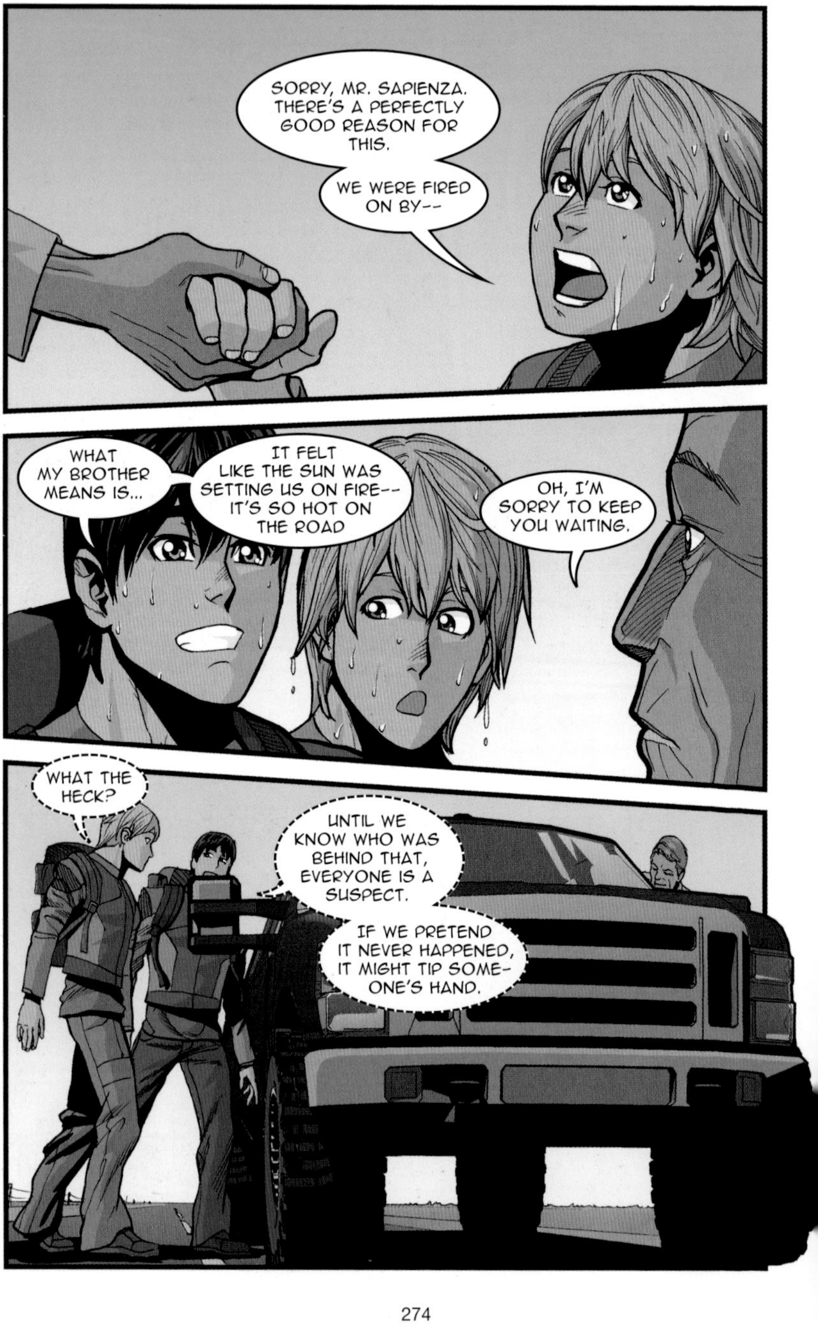
SORRY, MR. SAPIENZA. THERE'S A PERFECTLY GOOD REASON FOR THIS.
WE WERE FIRED ON BY--
WHAT MY BROTHER MEANS IS...
IT FELT LIKE THE SUN WAS SETTING US ON FIRE-- IT'S SO HOT ON THE ROAD
OH, I'M SORRY TO KEEP YOU WAITING.
WHAT THE HECK?
UNTIL WE KNOW WHO WAS BEHIND THAT, EVERYONE IS A SUSPECT.
IF WE PRETEND IT NEVER HAPPENED, IT MIGHT TIP SOME-ONE'S HAND.

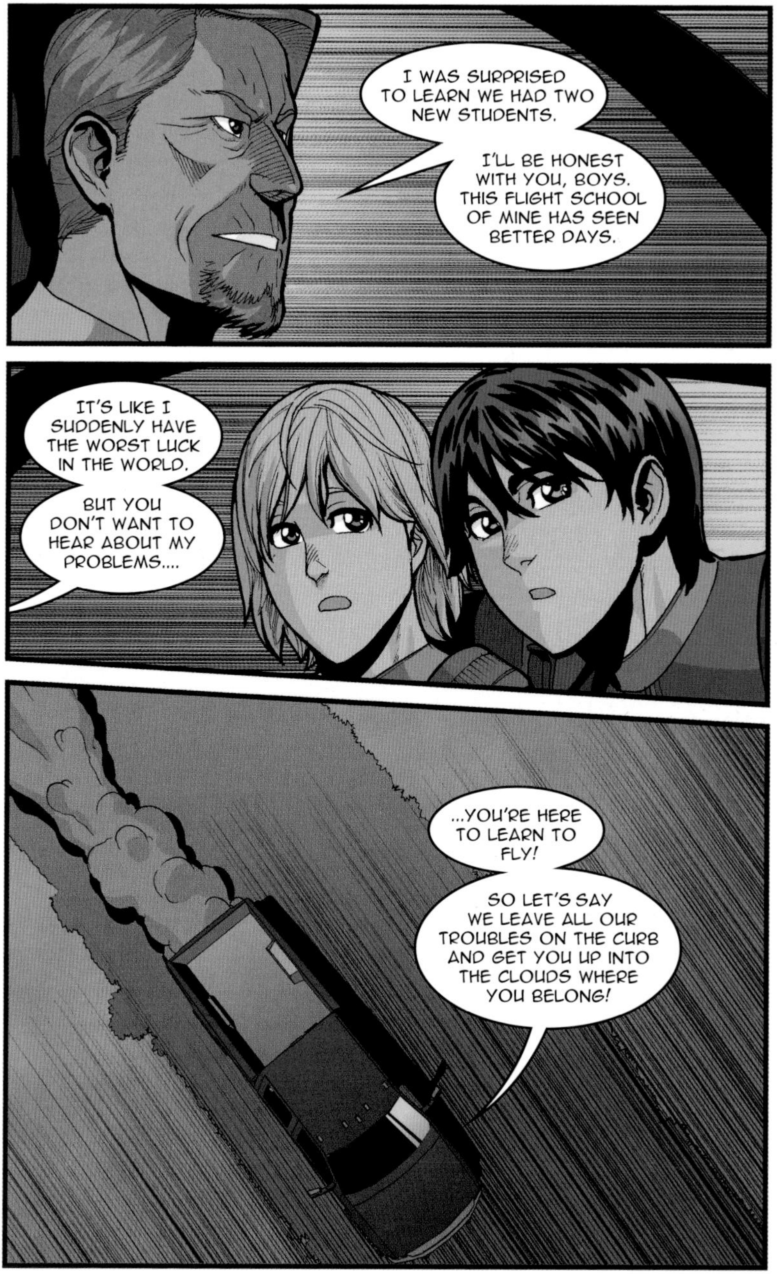
I WAS SURPRISED TO LEARN WE HAD TWO NEW STUDENTS.
I'LL BE HONEST WITH YOU, BOYS. THIS FLIGHT SCHOOL OF MINE HAS SEEN BETTER DAYS.
IT'S LIKE I SUDDENLY HAVE THE WORST LUCK IN THE WORLD.
BUT YOU DON'T WANT TO HEAR ABOUT MY PROBLEMS....
...YOU'RE HERE TO LEARN TO FLY!
SO LET'S SAY WE LEAVE ALL OUR TROUBLES ON THE CURB AND GET YOU UP INTO THE CLOUDS WHERE YOU BELONG!

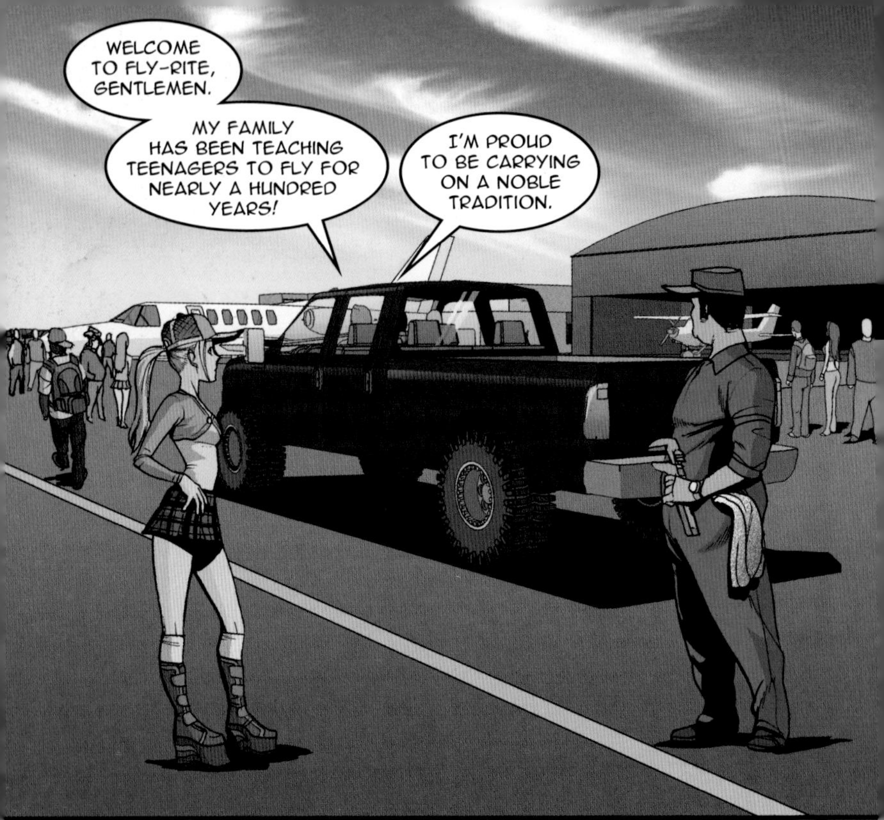
WELCOME TO FLY-RITE, GENTLEMEN.
MY FAMILY HAS BEEN TEACHING TEENAGERS TO FLY FOR NEARLY A HUNDRED YEARS!
I'M PROUD TO BE CARRYING ON A NOBLE TRADITION.

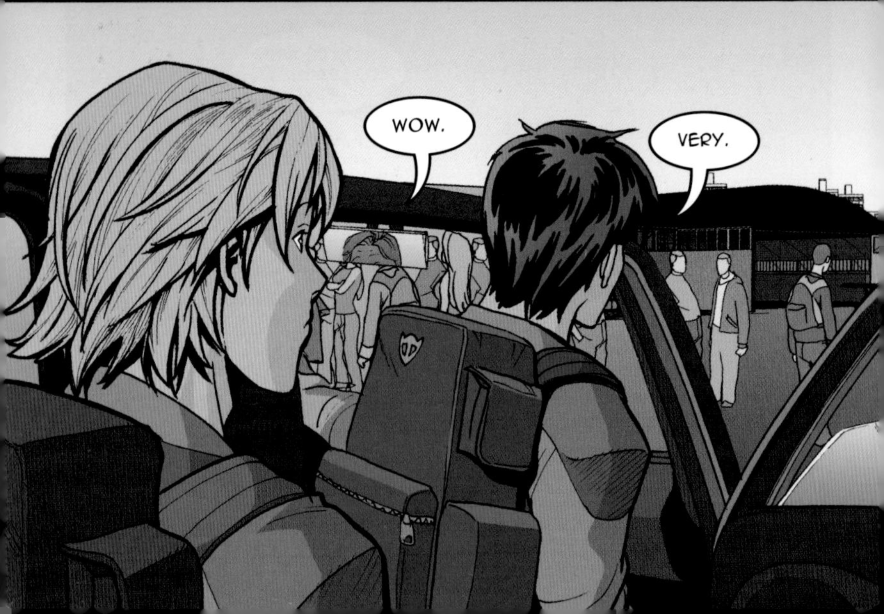
WOW.
VERY.

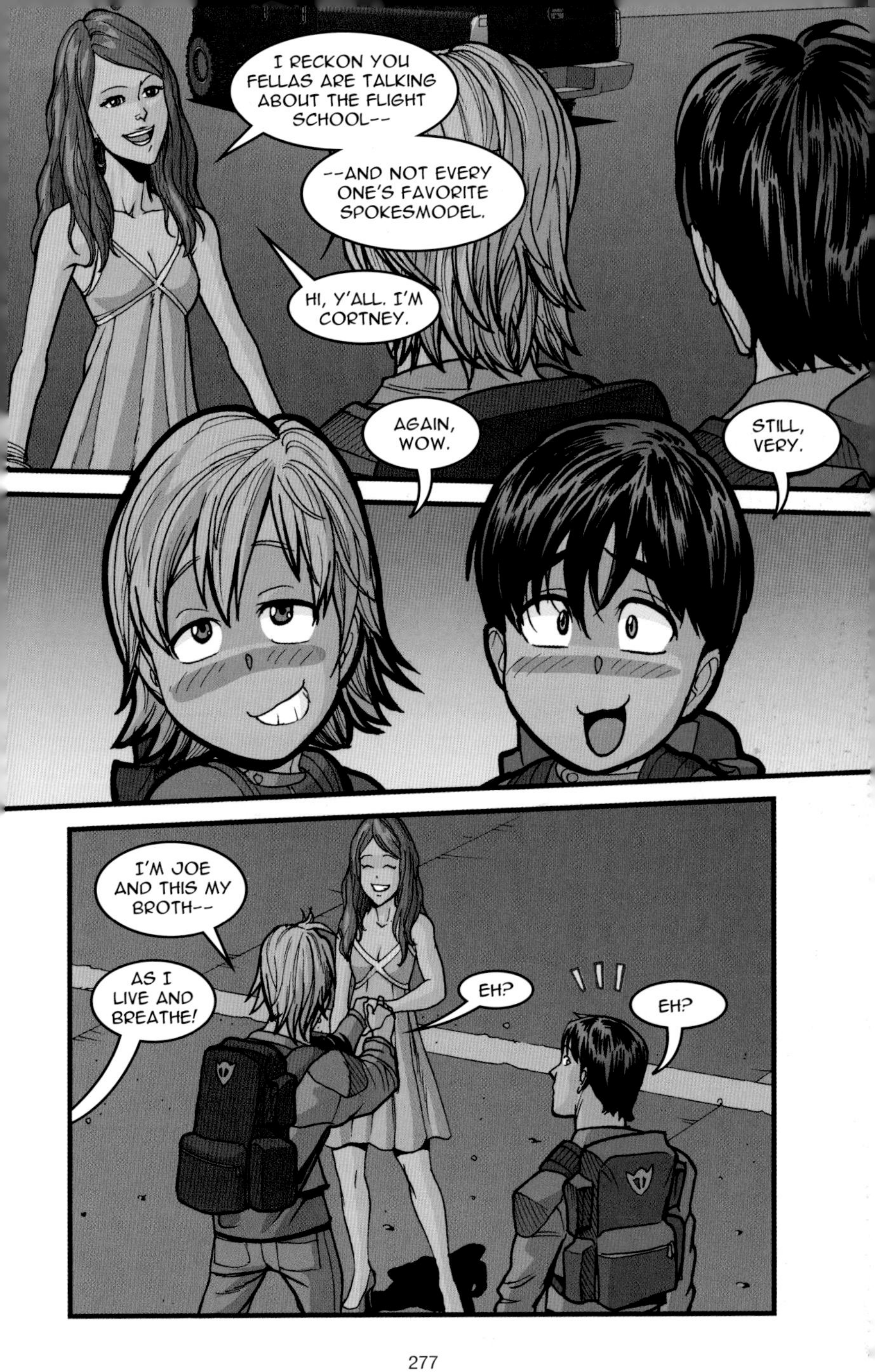
I RECKON YOU FELLAS ARE TALKING ABOUT THE FLIGHT SCHOOL--
--AND NOT EVERY ONE'S FAVORITE SPOKESMODEL.
HI, Y'ALL. I'M CORTNEY.
AGAIN, WOW.
STILL, VERY.
I'M JOE AND THIS MY BROTH--
AS I LIVE AND BREATHE!
EH?
EH?

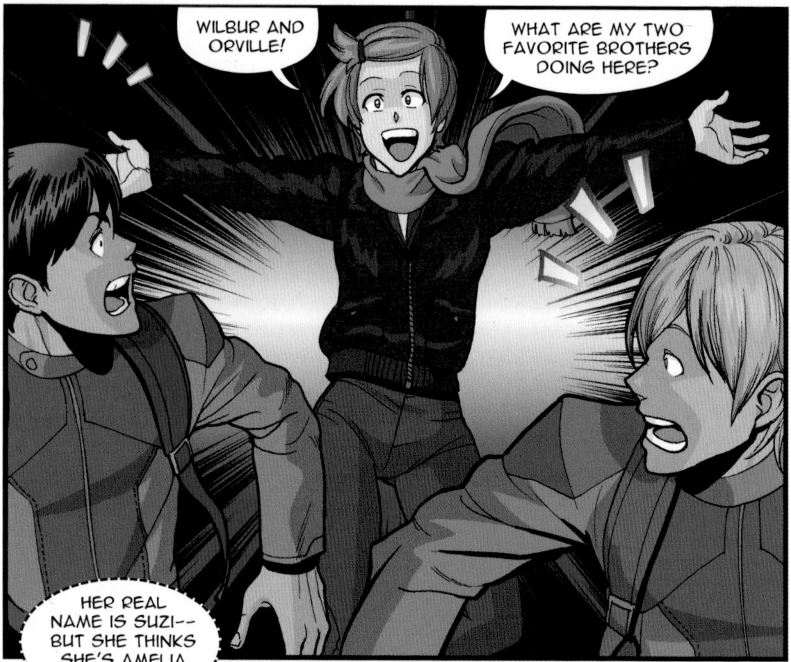
WILBUR AND ORVILLE!
WHAT ARE MY TWO FAVORITE BROTHERS DOING HERE?
HER REAL NAME IS SUZI-- BUT SHE THINKS SHE'S AMELIA EARHART.

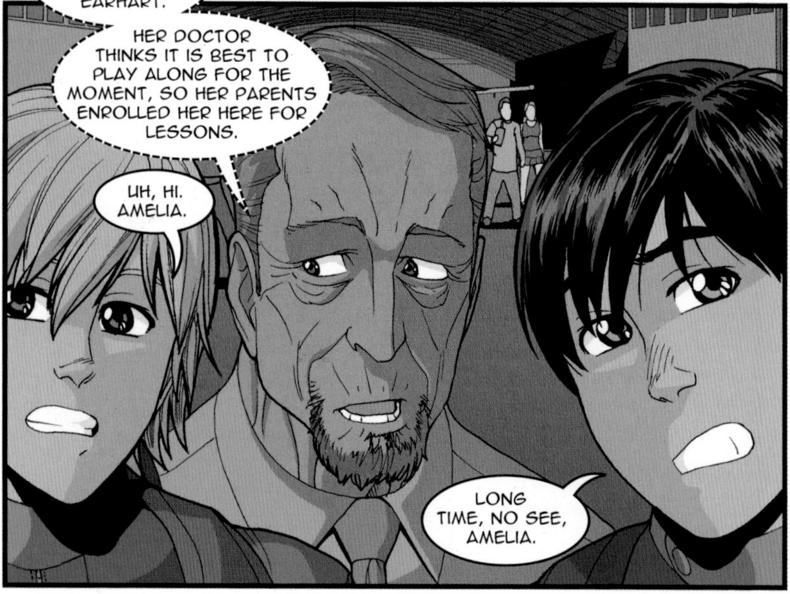
HER DOCTOR THINKS IT IS BEST TO PLAY ALONG FOR THE MOMENT, SO HER PARENTS ENROLLED HER HERE FOR LESSONS.
UH, HI. AMELIA.
LONG TIME, NO SEE, AMELIA.

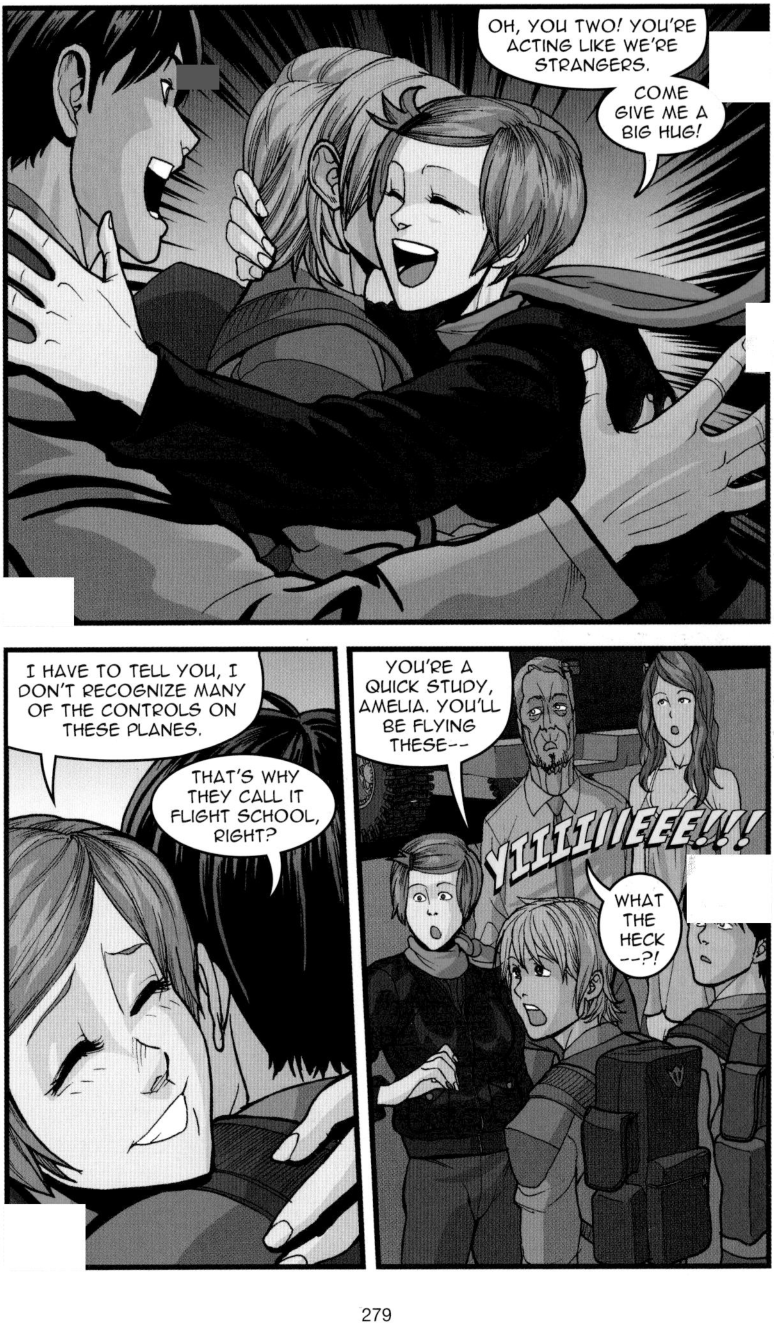
OH, YOU TWO! YOU'RE ACTING LIKE WE'RE STRANGERS.
COME GIVE ME A BIG HUG!
I HAVE TO TELL YOU, I DON'T RECOGNIZE MANY OF THE CONTROLS ON THESE PLANES.
THAT'S WHY THEY CALL IT FLIGHT SCHOOL, RIGHT?
YOU'RE A QUICK STUDY, AMELIA. YOU'LL BE FLYING THESE--
YIIIIIIEEE!!!
WHAT THE HECK --?!

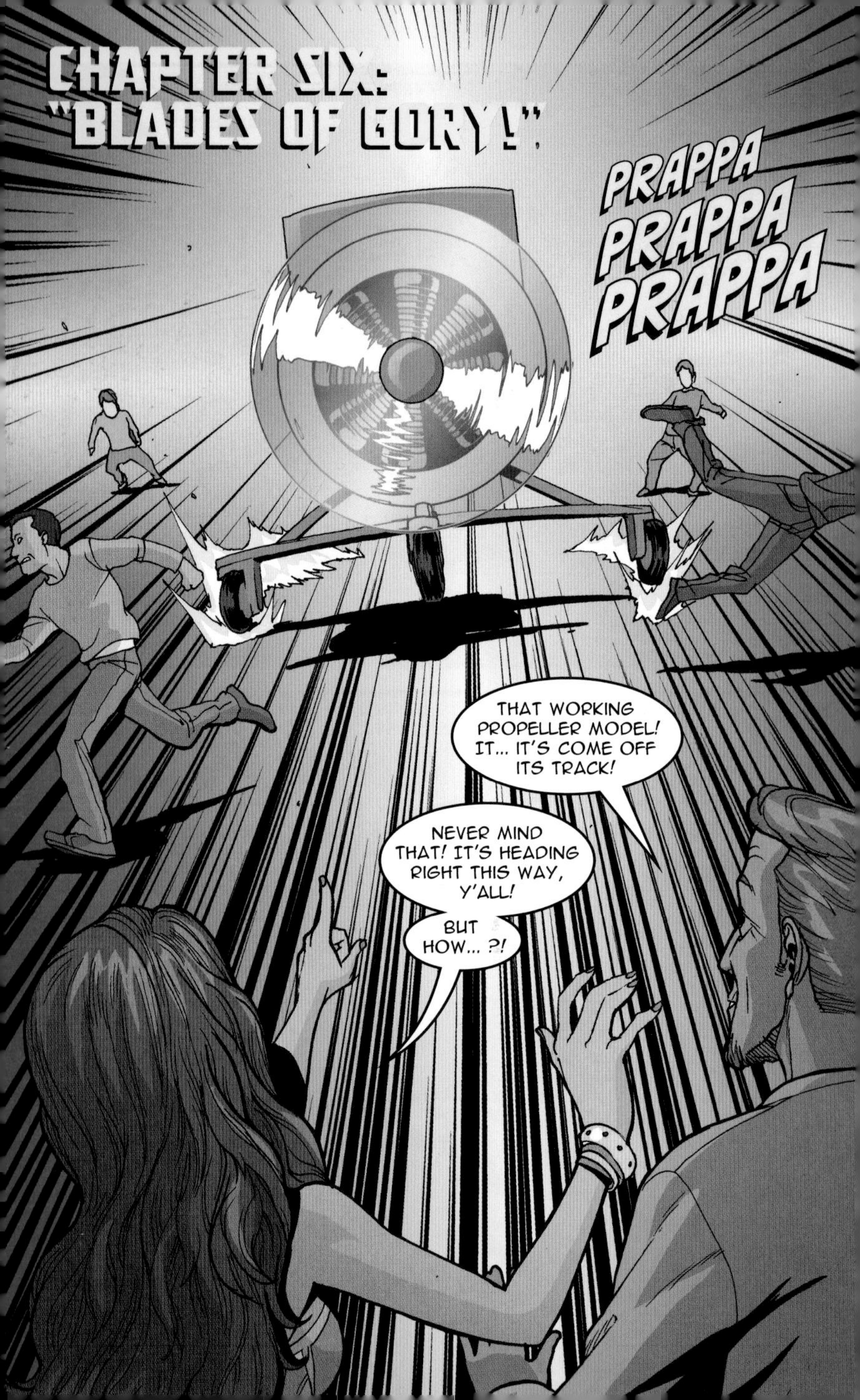
CHAPTER SIX:
"BLADES OF GORY!"
PRAPPA PRAPPA PRAPPA
THAT WORKING PROPELLER MODEL! IT... IT'S COME OFF ITS TRACK!
NEVER MIND THAT! IT'S HEADING RIGHT THIS WAY, Y'ALL!
BUT HOW... ?!

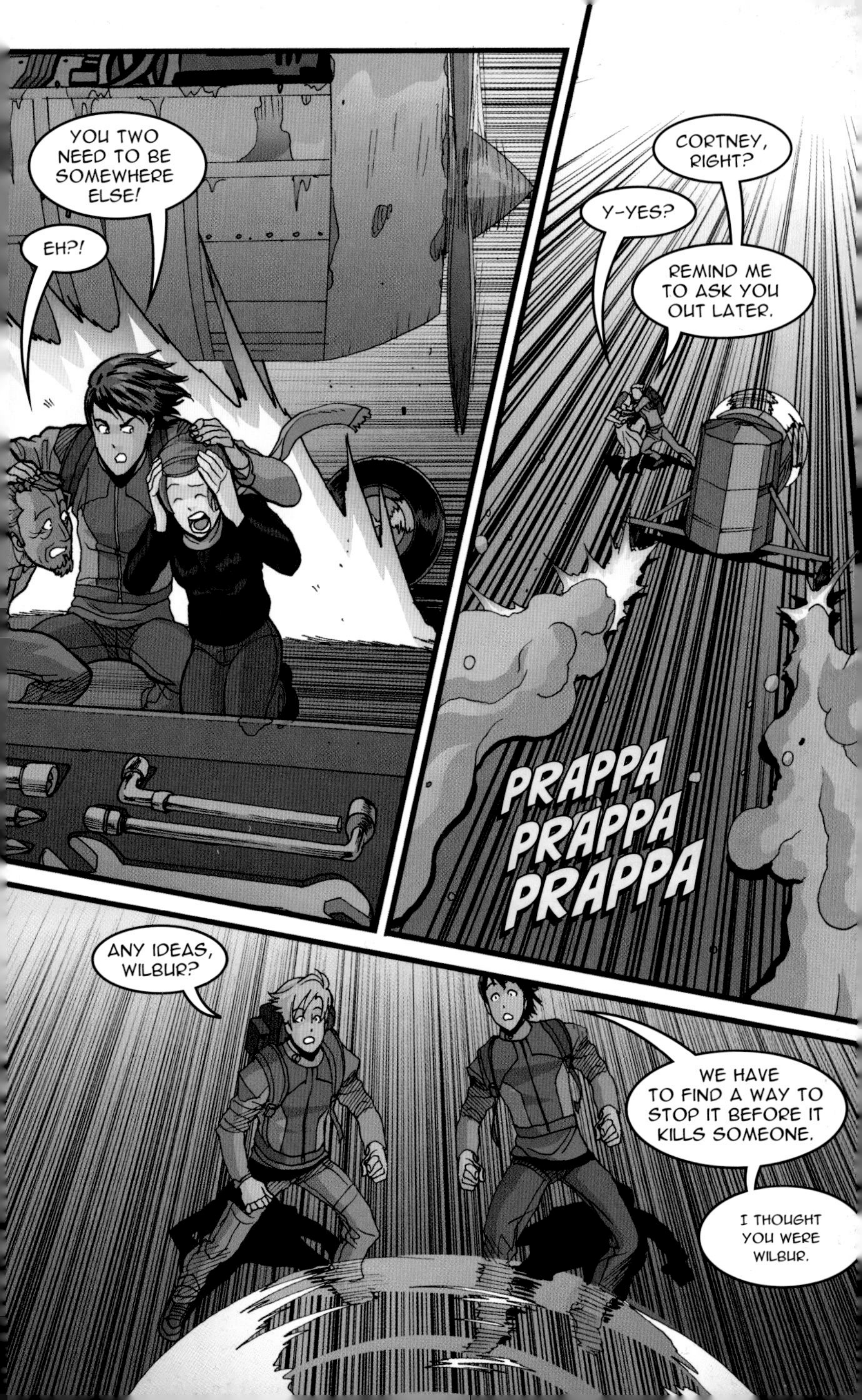
YOU TWO NEED TO BE SOMEWHERE ELSE!
EH?!
CORTNEY, RIGHT?
Y-YES?
REMIND ME TO ASK YOU OUT LATER.
PRAPPA PRAPPA PRAPPA
ANY IDEAS, WILBUR?
WE HAVE TO FIND A WAY TO STOP IT BEFORE IT KILLS SOMEONE.
I THOUGHT YOU WERE WILBUR.

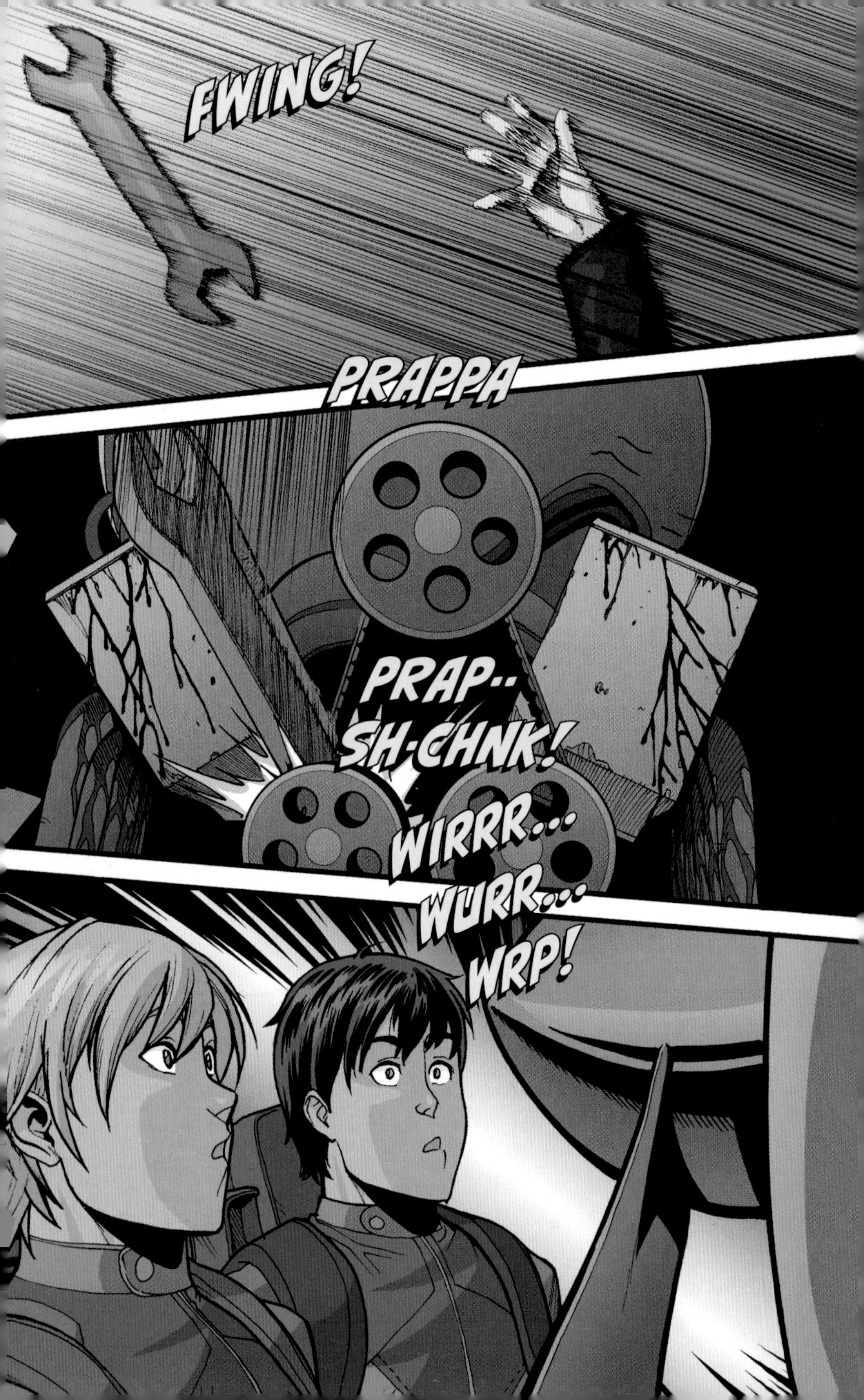
FWING!
PRAPPA
PRAP..
SH-CHNK!
WIRRR...
WURR...
WRP!

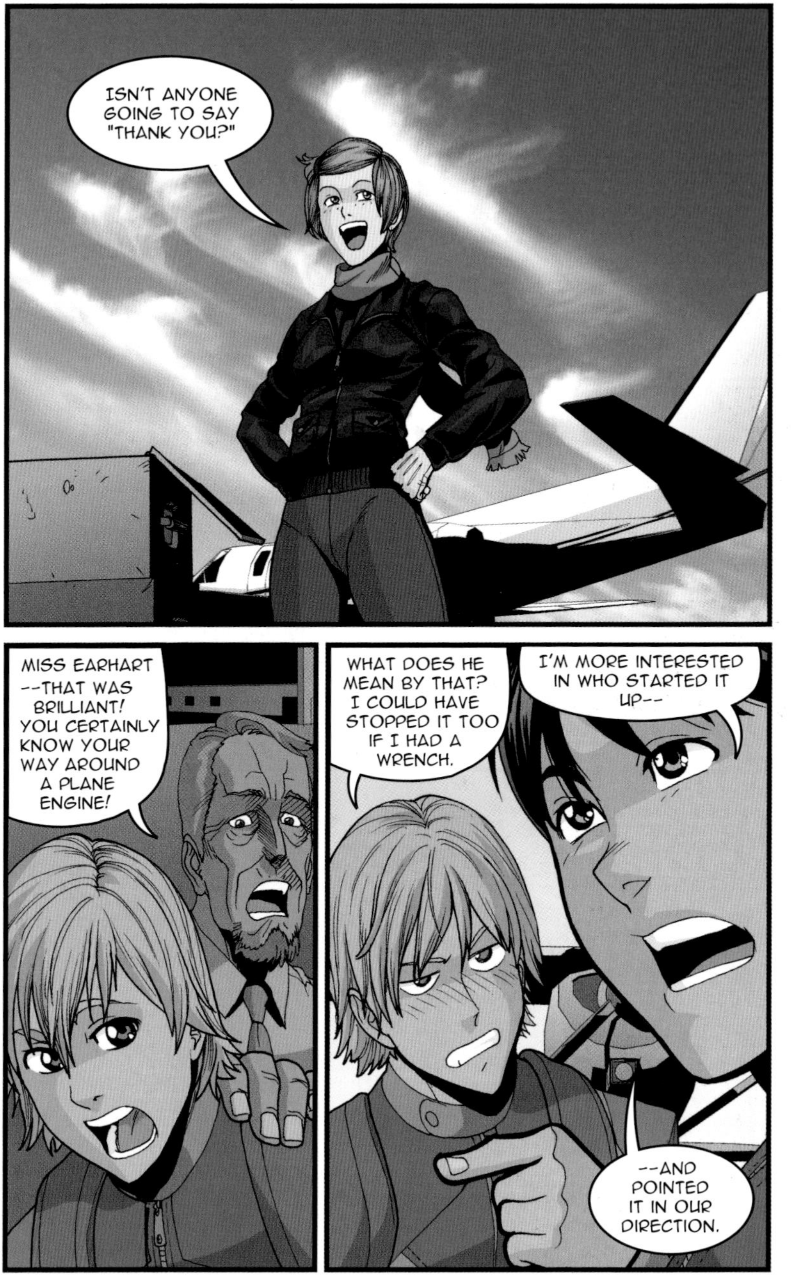
ISN'T ANYONE GOING TO SAY "THANK YOU?"
MISS EARHART --THAT WAS BRILLIANT! YOU CERTAINLY KNOW YOUR WAY AROUND A PLANE ENGINE!
WHAT DOES HE MEAN BY THAT? I COULD HAVE STOPPED IT TOO IF I HAD A WRENCH.
I'M MORE INTERESTED IN WHO STARTED IT UP--
--AND POINTED IT IN OUR DIRECTION.

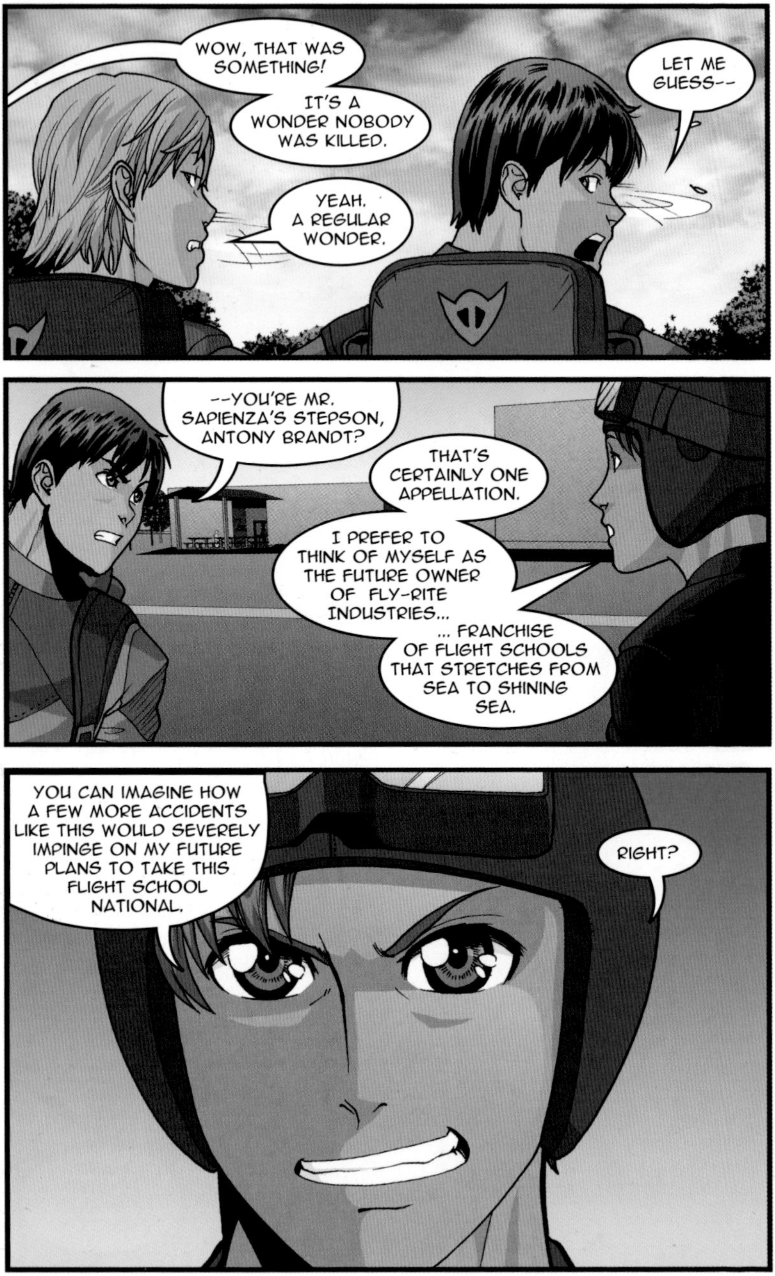
WOW, THAT WAS SOMETHING!
IT'S A WONDER NOBODY WAS KILLED.
YEAH. A REGULAR WONDER.
LET ME GUESS--
--YOU'RE MR. SAPIENZA'S STEPSON, ANTONY BRANDT?
THAT'S CERTAINLY ONE APPELLATION.
I PREFER TO THINK OF MYSELF AS THE FUTURE OWNER OF FLY-RITE INDUSTRIES...
... FRANCHISE OF FLIGHT SCHOOLS THAT STRETCHES FROM SEA TO SHINING SEA.
YOU CAN IMAGINE HOW A FEW MORE ACCIDENTS LIKE THIS WOULD SEVERELY IMPINGE ON MY FUTURE PLANS TO TAKE THIS FLIGHT SCHOOL NATIONAL.
RIGHT?

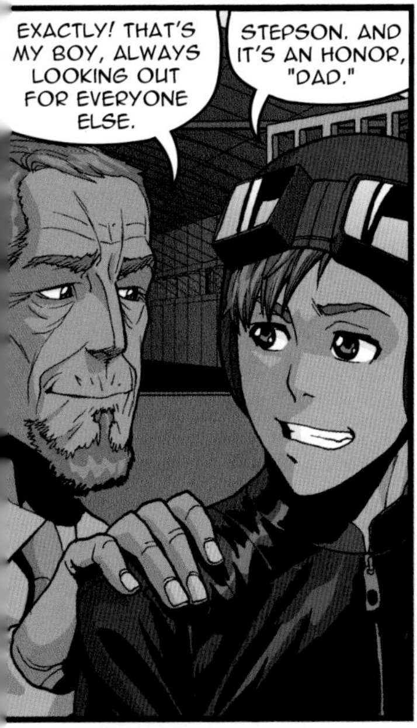
EXACTLY! THAT'S MY BOY, ALWAYS LOOKING OUT FOR EVERYONE ELSE.
STEPSON. AND IT'S AN HONOR, "DAD."

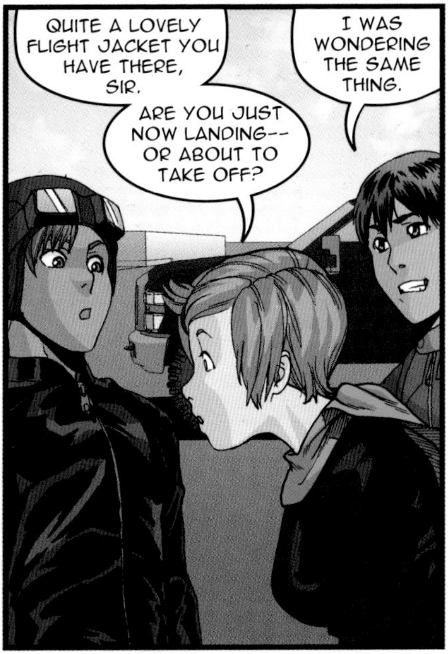
QUITE A LOVELY FLIGHT JACKET YOU HAVE THERE, SIR.
ARE YOU JUST NOW LANDING-- OR ABOUT TO TAKE OFF?
I WAS WONDERING THE SAME THING.

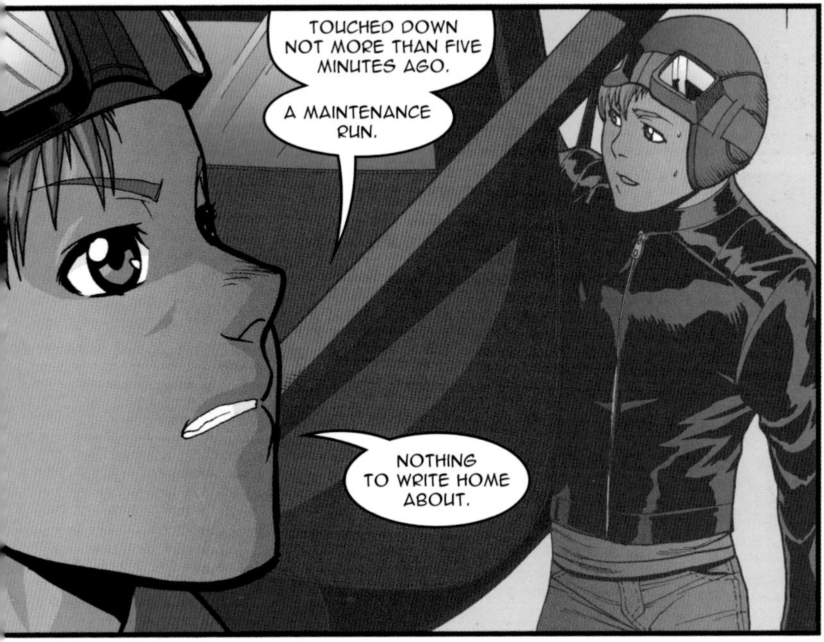
TOUCHED DOWN NOT MORE THAN FIVE MINUTES AGO.
A MAINTENANCE RUN.
NOTHING TO WRITE HOME ABOUT.

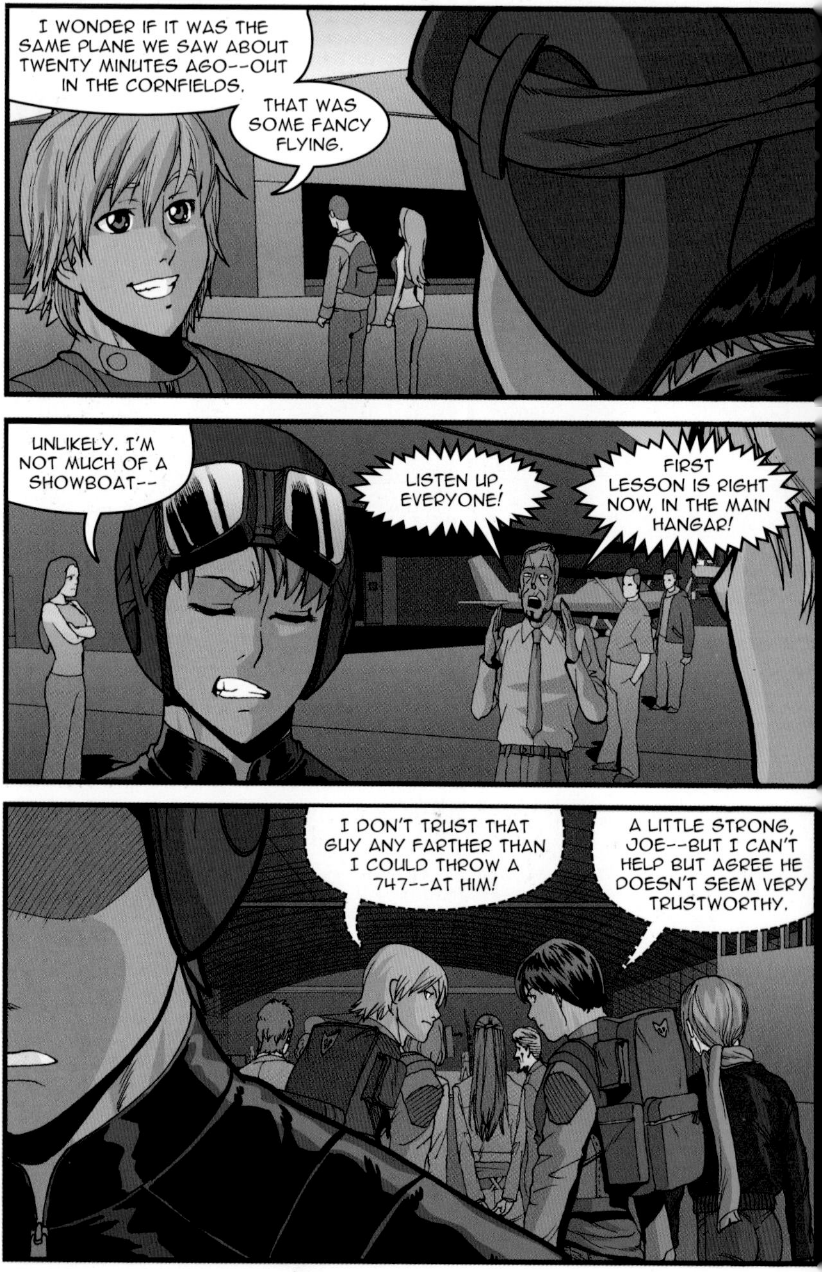
I WONDER IF IT WAS THE SAME PLANE WE SAW ABOUT TWENTY MINUTES AGO--OUT IN THE CORNFIELDS.
THAT WAS SOME FANCY FLYING.
UNLIKELY. I'M NOT MUCH OF A SHOWBOAT--
LISTEN UP, EVERYONE!
FIRST LESSON IS RIGHT NOW, IN THE MAIN HANGAR!
I DON'T TRUST THAT GUY ANY FARTHER THAN I COULD THROW A 747--AT HIM!
A LITTLE STRONG, JOE--BUT I CAN'T HELP BUT AGREE HE DOESN'T SEEM VERY TRUSTWORTHY.

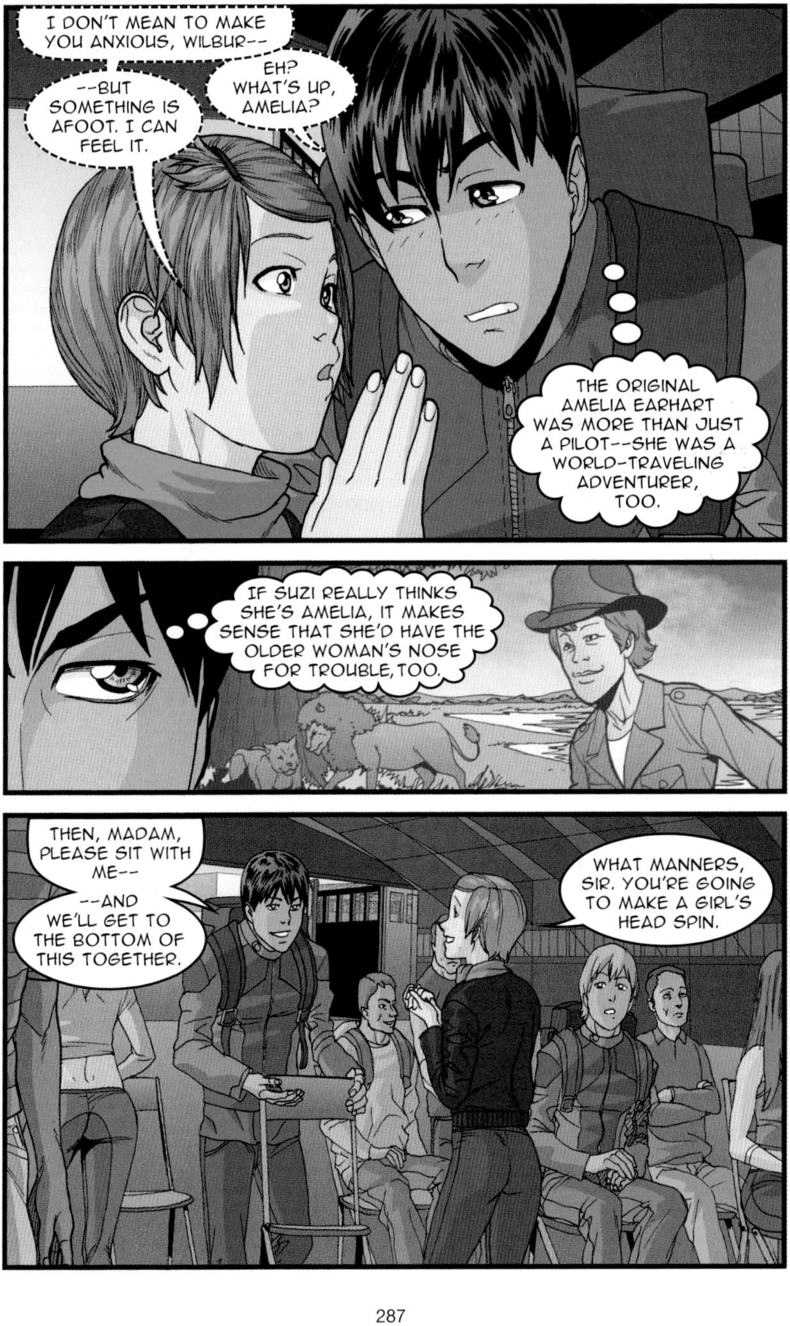
I DON'T MEAN TO MAKE YOU ANXIOUS, WILBUR--
--BUT SOMETHING IS AFOOT. I CAN FEEL IT.
EH? WHAT'S UP, AMELIA?
THE ORIGINAL AMELIA EARHART WAS MORE THAN JUST A PILOT--SHE WAS A WORLD-TRAVELING ADVENTURER, TOO.
IF SUZI REALLY THINKS SHE'S AMELIA, IT MAKES SENSE THAT SHE'D HAVE THE OLDER WOMAN'S NOSE FOR TROUBLE, TOO.
THEN, MADAM, PLEASE SIT WITH ME--
--AND WE'LL GET TO THE BOTTOM OF THIS TOGETHER.
WHAT MANNERS, SIR. YOU'RE GOING TO MAKE A GIRL'S HEAD SPIN.

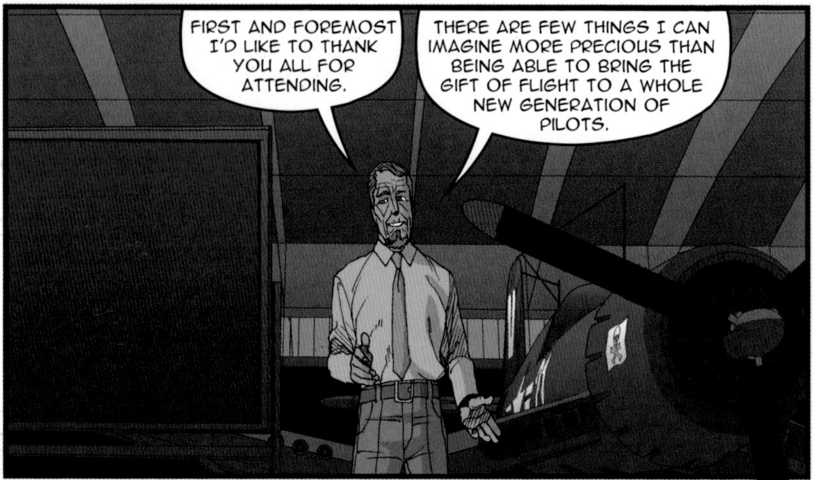
FIRST AND FOREMOST I'D LIKE TO THANK YOU ALL FOR ATTENDING.
THERE ARE FEW THINGS I CAN IMAGINE MORE PRECIOUS THAN BEING ABLE TO BRING THE GIFT OF FLIGHT TO A WHOLE NEW GENERATION OF PILOTS.

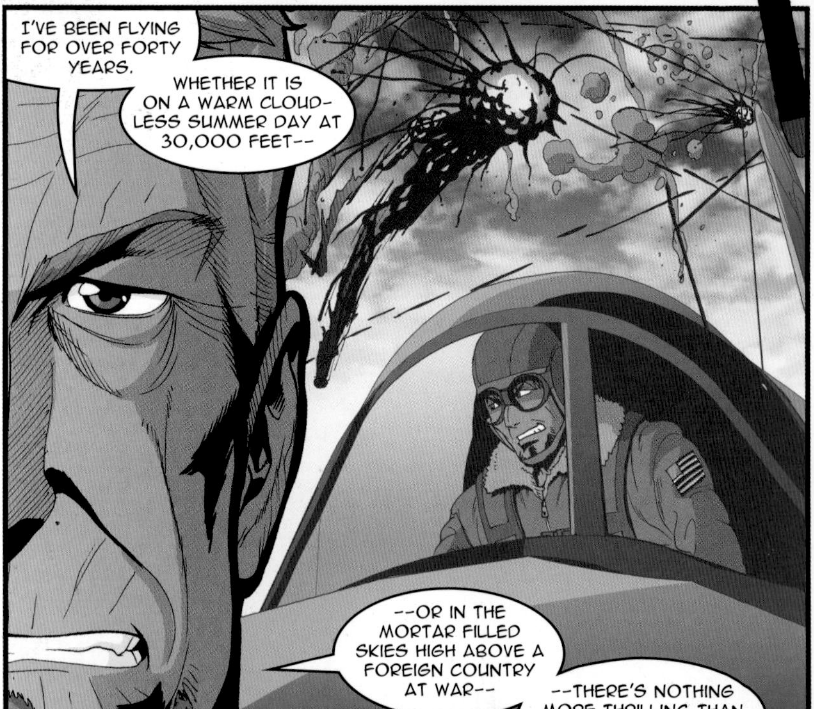
I'VE BEEN FLYING FOR OVER FORTY YEARS.
WHETHER IT IS ON A WARM CLOUDLESS SUMMER DAY AT 30,000 FEET--
--OR IN THE MORTAR FILLED SKIES HIGH ABOVE A FOREIGN COUNTRY AT WAR--
--THERE'S NOTHING MORE THRILLING THAN BEING THE PILOT OF YOUR OWN DESTINY.

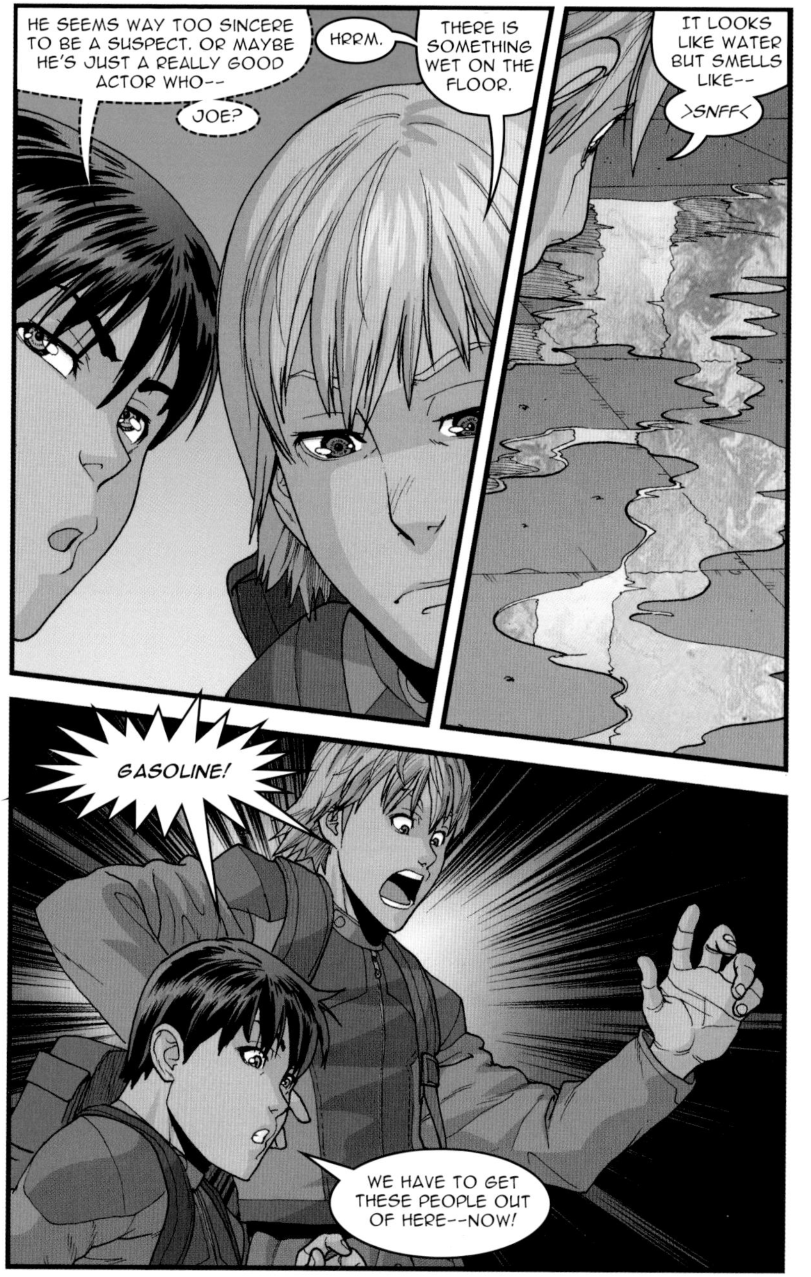
HE SEEMS WAY TOO SINCERE TO BE A SUSPECT. OR MAYBE HE'S JUST A REALLY GOOD ACTOR WHO--
JOE?
HRRM.
THERE IS SOMETHING WET ON THE FLOOR.
IT LOOKS LIKE WATER BUT SMELLS LIKE--
>SNFF<
GASOLINE!
WE HAVE TO GET THESE PEOPLE OUT OF HERE--NOW!

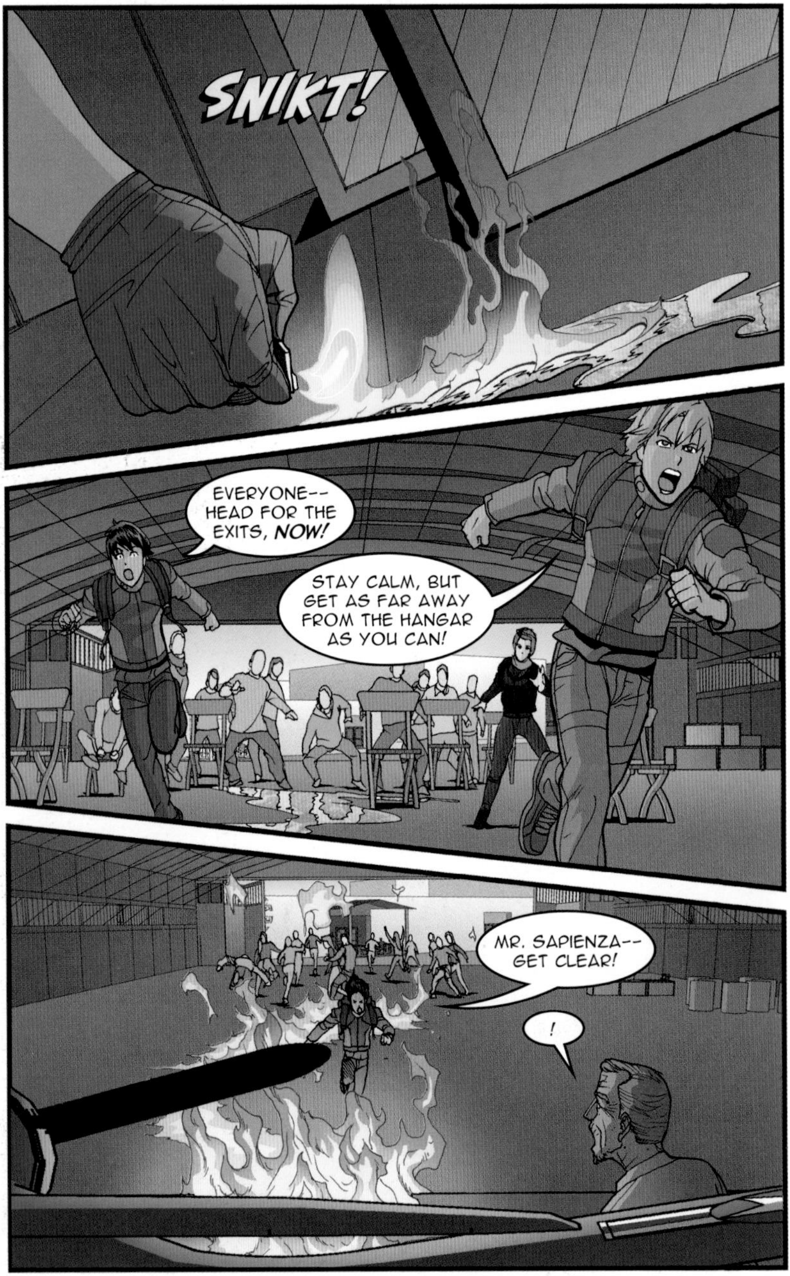
SNIKT!
EVERYONE-- HEAD FOR THE EXITS, NOW!
STAY CALM, BUT GET AS FAR AWAY FROM THE HANGAR AS YOU CAN!
MR. SAPIENZA-- GET CLEAR!
!

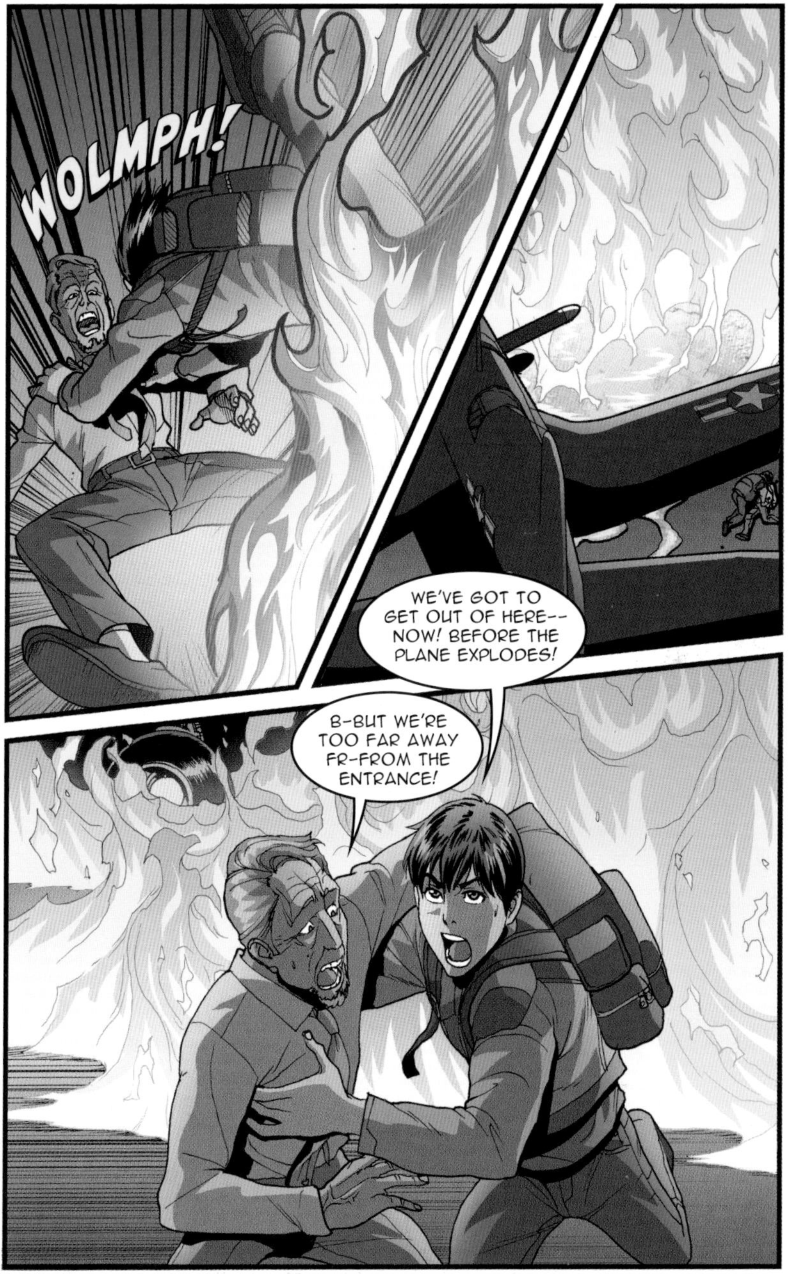
WOLMPH!
WE'VE GOT TO GET OUT OF HERE-- NOW! BEFORE THE PLANE EXPLODES!
B-BUT WE'RE TOO FAR AWAY FR-FROM THE ENTRANCE!

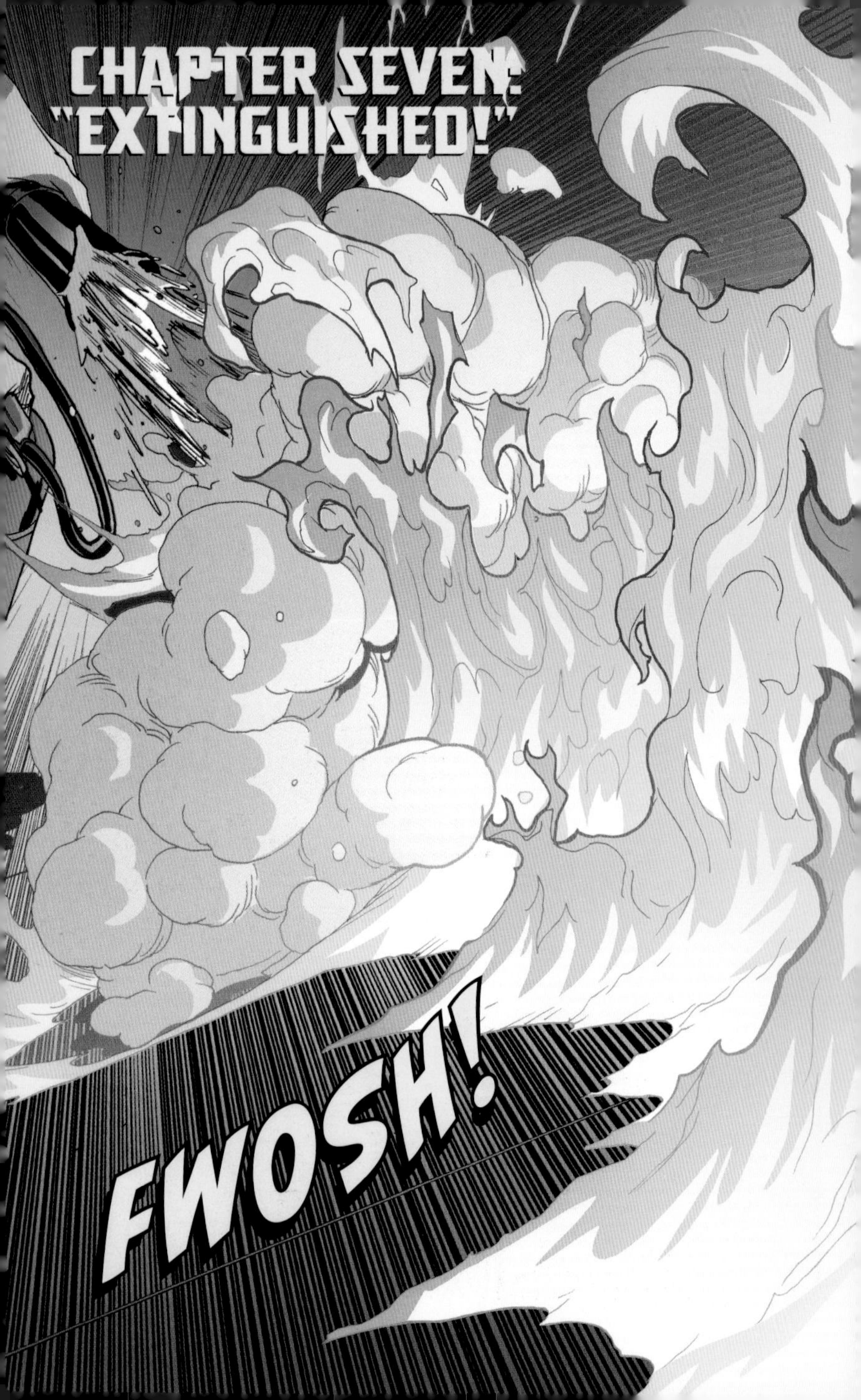
CHAPTER SEVEN:
"EXTINGUISHED!"
FWOSH!

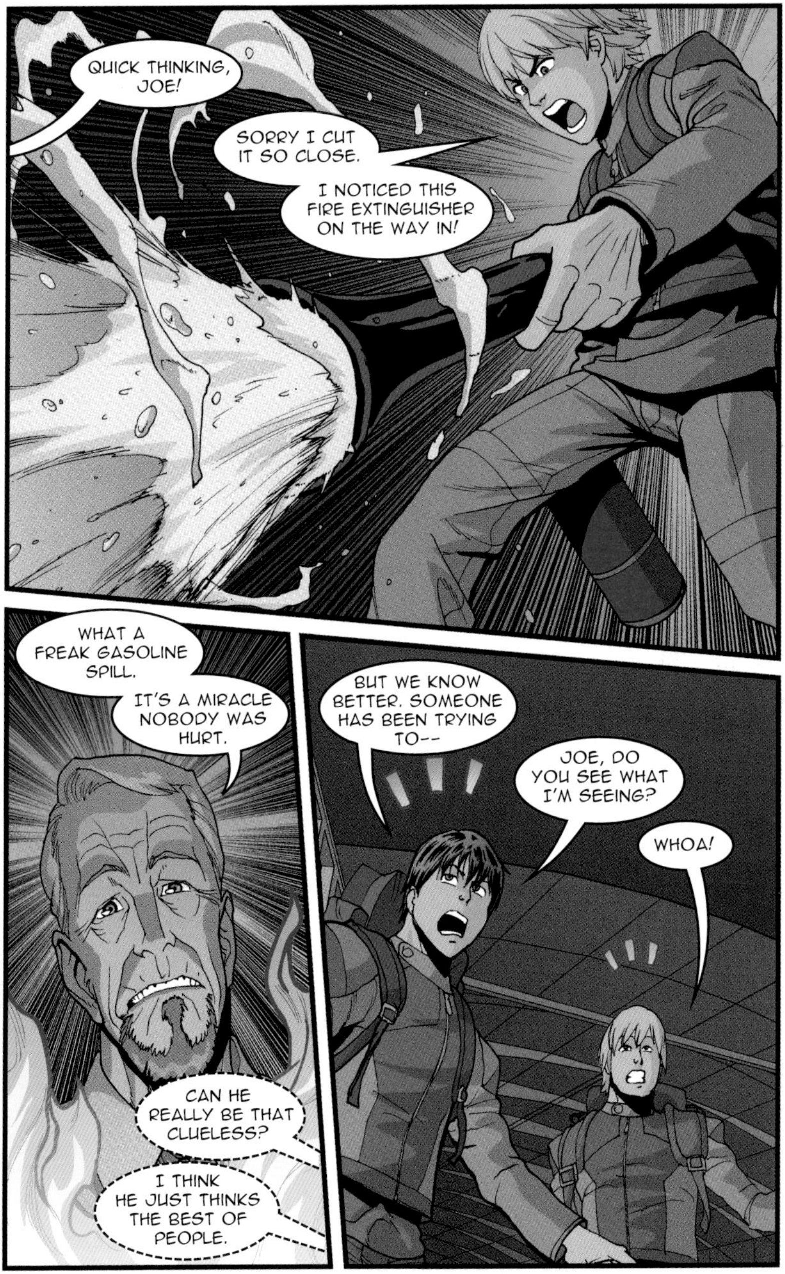
QUICK THINKING, JOE!
SORRY I CUT IT SO CLOSE.
I NOTICED THIS FIRE EXTINGUISHER ON THE WAY IN!
WHAT A FREAK GASOLINE SPILL.
IT'S A MIRACLE NOBODY WAS HURT.
CAN HE REALLY BE THAT CLUELESS?
I THINK HE JUST THINKS THE BEST OF PEOPLE.
BUT WE KNOW BETTER. SOMEONE HAS BEEN TRYING TO--
JOE, DO YOU SEE WHAT I'M SEEING?
WHOA!

CHAPTER EIGHT: "AIR HOSTAGE!"

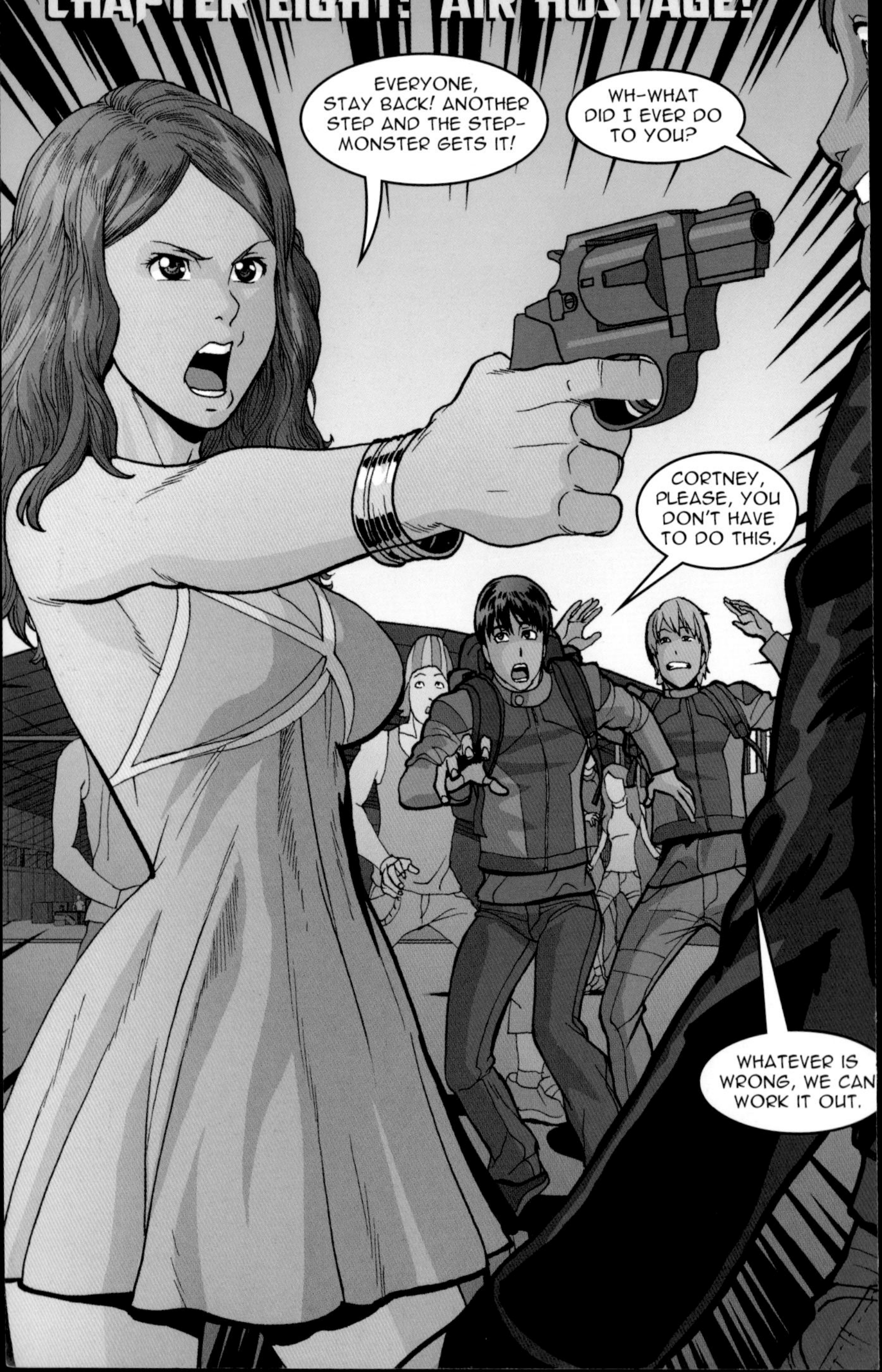
EVERYONE, STAY BACK! ANOTHER STEP AND THE STEP-MONSTER GETS IT!
WH-WHAT DID I EVER DO TO YOU?
CORTNEY, PLEASE, YOU DON'T HAVE TO DO THIS.
WHATEVER IS WRONG, WE CAN WORK IT OUT.

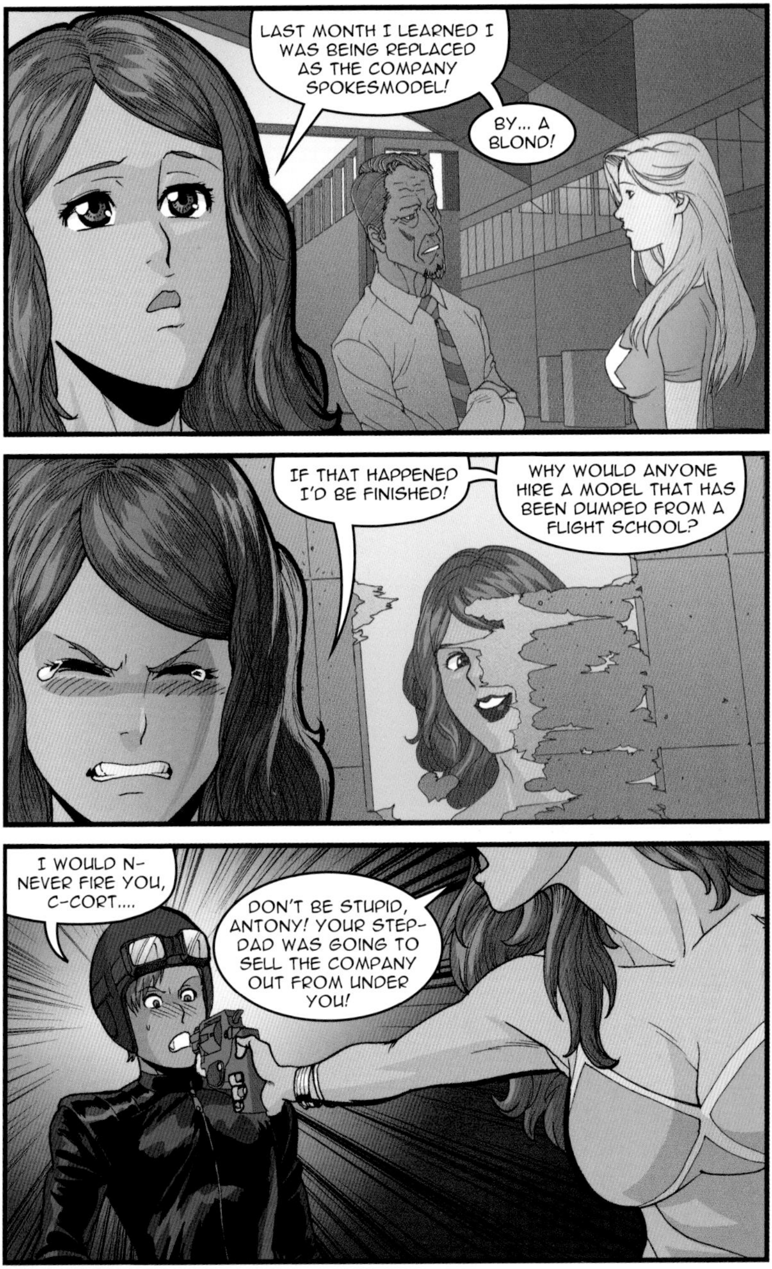
LAST MONTH I LEARNED I WAS BEING REPLACED AS THE COMPANY SPOKESMODEL!
BY... A BLOND!
IF THAT HAPPENED I'D BE FINISHED!
WHY WOULD ANYONE HIRE A MODEL THAT HAS BEEN DUMPED FROM A FLIGHT SCHOOL?
I WOULD N-NEVER FIRE YOU, C-CORT....
DON'T BE STUPID, ANTONY! YOUR STEP-DAD WAS GOING TO SELL THE COMPANY OUT FROM UNDER YOU!

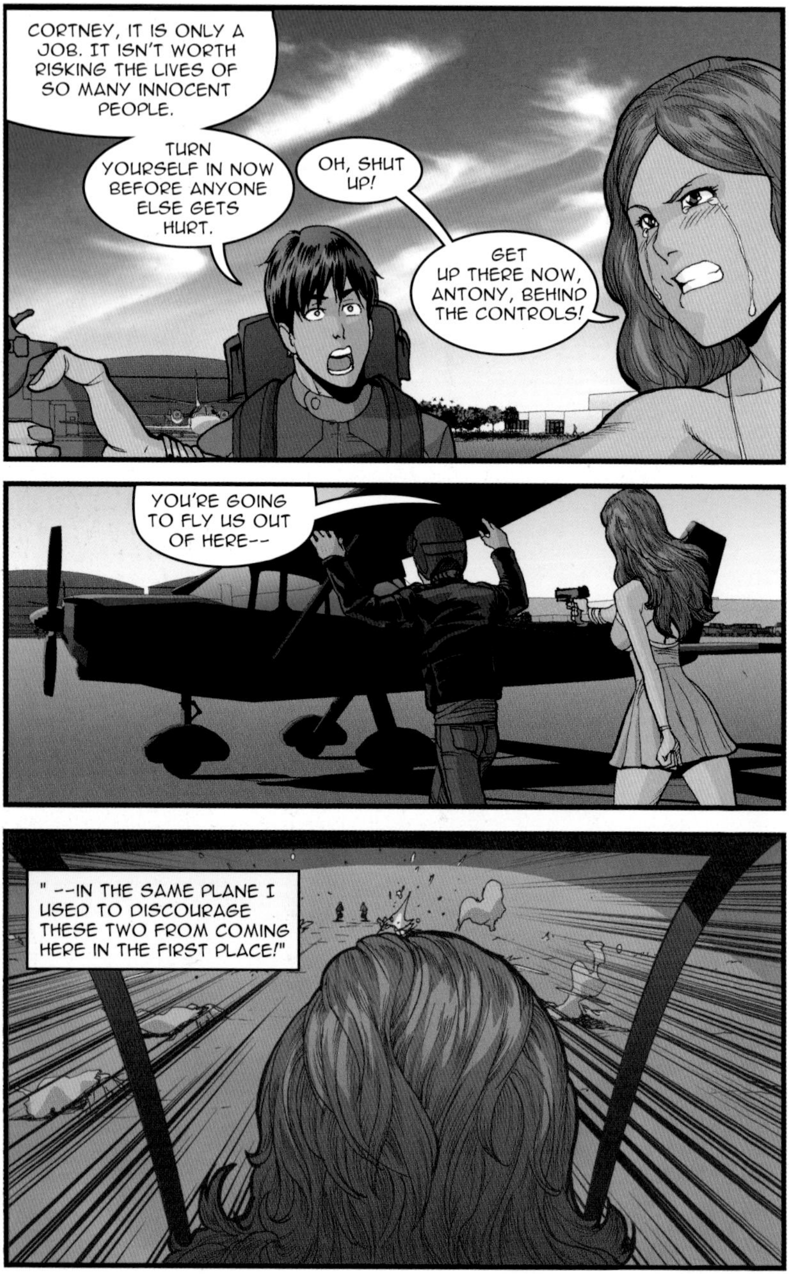
CORTNEY, IT IS ONLY A JOB. IT ISN'T WORTH RISKING THE LIVES OF SO MANY INNOCENT PEOPLE.
TURN YOURSELF IN NOW BEFORE ANYONE ELSE GETS HURT.
OH, SHUT UP!
GET UP THERE NOW, ANTONY, BEHIND THE CONTROLS!
YOU'RE GOING TO FLY US OUT OF HERE--
" --IN THE SAME PLANE I USED TO DISCOURAGE THESE TWO FROM COMING HERE IN THE FIRST PLACE!"

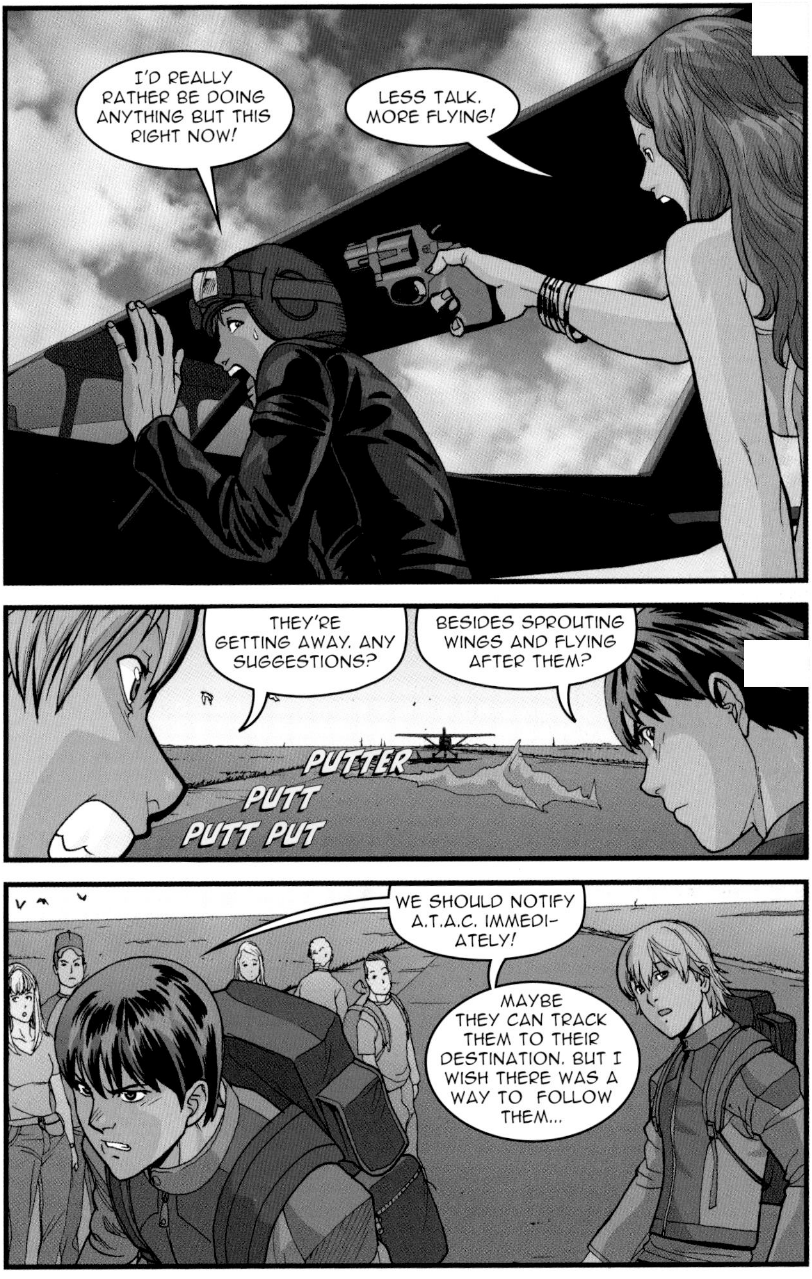
I'D REALLY RATHER BE DOING ANYTHING BUT THIS RIGHT NOW!
LESS TALK. MORE FLYING!
THEY'RE GETTING AWAY. ANY SUGGESTIONS?
BESIDES SPROUTING WINGS AND FLYING AFTER THEM?
PUTTER
PUTT
PUTT PUT
WE SHOULD NOTIFY A.T.A.C. IMMEDI-ATELY!
MAYBE THEY CAN TRACK THEM TO THEIR DESTINATION. BUT I WISH THERE WAS A WAY TO FOLLOW THEM...

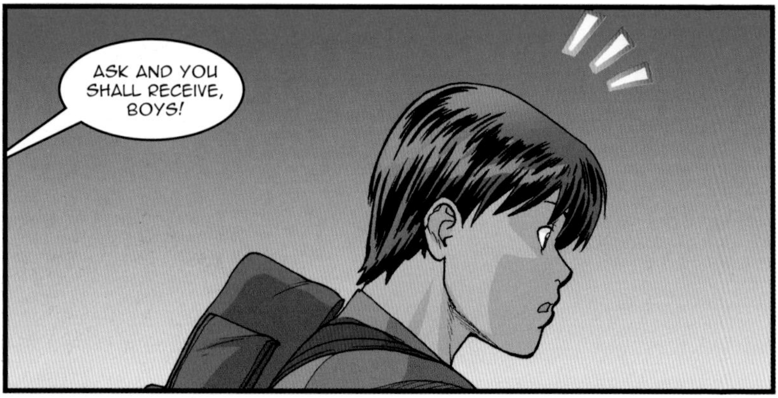
ASK AND YOU SHALL RECEIVE, BOYS!

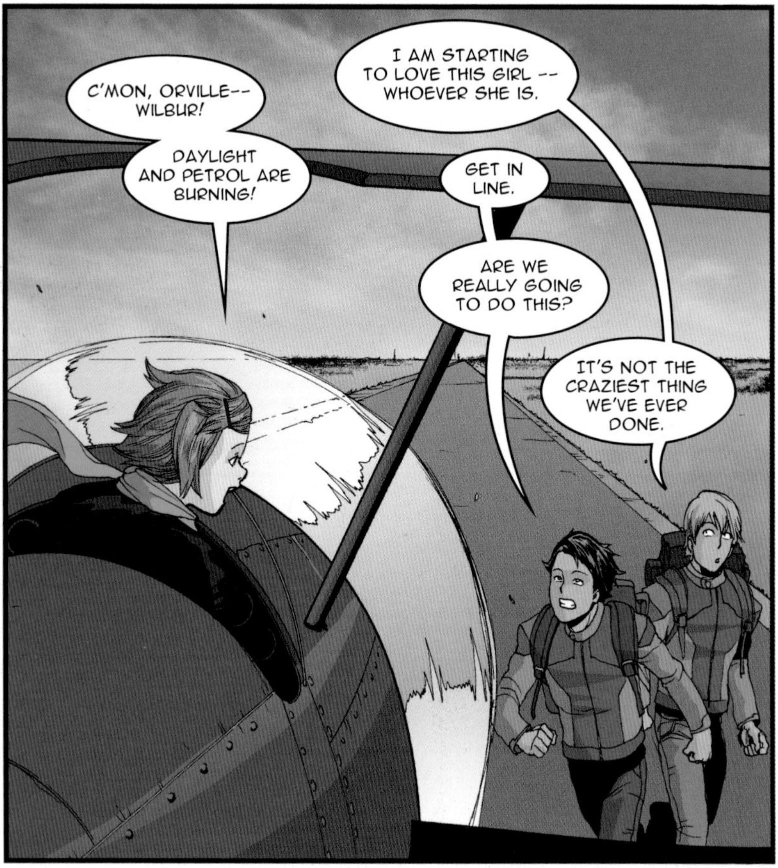
C'MON, ORVILLE-- WILBUR!
DAYLIGHT AND PETROL ARE BURNING!
I AM STARTING TO LOVE THIS GIRL -- WHOEVER SHE IS.
GET IN LINE.
ARE WE REALLY GOING TO DO THIS?
IT'S NOT THE CRAZIEST THING WE'VE EVER DONE.

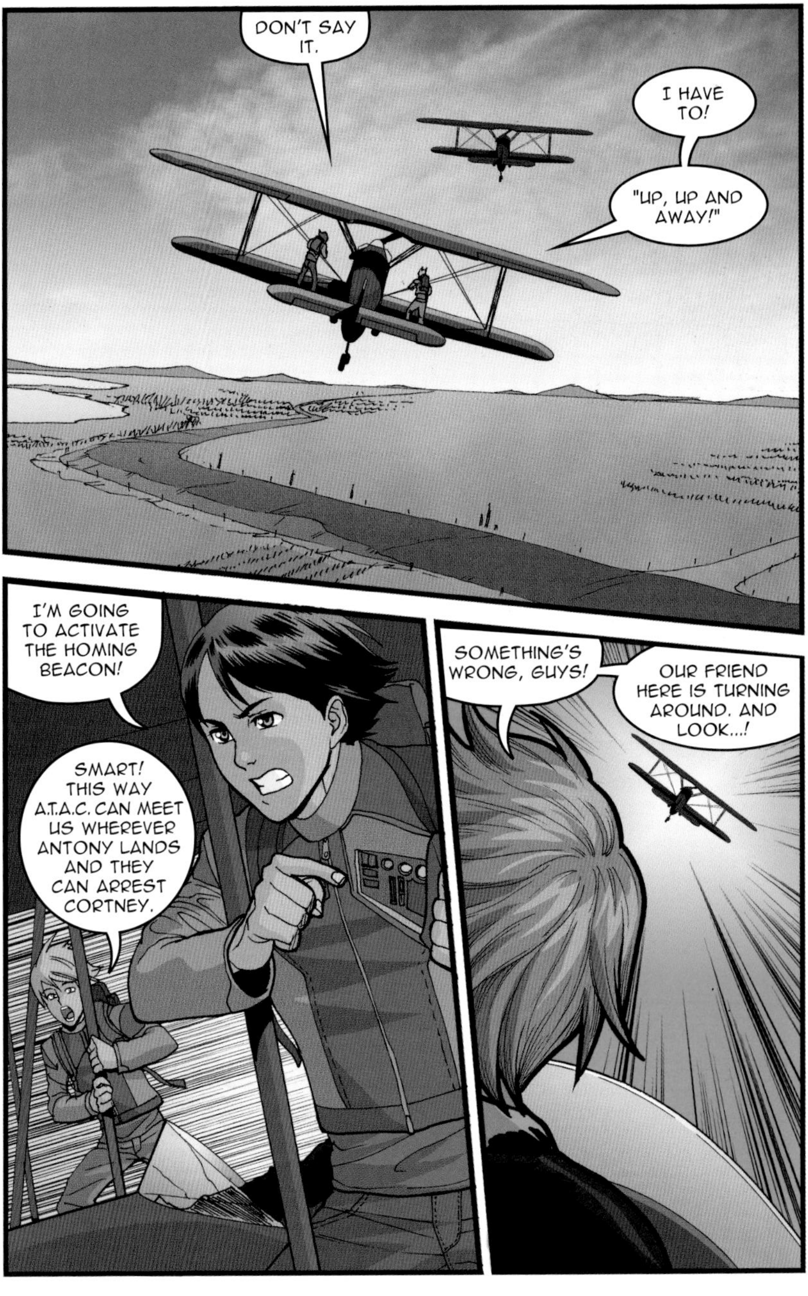
DON'T SAY IT.
I HAVE TO!
"UP, UP AND AWAY!"
I'M GOING TO ACTIVATE THE HOMING BEACON!
SMART! THIS WAY A.T.A.C. CAN MEET US WHEREVER ANTONY LANDS AND THEY CAN ARREST CORTNEY.
SOMETHING'S WRONG, GUYS!
OUR FRIEND HERE IS TURNING AROUND. AND LOOK...!

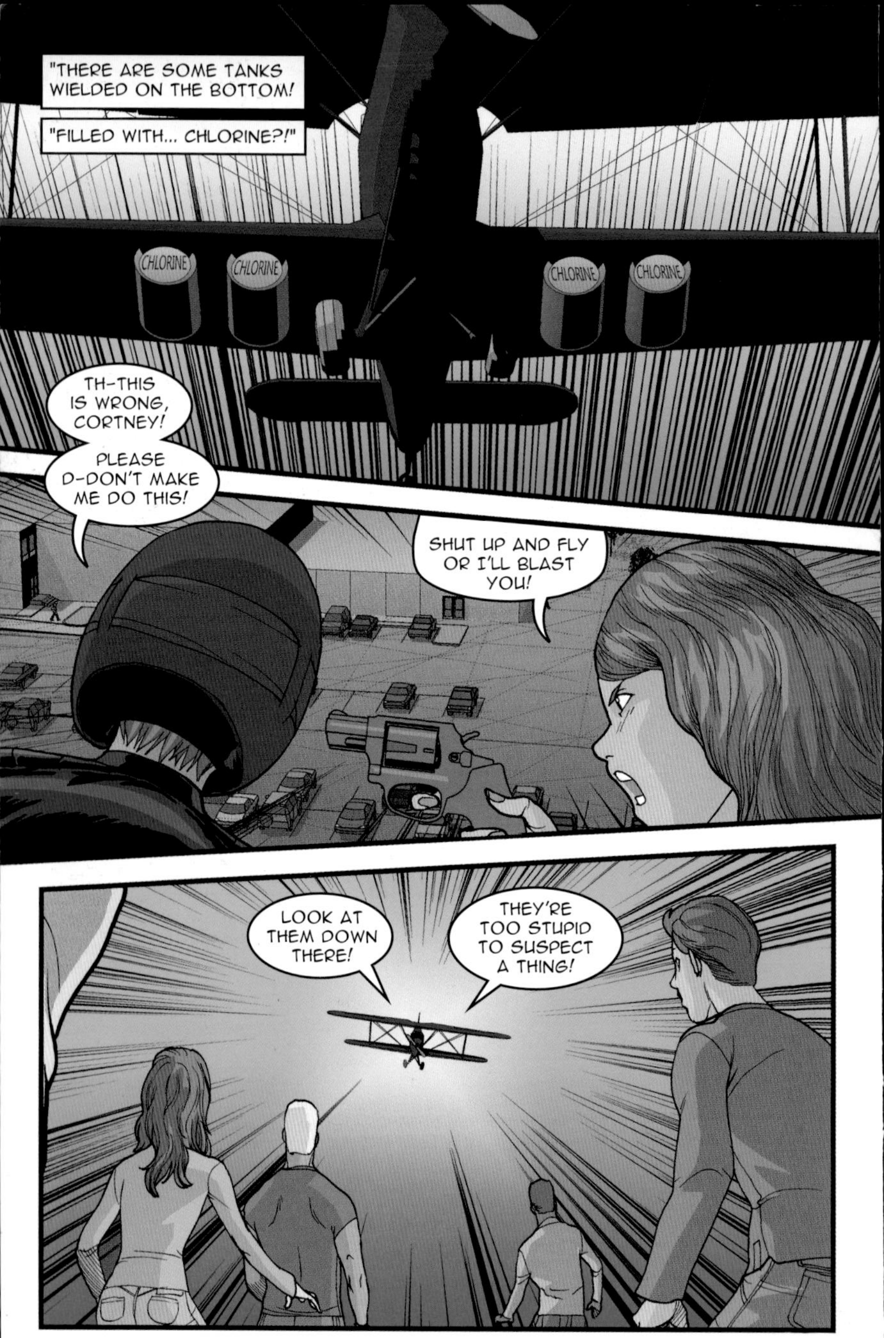
"THERE ARE SOME TANKS WIELDED ON THE BOTTOM!
"FILLED WITH... CHLORINE?!"
CHLORINE
CHLORINE
CHLORINE
CHLORINE
TH-THIS IS WRONG, CORTNEY!
PLEASE D-DON'T MAKE ME DO THIS!
SHUT UP AND FLY OR I'LL BLAST YOU!
LOOK AT THEM DOWN THERE!
THEY'RE TOO STUPID TO SUSPECT A THING!

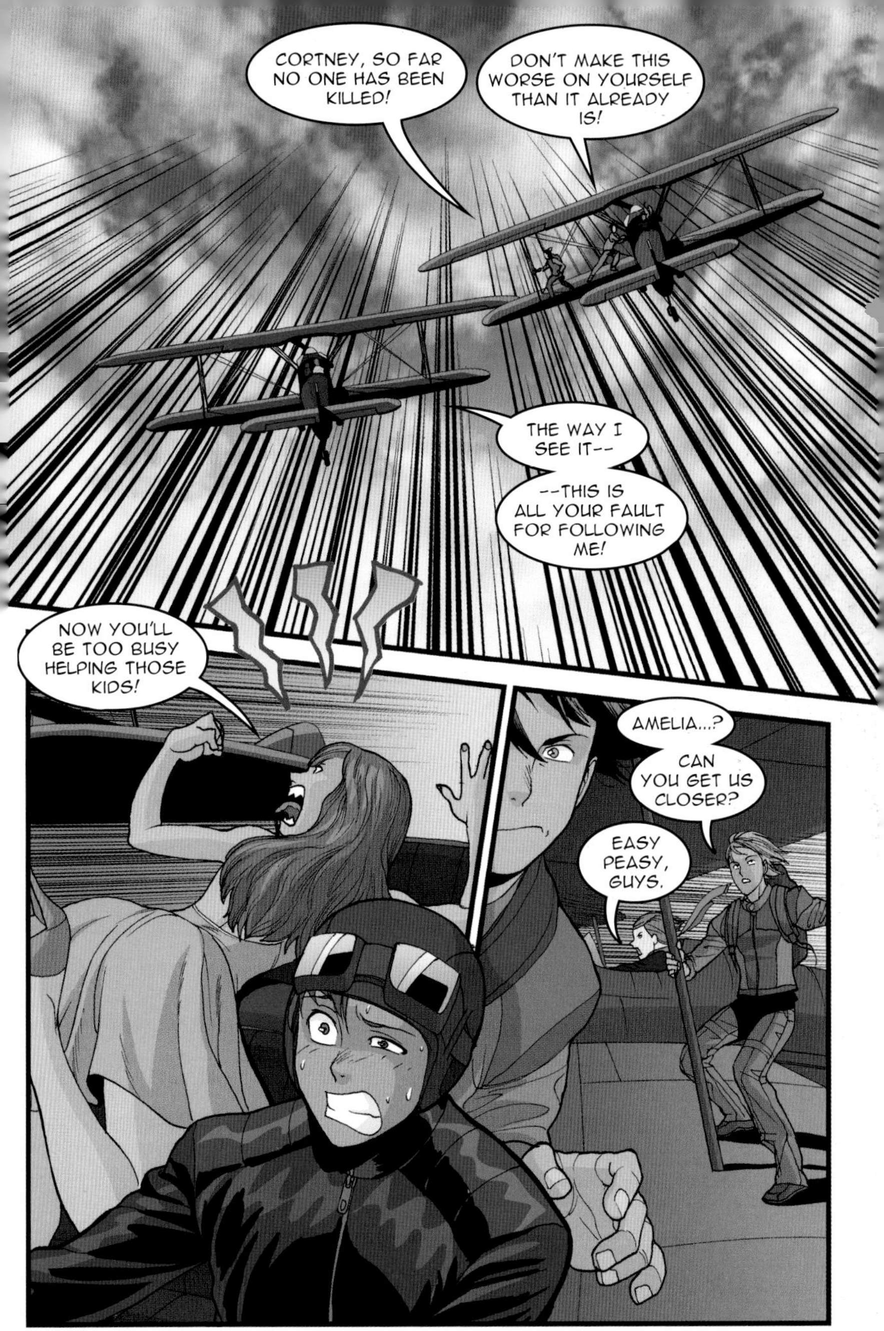
CORTNEY, SO FAR NO ONE HAS BEEN KILLED!
DON'T MAKE THIS WORSE ON YOURSELF THAN IT ALREADY IS!
THE WAY I SEE IT--
--THIS IS ALL YOUR FAULT FOR FOLLOWING ME!
NOW YOU'LL BE TOO BUSY HELPING THOSE KIDS!
AMELIA...?
CAN YOU GET US CLOSER?
EASY PEASY, GUYS.

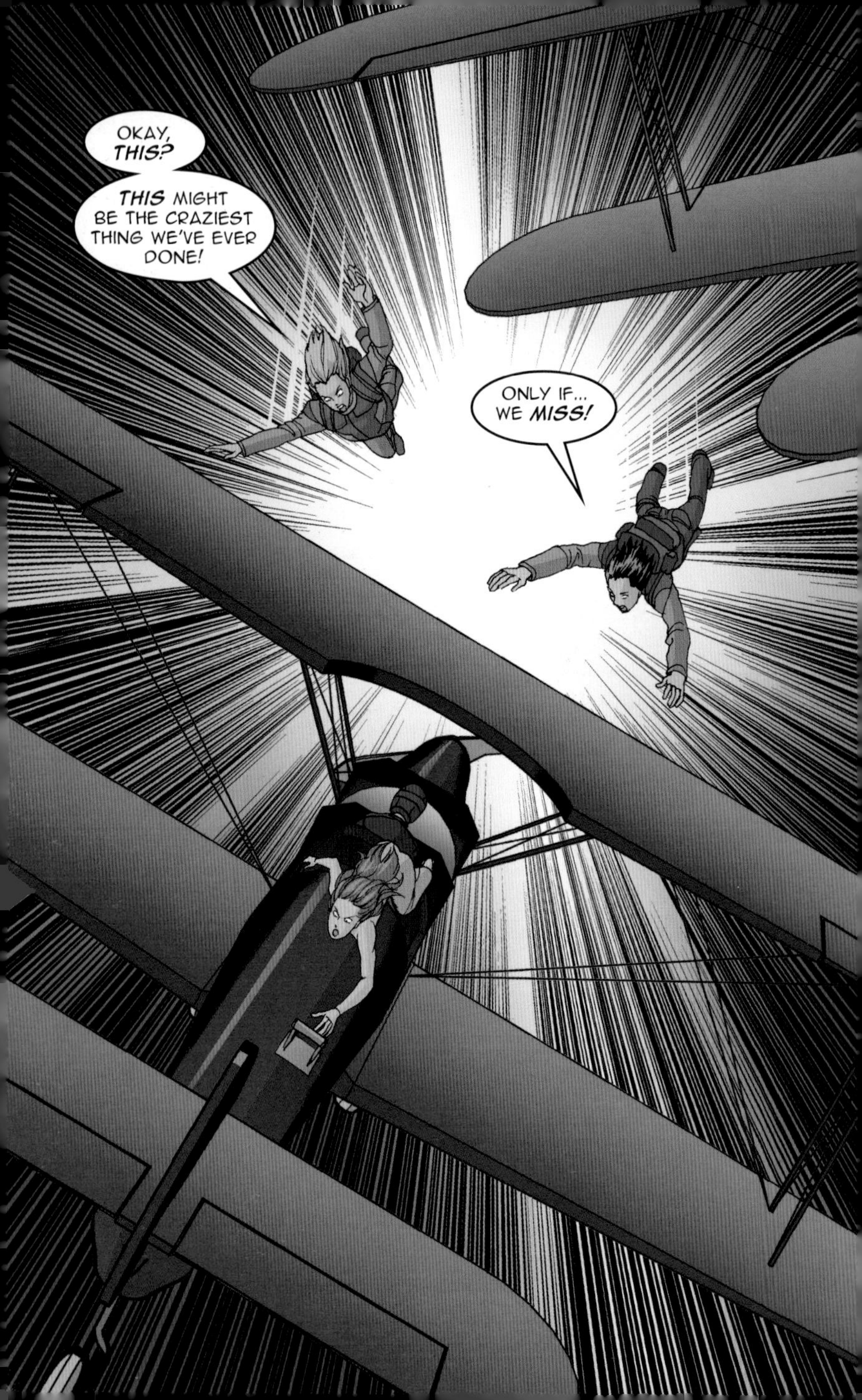
OKAY, THIS?
THIS MIGHT BE THE CRAZIEST THING WE'VE EVER DONE!
ONLY IF... WE MISS!

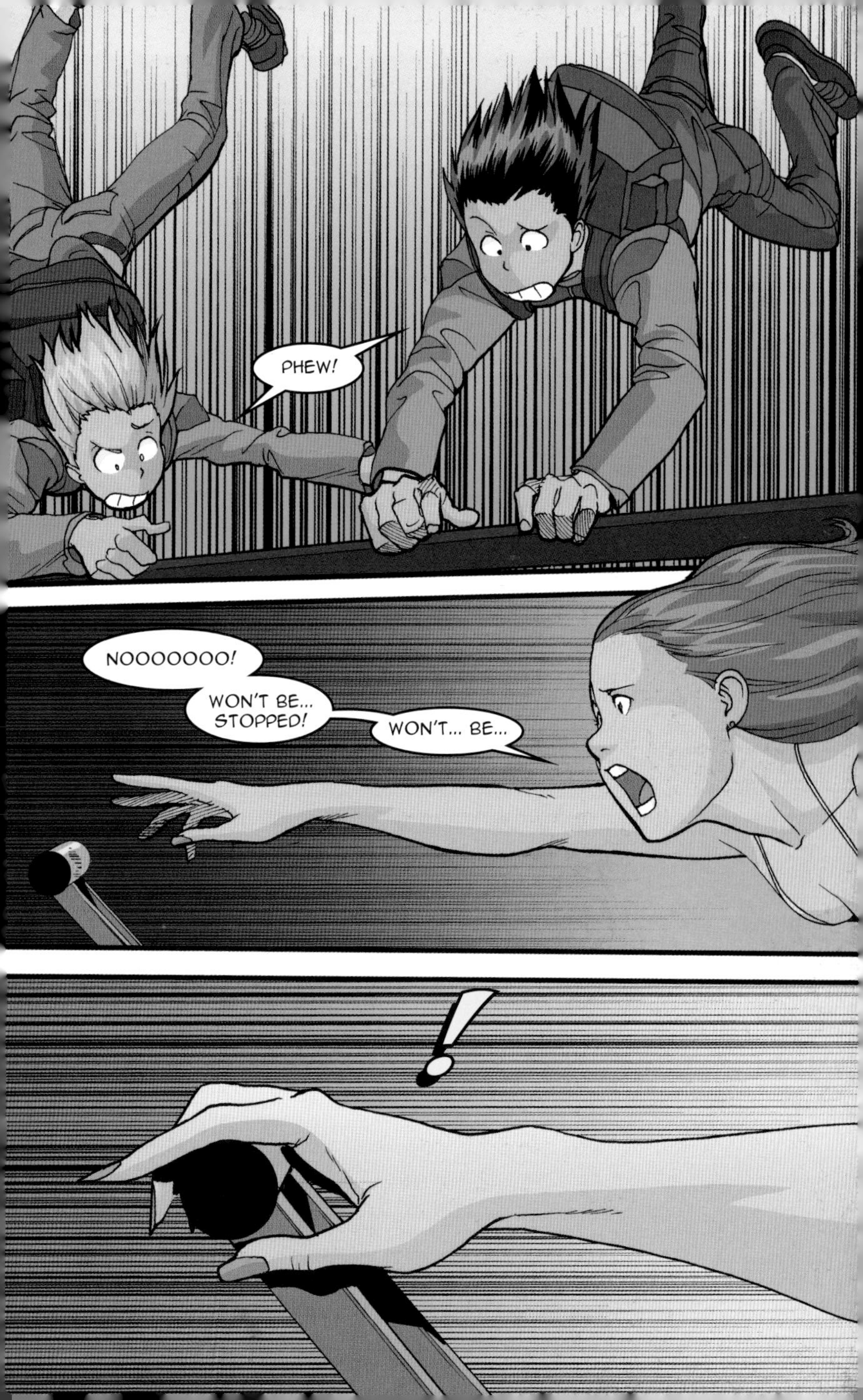
PHEW!
NOOOOOOO!
WON'T BE...
STOPPED!
WON'T... BE...
!

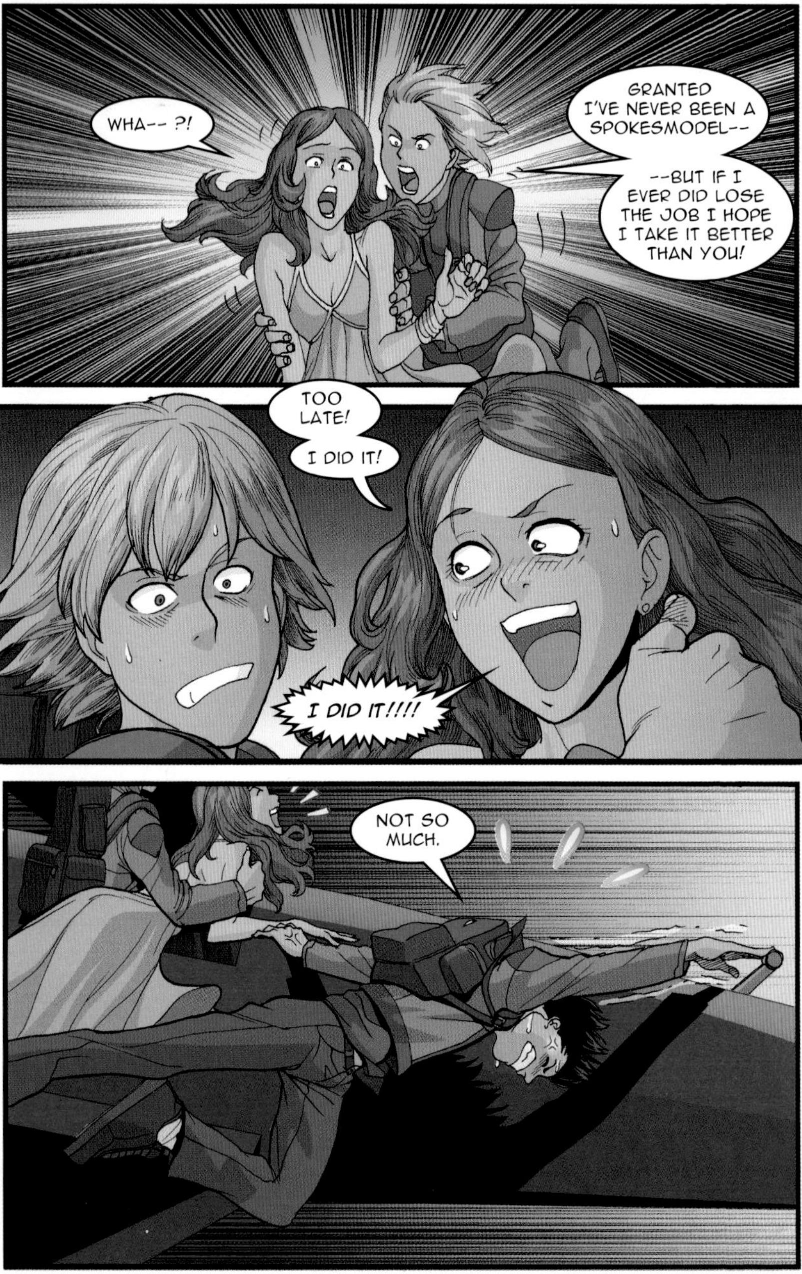
WHA-- ?!
GRANTED I'VE NEVER BEEN A SPOKESMODEL--
--BUT IF I EVER DID LOSE THE JOB I HOPE I TAKE IT BETTER THAN YOU!
TOO LATE!
I DID IT!
I DID IT!!!!
NOT SO MUCH.

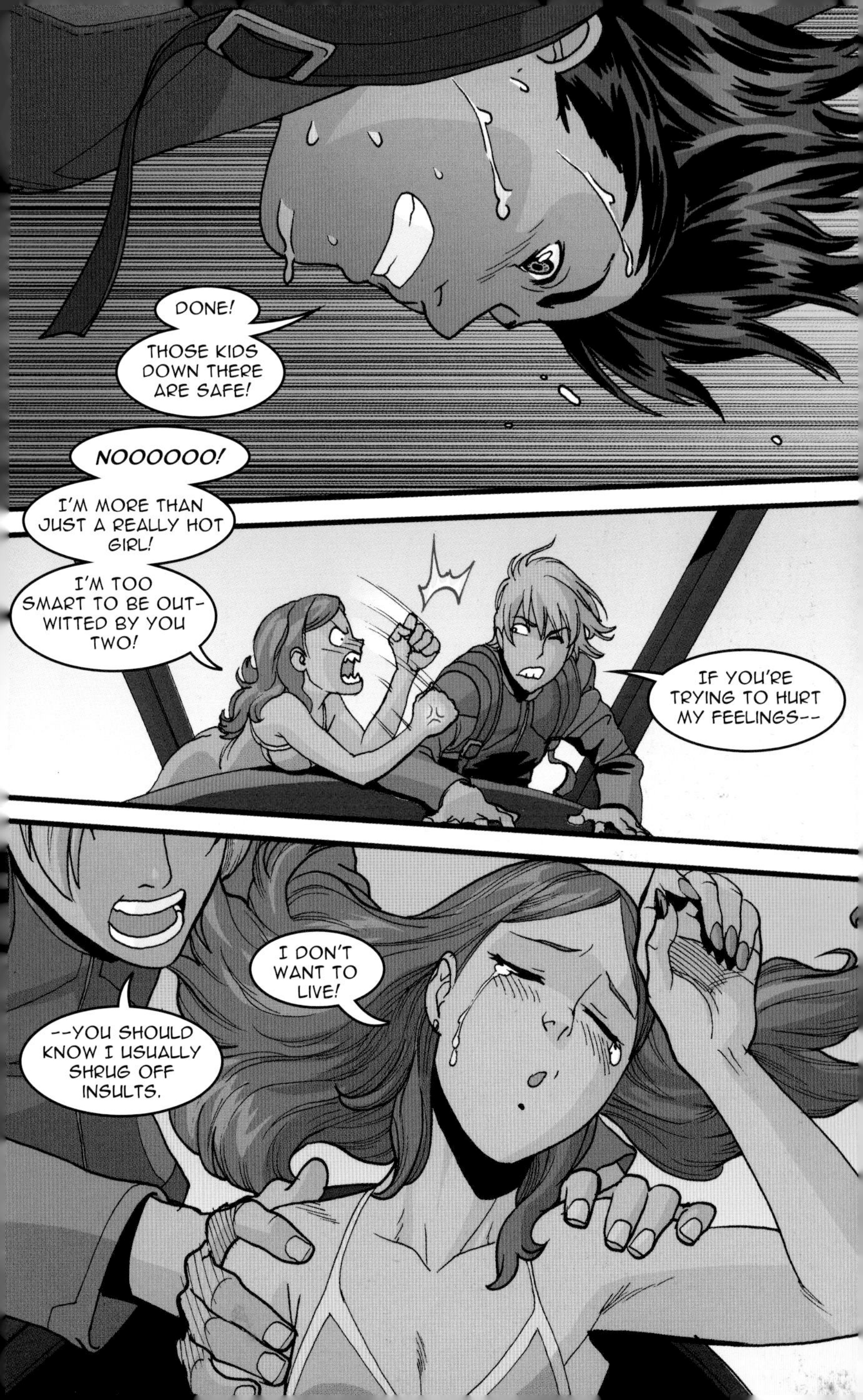
DONE!
THOSE KIDS DOWN THERE ARE SAFE!
NOOOOOO!
I'M MORE THAN JUST A REALLY HOT GIRL!
I'M TOO SMART TO BE OUT-WITTED BY YOU TWO!
IF YOU'RE TRYING TO HURT MY FEELINGS--
--YOU SHOULD KNOW I USUALLY SHRUG OFF INSULTS.
I DON'T WANT TO LIVE!

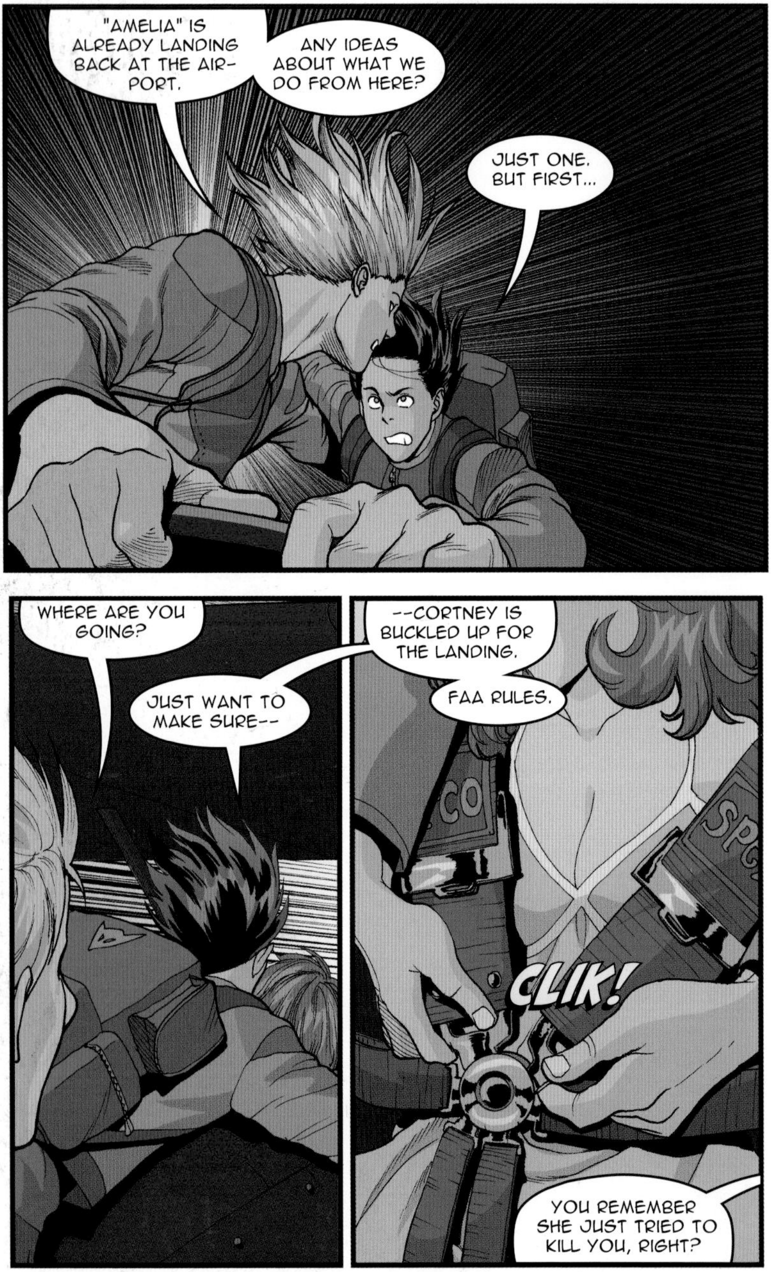
"AMELIA" IS ALREADY LANDING BACK AT THE AIR-PORT.
ANY IDEAS ABOUT WHAT WE DO FROM HERE?
JUST ONE. BUT FIRST...
WHERE ARE YOU GOING?
JUST WANT TO MAKE SURE--
--CORTNEY IS BUCKLED UP FOR THE LANDING.
FAA RULES.
CO
SPO
CLIK!
YOU REMEMBER SHE JUST TRIED TO KILL YOU, RIGHT?

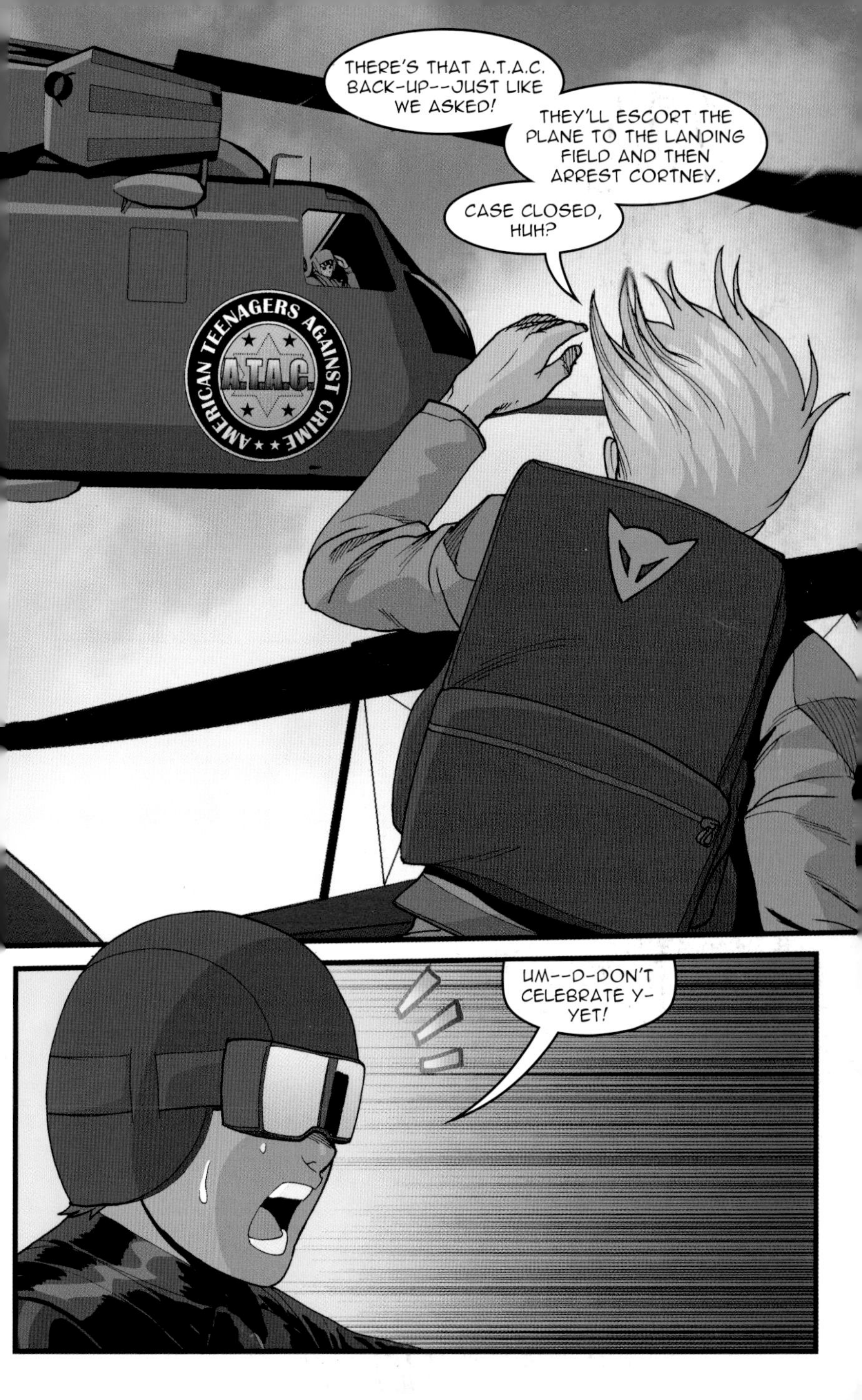
THERE'S THAT A.T.A.C. BACK-UP--JUST LIKE WE ASKED!
THEY'LL ESCORT THE PLANE TO THE LANDING FIELD AND THEN ARREST CORTNEY.
CASE CLOSED, HUH?
AMERICAN TEENAGERS AGAINST CRIME
A.T.A.C.
UM--D-DON'T CELEBRATE Y-YET!

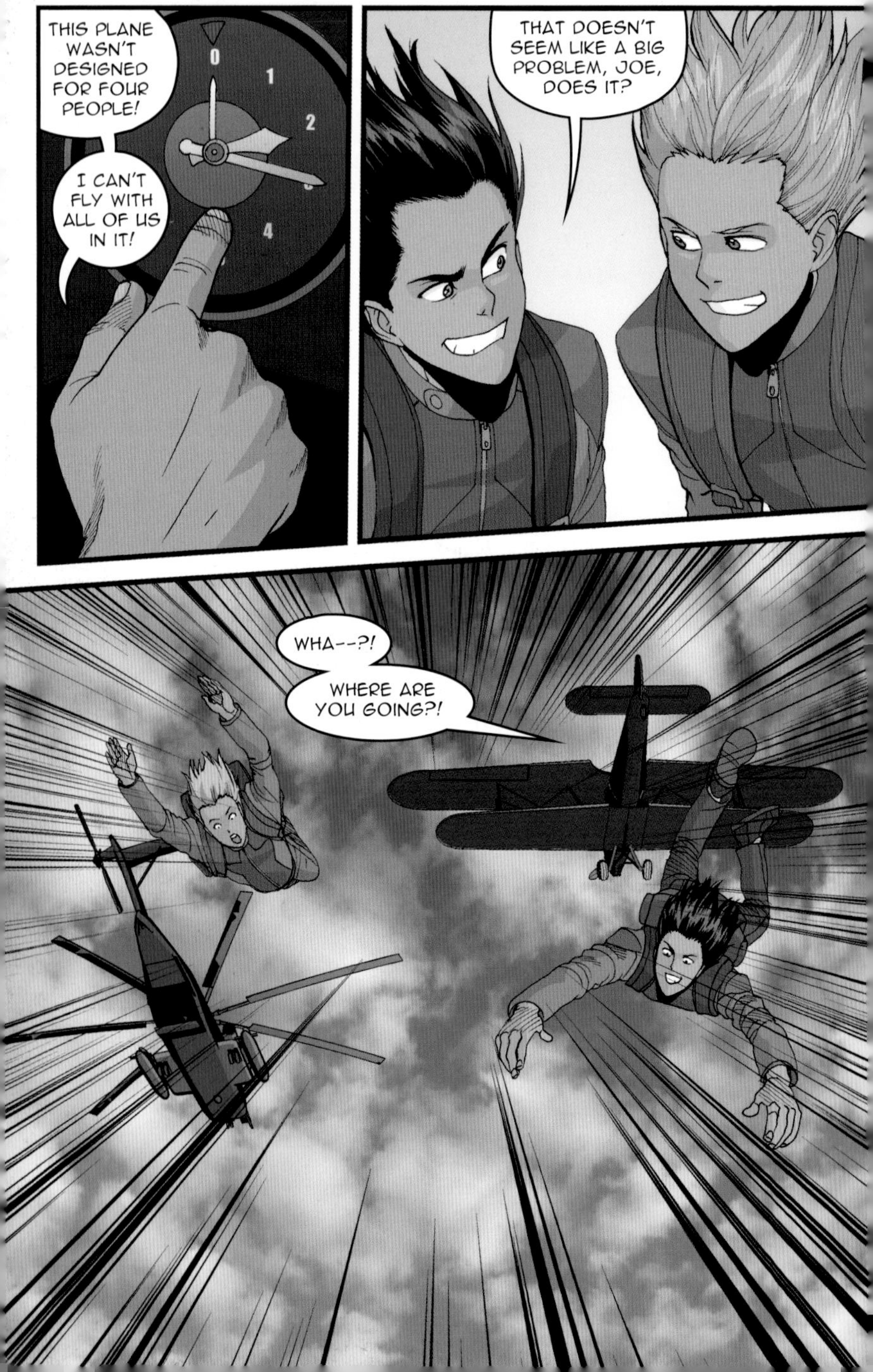
THIS PLANE WASN'T DESIGNED FOR FOUR PEOPLE!
I CAN'T FLY WITH ALL OF US IN IT!
THAT DOESN'T SEEM LIKE A BIG PROBLEM, JOE, DOES IT?
WHA--?!
WHERE ARE YOU GOING?!

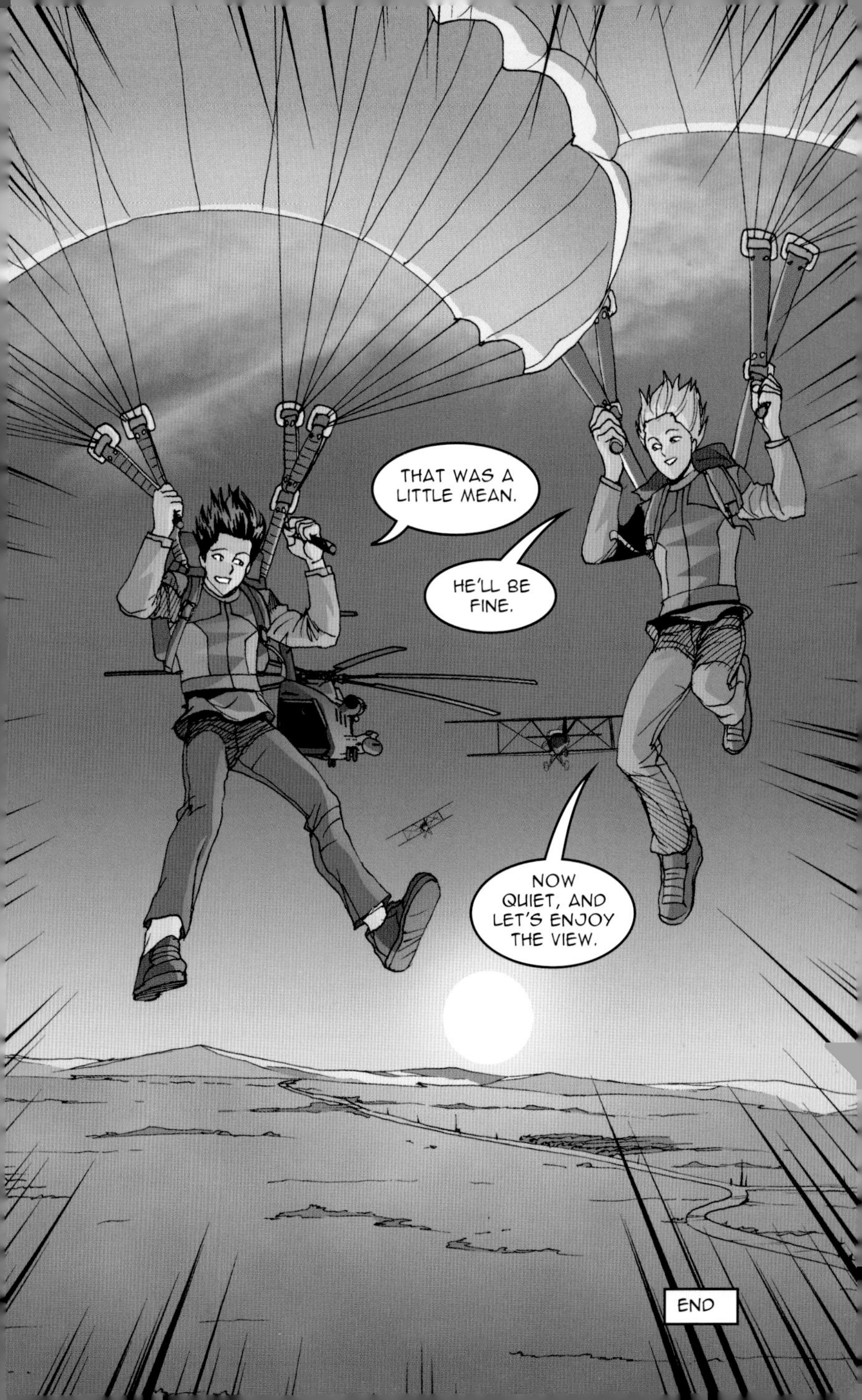
THAT WAS A LITTLE MEAN.
HE'LL BE FINE.
NOW QUIET, AND LET'S ENJOY THE VIEW.
END

WATCH OUT FOR PAPERCUTZ

Hi, mystery-lovers! Welcome to the third HARDY BOYS ADVENTURES graphic novel, filled with four stories featuring the return of the nefarious Noir Sisters, the brief return of Lindsay Rider, a cameo appearance by former President Barack Obama, the introduction of a talk-radio terrorist, and the shocking return of a long-lost aviation legend, all brought to you by Scott Lobdell, writer, and PH Marcondes artist, from Papercutz—those secret (literary) agents dedicated to publishing great graphic novels for all ages. I'm Jim Salicrup, the Editor-in-Chief and the proud owner of a NY Public Library card.

As you may or may not know, every volume of HARDY BOYS ADVENTURES is collecting four previously published THE HARDY BOYS UNDERCOVER BROTHERS graphic novels. This volume, for example, is featuring volumes 15, 16, 17, and 19. No, that's not a typo—we're skipping volume 18 for now, but it will be included in HARDY BOYS ADVENTURES #4. Why? Let's keep that a mystery for now and talk a little bit about the volumes that are included here...

Cazenove
William
The
SisterS
1 Just Like Family
PAPERCUTZ

First, we have "Live Free, Die Hardy!" that's notable for the return of Nicolina and Shira AKA the Noir Sisters. They're not to be confused with the stars of the new Papercutz graphic novel series starring Wendy and Maureen, THE SISTERS by Cazenove and William. Hey, that's not as far-fetched as it sounds. At first glance you may think these characters have nothing in common other than being female siblings, and you wouldn't be wrong. But while Nicolina and Shira are far naughtier than Wendy and Maureen, the fantasy versions of the grown-up Wendy and Maureen are a pair of costumed super-heroes! We bet they'd easily be able to hold their own, if not demolish, the Noir Sisters! We've only seen a few sequences of the grown-up girls in action in THE SISTERS graphic novels so far (the stories mostly focus on their misadventures when they were kids), but they've proven to be so popular there's an entire graphic novel coming up from Papercutz that'll be entirely devoted to THE SUPER SISTERS! Go to Papercutz.com for further exciting details! But back to the Noir Sisters, if you missed their dramatic debut you can still find it THE HARDY BOYS #7, or HARDY BOYS ADVENTURES #1, or the ebook versions of either of those two action-packed graphic novels.

In "Shhhhhh!" we reveal our love for libraries and librarians! While it does appear that wherever the Hardy Boys go, trouble follows, we assure you that libraries are generally very safe places. Many of the world's greatest writers, from Ray Bradbury to Neil Gaiman, would hang out at their local library reading just about every book they could get their hands on. I loved my local libraries when I was a kid, but back then I never dreamed that I'd be able to borrow comics and graphic novels from a library! Today, some of my favorite people in the world are librarians, and they do a wonderful job of introducing people to the many worlds that await you in all the awesome books you can find in your local library. Papercutz will soon be publishing comics and graphic novels featuring the world-famous clayboy, GUMBY, and one of his incredible powers is that he can literally morph into any book at all. While we can do the same thing figuratively, using our imaginations, Gumby can pop into a HARDY BOYS graphic novel if he wanted to and work side-by-side with Joe and Frank to solve a mystery! Wow, that would be fun!

"Word Up!" is about the power of words and free speech in general. While we're mainly about providing you with entertaining adventures starring the Undercover Brothers, sometimes these stories may reflect issues that are very important in the real world. We're not pushing a specific political agenda

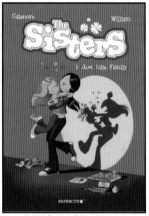

on you—we respect your intelligence too much to do that—what we're talking about are basic freedoms that have been an important part of our country since the beginning, and how we must be ever-vigilant to protect those freedoms.

In "Chaos at 30,000 Feet!" we get to see the Hardy Boys portray the legendary aviation heroes the Wright Brothers, while Suzi Shields plays the role of "aviatrix extraordinaire," Amelia Earhart. Everything's going great until Suzi gets hit by a loose screw on her head, and another ATAC caper ensues. It's funny how we take flying for granted these days. When I was a kid my dad would tell me how he dreamed of becoming a pilot when he was a kid—and he wasn't the only one. Flying off into the wild blue yonder was the dream of many of my father's generation back when they were young. Humans dreamed of flying since the very first humans walked the earth. In fact, even Smurfs dreamed of flying—in THE

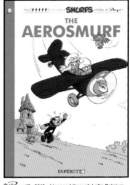

© Peyo - 2015 - Licensed through Lafig Belgium

SMURFS #1 (as well as THE SMURFS ANTHOLOGY Volume One, all published by Papercutz) we meet "The Flying Smurf," in THE SMURFS #16 we fly with "The Aerosmurf," and in THE SMURFS #7 (also in THE SMURFS ANTHOLOGY Volume Three) we take a giant leap for Smurfkind when we encounter "The Astrosmurf." I wouldn't blame Frank and Joe Hardy if, after what they went through in this graphic novel, they never wanted to fly again! But fortunately, they're very brave young men who simply seem to thrive on life and death adventures, so we're sure they won't hesitate to soar off into wherever a case will lead them!

As we said, these HARDY BOYS graphic novels were originally created a few years ago, so if you'd like to check out the latest work by super-star Papercutz artist PH Marcondes, we suggest picking up THE ZODIAC LEGACY graphic novels. Based on characters created by none other than comicbook legend Stan Lee, and written by Stuart Moore, we're sure you'll love these all-new adventures that fit into the continuity of the best-selling ZODIAC LEGACY novels. It's funny how things come full circle—Stan Lee, when he was a kid loved the original HARDY BOYS novels by Franklin W. Dixon, and it's fair to say it was one of Stan's earliest inspirations. So PH Marcondes has illustrated both the characters that inspired Stan and the characters that Stan has created in THE ZODIAC LEGACY. How cool is that? I also think it's fair to say that the creators of THE ONLY LIVING BOY, writer David Gallaher, and artist Steve Ellis, were also inspired by the countless comics created or co-created by Stan Lee. In fact, I just spoke to Mr. Gallaher, and he says he was also influenced by THE HARDY BOYS, which helped him increase his vocabulary. He specifically remembered looking up in dictionary the word "wryly," which he originally thought might've been a mistake, but discovered was a real word! Check out the previews of both THE ZODIAC LEGACY #3 "The Age of Bronze" and THE ONLY LIVING BOY #2 "Beyond Sea and Sky" on the following pages.

Finally, keep an eye out for HARDY BOYS ADVENTURES #4 coming soon to booksellers everywhere and, we hope, your friendly neighborhood library!

Thanks,

JIM

STAY IN TOUCH!

EMAIL: salicrup@papercutz.com
WEB: papercutz.com
TWITTER: @papercutzgn
INSTAGRAM: @papercutzgn
FACEBOOK: PAPERCUTZGRAPHICNOVELS
FANMAIL: Papercutz, 160 Broadway,
Suite 700, East Wing,
New York, NY 10038

Special Preview of THE ONLY LIVING BOY #2 "Beyond Sea and Sky"
by David Gallaher and Steve Ellis

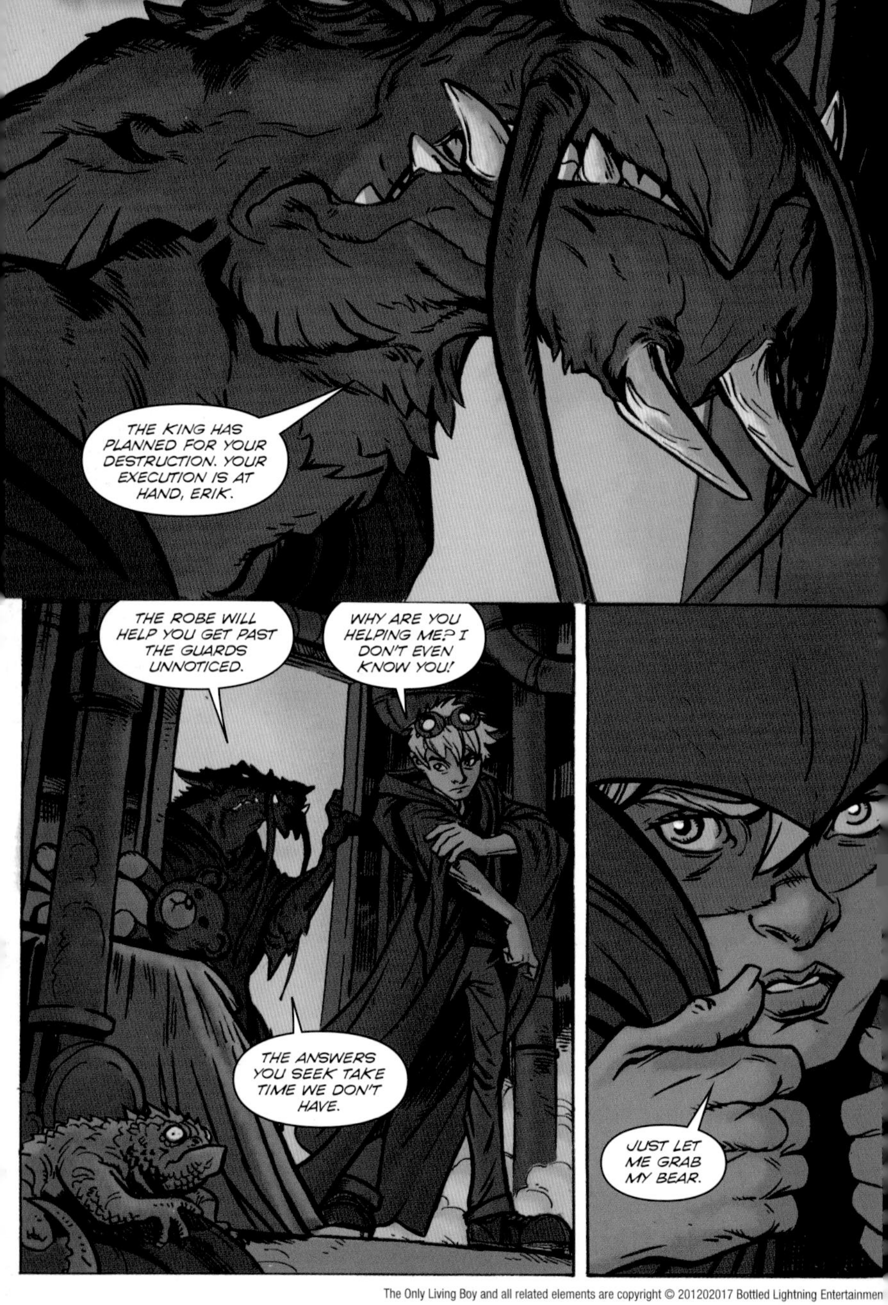
THE KING HAS PLANNED FOR YOUR DESTRUCTION. YOUR EXECUTION IS AT HAND, ERIK.
THE ROBE WILL HELP YOU GET PAST THE GUARDS UNNOTICED.
WHY ARE YOU HELPING ME? I DON'T EVEN KNOW YOU!
THE ANSWERS YOU SEEK TAKE TIME WE DON'T HAVE.
JUST LET ME GRAB MY BEAR.

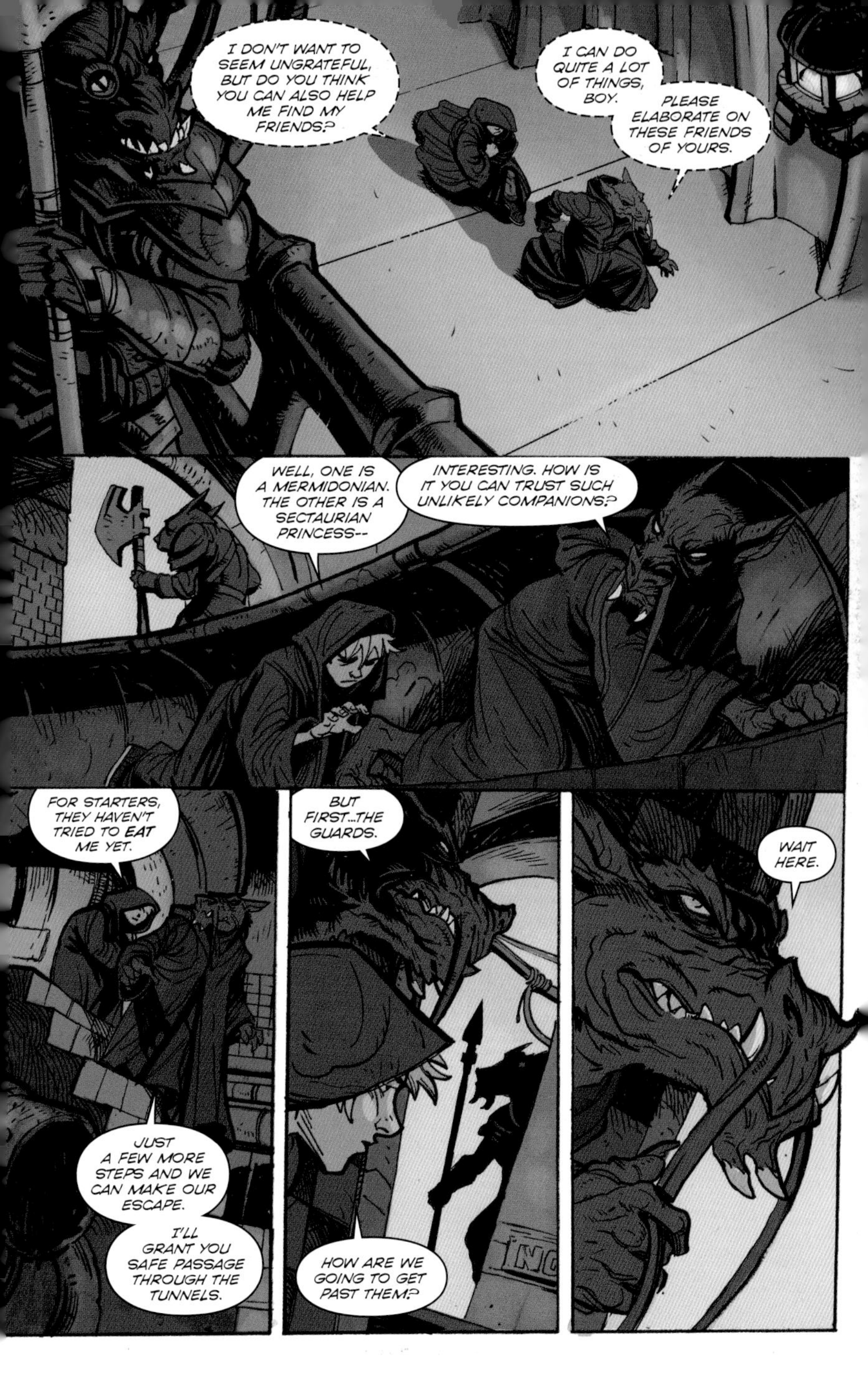
I DON'T WANT TO SEEM UNGRATEFUL, BUT DO YOU THINK YOU CAN ALSO HELP ME FIND MY FRIENDS?
I CAN DO QUITE A LOT OF THINGS, BOY.
PLEASE ELABORATE ON THESE FRIENDS OF YOURS.
WELL, ONE IS A MERMIDONIAN. THE OTHER IS A SECTAURIAN PRINCESS--
INTERESTING. HOW IS IT YOU CAN TRUST SUCH UNLIKELY COMPANIONS?
FOR STARTERS, THEY HAVEN'T TRIED TO EAT ME YET.
JUST A FEW MORE STEPS AND WE CAN MAKE OUR ESCAPE.
I'LL GRANT YOU SAFE PASSAGE THROUGH THE TUNNELS.
BUT FIRST...THE GUARDS.
HOW ARE WE GOING TO GET PAST THEM?
WAIT HERE.

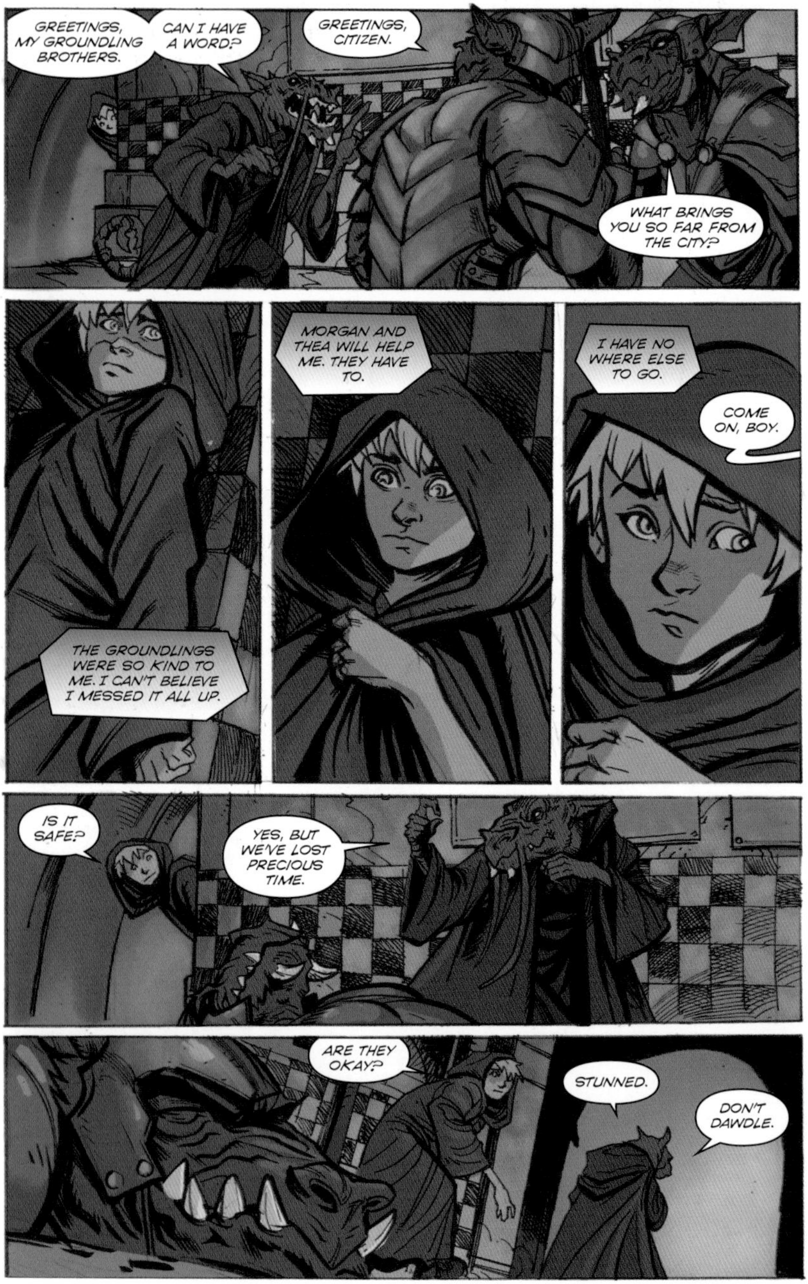
GREETINGS, MY GROUNDLING BROTHERS.
CAN I HAVE A WORD?
GREETINGS, CITIZEN.
WHAT BRINGS YOU SO FAR FROM THE CITY?
THE GROUNDLINGS WERE SO KIND TO ME. I CAN'T BELIEVE I MESSED IT ALL UP.
MORGAN AND THEA WILL HELP ME. THEY HAVE TO.
I HAVE NO WHERE ELSE TO GO.
COME ON, BOY.
IS IT SAFE?
YES, BUT WE'VE LOST PRECIOUS TIME.
ARE THEY OKAY?
STUNNED.
DON'T DAWDLE.

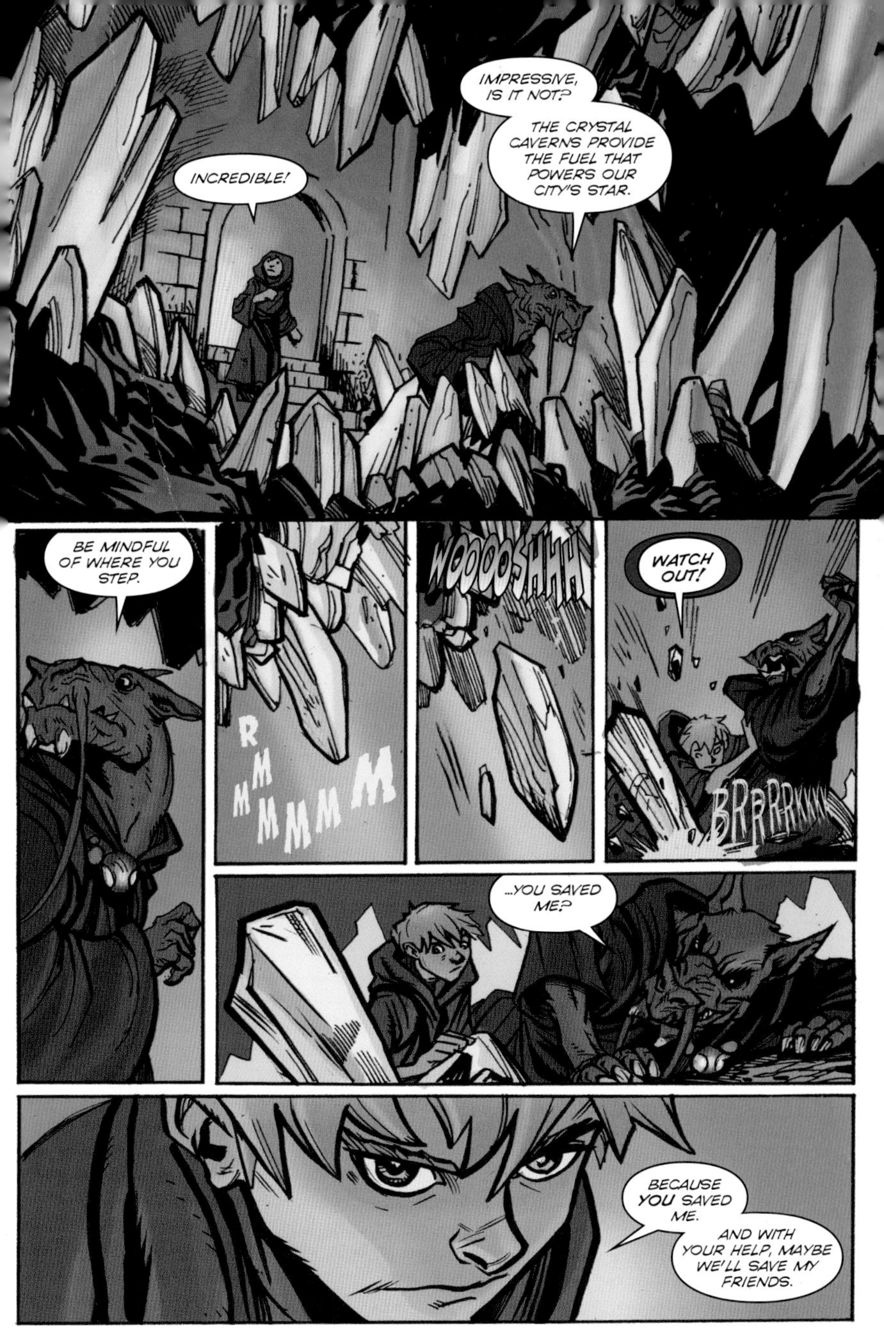
INCREDIBLE!
IMPRESSIVE, IS IT NOT?
THE CRYSTAL CAVERNS PROVIDE THE FUEL THAT POWERS OUR CITY'S STAR.
BE MINDFUL OF WHERE YOU STEP.
RMMMMMMM
WOOOOSHHH
WATCH OUT!
BRRRRKKK
...YOU SAVED ME?
BECAUSE YOU SAVED ME.
AND WITH YOUR HELP, MAYBE WE'LL SAVE MY FRIENDS.

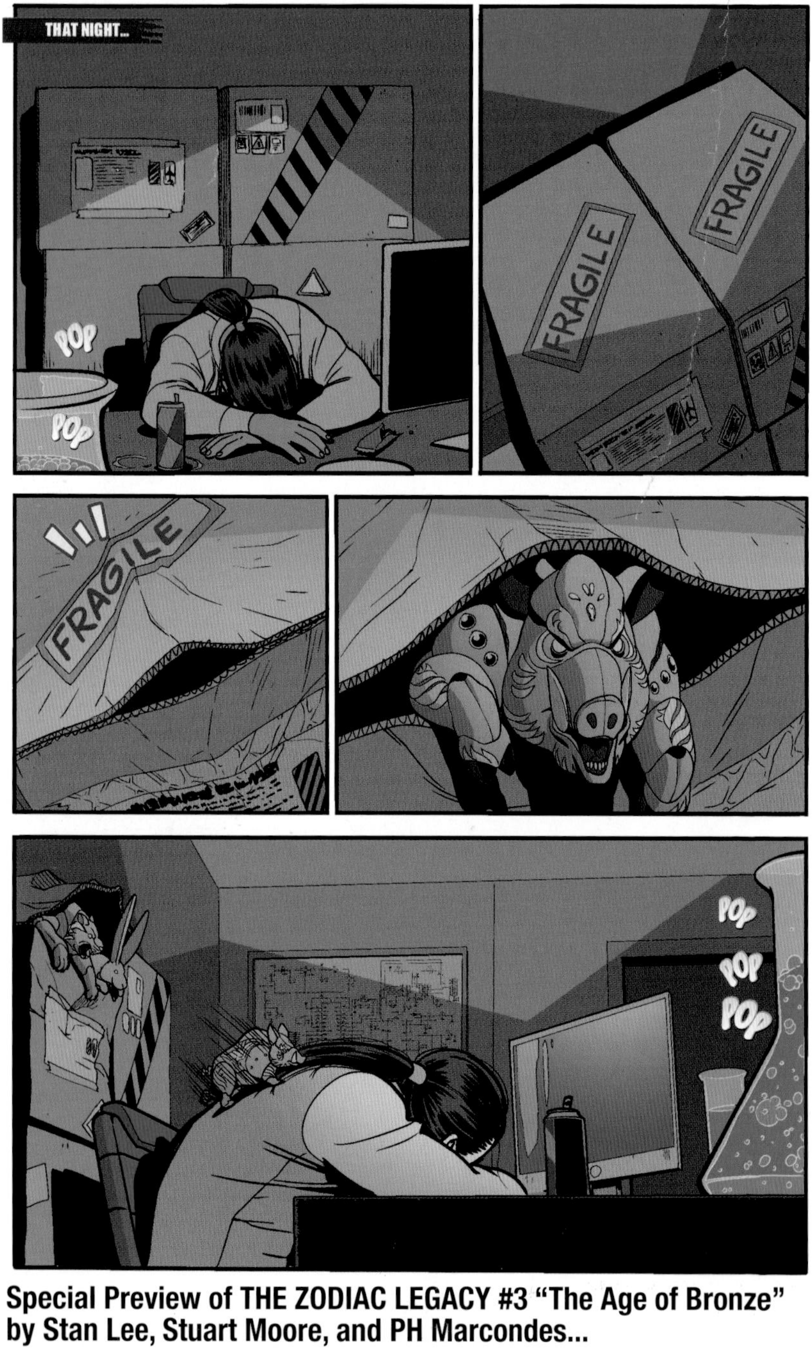
THAT NIGHT...
POP
POP
FRAGILE
FRAGILE
FRAGILE
POP
POP
POP

Special Preview of THE ZODIAC LEGACY #3 "The Age of Bronze" by Stan Lee, Stuart Moore, and PH Marcondes...

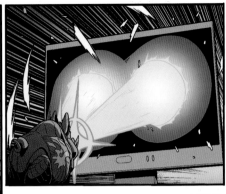

security lockdown
all doors sealed
silent protocol

MMM...

...HUH?

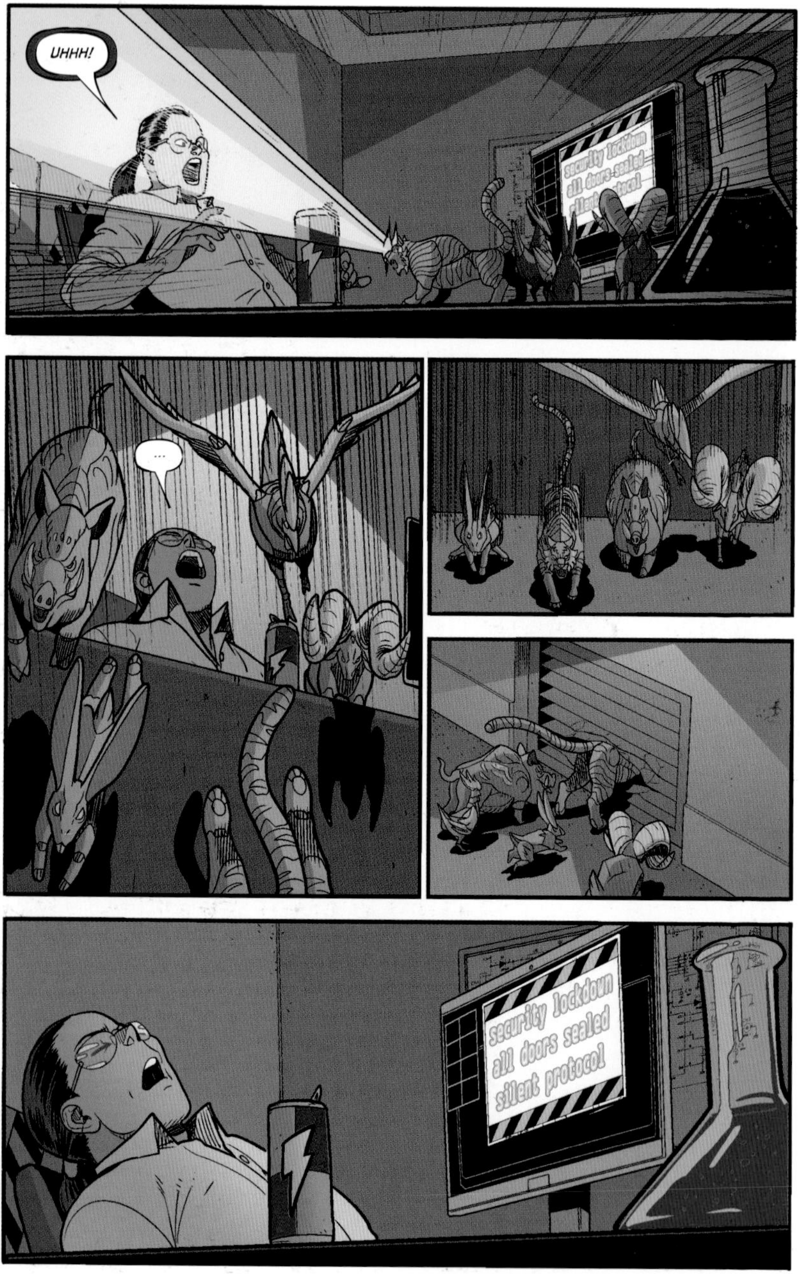
UHHH!
security lockdown
all doors sealed
...
security lockdown
all doors sealed
silent protocol

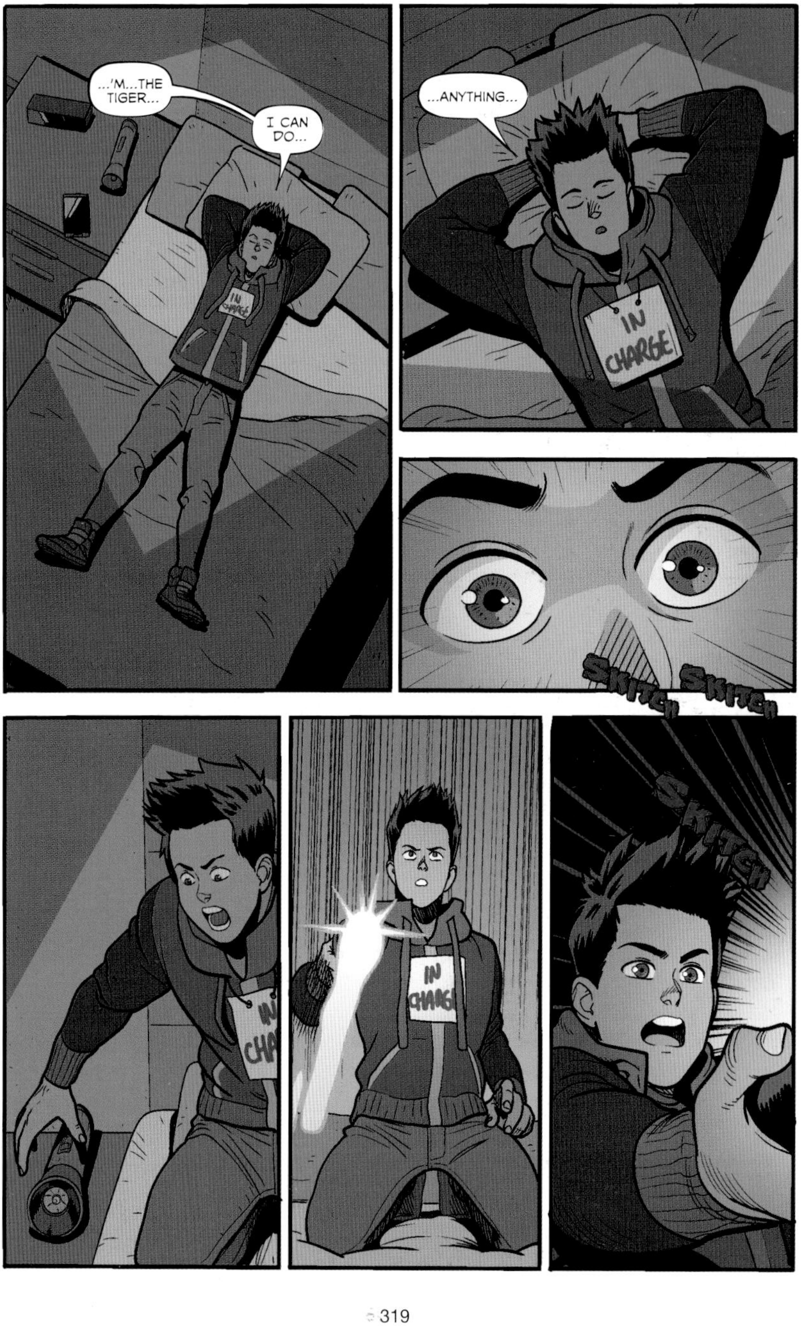
...'M...THE TIGER...
I CAN DO...
...ANYTHING...
IN CHARGE
IN CHARGE
SKITCH
SKITCH
IN CHARGE
IN CHARGE
SKITCH

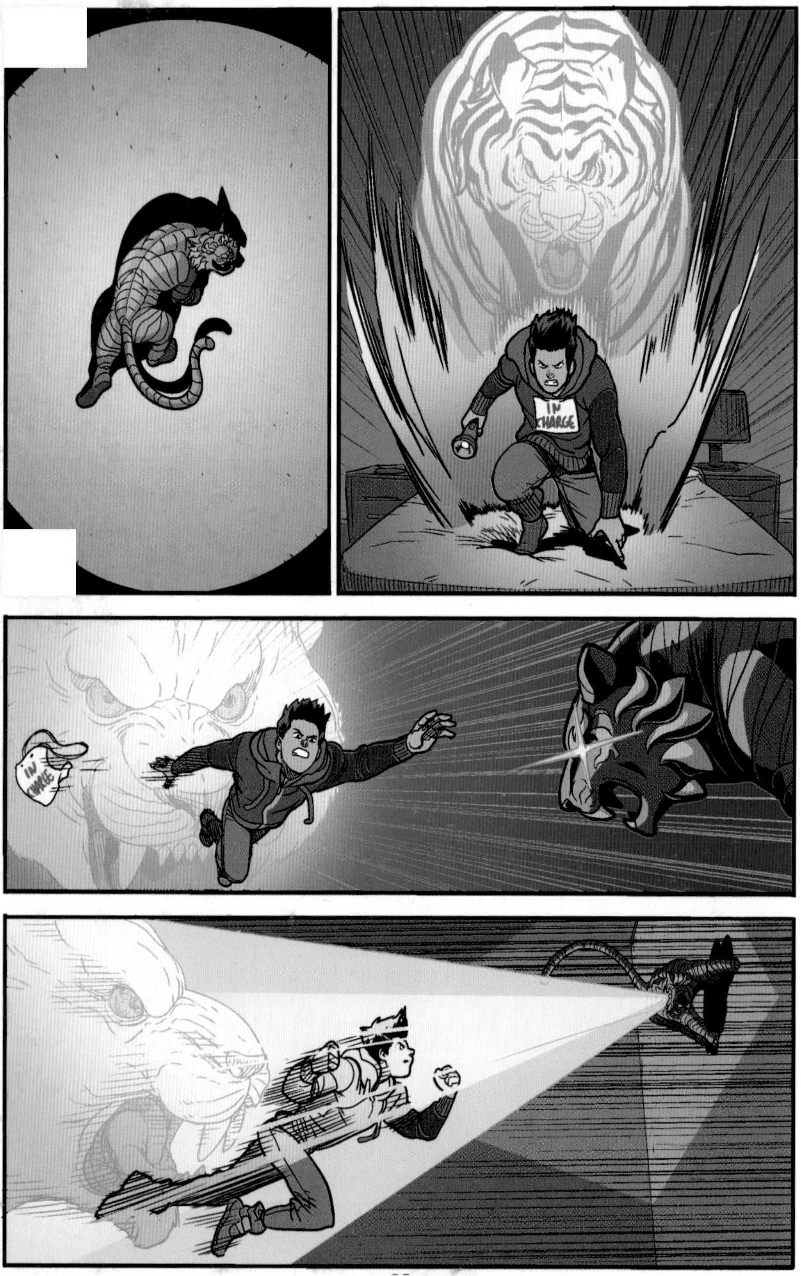
IN CHARGE
IN CHARGE

Special Preview of THE ZODIAC LEGACY #3 "The Age of Bronze" available now at booksellers everywhere!

HARDYBOYS
ADVENTURES™

THE UNDERCOVER BROTHERS
are dynamite detectives!

Four exciting adventures take Frank and Joe Hardy across the globe to solve dangerous mysteries! The fate of the world lies in the library? It does when the two sleuthing siblings need to provide security for the children of visiting delegates! What lengths will someone go to make the most explosive radio show of all? Tune in! What happens when the Hardy Boys are split up? Danger looms! And, what is Amelia Earhart doing flying around? The Hardy Boys are on the case!

HARDY BOYS ADVENTURES collects 4 great graphic novels that feature Frank and Joe at their best —in action, solving impossible mysteries!

PAPERCUT Z ™
Dedicated to publishing great graphic novels for all ages.

papercutz.com

$15.99 US | 22.99 CAN
ISBN: 978-1-62991-754-2